THE LEGEND OF
ELOH

THE FIRST TOME

ALAN DELAHAY

Library of Congress Control Number: 2020912436
Paperback: ISBN 978-1-7353304-4-0

Edited by Abigail Marks, Becky Markt, Mike Sandusky, and Joseph Brinnon
Illustrations by Grant Griffin and Serenity Henry
Layout and Formatting by Austin Marks
Cover Art by Kelly Carter
Author Photograph by Kali Moeck

MARKS MEDIA
Publishing Co.

thelegendofeloh.com

To the really important people.

To Keri – my lifelong love. You have been with me every step of the way with patience and thoughtfulness. Thank you for being so caring and loving. I love you more than I know how to say or show.

To my daughters - I love you and am so grateful that you have been able to help me and guide me along this winding way. It is not just in writing this book, but in all the ways that you are a part of my life. Thank You.

To Steve – You saw something in me I could not see in myself.

Thank you to the many voices and opinions given along the way. I am grateful.

Table of Contents

The Three Worlds

If you could, would you risk it all? Would you put everything else aside to find something that no one else is looking for, to go where no one else is going, to do what no one else has done? There is a place, a mountain where, it is said, the legend began. There, a secret is hidden, a relic from an ancient age. No one knows what it is or what it looks like, but the legend tells that whoever possesses it is given great power.

It was long ago in the vast celestial kingdom of Pardis, during the timeless age, when there were no old men like me living in the misery of decrepitness, and life had no counterpart, that the ancient relic, the Kleid o'Miht, was forged. It was given to one named Amik who had dominion over Tirnan, the smallest of the three realms of Pardis. Tirnan was a magnificent place, a wild land of abundance, teeming with innumerable species of creatures, great and small. They all lived peacefully together. The land was adorned with rivers, lakes, and great forests, mountain ranges, lush meadows, and fertile plains. To the west, bordering the lofty Alaya Mountains, lay the great realm of Assuk, the largest of the three realms. It was the most inhabited and beautiful realm, a land of opulent gardens, magnificently adorned. In the midst of Assuk, along the shores of the river, lay Anima, the home for all who lived in Assuk. South of Assuk, from the Telohm Mountains to the Great Sea was Shuk, a realm of mystery. It was the most rugged and uninhabited of all.

Pardis was a place where the principles of an idyllic world ruled in the hearts of every citizen. The Supreme Virtues were the guiding doctrines everyone lived by, without enforcement or demand. Of these, love, kindness, and humility were of the highest esteem. It was a place where there was no need, hunger, or poverty, where every citizen lived without guile or greed or want or corruption, life flourished.

Living in Pardis were the Theoscians, the Carascians, and the kerolus, all immortals of celestial origins. Of the Theoscians were Eloh, Alethia, and Shu. They were supreme and possessed absolute authority, though they had little use for such power. More than anyone else, the Theoscians understood and had command over the universe and the elements that made everything, seen and unseen. Above all else, the Theoscians possessed the force or essence of life, called the Elohan Essentia, which gave every living thing the fullness of life.

Eloh, the father of the Theoscians and of Pardis, could have had a kingdom, and sat as a ruler, but condescended to live as a husbandman, working the gardens, meadows, and forests of Assuk and living without distinction among all who inhabited Pardis. He was a friend to all.

Alethia, the daughter of Eloh, was beautiful, gracious, and above all else, wise. She, like Eloh, was humble, and yet, she was also strong. Shu was the son of Eloh. He had great compassion and kindness. He was especially loved by the kerolus who treated him as a brother. Together, the Theoscians gave life to all the living things that inhabited Pardis.

The kerolus were beautiful, giant, winged creatures, aerial guards, and keepers of the high places of the realm. They were skilled with bow and spear, capable with the sword, and some possessed magic powers. They were loyal friends, dedicated to Eloh and the virtues of Pardis. Of all who lived in Pardis, the kerolus numbered the most.

The Carascians were but two, Amik and Livia. They were the descendants of an ancient clan of mortals called the Cementars who perished in the high mountains save two, Amaya and Loani, both with child. They were the mothers of Amik and Livia. Shortly after giving birth, Amaya and Loani died. Amik and Livia were raised by the Theoscians who gave them immortality to honor their mothers and their people who were lost forever. Amik and Livia were humble but magnificent in appearance. They worked in the gardens of Assuk and became even more gifted in husbandry than the Theoscians. They nurtured their gardens, and the forests and meadows of Assuk, making them grand gems of perfection and beauty set against the backdrop of snow-covered mountains and unyielding forests.

Eloh decided to give the realm of Tirnan to Amik and Livia for their home, a place to have a family, and multiply. More than just living in Tirnan, Amik was given dominion over it, and it would be where he and his descendants would live forever. And so, it happened that Amik took Livia to be his wife and they journeyed to Tirnan. But not all was well in Pardis, for a strange wind began to blow throughout the realm.

There were three great arch-kerolus, who were chief among the kerolus clans. The first was Attar, the most beautiful. He was the chief musician and skilled in the magics. Remmel was the most powerful. He was faithful in service and friendship to Eloh.

Sargel was kind and gentle and gifted with visions. All three arch-kerolus were powerful, fearless, and noble, distinguished as the protectors of Pardis. All the kerolus clans had descended from the celestial realm of the stars ages before. They were creatures of magnificent form and great power yet had hearts like children, filled with loyalty, love, and genuine innocence.

There was one among the kerolus who became jealous. Attar opened the door of his heart to envy and became enraged over the gift of Tirnan and the Kleid o'Miht given to Amik. As the jealousy grew, so too did his vanity. Like a malignancy, the darkness spread to all parts of his being until Attar, a creature of light, from the stars, became a beast, corrupt and vile.

Attar secretly conjured dark magic to cast a spell over the waters of Eon, a place sacred to the kerolus. When they entered the waters to bathe, they were infected by the malice of Attar. Their hearts darkened with hatred and jealousy toward Amik and Eloh. The power of the spell and of their hatred began to change their physical form, making them deformed and grotesque. Worst of all, their beautiful wings shriveled and died, so they could no longer fly. All that was left were hideous stubs of protruding bone. Every kerolus who entered the poisoned waters, either by choice or by force, was subjugated under the will and power of Attar to become his slave.

Attar prepared his amassing horde of fallen kerolus to overthrow Eloh, take the Kleid o'Miht, and rule not only Tirnan but the whole realm of Pardis. To be sure of victory, he created another army of horrid, dark creatures called dakoons. Part fallen kerolus, part iron, they were giant flying beasts with grotesque black wings, framed in metal, and forged to their bodies through fire and sorcery. The wing frames were laid over with the skins of murdered kerolus who had tried resisting Attar and his cruel chiefs. The wings, though wrought of iron, were transformed into living appendages through blood and sorcery. The dakoons had heads like a crocodile with great teeth. Their hands and feet had only two long, sharp, hooked talons made of steel. Their skin was thick, rough, heavily scaled, and virtually impenetrable, and Attar gave them fire in their breath which they could spew upon their enemies. The transformation inflicted such excruciating pain and agony, it deepened their hostility and made every dakoon brutal, vicious, cruel, and merciless.

As Attar prepared to invade, Sargel had a vision. In it, he saw a black shadow and mighty black beasts flying out of the shadow, and on one of the beasts rode a kerolus. To Sargel, it was clear the vision was an omen of danger and the peace of Pardis, strong for more than a thousand millennia, was now in peril. Sargel flew to Eloh to warn him of the approaching danger. Eloh sent Sargel to sound the Horn of Shukeer, which called for the assembly of all kerolus.

When Sargel blew the giant stone horn, its deep, bellowing voice echoed into the valleys of Assuk and Tirnan, reaching into all parts of Pardis. From every corner, the kerolus army flew to Anima, appearing in the sky like an innumerable array of comets with long white tails of light trailing far behind each.

Far in the distance, in the high meadows of the Alaya Mountains, the moaning call of the horn approached Eon. Hypnotic, paralyzing, demanding, the great horn's call descended like a mighty hammer on the horde of those who had fallen prey to the spell of Attar. Every eye, ear, and mind turned to the sound, and for a time, every kerolus that had gathered with Attar stood in astonishment. Their instinct was to follow the call, but they were no longer free to go.

Even Attar felt the dogged authority of the horn's call. Seeing the power of Shukeer, he yelled out to his army. He boasted of his greatness and the power of the spell, declaring that the fallen kerolus would never again submit to the horn. He gave them a new name, a name which freed them from all former associations. They were gallues and they were to answer to no other master or to no other voice than his. The power of the horn was broken; it could no longer command them. They forgot everything they had ever known of their life as kerolus.

It was a kerolus named Jaroh who first saw the army of Attar advancing through the mountains and delivered the news to Alethia. If there had been any doubt, there was none left. With great sorrow, the Theoscians called upon the kerolus to form four armies that would surround and cut off the army of Attar. The four armies would engage the enemy in the Alaya mountains near Mount Ducapita. Remmel gathered a thousand legions of kerolus and set out to the west. Sargel gathered five-hundred legions and began the journey to Tirnan from the south along the river Aion. Eloh and Shu took two-hundred legions to the north and a fourth army stayed in Anima under the command of Alethia. Eloh also sent a small company of kerolus to protect Amik and Livia and the Kleid o'Miht.

Because timing and surprise were so critical, each of the armies was forced to travel on foot, for to take flight in such numbers would surely arouse suspicion, and they were certain that Attar did not know that they knew what he was up to. With speed and stealth, the four armies of Pardis clandestinely advanced toward the Alaya Mountains.

Jaroh was called upon to find and retrieve the Horn of War. Kept in a cave deep in the Impetus Mountains, the ancient Horn of War was like no other weapon ever made. Its voice was fierce and violent. It awakened unseen forces of the wind and the earth and the seas. Its power was indiscriminate and the forces it unleashed irrevocable. Jaroh was to take the horn to the summit of Mount Ducapita and sound it when he saw the army of Attar. He was to blow the horn long and loud with all his might until Attar's army was defeated.

After finding the horn, Jaroh traveled to where Attar and his army were assembled near the base of Mount Ducapita. He could see the black dakoons, thousands of them, and then he saw Attar sitting upon one of them. He knew then that it was time. Jaroh raised the horn into the air, put it to his mouth and began to blow with all his might. The twisted ivory and bone tusks of an ancient leviathan cried out a mysterious and haunting call with a piercing, sharp inflection, reverberating from the round, twin mouths of the instrument. Bellowing from one tusk and echoed by the other, the deep guttural voice of the horn blasted a swelling angry roar, *"WAR, WAR, WAR,"*. The terrifying call grew stronger and louder and, like an army, it marched throughout the skies and then descended upon the realm.

All the armies of Eloh rose up in flight. Thousands upon thousands of kerolus opened their wings and rose into the air, piercing the sky as if a great bow had been drawn, and a hundred thousand arrows were launched at once.

Soaring through the skies like great bursts of light, the flight of the kerolus was awe-inspiring, and yet, at that moment, to those who were the enemies of Pardis, their flight appeared like an immeasurable ball of fire and light composed of a million stars all descending at once. With spears in one hand and a sword in the other, the legions of Pardis descended with singular intent. The overwhelming force of the kerolus army combined with the power of the horn drove the army of Attar to react more like a band of rebels than an organized military unit.

When Attar saw it, he opened his black wings, and rose up into the sky, followed by the elite legion of winged dakoons. As the dakoons took flight, they filled the sky like a cloud of black crows. They flew brazenly into the aerial armies of the kerolus, spitting fire and gnashing at their enemies with their taloned feet. The dakoons fought savagely, sending kerolus after kerolus plunging to the ground. With a great thunderous noise, the clash of the aerial armies combined with the bellowing cries of the Horn of War began to cause the ground to shake and the mountains to crumble. All creation was embroiled in battle. Landslides and avalanches sent debris into the valleys. The waters of the Great Sea became violent, tossing great waves against the shores of Pardis. Dark clouds loosed frightful arrays of lightning and thunder, and a great shower of rain, driven by savage winds, began pouring from the heavens.

For six days and nights, the fight raged on. While the battle in the sky exploded, the realm of Pardis erupted in fire and lava as the mountains let go of their secret molten rivers. Fire and smoke, earthquakes, and floods threatened every part of Pardis as the whole of creation groaned in protest. The rivers began to overflow and the snow that covered the tops of the mountains melted from the heat of the battle and the echoes of the Horn of War. A great chasm appeared along the border of the Alaya Mountains. Like a garment being ripped in two, the land of Assuk pulled away from the Great Mountains, while at the same time, a coursing breach appeared south of the Aion River that flowed through Assuk. The Telohm Mountains started to shake, and the lower peaks crumbled; falling into the opening void of the crevasse. The Impastious Gorge that separated the realm of Tirnan from Shuk opened more deeply, swallowing the Aion River from the Zemorthra Falls to the sea.

Pardis was breaking apart, crushed under the weight of a struggle so great that no natural or physical thing would be untouched or unchanged.

The forces of Attar could not beat the legions of Pardis. One by one, the dakoons fell to the ground, consumed in balls of fire from their own breath like meteors, pummeling the world below. The gallues were hunted by the kerolus armies, captured and bound, if not destroyed.

Finally, Remmel rose to defeat Attar. He charged at Attar with tornadic force. The two great warriors crashed into battle, sword to sword and spear to spear, fighting to the death. Savage and violent was the struggle as

Remmel slowly overpowered Attar. Attar escaped into the upper heavens, but Remmel pursued and soon overtook him. With his great spear, Remmel wounded Attar, piercing him through his side. Remmel took his sword and went to finish the struggle with one final blow, but Attar blocked it. Again and again, Attar deflected Remmel's blows. Finally, Remmel flew, with great speed, straight at Attar, colliding with him. The two warriors fell from the sky like a meteor, a fiery ball of contention, descending at supersonic speed. Falling in sight of all the forces of the remaining armies, they wrestled and fought hand- to-hand until, with a great thunderous impact, they crashed into the base of Mount Ducapita.

The force of their descent and concussion was so great that it bore a great chasm into the rock, melting stone and ore and sending huge billows of smoke and ash into the sky. The fury of their struggle shook every part of Tirnan. Sending swells of shock waves through the ground and a sonic explosion into the air, the collision magnified the effects of the battle on the world of Pardis. Then the realm of Shuk broke away and began to spin into open space leaving a debris field of rocks and earth in its wake.

Tirnan, with a great convulsion, cracking and breaking away was pushed away from Assuk dragging with it, all the armies on the ground. The ground shook and quaked and the mountains erupted in fire as ancient volcanoes discharged hot molten rock and ore into the skies above. Each of the three realms continued to move further and further away from the others.

Broken and desolate, their lands were ravaged. The gardens of Assuk had fallen and the life and beauty of Pardis vanished away.

Seeing the magnitude of the devastation that the battle had caused to the lands of Pardis, Eloh ordered Jaroh to cease blowing the Horn. Attar, who lay wounded and defeated in the deep cavernous pit at the base of Mount Ducapita, was taken captive. Remmel wasted no time; he took molten rock and iron from the pit and forged impregnable chains and shackles, binding Attar to the walls of the pit. Eloh commanded that all the living and bound gallues be brought to the pit where they were held captive with Attar. Eloh took Attar's power and strength, leaving him with only his wit. Attar and his armies were utterly defeated.

A breathless hush fell over the three worlds. There was no celebration, no rejoicing, and while the armies of Pardis were victorious, their victory felt hollow and empty. For many months, there would be no song of the songbirds, no sweet aroma of the flowers, no laughter, no comfort, no satisfaction to either the conquerors or the conquered.

Sargel and Remmel forged enormous heavy iron gates, which they hung at the entrance of the pit deep in the mountain. Bound in the core of Tirnan, the rabble was sentenced to endless darkness. There were no guards or watches over the entrance of the pit, for the Gates of Abyssus and the iron chains for which there was only one key, would never fail to hold their captives.

Amik was given power and authority over Attar and the fallen gallues. Only he could loosen their shackles and open the iron gates for they were subject to the Kleid o'Miht. Eloh warned Amik to never open the pit, to never undo the shackles, and to keep the Kleid o'Miht safe for it held the power to rule over the realm of Tirnan. If it ever fell into the wrong hands, the realm would fall subject to its bearer.

For many ages, the Three Worlds remained scarred and broken from the catastrophe of the war, but over time, eons of time, the natural elements: the sun, the moons, the waters of the seas and the rivers and streams, the trees and flowers, soil and rocks, rain and snow, season upon season, healed the scars of the three worlds; they became whole again. Never would they be as opulent and grand as they once were, and for each realm, there would remain wastelands, vast deserts where no life would grow, dead seas, dried riverbeds, seasons without rain or with too much rain. The balance of Pardis, its perfection and beauty, had fallen; it carried the wounds of the war without repair.

Many seasons passed before the ruin of Amik which brought death to the Carascians. When Amik died, his body was laid to rest deep in the Telohm Mountains, in the Cave of Pelah, in the realm of Shuk. Many millennia passed until the pit and its darkness was forgotten, and the war was forgotten. Eventually, the descendants of Amik forgot him and Pardis. Eloh and the great war passed into legend and myth. The Kleid o'Miht and its power were hidden away in the darkness, lest it be found and all that had been done, be undone. Age passed into age, season into season until all the relics of Pardis were nothing but a myth, a faint memory carried on the wind and whispered in the song of the songbirds. Mount Ducapita, where the Gates of Abyssus hung, where the war began and the war ended, lost its name, forgotten through the ages, yet remaining, to this day, a sacred place, a forbidden mountain, where the secrets of Pardis are buried. Piercing the sky like the head of an arrow, it stood alone for generations until descendants of Amik found it again and gave it a new name. It is there,

Machapuchare, where the truth of the legend can be found.

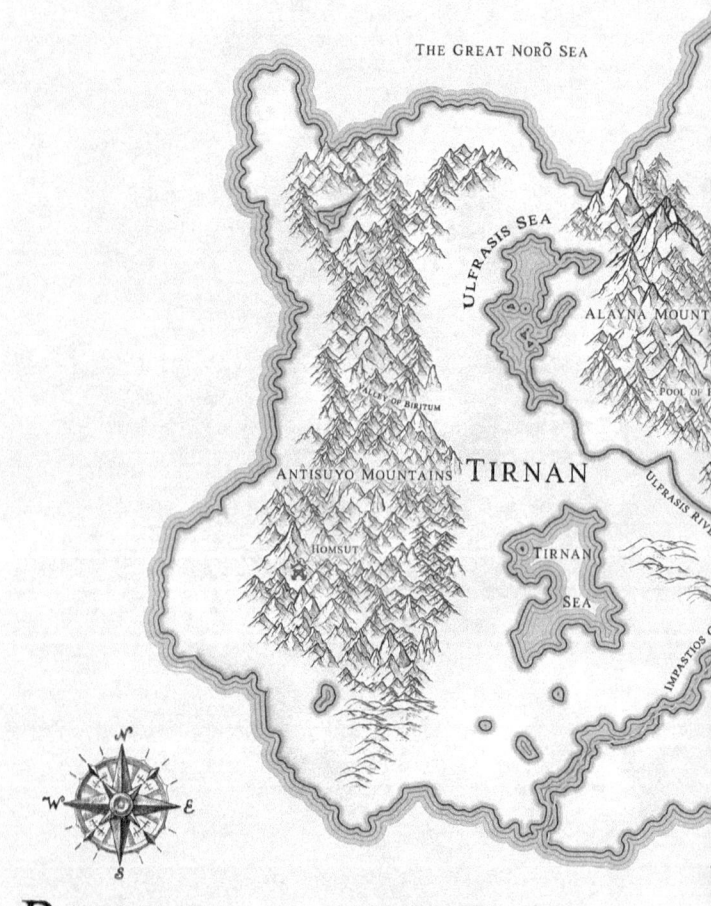

THE GREAT NORŌ SEA

ULFRASIS SEA

ALAYNA MOUNTA

VALLEY OF BIRITUM

POOL OF E

ANTISUYO MOUNTAINS TIRNAN

ULFRASIS RIVER

HOMSUT

TIRNAN
SEA

IMPASTIOS G

PARDIS

Chapter I
The Fall

"Daniel! Daniel!"

Had Ross's frantic calls been shouted anywhere else, they would surely have been heard, for the force and volume of them was great enough, but in a storm at nearly twenty-two thousand feet, they were immediately swallowed by the incessant, savage wind, which proved to be impartial to his immediate and desperate plight. Gust after gust, like waves breaking upon the seashore, the wind persisted, gnawing and biting at every inch of his exposed skin as he clung desperately to the side of the mountain. Alone and panicked on a narrow ledge near the summit of Ama Dablam, he was stalled by indecision. All he knew to do was call out and wait until he heard a reply, but fear encroached upon his mind and made him doubt.

"Daniel!" Ross yelled out repeatedly, while inwardly pleading, *Come on, damn it!*

Answer! You've got to be down there. Please!

He was angry with himself for not standing up to Daniel, for not taking the time to backtrack to a safer route. There had been so many times before, when Daniel, in his enthusiasm and ambition, led them into difficulty and Ross had gone along with him. They had veered off-course and descended to a blind ledge, hurried by the blinding conditions on the mountain and the impending night. Because of the engulfing storm, it was impossible to know how far off-course they were or to where on the dangerous mountain they had strayed.

"Why? Damn you! Why wouldn't you listen to me? Why?" Ross helplessly muttered.

Ross had dissented, but Daniel could not be persuaded; he did not want to climb back up.

Daniel insisted that it would save time. He argued that even if they did get back up, they would not be able to find their route in the blowing snow. Of course, it had made a degree of sense to Ross, but to him, it had seemed smarter to return. Daniel would not have continued without him; he would have turned around if Ross had demanded, Ross knew that, but sometimes he trusted Daniel's confidence more than he did his own. Except this time, unlike the times before when all turned out well, Ross faced a fear too fatal, too final, and his often-reticent sensibilities could not protect him from the squall of emotions rushing through his mind.

"Daniel!" He called again; this time, in defiance of the consumptive tumult. His voice was louder and stronger than before, yet there was still no reply or, if there was, the wind had swallowed it up. Rage rushed through the corridors of his mind like a wild beast, while at the same time, he could feel the cold breath of fear pushing deeper into his thoughts with each passing moment Daniel, his closest friend, was still missing.

It happened so quickly, so unexpectedly. Only moments before, a period that felt like a few seconds, Ross had heard Daniel shout, then the rope pulled tight on Ross's harness nearly pulling him away from the ledge and down the blind face of the mountain. Ross's footing had been rescued by a protruding section of stone on the narrow ledge. They had acted foolishly and hastily. Rather than set a proper belay anchor, they had trusted in their skill to descend roped together, and, as often is the case when caution is discharged by brashness, something unexpected and unwanted had happened. Ross feared that he would not be able to hold onto the ledge. Then, as quickly as the rope had tightened, it suddenly became limp and weightless, as if it had snapped or a piece of their gear had failed. Ross fell back against the wall of stone that extended up from the ledge. His immediate reaction was to pull frantically on the rope. For a few feet, it came with no resistance, as if unleashed; then it stopped. The rope became tight and refused to yield to his persistent pulling. It did not make any sense to him that the rope had gone slack but could not be retrieved. He looked over the edge into the white swirling fray below and screamed out as loud as he could, "Daniel! Daniel!" Ross pulled the rope again, but just as before, the rope would not yield.

Three hundred feet below fastened to the face of the mountain by a frozen grip, Daniel was pulled from his unconscious state by the robust wrenching of the rope that was still connected to his harness. At first, Daniel had no idea what had happened or even where he was. Only instinct and experience kept him from letting go of the frozen grip his hands had on the wall. As well, his boots were toed into the cracks of the mountain face, which, remarkably, had kept him attached to the wall. Slowly, Daniel's mind began to unpack the memory of where he was and what had happened. At the moment Daniel had taken purchase of the wall, a slab of rock and ice just above him, had peeled off the wall and fallen. As it came loose, Daniel had heard it and had looked up just in time to see the ice and rock falling straight toward him. He had pulled himself as close to the wall as he could but not before a large slab of ice crashed against his helmet. As it continued to fall, the ice snagged the rope and began pulling both climbers down the face with it. Inexplicably, the slab of ice broke free of the rope and fell several thousand feet. The force of the blow on his helmet was so powerful that Daniel had lost consciousness, though for only a few moments.

Blood ran down the bridge of Daniel's nose and dripped onto the stone wall. He cried out, "Ross! Ross!" but there was no answer. Still dazed, Daniel climbed a short distance up the wall, but he could still feel the rope pulling him, knocking him off balance. He suddenly remembered his radio was in his breast pocket, but he was unsure of his grip on the wall and needed to find a safer place to be able to free-up one of his hands. Daniel felt around the rock to find a place to set an anchor and tie-off.

Meanwhile, Ross was growing increasingly frantic. His mind flashed hysterically through a series of vivid memories as though they were super 8 movies playing on a white screen in his mind. The moment, though the span of a breath, felt as though time had stopped, and the raging of elements and emotions around and in him had been interrupted as if paused. He saw himself and Daniel as young boys, playing together in the front yard of Daniel's house. He then saw them as young men, chasing the thrill of their first face climb near their home. It was not anything massive or even remarkable for that matter, but it was their first attempt at a granite hill that could have killed them. Most vivid of the reels playing in his mind was the memory of an hour earlier, when they had stood triumphantly at the summit with their hands raised. Victorious, after two years of planning and raising money for the climb, they had finally succeeded. Now, only a couple of pitches below the top, something had gone terribly wrong and Daniel had vanished.

It is well known that a frenzied mind is an illogical and undisciplined mind, a mind incapable of making sound or reasonable assessments or decisions. The hysteria of fear freezes the thought process keeping it from functioning in a normal manner. For Ross, who was most often cautious and sound in reason, the fear of the moment had made him more like a mad man, irrational and neurotic. Eventually, he began to calm down. Now, whether it was due to a state of shock setting in, or of acute lucidity brought on by the mind's resignation to the worst of possibilities, it is hard to say, but for whatever reason, Ross finally realized he still had his radio. Hoping that Daniel would have his, he grabbed it and pressed the *PTT* button. He screamed desperately into the radio as the snow, driven by the relentless fifty miles per hour winds, stabbed at his cheeks, "Daniel! Daniel, are you there? Come back. Are you there? Damn it!

Where are you? Come in, please!" Ross hit the radio with his gloved fist, frustrated and unsure if it was working, "What's wrong with this fucking thing? Damn it! Daniel!" he screamed into the radio. Ross felt a sinking feeling in his gut. Tears began to roll down his face; before falling from his cheeks, they froze to his face. Daniel was his only friend. He could not be gone. The clarity of thought did not last for long; Ross's emotions quickly overwhelmed him again.

"Shit! Shit, you fucking idiot! Why? Why?"

Then, just as Ross was about to smash the radio against the rocks in a fit of rage, the voice of Daniel came over the radio. "Ross, do you read me, man? Hey Ross, are you there?"

Ross's hands were shaking, not from the cold or the wind, but from the sudden and unrestrained rush of adrenaline that can only be explained as relief. He fumbled with the radio for a moment and then wailed as tears poured from his eyes.

"Ross! It's Daniel! Are you there?"

Ross yelled back into the radio, "Daniel! Daniel! I hear you, man. Are you alright?"

"Yeah, I'm ok. I just about lost it, man. Whew! What a rush . . . gotta say!" Daniel's voice came across the radio as playful and unaffected, with not even a hint of the terror that Ross had felt in those brief moments. Before they could say anything more, the sound of the wind became even more deafening, to the point of causing pain, making it hard for either of them to hear anything.

"What? I can't hear you. Where are you?"

"Ross, I can't hear you. Don't move. I'll try to get back up to you. Can you take up the slack?" I'm coming up. Don't move!"

Though Ross could not hear much of what Daniel had said, he did hear the words, "Don't move". Ross quickly anchored himself to the face of the mountain and, though he could not hear instructions from Daniel, he instinctively took up the slack in the rope and belayed Daniel. While he sat on the ledge, he shook uncontrollably. The fear of being pulled off the ledge and losing his friend, coupled with the falling mercury and gusting wind, was more than his body could master. He felt weak and emotional. He took in a deep, cleansing breath, but it did little to relieve the convulsive shaking. As he waited for Daniel, he was unaware of the wind's sudden abatement or of the sun's rays that were beginning to reach across the sky as shadows crept incessantly upon the landscape. The bright, golden orb hung silently over the rugged horizon as if staring at him, waiting for him to turn and acknowledge its slow descent, just like they were two neighbors passing each other on a sidewalk. Ross never looked, and the sun set without notice, leaving behind only the fading alpenglow of a dying day to illuminate the empty sky above.

Slowly and methodically, Ross drew the rope through his belay device. Occasionally, he would draw too much rope and it would become taught, at which point Daniel would tug back. "Ross." Daniel's voice carried to Ross's ears, though at first, Ross did not acknowledge it.

"Ross, give me some rope."

Ross lifted his head and realized the wind had stopped and Daniel was getting close.

"Daniel!" Ross shouted.

"Hey, I'm almost there. Give me a little rope, man."

Ross let out some rope. Finally, Daniel reached over the ledge and found a crack in the rock near Ross's foothold which he could grip. Ross steadily kept his hand on the rope and waited for Daniel to clear the edge safely.

Tears froze on Ross's cheeks as he felt the rush of relief course through his body. He suddenly felt the harshness of the biting cold. He looked at Daniel who was, as usual, smiling, even with a bloody face. His wide, happy, ever-mischievous eyes reassured Ross that everything was alright.

"Man, that was awesome fun! Aye?" Daniel declared in an almost casual, undisturbed manner as if nothing dangerous had happened while hiding the fact that he had seriously been shaken.

"Are you mad?! You idiot! What the hell did you think you were doing?" Ross erupted angrily.

Daniel was known for his casual, almost carefree demeanor. He never took anything too seriously, and this was especially true during climbing. Ross, more cautious, felt that Daniel often took chances that were far too risky and reckless.

"What? I had it all under control!" Daniel exclaimed.

"Oh, bullshit!" Ross glared at Daniel, like a lion about to attack its prey. "You're an asshole sometimes, Daniel. Damn it! I just about pissed my pants. I thought that you were gone. . . fallen off the fucking mountain . . . thought you were dead, damn it! And you damned near pulled me down with you!"

"You worry too much, man. Calm down! We're OK. Everything is good."

Ross could see a glint in Daniel's eye; it was a look he had seen before, a look that made Ross unable to hold on to his anger or fear. Daniel had a way of disarming people and none more than Ross. Ross wanted to be angry, yet all he could do was close his eyes, shake his head, and chuckle. Though he tried, he could not prevent laughter from erupting from his smile. They embraced and laughed without reason until their eyes were filled with tears and their hearts had forgotten the terror. Sometimes close friends have a way of dealing with things, serious and dangerous things, that do not require words or explanations, apologies, or excuses. They find, between themselves, forgiveness without confession, reconciliation without the standard due process required by less intimate acquaintances. Daniel put his hand on Ross's cheek. "Thanks, Ross. You really came through."

As sincere as Daniel was, there was, in his eye, a sparkle, a glint of mystery that Ross could not ignore. Ross patted Daniel on the head and shook his own head insincerely.

"What are you thinking? You get that ridiculous look on your face every time you come up with some crazy scheme."

Before either of them had taken even a moment to process all that had just happened and all that could have happened, it became obvious to Ross that Daniel was making plans for their next misadventure. Ross shook his head in disbelief, pulled a headlamp from his bag, and affixed it to his helmet. "Crazy, huh? Well, it was my crazy scheming that got us here. Remember? You thought we would never have the chance and yet . . . We did it!"

"Yeah! We did. But we're not off this fucking mountain just yet, and you're making plans for something new. What's going through your head now? Everest?"

"Nah. Everyone climbs Everest. What about something no one's ever done?"

Ross looked at Daniel and shook his head. "No, no, no. You're still thinking about what that crazy old man said, aren't you?"

"Come on, Ross, think about it, to climb a forbidden mountain, one that no one's climbed before, one that's shrouded in mystery and legend!"

"You know, it's just another mountain. The only reason it's never been climbed is because it's illegal. It has nothing to do with some stupid legend about gods, ancient wars, some ancient artifact thing, and shit like that and you know it."

"So, you *were* listening. Ha! I knew it. Come on! You never know. It could be true and man, if it is, wouldn't that be so cool? We could climb a mountain that's forbidden and discover the secret of the gods!"

"Gods? There are no gods! You're just trying to find an explanation for why it's forbidden, just like that old man. Did you see how all those other people looked at him while he was talking? The guy's a fool and you're a fool for listening to him."

"Maybe, but you know you wanna climb it, legend or not."

"I'll think about it, after we get back home. Right now, we need to get off this mountain."

Daniel looked at Ross and smiled. He knew the hook was set and with only a little more time and convincing, he and Ross would be headed to the forbidden summit of Machapuchare.

The sun had fully set, so their way to camp in the dark would be several hours of a difficult, highly technical descent. Ross and Daniel made a few adjustments to their gear and set to the task of getting off the enormous slab of granite.

The terminal at the airport was eerily quiet as Ross, with his girlfriend, Eve, in tow, rushed toward the gate to catch the last flight of the day to Kathmandu. It had been over three years since Ross had been there. He had spent the last three days in the oppressively congested city of Calcutta, making final preparations and purchasing the gear needed for their climb; he felt anxious to escape to the mountains.

Eve's senses were accosted by the converging array of diversities that represented the cities and cultures of India. Racing through the modern metropolitan airport felt like a world in contrast to the noise and chaos of the one outside. It was for her a subtle reprieve from the foreign clamor. She raced ahead of Ross and yelled as she passed him, "See ya! Wouldn't wanna be ya! Ha-ha!"

Ross, who was fixated on the gate markers, was surprised and slow to react. "Hey, Eve! Slow down. Come on!"

They were looking forward to the end of airports and baggage transfers, tickets, and boarding passes. After all the commercial travel, the weeks to follow of hiking and climbing in the legendary Himalayan Mountains were, in themselves, a welcome and noteworthy reward. To the surprise of many of their friends, who had expected them to go for the summit of Everest, Ross and Eve were going to do some hiking and exploring and maybe a few lesser summits along the way. This, they said, was for Eve's benefit, as she had no experience of climbing in the Himalayas. However, they had lied, at least in part, for there was something they had not told anyone. The undisclosed purpose of their trip to Nepal was to do something Ross and Daniel had talked about many times since their return from Ama Dablam. Secretly, Ross and Eve had arranged to climb the forbidden peak, Machapuchare.

Machapuchare, though a respectable summit, at 22,943 feet, was, by Himalayan standards, a lesser summit. It was not ranked even among the highest 100 peaks in the world. However, the fact that it was officially unclimbed and certainly a challenge with its sharp profile, steep ascents, and sheer face, would have made it a jewel for any climber, especially if they could have earned the moniker of the first to summit. Eve had never met Daniel, though she knew the power of his friendship with Ross. She knew this trip was meant to be for the two of them and that she was, more or less, a substitution, though Ross would have never used that word. Eve never wanted, in any way, to compete with a friendship so deeply rooted in Ross's past.

Ross and Daniel had grown up together. They were nearly inseparable as boys, living next door to each other. Daniel's family was an average, middle-class family. Mitch, Daniel's dad, worked a nine-to-five day. He came home every night for dinner. He mowed his grass on the weekend, usually on Saturday, and was for the most part, as ordinary as anyone might expect a suburban father and husband to be. Meredith, Daniel's mother, taught second grade at the elementary school and loved to cook, shop, and do family things when she was home. During the summer, she spent many of her days in the yard nurturing her flowers. She had a prodigious array of wild mountain flowers which were arranged in such a manner as to suggest there was no plan whatsoever.

Ross's family, on the other hand, could not have been more different. Ross was only four when his father, Norman Blair, abandoned him, his little sister, and their mother. Ross still had memories of the night his father left, memories that often came to him in his dreams, memories he would have rather not remembered. His mother, Julie, had never adjusted well to being alone. Though Norman was abusive and spent most of the time either away working or high, Julie missed having a man in her life and had since been in several relationships with men whom she would meet at the bar where she worked nights. None of these relationships ever lasted long. Many of the men were brutish drunks, like Norman, or else interested in nothing more than one- night stands. The abuse and the loneliness were like competing demons, taunting her with impossible choices, so she turned to vice as a distraction to anesthetize the emotional pain and to help her forget. There were many times when Ross had found his mother either crying inconsolably or passed out on the living room floor.

Because of her worsening habit and accompanying depression, Julie often slept all day, leaving Ross and his younger sister, Tiffany, to fend for themselves. When she was not sleeping, she was usually intoxicated and unfit to care for them. It had proved to be a fortuitous twist of fate that no one had ever notified the authorities of their situation, for if they had, Ross would never have met Daniel or his family. It never occurred to Daniel's family to report Julie. They just felt compelled to help in the only way they knew, by taking care of Ross and Tiffany as if they were their own. The kids spent most of their days hanging out at the Yager's house. They ate meals, went wherever the Yagers went, and essentially lived as members of the family. It cannot be said, however, that it all ended well.

Daniel never seemed bothered by the presence of honorary siblings. Instead, it made him feel more connected to his own family and less alone. He had already known Ross from school and they rode the bus together. In fact, it was Daniel who had first told his mother about the situation at Ross's house. He had begged her to help them. Ross and Tiffany only went home when Julie had called asking about the children or had come to the house to collect them. This had become less and less as time passed.

As far back as Ross and Daniel could remember, climbing had been integral to their lives and relationship. As young, energetic boys, it had been their emancipation, a rite of passage, the first real adventure that had freed them from the restraints and confinement that all young boys seek to escape. It was the summer of their sixth-grade year when Daniel's father, Mitch took them to a climbing area called Flatirons, which was west of where they lived in Boulder, Colorado. Mitch had been a rock climber when he was young and had thought the boys would enjoy the adventure and challenge of the sport. He could not have foretold the overarching effect of such a seemingly inconsequential introduction or have predicted how influential it would be on their emerging adolescence. From that day until the end of summer, the boys made every effort, as often as it had been possible, to climb the rocks. Year after year during summer breaks, holidays, and weekends, the two spent every moment honing their skills and dreaming of climbing adventures in faraway places. Consequently, in those early days, they were shaped in character, idealism, and strength by the hard, impervious stone. They were also shaped by several meaningful, yet contextually benign events that occurred in the few years that followed. Some of these events were so memorable that they became the stories remembered and shared around the campfires and hanging camps of their climbing excursions.

As time passed and because of work and a busy schedule, Mitch stopped taking the boys to the Flatirons, so it was up to them to find their own transportation. Ross and Daniel often bummed a ride from a retired mechanic named Joe, who lived just a few houses away. The boys called him Ol' Joe. Ol' Joe was a spry, lonely old man with a round congenial face and short gray hair, though it was hard to see because he always wore a ball cap. He was always cracking a joke of some kind. He spent most of his summer days fishing and did not mind letting the boys ride along, nor did he mind going just a little bit out of his way to take them to their trailhead. The boys got a kick out of him and his jokes and all the stories he loved to tell. Each summer it was the same; from day to day, the boys would beg a ride from whomever they could, mostly from Ol' Joe, and head to the trailhead with their growing assortment of antiquated and often abused climbing gear, then spend the days climbing as many routes as possible. There were a couple of times when they found themselves having to walk the long route home because everyone else had left before they had finished. This happened only twice and was never forgotten by either of them. The first time they walked home, it was after dark, and when they finally arrived at the house, Daniel's mother was crying and hysterical, just short of calling the police. All her fears of the boys falling to their deaths, had come true in her mind. When Daniel and Ross saw it, they felt so guilty and expressed such remorse that their contrition swayed her from the resolve to never let them climb again. She let them go out the very next day. However, the second time, only two weeks later, would leave a much deeper impression upon their carefree and thoughtless young minds.

As they saw it, the long walk home should have been enough of a consequence for them being late. And of course, as they saw things, Daniel's mother would surely have forgotten about the first incident by then, or so they believed. Daniel fully expected to enter the house and see his crying mother so greatly relieved by their safe arrival, suddenly smile and grab them and kiss them both. To their surprise and considerable consternation, they came instead, face to face with one of the greatest terrors that any young man might ever face, the unappeasable fury of an utterly distraught mother. Daniel's mother, an otherwise patient and amiable woman, was no less angry than relieved at the sight of their casual entrance through the door. On this occasion, it was immediately apparent to Daniel that she was not crying, nor embraceable. She had a switch in her hand and her knuckles were white from the grip she had on it. She was red-eyed and shaking uncontrollably. She looked at the boys; her jaw was clenched so tight that the muscles in her face were quivering. Daniel stopped in his tracks and put out his arm to stop Ross from walking past him. He had never seen his mother in such a state, though it became immediately apparent to him that to step one step closer would be like entering the den of a distempered lion.

"Where have you been?" Her voice was nothing like the voice they were accustomed to; it was large, loud, and angry and had a growling resonance to it that sounded more like an animal than a human. They, of course, did not understand the reason for her anger. To them, she was just mad because they were late for supper again.

"We were just climbing and well, everyone else left, Mom. We didn't have a ride."

"What did I tell you, Daniel, the last time, huh?"

Meredith was wearing an old flannel shirt and a pair of dirty jean shorts. She had been working in the yard until it had become clear to her that the boys were once again tardy. She and Mitch had driven the roads that led to the trailhead and Mitch had walked the paths around the area yelling out for the boys. They had driven back to the house expecting to see the boys somewhere along the route, but there had been no sign of them. The boys, in their thoughtless youth, had not stuck to the roads and highways leading to and from the trailhead; they had cut across the open fields and through yards trying to shorten the distance. There was no doubt that at some point during the search, the Yagers had passed near the boys, which added to Meredith's frustration. All of it, the fear, the searching, the darkness, the danger of the rocks, their inconsiderate and thoughtless behavior, swirled into a massive storm of emotion and fear leading to an inevitable climax in the Yager's living room. Meredith slowly walked toward the boys, unconsciously slapping the switch against her bare leg. Each swish of the switch ended with a sudden, resounding slap, and each slap left behind it a long red mark on her leg. Daniel looked at her, first at her eyes, and then at the welts on her legs from the switch. He began to cry and at the same time tried to explain as he slowly stepped backward, Ross moving in synchrony behind him. "But, Mom, it wasn't our fault."

His feigning innocence acted only to impugn any possible defense that might have been offered. She became even angrier. "Oh! Really? And who's fault was it? And you, Ross Blair, don't just stand there looking at me like I'm some mean old hag! You know better than to be up on those rocks in the dark!"

"But, Mrs. Yager, I didn't know it was so late."

"That's what you said the last time! That's the best you can do?"

Meredith could not stop the tears; they began to well in her eyes, large drops that fell unintentionally down her cheeks. She quickly tried to wipe them away but not before more of them fell. Before she could stop it from happening, she broke into sobs and collapsed to her knees. She dropped the switch and with as much resoluteness and authority as she could manage, she bawled out, "You're both grounded! No more climbing! I don't care if you ever climb again!"

"But . . ." Daniel's importune reply almost overcame his normally good senses, not to mention underestimating the tension pulsing in the atmosphere around them, but he quickly shut himself up.

Meredith shook her head. She did not look at the boys, only down at the floor. "Nope! No more! I don't need to spend my days and evenings worrying about the two of you lying dead at the bottom of a cliff. I've told you!"

Of course, during this entire episode, Mitch Yager stood silently in the kitchen hoping that Meredith would not remember he was the one who had encouraged the boys to climb. She never turned around to see him or else she might have leveled a railing rebuke on him as well. After she had finished speaking, Mitch waved the boys away and took Meredith in his arms to console her. It was the only time Ross or Daniel had ever seen, or would ever again see, such a reaction from Meredith.

The boys were grounded for a week, though it was meant to be forever. Forever is a very long time when applied to young boys, Meredith soon realized. It became an interminable sentence filled with constant complaints and commotion, arguing and noise, as the boys overwhelmed her with an unyielding burden of dealing with all their misadventures and mischief, much closer to home than she might have otherwise desired. There are times when a punishment is more of a punishment to the punisher than to the punished, and this was one of those times. Whether the boys were intentional or not in their irritating behavior, the effect of it overwhelmed Mrs. Yager so greatly that she released them from their confinement and allowed them to go back to their climbing, if for no other reason than to free herself from their constant childish terrorism. It did seem, however, that after that, Daniel and Ross had gained an understanding or at least were able to recognize that Meredith was serious when she needed to be, for they made sure never to miss their ride again. Ross began to change after seeing the strength of Mrs. Yager's concern and care for them. It would be hard to know if it was this ordeal alone, a coming-of-age revelation, or the fact that no one close to him had ever shown him such concern about anything, but regardless, Ross felt different about their adventures and the dangers they posed. He was more careful, more conscientious after this.

It was the following year on a crisp Monday morning, the first day of summer after their freshman year in high school. The boys raced down the sidewalk and up the stairs of the porch, where they knocked on Joe's front door. They were full of excitement and anticipation to climb and for another reason altogether. In just a few weeks, they expected to get their drivers' licenses. In the back of their minds was hidden the hope that it would not be much longer before they could drive themselves to the trailhead.

Knock, knock, knock! Daniel was impatient. He knocked again. *Knock, knock, knock!*

"Where is he? It's getting late. Come on, Joe! What are you doing? Ross, go look in the garage. See if his car is in there."

Ross jumped over the steps and landed in the yard. He ran to the garage and peeked into the window. "Yeah, his car's still inside. Maybe he's still sleeping."

They stood on Joe's front porch knocking and waited for him to open the door, but Joe never came. After a few more minutes, they gave up and went to see if Mrs. Yager would drive them. They dreaded asking her, knowing she would probably complain about their climbing and lecture them about being careful, and of course, about getting a ride home and not being late.

Daniel had figured out that if Ross asked his mother for a ride, she was more likely to acquiesce. He looked at Ross who knew what was next. "Good morning, Mrs. Yager," Ross greeted her.

Meredith ignored his polite yet disingenuous entreaty.

"I was wondering . . . um . . .," Ross hesitated. His hands fidgeted in his pockets.

"What do you want, Ross?" she asked, without looking his way.

"Well, we went to see if Ol' Joe could take us climbing, but, well, he didn't answer the door. The car's in the garage, but no one seems to be home. So, we wondered, could you take us, please?"

"You boys! Hmmm, get your stuff in the car, and hurry; I have things to do," she answered with a tone of frustration. "Anyway, I can't have you two hanging around all day making messes and bothering me."

As they drove to the Flatirons, Daniel turned to his mother. "Could you check on Ol' Joe, Mom? Make sure he's OK."

"I will try," she replied, as they pulled up to the trailhead marker.

After returning home that day, Meredith and Mitch greeted the boys with solemn expressions. Mitch sat them down and broke the news that Joe had died the week before. Mitch explained that Joe's neighbor had come to check on him and found that he had fallen asleep in his recliner in front of his television and never woke up. As is the case for most youngsters, neither Daniel nor Ross had ever paid any mind to how old Ol' Joe might have been, nor had they ever asked.

Ross looked at Meredith Yager with tears in his eyes. "But, why? He was all alone."

Meredith sat next to him and put her arm around him. "I'm really sorry, Ross. He was an old man and it was his time, I guess. At least he went peacefully."

Ross wiped away a lone tear from his cheek. "What happens when you die?" he asked.

Meredith did not know what to say. The question and the tears surprised her. She had not realized that Ross felt so deeply for Ol' Joe. "I don't know, really." They all sat silently.

It was the first time that either of the boys had ever known someone who had died, and the loss had a deeply profound effect on both of them. For Ross, especially, losing Ol' Joe was like losing a grandfather. Ross had never known his own grandparents or any of his extended family, for that matter. Ol' Joe had filled a void that Ross had not known existed. Death had come and excavated a void, tearing open an expansive emptiness much deeper and darker than he had ever felt before. It is only time and the resilience of youth that softens such a blow, though the deepest wounds often never fully recover.

After losing Ol' Joe, the boys lost something else as well. They lost their enthusiasm for climbing--at least for a few weeks anyway. For Ross, the thought of going to the trailhead, of climbing on the rocks felt pointless, inane, but Daniel would not let him stay too long in his state of gloom. He tried incessantly to lift Ross's spirits, and did so successfully now and again. Eventually, as the wounds of loss, like scars, began to heal, and the indelible memories gave way to the harsh glare and demands of each present day, Ross and Daniel turned their thoughts once again toward climbing. They were resolute. If they could not find a ride, then they would have to make do with their worn out, second hand bicycles. They may have made it through their drivers' tests and earned their licenses, but neither of the boys had a car and their parents had been unwilling to let them use the family car except on a few occasions, and then, only on the weekends.

It was not until mid-August when the boys found out that Ol' Joe was ninety-two years old the day he died. It was his birthday. They would not have known this had it not been for a stranger that had come to the Yager house one morning. Ross was just arriving when a man wearing a suit and carrying a briefcase knocked at the door. While Ross waited quietly on the sidewalk, Daniel opened the door, expecting it to be his friend. He looked at the formally dressed man with a confused, wide-eyed inspection.

"Who are you?" Daniel asked in a tactless, yet curious manner.

"Daniel! Who is it?" Meredith Yager hurried to the door and gently moved Daniel to the side. She looked at him with scolding eyes. "You know better than to answer the door like that. Apologize!"

"Sorry. I just didn't expect . . ."

"It doesn't matter. Tell the man you're sorry for your impertinence."

"My what?"

Meredith lightly smacked Daniel on the back of the head with her open hand.

"Ouch, Mom! Sorry, Mr." Daniel looked at his mother with a scowl.

She looked back at him with an even bigger scowl. Daniel stepped back making room for Meredith to greet the man. "I'm so sorry for my son's manners. Sometimes it seems as if he's been raised by a pack of wolves, which of course he hasn't. May I help you?"

The man smiled with the kind of smile one exercises to avoid laughing. "I understand," said the man. "I've two sons of my own and they can be quite Philistinian at times." The man reached out his hand. "My name is Steve Brom and I'm looking for the parents of Daniel and Ross Yager. Would that be you, by chance?"

Meredith looked at Mr. Brom with a hint of confusion. "Well, I'm the mother of Daniel, but—" Before she finished, her eyes caught sight of Ross standing just behind the man. "Umm, my husband isn't home right now. It's a workday for him. What have the boys done now?" She rolled her eyes and looked at Daniel and then at Ross. Ross shrugged his shoulders, giving a look that was half-innocent and half-unsure of what he might have been guilty.

"Oh no. The boys have done nothing that I'm aware of. Sorry."

"Whew!" Daniel sighed.

"I'm an attorney representing the estate of Joseph Atwater."

Meredith lowered her brow in confusion. She could not recall knowing anyone named Joseph Atwater.

"Mr. Atwater lived just down the street, he passed away in June. The boys apparently knew him."

"Oh! Oh yeah, you mean Ol' Joe!" Daniel yelled out as if giving the winning answer to a gameshow host.

"Yes. Yes, I suppose that is what everyone called him."

"OK. I'm sorry Mr. Brom, but why are you here exactly?" Meredith could not understand why an attorney representing their neighbor was calling at their door.

"Mrs. Yager, if I might come in, I think I can answer any questions you might have. May I?"

"Oh my. Please, yes, please come in. I'm so sorry. I accused my son of being boorish, and here I am doing the same."

Mr. Brom just smiled.

They went into the living room and sat on the sofa. Mr. Brom opened his briefcase and pulled out a manila folder. "You see, Mrs. Yager, Joseph Atwater left a will, and in his will, he asked that his car be given to the boys."

Daniel and Ross had not followed Meredith and Mr. Brom into the living room, instead, they were talking about their plans for the day and where they were hoping they could convince Meredith to take them. However, when the resonant voice of Mr. Brom carried the news of their fortuitous inheritance to their ears, they were immediately interested and ran noisily into the living room.

"I'm sorry, Mr. Brom, did you say he gave them a car?" Meredith asked.

"Yes, Ma'am. I did."

"But, we cannot accept. Shouldn't the car go to his children? I mean, it's too much. They only just earned their drivers' licenses a month ago."

"Mom, what are you doing? And it's been almost two months now!"

"Shh! Do not interrupt me, Daniel!"

"I understand, Mrs. Yager, but Mr. Atwater was very explicit. And besides, his children all agree, the car should go to the boys. They want them to have it."

"But why?"

"Apparently, Ma'am, Mr. Atwater had grown quite fond of the boys. He told his daughter many times that it was nice having their company. The boys gave him a sense of purpose.

Anyway, that's what she told me. Both of his children worried that you might object but asked me to insist. So, I insist."

Meredith looked at Mr. Brom. Her eyes were kind and sincere. She smiled and looked at the boys who stood behind her with bated breath. Daniel labored to hold his tongue, afraid that the slightest misstep of candor or enthusiasm would somehow ruin everything, and the car would be gone forever.

"Hmmm," Meredith uttered. She sat with her back to the boys, with a mischievous smirk on her face, intentionally thinking long and hard, to cause the boys to agonize in suspense. She knew that as soon as she acquiesced, they would be like wild horses, whinnying and neighing, jumping, and running and wanting to go. It made her laugh inside to the point that she could hardly contain her own excitement, yet she also knew she needed to talk to Mitch.

"Well, Mr. Brom, I really need to talk to my husband. Can we get back with you tomorrow?"

"Of course, here is my card. Call me at your convenience. I'll get all the documents ready as soon as you give me the call."

Ross and Daniel were so excited they could hardly stand still, though they did try to contain it enough so as not to appear too eager before Meredith. She, however, knew without a doubt that they could hardly wait for Mitch to come home for they never left the house that day. They wanted to be there the moment Mitch pulled in the drive to tell him the news. Of course, Mitch was as excited as they were when Meredith told him, and just as she had expected, when they told the boys, they let out a loud and jubilant shout. They jumped up and down and asked the most inevitable question. "When can we drive it?"

Meredith and Mitch laughed.

On the day that the car became theirs, Ross and Daniel met Mr. Brom at Joe's house. Mr. Brom opened the garage and turned on the light; the car sat quietly alone. Daniel peered through the windshield, into the front seat, while Ross opened the driver's side door. The keys were hanging in the ignition, as they had always done. The car was mostly empty.

"Well, are you gonna back it out and take it home or just look at it?"

teased Mr. Brom.

"Oh, yeah, kinda weird that Ol' Joe isn't here," said Daniel quietly.

Ross sat in the driver's seat and turned the key. The old car started right away. Daniel ran around to the passenger's side and got in. Ross backed the car out of the garage slowly and drove it to Daniel's house. Mitch and Meredith were standing on the front steps of the house when they drove into the driveway. The boys were smiling with a smile that looked like it would never fade. Daniel jumped out of the car, but Ross sat behind the wheel for a few moments. Under his breath, he said, "Thank you." to Ol' Joe.

A couple of days later, the boys were loading climbing gear into the back seat.

"Hey, Ross, why don't we put some of this stuff in the trunk?"

"That's a good idea," Ross replied.

Daniel pulled the keys from his pocket, ran to the rear of the car, and opened the trunk. Ross, with his hands full of gear, was standing beside him when the trunk lid sprung open. Both boys stood looking down into the trunk and were unable to move. They were surprised to see Ol' Joe's fishing gear lying just the way he had left it the last time he went fishing. Three two-piece rods with reels, an old tackle box, and, set to one side, an old toolbox filled with mechanic's hand tools that Ol' Joe kept with him just in case he needed to work on something for either himself or someone in need.

The boys simultaneously took a deep breath, closed the trunk, and threw the rest of the gear into the back seat. They said nothing about the fishing gear; they just left it there as if Ol' Joe might come looking for it someday.

Having the car was, for Ross, a constant reminder of the man who had given it to them. It was also an antidote to the ache of guilt he sometimes felt. He had never given much thought to Ol' Joe, who he was, or what his story might have been, during those many rides he spent with him. He, in the narcosis of adolescence, thought only of himself. Now that Joe was gone and he was left to feel the hollow in his heart for the old man, Ross struggled with his own social ineptitude, the blinding indifference which kept him distanced from most who might ever try to care for him or love him. Driving Ol' Joe's car made him feel closer to the old man who was now further away than ever before. Unlike so many of the people in Ross's life who, though near at hand and very much alive, were, if truth be told, much further away from him than Joe was and would most certainly remain thus.

Several years later, when the motor finally gave up, Daniel and Ross pushed the car to the back of Daniel's yard, behind the garage. They never had the heart to get rid of it. Ol' Joe's fishing gear and toolbox were still in the trunk.

"Flight 3679 to Kathmandu is ready for departure. All passengers scheduled for this flight should check in immediately at gate 44," the voice announced over the intercom.

Ross, though not typically sentimental, felt a sudden sadness as he and Eve rushed toward the gate. Overwhelmed, tears filled his eyes as he passed a gift shop where he and Daniel had stopped during their last trip home from Ama Dablam. He could not have expected such deep and painful memories to come rushing in at the sight of a toy monkey hanging in the shop's window, but it stopped him in his tracks. Staring into the window through glazed eyes, his thoughts went to Daniel and the days they were both in college.

Ross had gone to college on the Pacific coast of Washington and Daniel had gone to Arizona State. Ross thought about how it had felt back then, not having Daniel around. Though living apart, they never grew apart. Every summer they met up, usually in an airport in some remote city near a new climbing destination. They bummed around, living off the money they had saved during the school year working at whatever odd job they had found.

Even when they were apart, they were analogous, like twins, as much as two boys from very different families in very different places could be. Whatever one would do the other did too, even if they had not planned it that way, like working at McDonald's or studying biomechanics and often reading the same books and loving the same movies. In their appearance and stature, however, they could not have been more different. Ross was less than six feet tall with a lean but muscular build. His hair was sandy-colored, fine, and constantly out of place. He was a good athlete, though not always motivated or competitive. Daniel, however, was tall and lanky, with long, sinuous muscles, coarse dark hair; he was considered to be quite attractive, which earned him a good deal of attention from the girls, though he gave neither the girls nor his looks much consideration. To accompany his charm, Daniel was daring, bold, and prone to pushing the limits of safety; he was not averse to taking risks.

Ross thought about his friend and all their adventures and what this trip, in particular, had meant to him. For more than six months, Ross and Daniel had made plans to climb Machapuchare. They had traveled to multiple climbing destinations and spent most of their waking hours on some mountain assault in training for the planned excursion. Their reasons for climbing Machapuchare were as different as their appearances. A first-to-summit title was especially enticing to Ross. He was not so much interested in the conquest as he was in the legend such a feat creates. Daniel, on the other hand, was drawn to the mountain's summit by something far more esoteric. He had become increasingly mesmerized by the mystique and legend of the mountain itself as if something inscrutable had rooted in his mind. Machapuchare was, for him, an incoherent obsession, an illusion of consequence that he could not escape. A myriad of thoughts ran through Ross's mind as he looked through the glass. For a moment he felt as if time had not passed, as if it was only a few days ago that he was standing there with Daniel, laughing with excitement, full of piss and vinegar.

Eve, who had rushed ahead, suddenly realized Ross was not with her. She stopped and turned to look for him. "Ross, what are you doing? We don't have time to stop and window shop?" she said in a playful tone as she hurried back to him. Eve looked at him and realized that Ross had not even heard her. Then, seeing him frozen at the window, she realized Ross had tears welling up in his eyes. She slowly put her arm around him and looked into the window with him. She saw the toy monkey, a marionette similar to the one she had seen in Ross's apartment. She thought it was something left over from his childhood. Eve leaned her head on Ross's shoulder and stood there with him in silence. "Are you ok?"

"Just remembering Daniel. We stopped here when we were headed home last time. I'd completely forgotten about that stupid monkey. Daniel thought it was cool and wanted to get it for me. He was always doing silly things like that. Man, I miss him."

"I know."

"Attention passengers. Would Ross Blair and Eve Bannister please report immediately to gate number 44? Immediately!" The voice over the intercom sounded frustrated.

"Oh, shit!" Exclaimed Ross. "We better get going! What the hell is wrong with me?!"

"Hold the gate!" Eve called out as the pair ran toward the flight attendant.

"Sorry. Sorry. It's my fault," Ross admitted to the middle-aged man at the gate who held out his hand for the tickets and boarding passes while giving the couple a stern, unfriendly stare.

They located their seats over the wing where Ross always liked to sit. Ross quickly moved to the window seat and Eve sat down beside him. "I hate the wing seats, Ross. Why did you get these seats again?"

"I like to watch from these windows. That way, if an engine falls off or bursts into flames, I can be the first to see it," Ross replied in a joking, somewhat sarcastic manner.

"What? Are you trying to freak me out? You know I hate flying and your flippant comments don't help at all!" Eve's voice was soft and honest with a hint of frustration.

Ross was not listening. His head was turned toward the window as if looking out, but once again he was thinking about the monkey in the window of the gift shop. His thoughts played across the screen of his memory like an old silent movie: *Ross, maybe you should take the lead on this one. I'm still feeling a little woozy from before.*

You'll be fine. Besides, you're already set up. It's fine. We have to get down. The sun is setting; it'll be dark soon.

Yeah, you're right. Later . . . .

Just five weeks before their scheduled departure date, while climbing in the Canadian Rockies outside of Banff, everything changed, forever.

There were moments, unexpected and haunting when Ross could still hear the deafening silence that loomed in the air after Daniel fell away from him that day. It was more than just a memory; it was a wound he felt over and over again, a wound that, on the surface, seemed little more than a scratch, but in the core of his being was a festering boil, deep, sore and oozing with bitter infection. The silence felt eternal as he hung alone on the face of the mountain. Daniel's smiling face had disappeared into the shadowy void without a single word or cry or sound whatsoever. Ross could only watch, stupefied, unable to stop it; it was irrevocable. He had replayed the moments before in his head many times, trying to understand, to remember what had happened, but it would never bring Daniel back or change anything that had happened. There was a part of him, a part vexed by the festering wound, that did not want to remember, but his conscience refused to let him forget.

The suddenness of the tragedy and the senseless finality of it was, at times, a crippling weight. Heart-broken, unable to reconcile any of his doubts and questions, and haunted by survivor's guilt, Ross had stopped climbing altogether. At one point, in an attempt to purge the guilt and anger, Ross had gathered all of his climbing gear and ropes, piled them in the yard, and set fire to them. On that clear, moonless night he had stood alone before the toxic plume, devastated and lost, while caustic black smoke ascended into the black night. He had cried, as memories of all the days of his life, as far back as he could remember crowded into his thoughts. Not one of them was without Daniel.

"Hey, you alright?" Eve's voice broke through the paralysis of his thoughts.

"What? Oh, yeah, I'm good."

Eve was not convinced. She could sense that the closer they got to Machapuchare, the farther Ross was drifting away from her. She reached out, took hold of his hand, and smiled. He returned her smile, but his eyes were full of tears. He turned toward the window to hide them from her. Though he often failed miserably to show it, Ross was comforted by Eve's tenderness. She had helped him find a way through some of the pain and guilt and, in a way that was beyond explanation, Eve had become the same kind of friend to Ross as Daniel had been; a fortune he considered implausible and therefore precious.

Eve had grown up near Portland, Oregon, the daughter of a wealthy real estate developer. Her father, Randal Bannister had always been an honest, hardworking man, though he had never given as much attention to his children as a father should. He had been too busy running a business, making money, and traveling, all things he had prioritized over fathering. Since Eve's mother had passed away when Eve was nine, Randal had left the child rearing to the nanny, Ms. Keri Edwards, or Ms. Keri, as Eve had called her. She had also lived in the Bannister's sprawling eighteen-thousand-square-foot home situated on some eight-hundred acres among the most pristine landscapes in the Pacific Northwest. Keri Edwards was a young, unassuming woman who had become a nanny during her last year of college. She had taken a job looking after and teaching three children to earn extra money for school. The job had suited her, so she had kept with it. She was a literature major and loved the classic poets. She had passed her love of poetry on to Eve, who had developed her particular forte for writing poetry. Eve's quality of character, her kind and tender nature, and her naïve sincerity were undoubtedly the result of the years Eve had spent with Ms. Keri, who had become more of a mother figure than a nanny.

Despite the time Eve spent with Ms. Keri, she had often been lonely. While Randal Bannister had been a loving and caring father and had treated Eve like a princess when he had been home, he had been absent most of Eve's formative years. It was suspected that Eve had reminded him too strongly of Lillian, Eve's mother. Especially in the first few years after Lillian's passing, Eve's remarkable likeness to her mother had been a constant infection to the deep, un-mended wound in Randal's heart. Lillian had been Randal's first and only love, and when she died, Randal lost his way in life. Though he had always been serious by nature, after Lillian's death, his seriousness had become a suit of armor he wore to protect himself from any memory of her, and from experiencing the vulnerability he had known with Lillian. Randal used his seriousness to avoid experiencing the level of vulnerability he had known with Lillian. He dulled his pain by overworking and traveling, eventually burying the sorrow that he felt along with the memory of Lillian. The exception was when he spent time with Eve.

Lillian Banister was a beautiful woman, small framed with long blond hair. Her eyes were piercing and bright, with a gentle innocence that made her seem somewhat naive to others. She was especially outgoing and gregarious, kind, and generous with disarming yet subtle confidence. Lillian possessed a natural beauty yet she was not vain and spent little time primping. In fact, her favorite outfit was an old pair of jeans and a loose-fitting button-up shirt with her hair either stuffed under a baseball cap or pulled back into a loose ponytail.

Eve was a striking and near-perfect image of her mother. Though her voice, her hair, her personality, nearly everything about her, reflected Lillian, she also held several of Randal's personality traits. She was strong, determined, intelligent, and could be quite opinionated, though she was not as forceful or overbearing as her father often was. Eve had anything one could ever want, yet she felt an emptiness inside of her, and she was looking for something or someone to fill it. When she went to college, this emptiness began to grow, expanding the already expansive void that had been hiding beneath the surface of her life. Having lost her mother and feeling the distance that Randal kept, she longed for affection and for an emotional fulfillment that she imagined would only be found in someone else.

Eve left home and went to the University of Washington when she was eighteen. She wanted to be a doctor. Her father did not approve of her choice of college and wanted Eve to attend his and his father's alma mater, Harvard University. Eve, who hated the thought of moving so far from home, resisted her father's manipulative ways. She applied for school loans and housing, choosing to make her own way in the world rather than live off the life her father had made for them. Randal Bannister may have been hardheaded and controlling, but for Eve, held a soft spot. He could not stand by and watch his daughter work a part- time job, live in a dilapidated dorm room, and eat Raman noodles for her meals as "most public college students do," he would say. However, Eve refused to change schools and eventually, Randal acquiesced and helped to pay for everything. It had been during her time at the University of Washington that Eve had met Ross.

As the plane taxied down the runway toward the terminal, Eve looked at Ross who was looking out the window. "One more flight, Ross. Whew! I'll be glad when this marathon of flying is over for a while. Oh, and I'm really glad we'll be taking a little more time between flights on the way back home. When does the flight to Pokhara leave?"

"Tomorrow morning at ten a.m. I'll be glad to have my feet on the ground for more than a few days in a row." Ross's voice sounded tired and dry.

"I can't wait to see the mountains, to see Machapuchare! I'm getting a little nervous, though. Ross, do you really think we can do this?"

"Oh yeah, no problem. This is a small mountain compared to some of the others around here."

"It doesn't sound very small."

"It's not that it's small, Eve. It's just smaller than some of the others around it. You'll see what I mean. Don't worry so much." Ross was suddenly struck with the memory of Daniel on Ama Dablam telling him, *"You worry too much."*

"Don't worry so much?" Eve snapped back. "Since when have you become so balmy about everything? You're usually the one telling everyone to be careful. Don't worry? Coming from you, it's hard to take seriously. You know? Maybe I should be more worried because obviously you're trying to hide something."

"I didn't mean it like that. Jeez. I meant you shouldn't worry about it now. Just enjoy each step of the trip. Don't think too much about what's ahead. We still have a long way to go yet."

"Well, thank you, Professor," Eve replied in an unusual manner. She was emotionally worn thin from the days of travel.

Ross took hold of Eve's hand, raised it to his lips, and gave it a kiss. "I love it when you're all worked up," he said with a mischievous tone and a smirk.

"Well, I guess I love you, too," Eve returned in a disingenuous tone.

In a more serious manner, Ross looked at Eve. "You know, I'll always be there for you. I'll always love you and take care of you. I won't let anything happen to you. You know that, don't you?"

Tears began to flow over Eve's cheeks then to drip off her chin. Ross reached over and gently wiped them away.

Sunlight bled into the small room through the worn curtains and landed on the pillow where Eve's head rested. Ross had his head buried in blankets. Eve rolled over, exposing her sleepy eyes to the rays of light. She opened her eyes, at first slowly and then, suddenly, she realized that something was wrong. "Oh, crap! Ross, wake up! Ross! We overslept!"

"What the hell?" yelled Ross, as he jumped from the covers and looked at his watch.

"Damn it!"

"I thought that you set the alarm." Eve's voice filled the small motel room as she ran into the bathroom.

"I did! I know I did! Damn it!"

"Well, you must have done something wrong. What time is it?"

"Let me look. It's ten till eight!"

"Well, I guess I won't be taking a shower," Eve complained, as the two of them rushed around gathering their luggage, dressing as they went and trying to get out of the hotel room as quickly as they could.

Ross stood in the street outside the motel waving his hands in the air to hail a cab. An old, dirty car with a half-lit light on the top pulled up next to him. "The airport, please, as fast as you can. Damn it, we're going to miss our flight."

"Don't worry, we'll make it. Everything will be OK." Eve tried to convince Ross.

They explained the urgency of their situation to the cab driver as best as they could and asked him to go to the airport as fast as possible. The driver raced through the crowded streets and, without a minute to spare, they made it to the gate and were off to Pokhara.

Chapter II
The Summit

"Do you think Psang will be here?" Eve questioned Ross as they exited the plane, still feeling hurried and anxious.

"He should be here. I told him when we'd arrive."

"Look for a sign. I only met him that one time. It's been a long time since, so I'm not sure what he looks like."

Eve pointed to the crowd of people standing near the entrance of the airport. Some were holding crudely fashioned signs with misspelled names written on them. "I think I see someone holding a sign with your name on it. Over there!"

"Oh yeah, that should be him. Hello!" Ross waved as he approached the short, dark haired man holding a cardboard sign with "Ros Blar" written on it in blue crayon.

"I guess he forgot to look at my name on the letters I sent him. Psang?"

"Yes. You Misser Ross?"

"Yes, yes that's me. Oh, and this is Eve. I told you she would be coming with me."

"Yes, yes of course. Miss Eve, tashi deleh, it's good to know you. Please, please, come with me, we find your luggage. Do you have much bags, Misser Ross?"

"A few."

Each step of the journey from Seattle had felt like a step back in time. The modern amenities and environment of the US gradually fell away as they travelled deeper and deeper into a world that was simpler and older than the one in which they lived. The airport in Pokhara was a small regional airport set in the valley. To the north lay the great mountain range of the Himalayas. Machapuchare stood as a sentinel over the region and was easily visible from anywhere in the area. Until 1960, outsiders had considered Pokhara to be a mystical city. There were no roads into the city and access was available only by foot. The evolution of progress and modernism had changed the region. As they drove through the city, Eve looked out through the dirty windows of the old van, seeing Pokhara for the first time. It was a modern city, a bustling metropolis, though the remnants of the ancient were still visible everywhere. Pokhara was a city of contrasts, of old and new, in a region where the tallest mountains in the world dominated everything. Although the modern world was attempting to take control, the ancient soul of the territory continued to eclipse all attempts at transforming the area.

Once they had arrived at the motel and checked in, Ross dropped his suitcase on the bed. "Thanks for your help, Psang."

"I will come tomorrow get you."

"What time?"

"As soon as I can. You be ready, yes?"

Ross had been here before and knew that time was considered of little importance to the Sherpa guides. "We'll be ready at first light." Ross closed the door, walked over to the bed, and sat down.

Eve looked around the simple, small room. As her gaze stopped at Ross, she said in dismay, "It's kind of strange."

"What's kind of strange?"

"Well, this place, it's so old and yet new, as if it's meant to be that way."

"Why wouldn't it be?"

"Well, I don't know. It just seems strange, that's all: carts drawn by mules and horses and men on the same roads as a Mercedes Benz or a BMW. What a contrast. And these people live as if there's nothing strange or out of place about it."

"Whatever," Ross remarked.

Eve hardly noticed Ross's indifference. She was preoccupied with her thoughts while she looked out of the window of their room seeing the sprawling city with snow and ice-covered Machapuchare towering in the distance. She pulled a leather-bound journal from her travel bag and sat down at the small desk under the window. She switched on the lamp and unwrapped the leather cord from around the journal. Within the cover of the journal was a pen tucked into the binding at the page on which she had last written an entry. Eve began to write:

We have finally reached Nepal and out the window in front of me, I can see the mountain that Ross and I will soon climb. It is unbelievably beautiful and big. I'm afraid. I've not told Ross, though. I just can't seem to shake the feeling that I am way out of my element. This mountain is huge and looking at it scares me. Ross keeps telling me that everything will be just fine, but I can see it in his eyes, he is afraid, too. I don't think he is afraid of the climb but of climbing without Daniel, and maybe, afraid of climbing with me. We have to keep everything a secret, which is so difficult. I almost wish we were climbing another mountain.

A lonely tear pushed its way to the surface as she stared out the window at the mountain. "Ross?" Eve softly spoke as she stared out the window, "Ross?" Eve glanced over at the bed. Ross slept on top of the blankets. She smiled at him and then wiped the lone tear from her cheek. "Hmm, figures."

In the twilight of predawn, Ross awoke to a dark room. He had fallen asleep in his street clothes and had not moved the entire night. Eve lay next to him, covered by the blankets and sleeping peacefully. Quietly, Ross moved toward the window of the small motel room. The glass had a film on it from years of cigarette smoke and neglect. Ross attempted to wipe away some of the film with his hand, then he stared at Machapuchare. In the dark silence, the early morning full moon illuminated the night sky, setting the shadowed form of the mountains against a deep blue canvas. Machapuchare was little more than a silhouette, but the hanging snow and ice fields glowed as if lit. Ross quietly stood at the window, mesmerized, spellbound and drawn inexorably by the illusion of immortality and fame, by the hope of leaving his mark on history as a great mountaineer. The possibility of such a reward had seduced him, like a man seduced by a woman. Ross had become irrationally obsessed.

There is nothing that will stop me now, he thought. Only he was becoming blind to the dangers, blind to Eve, and blind to reason. He remembered Daniel, remembered his reason for wanting to climb the mountain. As consumed as Ross was with conquering the mountain, Daniel had been even more consumed with the strange story told by the old man.

Ross laughed quietly under his breath at the absurdity of such a notion. Ross whispered into the silence, "This is for you, Daniel, legend or not."

The black night sky surrendered to gentle rays of morning light sneaking across the landscape, transforming it from black to dark blue and then to light blue as the stars, that had been shining bright, began to fade into the ambiguity of a new morning sky. The beauty of this moment was rarely witnessed, and Ross, for the first time in his life, saw it and felt its visceral impact. He saw the beauty of a vision that had been hidden from him. He saw the world draped in a new light through the window of his motel room. He saw life framed in the pane, and something at a subterranean level, something beyond intellect, beyond rationality, happened at that moment, something he was unable to fully understand. Ross pushed his emotions down, refusing to succumb to their raw, involuntary response. If there was anything that truly frightened him, it was losing control of his emotions.

Bang, Bang, Bang! Psang knocked at the door of the motel room. It was only seven fifteen in the morning and Eve was still sleeping. Ross, startled by the interruption, was jolted out of his introspection, which had transported him from the realm of shadowed night to morning's fresh arrival. Still sitting on the chair next to the bed, he had not noticed the sun, in full brightness, glowing eagerly through the window.

"Just a minute. Hold on. Who is it?" Ross hollered as he approached the door.

"Misser Ross, it is me, Psang. Are you ready to go?"

Psang heard the chain lock sliding on the metal track. He then heard the dead bolt turn, and the door was cracked open from the inside just enough for Ross to spy through the opening.

"Good morning, Misser Ross! I come as soon as I can, sorry to keep you waiting, Misser Ross."

"Wow! Um, you know, Psang, umm, we're not quite ready," Ross said with embarrassment. "Can you give us a little more time?"

"Oh yes, Misser Ross, no problem. I will wait here."

By now Eve was awake and out of bed. She was acutely aware, the moment the knock came at the door, that it had to be Psang. "I knew this would happen," she said in a cheerful but slightly frustrated tone.

"I'm sorry. I had no idea that he'd come so early. Last time Daniel and I came to Nepal, our guide didn't show up until almost noon. I kind of expected the same from Psang. Do you see my other boot?"

"It might be under the bed. You know, you just collapsed last night before even changing your clothes."

"Yeah, I know. Man, was I tired. Oh, here it is. Thanks."

"Will we be traveling very long today?" asked Eve.

"I think we'll be on the road for most of the day. Everything moves very slowly around here."

"Ross, I hope that all of our gear made it."

"Me, too. But you never can tell. That's part of what makes it such an adventure, you know?" Ross had a smirk on his face.

"Think you're funny, don't you?" Eve remarked.

"Psang should've picked it up. Hopefully, he has it packed for us."

Grabbing their bags, Ross and Eve left the small motel room and headed to the vehicle that would be taking them up to the trailhead. As they stepped out of the door of the motel room, they rushed past Psang who had been sitting just outside while they were packing. Ross stopped and looked around for Psang.

"What the?" Ross erupted just as he saw Psang sitting on the ground. "What are you doing, Psang?"

"Waiting for you, Misser Ross" "Where is the car?"

"There, Misser Ross. There it is." Psang pointed to a dirty, old Russian van sitting in the parking lot. It was covered in large patches of rust. The windows, layered with dirt and smoke on the inside and outside, were barely distinguishable from the gray color of the metal. The van had no hubcaps and the tires appeared to be bald, all four of them, and two of them were low on air. When started, the old van smoked and coughed like an old man with emphysema, the engine sounded as if it were only moments away from a total failure. All the gear for their trip was piled on top of the van and held in place by a complex network of ropes and cords crisscrossing their bags. The old vinyl upholstery was cracked and torn, revealing the yellow foam cushions which had become dry and hard from years of use and exposure to the elements.

"Come. Come. This very good auto," said Psang. "You see. Everything good."

Eve stood looking at the dilapidated old van, not so much disturbed or concerned but in sheer amazement. "You mean this thing is still running?"

"Oh yes, Miss Eve, very good auto, you see."

"OK, sounds good to me. I would not have expected anything less." Eve handed her bag to Psang with a cheery smile on her face.

The van was a treasure to Psang. Most of the Nepalese were too poor to own any kind of motor vehicle. In this part of the world, such treasures were only modestly cared for by their owners. Without much money or even parts for repairs, the owners of these chariots of rust had to devise their own means of repair, and as such, many of the vehicles were held together by wire and duct tape. This did not dissuade the owners, however, from using these vehicles in situations where most in the modern world would never consider using newer and more appropriately designed vehicles. Owning any kind of vehicle was a mark of distinction. Psang felt a great deal of pride to offer his clients a ride in his own private vehicle.

"Piece of shit," muttered Ross, who was not impressed, though he knew this was as good as it would get, especially considering his lack of financial resources and the secret nature of his journey.

Ross had met Psang three and a half years earlier when he and Daniel had descended from Ama Dablam. They had heard that one of the local Sherpas had just returned from the mountain and asked to meet him. Psang was that man. He had just returned from Everest. He was a simple man descended from a family of exiles who had fled Tibet in the early 1960s after China annexed the small nation. Nearly all the people around Machapuchare were from exiled clans. For the first several years, they had lived as refugees until they had been able to set up life in Nepal.

Psang was born in Nepal, so he had never known any other home or land. He was dark-skinned and short, as many of the Nepalese and Tibetans were. His hair was black and straight, and cut as if a bowl had been placed on his head and shears used to cut all hair hanging beneath its rim. His face was leathery and rough from a lifetime of exposure to the sun's powerful rays. His smile was broad and infectious, though his teeth were yellowed and crooked. Psang had been to Everest, the roof of the world, five years earlier when he had worked as a Sherpa for a German-led team, who had climbed to the top of K2 and to Everest a year later.

Though he had been to the top of the world and had climbed many of its highest peaks, climbing meant something very different to Psang than it did to Ross. Psang saw climbing as a way to feed his family. It was a job. He never expected notoriety or fame, just money. As such, Psang was a humble man with a clear sense of reality and purpose. He was not bewitched by the mountain gods or by a sense of accomplishment. This was an important trait for a Sherpa. Many men who had climbed the tall mountains had lost their sense of reason and objectivity, and it eventually cost them their lives.

This expedition was different, however, for Psang knew that climbing Machapuchare was illegal in the region. Machapuchare had been off-limits to climbers for almost as long as men and women had been climbing the Himalayas. The Nepalese people considered the mountain sacred and holy. It was believed that the god Shiva held the mountain as sacred; therefore, no man should contaminate it by stepping foot on it, though there had been some men who had, in the past, defiled the mountain. Shiva was also known as the Destroyer in some Hindu denominations, and many believed that his wrath might be demonstrated if anyone were to trespass on his sacred lands. Psang was not Hindu, however. His family was Buddhist and Psang was not a very devout Buddhist at that, but he was a believer. Aside from the legal aspects of climbing the mountain, Psang saw it only as another mountain.

Pulling away from the motel, the old van smoked and the gears of the transmission ground. The shock absorbers and the suspension were completely worn out. Riding in the van was like travelling in a cross between a small boat on a stormy sea and an old stagecoach with steel-rimmed wooden wheels. A steady stream of blue smoke trailed behind them as they journeyed toward their secret base camp.

Psang began talking to Ross and Eve. It was just chit chat really, until he came to the subject of his grandfather. "My grandfather tell me story bout the mountain. It a story told by the elders, passed down many generations."

"Really?" responded Eve, in a cordial if somewhat ambivalent manner, as she stared out the van window. Psang had been talking nonstop and she was finding it increasingly difficult to stay interested.

"Yes, yes. He tell me legend," Psang continued, but Eve's attention became immediately diverted.

"Ross, look over there. There, that old man, it feels like he's looking at me. He's a very strange person." Sitting along the side of the road, amid the chaos and busyness of traffic and people, one elderly man stood out. He did not stand out for any obvious reason, except that he looked straight into the dirty window of the van and into Eve's curious eyes.

Ross looked in the direction Eve pointed. "What man? There are hundreds of them."

Psang brought the van to a stop at an intersection, giving Ross enough time to find the man Eve singled out. "What the hell?" Ross muttered in amazement. His mouth hung open and his eyes fixed on the man.

"Isn't he kinda strange? It felt like he was looking straight at me!" Eve exclaimed. "I can't believe it!"

"What, Ross? What can't you believe?"

"That's him! That's the old man. What's he doing here?"

"What man? Who is he, Ross?"

"That's the man that told Daniel about the mountain. The crazy, old loon who got Daniel all worked up about some old legend and the mountain."

"Legend? What legend?"

Ross turned and looked out of the side window but did not reply to Eve.

Psang revved the motor and ground the gears until the van was moving again, while Eve and Ross sat staring out the window. Psang had noticed he had lost Eve's attention and had stopped talking. As soon as the van started moving and Eve turned toward the front of the van, Psang continued his story.

"My grandfather tell me legend, many in mountains believed. It a legend bout great Buddha who split one world into three. One world for the tribes of men, one world for their souls, and last world, place where great Buddha lives. He tell me that the mountain land was place where great Buddha spirits pass between the three worlds. Some say the great Buddha fight with evil Buddha. Evil Buddha lose fight and sent to third world where he is locked in cave in mountains. Evil Buddha promised to escape and destroy the great Buddha, but he forgot where secret passage between worlds, so evil Buddha still in this world. The great Buddha sent snow and ice and rock to hide way back from evil Buddha. It is only a story, I not believe it," Psang said with a grin.

"Really? Sounds a little like the story Daniel heard," retorted Ross with a bit of sarcasm in his tone, as he rolled his eyes dismissively.

Eve looked at Ross with surprise. She was immediately curious due, in part, to the realization that Ross had heard Psang's story and because they had seen the man before who had told the story. "You've heard about this, Ross? Why didn't you tell me?"

"It's nothing, just a stupid story. The people around here have all kinds of stories and beliefs. If you listened to all of them, you'd think that the world was full of all kinds of strange things. It's just a story. That's all."

"Really? So how did Daniel hear about it? And when?"

"Oh, come on, Eve! It's nothing. Really, it's nothing."

"You didn't answer my question, Ross."

"That old guy. He was sitting along the street. We were just walking along a couple of days before we were going to climb Ama Dablam. Out of the blue, this guy calls out to Daniel, you know, waves him in, like he needed help or something. Of course, Daniel, always one to lend a hand, rushes over to him, only to find that the guy just wants to talk. You know how old people are, always wanting to talk and give advice. It was crazy. Besides, the guy stunk. I mean he really smelled, and his clothes were filthy. I could hardly stand to be near him. But not Daniel. He sat down, right next to him and started talking to him. Told him we were going to climb the mountain. That's when the old guy looked at him and asked him some questions about taking a risk and shit like that. Then he started telling Daniel about this, umm, legend. I couldn't believe it, I mean for the next twenty or thirty minutes, maybe even longer, I don't know, the old guy goes on and on. Daniel sat there soaking up every word like it was all true. After that, Daniel couldn't let it go. He just had to climb Machapuchare. I don't know what he expected to find. It's just a mountain, not a legend."

"But you're sure bent on climbing it. So, there's something about it that's, that's more than 'just a mountain'. Right?"

"Eve, you know I don't believe in that sort of crap. I've wanted to climb the mountain for one reason, because no one else has ever done it. I just want to be the first, that's it. All this bullshit about legends and gods and evil spirits, it doesn't mean a thing."

Eve's attention went back to Psang. She knew Ross was not given to superstition and such, and he would not have given even the slightest consideration to village legends. Though she was apprehensive, her growing curiosity made her unable to ignore all she had just seen and heard. She was much more like Daniel than Ross, and as such, found it difficult to totally dismiss the legend.

"Why don't you believe it, Psang?"

"I been to many mountains all my life. I not seen secret places. It only old story told by old men," answered Psang with a slight grin on his face.

Eve, who was sitting in the back seat of the van, looked up at Psang. "Then why would you tell us about it?"

"Many who come, they like the stories. They do not believe, but they like to hear. Besides, many of the elders believe that the doorway to the other world was found on Machapuchare. That is why Shiva protects the mountain from intruders. It is good to know what others believe."

Ross spoke up, hoping to reassure Eve there was nothing to worry about. "What? Are you trying to scare us away, Psang? If so, it's not working. My friend, Daniel, wanted to come just because of the legends."

"No, no, Misser Ross. I just say what I have heard. I just tell stories."

"Hahaha! No worries, Psang, I know you're not messing with us."

Eve quickly spoke up. "I'd be interested in hearing more though. I think the old legends are interesting and sometimes hold a little bit of truth to them."

"Oh brother, Eve. You're a tireless romantic, aren't you? Just like Daniel." Ross dismissively protested, feigning indifference, though what she said had disturbed him.

"That's not such a bad thing, Ross," Eve responded, feeling a little mocked.

As the van passed the outer limits of the city, Psang turned onto a road that was more like a trail about as wide as his van. It was cluttered with potholes and its center was overgrown with weeds and grass. The road became steeper and more difficult to navigate the further they drove; however, Eve was distracted from the ride by her thoughts; thoughts of Psang's story, of the old man and the legend were causing fear to sink into her heart. She ruminated on what Psang said about Shiva protecting the sacred mountain.

"So, how does Shiva protect the mountain?" Eve asked in a semi-distracted manner, her attention split between asking the question and thinking about her growing fear.

"Many have gone to the mountain and have not returned, never seen again," answered Psang.

"What do you mean, never seen again?" Eve questioned him alertly, as she was jolted back into a state of full attentiveness. She looked at Psang with concern and leaned toward the driver's seat so she could hear every word.

"Yes, yes, never seen again. The mountain a very dangerous place, many ways to die."

"That happens all over the great mountains, though!" Ross objected, becoming aggravated with the conversation.

"Oh yes, you right Misser Ross. That why I not believe the stories. But many believe that Shiva protect the mountain and that those who do not return have offended Shiva in some way."

"It's all just fantasy, you know. You shouldn't be telling scary stories when you don't even believe them, and especially to paying clients. It's not good business. You might scare your dinner ticket away. Don't worry, Eve. He's just trying to get you worked up."

"No, no, Miss Eve, I not try to work you up. I just tell you story."

"It's fine, Psang," Eve tried to reassure him.

The undulating van slowly and steadily worked its way up the narrow road, through the jungle-like terrain. The subtropical environment experienced a great deal of rain each year especially during the monsoon season, which promoted dense vegetation along the sides of the road, as well as deep ruts. The trees and brush encroached more and more on the narrowing road making it impossible to see very far ahead. The constant side-to-side swaying of the overloaded vehicle combined with the fumes of the exhaust and the occasional whiff of unpleasant odors wafting in through the open windows were having a predictable effect on the couple. Ross began to sweat as he felt the sensation of his head spinning. Eve reached up to the seat in front of her where Ross was sitting and laid her forehead upon her arm.

"I'm getting sick, Ross!" Eve cried in misery.

"What?" belted out Ross, who felt as if he could throw up at any minute.

"Psang, stop! I'm gonna puke!" Eve commanded.

Psang quickly slammed on the brakes. With a jerk, the van stopped. Ross flung open the front passenger door of the van, jumped out, and threw up. Eve fought to keep herself from doing the same as she struggled to exit the van through the stuck sliding door. Psang ran around and worked the door open for her, but before she could get out, she vomited, too.

"Miss Eve? Miss Eve, you feel better?" Psang inquired, as he leaned over her.

"Give me a minute, Psang."

"Babe, you OK?" Ross asked.

"I'll be fine. Do you have something I can use to wipe my face?"

Psang handed Eve a slightly soiled and not-so-white terry towel. "Take, Miss Eve, take."

"Thank you, Psang. Thank you."

Slowly and reluctantly, they all got back into the van and continued their journey. For the next several hours, they wound up the narrow road. Just as the sun began to set, Psang turned off the un-kept trail onto one even more narrow and less traveled. There was no recognizable vehicle track on this narrow way and the brush closed in quickly around the van. The shine of the headlights was limited to only a few feet in front of the vehicle which was now moving more slowly than they could have walked. Pushing into the forbidding forest, the van finally emerged into a brief opening where a small, worn wall stood alone. In the yellow light cast by the headlights of the van, the structure looked almost the color of mud. There were holes in the walls of its canvas, and the bottom edges, while secured to the ground with rope and stakes, were worn and frayed. The entrance of the tent consisted of two pieces of wall tied together with string. Psang had put up the tent a few days earlier after confirming that Ross and Eve were going to come for the climb. This was intended as only a staging area, a place where the van would be left while Psang, Ross, and Eve, with a team of three porters, moved necessary climbing gear to a secret base camp further up the mountain. Once the gear was unloaded and moved to the base camp, the van and the wall tent were to be moved away from the trail head to prevent discovery of the expedition.

Psang stopped the van and turned off the lights. "Misser Ross, we here."

"This is the trail head?"

"Yes, yes, the trail just beyond. Tomorrow we go to base camp."

"And when will the porters be here?" Ross asked.

"In morning."

"Psang, how far is base camp?"

"Oh, not far, Miss Eve, not far."

"Hmm," Eve muttered to herself. Eve doubted that Psang was being entirely forthcoming.

She suspected Ross had told him not to reveal too much to her for fear she might back out. It was dark inside the wall tent and a musty smell hung in the air. Three old military cots were set up on one side of the tent, but there was no floor. A fuel lantern hung from a hook in the center, and a small camp stove sat on the ground in one corner. Psang lit the lantern. A soft yellowish glow began to fill the room. It was immediately apparent there was no heating stove, and they would definitely be using their sleeping bags for the night. The primitive camping accommodations were a bit disappointing to Eve, even though she knew before coming on the adventure, it was going to be rough.

Below, in the Pokhara valley, city lights glowed. They lit up the night sky, making Eve feel less isolated and alone. Though deep in the forest, high above the valley floor, they were not too far from the edges of civilization. The night was dark with no moon and the stars formed a magnificent display of sparkling lights stretching across the black celestial canvas. Eve and Ross decided to sit a while outside the tent. They were both tired from the day's journey but were not ready to turn in for the night. For more than a week, they had been in constant motion, except when sleeping. The relentless pace had kept them from having any meaningful time together, and sitting there, in the dark, without the drone of an engine humming in the background, they felt a sense of calm and peace they had forgotten.

As they sat and talked, Ross slowly opened up to Eve, sharing things he never spoke about. It came unexpectedly, even to him. The power of the mountain realm seems to do that; drawing buried, untended feelings to the surface and forcing self-examination. Until that moment, Ross had not realized just how important climbing had been to his personal journey. He always felt it was just something he and Daniel had done together, not that climbing or the wilderness were, in and of themselves, anything meaningful to him. Inadvertently, though, climbing, and all of its requisite dangers, had saved his life. The mountains, the wilderness, the adventure, in one way or another, had rescued him from a life that would have otherwise been a complete disaster. Climbing had been something he could do to escape, and the wilderness was a large enough for memories and emotions to exist without taunting each other. The mountains became a home to him, a place of refuge and safety, a place where he could count on almost everything always being the same. Now, they were not the same. They had changed, and the comfort they usually brought morphed into something more like the visions and memories he came to them to escape.

In all his years spent in the wilderness, Daniel had always been there, and now he was gone, forever. There was no way for Ross to separate Daniel from his memories and experiences of climbing. "I hate the sense of loneliness I feel right now. Don't get me wrong, I'm glad you're here with me and all, and I love being here with you. But without Daniel, I feel a kind of isolation that, I don't know, it . . . it scares me."

"Yeah, it is a lonely place, but I didn't know you felt so lonely here. I guess . . . I guess I thought you liked the solitude, the isolation. You almost have to love being alone to climb mountains, don't you?" inquired Eve.

"I suppose, but for most of my life I've felt alone, and I guess that feeling haunts me even more now, no matter where I am."

"But why do you feel so alone? Where does that come from?"

"When my mom used to leave me and my sister alone at night, while she went to work, I was always afraid that she wouldn't come back. Like my dad, he never came back, just up and abandoned us. I remember the last night that I saw him, you know?"

"Really? But you were only a little boy, weren't you?"

"Yeah, about four I guess, maybe five, but I still have that picture in my mind: the Christmas tree lying on the living room floor, glass and broken Christmas lights scattered everywhere and Mom standing by the front door crying. I even remember the smell of beer on my mom's breath and in the air as it soaked into the carpet. Strange, the things you remember. She didn't even seem to notice Tiffany and me standing there in the room crying, afraid. I don't think our mother ever noticed us again after all that happened. It was like she died that night, died inside. Sometimes I wished they both would've died that night. Life would've maybe been better, definitely different."

Eve sat quietly. She did not want to say too much or try to make his feelings less palpable.

Ross went on. "I've spent most of my life, until now, feeling alone, feeling lonely, and feeling somehow broken. When mom died, I cried. I don't even know why I cried. I guess her death took me by surprise. It was so unexpected. But, well, it shouldn't have been. She was so messed up."

It was in July, and Ross had just graduated from high school. It was on one of the rare occasions he had gone home, or at least to the house his mother called home. It was on impulse, really. If anyone had asked him why he had gone home that day, he could not have given an answer. He had walked in the front door and found her, as he had several times before, passed out, half on the couch and half on the ground. With her face against the floor, vomit had pooled around her mouth and cheek. Ross's call for an ambulance had been too late. Julie had aspirated during an alcohol-induced sleep and suffocated.

"The coroner told me she must have tried to sit up when it happened, but was too drunk to do much more. She died alone."

"I'm so sorry, Ross. That's awful, and for you to find her." Eve had never heard the details of Julie's death. She felt bad for Ross and couldn't hold back her tears.

"But then," Ross continued, "when Tiffany died, I felt more alone than I've ever felt. I guess I didn't realize how much a part of me she truly was. She was so young, and I wasn't there for her, either."

Ross had received a call one Sunday morning in September from Tiffany's roommate. After graduating from high school, Tiffany moved into an apartment near Boulder with one of her friends from school. The friend, Ross could never remember her name, told him Tiffany had been involved in a car accident on her way to work. She experienced serious injuries when a truck struck her side of the car after running a red light. The driver was drunk from a long night of partying. He survived. Before Ross could arrange to get back to Colorado from Washington, Tiffany died.

"And then, Daniel, man I miss him. When he fell, I wanted to fall with him." Ross's voice was soft and his lips stammered with each word, as he tried to push down the deep pain and emotions. "Everyone I have ever loved or needed is gone. I'm so afraid to love someone, to love you. I wonder how you can even love me. I'm such a mess. So broken. My whole life's been fucked up, it seems."

Eve took hold of Ross's hand. She swallowed, struggling to keep herself from crying more. It was the first time Ross had spoken of his family in such tender terms. She said nothing, knowing Ross was not looking for comfort from her. She knew he was not asking her to give him some simple, well-intentioned platitude. She knew, at this moment, Ross only needed her to listen, to let him talk. She sat in silence, pushing back tears of sadness as the man she had fallen deeply in love with struggled to make sense of his life, of his severely broken heart.

In a strange, inexplicable way, Ross felt he was the reason for these tragedies. Over the years, others had tried to tell him these things in his life, circumstances that went bad, were not his fault. In some cases, Eve had also heard them, the insipid platitudinous offerings like, "you have to move on, to forgive yourself, to forgive your dad, your mother." Ross had heard it all before, and though it was meant to help, it had the opposite effect, making him more embittered, more angry, and more hurt. Eve had once made the mistake of doing what everyone else did, but, before the words were fully out of her mouth had seen their effect on Ross. He turned away, not physically, but in his soul. She had crossed an invisible line and had feared she would never be able to go back.

For Ross, that evening in Canada, watching Daniel, his best and only friend at that time, fall from the mountain to his death, caused the pain of all the losses of his life to reawaken in the worst imaginable way. It was as if a dark evil spirit suddenly arose to the surface, a spirit that had been locked away in a dark hole beneath the synthetic crust of life. A pit of pain and torment, deeper than any darkness had opened and the beast was out, free to infect him with bitterness and to remind him of all of life's cruel inequities.

Now, as Eve sat in silence next to him, she remembered the first time she had heard about the accident. She could not imagine how anyone could ever get over a loss like that, especially the loss of such a close friend. It might have seemed natural for Ross to find comfort through family, but he had none other than Daniel's family, and though he considered them to be his only family and continued to stay in touch with them, their relationship was never quite the same, mostly because of Ross's inability to reconcile his own sense of guilt. Everyone knew Daniel's death was not Ross's fault; however, it seemed, at times to Eve, there was something Ross had not told anyone about the accident. It was not that Eve, or anyone else for that matter, expected there to be some terrible secret. It was the way Ross avoided any of the details of the incident. It seemed strange to her. She never pushed for any kind of information or explanation; she felt that eventually, Ross would tell her what really happened on that mountain that day.

Ross struggled to hold back his emotions as he remembered his friend. Everything around him was resurrecting the deepest of memories he had been working to bury. "I'm sorry," whispered Ross. "I don't know where all that came from. I didn't realize how much I missed him. It kind of caught me by surprise."

"He was your best friend. It was the right response, to cry for him. Don't be ashamed of your tears or your love for him. I get it. I would feel the same."

"Yeah, I guess so. It's just so painful to encounter these feelings again."

"Pain reminds us we are human, that we have feelings"

"Maybe," whispered Ross.

"I wish I could have known him."

"Yeah, me too. He would have liked you."

"Ross," Eve began. "Ross, I love you. I love you so much."

"Even when I cry?" asked Ross, with just a modicum of levity, trying to break the tension of the moment.

"Especially when you cry." Eve stood and turned to Ross. She wrapped her arms around his neck and pulled him close. "I will love you always," she whispered tenderly into his ear.

Psang rose early and, as usual, prepared breakfast for everyone, knowing what lay ahead was a difficult slog to their basecamp. It was not a long hike in terms of distance; however, it was a treacherous route with no established trails, and much of the lower section would require bushwhacking. It would take them at least three hard days. The Siti River which flowed through the area, with many narrow gorges and cold glacial tributaries flowing into it, made the way hazardous, and all would have to be done carrying full packs.

To catch a few more moments of rest, Eve turned her head away from the encroaching light. It seemed, however, that one stray beam of light had come with the singular intent of rousing her from her sleep. When she turned her head, the radiant shaft, as if trying to sneak up on her, moved across to the other eye. "Arggh!" howled Eve. She wrestled with the impending thought of getting out of her cot to prepare for her day. The beam of light seemed fixed on her every move while she lay on her cot. After a few minutes of cat-and-mouse, Eve sat up inside her sleeping bag. "Of course!" she moaned, lamenting her circumstance and envying Ross's still-peaceful sleep.

The smell of the food cooking outside meandered into the tent, arousing pangs of hunger. As she stumbled around the tent to find something appropriate to wear, Ross shifted in his cot and complained in a deep tired voice. "What're you doing? I'm trying to sleep!"

Eve's efforts to be quiet were immediately thwarted. Ross's complaint incited a response of ornery playfulness. She grabbed a pillow from her cot and hurled it, hitting Ross squarely in the face. "Hey, sleepyhead! Time to get out of bed!"

He rolled over in an attempt to ignore her command.

Eve finished dressing and stepped out of the canvas shelter into the thinning mist of the morning. She intentionally left the curtain-like door agape, allowing the sunlight to chase away the shadows.

"Good morning, Psang," Eve greeted in a cheery and seemingly renewed tone. She peeked back at the tent with a mischievous smile on her face. "It's a lovely morning. I'm famished. What smells so good?"

"Good morning, Miss Eve." Psang politely returned her greeting as he handed her a bowl. "Tsampa porridge, tea, and bread. You like, you like." Psang had also set out some fruit, bread, and honey for the meal. Eve helped herself to the homemade bread and poured some honey over her porridge.

After stumbling around trying to find his clothes and the one boot that appeared to have walked itself out of the tent, Ross slowly made his way out and stood alone on a clump of grass about twenty feet from the entrance. He glanced at Eve, who tried to look away before revealing a guilty grin. Ross, however, spied the irrepressible glint in her eyes, which confirmed what he was beginning to suspect. Slowly, Ross walked through the dewy grass, grabbed his boot and, without saying a word in response, carried it over to where Eve and Psang quietly rested and sat down with them.

"Good morning! Finally decide to wake up, did ya? Ha-ha-ha!" Eve could no longer contain her delight.

"You'll get yours. It'll come; I promise," Ross bantered with a smile on his face.

"Psang, when do you expect the porters?"

"Soon, very soon, Misser Ross, very soon."

"Good. We have a lot to do and a long way to go." Ross seemed impatient. He got up and walked around the small camp looking at everything, mumbling to himself as if he was dictating an inventory of gear.

"Ross, you should eat something before you get started with that. Come on, sit back down," Eve encouraged enthusiastically.

"I will, just trying to go over everything . . . hope we have it all."

"Looks like a lot of stuff to me. Maybe too much. Anyway, doesn't matter now if we don't have it. It's not like we can run to the store and get it," Eve remarked with a smirk on her face.

Ross glanced at her and smiled. He acted the same as he always would at the beginning of any expedition: focused, anxious, and eager to go.

It was not long before the three porters arrived. Together, the team got ready for the arduous hike: organizing, packing, and making sure all the necessary supplies were accounted for. Ross double-checked everything. With packs full and ready, the group embarked on their first day of hiking. Psang and Ross took the lead and carried machetes, which they used for clearing the undergrowth. Progress was slow as the team pushed deeper and higher into the subtropical rainforest.

Each of the three days of hiking to base camp was a trial of endurance and resolve. Tested by heat, water, rock, and altitude, the climbers pressed on hour after hour. First, they hiked through the dense forest, and then, higher up, over the rocks and across gorges, through the river and its tributaries and up steep mountain walls. Each night, under the cover of darkness, they set up their camp and climbed into their tents exhausted. Each morning, they arose to a new and even more difficult leg of the journey burdened under the oppressive weight of packs that seemed only to increase with each step they took.

It was during these days of intense hiking and climbing that Eve proved her mettle. She showed Ross and the others she was very capable as a climber, and that she was strong and determined. Though small framed and softly spoken, Eve was earning the respect of the porters and of Psang. Of course, Ross knew her strengths; he had hiked many times with her, and it made him proud to see her show such grit against this inhospitable landscape. At one point, later on the second day, Eve found an unexpected reserve of energy and, without realizing it, took the lead, even out-pacing

Ross. It was not long before Psang realized Eve was far out front and moving as if she was a machine.

"Misser Ross, do she know where she go?"

"Huh? What do you mean?"

"Miss Eve, she way ahead. I can't see her. Do she know where she go?"

"Eve! Eve!" Ross yelled. "Eve! Wait up!"

"What?" Eve's faint response could barely be heard through the bush.

"Wait up! You're going too fast. Hold up!"

Eve stopped and leaned against a tree as she waited for the others to catch up. As she caught sight of Ross, she shook her head and smiled. "You guys are slowing down. Come on! We have a long way to go. No time for lollygagging. Ha-ha-ha! Want me to take some of that pack weight from ya? Maybe you'll be able to keep up, huh?"

Ross just looked at her with a weak grin. His thoughts went quickly to the first time he had seen her and how unlikely it seemed for them to be together. There was something amazing and almost precious about her, something that took hold of his thoughts and his heart. It had been the month before Daniel fell. Ross had been out alone on a climb at Mazama in northern Washington. During the two-day outing, he met Eve, who had been climbing some of the single pitch crags in the area. They had decided to do a multi-pitch climb together, since they were both soloing for the weekend. Ross was impressed with how well she moved on the rock and how calm and in control she behaved in some very technical areas of the wall, as well as how strong she was in spite of her appearance. At times, Ross had even needed Eve to coach him over some tricky sections of the climb, and she had taken her fair share of leading on the rope. Eve had been free climbing for several years, but was not a mountaineer, and had never climbed anything above fourteen thousand feet. To her, the opportunity to summit Machapuchare seemed both exciting and daunting at the same time.

After that weekend with Eve, Ross had returned home to focus on the summit bid to Machapuchare with Daniel. He had told her he would like to see her again and she had been interested in another outing. However, before either Ross or Eve could try to arrange for a second climbing date, tragedy struck, and Daniel had died. The shock left Ross emotionally distraught. He lost interest in everything, including climbing, and had forgotten about Eve.

The news of the tragedy traveled quickly through the relatively small community of mountaineers and rock climbers. Eve heard about the accident. She was, however, unaware that Daniel and Ross were such good friends. Had she known, she would probably not have tried to reach out to Ross the week following Daniel's funeral.

She had not heard from him since their climb together more than a month before and had hoped to set up another climbing date. Eve had been shocked and horrified after a very short and painful conversation where Ross, fighting back tears, told her that Daniel was not only his best friend but, he had been with Daniel the day he fell to his death.

Hanging up the phone in total disbelief, Eve felt her light-hearted invitation seemed terribly inappropriate. She doubted whether she would ever hear from Ross again, and yet several months later, to her surprise, she received a phone call from Ross.

Their second weekend together was the beginning of the first, meaningful friendship Ross had ever had with a woman. Women actually scared Ross a little, and his fear caused him to avoid them. Eve was different, though. She was disarming, gentle, and sincere, which was refreshing to Ross, for so many people he had known, aside from Daniel, were disingenuous posers.

Eve gave Ross all the time he needed to heal; she never pushed him to move on. In fact, she encouraged him to hold on to his memories, to embrace them, to remember Daniel, and to let the pain of his loss remind him of the preciousness of an honest true friend. The kindness, vulnerability, and love Eve showed worked like a balm to heal the wounds in Ross's heart.

"Hmm, don't make me regret bringing you along," Ross joked back.

"You couldn't make it without me and you know it. Slowpoke!" Eve teased.

They both laughed.

At the twilight of the fourth day, with great relief, they arrived at base camp. It had taken them an extra day because one of the porters had slipped on a nasty section and fallen into the river when they were just half a day from the camp. The river flowing through the gorge swept the porter downstream, requiring the team to backtrack to rescue him and recover their gear. He was pulled out with only a few scrapes and bruises. The accident had shaken the whole team, making them more cautious and deliberate in their approach.

Eve quickly dropped her pack to the ground and squatted on a stone. She put her head in her hands and began to cry. The tears were not from sadness or exhilaration but from sheer exhaustion. Her body could not restrain the emotional eruption.

"You alright?" Ross asked.

"Yes! I'm just great! Absolutely elated! Can't you tell?"

"Then why were you crying?"

"I'm not crying. These are not tears, silly. I just have seriously sweaty eyeballs, probably the altitude or something. Leave me alone!"

"Yeah. That's probably it, the altitude." Ross dropped his backpack, walked over to where Eve was sitting and gave her a hug. "You did great these past few days. I'm really proud of you. I love you."

Eve smiled and touched his cheek.

Below the east face of Machapuchare, amid rocks and scree, they looked for a place to set up their base camp. Dwarfed by the hulking monolith of towering granite rising more than two miles above them, Machapuchare's twin summits stood austere and indomitable in stark contrast to their utter finiteness. Surrounding the area was a large basin flanked by four gigantic mountains: Annapurna II, Annapurna III, Gangapurna, and Machapuchare. The basin was more than two miles across, with three valleys flanked by three lesser mountain ranges with peaks of twelve and thirteen-thousand feet. Many streams ran down through the basin. Their source was the glaciers that had carved out the valleys of the basin eons before. The streams eventually ran together to form the Siti River, which carved out the deep gorges that scarred the descending landscape to the south. Clawing its way down the eastern face of Annapurna III, an unnamed glacier cut its way along the east base of Machapuchare before it surrendered to the inevitable fluid transformation of all glacial flows.

Ross looked over the landscape. It was so different than he had imagined. The maps he had studied could not have prepared him for the rugged enormity of everything. He wondered what it would have been like to be standing there with Daniel. "Hey, Eve! What do ya think, maybe we call this basin 'Daniel's Basin'?"

"Seems kinda fitting. Sure, 'Daniel's Basin'."

"Great! He'd like it, I think."

Psang situated the base camp at the outlet of the central valley, near the conjunction of four of the tributaries at the outlet of Daniel's Basin, and for the next several days, Ross and the others rested up while they acclimatized and worked on the base camp. On the morning of the fourth day, the porters were ready to return down the mountain to the van. Psang had arranged for them to return once they finished their summit bid. All he had to do was radio, and they would return to haul the equipment and gear back down to the van. Of course, Ross was very emphatic the porters not mention any details to anyone, including their location and what they were doing. He knew it was illegal to climb Machapuchare and he did not want the local authorities to get wind of their plans and come looking for them.

"You're sure you can trust these guys, Psang? They won't say a word, right?"

"Oh yes, Misser Ross. They reliable, very good friends."

"You told them to move the van, to get it away from the trailhead, right? Did you give them the keys?"

"Yes, Misser Ross. Yes, Yes." Ross looked at the porters who smiled at him with naïve, almost childlike grins, which did little to reassure Ross, but there was little else he could do to guarantee their secret was kept safe. Ross focused on one of the porters whom he had talked to many times over the previous days. "You won't tell anyone, right?"

The porter smiled and nodded his head.

"OK, OK." Ross nodded his head and smiled nervously.

The porters turned and headed back the same way they had come. It was not long before they disappeared into the thick forest and Ross, Eve, and Psang were left alone without support or assistance.

Psang had come to assist on the climb, not lead, though he was the most experienced climber of the three. He looked forward to climbing the special mountain and though none of them could divulge their conquest, should they succeed, the chance to do what no one had done before was a very intoxicating motive, even for a humble Sherpa such as he.

The eastern face of Machapuchare gained immediate and steep elevation from the basin floor. A sixty-five-degree channel of ice and snow, scree and boulders, a couloir, ran down the mountain to the basin. Ross determined that climbing the couloir to just over sixteen thousand feet would put them at the final and most difficult section of the climb, a six-thousand-foot vertical wall to the top. From their low vantage point at base camp, it was impossible to see the summit or the true difficulty of the six-thousand-foot wall. It is always that way in the mountains; one is never truly able to assess the dangers from below. Often a route looks feasible and yet, once in its midst, climbers can find themselves stuck and needing to change direction or descend.

"We need to get higher, Psang. We'll have to find a better vantage." Ross looked across the glacial basin for a peak to climb, which would give him a better view of the wall, the last section of the climb. "Tomorrow we'll need to climb to that summit over there. I need to get a better view." Ross pointed to a distant summit that was a couple of thousand feet higher than base camp. "You up for it, Eve?"

"What summit are you talking about?"

"That one there. It should give us a great view of the wall and help me find a good route up."

"Oh, that one. Yeah, it'll be fun, and good practice, too."

The next morning, they loaded up daypacks and headed off. Most of the basin that lay between them and the mountain was covered in scree and boulder fields, with the occasional creek breaking up the landscape; all of which made progress slow. By mid-day, they reached the summit of the mountain. On any scale, the challenging summit would have been meaningful for the acclimatizing mountaineers, but, set against the Himalayan range, it seemed hardly more than a grain of sand against a sand dune.

Ross took his binoculars from his pack along with the topographical map. He quickly oriented the map and began to study the wall of Machapuchare. He made some marks on the map as he studied the terrain. Eve looked up at the mountain and felt, deep in her soul, that the mountain was something more than stone, and ice, and snow. Her first impression of the naked wall was that the dark gray face of granite staring down at her was almost alive, breathing out great clouds of frozen breath from its summit like the fog of her own breath. It did not respect anyone, regardless of their skill. It felt cold and indifferent, unwilling to notice her intended trespass. To her, Machapuchare displayed the quiet confidence of a monarch, assured of its authority and power, unmoved by their intended assault or by their ambition. They would not, however, receive any help from the mountain: no directions, no breaks, no mercy, and yet, it seemed too, that the mountain was not opposed to them being there. Many of the people in the Himalayas believed the mountains either blessed or opposed your journey, and this was mostly a matter of opinion. Psang, though not a devout believer, had sensed a friendly ambivalence from Machapuchare. His reassuring interpretation, however, did not completely dispel a menacing sense of concern growing within Eve's heart. She may have just been intimidated by the overwhelming scale of the mountain since she had not been on such massive summits before. Yet, to her sensibilities, the growing angst she felt represented something more imminent than fear, but she said nothing to Ross or to Psang.

After examining the face of Machapuchare, Ross estimated the climb would take about four to five days. At the end of each day of climbing, the team would set up a hanging camp on the face. Their only major shortcoming on the final ascent was not having good weather information. This was a big risk which could prove to be very dangerous.

While at basecamp, the team was able to monitor both current and incoming weather conditions. They were waiting for an opening of four to five days when the weather would be the most agreeable for their climb. After eleven days at base camp, a favorable pattern developed and the team began to discuss the final preparations for their ascent.

"Yes! That's it! We go tomorrow. Finally!" Ross shouted with enthusiasm.

Eve looked at him and smiled. "You're ready to go, aren't you? Can't wait?"

"Totally ready! Waiting and acclimating is the hardest part of every climb. I'm ready to get on the wall and summit this bitch!"

"Misser Ross, you not say that to mountain! She not favor disrespect!"

Ross looked at Psang with an audacious glare. "Really? You've got to be kidding me."

Eve could not believe the impudence. She had very little tolerance for rudeness and brazen arrogance, especially from Ross. "Ross, how dare you talk to him that way. What are you thinking?"

Ross looked at her and walked away. "Whatever . . ."

Eve was aghast and looked at Psang. She apologetically said to him, "He shouldn't have treated you like that. I'm sorry."

Psang smiled. "We friends. It fine, Miss Eve."

The weeks of close quarters and shared spaces had developed tension between them, tensions each of them secretly hoped would find relief once they were on the mountain. They were ready to climb Machapuchare and climbing her would be the cure for all that ailed their strained, though dependent companionship. If the weather forecast held, the next morning was to be their first day of climbing the behemoth they had come to assail.

In their separate ways, they spent the rest of the day preparing for the four- to five-day climb. It was quiet around the camp, quieter than usual, and for each of them, the exhilaration of what was to come was mixed with deep soul searching. The quiet atmosphere was less about the sharp words that had been exchanged or the offense that might have been taken than it was about the contemplation of possibilities. The question of whether or not they would make it back hung in the air. More than the summit, or the climb, or anything else, their thoughts, though private and certainly unspoken, lingered on that one unified fatal consideration. Each of them was working through their own fears in order to muster up the courage they believed the others to have.

It was getting dark when Ross called out to Eve and Psang. "Hey, I think we need to talk about tomorrow. Can we talk over by the fire? Please?"

Psang, the first to reach the fire, seated himself on a large stone and stared into the flames. Ross walked over and sat across from him and looked at the fire as well. Eve came from around the tent, putting her arm into her jacket as she walked. She settled next to Psang and resisted looking at either of them.

"Hey, I might have said some things that were out of line earlier, and I'm sorry. My mouth, sometimes it just . . . " Ross's words failed him.

Eve looked at Ross across the fire then she looked at Psang. He smiled. "We good Misser Ross."

Eve allowed a timid smile to spread across her face.

Now slightly encouraged, Ross spoke, "We need to talk about our plan. I know, I know we discussed it before, but I think we need to do it again."

"Yes. Yes, Misser Ross, we should."

"Great. Are you OK, Eve?"

Eve looked at Ross and smiled. "Of course."

"I'm sorry for earlier, you know?"

"I know. It's not really about earlier. Just a lot of thoughts going through my head, that's all."

"Yeah, me too," Ross agreed. "OK, considering the weather forecast looks good for the next several days, it looks like this is it. We are going for it in the morning. Everyone good with that?"

"Yes, I ready," Psang quickly answered.

Eve just nodded her head and smiled.

"Great! OK, so here's the plan. The first section of the climb is up the couloir to camp one, it will be just over sixteen thousand feet. It will be a long day, but I think we can do it. If not, then we'll set camp early enough so that we're not setting up in the dark. Psang, I need you to make sure I don't push the clock. If it's getting close, we stop. Got it?"

"Yes. Yes, Misser Ross. You count on me."

"Most of the heavy gear, a couple of small tents, and supplies should be ready and in our packs. Did you guys look over your lists and make sure everything is in your packs?" Ross cast a slightly skeptical glance toward Eve.

"Of course. I read the list and checked it twice. Now I sound like Santa Claus. Shall we discuss who has been naughty and nice as well?" Eve looked at Ross with a mischievous grin. Ross and Psang both laughed. The laughter changed the solemn mood, lifting their spirits for the first time in days.

"OK. Let's get back to it. It's getting late and I'm getting hungry," Ross said with a smile. "We'll stay the first night at camp one, then the next day we will start section two, up another thirty-five hundred feet to just under twenty thousand feet. Now it's possible that any one of us could start to feel the effect of the altitude. Eve, you've never been that high, so if you begin experiencing any of the symptoms we've discussed, don't hesitate to say something. Got it? No being tough."

"Got it. No being brave about being sick. What about climbing a twenty thousand something foot mountain? Is it OK to be brave about that?"

"Funny! You're really funny!"

"I try. Maybe you could give it a go once in a while." Eve had a very satisfied smirk on her face.

"I'll be funny at the top. Until then, I'll leave the funny to you. Camp two will be a hanging camp on the east face, so we can't set it up too late. Again, Psang, keep track of the time and the sun. The last section of the climb is the summit. If all goes well, we should be there on day three. Based on the maps and altitude projections, the summit is just over two thousand five hundred feet from camp two. Once on the summit, we can only stay a moment, then we'll make a quick descent back to camp two where we'll stay the third night. On day four we'll break camp two, descend to camp one, and if all's good and time affords, we'll break camp one and make the final descent to base camp. It's a very aggressive plan, but the weather is difficult to predict beyond four or five days. I think we'll be good. Does that sound like a plan?"

"Very good plan, Misser Ross. Very good plan."

"Sound good to you, Eve?"

"Yep. Sounds good to me. Sound good to you, Ross?"

Ross laughed and shook his head. "Looks like a day alone makes you a very feisty girl!"

Eve just smiled. "Let's eat!"

After eating, Ross and Eve sat together by the fire. Ross looked at Eve and his heart was filled with a sudden, unexpected satiation. He was glad she was there with him, but it was more than that. In that moment, he realized in all the time he had spent with Daniel in the mountains, he had never felt as completely alive as he did with Eve. The feeling of it washed over him slowly, like the warm water of a shower. He felt choked up for a moment but shoved down his emotions. "Are you ready for this?" Ross said.

"Yeah, I think I'm ready." Eve looked at Ross and immediately noticed the glassiness of his eyes and wondered to herself what he was feeling.

"You don't sound so sure, Eve."

"It's not that, it's just, well, I take all this very seriously, no playing around, no games, you know what I mean?"

"Hmm. Yeah, I do."

"Ross, do you have any doubts?"

"Always, I always have doubts now. I don't doubt myself or my ability as much as I doubt the things I can't control. It's always the things we can't control."

"There's almost nothing you can control, Ross."

"Yeah, I know. Maybe that's why I doubt so much more now than I did before. I can't control anything, but I can try, or at least I can be ready for anything."

"Why do it then? Why climb?"

"Cause it's something I do well, and it puts me on the edge of life and death in a way that's more, I don't know, more recognizable than other things."

"What do you mean?"

"Well, we live on the edge of life and death every day, only most of the time, we don't see the edge. At any minute something catastrophic could happen and we could perish, only we aren't expecting it: a car crash, an aneurism, a city bus running us over, whatever. At least with climbing, I know where that edge is. It wouldn't be such a surprise, and that gives me the feeling of having more control. It also makes me feel more alive. Life has more meaning when death is so close."

"Wow, you seem to have truly given this some serious thought."

"I've spent a lot of time alone over the last few years and my thoughts seem to dig deep when I'm alone. Plus, I think a lot when I'm on the wall, not just about climbing but I contemplate life, my life and what it means."

"So, do you think there is some meaning to life, then?"

"Not really. You just have to live it, I guess. Too much stuff, stupid stuff, pointless stuff has happened to think there's meaning to our lives. Anyway, that's what I think. What do you think? Is there some bigger purpose to all this?"

"I'd like to think we're not all just going through the motions without any real reason or meaning. Too many bad things have happened to good people to not hope that it's all for something. Can you agree?"

Ross threw a stick into the fire. "I don't know, Eve. I don't want to know. Purpose or reason can't change all the shitty things that have happened. It can't bring Daniel back; it doesn't change what's happened. So it doesn't seem to matter much. Not to me, anyway."

"So this is about Daniel, then, this whole living on the edge thing?"

"Maybe. Maybe not. I'm not really sure. I actually think it's about everything. You know, the sum of all your parts." Ross feigned a smile as if trying to lighten the weight of the conversation, but Eve was not yet ready to let it go.

"You mean, the whole is better than the sum of all its parts, thing?"

"Well, I'm not sure. It's more like the sum of all your parts is what makes you whole. Whatever happens to you in life affects who you are and what you become."

"So, it's not just about Daniel?"

"No, it's everything. Some parts are definitely more relevant than others, that's for sure. I feel like I've lived on the edge my entire life, and most of the time I wasn't even conscious of where the edge was. There never seemed to be any reason for hardships, dreadful catastrophes, or distress. It's hard to believe in reason or purpose when everything seems so random and chaotic. Quite purposeless."

"Hmm. Yeah." Eve's thoughts drifted back to when she was young before her mother died. She still remembered her voice, and her touch, and especially her smile. She also remembered how her death felt and afterward, how her life seemed so broken those first few years. The pain of it was still palpable, though not as sharp. In one way or another, her mother's voice always came back to her, always whispering in her heart the same simple words she had heard her say so many times, *We can't always know the reason, only that there is one.*

Eve looked at Ross. "Maybe. Maybe you're right, but I'm not sure I like the potential outcome if that's the case. I don't like the idea that we're slaves to our circumstances and that we have to be formed by them, shaped into someone that we may not like being."

"But don't you see? If there is a purpose for our lives, then it's the same. We have no control over who we are or what we're meant to do. In either case, it feels like we have no choice. At least by choosing to live on the edge, I get to choose something. I get to decide how daringly close to falling I will be. No one chooses for me."

For Eve, the conversation had taken a wrong turn, gone down a dark alley. It made her feel a sense of conflict and anxiety she hadn't felt before. She felt worried about their relationship. Quickly, in an effort to avoid overthinking it all, something she was often intentional about, she took a deep breath and exhaled demonstratively. "Whew! How did we start talking about this anyway? Way too serious for a romantic moment by the fire under a starry sky. Don't you think?"

"Ha-ha! Yeah, you're right," Ross agreed. He leaned closer to her and kissed her. "I love you." Eve smiled and laid her head on his shoulder.

As they sat in silence, Psang walked up to the fire. "Misser Ross, everything ready for climb tomorrow. We leave early?"

Ross scowled at Psang for interrupting. He felt a rare, sharp stab of jealousy for the loss of the tender moment alone with Eve. It had been weeks since they had spent any meaningful time alone. Psang had an uncanny way of showing up at just the wrong times. Ross replied in frustration, "Of course we will leave early, Psang. We discussed this already."

"Good, good." Psang backed away graciously and went to the tent.

Eve looked at Ross and smiled. She did not like the way Ross had spoken to Psang, but she, too, wanted to be left alone for a while longer.

That was not to be. Ross stood to his feet. "Well, I suppose we should get to bed."

Eve hesitated, hoping Ross would sit back down beside her.

"Come on." Ross held out his hand.

"Yeah, yeah, I guess you're right."

The early morning sky was clear, though dark and star-filled. Eve turned on a lantern. Soon Psang's tent was glowing like a yellow paper lantern. Everyone began shuffling around, preparing for the first leg of the climb. They moved quietly as if in a trance; anticipating what they were about to do. The whirring sound of a zipper broke the uneasy silence. Psang was the first member of the team to exit his tent. Pulling his gear out with him, he began carefully arranging it in his backpack under the glow of his headlamp. The ritual of packing one's backpack was very personal and deliberate. Everything was systematically accounted for and situated so the climber could locate what they needed, quickly and conveniently.

The whir of another zipper cut through the quiet, and Ross stepped out of his tent. Eve followed and silently, the two began the final packing of their gear also under the glow of their headlamps.

"There, I'm ready. You guys better get a move on or you'll get left behind," Eve encouraged cheerfully, hiding her anxiety. Aside from the internal fears she had been having about the mountain, Eve was very excited to finally step onto its towering walls.

For the next four days, the trio would share one small tent and a small sleeping platform, attached to the face of the mountain with anchors, webbing, and robe, they called, hanging camp. This was so they could minimize the weight and bulk of their gear while climbing. When climbing, they hooked a rope to a gear bag, which had all their camping and sleeping gear, and pulled it up behind them as they made their ascent.

Eve shouldered her backpack. She clipped her waist belt and pulled it tight. "Are you slowpokes ready yet? Come on!"

"Just about. I need to double-check a couple of things."

"Psang, are you ready? Men, always primping," Eve said facetiously. "Funny!"

"Yes, Miss Eve. I ready."

As the sun rose over Annapurna II, it began to warm the dark gray rock of Machapuchare. In the darkness, they began to climb.

The team moved slowly and methodically up the couloir, trying to stay mostly to the sides where there was more solid rock on which to gain purchase. Because the couloir acts like a steep gutter for snow, water, and debris, the base was very loose with gravel and boulders, which could be very dangerous if dislodged. Climbing precisely and in as straight a line as possible, they moved with determination. As they gained elevation, the thinning air caused their lungs to burn and their breathing to become heavy; their bodies struggled to gain essential oxygen. Every movement became more and more laborious the higher they climbed, but they moved well together, ever upward.

After fourteen hours of constant climbing, the darkness was beginning to settle over the range. Psang, who was taking the lead, looked down at Ross and cried out over the wind. "Mr. Ross, we need to make camp soon."

Ross hollered back up the three hundred feet separating them, "Do you see a good spot?"

"Oh, yes. A good place just ahead, not too far, come, come."

They reached the place for camp one, a minor outcropping of stone, hardly large enough to hold their small tent. When Eve finally made it to the site, she laughed in disbelief. "What? This is your idea of a good campsite, Psang? Most birds wouldn't feel safe on this ledge."

Psang looked with a confused expression. He could see that Eve was smiling at him, so he quickly realized that she was only joking. Psang smiled back and playfully teased her, which was not his norm. "Your palace, my queen."

Eve laughed and patted him on the shoulder.

"Man, that was a long climb, but it went a lot faster than I thought it would. I mean, it seemed like it went a lot faster. I'm bushed," Eve admitted.

"Me, too. You did great today, Eve."

"Thanks!"

As they sat together in the close confines of the tent eating, fatigue began to settle upon their bodies. There was little conversation between them. Once they finished their meal, they climbed into their sleeping bags, turned off their headlamps, and without a word, fell asleep.

The next morning came much more quickly than any of them could have expected as the alarm clock's unapologetic clatter filled the small tent. After silencing the alarm, Eve rolled over and covered her head with the hood of her sleeping bag. She began to think about home. She thought about her father and wondered what he might be doing at that very moment. As she was thinking about him, she could hear Ross, snoring. She smiled and turned over, then sat up. She reached for her headlamp and turned it on.

"Hey, sleepyhead, it's time to get up," she said in a playful and altogether excessively energetic tone, especially considering how early it was.

"How can you be so full of fun? Aren't you tired?" Ross asked as he rolled over.

"Nope."

Psang was next to sit up. He unzipped his bag, grabbed his headlamp, and began dressing for the day. Eve noticed, as Psang was moving around, that his breath appeared as large white clouds in the tent. It was very cold. She felt the bite of the cold for the first time and quickly added another layer of clothing. Ross was the last to emerge from his sleeping bag, and he quickly dressed and turned on the stove to boil some water for breakfast.

By the time they had finished dressing and eating, the yellow glow of the rising sun was warming the side of their tent. They would need good light for climbing the next two sections of the wall if they were to be safe, so they timed their exit of the tent for the arrival of the morning light.

While prepping the gear bags, Psang sang a little tune to himself. As he sang, Eve began to realize that her head was aching and rubbed her forehead.

"Are you feeling alright?" Ross asked.

"Well, I was, but now my head is starting to hurt."

"Just now?"

"Yeah. I was fine a minute ago. It's not that bad. I should be OK."

Ross was concerned that she could be developing AMS, Acute Mountain Sickness.

"Don't worry, I'll take some meds, and everything will be just fine. I haven't had any trouble so far," Eve insisted. She knew Ross would overreact if she said too much.

"Yeah, but we haven't been this high before. You sure you're good to go on?"

"If I have any other problems, or if the headache persists, I'll let you know. I know how much you want this."

"I can go without you from here. Psang and I can go on if you would rather stay back."

"No way! Are you insane? I didn't come this far to sit in a tent on a ledge for a few days while you're climbing! No! No, I'm good."

Leaving the small tent and a few of the supplies behind for the return trip, they began day two. Three thousand five hundred feet up the face: this was where the real climbing would begin. Slowly at first, they moved pitch by pitch, each member taking their turn as the lead and sharing in the belay work. The three climbers moved up the face of the behemoth like a three-legged spider. Linked together by a ninety-meter rope, the team worked as a unit, hour by hour.

As the sun began to set low on the horizon, they were still five hundred feet below their goal for the day. If they were to make the summit and get back down to camp the next day, they had to make it the last two pitches. Ross took the lead on the next-to-last pitch, moving like a monkey up the face from handhold to handhold. He set his anchor, connected the rope in with carabineers to the anchors, and moved to the next handhold. Once he reached the end of the pitch, he set up to belay the other two climbers as they came up. With one pitch to go, the trio decided to press on. They turned on their headlamps and began their last pitch. An hour later, they reached 19,847 feet and set up the hanging camp. After twelve pitches and another grueling fourteen-hour day, all three of them were approaching total fatigue. It was the kind of fatigue that keeps a person from resting.

Every bone, joint, and muscle ached, and of the three, Eve was feeling the worst.

Throughout the day, she had continued to deteriorate. Her headache had only intensified, and she was also losing her appetite and feeling nauseous; however, she did not tell Ross or Psang. She hoped that some rest and a cup of hot soup would help. She also desperately longed for a good night's sleep, despite the cold, the wind, and the thinness of her sleeping mat, which caused her to feel pressure on every bone and muscle.

In the tent, the team discussed the final day's climb. Ross, who had studied maps of the mountain, described the final ascent that was to come. As he talked, Eve lay in her sleeping bag, struggling to stay awake.

"We have about three thousand feet to go tomorrow. The last fifteen hundred feet, though, begins to taper off, so the climbing should be a little easier. Up until that, we have some very difficult mixed climbing. We need to be ready. I'll take the lead, and we need to move at least as fast as we did today."

"Misser Ross, are you sure we have enough time to get to the top and back down to camp?"

"Well, I certainly hope so. I don't want to drag that damn gear bag up to the top. Do you?"

"But Ross, what if it gets dark before we get back down? What will we do then?" asked Eve.

"We should be OK. We'll be rappelling, so things should go much faster on the way down. Getting back to camp two is crucial. We won't be able to hang on the face during the night, and if the weather were to go south on us . . . well, it won't. We should have good weather if our intel is correct." Psang and Eve both sensed that his confidence was wavering slightly.

The glow of their hanging camp on the face of Machapuchare was like a firefly sitting on a skyscraper: small, indefensible, and nearly invisible. As they sat discussing plans for the next day, the wind started to blow against them, and the air began to feel icy, but no one noticed because of their conversation and their fatigue.

"Eve, how're you feeling?" inquired Ross.

"I'm doing OK. I'll be fine," Eve responded while turning her head away, hoping Ross would not keep asking. She just wanted to go to sleep. Of course, Ross did not really want to know if she was not feeling well. He knew, in good conscience, he could not leave her, and he did not want to turn back.

"OK then, we better hit the hay. Big day tomorrow."

Lying in her sleeping bag, Eve's thoughts turned again to life back home. She was missing her friends, the ocean, the smell of saltwater and fish; she missed her cat, her apartment overlooking the bay. Moreover, she missed her dad, whom she had not seen for almost a year. She had called him the day before she left for Nepal.

"Don't do anything dumb," he had said to her. However, Randal Banister had not imagined just how risky this journey would be. She could not have explained it to him even if she had wanted to, for she had not possessed any idea of the dangers. Lying in the dark, suspended three thousand feet in the air by a few ropes and a canvas platform, she felt that she may have made the biggest mistake of her life. She could not sleep. Her head was thumping and her entire body was vibrating with chills. A tear welled up in her eye and froze to her eyelashes. Eve rolled over onto her side, facing Ross, who had his back to her. Exhaustion finally overtook the altitude sickness, and she slept.

Ross imagined the top of the mountain. He pictured the climbing and each step the team would have to take to reach the top. His mind was fixed on the summit. He had asked Eve how she was doing, but he had asked because it seemed like the right thing to do, not because he was genuinely concerned. He had grown indifferent to her, to the possibility that she might be sick and might not be able to make it to the summit. He had become dismissive of the danger and of the potential for disaster. Ross lay in the dark, obsessed with the idea of success, possessed by the illusion of conquering the mountain. He saw success on the mountain as a kind of redemption, redemption from the guilt and self-indictment that he felt over Daniel. He had never spoken to anyone, not even to Eve, about what happened the day Daniel fell.

Lying next to Ross, in the thick darkness that made everything seem a million miles away, Psang stared at the blackness; his thoughts fixated on his wife and four children who waited for him back home. Ross was paying him well for his help and finishing this job would mean that he would be able to provide for his family's humble needs for many months. Psang loved his children and every time he had to leave them, he felt deep pain and sadness. It had been several weeks now, and in just a few more days he would return. The thought of them elicited a smile that broke across his face. Quickly, his thoughts returned to the mountain. Psang had climbed much higher and more dangerous mountains before, so the circumstances of this climb should have concerned him less; however, Psang was a superstitious man, not because he was particularly devout, but because he was a man who took the possibilities of the unseen seriously. He noticed that Ross had changed since they had arrived at base camp. At one point, Psang had tried talking to him about it, but he dismissed him and his concerns and offered him an ultimatum. Ross's words echoed in Psang's mind, *"If you don't want to continue working with me, then you can leave, and I won't pay you anything since you would be breaking our agreement."*

Although Psang had wanted to walk away, he needed the money and felt he could not back out of the expedition. Desperation dilutes even the most resolute ethic and erodes the strongest will. Psang could feel the constant and palpable grip of privation threatening his family. He could not let them down, no matter what it cost him.

Psang lay awake after a cold night of restlessness and unease. He was unsure whether anticipation, nerves, or anxiety was the culprit, robbing him of these precious hours of sleep. Thinking about the final ascent, worrying about the changing weather, and being plagued by the superstitions of his fathers, opened a wide doorway of wariness and fear in his mind. He lay there trying to make himself move, to shake off the menacing thoughts that were paralyzing him. Finally, he reached around searching for his headlamp.

At the push of a button, the small hanging tent was aglow with the soft illumination of the small light. To Psang's surprise, Ross and Eve were also awake, lying in their sleeping bags with their eyes wide open, staring at the dark nothingness, silent and contemplative. No one spoke a word; they just began the morning ritual of warming soup and water, all of which had frozen during the night. As they sat up wrapped in their sleeping bags, a fog of warm breath collected in the cold, cramped space. Slowly, as the small stove heated up the soup, each of the team stirred about, putting on layers of clothes, while the room of nylon walls began to slowly thaw.

Outside the tent, the morning sun rose over the mountain peaks, casting light and warmth upon the hanging shelter. From the start of the day, time was not their ally; it moved forward impatiently, unwilling to wait for them. Minute by minute passed, and critical moments slowly moved further and further away as each member of the team rushed about the hanging camp putting on their frozen climbing gear, crampons, and gathering ropes. With ice axes in hand, one by one, they exited the tent and began their assault of the mountain. Ross took the lead in the biting cold as the wind howled about him making each move slow and clumsy.

The wall of the mountain was covered under a blanket of snow and ice. The night's storm had left the wall with a thin layer of translucent ice. A dusting of snow topped the ice, requiring even more precision with each step and reach of their ice axes. The climbers used the front spikes of their crampons, placing them courageously into whatever hold they could find.

At first, the climbers were slow, cautious, and methodical, but as they warmed up from the adrenaline coursing through their bodies, they were able to relax and they gained confidence on the rock. As the rays of sunlight struck the black granite wall, the ice began to melt, and the dusting of snow disappeared, making the task of finding purchase on the face much easier.

On the second pitch of the climb, Eve took the lead. Only a few hours before, she lay in the tent contemplating retreat, but for some inexplicable reason, she was feeling better than she had for days. Climbing as good as any climber, Eve moved with precision and speed that surprised Ross and Psang.

"What's gotten into you?" shouted Ross, who was nearly ninety feet below.

"What do you mean?" She knew what he meant but chose to make him admit to the fact that on this day she was King of the Mountain and the strongest climber on the wall.

"I've never seen you climb like this. I'm impressed!"

"Thanks. I've been waiting for just the right moment to show you up. This is it!"

Eve moved farther and farther up the face, leaving the other two climbers lower down the rope.

"She a very good climber, Misser Ross!" Psang exclaimed.

"Yeah, I know. She's way better than I am. I've just never told her so. She's strong and she moves like Daniel used to move on the rock. It's kind of irritating."

"I glad she with us; she good climber," Psang cheered.

"Me, too!"

"It a good day. Huh, Misser Ross?"

"Yes, it is Psang. Yes, it is," Ross said as he smiled.

The hours passed as they made their way to the top of the mountain. Eventually, they came to the section that tapered off and the wall became less and less steep, only one thousand feet to the top and to their prize. Their progress was slowed by deepening snow and gusts of wind that blew fiercely. From the west, the wind blew, and a plume of snow sailed from the top of the peak, looking like the veil of a bride blowing in the air. It was a beautiful sight from afar, but a menace to the climbers, for the blasting snow beat against their faces like sand, stabbing them and blinding them. Seeing their final destination just above them, they persisted.

On the peak, they could see a massive cornice, formed by the blowing snow. For the climbers, this was a serious danger because it made the actual ridgeline and peak hard to find. If one of the climbers were to step onto the cornice, they would likely fall through the snow into thin air and to their death.

Pushing through the deepening snow with the wind assaulting them at every step, they closed in on the summit. The sun moved closer and closer to the horizon, and each of them secretly knew they had pushed the limits and were sure to be descending in the darkness.

"Ross, do we have time?" questioned Eve.

"What do you mean? We're only a few hundred yards away. We can't turn back now!"

"But, Misser Ross, we have to turn back now. It too late. We be out here in dark and cold!" reasoned Psang.

"No way! There's no way we're turning back, not when we're this close. We can do this. Come on! Let's finish this!"

Eve looked at Psang, then took another step. The headache that had kept her awake the night before had returned and with it a sick feeling in her stomach. She doubted she could make the summit but would not give up. As she pressed on, she was finding it hard to concentrate. At times, she suspected she was not thinking straight, and her coordination was suffering as a result.

"Yes! Finally!" shouted Eve who led the team on the last stretch to the summit. She knelt in the deep snow and put her hands on her head, which felt as if it would explode at any moment.

"Woo-hoo!" shouted a jubilant Ross.

"Misser Ross, we need to hurry down," entreated Psang, who did not wish to waste any time on the summit.

"Give us a little time Psang. Just a few minutes to soak it in," responded Ross.

Ross unclipped himself from the rope that had leashed the three climbers together and walked to the summit of Machapuchare. As he stood there, surveying the world around him as if he were some great conqueror reveling in his conquest, the wind settled down, and he was able to remove his goggles and hood and let the sun shine on his face. Tears filled his eyes. He thought about Daniel and whispered, "This one's for you, this is your mountain."

From his pack, he pulled out an ice axe he had been carrying. It was Daniel's pick, the one he had been using the day he had fallen and died. Ross had kept it for this moment. He took it and thrust the spiked handle into the snowcap of Machapuchare. Ross pushed the ice axe farther into the snow until the head of the axe was all he could see. The dark red leash of the axe, which was laced to the head, lay on the snow like a flag, fluttering in the light breeze. "This is for you, buddy. We did it!"

Just a few feet away, Eve stood watching Ross say good-bye to his best friend. Until that moment, Ross had never been able to say goodbye and watching it, Eve realized just why this climb meant so much to him, why he was so driven, so focused on this mountain. Eve took her small digital camera out of her pack and snapped a couple of shots of Ross against the backdrop of countless mountain peaks and the endless sky. Psang looked over at her and quickly asked if she would like him to take a shot of her and Ross together.

"Of course, Psang. Thank you. Let's wait until he's done over there. The sun feels glorious right now, don't you think?"

"Yes, Miss Eve, very nice."

Ross turned and saw Eve and Psang standing together watching him. He waved at them and then started walking toward them.

"Psang is gonna take our picture," Eve yelled.

Ross nodded his head and smiled. Together on the summit with their arms around each other, they looked at Psang. Eve removed her hood and smiled. Her blond hair took flight in the breeze as she turned and kissed Ross on the lips then leaned her head on his shoulder. Psang took the small digital camera and took a close-up picture of the couple.

The light was fading quickly as the sun set in the sky. To the east side of the mountain, the shadows were growing long and dark; the night was fast approaching.

"Psang, can you get the background in the photo so others can see what we are seeing? Oh, and the sunset?" asked Eve, almost as if they were on vacation asking a local to take their picture.

"Oh, yes, Miss Eve, yes." Psang stepped away from the couple to get the sprawling landscape that lay behind them in the photo with the couple standing to one side.

"Don't get too close to the . . ." Eve warned Psang as a loud cracking sound ripped through the air. It was not the sound of thunder; it sounded more like a large tree branch breaking under the weight of heavy snow.

Suddenly, the ground where Psang was standing collapsed, and without any other warning, the cornice that had been building from the summit fell away, taking Psang with it. Without even being able to shout a word for help, Psang disappeared into the void.

"Psang!" Ross yelled, while he ran and dove for the rope attached to Psang's harness.

"Ross!" Eve's scream carried through the air like the resonant shriek of an eagle, but he did not respond; he chased recklessly after Psang. When Ross had unclipped from the climbing rope, he had attached another rope to his harness and then to one of the ice axes he had driven into the snow on the summit. If he was to slip on the snow or ice, it would arrest his fall. He assumed that Psang and Eve had done the same. They had discussed it the night before.

Diving for the rope was instinctive and reactive; Ross hoped he could hold on to it long enough to stop Psang's fall. However, Ross missed the rope. He frantically scrambled on his hands and knees toward the edge of the cornice trying to grab it, but the rope was falling away into the void faster than he could race toward it, and soon there would be no edge to keep Ross from falling.

Unexpectedly the rope began to grow tight and Ross felt a sudden sense of relief thinking that Psang had anchored himself to the mountain, but out of the corner of his eye, he saw the rope was still hooked to Eve's harness. She was the reason the rope was getting taut. She was Psang's anchor. He turned toward Eve, who was standing all alone and in shock, motionless and completely unaware that she was about to be pulled from the summit by the weight of Psang's body falling into the void.

"Eve!" Ross screamed as he frantically tried to get up and intercept her, but by then, she had been jerked from her frozen stupor and was shrieking for help while being pulled toward the void. Reeling from the severity of her headache and confusion, Eve had not anchored herself to the mountain either.

"Ross! Ross, help me! Help!" Frantically she scratched at the snow and ice, flailing at the mountain, trying to stop her fall.

Ross cried out to her, trying every way he could to reach the love of his life, but he was too late. "Eve! Eve, your axe! Use your ice axe!" But Eve had dropped her ice axe in the snow when they were taking the photos.

"Ross, Ross! Help! Ross!" Eve cried out as she was inexorably pulled toward the edge, into the black abyss.

Ross managed to get to his feet and made one last frantic effort to save her by diving toward the edge, but she was gone. "No-o-o! Eve!" bellowed Ross. "No! No! No!" he wailed repeatedly. Ross lay on his stomach crying hysterically, beating the mountain with his fists as if it were able to feel his blows.

The memory of Daniel falling away from him coursed through his mind. Images of his life, of his mother and her boyfriends, of his dad leaving them, of his sister, of all the people that had ever meant anything to him flashed before his eyes. The weight of his grief grew and grew; he could feel his heart beating in his chest with the same intensity he was beating the mountain with his fists. Sobbing, he lay in the snow at the summit of the mountain he had dreamt of conquering, but it had conquered him. He could feel death in his bones; he felt it in his thoughts, in his breath, the death he had taunted, that he had dared to challenge.

Silence surrounded him, innocuously swallowing up his cries, leaving the intrepid darkness to close in around him like a black cocoon, isolating him from the rest of the world. Frozen, unable to leave the spot where he had last seen Eve, Ross, now emptied of tears and filled with grief and rage, lifted his head to see a black sky. He had no idea how long he had been lying there, but he could not make himself move. Waves of sorrow and tears came and went. He was alone, alone again on a mountain surrounded by darkness and death.

Slowly and reluctantly, Ross rose to his feet and walked back to where he and Eve last stood together, to where the picture had been taken. Something was glowing in the snow a few feet from the edge of the cornice. Ross shuffled towards it and reached down into the snow. He pulled out the camera Psang had used to take the last photo. Psang had dropped it when the cornice fell away under his feet. Ross thought about Psang, how he had just disappeared, how he had never heard Psang yell or scream. All he heard was the almost imperceptible sound of the rope being pulled through the snow. He brushed it off and turned it over. It was still on. Ross saw the photo, the close-up that Psang had taken of him and Eve with her head on his shoulder. Tears swelled in his eyes, tumbled out, and froze on his cheeks. A wave of nausea came over him; he began to sweat from his brow and his eyes could not make out the photo through his tears. The deafening silence amplified every one of his movements. The sound of the crunching snow under his feet, his breathing, even his heartbeat, seemed amplified in his ears. At that moment, Ross felt more alone than at any other time in his life.

He walked slowly to the spot where Eve last stood. He saw her ice axes stuck in the snow and the backpack she had been wearing lying beside them. His thoughts began to spin; suddenly he felt dizzy. Ross started to reach out for her backpack and stopped. The spinning in his head was accelerating, and the gut-wrenching-pit-of-the-stomach nausea, started to intensify. Suddenly, Ross vomited in the snow. The force of the expulsion brought him to his knees, and for several moments, he knelt in the snow puking. The spinning in his head turned into a massive headache.

Still kneeling, with a puddle of vomit staring up at him, Ross could hear the sound of Eve's screams. He could see her falling away from his outstretched arms, he could see her eyes looking helplessly back at him as she clawed at the frozen summit, and then he could see her no more.

Ross could not imagine or accept living without her. Impulsively, he rose to his feet, and with a jolt, raced as fast as he could to the edge of the cornice and jumped into the dark, night sky. Hurling his body into the void, he closed his eyes and waited for his body to be crushed by the force of the six-thousand-foot fall. As he was falling, time slowed, and in his mind, he saw Eve, he saw Daniel, he saw Psang, he saw them all together, and in a moment, he would be with them forever. Death would win.

Then, with a sudden, violent, and painful jerk, Ross was yanked out of his trance and away from his hope. His fall into the abyss was arrested by the rope he had anchored to his ice axe earlier in the day. Slammed against the towering granite wall of Machapuchare by the pendulum effect of the rope, he was nearly knocked unconscious. Hanging more than two hundred feet from the top, in the black void, Ross swung from the end of the rope tied to the harness around his waist.

Barely conscious and hanging upside down, Ross considered closing his eyes and going to sleep, knowing it would be his final sleep. If he could just sleep then he would be free and not have to face the loss, the pain, the grief, not have to face himself. He hung there like a corpse, limp. Finally, too exhausted and cold to stay awake, he closed his eyes and fell into the chilly arms of hypothermia, knowing he would eventually cease to live. He was ready to die. He wanted to die. He imagined himself falling into darkness, falling deeper and deeper into nothingness, a nothingness he hoped was death.

As the darkness wrapped itself around his fading life, the chill of its touch wounded him.

He waited, alone, for the abysmal shadow to consume him.

"Awake, my heart, to be loved, awake, awake!"

He could hear the words, they sounded distant and the voice familiar. They came again, and closer:

Awake, my heart, to be loved, awake, awake!

Lo, all things wake and tarry and look for thee.

Though soft and familiar to him, the words were, at the same time, discomforting, for they made him struggle against his resignation and would not be silent. Ross moaned and lifted his head. Death was upon him; it stole away all his will, but the voice drew closer and became more insistent. Ross tried to open his eyes, to see who it was. The voice seemed so real, so close, so familiar. He wrestled with his thoughts, thoughts of Eve, of the voice being her voice, but the thought of it made him wretch with soulful pain and despair, for he knew what he had witnessed, and he knew she was gone. Louder and more passionate, the voice echoed in his ears. He could almost feel breath on his face. He could feel the words as they surrounded him, like the wind, swirling around him, at first far away and then, touching him, kissing him, breathing life into him:

Awake, my heart, to be loved, awake, awake!

The darkness silvers away, the morn doth break.

Ross remembered the words. They were from Eve's favorite poem;

one she had known since she was a child, and he knew, in his heart, it was Eve's voice speaking the words. He wanted to forget, to push it away, but before he could close his mind and heart completely before death could take its final hold, the voice came even closer and whispered into his ear, "Ross, wake up!"

Ross heard it as though he were a drunk man being shaken from a stupor. He opened his eyes. He was unable to see anything, but he could feel snowflakes falling on his face and the cold biting his nose and ears. He was only slightly conscious but enough to wonder how long he had been hanging there. However, he soon drifted back into unconsciousness, consoled by the warm arms of sleep, by the thought of death, and by the hope of joining Eve.

"Ross, Ross, wake up. You have to live," called out the voice.

He heard it again, and despite his delirium, Ross realized there was something very pure and authentic about the voice. He wanted to believe it was Eve, but another part of him rejected this possibility. Opening his eyes, he saw her standing over him, except there was no ground for her to stand on. It was as if she was floating in the air. Her eyes were focused gently on him, and she had a comforting smile on her face. She held out her hand to him. Ross's eyes followed her hand, then up her arm, then he noticed she was not dressed in her climbing gear. He believed this had to be a hallucination, or he had, in fact, died. She stood in the howling wind, bare-footed and in a long, flowing gown that was blowing like the sail of a ship. She looked like a ghost as she called out to him, reached her hand toward his, reached down to his suspended body.

"Ross, listen to me. You must wake up! Wake up, Ross!"

Ross could see her looking into his eyes. "Are you real? Is that you, Eve?" His voice was weak, and his breathing was slow and forced.

"Ross, you cannot go to sleep. Awake, awake!"

He looked at her. "I can't. I'm too tired. Please! Please let me come to you! Let me be with you, Eve! Please!"

Ross saw her hand come close until just one of her fingers touched his frozen face. The frost and snow that was building upon his cheeks and eyelashes and around his lips began melting away. Ross felt the warmth of her touch push into his skin and then deeper into his body, from his head to the soles of his feet. He felt life forcing itself into his bones as if a war were being waged right there within his frail, broken frame. Life and death were fighting for the right to take ownership of him. "No, I can't, I can't go on without you!" Ross cried. "Don't make me," he pleaded.

"You have to wake up," she whispered. "You have to live. Ross, wake up."

Ross stared through the tears into her eyes. He looked deeply at the woman who had rescued him from loneliness, and anger, and his own self-destructive ways, the woman who had loved him just the way he was. Ross saw her looking back at him, seeing something that he could not see for himself. She stood over him like a ghost, calling him back to life, refusing to let death cover him in its sallow cloak.

He was confused. Rationally, he knew what he had seen; he knew that Eve had fallen and was dead, and yet to his eyes and his heart and the newness of life he felt in his body, he could not deny that she was standing, like an angel, over him. Then Ross remembered his promise to her. He remembered what he had told her just days before, *"I will always be there for you, I will always love you."* Ross remembered his vow, how he had promised to protect her. He felt a simultaneous conviction of guilt and urgency. He felt that he had completely failed Eve, and yet, at the same time, that he had to live, though he could not find a reason.

"Awake, my heart, to be loved, awake, awake!" she said to him.

Ross knew that death would come soon if he did not do something. He felt blood running into his eyes and he tasted it in his mouth. With a cough and then another louder and harder choking cough, Ross struggled for air. He began gagging and choking on his own blood pouring out of his nose and a broken lower lip. Thoughts of Eve came flooding back into his mind, filling him with guilt and loss. He looked around for her, but she was gone.

Helplessly he hung in the bitter night air, alone, freezing, wanting more than anything to go back in time, to retrace his steps, wishing he had never gone to Nepal. In a state of dazed confusion and palpable sorrow, Ross thought about the voice of Eve, calling out to him and he called out to her in reply.

"Where are you, Eve? Eve?" He could still feel the warmth of her touch on his face. He wondered where she was or if it was just a dream, but he hoped, in between the tide of confusion and the anguish of grief, in the ebbing solace between consciousness and delirium, that it was not a dream and that she was real.

Ross reached for the rope and pulled himself upright. In all directions, there was nothing but darkness. His heart ached with sorrow. He looked to the summit and could see a faint glow emanating from the snow above him where the cornice used to hang. The rope had cut a deep groove into the snow. Using his ascenders and some webbing, he began to work his way up the rope until he reached the edge of the cornice. His freezing hands struggled to hold onto the devices. His mind was of no help; he had to rely on instinct and the hundreds of times he had done it before in order to work his way up the rope. He was just aware enough not to create too much swing on the rope, fearing that the ice axe, to which the rope was anchored, might break loose.

With each foot of rope he ascended, Ross became more determined to live. He was fighting a battle in his mind. He was unsure whether the voice and the spirit of Eve were real or just part of a delusion, if he was actually alive, or if he was still in some dream state. If he was alive, would he survive, even if he did make it back up to the summit? Nevertheless, he slowly worked his way up the rope several more meters, then he stopped.

In the back of his mind, out of the shadows of thought, an unsettling memory forced its way to the forefront, like a haunting spirit taunting him. He remembered something that Eve had said to Psang: *"old legends sometimes hold a little bit of truth to them."* Ross was once again disturbed by the seemingly naïve, not to mention, absurd notion, yet his mind could not stop thinking about what she had said.

He swallowed, took a deep breath, and then exhaled. He closed his eyes for a moment, trying to see if the vision would return, but it did not. All he could see behind his eyelids was darkness. He listened, hoping to hear her voice again, hoping to hear her tell him to live, but all he heard was the wind. Slowly he extended his hand up the rope, locked the ascender, and began to climb again.

Chapter III
The Pit

The wind blew stronger and the snow fell heavier as a storm blew over the Himalayas. The season of monsoons had closed in with a fierce crushing grip as Ross desperately worked his way up the rope. Freezing and bleeding from the gash in his head, he worked methodically, as if in a trance: one hand and then a foot and then the other hand, over and over, he ascended the narrow thread of nylon. The darkness of the night compounded by the thick storm clouds and zero visibility made his solitude desperate. Forcing himself to keep going, Ross reached the edge of the thick drift of snow where the rope had cut a deep groove. With a strong thrust of his right leg, Ross pushed his fatigued body up to where his hand could reach over the crest of the edge, and with a Herculean effort, crawled away from the edge, again reaching the summit.

There was no shelter, no place to hide from the freezing attack. The peak of Machapuchare was fully exposed. Death would have been a welcome reprieve. More than a foot of snow had fallen and finding his gear and Eve's backpack in the near blizzard proved to be a task he was barely able to perform. Pushing his way through the pain, he dug at the ground to find their packs and other missing equipment. Ross could still hear the voice of Eve telling him that he had to get down off the mountain. He moved like a man drunk with delirium. With every part of his body urging him to lie down and sleep, Ross trudged on. He pushed himself in the same way he had done many times before, with a will to survive, fighting less against the elements than against himself. Pulling on his buried axe, frozen in the ice, was proving too much for him, but Ross knew for him to get off this mountain, he had to have it. Finally, it broke free and he began his descent. As he moved through the snow, Ross tried to get his bearings. He knew he was far from safe, and one wrong move could send him falling into the abyss.

Cautiously, he headed in what he hoped was a northern direction, toward the shoulder of the ridge. He crept down the steep north ridge, pressing onward through the most violent storm he had ever experienced. The only thing Ross could feel was the stabbing grip of the cold piercing into every inch of his body as if he were wearing nothing at all. The image of Eve led him at every step and her hushed voice urged him to "get off the mountain". Losing his grip on reality, Ross drifted in and out of his thoughts, seamlessly moving from reality to illusion.

Ross and Daniel hung together in clear skies from their anchored ropes and got ready for their first rappel off Mount Robson. *"I'll take the first drop so you can see how it's done."* Daniel taunted Ross before he leaned back and fell away into the void.

As Ross had watched him fall, he had seen him smile and wave and heard him call, *You worry too much.* Ross hung there in silence, watching him fall into darkness.

"Ross, Ross, you have to get off the mountain!"

"Ross, you must get off the mountain. Ross, wake up!"

Again, the voice of Daniel and then of Eve rang in his ears, startling him back to consciousness and out of his dream state. Ross opened his eyes in the thrashing winds, the snow biting at his skin like a swarm of carnivorous flies. He stumbled along the ridge as if following an imaginary escort who led him like a dog on a leash.

For what seemed like hours stretching into days, Ross descended through the unrelenting storm. Blind and freezing, he inched down the ridge, not knowing how far he had come or how far he had to go. In moments of lucidity, when he tried to eat or drink, his hands, almost frozen, were unable to feel anything, making even the simplest tasks near impossible. His water was frozen, and the symptoms of dehydration were beginning to have their effect on him. Soon, if he did not get out of the storm, he was going to die.

Reaching the edge of a sheer drop, Ross stopped; he looked down and let out a long sigh of defeat and fell to his knees. A rappel over the edge, in his current condition, felt suicidal. Everything seemed opposed to his escape. Under his breath, he mumbled, "Why? Why, why, why?"

Ross lowered his head into the deep snow. There was nothing left in him. He shook his head and thought about giving up. *It would be easy*, he thought. Nevertheless, something about giving up like that disquieted his resignation. He had known a few climbers who had died, who had laid down and froze to death. He had seen the bodies frozen into the ice and snow on the side of a mountain and shook his head in utter disbelief. *How could they have just given up like that?* he had wondered. Ross lifted his head and brushed the snow from his goggles. He struggled to his feet. His instincts as a climber began to take over, and he set up an anchor point from which to rappel down the face. His fingers were cold and frostbitten, making the setup arduous and challenging. Ross feared he would not be able to control his descent. As he looped the rope through the rappel device and clipped it to his harness, he considered that should he fall, he would not be any worse off than he was already. He was not afraid to die.

The last time Ross had leaned back on a rope alone was after Daniel had fallen from Mount Robson in Canada. An eerily familiar feeling oppressed his thoughts as he leaned on the rope and took his first drop. Without realizing, Ross, in the blinding fury of the storm, had set out to rappel a wall that was several thousand feet down. Rappelling slowly down the rope into the unknown, Ross reached the end of his rope, and the base was nowhere to be found. As he clung to the face of the mountain, he tried to see if there was a ledge where he could set up a second rappel, but the blowing snow limited his ability to see any distance. "Damn it! Can't I get a break?"

He knew that he had no strength to ascend the rope. He fumbled for an ice screw on his harness, forcing his frozen fingers to work the screw into the icy wall. He was able to set up a new rappel point on the wall by securing himself to the ice screw. Pulling the rope from the first rappel, Ross set up to continue his descent. As he continued down, he came to a ledge that was no more than five or six inches wide and covered in ice. He examined the ledge carefully and noticed that it led to a large crack in the wall where it looked like he might be able to get out of the battering wind. Ross took his ice axes and worked his way cautiously along the ledge. He faced the wall making sure he was secured to the ice with each axe before taking a step. Carefully, Ross kicked his crampons into the icy ledge, checking that each foot had a good hold before he moved one of his ice axes to the next point. Each movement was slow and methodical—the motions of a skilled climber. Reaching the crack, Ross found it to be much larger than he had originally thought. He sat down and rested, sheltered from the elements.

After several minutes, Ross started shaking uncontrollably and had to stand up again and move around. He noticed that the crack ran along the face of the mountain. Using his headlamp, he could see that it was not a crack in the mountain, but an opening; like a gap between two massive slabs of stone, one leaning against the other. It was triangular, like a shard of glass, and as much as fifty or sixty feet high. The base, where Ross could walk, was only about three to four feet wide. Cautiously Ross moved through the gap to see if the other end might have a more hospitable route for him to escape. At the other end of the gap was a large slab of ice hanging on the wall. Above the ice slab, Ross could see the ridge that he had lost in the storm. Believing the ridge was a safer route down the mountain, Ross decided to gather his gear and go that way. First, he would have to climb the ice slab, which rose high above him. Below was an approaching darkness, hungry to swallow him up in another night on the mountain.

Ross doubted whether he would be able to climb up to the ridge. His hands were numb, and his feet were stinging from the stabbing chill of the sub-zero winds. He was weak and tired, and every thought tried to persuade him to give up. *You can't go on. You're going to die, and there is nothing you can do about it. You're a fool; you thought you could conquer the mountain. What has it cost, and who is going to care anyway? No one will miss you, hell, they won't even notice you're gone. You killed your best friend; you know you did. It's your fault. You should have told him. You saw what was going to happen. You deserve to suffer. You never really loved her, you know. Not really. If you had, you would have saved her, you would have done more. You failed. You've failed at everything in your life . . . you're a total failure. No one loves you, not really. Your dad could not stand you; that's why he abandoned you.*

Huddling down in the darkness, Ross struggled to make himself keep going. He had lost the will to live. Alone and no longer afraid to die, he sat shivering. He had never taken the easy way; he was a fighter, a man who had known heartache and sorrow. Though he felt the emotions deeply he had always been able to keep moving on, through life, hoping that eventually, he would find something better. He was driven by this hope, and in his darkest moments, it kept him going.

He wondered, at times, what right he had to hope for such things, what right he had to expect a happy life, full of adventure and excitement. He wondered how anyone could accept anything less than all the good that life could give and yet he had never experienced it himself. It was naïve, but he believed he was meant for something better, something more, though all the good things he had ever received came at a great cost and were gone before he had time to fully experience them.

This mountain, this trip, this dream had cost him the most. Sitting alone, Ross replayed every failure, every mistake like a picture show in his thoughts, from his boyhood to that pivotal moment in the gap of the mountain. He watched, what he felt was, a meaningless life playing out before him. And yet, there was one thing kept coming to him, which counteracted the poison of his self-contempt and that was the sound of Eve's voice. Whether a memory, a dream, or some inexplicable apparition, her voice and her words echoed deep into the corridors of his heart, pulling him from the edge of surrender.

Like the voice of an attorney calling *objection* in the courtroom, her voice resonated, reminding him that he was better than all his failures and stronger than his weakest moment. Eve had believed in Ross and loved him deeply and unconditionally. She may have been the only person in his life, besides Daniel, who knew his heart, and she never failed to tell him so. Her voice was the voice that woke him from his despair.

While the memory of Eve broke his heart, it also gave him strength, life, and hope. With her image appearing to him, reminding him, Ross could not concede to death. Standing to his feet, he gathered all his gear and moved to the edge.

Exposed and in the dark, Ross swung the ice axe into the frozen wall. Kicking the toe picks of his crampons into the ice, he lifted his body away from the protection of the ledge and set himself against the icy granite face. Slowly and skillfully, he moved away from the ledge, until he was fully exposed on the wall of the mountain with nothing to save him should he fall. Climbing like a spider up the wall, he saw the ridge getting closer. He swung his axe into the ice wall. A hollow thud echoed through the air. Ross hesitated for a moment and then pulled the pick from the wall. Swinging a second time, he heard a crack that pierced the silence like the clap of hands. He realized that the slab was hollow and saw a jagged line moving toward his face and continuing below him. The ice was cracking like a piece of glass. Hanging precariously over a great dark void, Ross was unable to do anything. The ice began to fracture and shift, breaking away above him.

With limited sight, Ross leaned hard against the ice hoping it would hold and the shards falling around him would not strike him. The ice collapsed into the mountain dragging him with it.

Ross was falling through the dark. He prepared to die, as much as it was possible. He felt a sudden calm pour over him. He thought he was falling down the face, though he was actually falling into an opening in the wall of the mountain. Crashing against the stone floor of the opening, the ice shattered with a thunderous roar. The air was forced from his lungs as he landed flat on his stomach. His face struck hard against the same ice he had been clinging to just moments before. The ice that hung over the opening collapsed behind him, entombing him in the tiny cave. Suddenly there was absolute silence. Ross moaned as he tried to catch his breath. The fall left him stunned. Slowly he rose to his knees and looked around only to see total darkness. He reached for his headlamp and then realized it had been broken by the abrupt impact of his face against the granite floor. He pulled his pack off and rolled over onto his back.

After a few moments of rest, Ross grabbed his gear and began to move around in the darkness hoping to find a way out. Ross felt his way around the cave by touching the cold, dark walls. The floor of the cave was icy and slick, but Ross's crampons kept him from slipping or falling. He was unsure whether he was moving in a circle or if he was moving away from the spot where he had landed. Suddenly, Ross felt himself falling, tumbling down and down, unable to stop himself. Holding his head in his hands and tucking his body, Ross did all he could to protect himself from further injury, but once again, he was aware of his helplessness in the face of such danger and was certain he would die.

For what seemed like ages, he felt himself plunging deeper into the hollow of blind emptiness. With a jolt, Ross was surrounded by unexpected warmth pouring over his frozen body. It wrapped around him like a molten blanket sealing around his face, gradually robbing his breath. Ross realized he had landed in a deep pool of water, and the weight of his pack and gear was dragging him under. Thrashing about in the pool, not knowing where the surface or shore might be, Ross struggled until his head broke the surface and he began to swim to safety. He did not know which direction to swim and was aware that he could not swim far clothed and with his gear and backpacks fastened to his body. He reached as far as he could with each stroke until his foot hit something hard. Pushing his crampon-laden feet under him proved to be difficult, for when he would bring his foot forward the sharp tines of the crampons would arrest his progress, and he would fall face-first into the water. He lifted his head out of the water, gasping and coughing because of the fluid he had inhaled. He tried again to stand up. Finally, his foot planted on the rocky substrate, and he stood waist-deep in the pool.

Ross walked carefully out of the water and sat down at its edge, unsure where he was or what to do next. Soaking wet, but warm, he began to remove his gear and clothing.

When Ross had found Eve's backpack under the snow on the summit, he had stuffed it into his own pack. Ross remembered that Eve's headlamp was in it and began fumbling through the different items. He felt several pieces of her climbing gear, her journal, and then her camera. Feeling the camera made him pause for a moment. He was relieved to find that it was dry like most of the other items in her pack. He moved it aside and continued his search. "Gotcha," he said with relief, as he pulled the headlamp from the pack.

Ross quickly put it on and looked around as he knelt on the floor next to the pool. In every direction, he could see nothing but more darkness. He had fallen into a hollow, a huge cavity deep in the core of the mountain. The beam of light from the headlamp could not reach to any wall on its perimeter. However, he could see that where he knelt was a high plateau rising above the floor of the cave. He rose to his feet to look further. The pool was about one hundred feet or so across and almost perfectly round. He scanned for a way down off the high rock table. Cautiously moving toward the edge of the plateau, he discovered that it rose precipitously for what seemed like half the length of his climbing rope. In the light of his headlamp, he could faintly see the rock below. It seemed there was no other way down than for him to rappel over the edge. Ross continued to assess the situation and determined that before he moved off the plateau and away from the pool of water, he should check his food and water supply. He found several energy bars and a bag of nuts in his pack, along with a package of trail mix and more energy bars in Eve's pack. He also found half a candy bar and his survival kit, which contained various supplies for extreme circumstances.

For the first time in several days, Ross realized the extent of his hunger and seeing the food made him behave like a wild animal. He devoured one of the energy bars, then guzzled some water he had taken from the pool. The water, however, was not treated for microbes, which could have made him sick. Realizing his mistake, Ross tried to spit out the water but had already swallowed more than enough to make him sick. Gathering his wits and controlling his urge to act irrationally, Ross filled his bottle with new water and added tablets to purify the fluid.

The hunger pains continued to intensify, and Ross consumed another energy bar and some of the trail mix. Everything Ross did, from drinking the water to eating the energy bar, ushered him one step further into the realm of reality. The awareness of his circumstance grew more acute by the moment as Ross wrestled with deep, minacious fears. On one hand, he was returning to a sobering state of reality, yet on the other hand, he found himself in the darkest of nightmares.

He could feel strength and life returning to his body and mind. Thoughts and memories were becoming more lucid; Ross remembered the vision he had seen while hanging from the summit on the rope. He contemplated the figure of Eve hovering over him, speaking to him, calling him off the mountain. He remembered she had touched him on the face, he remembered how it had felt, life pushing into his bones, the same feeling he had just experienced while eating the bars and nuts. It had seemed so real, and yet to his pragmatic way of thinking, it could not have been. Eve could not have been there in that storm hovering over him, touching him, calling out to him.

Ross reached up and touched the same cheek that Eve had touched as though he could still feel the sensation of her touching him. Dazed by the memories, by the vision of Eve, Ross lay down on the rock at the edge of the pool and closed his eyes.

"What are you doing?"

"Come on. Let's enjoy the moment. Come sit down with me."

"Oh, what's this we have here? A picnic on the lawn? Ross, what's the occasion?"

"I just thought we could relax a little and have a glass of wine."

"You never want to be romantic; don't you think this is kind of a strange place to start?"

"I have something I want to ask you. Come on, Eve. Sit down with me. Relax."

"Oh, alright. But let me change out of these climbing clothes first."

"Hurry, Eve, we don't have much time, you know."

"You're always trying to rush me, always in a hurry."

"I really like that dress. Where'd you get it?"

"You got it for me, silly. Don't you remember?"

"No, not at all. Where'd you get it?"

"Oh, never mind."

"I . . . I have something to ask you, Eve."

"Really, what is it? This is very good wine."

"I want you to marry me. Will you marry me, Eve?"

"Of course, I'll marry you."

"Will you marry me now? Right here? Today?"

"Ross! What is the hurry?"

"We don't have much time, Eve . . . We don't have much time."

"Right here and now. But there's no one to marry us, Ross."

"Oh, yes there is. I have brought a priest to take care of everything."

"But I'm not ready: I have no shoes or dress for a wedding."

"You look great. Really, you do. The dress you have on will do just fine."

"How'd you find a mountain-climbing priest, Ross?"

"You know, Psang. He is a priest."

"Psang! He's no priest."

"Look, Eve, all of the flowers and the runner; we have everything we need. What do you say?"

"How did you get all this stuff up here? Did Psang bring it in one of the packs?"

"You worry too much, Eve."

"Now you sound like Daniel."

"Daniel, Daniel who?"

"Your best friend, silly. Don't you remember? You let him fall off Mount Robson."

"Oh, yeah. That Daniel. I remember now."

"Well, Ross, are we going to do this or not?"

"Yes, just as soon as I tie off to my ice axe."

"Maybe I should tie off, too. What do you think?"

"I think you worry too much. After all, what could happen?"

"Yeah, you're right."

"Did I tell you how pretty you look?"

"No, no you didn't. You should have though."

"I wish I had. I sure do miss you, Eve."

"I miss you more."

"Ross . . ."

"What is it, Eve?"

"Ross, you need to wake up."

"I am awake."

"Ross, you need to wake up, my dear."

"But I am awake, Eve."

"Ross, wake up. Wake up, Ross!"

Cracking one eye open, Ross realized he had fallen to sleep. The glow of the headlamp was fading. Cast upon the still, black water of the pool, its light reflected upward, and for the first time, Ross turned his gaze to the endless darkness above him. His eyes had adjusted enough that he began to see faint specks of light shining off the walls, ceiling, and floor of the cave. Like the ceiling of a planetarium, the tiny sparkles of mica, silver, and gold specks, held captive in the black granite, began to reveal themselves in all directions around him. The water of the pool mirrored the tiny sparkles, creating a magnificent display that rivaled the most spectacular starry night. Ross turned the headlamp off.

Mesmerized by the sight of innumerable sparkles of light and still thinking about the dream he had woken from, Ross listened. The silence was impenetrable. He thought about Eve's voice that had again woken him from his sleep. Where was the voice coming from and why could he not hear it now? Was it all just a dream or a figment of his imagination? She had touched him, and he still felt her hand on his skin. For a moment, Ross questioned whether he was awake, asleep, or even if he was alive. He wondered if, he was in some kind of alternate state of consciousness, like in a coma. He doubted everything he had seen and done to that point, for nothing made sense. *Is this how it is then? Is this how I'm going to die, in this cave alone? Maybe this is how it should be, maybe I deserve it. I'm such a damn fool . . . a selfish idiot. I suppose I do deserve this, but Eve didn't . . . She deserved better, better than me . . . I wish I could've told her how much I loved her . . . I love you, Eve . . . so, so much.* Ross's thoughts began to echo in the hollow before he realized they were not just thoughts; he was also mumbling to himself what he was thinking. The sound of his indistinguishable maunder returned to his ears, strange and foreign. For a moment, Ross stopped speaking to himself and listened to the repeating echoes reverberate around him. Soon he heard the strange murmurs again, as his thoughts escaped faintly from his tongue. For a moment, he thought there was someone else in the cave with him, but he soon realized it was again himself speaking aloud. "What's the point of trying if I'm just going to die anyway? There is nothing to live for, nothing. I messed up. I really, really messed up this time. Maybe I deserve this. Maybe Eve would be better off without me. Maybe she'd be happier with someone else. Maybe."

He slipped in and out of reality as his fatigue and sleep depravity made him delirious. Rambling on about Eve, as if she was still alive, he lost all sense of his surroundings and began to drift off again.

"Are you sure we can climb this? I mean, it's so big."

"Of course, we can. Don't be silly."

"Daniel, you need to be more careful; you could die, you know?"

"What's the point of living if you can't have a little fun?"

"But if you kill yourself, what's the point in that?"

"Ross, I won't kill myself. We're just having fun. Can't you just have a little fun without worrying so much?"

"I guess you're right."

"Hey man, I'll take the first rappel. Is everything set?"

"Yep, everything's good to go."

"See ya!"

"Wait!"

Startled, Ross opened his eyes at the sound of his own voice screaming Daniel's name. The memory of Daniel's fall haunted his dreams, waking him every night. Now he would have two dreams disturbing his sleep.

In the distance, he heard a faint, short sound. He listened intently without moving and tried to decipher its source. After several moments, he heard it again. He barely breathed for fear of not hearing it again. Softly, like a single beat, the sound came again. Ross sat up and looked around for any sign of life or light or movement, or anything that would tell him what the sound was and where it had come from. Excited, he leaped to his feet, and once again, the sound came to his ears, but its faint echo bounced off the hard, stone walls, disguising its origin and identity. Never louder, never nearer, the sound repeated in unchanging cadence.

The sound was only significant because it reassured Ross he was alive and awake, that what he was experiencing was all real. He wanted to discover the source of the sound. Maybe it led to a way out of the cave. He grabbed the headlamp and turned it on, but the light was dim. Knowing it would not stay lit for long, Ross dug for some matches in Eve's survival kit. In the kit were a compass, matches, a candle, first aid supplies, an emergency space blanket, and water purification tablets. Ross struck one of the matches against the stone floor and lit the candle. The tiny flame radiated with the faintest soft yellow glow. The flame's insolent attempt to illuminate the massive room was received with contempt by the mocking blackness. Undaunted, the defiant flame burned, sending its soft aurora into the shadows.

After turning in place, hoping to pinpoint the sound, Ross finally stopped and faced the pool of dark water. It dawned on him that the sound may have been from water dripping off his backpack onto the hard-stone floor. As he stood straining to see any distinguishable feature, the flame lit the surface of the pool. Falling like morning fog on the landscape, the glow touched the surface of the pool and kissed it with light. Upon the water's surface, a strange, unearthly phenomenon began to unfold. The light appeared to ignite, not into flame, but into liquescent molten droplets of pale blue, white, orange, and amber. The droplets hovered just above the surface of the pool, folding in and out of one another, growing larger and then smaller until the whole surface of the pool was aglow in a flameless fire of light. One by one, the droplets descended; sinking like pearls into the pool, creating more light. Like a million tiny jellyfish swimming in the ocean, the life-infused light took form and began to swim about. Growing in brightness and mass, the light erupted into great streaks of colors, like the *Aurora Borealis,* dancing in the deep dark waters.

Witnessing the display beneath the surface both startled and confused Ross. Just moments before, he had shone his headlamp on the water and had seen nothing; now the light was coming to life in the pool beneath him. Ross could see a single ray of light shining from the flame of the candle into the pool as if this tiny flame were the source of this unimaginable display.

"What the—?" Setting the candle on a stone next to the pool, Ross tentatively reached down to touch the water. *"Extraordinary!"* He couldn't comprehend it. There were no flames, no fire. The small droplets of light disappeared in his hand as he tried to lift them out of the pool. He smelled the water, but there was no odor. He tasted it again, but there was no flavor. In every respect, the pool appeared to be water, and yet, the droplets of liquid light were not only in the water but also of the water.

An almost imperceptible mist began to rise from the pool like the fog that lifts off the warm surface of a mountain lake in the early morning. The mist was infused with droplets of light, and as it rose above the pool, it began to illuminate the pit. From the depths of the pool, the droplets rose higher and higher into the tower of light and mist, growing brighter and brighter until rays of light began to pierce the infringing darkness in every direction. The darkness began to flee, and for the first time since he had fallen, Ross was freed from its oppressive grip. The mist rose higher and higher until it formed a transparent tower of vapor and light from the surface of the pool to the ceiling. Ross stood amazed and terrified at what he saw. The darkness fought for its position, pushing in on the tower of light in all directions, unwilling to yield its reign over the pit.

The tower of light became brighter and shone farther into the darkness, exposing a massive subterranean chamber that stretched in all directions. Ross stood alone, overwhelmed by the vastness of space around him. Great walls towered hundreds of feet above him and massive slabs of stone of every kind jutted in every direction. Jagged and sharp slabs of stone were pitched in huge piles here and there as if some primordial giant had hurled them. The plateau where Ross stood rose in the middle of the great hall. Standing two hundred feet above the floor, it was solid black granite that appeared to have been formed by cutting away the stone around it, as if it were some ancient altar. It was perfectly circular. In one direction, Ross could not tell if it was north, south, east, or west, but in that direction, there was a stream running from the base of the plateau, around and under the malformed stone debris. The water glowed just as the waters of the pool and from its surface raised the mist of light, exposing what looked like a passage in the wall.

Above him, Ross could see the small hole from where he had fallen into the cave. It appeared to be in the center of the tower of light. His fortune in falling into the pool had not been realized by him until that moment, for the height of the opening in the ceiling could not have been less than a few hundred feet. How anyone could have survived a fall from such a height, even though landing in water, was beyond Ross's ability to comprehend.

Everywhere were great shards of granite rising high above the cave floor like spires. Beholding the sight caused Ross to feel very, very small and insignificant. An ominous feeling came over him as he, at first, observed the spectacle and then, as he considered the possibilities of what this place had been. A contradiction of elements seemed to exist. The walls, floor, water, and space were inky black, and the opaque shadows of the pit emanated an atmosphere of fear and oppression yet, from the midst of this dark hole shone a beautiful and glorious luminous display.

On the stone floor around the pool there was a carved inscription of some sort. Ross looked at it and realized that it was an ancient script. It puzzled him as to why or how anyone would have put it there, and why it would be placed in the stone here at an entrance into the pool. Ross had escaped the waters at this same spot, but before the light of the tower, he had not seen the engravings. The letters, if they were indeed letters, were three feet from base to top and in a single line approaching thirty feet long. Ross remembered Eve had carried a journal in her pack. He dug it out and flipped to the first empty page. With the pen with which she had written her last entry, Ross carefully copied the inscription, thinking it might be important to someone.

It was something Eve would have done. He knew she had loved archeology and had studied it in college. Why he took the time here and now to make note of the thing was strange even to him. Before he could be tempted to read Eve's journal entries, Ross quickly closed the journal and tied it with its leather cord.

The light in the pit had finally pushed the shadows into hiding, though, considering the source of the light, it seemed a tenuous and momentary victory. In the distance, at the opposite end of the pit from where the stream flowed, Ross saw what looked like great, black iron gates, installed into the walls of the pit. There was no light beyond the gates, but Ross could see that massive boulders had fallen onto its bars and hinges. It appeared an avalanche may have closed the entrance or that the mountain had collapsed onto the gates at some time ages in the past. The way to the gates looked impassable, blocked by sharp rocks, and strewn with piles of boulders everywhere. A strange chill fell over Ross as he looked at the gates in the distance. The more he observed it, the more he felt fear and danger creeping into his thoughts.

Like a young boy with an overactive imagination, Ross began randomly considering the possibilities of the pit. As a boy, Ross had spent many a day in the principal's office for daydreaming during class and making up outlandish stories that he would tell his classmates instead of concentrating on his studies. His imagination was not only active but also vivid. Even as an adult, Ross possessed a very creative imagination, which was a trait Eve admired and was attracted to.

Breaking the spell of his daydreaming, Ross began to wonder how long the glow of light would persist. He wanted to get off the plateau and thus began setting a rappel point to lower himself and his gear over the edge. Though it was hard to resist the urge to investigate the iron gates, Ross determined to find a way out of the pit. Carefully he attached himself to his rope.

"Let me show you how it's done." Daniel had told Ross many times during their adventures together. Eventually Ross, almost superstitiously, made the statement every time he rappelled. It had become a kind of joke between friends.

Ross unclipped at the bottom of the plateau. Retrieving his rope and pulling the headlamp from the pack just in case it got dark again, he followed the small stream that flowed from the base of the plateau and through the jagged rocks. It was strange to Ross that there could be water in the pool above him and water from that pool flowing in the stream away from him at the bottom.

Why doesn't the pool drain out? Ross thought. He stood watching as the stream continued to flow without restraint.

The opening that Ross had seen in the granite wall from where the stream flowed led him a mile through slick, jagged rocks making his journey slow and challenging. After what seemed like hours, Ross reached the opening. It was not a carved opening, as he had first thought; it was a large crack in the wall that was little more than a few feet wide. The crack, however, ran up the wall of the pit to its ceiling. Like a slot canyon, the walls of the opening were sheer and imposing. The passage between them narrowed, making it difficult to negotiate in certain places and forcing Ross to walk in the stream. His feet were surrounded by the drops of liquid light; it felt as though they were carrying him to safety.

The light in the crack of the mountain was not as strong as the light of the mist towering over the pit. Ross could feel the chill of the pitch-black that struggled to overcome the glow of the stream. Just feet above his head, the darkness hovered like a hungry beast waiting for just the right moment to pounce on its prey. The antagonism of the darkness drove Ross to push himself longer and harder to safety. He had no idea how far he would have to go or how long it would take him to find an escape from the passage. He felt weak and his physical condition worsened as he followed the stream hour after hour.

Back in the pit, the flame of the candle began to shrink before it extinguished entirely. Ross noticed that things were becoming much more difficult to see, and before he realized it, the light of the stream faded into darkness. Closing in, the black surrounded him like a tomb. He reached for the headlamp and hoped it would have enough life in it to get him out of the mountain.

The light of the headlamp was weak, barely able to illuminate even the stream at Ross's feet. Anger and frustration began to overpower his hope. He wanted to kick himself for leaving the light on earlier. Now, when he needed it the most, it seemed sure to fail before reaching the end. Soon, he could hardly see anything at all. The light of the headlamp faded slowly and then quietly went out. Ross halted and knelt, resting for a moment. His feet were soaking wet and he was beginning to panic. Trying to regain composure, he paused in the dark, pressed in on either side by massive walls of stone with only the narrow slot and the running stream as a guide. In the silence, a strange sound came to his ears. It was the sound of water, but not of the stream running around his feet. It was the sound of water falling nearby. Ross rose slowly and listened, moving toward the source of the noise.

Feeling ahead with his hands and carefully taking each step, Ross restrained his compulsion to dash for the end. As he drew closer to the sound, he could see a different shade of darkness than what he had been seeing. In front of him, rising immeasurably, was a dark shape like a knife. Ross squinted his eyes, trying to make out what he was seeing. Closer and closer, he moved toward the sound while the giant dark figure became larger and larger. Stopping to look, Ross noticed a tiny sequin of light at the top of the dark figure. Then he saw another light and another and another until finally, he realized what he was seeing. The figure of the knife was actually the night sky framed by the towering granite walls of the slot. Slowly, his eyes began to adjust, and he could see reflections of stars shining on the surface of the stream. Moving closer and closer to the night sky, Ross stepped out from the slot and into a coal-black night sky. The stream flowed just feet beyond and over the edge. A waterfall fell away from the mountain, the sound that led him to freedom.

Exhausted, Ross collapsed onto the soft ground just beyond the slot. He was alive, and though he wondered if he was safe, for the moment it did not matter. He was out of the pit and off the mountain.

Kumél

Chapter IV
An Epiphany

"What're you doing? Where're you going? Eve! Come back."

"Come on, silly, what're you waiting for? Let's get in the water."

"It's too cold!"

"Yeah, but the sun is shining; it'll warm us back up. Come on you lazy bum."

"Oh, alright. You sure are pushy, you know."

"No, I'm persuasive. There's a difference."

"Pushy, persuasive, hmmm, sounds the same to me."

"Oh my God! This water's so cold."

"I told you it would be."

"Come on, get in. It's great after you get used to it."

"Oh shit! It's colder than I thought it would be. Stop! Stop splashing me, Eve! Stop splashing me."

"Well, I'm out of here. Enjoy your bath."

"So, you drag me out here just to leave me."

"The sun is shining, it's warm and cozy on the grass. And I didn't drag you out here; you came of your own free will. Doesn't the sun feel so good after being so cold? It's one of the most amazing feelings in the world."

"Ahh, yes, you're right. It feels so, so good shining on my face. I could lay here like this forever."

"Ross, you can't stay here forever."

"Why? Let's just stay here, just like this forever."

"We can't, you silly man, you know that."

"Please, please? Can we stay for a while longer?"

"Ross. Ross! You have to wake up, my dear."

"No! No, no! I don't want to wake up. I want to stay here, right here with you."

"Ross! Wake up. Wake up, Ross! You don't belong here."

Ross's eyes sprung open. Without moving a muscle, he looked around. Shining on his face and body was the diffused light of a cloud-cloaked sun, warm and soothing to his body and to his soul. Listening to the sounds of birds singing and insects buzzing around as he lay on a soft bed of grass, Ross tried to remember what had woken him from his sleep. A gentle breeze moved through the trees rustling their leaves. The sky was muddled with light and dark clouds and the playful sun peeked in and out through the overcast veil. Yet, amid the pastoral tranquility that surrounded him, Ross was discomforted by something, something he heard in his dream, something Eve had said. *What had she said? What was it?* He lay still hoping the words would form in his thoughts. Unable to remember what it was he thought he had heard, Ross sat up. He could not tell how long he had been sleeping. He did not know if it had been a day or several days, but he knew he felt better than he had felt for many, many days. Ross reached for his backpack. In a pile behind him lay the rope, packs, and miscellaneous supplies and climbing gear. Ross grabbed two energy bars and the bottle of water, which he had refilled just before the light went out in the crack of the mountain.

He began to take in the view of the landscape that spread before his eyes. He could see far into the distance, but he was unsure how far. The land he saw seemed strange to him, unlike the valley below Machapuchare. He had expected to see some signs of a city, or roads or of some civilization, and yet all he could see in every direction were vast forests and valleys, flanked by mountain ranges. Assuming he had come out from the belly of the mountain on another side where things must surely be different from where he had started, Ross wondered how far it would be to a city or town. The more he looked out on the landscape and then closer, at the vegetation, trees, and plants that surrounded him, the more he became confused, for nothing looked familiar.

The panorama that lay before his eyes was as shocking as it was beautiful. There were grand expansive valleys rimmed by towering snow and ice-laden peaks, mountain ranges stretching infinitely in every direction, rising into the clouds, proud and indomitable, valleys lush and green with expansive meadows and forests adorned with flowering bushes, plants, and trees of indescribable variety and color. It was like an immaculate garden, only it was more than a garden and greater than any human could have ever created or even imagined.

Ross was amazed and spellbound by what his eyes were seeing. In all his years, in all the wild places he had seen, he had somehow missed what it was he was seeing here, at this moment. Awestruck, he whispered under his breath, "Beautiful. How'd I never see this before? How could I have missed all of this?" The majesty of the scene in front of him brought unexpected, uninvited tears to his eyes. He stood staring, motionless and transfixed.

As his circumstances became more apparent and as he began to recall the events that had brought him there, Ross realized he might not yet be out of trouble. Looking around, he saw that where he stood was at the end of a massive ledge, suspended several thousand feet above the valley floor. Straight out from the mountain, the ledge extended some forty or fifty feet, then dropped straight down. Ross could see the place where the stream fell to the valley below. Strangely, though, the stream had stopped flowing and only a wide, shallow little rock bed remained with puddles of water scattered here and there.

Ross turned and looked back at the mountain from where the stream had flowed. His eyes grew wide as he became troubled, for what he saw defied everything he thought he remembered. The narrow crack he had used was now closed. Ross walked toward the wall of stone trying to understand how it was possible for him to have followed the stream through the mountain where there was now no exit. Reaching out and touching the wall of the mountain, he tried to fit his fingers into the narrowed opening. Before, he had been able to slide through the gap sideways, but now all he could feel was solid rock. Confused, he stepped away from the wall and began to inspect it more closely. The stream bed that had led to the rim of the ledge emerged from solid black granite.

On the opposite side of the streambed, the ledge extended about one-hundred feet, narrowing dramatically in its relief from the face of the mountain, until it disappeared. Next to the place where Ross had slept, there were bushes and several trees that were small in diameter but stood thirty to forty feet tall. The ledge in that direction broadened and sloped steeply toward the base of the mountain. Ross could not see if there was a way down from the ledge through the trees and bushes, but he knew if there was, there was only one option.

In his many years of climbing, Ross had attempted to escape mountain heights through similar innocuous routes only to discover they eventually led to impassable and dangerous sheer drops. Like hanging gardens clinging to the face of the rock, they flourish as inescapable fortresses.

Gathering his gear and supplies, Ross prepared to descend the steep, green ledge. He wrestled with leaving the quiet, accommodating ridge. Looking up, he could see the sky growing dark, and the winds were beginning to pick up. It looked as if it might rain at any moment. Ross began to make his way through the dense, green vegetation.

The plants that grew on the slope were knee-high with broad leaves and beautiful blue flowers. Ross tried to walk through the thick growth but found quickly that his boots were becoming entangled in the thick, long stalks making his progress both slow and menacing. Several times he almost tripped, which would have sent him headfirst tumbling off the ledge. Beneath the thick cover of the plants were loose fist-sized rocks interspersed with larger boulders. The larger boulders dislodged and tumbled down the steep ledge, bouncing and hopping as they went until Ross could see them no more.

His progress down the slope was painfully slow, and one thing loomed heavily; if this was not the way down, he could become stranded. The ledge began to descend into the unknown, and the vegetation began to thin as he came to a steep, rocky section. Sliding over the surface of the ledge, Ross kicked the loose rock in front of him, letting it fall away to secure his passage. Farther and farther down the slope, he descended until he heard water flowing. At first, the sound was faint and somewhere below him, but soon it was right under him. Out from the rocks flowed a rushing stream over the surface of the ledge. The route he had chosen had suddenly become even more treacherous.

Using his ice axe as an extension of his arm, Ross pushed it into the rocks below him, then slowly lowered himself down. The stream became stronger and swifter the farther Ross moved down the ledge. The debris disintegrated with his descent. Rocks, large and small, were tumbling down the ledge, causing other rocks to dislodge and tumble to the bottom. Finally, Ross reached a vantage point that allowed him to see the bottom of the ledge. Unfortunately, he also saw a massive boulder hanging over his only route down. The stream flowed under the great stone, then out below it onto the base of the mountain.

The overhanging boulder hung near-vertical, only a few feet above the ledge. Beneath the cascading stream was a smooth, greasy slab of granite with no holds for Ross to control his descent. If Ross were to lose his grip, the two-hundred-foot drop to the bottom would have been to his death. With cold mountain water flowing over him, Ross put his back against the slick, wet slope and used his hands and feet to push against the overhanging boulder. He inched his way down, sandwiched between the boulder and the slope. Soaked and frozen, he emerged from the slot and set his foot on a solid rock step that lay only a few feet above the base. He climbed down from the step and worked his way out from the base of the mountain to a spot near the tree line where he could rest.

Ross began shivering. His clothes were wet, and the sun's warmth was hidden behind thick clouds, robbing him of its gift. Ross stood up and continued his descent. He figured the best way to stay warm was to keep moving. Finding a massive old tree with low-hanging branches that reached extensively in all directions, Ross sat down under its cover. At the base of the tree were large mounds of bright green moss, which grew in the shelter of the tree, protected from the sun and other elements. Like a carpet, the moss covered the ground and grew up the trunk of the tree. Spongy and soft, it formed a perfect place for Ross to set up a camp. There were many more of the massive trees all around and leading down the mountainside. They rose like skyscrapers above the forest floor. The gargantuan ancient mossy and twisted trunks stretched their roots out like a great, powerful hand, grabbing the earth. The canopy of the forest spread for miles and miles through the hills and valleys, broken only by vast meadows where the streams and rivers flowed. The sounds of life came from all directions, sounds Ross had never heard before. Birdsongs rose on the breeze with soothing, hypnotic tones. The world that spread itself before him had never seen a man before. Uncivilized, unmolested, the world seemed new and ancient at the same time. Though transcendent and beautiful, the landscape was filled with a strangely haunting ambiance.

As the day ebbed into evening and the setting sun was slowly embraced by the horizon, darkness began to close in over the land. Gathering sticks and pieces of old wood for a fire, Ross wandered through the forest. In the dwindling light, he quickly made his way back to the old tree, the place where he would spend the long, dark night.

The soft yellow glow of the fire warmed the ground and kept Ross comfortable as long as he fed the flames. The night air became chilled and damp, and as Ross watched, an eerie mist rose up from the ground and climbed into the night sky like the smoke from his fire. The sky was dark and mysterious. Whenever the clouds momentarily pulled away from each other, the light of the heavenly sky shone through, stars and moons cast their soft lucent glow down upon the rising mist.

It was like nothing Ross had ever seen. It held his imagination captive for hours as he sat watching the night sky interact with the world around him. Then, an uninvited realization began to overcome the hypnotic, heavenly spectacle. Two moons hung in the sky. He looked at them, then closed his eyes. When he opened them again, the two moons were still there. Ross sat up keeping his vision fixed on the two mysterious moons. He could not understand how there were two moons in the sky, but before he could think about it any further, he noticed that it was strangely quiet, uncomfortably quiet. It was possible that he might not be alone. Chills ran across his back and down his arms. He suddenly felt very vulnerable. Ross moved closer to the flames and added more wood to stoke the fire in hope that if any wild animals were near, the fire would keep them at bay.

Hunkered close to the fire, Ross listened intently for any sound or noise, but there was none, not a single sound from wind, creature, or insect. Ross tried to distract himself from a torrent of fears. Images of wolves or bears or some other dreadful beast waiting for just the right moment to attack tried to push their way into his already-tormented thoughts. *If I keep the fire going and keep my back to this root so that nothing can surprise me from behind, I should be OK. It's probably nothing, nothing at all. Maybe there are no animals this high in the mountains. But no bugs? No crickets or mosquitos? Maybe it's too cold . . . Yeah, that's it, too cold. What was that? I sure do wish I had my knife . . . I could at least fight it off. But, but what if it's a bear? A knife won't stop a bear or worse a pack of wolves. Oh, shit! Wolves! There are no wolves up here; I would've heard them howling. It must be a bear.*

Hoping to distract his attention from the whirlwind of uncontrollable imaginations, he began to hum "Ain't No Sunshine When She's Gone" softly to himself. He could not remember the words, but the melody had always stuck with him. Ross repeated the tune in a soft cautious tone. Before, when he could remember the words, he had sung it to Eve. It had become their private love song. When they were apart, he sometimes hummed it to himself. Ross did not know many songs by heart, so it was the only one he could think to sing other than "Itsy Bitsy Spider" which he started to sing, however, he thought that if anyone did find him, he did not want to be found singing a child's song. Rarely did Ross get the lyrics correct, and rarely could he sing the melody on-key but humming the song brought him comfort and peace. After a while, Ross lay his head on the ground and drifted off to sleep.

"You don't belong here!"

"You don't belong here!"

"You don't belong here!"

Again and again, the words haunted Ross in his sleep. He could hear them echo in his ears like a ringing bell. The voice came out of the dark. They were not accompanied by any sort of vision of the speaker; only the words. In his dreams, Ross tried to find the voice; he tried to reach out and to call out, but it was to no avail—there was no one there.

"You don't belong here!" The voice in the dark spoke in a demanding, restrained tone, hushed but sharp. Closer and closer, the voice and the words approached through the dark shadows of Ross's subconscious incubus. Slowly, in his dream, he saw a figure emerge from a featureless shadow. The figure was dark and mysterious. Fear began to grip him and he found himself trying to run from whatever it was or was not. Terrified, he could not move; it was as if he was restrained or cornered. In every direction, there was nothing but a wall of darkness. A beastly figure was drawing near muttering over and over again. *"You don't belong here! You don't belong here!"*

Ross watched as a dark, scaled hand, boney, with long dirty nails, like talons, reached out of the shadows. Suddenly, the creature lunged towards him. Ross was surrounded by beastly, squid-like tentacles. He was unable to move away from the dark hand.

Ross lurched backward, hard against the root of the giant tree. "Ouch!" He cried out from the pain of his head smashing against the root of the tree, waking him from the depths of his nightmare. He reached up, grabbed his head, and rolled away from the root, closer to the hot coals of the dying fire.

"Damn it!" Regaining his senses and realizing that he had been dreaming, Ross sat upright with his hand still holding the right side of his bleeding head.

"Ye dunna b'lung haer!" Ross stopped, frozen by the words and the reality that he was not alone. He knew he was awake, and he was not dreaming, nor was he hearing things. They were real words from a very real and close and unwanted stranger.

The voice was quiet and raspy with an almost sinister tone, breathy, deep, and precise. Ross, afraid to move, pushed his back against the root of the tree and slowly looked around without moving his head, only moving his eyes in their sockets. From side to side, then up and down, Ross cautiously studied the darkness around him. Ross sat motionless for, what felt like, ages

"Wut fur bae ye haer? Wut fur ha ye com?" The eerie voice spoke as if both cautious and agitated, forceful but tentative.

"Who ... who's there?" Ross, almost too afraid to know the answer, but wanting to know where the voice was coming from, spoke out with trembling lips, his heart beating rapidly.

"Wut fur bae ye haer? Ye dunna b'lung haer!" The voice of the unseen stranger became increasingly agitated, even hostile. The caution and fear that Ross had sensed at first were quickly disappearing, as the voice moved closer and louder.

"I'm lost. I don't know where I am. Who are you? Where are you?"

"Kumél. Mae nam bae, Kumél. Wut fur ha Amik returned frum da grave un com t'Shuk?"

Ross struggled to understand what the strange voice was saying to him. The accent was strong and the language broken. "Who's Amik? What's Shuk?"

"Ye! Ye bae Amik."

"No! No, you've got it all wrong. I'm not . . . I don't know any Amik!"

"Uf yer nut Amik, thun who ye bae? Whae d'ye cull yersaelf?"

"Huh? Oh . . . Ross, my name is Ross."

"Ross? Hmm, bae u strange nam. Ye luk lik Amik. Ye bae o'ees clan?"

"I . . . I've never heard of this Amik guy or his clan. Honestly."

Ross could feel that the one in the shadows was slowly circling his position. Each time the voice spoke, it came from a different direction. For a moment, Ross thought he was surrounded by a group of men, but he soon realized it was only one voice and there was something vaguely familiar about it. It reminded him of an old Scotsman he had met during his travels, who spoke with a heavy brogue.

"Show yourself!" Ross carefully picked up a small branch and placed it on the glowing embers of the fire. He realized the intruder did not intend to do him harm and hoped that by stoking the fire he might catch sight of the person hiding in the dark. Soon the wood caught fire and the flames quickly illuminated the area around the makeshift camp.

Squatting down on a large root, directly opposite Ross, a large figure barely came into view. He did not seem bothered by the fire or the light it gave off, although he did seem to prefer the dusk of concealment. Motionless, he stared at Ross. His eyes were ebony and set deep in the sockets of his face. The stranger's skin appeared rough, scarred, and of different shades. His head was oversized with only a tuft of black hair, several inches long, growing from the top of it. Ross squinted, trying to make out more physical details. He could tell that whoever was sitting across from him was exceptionally large and possibly inhuman. Ross leaned on his rational thinking, dismissing his suspicions, and convincing himself there was nothing extraordinary about the stranger, despite what his eyes were witnessing. He knew eventually the sun would rise and what he could not comprehend now, he would understand in the daylight.

As the fire burned, Ross continued to sense he was in no immediate danger from the intruder. He threw more wood on the fire, hoping to have a better view of his visitor.

"Where are you from, Kumél? I'm from Washington, in the US. Have you heard of it?"

"Wush-ee-ton-in-da-yoo-es. Long nam. A naer haerd o'ut afore."

"Are you from here in Nepal or from India? Where are you from?"

"A dunna know o'Nee-pal."

"Well, I've come from a long way, several days journey and thousands of miles."

"A com frum Pardis."

"Pardis, hmmm. I've never heard of it. Is it a city?"

"Pardis bae no ceetie. Dis da realm o'Eloh."

"Eloh? What is Eloh?" Ross was aware that the locals in the remote villages and cities often had names for places that were handed down from generation to generation and were thus different from what the outside world knew or used.

"Haer bae Shuk."

"Ah, ok. So, you are from Shuk."

"Nae! A com frum Pardis. I bae exiled haer. Dis bae no home fur mae."

"Oh. Wow! Exiled, huh? I've never met an exile. What did you do to get exiled?"

"Ye ask muny tings. Tae muny."

"Just trying to be friendly, that's all."

"Ye ha nut answered mae; wut fur bae ye haer?"

"I'm trying to get back home. I've been climbing the mountain and . . . well, some things happened. I just want to get back to Pokhara, so I can catch the first flight back to the states."

"Poookhaaaarrrra . . . wut bae ut?"

"It's a city in Nepal, where I need to go. You've never heard of it?"

"Nae."

"Great! I assumed all the locals knew of Pokhara. It's an ancient city."

"Dar bae no cities un Shuk. Whit wae dud ye com frum?"

"You mean how did I get here?"

"Aye."

"I'm not really sure, but I came from the mountain. I guess I'm still trying to figure out where 'here' is."

For the entire time Ross spoke with Kumél, Kumél did not move from the spot opposite him. Never moving closer or out of the shadow, Kumél seemed to favor the darkness and the comfort of his distance from Ross.

Ross and Kumél were wary and untrusting of each other; Ross could tell Kumél was unsure of him and that he was skeptical of all he had told him. Both seemed uneasy about the conversation, but they managed to carry on even though neither of them had held a conversation with another intelligent being for some time. Ross wanted to ask more probing questions but feared he might become offended. Kumél, on the other hand, seemed only tentatively interested in Ross, returning often to the question of why he was there and telling him repeatedly, "You don't belong here."

"I've heard that before, you know."

"Haerd wut?"

"That I don't belong here."

"Aye? Who told ye?"

"In my dreams, I heard it just before I woke to find you here. I heard Eve. I heard Eve tell me that very same thing when I was on the ledge above. She was in my dream . . . Why do you keep telling me that?"

"Dis bae no place fur u Carascian. Ye dunna b'lung haer. Uf da gallues waer t'sense ye, dae wud hunt ye down un kull ye."

"The gallues? What're gallues? And what're Carascians? Why do you call me a Carascian?"

"Ye shud gae buk t'waer ye com frum."

"Believe me, if I could go back, I wouldn't go that way. It would be impossible, anyway."

"Wae?"

"The way is closed. The mountain I came through closed behind me. There's no way back. Besides, there was no other way out of the pit that I could see, except for, well, possibly through the iron gates."

"Iron Gates, wut iron gates?"

"I thought you weren't interested?"

"Wut iron gates!" Kumél's tone was impatient.

"I don't know, the ones inside the mountain. They were too far away; I didn't really see them very well. Looked like they had been there for a long time, though."

"Da Gates o'Abyssus." Kumél whispered the words in an alarming tone.

Ross could detect an ominous sense of concern in Kumél's voice as he said the words, then looked away, as if in deep thought. It was the first thing that he and Kumél were able to mutually recognize.

"Ye ha bun t'da Pit?"

"Yeah. Yeah, I told you all that. Why so interested now? What's the big deal?"

"Waer ye saen?"

"Seen? There was no one there to see me; I was alone."

"Hmm."

The conversation between them faded as Kumél sat silently in the shadows.

As the sun rose over the mountains, casting a soft yellow glow upon the landscape, Ross sat staring at Kumél who was becoming more visible, his features becoming illuminated. The frightful realization that he was not, in fact, human, overwhelmed Ross. While previously cloaked by the shadows, Ross could not have suspected that Kumél was this huge, monstrous beast. Now, as the sun's rays began to reveal the truth, Ross began to panic. His eyes were fixated on Kumél, his heart raced, and a nauseous feeling came over him. He could feel the blood draining from his face; his skin turned pale and clammy, and the world around him spun uncontrollably. Ross's breathing became quick and shallow; he could feel himself going limp as he was about to pass out. He tried to regain his composure by taking several deep breaths and slowly releasing them. He never took his eyes off Kumél, though. Every instinct in him wanted to yell, scream, or cry out. He wanted to escape, to run and hide, yet he couldn't move a muscle. He was frozen in place.

The terror consuming Ross finally began to subside. It dawned on him that for most of the night, he had calmly sat across from Kumél, unafraid. He realized Kumél could have already harmed him, but he had not. Though this thought helped ease Ross's fears, it did not reconcile the inexplicable contradiction between his own sensible reality and the present, albeit unbelievable, beastly reality watching him. To disguise his trepidation and astonishment, Ross rose to his feet and turned away. Trembling and nauseous, he leaned against the giant tree and cradled his head in the narrow space between his forearm and bicep, letting the sensation of sickness pass. Momentarily, Ross turned back to look at Kumél. He stared at him extensively, trying to gather his composure and his wits, letting a new reality find its way into his mind.

Ross studied Kumél's strangely deformed body, trying to gain some point of view that would offer a meaningful explanation for what he was seeing. Kumél's appearance was like nothing he had ever seen in his life. The fact that the creature was real and could communicate with him with such clarity made comprehending the situation even more difficult. At first glance, Kumél appeared to be human-like. He was marked with strange tattoos over his entire body and head and was clothed in a ragged kilt with a golden belt and shoulder strap. It appeared to Ross that Kumél might have stood fifteen feet tall, though it was difficult to see. On his belt was a long iron sword, sheathed in worn animal skin. On the shoulder belt was a bone- handled dirk, long enough to be used as a sword by a man. Kumél was anatomically built mostly like a man. He stood upright on two large muscular legs, he had two strong arms and so forth, but his size, the colors of his skin, and the markings on his body were so unhuman-like, that one would not know how to explain what they were seeing. When he turned away or to the side, Ross could see a huge bulge on his back that started at his shoulders and extended down toward his waist. From the top of the bulge protruded two skeletal-like appendages, which extended up and out from his body. They were about four feet long, like bent or curved shafts, differing in height.

The ends of the two appendages were rough and fractured as if they had been broken off something much larger. Lower down his back were another pair of similar boney-looking shafts, which extended downward. Ross wondered if the beast, at one time, might have had wings, though he could not imagine such a huge beast flying.

The skin of Kumél was the most unexpected feature about him. Dark and light as if he was, at some time, burned with fire. The dark parts of his skin were hard and scaly, reptilian in texture. The light spots were iridescent, reflecting the spectrum of colors from the sun's rays. Glowing and beautiful, these irregular patches of skin were in complete contrast to the dark scaly parts. His face was a mix of the two skin types. Veins in his legs, arms, neck, and head were exposed, and running through the veins was yellowish-colored blood. His hands and feet were large with four digits on each, and from the ends of the digits were sharp black talons.

In spite of his startling appearance, Kumél had a kind face. His eyes were round, and gentle compared to his forbidding and grotesque physical form. At the top of his head was a gold band wrapped around a large tuft of black hair. The hair was only a foot or so long, though not uniformly cut. From one side of his mouth, where the light iridescent skin was, grew a long lock of hair extending down his face and chin. When he spoke, Ross could see that his teeth were yellow and broken. So scarred was his body, so mangled with damage, that, despite the terrifying first impression, Ross began to feel compassion for Kumél.

Even so, the realization that Kumél was not human was not the only alarming epiphany Ross was confronted with. Mental images began to flash in and out of view: Eve in an ivory gown, the pit, the column of light, the stream, the crack in the mountain wall, the iron gates, his fall into the pool from more than a thousand feet, the ledge, the dried-up stream, the closed mountain, and Kumél. Images were racing in and out of his crowded mind, all trying to tell him something his rationale refused to accept. However, it all began to fit together. In a strange mosaic of images, all the pieces of the puzzle collided into each other until finally, Ross had the most dreadful and petrifying realization: *I've died and gone to hell. I'm dead, there's no other explanation. Damn it! Shit, shit, shit! I knew it. I knew there was no way I could have fallen into that pool and survived. The damn rope must've broken. Maybe I'm not in hell . . . yet. Maybe this is some kind of holding area and this demon has been sent to test me. Maybe there's still a chance. NO! NO! NO! This can't be it; this can't be what death looks like . . . can it?*

The images kept replaying, over and over; they ran like an old family movie projected onto a white sheet hanging on a living room wall. Ross was frozen from the chilling visions of his possible demise. He remembered the gash on his head and the blood that had flowed from it. He reached up and felt the wound with his hand. A scab had crusted over the gash, but the wound was still tender to the touch. He picked at the scab which made the wound bleed again. Blood slowly leaked from beneath the scab. He took his finger, touched the blood, and then he looked at it on his finger. He could feel it begin to dribble through his hair, warm and thick. *I'm alive! I'm alive, not dead. This can't be hell. This can't be hell or heaven. But it can't be earth, can it? Where the hell am I?*

Slowly his blood began to flow again, and the color began to return to his face. Ross glanced over at Kumél, who was still unaware of his acute mental collapse. Ross tightly squeezed his eyes shut. He hoped that, maybe, when he opened them, Kumél would not be there. He hoped he had been delusional or having a nightmare, but no matter how many times he blinked his eyes, Kumél remained in front of him. Ross knew for the very first time, with absolute clarity, that something strange had happened to him. He knew this place was not the place where he wanted to be, that Shuk was not a province in Nepal. He also knew he was far, far from home and not on planet earth anymore.

His eyes turned back to Kumél, and he looked at the giant creature with wonder. It struck him that his fear, the sudden terror he had felt, was slowly subsiding. As grotesque and horrifying as Kumél looked and as inhuman as he seemed, Ross knew Kumél was not going to harm him. With a quivering but sincere voice, Ross spoke to him. "What happened to you?"

Kumél, still lost in thought, did not notice Ross was speaking to him. "Hey, what happened to you?" Ross gently repeated.

"Wut ye maen?"

"How did you get that way? You know, all scarred and broken."

"T'was lung ago un nae concern t'ye."

"Are there many like you out there?"

"Lik mae? Nut muny."

"That's good. I mean, I ... I don't really know what I mean."

"Hmm."

"Where exactly am I? I think you're right; I don't belong here."

"Yur un da raelm o'Shuk."

"Haven't you seen anyone like me before?"

"Lung ago. Amik, ee waer lik ye. Wae waer fruns." Kumél's voice became soft and Ross could see tears welling in his large, gentle eyes. Though powerful, he could not withstand the force of his emotions. Ross could see that the memory of his friend, Amik, was still a painful wound.

"What happened to Amik? Did he die?"

"Aye, ee dud die, but nut afore A b'traed eem, eem un all mae fruns."

"I've lost a good friend; I still miss him. I've also lost the only woman that I've ever loved. What happened to both of them was my fault. I miss them both, every day. I wish I could go back, back and do it all over again."

"Ye cun nae'er gae buk. Wut bae b'hind ye bae gone fur gud."

"I hope not. I really, really hope not. I keep having this dream of Eve. She comes to me and tells me that I have to get home, but I just want to die. I don't want to move, to do anything, but she's there, in my darkest moment. *'Ross, you have to make it home. You have to get back home.'* Ross recited. Eve saves me."

The pain of loss was still very acute, and he had to force himself to tell the story. Kumél sat staring at him, watching the brokenness of Ross's heart seep out from his eyelids and flow down his face. "A used t'bae u kerolus. A waer u frun t'Eloh un Amik. A work'd aside Amik un da garduns o'Assuk, afore da treachery o'Attar, afore A lost mae wings." Ross looked at him with an uneasy stare. Before he could say anything, Kumél continued. "A bae un aposta, now, for A ha forsaken both Attar un Eloh."

"What do you mean, forsaken? Did you have a choice?"

"Nae, ut matter nut. Dar bae nae furgivness fur mae, fur ony o'us."

"But, have you ever tried to ask or go back to your home? Surely they can't blame you?"

"A bae lost from thut life, an thut world. Dar bae nae wae back. Da war splat da realm apart, un da wae bae gone. Eloh wud nae'er furgiv mae treason. Dar bae nae redemption fur traitors."

"Who's Eloh? Why wouldn't he forgive you?"

"Ee bae da one thut Attar hates, da one thut da legend tells wull com un break da rule o'Attar. But ut waer muny ages ago. Ee wull nut com agan."

"He might. What happened to you?"

"A, un mony others lik mae, waer led t'da Waters o'Eon, thut waer bewitched bae Attar. Muny o'mae own kin bathed un thum fur days. U horrible transformation b'gun. Dae cried out as Attar stood o'er thum casting ees spell. Ees malice un hatred b'gun t'strip way deir beauty, un deir wings ... lik u d'sease. A ha nut entered da waters afore da firs signs o'da treachery b'com claer ... But ut waer t'late ... Da waters waer splashed on t'mae body un dae b'gun t'aet at mae flesh. Da enchanting words o'Attar, mixed wit da poisoned waters, b'gun t'deform mae. A, un four others escaped unto d'mountuns o'Tirnan, un thun t'Shuk."

"Were you the only ones to escape?"

"Dar waer muny others who tried, muny who refused t'enter da pool, but afore dae cud escape, Attar murdered thum."

"You can't blame yourself for the evil of another. You didn't mean to do anything wrong. Do you honestly think this, Eloh, would hold you accountable for the treachery of this, Attar?"

"Ye dunna know wut followed. Dar bae so much mur thut cunna bae undone."

"Have you ever tried to tell your story to Eloh or the others? You know, tried to make it right?"

"A ha nae'er ha da chance. Eloh dunna com t'Shuk un A canna gae buk t'Assuk."

"How long have you been here, in Shuk?"

"T'lung, far t'lung."

"The others, who escaped with you, where are they?"

"Two o'thum bae captured bae da gallues, who rule over Shuk. One naer saen fur muny ages. Un da other livs un da hae mountuns."

The more Kumél talked and the more he said about himself and Shuk, the more Ross began to wonder about the legend the old man had told Daniel. He was surprised that some of the things Kumél was telling him sounded vaguely familiar. There were many things that frightened him, and one thing that kept bothering him was hearing the word "rule." He felt a knot in the pit of his stomach when he heard it. It was a concept that he had no context for, no experience with, something, which seemed archaic and beyond the realm of being acceptable.

He looked at Kumél. "Rule? Who do they rule over?"

"Da nephesh."

"Nephesh? What are nephesh?"

"Dae bae da embodied souls o'da Carascians captives o'Attar guarded o'er bae da arch- gallues."

"Captives? You mean held captive, like prisoners or slaves?"

"Aye."

"Why? Where'd they come from?"

"Da nephesh bae stripped away frum da Carascians afta da ruin o'Amik. Dae bae vary powerful, da Elohan Essentia o'da Carascians, but apart frum deir sapiens dae ha no wae o'escaping Attar or ees cruel captains."

"The sapiens?"

"Da sapien bae o'da Carascians, descendants o'Amik. Dae liv un Tirnan under da captivity un rule o'Attar himself."

Ross did not understand much of what Kumél told him. He was confused and afraid that it was more real than he wanted to believe.

"Dar bae much thut ye dunna know, much thut ye maet nut wish t'know."

"Well, that's something we can certainly agree upon."

Ross sat down on the lush grass and considered the things Kumél had told him. Ducking under the overhanging branches of the ancient tree, Kumél walked over and sat down near Ross.

"Dar bae u reason thut ye ha cum t'Shuk. Dis bae u lund fulled wit mystery. Dar bae muny tings thut happen thut few cun know. Uf A cun haelp ye, A wull."

"Will you help me find my way home?"

"Mubae ye foun mae so ye cud fin yer wae home. A wull haelp ye uf A cun."

"I really don't know where to begin, though."

"Dar bae u place t'da norõ, un da Gershom Forest, hae un da hills. Wae shud gae dar firs."

"The Gershom Forest? How far's that?"

"Tis muny days frum haer. Wae wull ha t'cross da Black Valley un climb da Pass o'Borak afore wae cun reach Gershom."

"Will we be safe there?"

"A cunna say. Gershom bae u mystic place. Tis rumored thut u celestial empress visits dar. She knows muny tings."

Ross looked at Kumél with skepticism and doubt, lowering his brow in disbelief. "Do you think it's true?"

"A ha naer bun t'Gershom. Ye wull fin answers dar. Wae mus go t'Gershom."

"Well, if there are no other options, let's go."

Zoësh

Chapter V
Two Dead Mēgs

Throughout the valley lands of Shuk, hidden in the shadows and darkness, were the snitches of Shuk, lost nephesh who had become willing slaves to the arch-gallues. Willing to tell of any news, of any disturbances in the land or to assist in the capture of their own, these shadow dwellers were despised and hated by all the nephesh who lived under the captivity of The Twelve, the group of arch-gallues who ruled the realm. Having betrayed their own kind, the snitches of Shuk were an outcast group, untrusted by all. Even the gallues hated and distrusted them. These treacherous creatures exchanged lives and information for privileges and leniency from The Twelve.

It was known to those who wandered the highlands of Shuk that the snitches were always on the prowl, looking for information that would gain them favor with the arch-gallues. It was for this reason that many had chosen the solitude and refuge of the highlands, including Kumél. The dangers of crossing the valley lands were very real; anyone caught by the gallues would be enslaved and tortured and possibly murdered. For Kumél, chancing an encounter with any occupant of the valley lands could mean death, slow and painful.

It had been many ages since Kumél had ventured into the valleys. The last time he had traveled there, he had come close to losing his life at the unforgiving talons of the arch-gallue, Gubrone, who ruled the twelve domains of the Valley of Souls. Many of the scars Kumél bore were from encounters with snitches and gallues, but the worst were from his struggles against Gubrone.

Not every valley land in Shuk was a place of danger, yet it had been rumored that the arch-gallues had been spreading into more and more of them, seeking the nephesh who had taken refuge there. One of these valleys that had become overtaken by the gallues and their snitches was the Atramentous Valley, which wound through the impenetrable highlands of western Shuk, starting in the highlands of the north, and running south, to the Plain of Haemus. This long, narrow valley formed a barrier to Gershom Forest in the east. Flanked on either side by gargantuan mountain peaks, the only way to get the other side was to descend into its dark, shadowy cover.

It was with great trepidation that Kumél began the journey to Gershom Forest knowing that the way lay through the dark valley. There was, however, a strange, inexorable force drawing him to the aid of Ross, a force he had experienced before, a force he had forgotten he could feel. Kumél had been alone for so long he did not realize just how lonely he was. Ross reminded him of something he had forgotten, something that, a long time before, had meant a great deal to him: friendship. Kumél had no friends, but it had not always been so, for Kumél was once a close friend to Amik. Long ago, Kumél abandoned all thoughts about his past life. When the memories did surface, they overflowed with the pain and guilt of his betrayal.

Kumél was often given to deep introspection. He found, in himself, dark and inexplicable feelings of anger and hostility, which, though he knew were unjustified, existed in his mind and heart, like a splinter, infected and sore. His life of solitude opened him up to unedited feelings of hatred, jealousy, and even murder, but where they came from, he could not fathom. He had thought the inner struggle between his true self and the self he had become had ended ages ago when the kerolus he had once been was slain by the monster and traitor he had become. There was no forgiveness, no redemption for him, and even if there was, Kumél could not accept either. There may be no greater pain than the pain of self-betrayal, and Kumél believed he had betrayed his friends and himself. For ages, Kumél had known only darkness, but this young foreigner, who had come from the mountain, brought with him an invisible light that began to shine in his heart.

What lay ahead worried Kumél. It was not the looming dangers or the possibilities of capture that worried him, exactly; it was not the evil but the good. He usually feared nothing and yet, what he knew about Gershom Forest made him hesitant, even afraid. Quietly, introspectively, and cautiously, Kumél headed toward the east, taking Ross to Gershom Forest.

The upper region of the Atramentous Valley was crowded by ancient towering trees. The forest was so thick and overgrown that the diffused light of the ever-overcast skies rarely touched the soil. With constant melt-off from the high mountains, the ground beneath the canopy of trees had become marshy and soft with dangerous sludgy mud pits and bogs. The undergrowth was a combination of blackstalk, a black-stemmed, gray-leafed shrub that had long, sharp needles growing on the stalks of the bush, and xanthic, a broad-leafed tawny vine growing in tangles and knots up the trunks of the trees. The needles of the blackstalk were as long as a man's finger, thin like a sewing needle and very sharp. The shafts of the needles also had dozens of imperceptible barbs that curved away from the point of the needle, making extraction difficult and excruciatingly painful. The needles would break off in the skin and work deep into the tissue, becoming infected within just a few hours. The large, dark green leaves of the xanthic were sharp with knife-like serrated edges, which could shred both clothing and skin with relative ease. The leaves of the xanthic were also poisonous to the touch. Both plants had adapted to the unwelcoming environment so well that they thrived without sunlight and had thus overgrown into thick, impenetrable hedges. As the plants died, then decomposed, the rotting mulch emitted a vile stench, which for anyone near, could induce vomiting, hallucinations, and eventually unconsciousness. No living creatures chose to dwell in the upper regions of the Atramentous Valley because of this unruly flora.

Even the waters of the upper marshes had become caustic from ages of decomposition of the two plant species. To drink the water would mean certain and painful death. Negotiating through the upper marshes meant avoiding the pools and small streams of water as well as the hedges of the undergrowth. There were not many ways to pass through the forest's upper regions, no paths to follow, and once under the forest's canopy, it would not be possible to use the sun or the stars for navigation.

The lower region of the valley was less hostile, but much more dangerous because of the presence of the gallues and snitches. Hoping they would be able to negotiate a route through the blackstalk and xanthic hedges, Kumél headed north toward the upper marshes. "Whaer wae bae headin bae vary dangerus. Muny ages ago, A com through da valley, lung afore da gallues foun out. Fur muny ages ut waer u refuge fur da nephs who waerna enslaved. Now ut bae overrun bae da snitches un gallues."

"Overrun! So, what you're saying is . . . we're heading for trouble."

"Aye, ut bae u stronghold, un trouble bae dar t'fin ye.

Ross stopped. He took a deep breath. Kumél glanced back and stopped also. "T'is da ony wae t'Gershom Forest . . . Uf ye'd rather nut gae, A wud bae quite satisfied t'laeve ye right haer un bae on mae wae."

"No, but if it's overrun, how are we going to get through without someone seeing us?" Ross looked at Kumél, a hulking beast and could not see how it was possible for them to be missed. For a moment, he doubted Kumél's intentions, and Kumél knew it.

"Dar bae mur at stake thun ye realize, un A d'nut plan t'gut caught bae da gallues. Ye shud know, Shuk bae u vary dangerus place. Eary whaer ye gae bae risky. Uf ye wanna gae alone, A wull point da wae."

"No, No! That's not it . . . I'm sure you know what you're doing, but . . . never mind." Ross lowered his head and breathed out a great sigh. "I'm not sure about this. It seems like everything I do gets me into some kind of trouble . . . Guess I have no choice, though, do I? I have no choice but to follow you."

Kumél sat down on a rock with his back to Ross. "Nae, ye cud gae alone." Kumél pointed toward the valley. "Dar, thut bae da way."

"You're crazy! I don't know where the hell I'm going or what the hell I'm doing here!"

"Aye, ye dunna, but A do."

"Come on then, damn it! Let's go before I change my mind and do something more stupid than what I'm about to do."

Kumél stood back up. He glanced back at Ross and asked sarcastically, "Ye dun' have mony fruns, do ye?"

"Fuck you. You're not one to talk now, are you?" Ross grumbled under his breath, knowing that if Kumél wanted, he could surely make him regret his harsh words. Kumél just chuckled as he walked away.

The atmosphere between the two had become cold and the air was silent as they made their way across the high shoulder of the mountain toward the edge of the valley. Kumél was concerned that they might be seen traveling into the valley floor because the upper portion of the mountainsides were mostly bare of foliage, leaving them exposed to any watching eyes. Strewn over the sides of the mountains, above the timberline, were massive rocks and boulders of every size and shape. Not only were they concerned about being seen, but also about the difficulty of the descent through the steep boulder fields.

"Wae'll wait haer, til da sun bae down un da dark night bae upon us."

"Why? We have plenty of daylight left. We could cover a lot of ground before dark, especially these damned boulder fields," Ross sharply protested.

"Wae naed da cover o'darkness t'kaep us frum watching eyes."

"Hmm, I guess maybe you're right, but it seems crazy."

"Aye, ut ma bae . . . tis better thun travlin wun wae cun bae saen . . . un caught." Kumél's words had a mischievous tone to them, revealing he had a slight sense of humor. The banter helped to break the tension that had grown between the two of them.

"Ok, great. I suppose you needed a rest, anyway, at your age and all."

"Hmm," grunted Kumél turning away, without giving Ross the satisfaction of a defensive rebuttal.

Everything seemed too quiet, too peaceful, which made Kumél feel uncomfortable. Finding cover under a pile of large stones, the pair sat waiting for the long day to turn into night.

"So, tell me, what exactly might we be up against in those woods?"

"Gallues an' snitches, an' maybe u mēg or two."

"Gallues? You mean more beasts like yourself?" Ross's reference to *beasts* was intended as a friendly jab.

"Ha! Des gallues bae far worse thun A. Dae ha completely lost deir true saelfs un b'com creatures o'darkness. Dae bae very strong un corrupt."

"Are they as . . . large as you?"

"Aye."

Now, most of the gallues were similar to Kumél, though only in the most basic sense, such as their size and general physical form. Kumél had

135

not been fully transformed, and so he more closely resembled his former kerolus self. Therefore, his skin was patchy with spots of black scales and areas of iridescent skin, but the gallues were dark, almost black and they often smelled of rotting flesh. Many of them were so deformed that they could not walk upright and had to move about on all fours. However, the strongest and most dangerous gallues stood upright and commanded the lesser gallues about as slaves. All of them had misshapen, mostly bald heads, wrinkled faces, dark, lidless eyes, and a broad snout like a boar. They had tusk-like teeth, black and sharp, two on each side of their mouth. They did not resemble their former selves in any way.

"Dae bae vile, heartless killers." Kumél's words cut through Ross's thoughts.

The caution he had felt before, began to turn to fear as the gruesome images of the gallues began to form in his imagination. He tried to distract himself from thinking about them and kept talking. "What were you like before?"

"Ut bae haerd t'rumumber wut A use t'bae. A ha bun lik dis fur so lung. Dar bae u tam wun A waer beautiful, wun A waer unscarred, magnificent, an frae. Dat tam bae lung gone."

Ross passionately defended Kumél. "But, you're free, aren't you? Who do you answer to? You come and go at will. Isn't that freedom? Not all has been lost, has it?"

Kumél looked at Ross with eyes that were filled with both contempt and pity. "Ye know notin o'fraedom. Ye tink thut baein frae bae com'n or gaein at will? A live wit da chains o'guilt, o'sorrow un o'rugret eary day. A ha mur sins thun ye cun draem. A ha bun u slave t'mae treachery un rebellion. A wake t'da shadows o'da world thut bae lost, thut bae ripped apart bae war un violence, haertbreak un b'trael. D'ye raely b'laeve thut bae wut fraedom luks lik? Nae. A bae nut frae . . . un nae'er bae ye. Wae bae prisoners, boun bae chains un bars thut wae ha forged wit our own hands."

The passion that enveloped Kumél's response surprised Ross. He suddenly felt smaller than ever, and for the next several hours, was unable to bring himself to speak. The words that Kumél had spoken were words that he had never heard before, and even if he had heard them before, they would have passed over him. Ross was not one to engage in deep or meaningful conversations unless he was required to. There was something sharp, yet gentle about Kumél's words: sharp because they pierced his normally impenetrable sensibilities, gentle because they seemed less intended to wound than to heal.

The sun began to set over Shuk, and darkness closed in with sudden, unrelenting determination. Picking up their belongings and exiting the stone shelter, they began the daunting descent into the valley below.

The darkness brought both a notable advantage and a disadvantage. The disadvantage looked to be the greater of the two, for navigating silently through the steep rockslides and fields was slow and dangerous without the light of a lantern or of the sun. However, the darkness offered an advantage they had not anticipated. As they descended toward the dense forest, they could see the light of fires glowing faintly through the canopy of the trees. In some places there were clusters of several fires, indicating that there were groups of gallues and snitches gathered together. To their satisfaction, they saw that the way of the upper marshes was absolutely black during the night with not a single fire in sight. The revelation was both comforting and ominous, for the darkness of the upper marshes was itself a formidable deterrent to passage. The comfort was mixed with dread and for Ross, fear.

"Dae cun fael yer fear ye know." The hushed words of Kumél broke the spell of silence that had been cast between them by the curtain of darkness.

"I don't know how not to be afraid."

"Ye mus fin courage. T'is in ye, A know ut."

Kumél's words shocked Ross, and for a moment he believed them. Maybe it was Kumél's size, his massive frame, that made Ross feel so small and vulnerable, but having Kumél say such things made him suddenly feel less small and less afraid.

"What about the snitches? What are they?" Ross began asking Kumél about the enemy they were sure to face. He was not exactly sure he wanted to know much more, but he could not think of anything else to talk about.

"Oh, dae bae harmless, most o'thum, except dae wull tell earyting thut dae sae un haer t'da gallues. Ye cunna trus um, ony o'thum."

"So, how do you know the difference between a nephesh that is a snitch and one that's not?"

"Dar bae no difference thut ye cun sae . . . so stay wae frum ony o'thum. Take no chances, ye haer? Ut mae cost ye yer life."

"Better safe than sorry then, huh?"

"Aye. Better safe"

"Who's there?" A voice whispered out of the darkness.

Ross and Kumél stopped and looked at each other. Kumél put his finger to his mouth, signaling for Ross to be quiet. Ross's heart began to race with fear as he slowly looked around. Kumél slowly squatted low to avoid being seen.

"Who is there? What are you doing here?"

"Who is that?" Ross whispered to Kumél.

Kumél's stance was low on all fours, like a lion ready to pounce on its prey. Ross crouched down next to a large boulder and waited, hoping they had not been seen or heard and that whoever was out there in the darkness would move on.

"Well, are you gonna answer me or not? Please, if you can hear me, show yourselves." The voice in the darkness spoke softly and yet with urgency.

Kumél began to sniff the air like a hungry beast. Ross could hear him sniffing but could barely see him crouched there, tense and alert. Ross slowly arose from his squatting position. He looked behind him and, in every direction, possible until he could peek over the edge of the boulder where he was hiding. He waited for the voice to speak again, hoping he might decipher its location. "Who is there?"

Hearing the words startled Ross again. However, this time it shocked him because it came from immediately behind him. Startled, Ross turned and stood face-to-face with another being that he had never seen before.

Kumél, like a wolf, reared around and pounced on it. He raised his powerful right arm ready to deliver a fatal and final blow with his powerful black talons. The intruder, a female, barely a third of Kumél's size, reached up and halted the powerful blow with only its outstretched arm, as if Kumél were a child at play.

"Stop!" Ross almost yelled but was able to control his volume.

For the first time, Ross reached out and grabbed the already-stayed arm of Kumél. The sensation of Kumél's skin in his hands made Ross quickly release it and step away. Afraid of the giant's reaction, Ross quickly ducked down. Kumél, equally surprised by Ross's touch, seized his instinct to kill and instead lowered his hand slowly, but he still refused to let go of the intruder, though it appeared that the intruder could have escaped of its own volition.

"Wut d'ye wanna frum us?" Kumél's deep, raspy voice, restrained to a hiss, descended upon the ears of the intruder with threatening intent.

"Please, please, let me go."

"Yur u snitch!" Insisted Kumél.

"A what! No! I'm not a snitch."

"Liar, Yur u snitch. A know ut."

"I don't know what you are talking about. Let me go."

"A shud kull ye afore ye laed da others t'us."

"Kumél, Kumél!" asserted Ross, still trying to keep his voice low.

"Wut?"

"Let her talk. Hear her out."

"Wut d'ye maen, haer her out?"

"Listen. Hear what she has to say. Maybe she's not a snitch, maybe she can help us."

"Bae ye u snitch? Unsaer mae!"

"No, No! I am not a snitch. What makes you think I am a snitch anyway?"

"A dunna trus ony o'ye nephs. Ye nae'er cun tell."

Ross stood staring at the intruder, mesmerized and confused, for what he saw was not a menacing beast or an evil enemy, but a beautiful, innocent, and guileless creature similar in appearance and form as himself.

"What the hell is she?" Ross's words rolled out of his mouth like an uninhibited drunk man, exposing his thoughts.

"A nephesh. Ut bae u neph, un mubae u snitch."

"Oh, so that's a nephesh . . . Don't hurt her."

The nephesh were the most unique and mysterious of all the creatures of Shuk for they were the personification of the Elohan Essentia. Few have ever truly understood the mystery of the nephesh and their relationship with the sapiens and as such, few have ever been able to understand the fate of the Carascians. It was Attar who conjured the dark magic and broke the bond between the nephesh and the sapiens, bringing death upon the Carascians.

Over the ages, the sapiens, who inhabit the realm of Tirnan, have forgotten the nephesh. The nephesh, however, have never forgotten them, and so they continue their search for wholeness, to reestablish the line of Amik and of the Carascians. It is for this reason that Attar hunts them and enslaves them. That is why the nephesh have been exiled to the realm of Shuk where they are physically separated from the sapiens.

Ross looked at the nephesh in amazement. "Who are you? What is your name?"

"Zoësh. My name is Zoësh, and how is it that you are here? You don't belong here."

"So I've been told."

Zoësh was tall, slender, and pleasing to look upon. Her attractiveness was not merely derived from her outward appearance but from something beyond physicality. There was a radiance that emanated from all nephesh, coming from a mysterious, hidden persona that made them most alluring. Many nephesh disguised themselves beneath raiments fashioned from organic materials in colors of grass, earth, sand, and stone. These garments helped them blend into the environment so they could hide and move without being seen, much like chameleons. Having developed these special abilities to transform the flora of Shuk into superb but inconspicuous garb, the nephesh adorned themselves skillfully but modestly. They were so skilled at this craft, that if Zoësh had wished to be undiscovered by Ross and Kumél, they would not have been able to recognize her form against the surrounding milieu. Their shrouds were so form-fitting, they seemed more like skins than garments. Initially one might have thought that the coverings were applied like paint on a canvas. This made them very agile as well as unencumbered. The nephesh who were captured and enslaved by the vile gallues, were cruelly stripped of their stunning, protective coverings.

The only part of their skin that could be seen was their face and head, which was uncovered unless concealed when wanting to be completely camouflaged. Some were dark while others were pale, but all had smooth, nacreous skin that was pearlescent and glowing as if with some inner luminescence. Their oval-shaped faces were youthful with small, attractive features. The most striking and dominant features of the nephesh were their eyes, bright and gentle, blue and piercing.

Their hair was usually long and fell down each side of their face and was finished by a bronze headband. Each fiber of hair was like a long shaft of fluid glass, which allowed the colors and shapes of nearby objects to show through, aiding their disguise when needed. Each shaft of hair would also absorb the light of the sun, or the moon, or even a candle, becoming illuminated and making the nephesh appear to glow. It was this aspect of their beautiful locks that made them especially susceptible to capture, for the enemy could see them from afar. Many of the nephesh who were on the run had chosen to cut their beautiful hair or at least to cover it. Zoësh's hair was long but covered. The bronze headband was worn by all the nephesh, even if they had shaved their heads. On the front center of the headband was an engraved mark, a sign called the mark of Eloh.

Zoësh carried a sharp, single-edged falchion, which was about three feet long and sheathed in materials matching Zoësh's raiment. The sword was not a common tool for the nephesh, but it was necessary for protection against the gallues. Zoësh's sword was actually a gallue dagger she had stolen. The gallue it had belonged to was murdered by Gubrone for losing the weapon to a nephesh.

At no time during their encounter with Zoësh had Ross or Kumél noticed the falchion nor had Zoësh made any attempt to brandish it for protection or defense, even though Kumél's attack would have been a perfect reason.

"She brangs danger. She bae u spy o'da gallues."

Kumél was insistent, though, for the moment he seemed less convinced and even less convincing.

"But, what if she's not a snitch, what if she's just another nephesh that needs help? You know what the gallues will do to her if they capture her."

"Uf shae bae u snitch, shae wull brang others un da gallues wull follow."

"But you can't just kill her, can you? Aren't you better than that, better than the gallues?"

"Arg," objected Kumél. "Shae wull slow us down."

"She could help us, too."

Zoësh did not seem to fear Kumél or Ross. To the contrary, it seemed that the attack was of no significance to her whatsoever.

"Aye," protested Kumél, as he rose from his position over the nephesh, though he kept one hand firmly clasped around her arm so she could not escape. "You needn't worry. I will not leave you."

"Hmm . . . A bae nut sur A cun b'laeve ye. Ye maet yet bae u spy."

"I assure you; I am not. I am in just as much danger as you. I have seen them, the gallues, they hunt me. I am not with them."

"How bae ut ye ha nut fallen captive? Dae bae very skillful hunters," Kumél continued to interrogate Zoësh.

"I've seen them capture others. I was their captive once . . . some time ago . . . but I escaped. At least for now, it would seem they haven't found out where to find me."

"Wut d'ye maen? All da nephs bae slaves t'da gallues or else deir snitches. How bae ut ye bae free?"

"Not all of the nephesh are slaves or snitches. Some have not yet been captured, and some have escaped."

Kumél looked at Zoësh with a furrowed brow and suspicious eyes. He did not trust her even though he could not truly justify his apprehension. He saw the sword she carried and knew that snitches did not carry swords. Kumél was, however, invariably suspicious. Ages of being hunted and living in solitude had forged a previously gentle and trusting nature into a harsh and unrelenting wariness. Kumél turned and walked into the darkness without another word.

As they worked their way toward the valley, Ross talked with Zoësh. His curiosity about her and what she was and where she had come from was such that he was unable to keep himself from inquiring.

"So, you're a nephesh?"

"Yes, I am. Why do you ask?"

"I just . . . well . . . I've never seen one before."

"Alright, and you, what are you?"

"Me? I don't know . . . just a man, you know?"

"A man, huh? That's what you call it? You look like what I imagine a sapien looks like. What's a man?"

"What do you mean? I'm a man. Haven't you ever seen a man before?"

"I have not."

Ross was dumbfounded. He scratched his head in confusion as he tried to understand how it was possible for her to have never seen a man before. He also thought it was odd that she assumed him to be a sapien, which, of course, meant nothing at all to him.

"So, you've never seen anyone like me before, ever?"

"No, never."

"You said you thought I was a sapien. What's a sapien?"

"Long ago before I came here, in my memories, like a vision, I saw her."

"You don't see her anymore?"

"No, my sapien has passed into the shadows. I am a waif now, alone, abandoned, with no one to go to."

"'Passed into the shadows.' What does that mean?"

Ross acted confused by what she had said about the shadows, but he understood. "I am unable to see my sapien any longer. She has passed out of my vision, into darkness."

"Ut maens dae bae dead"

Kumél spoke out in an indifferent, almost rude tone. He was becoming weary of the conversation even though he was not in it. Ross continued as though he had not noticed Kumél's impertinence.

"I'm sorry for your loss. What happens to you now?"

"Maybe we shouldn't talk about it right now."

"Now thut yer sapien bae gone, da gallues wull hunt ye down un turn ye, muk ye u snitch or u slave or worse."

"How do they know that my sapien has passed out of the light? Why do I matter to them now?"

"Dae know. A bae nut sure ha dae know, but dae know. Ha ye nae'er bun un da Valley o'Souls?"

"Of course, I have. When I was born, I was sent here to Shuk. I was captured by Gubrone and held in the valley, but I escaped, and I have been hiding from the gallues and their mēgs ever since."

"A ha saen da mēgs, but nae'er dis far frum da Valley o'Souls."

"Oh, they're here. The gallues have been training them to find escaped nephesh like me. The vile creatures are loyal to their masters and go wherever the gallues go. There are many of them in the valley below."

Ross listened to Zoësh and knew, by her tone, that whatever it was she was talking about was very serious. "What's a mēg?"

"Mēglydaims, black beasts. We call um mēgs—very dangerous creatures."

"Nae'er ye wery bout thum," Kumél tried to reassure Ross.

"Well, you'd better worry about them. They'll tear us to shreds if they get the chance. They're monsters, dark evil beasts with no qualms about killing whoever or whatever they find, save their precious masters." Zoësh's voice cut through any ambiguity that might have lingered in Ross's mind. She was serious and meant to make it plain to both Ross and Kumél. Ross began to feel real fear.

Kumél could see that Ross was becoming very worried and unsure. Zoësh also sensed Ross's fear and doubt. Zoësh tried to warn him. "They will sense your fear. You have to be strong."

"Yeah, I know. Kumél told me."

"You're only beginning to open your eyes. There is much more that you don't yet see."

The words of Zoësh bore a hole into Ross's heart. He could feel the piercing thrust of dread penetrating his consciousness, pushing deep into the inner parts of his being. Eve had told him once that he was blind to the world around him and that there was so much more to life than what he understood. However, her words had meant nothing to him at the time. They seemed like some strange cult philosophy fresh out of the mouth of a rookie college professor, but now, in this place, after all that had occurred, Ross was beginning to comprehend. It was all he could do to keep from running away into the darkness. Nevertheless, Ross knew he had no choice but to stay with his strange new companions.

Slowly and quietly, they continued down the steep, rocky slope into the valley below. It was imperative that they reach the forest before daybreak. Zoësh wanted to change the mood between them to lighten the weight of anxiety and fear. She spoke out in a friendly, affectionate manner. "You haven't told me your names."

"Ye dunna ask."

"I'm asking now."

"Kumél."

"Kumél, I've heard of you. You're a warrior, the one who battled Gubrone and lived."

"Aye, thut bae mae. Baen u lung tam ago."

"And you, Carascian, what's your name?"

"I'm not a Carascian. My name's Ross."

"That's a strange name."

"That's what Kumél said. I don't find it at all strange considering . . ." Ross held his tongue, realizing he was not only out-sized, but also outnumbered.

They moved through the darkness discreetly, descending deeper into the valley. The closer they got to the tree line, the darker the night became, and though they could see the alpenglow of the morning sun hinting its arrival, Atramentous would soon envelop them in its daunting shadows.

Picking up the pace in order to find shelter from the revealing sunlight, the trio moved swiftly through the upper tree line. Twisted and deformed, the first trees stood exposed and alone, like sentinels keeping watch over the valley below. Their long, pointed needles, in shades of green and brown, reached longingly toward the first rays of daylight, eager for the caress of the warm aurora of dawn.

The spectacle of morning's arrival was, however, short-lived, for the gray impenetrable overcast quickly swallowed the virgin sunlight. Snow began to fall over the mountains. Softly, the stark, white flakes drifted down landing upon whatever surface they found. Covering the rocks and grass, trees and bushes, the gentle flakes were a contrast to the austere world on which they descended. Like the travelers descending into the dangers of Atramentous, the silent snowflakes fell to a world that would soon consume every trace of them ever having been there.

Entering the dark woods, the small company was greeted by a lush and surprisingly placid environment. At the upper reaches of the forest, above the marshes, the canopy was sparser and more broken than deeper down in the valley. Here, the ground was covered in tall grasses and moss, with an assortment of high mountain flowers coloring the ground in patches of yellow, blue, purple, white, and orange.

Cautiously Ross, Kumél and Zoësh moved through the shadowy woods. Kumél led and was more alert than usual. Ross, seeing how Zoësh could disappear into the scenery, began to realize that if the snitches were anything like Zoësh, in terms of their ability to cloak themselves, then, at any point they could find themselves being spied upon, and their covert mission would be revealed.

Slowly surveying and sniffing the air, Kumél moved with careful deliberateness, like a hunter stalking its prey.

Zoësh, who was especially keen to the movements of the nephesh, followed in second place, watching for any sign or movement in the dark woods. "Shh!" All three halted and remained motionless. "Kumél, I saw something just ahead. Do not move!" Zoësh quietly stepped around to the right side of Kumél but remained near him for cover.

Ross could not believe his eyes. As Zoësh moved near Kumél, her appearance began to change, taking on the colors and shapes of Kumél. One moment Zoësh was there, and in the next, Ross could hardly detect the nephesh's presence at all.

Ross saw something out of the corner of his eye. It was a flash of movement about twenty or thirty yards out. The sudden revelation that they were not alone sent chills up his spine, and his heart began to race with fear.

"Down, get down!" Zoësh moved away from Kumél and stopped a short distance from Ross near a group of small trees. Suddenly another nephesh, or rather a snitch, stepped into a clearing not far from Zoësh. Ross held his breath as he knelt behind a moss-covered stone, peeking over its top. The snitch was unaware of the presence of Ross, Zoësh, and Kumél though it would not have taken much for it to discover the hulking Kumél. Kumél fought back the instinct to attack the snitch for he sensed that there might be others around.

Ross felt the presence of something to his left. Carefully he turned only his eyes to see what it was. Just a few steps from him stood another snitch, which had not seen him crouching next to the rock. Fortunately, there were ferns and other plants growing near the rock that were obscuring Ross's position. The snitch moved toward the spot where Kumél was hiding.

Kumél became aware of the approaching snitch and held his breath. He was crouched low next to a large tree that had low-hanging boughs and tall undergrowth around it. Because of his size and the color of his skin, he should have been an easy mark for the snitches to see, however, the snitches seemed more focused on each other than on anything surrounding them.

Voices began to resonate through the forest. The two snitches met up and greeted each other. A few moments later, another three snitches came from deeper in the woods. Together they spoke while standing in a clearing close to where Ross, Kumél, and Zoësh were hiding. "Morak said there were rumors circulating. The escaped one may be near here."

"I've seen nothing. We have been too long in this nasty marsh and not a sign of her anywhere."

"Maybe we have come too far north; maybe she is farther south. They never come this high, you know?"

"Maybe, but that is what Morak said, and you know him. He thinks he's never wrong."

"How did he let another one get away. We showed him the exact place to set up the trap, and still, she got away. The gallues are nothing but barbarians."

"I heard that the rebel Zoësh has been seen again."

"Zoësh? I would rather not find that one. Let someone else handle her."

"The reward is pretty big, though. Maybe we should, I don't know, offer our services."

"Oh yeah, that sounds like a real good idea. Have you forgotten what happened the last time a gallue tried to capture Zoësh?"

"What?"

"He's dead! Not to mention Zoësh took his sword. Armed and dangerous! That is what that one is, and I for one am not interested in knowing just how sharp the edge of that blade is."

For a long time, the five snitches talked while Ross, Kumél, and Zoësh waited for them to move on. Ross noticed that the snitches were not as well-disguised as Zoësh. All five snitches bore scars on their faces, backs, and arms from the unrestrained beatings inflicted on them by the gallues, most likely by the chief-gallue, Gubrone.

Gubrone was known for the cruelty and malicious brutality he often unleashed upon the nephesh and, especially the snitches. While Gubrone used the snitches for his purposes, he also deeply hated them, knowing they were untrustworthy and devious. Gubrone whipped and tortured the snitches regularly to make sure they remained afraid and loyal to him. The snitches were too terrified of Gubrone to ever try and countermand his will.

"Have you seen the others?"

"They have already turned suõ to the camps. They reported that they have searched the upper marshes as well as can be expected and have found no trace of the she-neph."

"Then let's follow them to the camps. There is nothing here either."

The snitches left and headed to the south, into the lower forest where the gallue camps were set up. For a long time after, Kumél, Ross, and Zoësh remained still and hidden just in case there were others who guarded the perimeter. Once they were sure they were safe, Zoësh and Kumél stood up and walked toward the clearing.

"What's a she-neph? I thought that they were hunting for you?" Ross asked Zoësh.

"I'm a she-neph. A neph is what most call a nephesh. I thought they were looking for me, too."

"I guess I should've figured that out." Ross admitted as he rolled his eyes.

Zoësh smiled at Ross.

"Dar bae anoter neph on da luse, huh?"

"It sounds like it, and they're on the hunt for her."

"Let's get out of here before they come back," Ross urged impatiently.

"They won't be coming back here."

"How do you know that?"

"I just do. They may be sneaky, but they aren't that smart. Besides, you heard them; there's nothing here to find." Zoësh grinned and winked at Ross.

The fatigue from a night of careful trekking and from the tension of near discovery started to take its toll on the three, so they began to hunt for a safe hiding place where they could rest for a while without the worry of being discovered. Zoësh found a large tree with a massive root ball that had several large hollows, like small caves or dens dug out by some animal long ago. The entrances into the hollows were draped over with moss and thin, string-like roots. Inside the hollows, there was enough room for them to lie down and rest without the worry of being seen by unwanted eyes. Kumél did not like being on the ground. He worried that they would be vulnerable and indefensible. Nevertheless, because he could see no better obvious place, he relented.

Meanwhile, sitting around a fire in the belly of the dark Atramentous Forest, Morak, Jekkid and six other gallues waited for the darkness to descend.

"Gubrone demanded thut wae return wit da escaped one."

One of the other gallues spoke up in a malicious, almost quarrelsome manner.

"Jekkid, ha dud da neph slave gut u blade."

"A ha un idea, Morak. Wae shud, jus dis once, lut da mēgs ha deir wae wit er, jus dis once."

Several of the gallues laughed with him in a loud, unruly manner. Another of the gallues quickly chimed in. "Ut cunna bae thut haerd t'capture u lone neph slave."

"A ha sent da snitches out t'search da woods. Da she-neph wae seek ha kulled mur thun twelve mēgs wit one o'our own swords. Ut bae u problum wae need t'fix, once un fur all." Morak's words were sharp and demanding.

"Aye, lut da mēgs ha deir wae wit er."

"Gubrone wull ha ees wae wit us. Thut'd bae worse thun sittin out haer un da dark waitin."

"How cud one lone neph kull twelve mēgs? I ha nae'er saen u neph thut had ony rael fight in thum."

"Dar bae u few, rael rebels."

"Wut d'ye maen? Dae bae no match fur us un da mēgs."

"Dunna bae so sure! Dis one bae quite capable . . . quite capable indeed."

"Ye sound as uf ye ha som respect fur dis one. Bae ye gaein soft, Morak?"

"Nae, ut bae nut softness, uf ye dunna ha u bit o'respect fur yer enemies thun yur bound t'lose yer haed!" Morak's words penetrated the hardened minds of the gallues, making them a little less confident in themselves. "Soon wae'll lut da mēgs out t'hunt."

It was during the dark hours that the gallues sent their mēglydaims to hunt for the nephesh. Specially bred to hunt in the dark, the mēglydaims were shadow-dwelling creatures; their eyesight was specifically suited for the low, dim light of twilight and nighttime. The only time they could hunt during the day was under heavy cloud cover. Even the soft glow of the campfire was often too much for the wretched beasts. Unlike the gallues, the mēglydaims were mortal beasts. Their mortality, however, did not make them vulnerable or weak. Killing a mēglydaim was extremely difficult and dangerous. Rarely had any of the hunted nephesh mounted a defense against the creatures, much less attempted to kill them.

The mēglydaims were a crossbred creature, bred by the arch-gallues for the purpose of hunting and capturing the nephesh. The arch-gallues had witnessed the fearless ferocity of the lion, the pack nature and intelligence of the wolf, and the cunning and size of the saber tooth and had crossbred these predators into a mongrel beast. Then they used their dark magic to breed them with their gallue slaves. Eventually, the first mēglydaim was born. However, the arch- gallues had not been able to find a remedy for their greatest problem. Their specialized creations were born sterile. There were only a few breeding pairs that had been able to bear the hideous creatures, and every mēglydaim born nearly destroyed its host.

The mēglydaims had large heads that were mostly hairless except for a narrow mane that ran from their foreheads, between their ears, down their necks and backs to their long, bald tails. Their tails, about the same length as their bodies, and dragged along the ground as they walked.

At the end of their tails were sharp, boney points, like daggers, that the beasts used with skill to thrash and slice their victims. Their large head, face, and most of their bodies were covered with black scales from the gallues. They had cat-like eyes, large and yellow, with black, slit-like pupils, which gave them excellent vision in the dark. Their snouts were short and broad with large, black, leathery noses that gave them an excellent sense of smell, having been adapted to specifically sniff out the nephesh. From the top of their jaw were two saber-teeth, one on each side of their faces, extending over their lower jaws and below their chins. From the lower jaws, just behind the saber-teeth were black tusks inherited from the gallues, two on each side, which extended up over the upper jaws to the bridges of their noses. Like giant steel traps, the mēglydaims could crush bones in their powerful jaws and, with a single snap, tear off a limb or even kill their opponents. In front of the saber-teeth, on the upper jaw and the lower jaw, were razor-sharp front teeth, like spikes, used for tearing and cutting.

Their necks and bodies were large and muscular with short, powerful hind legs like the wolf and lion. Their mighty front legs were thick yet agile, like the front legs of the saber-tooth. All four of the beasts' paws were large and hand-like, not resembling either cat or dog but almost human with three long, finger-like digits extending forward and one rearward extending digit.

Extending from the ends of each finger were long, black talons, extending a palm's length; as sharp and as hard as iron. While on all fours, at their shoulders, the mēglydaims stood six feet tall. From their noses to the tips of their tails, the frightening beasts were more than twelve feet long.

Hunting the nephesh had become a specialty for a few of the gallues. Like bounty hunters tracking down escaped or wanted criminals, the task of collecting rogue nephesh fell upon two especially talented gallues named Morak and Jekkid. The two hunters possessed a pair of mēglydaims each, which they had trained particularly well. It was important to the arch-gallue, Gubrone that the nephesh be handled without molestation by either the hunters or their vile beasts and that they were brought into the Valley of the Souls unharmed. Few of the hunting gallues shared this concern for the well-being of the nephesh, but only because they were unaware of the consequences if this order were broken. Gubrone, more than any of the twelve arch-gallues who ruled Shuk, well understood that Attar had commanded this careful handling of the nephesh for fear that an indiscretion on this level could attract the undesired attention of Eloh and his kerolus armies.

Since the beginning of the Covenant of Elements, many ages ago, the land of Shuk had been set aside as the domain and safe refuge of the nephesh. Without any suspicion or hint of nefarious activity, the Theoscians had relegated Shuk to the nephesh, not realizing that the nephesh had, in time, become captives there, enslaved by the gallues. However, news of the atrocities against the nephesh and against the land itself had finally reached the realm of Pardis and the Theoscians. The eyes of Eloh had once again fallen upon the realm of Shuk.

Slowly, one at a time, Kumél attempted to open his eyes. One eye struggled to find the will to open, while the other fought a more dogged opponent that had sealed his lids closed. Eventually Kumél reached up and pulled the two lids apart allowing his eye to see what his other eye had already discovered. Darkness had overcome the company. Kumél was surprised by his pitch- black surroundings and immediately sat upright.

Shortly thereafter, Zoësh awoke to the same unexpected revelation. "We overslept!"

"Aye."

"Aye?! That's all you can say. This isn't good. We won't be able to find our way through the thick forest in the dark—and the mēgs—they'll be out hunting before long."

"Aye."

"Is that all you know how to say?"

"Aye, but ye maet wanna kaep yer voice down."

Kumél and Zoësh decided to crawl out of the den and take stock of the situation. Both were beginning to feel claustrophobic in the confined den.

"Wut fur u neph ha u dagger, da dagger o'u gallue?"

Kumél had seen that kind of dagger before, it was much like his own, but he had never seen one in the possession of a nephesh.

"I took it from a gallue, a gallue who is now dead."

"Ye lie. Ye cud nae u kulled u gallue wit thut dagger."

"I never said that I killed it. Gubrone did that for me."

"Wut ye maen? Gubrone kulled ees own gallue fur ye?"

"Not for me, but because I stole the dagger, Gubrone killed him. As you know, there's no forgiveness with Attar or his chiefs."

"So, d'ye know ha t'use ut?"

"I've used it a few times. I can take care of myself. Didn't you hear the snitches earlier? They were talking about me." Zoësh showed a few of her skills as she talked to Kumél.

"Weel, thut wud bae u firs. A nae'er giv much attention t'da snitches or t'wut dae say. Dae bae liars, ye know."

Now Ross lay sleeping deep in the cover of the tree's roots, unaware of the conversation between Kumél and Zoësh.

"How is it that a Carascian walks in the realm of Shuk. I didn't think that there were any left since Amik."

"A dunna know. Ee says ee coms frum da mountun, thut ees baen un da Pit."

"The pit, you mean *The Pit*?"

152

"Aye, tol mae ee saes da Gates o'Abyssus."

"He's seen the iron gates? Hmm . . . How did he find his way out of the pit?"

"Ee says ee waer led frum da pit bae u straem . . . u straem o'light thut flowed frum u pool."

"You don't mean the fire-falls that were falling the other night, do ya?"

"Aye. A saes da straem fallin down da mountun un A dud gae dar t'sae wut ut waer. Thut bae wun A foun eem asleep unner u tree."

"So he came by the Aurora Path. Only the nephesh have ever followed that path from the pit."

"Aye, but tis wut ee says."

Zoësh looked at Kumél with confusion in her eyes. She did not doubt that he was telling her the truth, but she wondered about Ross and how the things that he had told Kumél could be true.

"Do you believe him? I mean, how did he . . . how could he? Umm, how could he come from the mountain, from the pit? It's not—"

Far in the distance a strange, savage call echoed through the valley, breaking the stillness and silence of the darkness. The sound of the mēglydaims' howls was like a roar, a screech, and a scream combined.

Kumél and Zoësh stopped talking immediately. Ross jolted awake as the eerie calls of the mēglydaims ripped through the peaceful blanket of sleep that he had been under. He sat up, wide-eyed and troubled. The three of them sat in tenuous silence, not moving, not breathing and not even blinking. They said not a word to each other. The horrific howls reverberated through the valley unyielding in their terror and intent. The evil mēglydaims were on the prowl, hunting for the unknown nephesh and hunting for Zoësh.

Eventually Zoësh whispered to Kumél, "We should move deeper into the marsh forest."

"Ut bae t'dangerous un da dark! Da blackstalk un xanthic bae t'thick."

"But we'll be safer there because the mēglydaims have no defense against the poison either."

"Aye, but da mēgs ha thuk skin, un ha hunted un da marshes afore. Wae'll wait haer as lung as wae cun."

"They can't hunt in the light. If we can survive until the sun rises, then we can make for the marshes."

Ross sat in the darkness, listening to Kumél and Zoësh strategize. He did not say a word, nor did he want to. Zoësh whispered, "Ross, you awake?"

"Uh-huh. I'm awake."

"We'll be alright."

The howling of the mēglydaims moved farther and farther from them, and for a while, the trio sat feeling confident. Yet, out of the darkness, Kumél heard a cracking sound coming from the woods outside the hollow. Feeling indefensible inside the hollow, Kumél quietly exited the root cave. Carefully he looked around, but because of the darkness was unable to see anything at all. Hoping to hear or see some sign of movement, he knelt down and waited quietly.

The mēglydaims were highly intelligent creatures and had, over time, adapted very clever hunting techniques. Recently they devised a tactic that involved the large pack splitting into smaller packs. They would howl to others to signal their location and if they had found anything. The gallues called these 'the howlers'. The other packs would hunt in silence away from the howling pack. These were called 'the silent stalkers'. This tactic would fool potential prey into assuming that the pack was thrown off their tracks or was a long distance away. Once the hunted began to move away from the howling they would walk into the trap of the silent stalkers.

Kumél listened to the howling but suspected that something was not right. He had had little experience with the mēglydaims, but he was a skillful hunter and not easily fooled. He knew that the mēglydaims had a very good sense of smell and superior eyesight in the dark, so he became concerned that there was a very real chance that they had been scented by the beasts and that one or more of them were lurking very close by even though their howling suggested that they were far off. Not sure whether to stay or make a break for the thicker woods and marsh, Kumél watched for anything that moved.

Zoësh sat on the ground under the cover of the tree roots in a position that blocked Ross's way of escape. The location of their hideout had become a certain liability should the mēglydaims find them, for there was only one way to get out once they were in the hideout.

Zoësh turned to Ross. "Have you a weapon?"

"Me. No! No, I have nothing but, well, I have this ice axe. That's about it."

"You may need to use it." Zoësh pulled her sword from its sheath. "We may not have much time. Get out now, or you might be left with no escape!"

"Can't we take our chances in here? Wait it out?"

"If they come, they will not let you out of this hole. You will become meat for the dogs."

"But I thought that they were after you, not me."

"Doesn't matter! They'll take us all and you may become a treat for the mēgs."

Ross just looked at Zoësh.

Kumél could smell the rank odor of the mēglydaims. He could not be sure if there was one or more, but he had smelled them before and knew that at least one was close. Kumél's vision at night was no better than Ross's, whereas the mēglydaims' night sight was as good as Kumél's day sight. Kumél began to move away from the hideout. Slowly and without making a sound, he crawled on his hands and knees away from the opening. Sniffing the air, Kumél could tell that the mēglydaims were closing in.

Zoësh exited the hideout making sure she was fully covered and disguised with the surroundings. Zoësh could see Kumél who had found a position near a giant tree with a trunk as wide as he was tall. Kumél reached up and took hold of a large branch and pulled his hulking body up into the tree. Zoësh stepped away from the entrance and motioned for Ross to follow. Ross reluctantly crawled out from the back of the hideout clutching his ice axe in his right hand and breathing hard, almost panting. The tension in the air was thick, and the darkness was oppressive, deepening Ross's sense of terror to the point of near panic.

Out of the darkness, just behind Ross, the growl of a mēglydaim pierced the blackness. Ross stopped dead in his tracks. Zoësh turned to see the white saber-tooth fangs of a giant mēglydaim shining through the dark. The night air was cool, and a light snow fell from the sky. A frozen cloud of breath rose from the mēglydaims awful mouth. The dark eyes narrowed as the beast drew back the skin of its lips, exposing a full jaw of sharp, deadly teeth. The creature was crouched and ready to pounce, positioned on top of the roots that had been their hideout. The mēglydaims were trained to not hurt the nephesh, but to any other creature or being, they were unbridled in their violence and ferocity.

Kumél could see the vile beast as it leaned closer to Ross. Kumél listened and sniffed the air to discern if there were other mēglydaims nearby or if there were gallues afoot. A sound was heard to the right of the first mēglydaim. Kumél sniffed the air again and realized that there was now another mēglydaim closing in. Two faint echoes of distant mēglydaims rang through the air. Kumél knew there were more prowling, but he still could not tell just how many were near them. Kumél waited for the other mēglydaim to close in so that he could see it and held his position in the tree, hoping he had not yet been seen.

Zoësh was now fully camouflaged, though the mēglydaims were not often fooled by this defensive act. The sword, however, was not hidden and gave Zoësh's position away. As the second mēglydaim closed in, Zoësh moved toward the first one. Zoësh knew that if the beasts let out their terrible howl, then the others would soon come. The mēglydaims had a different howl for a capture than for a call, and the gallues knew the sound of the capture howl. Zoësh knew that if they were going to act, it would have to be soon, or else they would be in even more trouble against an unknown number of assailants.

For just a moment, Zoësh dropped her camouflage and moved toward the first mēglydaim, hoping that Kumél would see and know to make a move on the second beast. Kumél saw Zoësh step closer to Ross with her sword extended toward the beast and the other hand clutching something that Kumél could not see. Kumél turned his attention to the second mēglydaim who was closing in and whose figure was completely exposed to Kumél and to Ross as well. Ross had not seen the first beast that was behind him and at the moment he saw the second mēglydaim, panic overtook him.

Suddenly, Ross dove back into the hideout, which to the complete surprise of Kumél and Zoësh, distracted the two mēglydaims. Zoësh raised her sword into the air and, at the same time, with her other hand, pulled a long cylindrical object from a fold in the front of her attire. The object suddenly began to glow with a brilliant, clear white light that, to unexpecting eyes, shone as bright as the morning sun. The veil that Zoësh wore protected her against the sudden brightness, but Kumél was less prepared and was temporarily blinded.

The mēglydaims were momentarily paralyzed by the unexpected light. Zoësh, moving swiftly with skill and experience, sprang into the air above the mēglydaim and swung the gallue sword with strength and speed, landing its blade square on the neck of the mēglydaim and lopping its head off. Kumél brandished his broken sword and, with speed unexpected of a creature so large, split the head of the second mēglydaim clean in half from nose to neck.

With a revolting cry, short and quiet, the second mēglydaim fell to the ground in a pool of its own blood. For a moment, its legs flailed and pawed the ground as if trying to get back up and run. Kumél lowered the sword one last time onto the neck of the giant beast and took off its head.

For a moment, the two warriors stood alert with swords ready, but there were no other attacks, no other mēglydaims, no gallues. The fight was over as quickly as it had started.

"We must move fast before the others smell the blood."

Ross crawled back out of the hideout cautiously and looked at the two fallen creatures. He suddenly felt quite ill seeing the severed heads of the mēglydaims and the swords dripping with blood.

"We must move! The others will come to the smell of the blood. Quick! Wipe it off so they won't follow us, at least for a while."

"Wae wull gae t'da norõ. Stay out o'da marsh 'til firs light."

"Get your belongings. Leave nothing behind." Kumél knew that the gallues would find the dead mēglydaims eventually and that they would also find their scent and track them down. It was fortuitous that sunlight was so close, for this would give the trio at least an extra day's head start.

"Do you think that they will follow us?" Ross hoped that they might be free of the creatures and their keepers.

"They will if we don't get far from here. The gallues have very good noses. Ask your friend there." Zoësh pointed to Kumél.

"Aye, dae cun smaell ye u lung wae off. Luts gae!" Kumél led Ross and Zoësh through the dark woods, skirting the marshes and distancing themselves from the two dead mēglydaims. In the distance, they could still hear the chilling cries of the other mēglydaims echoing through the valley.

Mēglydaim

Chapter VI

The Foreigner's Weapon

As the sun's first rays began to spread over the dark valley, and fog and mist filled the gray sky above, suspicion began to arise concerning the whereabouts of the other two mēgs. Morak and Jekkid soon realized that there was something wrong, that trouble was afoot.

The gallues began to fight about the missing mēglydaims, inciting a brawl between Morak and Jekkid. As they fought, the other gallues, brawlers by nature, watched and goaded them on. They craved a good fight and often engaged in riotous skirmishes amongst themselves for no obvious reasons.

They rolled around on the ground, violently throwing and pushing each other until finally, Morak was over the top of Jekkid with his sword drawn and its point pushed into his throat. It would not have been unheard of for Morak to run his blade through Jekkid's neck, but this time he paused, distracted by a sudden scent carried on the breeze from the north, filling his nostrils. Morak released his grip and pulled his blade away. "Hmm, somting bae foul. Dar bae death un da air. Blood ha bun spilt."

"Aye. Tis da blood o'u mēg," Jekkid announced.

"Com on!" Morak barked the order to the others, and they all began following the scent. The gallues sprinted through the forest like animals chasing prey, stopping only long enough to sniff the air for the scent. Eventually, their noses led them to the carcasses of the two dead mēglydaims.

Jekkid became enraged. "Who dare raise u hun agan mu mēgs?"

"Ut mus bae da she-neph, da one who kulled mēgs afore," Morak quickly accused.

Sniffing the ground and the air, the gallues tried to find any significant scent of the killer or killers, but the blood of the Mēgs was so rank they were unable to smell anything else but it.

Morak knew they needed the other mēgs to track the killer. They had a better sense of smell than the gallues and could find any scent left behind. Morak turned to the others. "Wae naed da other mēgs. A wull return un fetch thum."

"Gubrone wull kull us fur dis," worried Jekkid. "Nut uf wae fin um firs."

"Wae cunna gae buk less wae do!"

"Aye, A know. Wae wull fin um," Morak assured him.

Kumél, Ross, and Zoësh reached a stream that divided the upper woods of Atramentous and the marshes of the valley. They entered the stream and waded through the cold waters for half the day hoping to leave no trace of their scent. At points along the way, Zoësh and Ross had to let Kumél carry them on his back because the stream was either too deep or running too fast for them to continue. Eventually, feeling certain the mēglydaims could not follow their scent, they found a rocky bank where they could exit the water and continue into the dark marshes.

They had not said a word to each other since escaping the mēglydaims. Silently clinging to Kumél's back, Ross had been thinking about the encounter with them and how close he had come to death. As Ross and Zoësh climbed down from Kumél's back, Ross looked at Zoësh. "Thank you."

"For what?"

"For saving my life back there."

"I didn't save your life, I saved mine."

"Maybe, but you saved mine as well," Ross contested.

Zoësh smiled at Ross, then without saying a word, turned and followed Kumél who was almost out of sight. Not wanting to be left behind, Ross ran after them.

After a long, rigorous push through thickets of spiny bushes, Kumél reached a clearing on the edge of the marsh. Hoping they were beyond the detection of the gallues and the mēglydaims, Kumél stopped. Ross and Zoësh were close behind, and when they stepped out of the bushes into the small clearing, the sight of the marsh arrested them. Ross looked up at Kumél and then at the foreboding landscape that stretched out before them. He wanted to say something, yet words would not come to him, only the silence of disbelief. Kumél looked at Zoësh, then at Ross, and then began the long journey through the marsh of Atramentous. There would be no passage in the darkness, so they knew that they had to make it across the marsh before the sun set. The only positive was that the marsh treated everyone with the same inhospitable rancor whether gallue, nephesh, or mēglydaim; the marsh was indiscriminately malevolent.

Over the years of his adventures in climbing, Ross had explored many high mountain meadows. Most were a maze of oak brush and willow, growing in tangles along the banks of small streams and beaver ponds. Underfoot, there had been little solid ground, and there never had been a clear or easy path through. Ross had found these to be somewhat friendlier to him than to the others. He had always had a knack at finding ways through the dense brush and seemingly impassable bogs. Looking at the marsh before them, Ross began to see a route where the others could not; however, he said nothing and kept following Kumél and Zoësh. As they struggled through the brush, Zoësh began talking to Ross. "You know, you're stronger than you think. Why do you doubt yourself?" She could sense he had a fear that was buried deep in his soul, fear that had been a part of his life for longer than he could remember.

Ross thought it an odd thing to say. How could she presume to know that about him? He resisted commenting for a moment, as if not intending to reply, but her words continued to echo in his thoughts and reminded him of something he had heard before.

"Why would you say that?" His delayed response was less about what she had said and more about who he had remembered saying it. He recalled sitting on the old wooden steps of his apartment with Eve, after Daniel's death. He had intimated to her that he did not know if he could keep going—he didn't think he had the strength. Eve had put her arm around him and had told him that he was stronger than he thought. She had said it many times. The words themselves had landed on his heart like a feckless platitude and would have made him angry, except that it had been Eve who had said them. Coming from her, he knew they had been honest and deeply sincere. He sensed the same sincerity from Zoësh. Without intending to, she had touched an open wound. Thoughts of Eve flooded into his mind and with them, the weight of guilt and loss.

Zoësh could see the pain and sorrow in his eyes. "I don't know what you've been through, and I'm sorry for the pain you're feeling," she consoled sympathetically.

Ross closed his eyes and waited for his emotions to subside. He did not want to let them out, to expose them to her. After a few moments, he lifted his head. He looked at Zoësh and tried to smile. "It's OK . . . sometimes . . . I don't know . . . I think, why did I take her? Why didn't I make sure she was safe? Why didn't I do what I promised? I failed."

Zoësh looked at Ross. He could see compassion and kindness in her eyes. "You worry too much about things you cannot change."

In a strange, unpredictable twist, Ross felt, for that moment, released from the guilt. It was something she had said. He smiled as he remembered the day they had been on the face of Ama Dablam and Daniel had said with a grin, "You worry too much man." Ross laughed aloud. It was the first time he had been able to think about Daniel without tears.

"What is it? Why do you laugh?" Zoësh asked.

"Just remembering something a friend told me once. Kinda funny now, in a strange way."

Ross grabbed the shoulder strap of his backpack to make sure it was still with him. He remembered the camera. He wanted to get it out, to see Eve again. He could not put everything together, but there was something in the things Zoësh had said, something he had heard before from good friends, that had helped him.

Their short conversations inspired him and made him wonder about those strange, spiritual things that he refused to believe. He felt a sudden urgency to do something, to be more than the weakest link. "Hey! Kumél, I think I can find the way through this mess. Let me take the lead for a bit."

"Ye bae sure?"

"Yeah, let me do something to help." Ross rushed around Kumél. He had a new vigor in his step, and as he guided Kumél and Zoësh, for the first time in too long, he felt capable. When he kept his eyes on the environment, on the mountains and meadows and streams, Ross became confident. These were the places he always felt at home, where he felt safe, even though they were inherently dangerous. Shuk may have been another world, but it was a world of trees, mountains, streams, and lakes, all of which Ross knew well, all of which, with sweet memories, brought him peace.

They weaved through the marsh, avoiding dangerous tangles of blackstalk and xanthic; however, the night was quickly closing in and concern began to increase. Ross stopped and turned to Kumél and Zoësh. "We may have to find a place to spend the night. It won't be long before we won't have enough light to set up a camp. I'm sorry. I really thought I could get us out."

"How much farther do you think we have to go?" Zoësh inquired.

"I can't tell. The brush is too thick and dark, but if we don't find a safe place to spend the night, we'll be in a very dangerous situation very soon." Zoësh and Kumél could tell that Ross knew what he was talking about.

Kumél could see just a little farther than the other two and saw a place that could work for them. He pointed to it. "Dar bae u wee opening unner thut ol' tree. Mubae wae cun fin u place t'hide fur da night." Kumél pointed to a massive, old tree that reminded Ross of the giant cypress trees he had seen in the swamps and marshes in South America. At the base of the tree was a small plot of grass-covered ground, high enough out of the marsh that it was dry. The trio moved carefully toward the cover of the tree; it branches hung low with mossy vines draping to the ground.

Darkness fell heavily on the marsh as they readied for a long and uncomfortable night. While getting settled, each of them had only one thought on their minds: they hoped that the gallues had not yet discovered the dead mēglydaims.

Kumél noticed that there were stars shining in the sky. He could see the clouds rolling in and out like the tide of an ocean, and he could see that they were getting thinner at each break. From the east came a soft, white glow over the ridges of the mountains. As the clouds renounced their reign over the sky, another soft white glow began to appear to the north.

It would have seemed that Kumél, Ross, and Zoësh had favor, for the night sky opened wide and clear of its usual overcast, and there, hanging in the starry sky, were two full, glowing moons lighting the whole realm of Shuk, like twin morning stars. The bright moons not only lit the way through the menacing marsh, they also, more importantly, acted as a shield against the mēglydaims, who would not be able to hunt on that night. This gave the trio even more advantage over their pursuers.

Once the light fell through the canopy of trees and upon his camp, Morak cursed the moons as he sat in the glow of their twin lights. The mēglydaims erupted with loud howls from their dens of darkness. Back with the dead mēgs, Jekkid and the other gallues realized that Morak would be unable to bring the mēglydaims from their dens and, as such, were resigned to wait out the night until they could hunt again.

"With the light of the twin moons shining so bright, we can keep moving and get out of the marsh before morning light. The mēgs won't be able to hunt tonight so we must leave now!" Ross declared to Kumél and Zoësh.

"Aye, luts bae quik bout ut," Kumél agreed.

"I can get us out of here tonight. And I hope what is to come is better than what is behind us." Ross's voice had a ring of optimism in it.

The thought of creating more distance between themselves and the mēglydaims motivated the company to move fast, without rest. Through the night, they wove their way through the maze of the marsh and, at the break of day, as the sun's morning rays rose bright and unencumbered upon the landscape, Ross, Kumél, and Zoësh reached the slopes leading out of the Atramentous marsh and up to the Pass of Borak.

The Pass of Borak, a rugged, difficult passage, was the only way into Gershom Forest from the west. The slope leading up to the pass was a steep, narrow, rocky couloir with long fields of falling boulders and broken stone. At points along the way, the slope was so steep that the giant boulders littering the route seemed to be hanging by invisible wires. At the top stood an imposing wall of ice that was pressed between two solid walls of black stone, as if it was attempting to push itself free. Beyond the wall of ice, there was the long, monolithic body of a glacier, which spread out wide and far, covering the saddle between the black ridges of the mountains like a petrified sea of white clouds. From one end it was impossible to see the other, and the way through was strewn with treacherous fields of rock and ice that had fallen from the surrounding peaks. There were also innumerable crevasses that scarred the glacier across its entire range.

For ages, the glacier had been alive and active, flowing from the high parts of the surrounding mountains through the narrow walls framing the couloir and then down toward the dark valley. Now it was dying, having receded out of the lower valleys. It laid over the pass, mostly asleep, like an old man napping, on occasion waking to shake off some of its frozen self, calving blocks of ice down the mountain.

This unpredictable element made the already challenging way to the pass even more daunting. From a long distance below, the glacier's wall of ice was visibly imposing. In addition to its physical enormity, there were the loud groaning protestations and thunderous cracking noises uttered by the gigantic ice field, which haphazardly roared down through the couloir, threatening the way below.

Ross's stamina surprised Kumél and Zoësh. He had moved through the dark marsh like a machine, pushing his body to its maximum, trying to escape the complex and dangerous mire.

Arriving at a high mountain lake just above the marshlands, Ross finally stopped to rest. His body was becoming weak, and the increasing altitude was having its effect on him. Breathing hard, Ross sat on a large boulder with his head between his legs.

"Ross, you must rest. You can't go on like this much longer," Zoësh warned him.

"I know, I know. I just wanted to be out of that awful place and as far away from those monsters as possible."

"But you must rest or you won't survive it. We should have a good day's advantage by now."

"Dunna lut yer guard down. Snitches bae sure t'bae bout. Dae lik des woods."

"Yes, but we should rest a while," Zoësh advised.

"Aye. Kaep yer eyes open. Ye nae'er cun bae sure."

Once they left the upper forest of twistbranch trees, the hike to the pass would take the trio another two days and would be over mostly open steep terrain, laden with boulder fields. The twistbranch trees were the oldest trees in Shuk, growing only at the highest elevation a tree could grow. The behemoth evergreen topiaries were shaped and sculpted by the relentless winds that blew across the upper mountain regions. Like stalwart sentinels standing watch over the kingdom, the antediluvian woods stood undaunted at their high mountain posts.

As they walked among the trees, they could see the faint glow of morning sun rising over the mountaintops. The greens and browns of the trees, along with colors of all kinds from countless plants and flowers began to appear in the soft light.

"I've always loved the shape of these trees. Like a flag blowing in the wind, the branches reach out over the land. It's an amazing feat that they grow at all, way up here," Ross said, admiringly.

"I didn't know that you had seen the twistbranch before," Zoësh told him.

"We don't call them that back home. We call them flag trees. It's said that they are the oldest living thing. They grow in every part of the world—all from a small seed—living more lifetimes than one can remember or count. Like a father, they're in every part of our lives, growing and changing, living and dying. They offer their shade freely, their fruit, and their stalk. There's no part of our lives where trees are not there, and yet, so often we never notice them. If they could talk, I wonder what stories they could tell."

Ross rose to his feet and walked over to an enormous old twistbranch tree whose bark was smooth and hard. On one side of the trunk, the bark had been peeled away by the wind exposing the hard, wooden core. Ross reached his hand out and touched the tree's trunk, then took hold of its short green needles and gently pulled his hand over them as if petting an animal. He stood looking up into the twisted branches contemplating deep thoughts.

"Ut tis jus u tree," intruded Kumél.

"No, it's not just a tree. It's a living being, a beautiful living creature in its own right," argued Ross.

"Sounds lik Amik. Sur' yur nut eem?"

"I'm sure, Kumél. I'm not Amik. Eve taught me to appreciate the wonder of life that exists in nature."

"Eve? Who is Eve?" Zoësh asked Ross.

"Someone . . . someone very special."

"Where is she now?"

Ross looked down to the ground but said nothing.

The moment was sober, tender, palpable. Even the wind stopped blowing. The air became calm and the mood reverent. Without having to explain what he was feeling or what he was remembering to Kumél and Zoësh, they understood the unedited emotions that were erupting from his heart. It may have been the exhaustion or danger or the stress that had unlocked the deeply confined memories from his soul. Or it had been the crispness of the air or touching of the bark of the twistbranch trees that aroused his heart's tenderness. Whatever it was, a tide of tears erupted from his eyes and poured down over his soiled, weathered face. Convulsing in sorrowful wails and irrepressible bawling, Ross crumbled to the ground beneath the boughs of the twistbranch tree.

"I'm sorry. I'm sorry." Over and over Ross murmured the same agonizing lament.

The hulking frame of Kumél melted. The normally strong, unaffected warrior felt a pain unlike any other he had known. As if slain by some invisible sword, Kumél slowly knelt to the forest floor. His eyes focused on Ross, and for a moment, he wanted to reach out to him and console him, but something in his own heart stopped him. A single, bold tear sprung from Kumél's left eye and trailed down his scaled cheek. He reached up and caught the tear in the palm of his hand before it had a chance to fall to the ground. He had not shed a tear since before his hideous transformation. Some part of the giant creature's past began to come to life again as he felt the crushing pain of a mortal man who had become his friend.

In his giant hand, the solitary tear lay, clear and warm. Through the tough scaled palm, the sensation of its warmth and moisture penetrated Kumél's otherwise hardened shell. Memories of Pardis came rushing back as he stared at the anomaly. He remembered Eloh, who had always been a good friend, Sargel, who was his closest friend, and then Amik, who had chosen him to share in the forestry and husbandry of Pardis. The memories flooded in, and then, as if he was dreaming, Kumél began to see the life he had once known, long ago, before the war, before Attar's curse.

Suddenly and unexpectedly, the voice of Eloh spoke into his heart. It was not just a memory, though, not just a daydream; it was a whisper that penetrated his thoughts and his subconscious. "Kumél, hear my words and know that it is I, Eloh, who speaks to you this day. It has been a long time since you last heard my words, and so you may be unsure, but know, know in your heart that I am with you. I have sent Ross to you and you are to bring him to the Well of Veritus in Gershom Forest. Do not hesitate or linger too long here, for danger seeks you out."

The message of Eloh caused Kumél to tremble. Opening his eyes, unsure how much time had passed, Kumél looked to see Ross still kneeling under the twistbranch tree and Zoësh standing near him.

"Ross." Kumél began to speak softly to the broken man hunched over on the ground.

Zoësh reached out and touched Kumél on the shoulder stopping him. "No. Let him be; he has needed to do this."

Zoësh, too, felt deeply moved by the moment. Removing the cloak that covered her radiant hair, she stood as if in respect, not only for Ross but for those whom Ross mourned and wept. Zoësh knew that the tears Ross cried were not only tears of sorrow but also tears of memories, tears that were born out of the deepest of places, tears that cleanse the soul of the guilt that has stained the conscience. From sorrow to pain to grace to emancipation, the tears finally began to flow from a new place in his soul, a place of life. Bringing to his heart a new, untarnished vision, the cleansing flow washed over, not only his memory but also the moments that exist between the past and the future.

The pain of his loss would never be forgotten, nor should it be. The tears could not wash away what was meant to be felt, but they could wash away what could never be understood. Life stalls at moments when things stop making sense. Understanding is often a wall too high to climb. The river of his tears carried Ross away from the dark ruins of sorrow out into an infinite sea where memory floats unmoored to affliction.

In silence, the three of them sat for a long time. Not one of them seemed anxious to move on from that place or that moment. There was something precious about what had happened, and it had happened, not just to Ross, but to all of them.

Kumél looked at Ross. He stared at him for a long time until Ross was composed. Then, hesitantly, respectfully, he put his hand on Ross's shoulder and spoke softly. "Wae better bae off or wae wull lose our advantage."

"Yep." Ross rose quickly to his feet, grabbed his backpack, and stood ready to move on. He gazed up at the sun for a moment, which appeared as if it was cradled between two black peaks. "I'm so glad to see the sun. Can we get to the pass today?"

"Nae. Tis mur thun u sun t'da pass. Wae cun try, douh."

They began the climb out of the forest, up toward the pass. At the tree line, they entered a long, winding glacial valley that led to the base of Borak Pass. For Ross, the climbing was easy. Though sections of the route were steep, they were manageable without ropes or technical gear.

The valley was a wasteland of rocks and boulders lying in heaps everywhere, which they had to negotiate at each step of the way. By nightfall, they reached the point of total exhaustion.

As the last rays of light peeked through a narrow slot in the high mountains above them, they stumbled upon a place to rest for the night. It was not long before the twin moons began to rise above the enormous shoulders of the mountains and the sky was crystal clear and filled with stars. The mēglydaims would not be hunting. Ross, Kumél, and Zoësh fell asleep.

Morak had spent the day impatiently waiting for the night and then the night came and so too did the twin moons. Casting their bright glow over the land, the two moons sat proudly in the night sky. Realizing that the Mēgs could not hunt again and that the killers were getting even farther away, Morak decided to leave the pair of Mēgs in the den and head back to where the other gallues were waiting. They would have to come up with another plan or else abandon the pursuit altogether. However, Morak was not willing to abandon anything. He knew that Gubrone would surely crush them if they did not find the renegades.

Jekkid and the other gallues had become impatient. Waiting was something they never did very successfully and here, the stench of the two rotting mēgs had become rank even to ones such as they, who, themselves, stank. "Hae lung d'wae ha t'wait haer wit des stinkun mēgs?"

"Shut up!" Jekkid was becoming agitated with the other gallues who had spent the day ceaselessly fighting and arguing amongst themselves. "Uf wae dunna capture da one who kulled da mēgs, thun wae wull b'com fodder fur da mēgs o'Gubrone."

"Wud ye shut thut gapin hole un yer face? A says wae forgut Morak un des stinkun corpses un gae afore dae gut t'da Plain o'Haemus."

"Wut muks ye tink dae bae headin t'Haemus?" Jekkid asked the impudent gallue.

"Whaer else? O'er da pass o'Borak?" The gallues laughed loudly with contempt. They knew that crossing the pass was plagued with hazards. The notion seemed absurd.

At that moment, the sound of breaking twigs interrupted their conversation. They immediately reached for their swords and stood to their feet. They had been so engrossed in their conversation that they had not noticed how dark it had become. The twin moons had disappeared behind heavy, dark clouds, and their fire was not enough to illuminate the shadows. They all peered into the forest to locate and identify the intruder. Jekkid hollered, "Who goes dar?"

A familiar voice called back to them, "Put yer weapons down, ye fools. Ut bae mae, Morak."

"Wut ye doin? Snaekin up on us lik thut?" the impertinent gallue protested.

"A highly doubt thut. Yur so noisy thut earyone knows ye bae haer."

"Whaer bae da mēgs?" demanded Jekkid.

"A luft thum un deir dens."

Kumél observed the valley below. He could feel the imminent storm and hoped the rain would wash away any trace of their scent. Kumél was confident that the mēgs could not have been on the prowl through the night but, now that the clouds had moved back in, he knew it was imperative for them to get over the pass and down into the safety of Gershom forest before nightfall.

Zoësh felt the gentle touch of the falling snow landing softly upon her face. Joining Kumél on a large boulder, the two sat in the snow staring at the path they had journeyed on the day before.

"What are you looking at?" Ross's voice pierced the still silence of the moment.

"Shh!" Zoësh put her finger to her mouth and looked at Ross with an intense glare. Ross felt his heart begin to race as he moved quietly toward her while, at the same time, looking around to see what they were so focused on.

"What? What is it? What do you see?"

"Dar bae somting comin."

"What the hell? How? How could they have found us up here?"

"I don't think it's them. I think it's a nephesh." Zoësh quietly answered. "Or a snitch. You can't tell, you never can, especially not from this distance."

"Where is it now? I can't see anything? Are you sure?"

"Aye."

Ross paced anxiously behind the stone where Kumél and Zoësh sat. The thought of the mēgs coming made him truly afraid. Nevertheless, Ross was not as afraid as he had been. "Maybe we should set up a trap for it."

"A trap? I thought that you might rather make a run for it." Zoësh offered. "I'm tired of running, of feeling afraid."

"Faer bae how wae all survive."

"So, what's your plan? Sit and wait for it to say hello?" Ross wanted to know. "Hellooo? Wut bae thut?"

"Oh, never mind. Wut ar we gonna do?"

"If it's a snitch, then it hasn't seen us yet, or it wouldn't be coming toward us. But, if it does see us and it is a snitch, then it will find the gallues and tell them where we are." Zoësh explained to Ross.

"But if it's just another nephesh, like you, then maybe it could help us."

"Maybe, but we have to know fur sure before it sees us and is able to escape."

"So, I was right then. We need to set a trap and catch it. One problem, though . . . actually two problems . . . actually maybe there are more problems than two, but . . . anyway . . . "

"What's the problem?"

"Well, how do you catch a nephesh? And if you catch it, how do you know if it's a snitch or not?" Ross questioned.

"Wae ha t'hurry or else ut'll fin us afore wae ha u chance t'set u trap."

"I have some rope. Can we catch it with rope?"

"Nae. We cun trap ut un da rocks. Wae wull ha t'hide an' wait fur ut t'com."

The trap was a long, narrow space in the rocks that was surrounded by towering granite walls and had only one way in or out. Like a dead end in a maze, it was a perfect place to trap the nephesh. The approach to the trap was a thin ravine that wound through the boulders as if it were the remains of an old streambed that led down the valley for some way until it suddenly disappeared under a massive pile of glacial boulders.

"How will we lure it?"

"Ye, ye'll bae our bait."

"Me? Why me?"

"Ut dunna know wut ye bae. Ut wull bae curious, lik A was."

"Well, I'm certainly glad that I was a curiosity for you to amuse yourself with."

"It's a good plan, Ross. You're the one who said we need to catch it. What were you thinking would happen?"

"I don't know. But I wasn't planning on being bait for the trap."

The unknown nephesh moved cautiously up the valley toward the trio and their trap. Kumél watched it carefully as it closed in on their location. It appeared to him that the nephesh was alone. It was not following them at all. It followed something else. Maybe it had heard the howling of the mēgs and was trying to get as far away from them as possible. Maybe it had its own hiding place up in the glacial valley amid the rocks.

The plan was to wait until the nephesh was close to the trap and Kumél was in a position behind it. Once the nephesh was close enough, Ross would show himself and run into the rocky ravine. When the nephesh followed, Kumél and Zoësh would block off the escape route and box it in.

Zoësh hid behind a pile of large stones near the trap's entrance above the ravine. Kumél circled back behind the approaching stranger and Ross watched as it approached within eyeshot. Ross quickly climbed to the top of a stone plateau that was in clear sight of the nephesh and made sure that it could see him. Moving into the ravine, Ross made his way through the twisted route toward the trap as if having no idea that the nephesh could see him. Ross tried to resist the urge to move too quickly though everything in him wanted to run for his life.

The nephesh stopped suddenly when it saw Ross on the rock plateau as if it were afraid. It quickly squatted down trying to hide from him. Kumél watched and became worried that it would not take the bait. Zoësh had assured Kumél that the nephesh would follow after Ross to better see what he was. Kumél readied to overtake the nephesh if it did not follow Ross.

Slowly, the nephesh rose and carefully looked toward the place where Ross had been standing. The curious nature of the nephesh compelled it to follow as if it could not help itself. By now, Ross had been out of sight for several moments; nevertheless, the nephesh slowly moved deeper and deeper into the stone trap until, finally, it came upon Ross standing in a shadowed corner.

The nephesh was in full camouflage and entered into the space where Ross stood. At first, Ross could not see it approaching him. "Who are you?" A soft, gentle voice, barely audible, spoke to Ross.

Ross jumped, then froze, looking in the direction of the voice.

"Where are you? Who are you?" Ross's voice quivered at first, then he regained his courage and spoke firmly.

The nephesh stepped closer to Ross and, at the same moment, changed its appearance, allowing Ross to see it. Kumél and Zoësh had already closed the way of escape and stood watching Ross and the nephesh, who were both spellbound for the moment.

"Where have you come from?" The suspicious tone of Zoësh's voice carried through the enclosed space with the faintest echo. The nephesh jolted out of the suspense of the moment and spun around to face Zoësh. Zoësh stood calmly and tried to speak reassuringly. "I am Zoësh. Where have you come from? Why are you here?"

"Please, please don't hurt me."

"Where have you come from? Who are you? Why are you here?" Zoësh spoke kindly but insistently to the stranger.

"I ... I am lost ... trying to find my way home."

"Me, too," said Ross, still frozen in place. "What's your name?"

"Seerae. I am called Seerae."

"What are you doing here?" Ross asked her.

"I am looking for you," Seerae answered.

"For me? What do you mean, you're looking for me?"

"I saw you come out of the mountain. I was there with you on the ledge."

"Wait a minute. I don't remember seeing you. What were you doing there?"

"I came out of the mountain just before you did. I was in the pit where you were."

"But . . . but why didn't I see you? Why didn't I know you were there?"

"We hid from you."

"You hid from me?"

"We? What do you mean, we? Were there others like you there?" interrogated Zoësh, as she moved nearer to Ross and Seerae.

"Yes. There were many there."

"But where are the others? Where have they gone?"

Seerae's glance fell to the ground. "They were captured by the gallues."

"What gallues?"

"The ones who are looking for you. The ones who owned the mēgs that you killed in the marsh."

"Ye saen us un da marsh?"

"No. I was trying to find you when I came upon the dead creatures."

"How'd you know we killed the mēgs?" Ross was seriously perplexed.

"Your trail. I was following your trail, and it led me to that place. Bloody mess."

"Nae! Ye cud nut ha bun followin our trail. Wae luft none!"

"Oh, but there is. I have been following it right up to this very place."

"But we have left no trail," insisted Zoësh.

"Aye. You and the large one haven't. But him—he has—and I have been trying to catch up with him for many suns now."

Kumél began looking for any sign of their movements, like a trail. "A cun sae no trace o'tracks, no trace ut all!"

"Show me what you mean." Zoësh was looking everywhere for tracks as well.

"The snowpetal—can you not see it? It grows everywhere he goes."

As their eyes searched in all directions, they saw rocks piled upon rocks. In the cracks of the rocks and on the sandy floor of the valley between the rocks, grew small clusters of tiny, white flowers known by some as snowpetal. They grew on slender, green stalks with thumb- sized leaves. The flowers themselves had five tiny, white petals with lavender centers. From a distance, a field of them could appear as snow covering the ground, and they grew when the snowflakes fell from the sky and landed on the soil.

"Snowpetal, but it's said to grow in the high mountains when the snow falls?"

"Aye, but come with me. I will show you what I mean."

"Come with you where?" asked Ross, warily.

"Not you, you must wait here for just a moment. You, the large one, come with me. I will show you what I mean."

Kumél followed Seerae away from the entrapment and over a small ridge.

"Look. Do you see any snowpetal?"

"Nae."

"Call your friend over to join us; keep your eye on the land as he comes."

"Ross, cum haer."

Ross and Zoësh walked up toward the ridge to meet Kumél and Seerae. Kumél watched as Ross came closer and closer but nothing happened.

"Wait, it takes a bit. Just wait here and watch."

When Ross and Zoësh reached Kumél and Seerae, they turned back to see what they were looking at. Almost imperceptibly, a couple of moments after Ross passed a barren area, frail green stems began to grow out of the cracks and the soil, wherever he stepped. The stalks rose gently, then leaves began to unfurl from the tender stems, like tiny sails spreading out to catch the wind. Small, white bundles of flowers spread their petals, reaching wide like little hands to catch the falling snow. In no time, the rocks and the valley floor that had been barren were alive with snowpetal.

"Do you see what I mean?"

"Aye."

"Yes."

"What does this mean?" Ross questioned, uncertain that there was an answer, or that it even mattered if there was one. "If you could find me, then they can find us, too!"

"Not quite; the snowpetal only stays in bloom for a day or two after you've left the area. That is why it took me so long to find you. I lost track of you when the others were captured. I just happened to see the snowpetal from quite a distance a few suns ago, and I've been trying to catch up to you since then. I knew I was close when I reached fresh blooms. As long as you remain in a place, the snowpetal will grow."

"So, da gallues mus nut know. Thut maens da mur distance wae put between us, da better. Wae naed t'kaep movin."

"I don't understand. Why would the snowpetal grow around me? I don't even belong here. How did you know about the snowpetal?" Ross begged Seerae to make sense of all this.

"I had a dream, and in my dream, I saw the snowpetal growing from a pile of rocks, then a voice spoke in my heart and said, 'The way is blooming and life is growing. Let the little snowpetal lead you.' So, I began to follow them."

"What did you hope to find?"

"I didn't know. I suppose I hoped to find whatever they led me to."

"But why me? Why would they lead you to me?"

"I don't know. Really, I don't know. I just know I was supposed to follow them."

"Zoësh, how could you have not known. I mean Seerae is the same as you, a neph. Did you know about the snowpetal?"

"Maybe I should have, but no, no I didn't."

The new development troubled Ross. It worried him that the gallues and, especially the mēgs, could be tracking them, just as Seerae had. He looked at Zoësh. "It's more important than ever that we keep moving. As amazing as this is, it's not good news right now."

"Dis cud lead da snitches t'us, uf dae fin out."

"Maybe they won't," Ross said with more confidence than he felt. "Let's get our stuff and get over the pass."

"May I come with you, please?" Seerae pleaded.

"Aye. Wae cunna leave ye haer. Uf dae fin ye, dae wull muk ye talk." Kumél was untrusting of Seerae, but he mistrusted everyone, of course.

Making sure not to leave any trace, they began moving quickly over the rocky terrain toward the pass. In the valley below, the rain fell, and the rain clouds moved upward toward them. There were advantages and disadvantages when it came to the rain. It was an advantage because it would wash away their scent and slow their enemy's pursuit of them. It was a disadvantage because in the higher altitudes the rain would be turning to snow and, at the rate it was falling in the valley, the snowfall on the pass would be heavy and deep, so it could also slow their escape. Kumél considered the snow their friend. He believed that although it could hinder their progress, it would also cover up any trace of them ever passing that way. He also reckoned that the gallues and mēgs would not be able to find any scent or sign of their tracks in the blowing icy powder. Kumél hiked toward the pass with confidence.

Three days had passed since the mēgs had been killed and because of the unusual events of the twin full moons, the gallues had been unable to track Ross and his small band. On the fourth day, as the sun had risen over the valley, the storm clouds that had delivered the rain during the night rested over the valley below but were migrating toward the pass. Morak, Jekkid, and the other gallues had sat in the downpour of the rain throughout the night waiting for their chance to hunt again. They were soaking wet and frustrated that any sign or scent they could have tracked was already washed away. They were further dismayed by the arrival of the freezing freezing wind and snow mixed with rain that had started falling just as the morning sun had risen to illuminate the landscape.

Morak remained silent as the other gallues discussed what might have transpired with the killer (or killers) and what would ensue when Gubrone found out about the mēgs.

"Hae wull wae er fin who kulled da mēgs now?"

"Ut bae as uf dae ha somon on deir side haelpin thum."

"Dunna bae u fool, ut's jus da storm. B'sides, who wud haelp da enemies o'Attar?"

"How wull wae know whaer t'search? A say wae gae t'da suõ, t'da Plain o'Haemus. Dae wud nut gae t'da ushus, o'er da pass. Dar bae notin fur thum dar."

One of the gallues, Lyzop, tired of the wet snow falling, crawled into the den where Ross and the others had hidden. As he tried to find a comfortable place to lie, he discovered something sticking up out of the moss. At first, Lyzop gave it no thought, but curiosity overcame him; he reached out his sharp black talons and pulled the object from its cover. In his hand, the gallue held something he had never seen before. It was not from Shuk. Lyzop looked curiously at the object. "A foun somting." Lyzop crawled out from the den and handed the object to Jekkid. They studied it with puzzled expressions.

Morak grabbed the unknown object from Jekkid. "Ut bae u weapon. A weapon o'da one who kulled da mēgs."

"Nut u vary big weapon. Nut vary sharp."

"Thut ting cud nut o'kulled da mēgs."

"Ut tis nut u vary gud weapon."

"Wut er ut bae, ut bae nut frum Shuk. Somon ha com t'Shuk thut dunna b'lung haer," Morak grimly stated.

The discovery changed everything for the gallues. Now, instead of searching for a nephesh or an aposta, they were on the hunt for a foreigner. The gallues believed that this was meaningful and that once Gubrone was told, he would no longer be interested in the dead Mēgs. After some quarreling and a few blows from Morak, it was decided that he, himself would take the object to Gubrone. The other gallues were to split up. Jekkid, Ourdïs and Slŷteeg, went to the Valley of Borak to search for any signs of the foreigner. The others, including Lyzop, went south to the Plain of Haemus to wait until Morak contacted them.

Lyzop, however, disagreed with the plan and issued a resounding protest. He objected to Morak giving them orders and demanded to be the one to take the object to Gubrone since he was the one who found it. Morak took a measured, deliberate stride toward Lyzop and at the same time tightened his fist. With all his might, Morak struck Lyzop square in the face, knocking him backward to the ground. Lyzop did not have time to react; Morak leapt upon him while he was down and held him there with his foot pressed against his throat. "Ye wull do wut er A says, or ye wull bae luft haer wit da mēgs, dead lik um."

Lyzop just nodded his head. Morak stared at him with fierceness in his eyes. "Uf ye er defy mae agan, A wull rip yer throat out!"

Kumél could see that the steep approach to the pass was only half a day away. However, before they could reach the slopes, they would have to negotiate the ice fields of the dying Borak Glacier. The valley of rocks and glacial debris they were negotiating was opening into a wide amphitheater or cirque with a network of small glacial streams meandering around giant shards of ice and rock that had calved from the face of the glacier. The towering ice fragments stood like sculptures carved into abstract forms, melting slowly.

By midday, they reached the base of another steep couloir. Ross looked up at the route and could see the overhanging ice of the glacier far above them. Though he questioned the sanity of climbing this route, as he looked around, he realized there was no other way for them to advance. To make matters worse, it was snowing. Large, wet flakes were landing on each one of them, sticking to their clothing. The wind had increased, churning the snow into a blinding blizzard. It seemed the inclement conditions would hinder or halt their climb, but none of them were willing to quit.

Convinced that he was the best one to take the lead, Ross prepared for the daunting climb. The near-vertical slide of gravel and unsecured boulders he could see above them was worrisome enough, but of greater concern was the ice face they had to negotiate without adequate tools. Ross only hoped they would discover a climbable route once they reached the ice. Leaning against a rock, Ross pulled his backpack off and reached for his ice axe; it was gone. "What the hell?"

Zoësh heard the consternation in Ross's voice. She looked over at him.

"What is it, Ross?"

"My ice axe—I had it when the Mēgs attacked us. I thought I had it here on my pack. I always strap it right here."

"Did you look inside?"

"No! No, I didn't. I wouldn't put it inside the pack!" Ross's temper was beginning to rise, and his face was turning red with anger. Reluctantly, Ross looked inside the pack, but the ice axe was not there either.

"Why do you need it?"

"It helps me climb these steep slopes, especially the ice. Damn it! Where could it be?"

"I hope you didn't leave it back with the Mēgs," fretted Zoësh.

"Aye, Uf da gallues fin ut, dae wull bae suspicious. Dae wull hunt us down fur sur."

Ross's frustration quickly turned to genuine concern for all their safety.

"What did it look like? Maybe you dropped it along the way. We could look for it," Seerae offered.

Insistently, Ross replied, "No! It wouldn't have fallen off of my pack. I must've left it back there in the den. Shit! I can't believe I did that, of all the stupid things to do."

"Maybe you've lost it since then," Zoësh proposed.

"I doubt it, but either way, it's lost and someone, anyone could find it."

"We must keep moving on; we can't wait here anymore," Zoësh said.

"I know, I know. Damn it! I can't believe I did that!"

Ross had a hard time excusing himself for having done something so careless. Losing the ice axe and the serious ramifications that it could have on him and the others sank deep into his heart. The weight of his situation intensified as he contemplated the strange reality that had beset him. He had lost count of the days since he had stood with Eve on the summit of Machapuchare. The image of her face was fading from his memory as thoughts of danger and unique creatures in a strange world buried the memories of his other life. The only positive thing that had developed from the danger was that it had helped to dim the sorrow and pain he felt over Eve's death.

At times, Ross became so absorbed by the danger and the task of staying alive, that he forgot what he was trying to do, that he was endeavoring to get back home. When he thought about home though, he often wondered if he truly wanted to return. *"Go back to what?"* he thought to himself. The feeling of aloneness pushed deep into his soul as he realized there was no one left at home that he wanted to return to. There in Shuk, he was also alone, alone as a human, as a man. So, no matter where he was, he was alone, and the thought of that began to temper his inner being, hardening his essence, making him stronger, and yet, at the same time, cold.

The only aspect of his life that continued to resist the hardening was the fading image of Eve that came to life in his dreams. Her voice, her touch, her love, all of which he could feel when he closed his eyes, melted the steely shell that tried to close in around his heart. It was Eve who kept him going, step-by-step, day-by-day. The thoughts and memories of her were keeping his weighted, broken being afloat in the unfathomed waters of gloom.

As an act of utter defiance against despair, against the dark, undulating tide, Ross did what he knew he could do, what he had to do: he climbed. Ross led the others upward toward the ice wall. The higher they climbed, the heavier the snow fell. With every step, every grasp of the hand, the sky was becoming darker and the air sharp and chilling. With no place to retreat, no place to hide or rest, they kept climbing. As they reached the bottom of the ice wall, the dark night was closing in around them, and fear began tormenting Ross. He remembered another icy cold night, alone on the summit, hanging over a black void. Without ropes or gear, Ross could not climb this ice wall. He looked desperately through the deepening darkness, trying to find a way around the wall. The fading light disguised the features of the terrain. He examined each side of the wall multiple times. As his eyes adjusted to the surrounding darkness, a faint glimmer appeared over his right shoulder. Ross blinked, then squinted as he tried to improve his focus. To his surprise and relief, a narrow gap between the ice wall and the granite wall came into view. Ross carefully made his way over to the gap and looked up. For as high as he was able to see in the diminished light, the chimney-like gap rose straight up. Ross knew that they had no choice but to climb the gap. He reached up, took a hold of a slick, but solid rock, and climbed. The others followed without question. They, too, were tired, afraid, and knew they had no other choice. They put their trust in Ross and his ability to get them to the pass.

In the middle of the stormy night, fatigued and shivering, they crested the ice wall and reached the Pass of Borak. The night was black and plagued by high winds. As far as they could see, there was nothing but snow, ice, and the unknown dangers of crevasses. Unable to find any place to shelter, they pressed on, hoping to find somewhere to weather the storm. As they fought their way across the glacier, a subtle glow began to reach out across the ice floe. Kumél turned and gazed into the sky. The snow began to subside, and suddenly everything became calm and quiet. They peered back from where they had come. The light reflecting on the deep snow revealed there was not even the slightest trace of their footsteps. One-by-one, they turned and looked forward and discovered they were more than halfway across the frozen pass. Ross scanned ahead and was able to see that the way before them was sloping gently downward.

Pushing through waist-deep snow, they were all exhausted and needed to rest, but because they were so close to Gershom, they elected to continue moving through the night. They would recuperate for as long as they needed once they reached the safety of the forest.

It was daybreak before they arrived at the edge of Gershom forest. "Finally!" Ross's voice broke the silence. There were no responses from the others, for words required too much effort. Kumél sat on the trunk of a fallen tree, lay his massive body on the giant beam of wood, and closed his eyes. Ross chose to lay on the ground, which was soft and lush with thick grass. Zoësh took refuge under a tall evergreen, leaning against its smooth trunk, and Seerae found a spot close to Ross. They all fell fast asleep.

Alan Delahay

SHUK

THE AURORA PATH

THE SEA OF THE WES

THE PLAIN OF HAEMUS

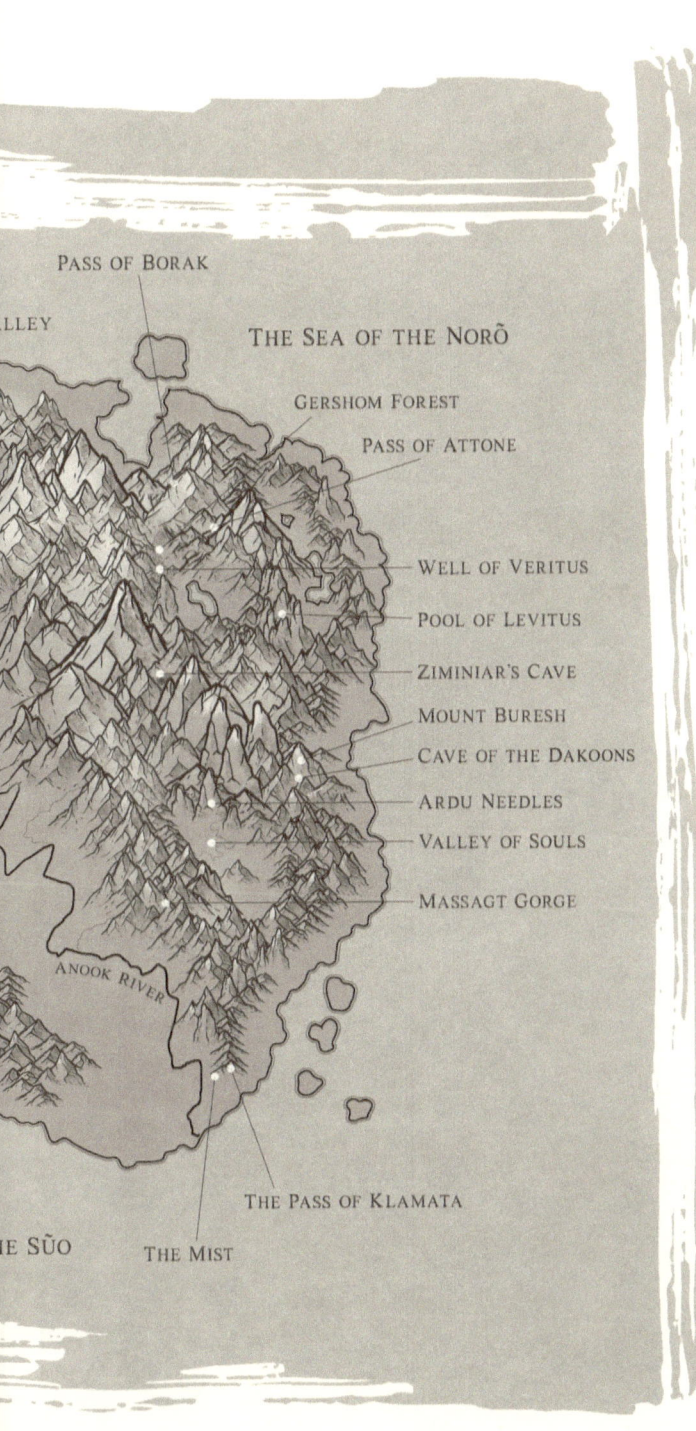

PASS OF BORAK

..LLEY

THE SEA OF THE NORÕ

GERSHOM FOREST

PASS OF ATTONE

WELL OF VERITUS

POOL OF LEVITUS

ZIMINIAR'S CAVE

MOUNT BURESH

CAVE OF THE DAKOONS

ARDU NEEDLES

VALLEY OF SOULS

MASSAGT GORGE

ANOOK RIVER

THE PASS OF KLAMATA

IE SÙO   THE MIST

Chapter VII
The Ruin of Amik

For more than a thousand years after the great war, the realm of Tirnan rested, quietly tending to the wounds inflicted upon it. Amik and Livia worked the land with the help of the kerolus who stayed in Tirnan with them. Eloh came, just as he promised he would, and helped them rebuild the land and restore life to the war-ravaged region. Eventually, Amik and Livia moved away from the Alaya Mountains to the west into the Valley of Biritum. There they worked the soil and created a vast and beautiful garden rivaling those in Assuk.

Amik and Livia were passionately in love and from the depth and strength of their love their children were born. The children of Amik grew to be strong and adventurous, full of curiosity and imagination. Like their father and mother, the children were good with the land, and the land was good to them. The flora and fauna came alive at the touch of their hands and grew up before them like children growing up before their parents.

For many seasons, Amik and his family lived happily in the valley, but Amik missed the high mountains. From the first sight of them, Amik felt their silent, majestic lure inexorably drawing him into their vast, mysterious domain. Being away from them provoked a deep longing that nothing else could satisfy, so Amik would often journey back to the Alaya highlands to meet with Eloh, and they would explore the heights together as they had in Pardis. As time continued, Amik spent more time alone in the high mountains, exploring their raw, hidden beauty and making plans to bring that beauty to other parts of Tirnan. It was during one of those solitary adventures when the first breath of a foul wind descended into the valley of Biritum.

Attar discovered that Eloh had given the Kleid o'Miht to Amik which locked the iron Gates of Abyssus and secured the impregnable chains of iron that bound him to the pit wall. The Kleid also gave Amik dominion over the whole realm of Tirnan. Whoever possessed the Kleid o'Miht could rule the realm. Attar, whose corrupted heart lusted for power, strongly desired the Kleid, and so he set his mind to acquiring it.

There were many in the pit with Attar—gallues who had not been destroyed in the war, cast there as prisoners. These brutish gallues, lacking tact and shrewdness, wanted to take a more direct, less cautious approach. They were impatient and wanted Attar to take the Kleid by force, avoid all the illusions and deceit, and then kill Amik and his descendants. Of course, they had no plan for freeing themselves from the pit and, as such, could only spout off about what they would do. Nevertheless, Attar was much too clever and patient to take the Kleid by force, even if he could. To do so would mean that Eloh and the kerolus armies would return to Tirnan and destroy him and his minions. Attar knew that his ability to rule over Tirnan had to be legitimized by his rightful possession of the Kleid o'Miht. There was no better way to that end than for Amik to surrender the Kleid willingly.

In his cunningness, Attar devised a subtly devious scheme, a plan that, if successful, would have Amik offer the Kleid o'Miht to him, even insist upon his taking it.

Attar was the most skillful of all musicians. His talent with wind instruments was unequalled. No one else had ever played with such passion and enchantment. His music was more than precise and skillful technique; it flowed into the ears like breath into the lungs, into the thoughts like sunlight into the shadows. Attar's music resonated with a force so strong, so enticing, that even those elements of the natural realm without ears, heart, or soul felt its touch. This was how Attar intended to draw Amik into his scheme, to cast a spell on him. Attar set to playing a wooden pipe called a dukwán, whose moaning, seductive voice he set upon the wind. Floating over the mountains and meadows, over streams and forests, and eventually into the Valley of Biritum, the seductive voice of Attar's song searched for the tender, unsuspecting heart of Amik. As if a lure had been cast into a stream, so the song of Attar was sent throughout the realm of Tirnan, floating on the currents of the wind until it would catch the heart of Amik.

It was in the year of the Red Crescent Moon, in the season of bloom, when the cold, frosty winds gave way to the warm, tropical breezes, and the morning sun caressed the earthen canvas that Amik first heard the enchanting sound of the music. It came to him like an intimate whisper. Carried on a cheerful breeze, the melody crept into Amik's hearing. It softly kissed his cheek with full, warm, velvety lips and made his heart race with intrigue and a new, strangely illicit excitement. Amik felt surprised by his reaction, even uncomfortable at first, but the song of Attar was strong, seductive, and mesmerizing. It was not long before Amik began craving the sound of the pipe's melody and started seeking its source.

The Valley of Biritum lay far away from Mount Ducapita and the pit, requiring Amik to travel far and long, for more than a season's length, in search of the music's maker. Season after season, Amik journeyed to the east, searching the mountains and valleys, following the song that whispered in his ear.

Attar could not know with certainty that his scheme would have its desired effect, but, because he was patient, Attar kept playing, waiting for Amik to come.

With the wooden pipe, Attar played haunting, mournful music that reached into the inner being of Amik. The bewitching song reached into his deepest parts, enticing an unquenchable thirst and a ravenous discontent. It drew him further and further from his home in the valley. For longer and longer periods, Amik was gone from the valley and from his family. Slowly and methodically casting its spell upon him, the music became more than a curiosity; more than a mystery to be solved, the music became a seductress, a mistress, and Amik became subject to her power. Each new season, Amik left Livia and their children to journey far away on his quest to find his secret siren.

In the third year, Amik came to the Valley of Dolus. There he saw the huge gaping entrance of the pit again. Guarded by the iron Gates of Abyssus, the black granite entrance was situated at the base of a towering pyramid-like stone monolith, soaring thousands of feet above the surrounding landscape. At first sight, Amik felt the urge to flee, to run away from the dreadful sight, for there was a strange, lurid darkness inhabiting the area. As he surveyed the landscape, Amik remembered the war and what happened long ago. Something dark and dreadful seemed to emanate from every stone. However, while he felt the urge to flee, he also heard the song calling from the dark entrance of the pit. Conflicted by converging emotions of fear and desire, Amik stood, unable to move. He sensed that someone or something was watching him. He then realized that the music was fading away. Fear began to overtake his senses causing him to shiver in the full sunlight of the hot day.

A voice spoke out of the dark pit. It spoke in calm, soft, enchanting tones. For a moment, it sounded vaguely familiar, for the accent and dialect were like those of the kerolus, and yet, at the same time, it was strangely similar to the music he had been following. In his ears he had heard only the music of the pipe, but in his thoughts, he heard a voice like the one speaking from the pit. "A ha baen waitin. A hoped ye wud com."

Amik looked around, for the voice echoed around him. "Who is there? Where are you?"

"A bae da musician who plays fur ye. Shall A play mae pipe fur ye, Amik o'Tirnan."

"How do you know my name?"

"Ut's taken ye quite u lung time t'gut haer. A ha played mae music fur jus yer aers."

"But why? Why do you play for me? Who are you and what is this place?"

"Ye ask muny questions. Bae ye sure ye ask da right ones?"

"What do you mean, the right ones? What is the right question?"

"Why bae ye haer, Amik? Thut bae da rael question. Why ha ye com, kaeper o'da Kleid, frun o'Eloh. Dar bae u raeson thut ye ha com. A raeson thut bae mur thun mae music. Ye bae lukin fur somting, somting thut wull satisfy ye."

"I thought the music drew me."

"Da music? D'ye tink mae music bae da one ting thut yer haert desires? Nae, da music ony excites yer hunger. Ut awakens yer thirst!" As the voice spoke to Amik from behind the darkness of the gates, it patiently drew him closer and closer to the black entrance. The sound of Attar's words penetrated Amik's thoughts and soul just as the haunting voice of the dukwán had. Amik became spellbound by the words and hypnotic intonation of Attar's voice. Casting off caution and memory, Amik crept nearer the gates to find the owner of the voice.

When Amik was close enough to touch the large iron bars of the gate, he looked beyond them, into the darkness that hid behind. At first, Amik could neither see nor hear anything. His senses began to override his obsession and forbade him to speak. Silently, Amik peered into the pit, and silently, the darkness behind the bars glared back at him with invisible eyes. Then, out of the blackness, two yellow eyes with dull black pupils appeared, as if they had been closed and, just in that moment, had opened. Amik stepped back from the gates, startled by the unexpected attention.

Attar's lust for the Kleid o'Miht was every bit as strong as Amik's desire for the music, and it began to ignite his impulsive nature. Attar wondered if Amik had the Kleid with him. As he stared at Amik in silence, his ageless contempt and thirst for power tried to overtake his cunning. Everything in his being wanted to leap forward and grab Amik, destroy him, and take the Kleid. Yet Attar knew that even if Amik had the Kleid with him, he could not steal it or take it; the power of the Kleid came only through the one to whom it was given. The earlier words of the gallues kept assaulting his mind, trying to coerce him to act, but he restrained his violent propensities. He had waited for too long to be impatient now; waiting a little longer seemed a small sacrifice. The gallues hiding in the pit could sense the conflict of his resolve. They watched as he struggled within himself to tame the wildness of his aggression. Yet, before he was able to tame his temper, the aura emanating from him corrupted the atmosphere surrounding Amik with hostility and violence. With stammering lips, Amik spoke to his unknown observer, "Who's there? Who are you?" At first, there was no reply, and the eyes did not move or change in any way. Amik took another few steps back. "Why won't you answer me? Who are you?"

"Whae d'ye faer mae now, Amik?"

Amik hesitated while fear greater than he had ever felt before, coursed through his body like a current of lightning. The hair on his neck stood up, and his eyes revealed the growing trepidation that was trying to overcome the power that had dulled his sensibilities.

Attar could see that Amik's mind was breaking free of the spell, so he stepped out of the darkness allowing Amik to see him. Attar was still powerful and capable of great deception. He used his craft to blind Amik to

193

the terror of his appearance. Deceiving Amik's eyes, Attar appeared as a creature of beauty. As he stepped into the faint light sneaking in through the bars, the sound of the heavy iron chains echoed through the pit, ringing in Amik's ears. Before Amik could think to ask about the gates or the chains, Attar spoke to him. "Whae ha ye com t'mae? Wut bae ut ye wunna?" Every word that Attar spoke, every syllable of every word, was filled with the power of his magic, and like the song of the pipe, they transfixed Amik, seducing him to desire the music of the pipe above all else.

"I . . . I came in search of the music and of the one who plays it."

"Ye ha haerd da soun o'da pipe ha ye? D'ye know wut ut saes?"

"What it says? It has no voice or words."

"Ye ha nut listened close aenuff, thun. Nor ha ye listened t'yer own haert, or else ye wud ha haerd da words tell ye wut ye lung t'haer."

Amik was unsure what Attar meant about the voice of the pipe or of its words and did not know how to answer. So enraptured by desire and consumed by hunger, he was incapable of discerning the guile lurking in every word and note. Forgetting the fear that he had felt only moments earlier, Amik responded naively, like a child, innocent and, as yet, uncorrupted. "Are you the one who plays the music?"

"Aye, ut bae mae song thut ye haerd."

"Can you teach me to play?"

"Nut all cun play da music o'da pipe. Ut bae u very special gif. Wud ye lik t'sae mae pipe?"

"Yes. Yes, I would."

"Ut bae haer. A wull play fur ye, but ye mus open yer haert un listen closely t'da voice o'da music." Attar took the wooden instrument to his lips and began to play. As the music leapt from the pipe, it surrounded Amik like a thousand beautiful dancers. Carried away into a dreamland of ecstasy, where all his thoughts of life and Livia and Tirnan were left behind, Amik was lifted up in an illusion of pleasure. For hours that flowed into days, Attar played the pipe, bathing Amik in a sordid melody, conjured, not only by the pipe, but also by Attar's dark magic. The notes came alive. Out of the opus rose the melodic whispering of a soft, poetic refrain that was almost imperceptible. The words of the whisper began to fill Amik's heart and mind with envy and lust, speaking to him of pleasure that could be his. Attar played the pipe until Amik had forgotten even those things that he had been told by Eloh, things about the pit and the Gates of Abyssus, things about the war and the treachery of Attar. Amik forgot about the gallues, he forgot who he was, and fell deep into the shadows of Attar's enchanting melody, which made him hunger for something that would never satisfy. The delusion that was cast over Amik made him desire the music more than anything else in life. It made him crave the song of Attar with such urgent want that he would trade anything he possessed to have it.

Rumors had begun to surface, throughout Tirnan and beyond, about Amik's wanderings. Even Eloh heard that Amik was going on long journeys into the high mountains where he was often gone for many seasons. Eloh was not concerned at first, for Amik had always been one to journey into the mountains. However, when Eloh came to Tirnan in the spring of the third year and could not find Amik, he became suspicious. Summer and fall came and went, and there had been no report of anyone in the realm having seen Amik. Livia and her children and those kerolus who dwelt in the valley began to worry. The winter winds were beginning to blow in the high mountains and still Amik had not returned home.

Gamlak, the kerolus who had been with the Carascians from the days of the war, warned Eloh of a foul wind and strange song blowing through the realm. When Eloh heard of it, he knew that it had to be the song of Attar.

Eloh knew the power of Attar's music and especially of his lyrics. He remembered how strong the spirit of Attar's pipes was, how compelling it was, even to his heart. He was greatly troubled by the thought that Attar might be playing his pipe. Eloh turned to Gamlak. "You must find him. Fly to the ushus, to the gates, if you must. Find Amik and bring me word when he is safely returned."

After three days, Attar stopped playing the pipe. Standing alone with heavy wet flakes of snow falling on him, Amik awoke from the trance cast over him by the song of Attar. Attar looked at Amik and whispered to him, "Wut wull ye giv mae fur mae music?"

"What is it that you want? I will give you anything I am able." Amik had become so intoxicated by the melody of Attar's song that, though he was willing to do anything to hear it again, he was unable to think of anything to offer.

"Ye mus ha somting ye cun giv mae?"

"I could give you my services. I am very good with the elements. I am a husbandman, a very great one."

Attar knew he had Amik hooked, that all he had to do was help Amik realize what he should offer. He refused everything Amik offered, waiting for the one thing he most desired. "A ha no naed o'yer services, husbandman. Ye cud bae mae slave un A would nae'er giv ye mae music. D'ye hav onyting thut ye brung wit ye? Onyting ye cud giv mae?"

"All that I have with me, I have offered. Everything else I left behind."

"Thun gae, un dunna com buk t'mae until ye ha somting t'giv mae. Thun A wull play fur ye."

"But—?"

"But wut, Amik? Wut bae ut ye wanna?"

"I will not be able to return for a season!" Amik collapsed to his knees and cried out in desperation.

"Brang mae somting A wunna an A wull play fur ye, not afore."

"I will! I promise."

Now that Attar was sure Amik was not carrying the Kleid o'Miht with him, he considered how he might persuade Amik to bring it on his return. Attar also wanted to be sure that Amik did not fail to return, so he took from among the many unseen things hidden with him in the pit a black triakis. He held the stone in his hand and whispered an incantation over it. The triakis had veins of gold, silver, and quartz which began to glow, illuminating the stone as Attar whispered over it. Several times, Attar said the words and each time the veins of the triakis glowed even brighter. Attar gave Amik the triakis as a keepsake to take with him that would remind him of his promise, a keepsake that had a powerful spell. "A wull giv ye dis one ting, Amik o'Tirnan. A wull giv ye dis stone."

Attar passed the black stone through the iron bars. Amik reached out and took hold of the triakis; it was the size of his palm and was much heavier than he had expected, than its size would have suggested. As the stone was transferred, Attar took hold of Amik's wrist and pulled him close. "Dis bae u gif t'Livia, yer wife. Take it t'er. Tell er it bae frum ye, thut ye ha brung it frum da mountains."

"What is it?"

Attar released Amik's hand. "It bae an oracle o'song. It wull play da music o'da pipe."

"But how? How does it play?"

"Breath upon it." Amik looked at Attar doubtfully. Then he looked at the triakis in his hand and blew a breath into his palm and over the black triakis. The veins of gold, silver, and quartz began to glow, and from the triakis, a song began to lift into the air and into Amik's ears. It continued for a long time. Amik stood spellbound by both the beauty of the song and the alluring beauty of the triakis. Amid the sound of the dukwán emanating from the triakis, there came a subtle voice, a whisper in a tongue that Amik had never heard. Amik listened; he closed his eyes and meditated on the words. Over and over, the words repeated.

Amik opened his eyes and looked at Attar. "What is it saying?"

Attar simply looked away. "Go home, Amik o'Tirnan, un dunna com again, less ye ha somting t'giv un return fur wut ye wanna."

"Thank you! Thank you very much. I will come again in the season of bloom."

Amik put the triakis into his bag and began the long trek home in the heavy snow. As he traveled the many months toward the valley, to Livia and his family, he could not forget the music of the black triakis. He often stopped to retrieve it from the bag and blow upon it. Amik was giddy like a child who had just received a gift on their birthday. Skipping and jumping and running toward his home, he felt like he had found something greater than anything he had ever found before. Amidst the elation, lingered an unanswered question that bore into his thoughts. He wondered what he had that Attar would accept from him in exchange for his music. Amik's thirst for the song of Attar had become an addiction; his every thought became consumed by the melody and his want of it. Amik desired more than the song itself, he desired to become a creator of the song, to play the pipe as Attar had played them.

Attar had cast a dark spell into the black granite triakis, that Amik unwittingly released over his family. The spell was strong and unyielding and yet was nothing more than a suggestion, a hint that would lodge itself into the minds of everyone who heard it. It lingered in the notes of the song and entered the heart of Livia and her children like soothing words. Beyond their understanding, the song sang, *"Only to the Kleid will he agree."*

Without realizing it, Amik's family would become complicit in the demise of Tirnan. The whisper would convince them to persuade Amik, to encourage him to offer the Kleid o'Miht in exchange for the music. With their mouths they would reveal the one thing the musician desired, and

Amik, in his inebriation, would excitedly agree. All Attar had to do was wait until Amik returned in the spring, and freely surrender the Kleid.

It was late in the winter when Amik finally returned to his home. Upon arrival, Eloh greeted him. "Amik, my friend, I have missed you."

"Eloh, this is an unexpected pleasure." Amik's tone was less than enthusiastic.

"Is Gamlak with you? I sent him to find you. Have you seen him?"

"No, I have not seen him. How did you know where to send him?"

"We did not know. We only hoped that you were well and that if not, he would find you. Everyone was worried. You have been gone for such an extended time. Where have you been?"

"Wandering, looking for new meadows and valleys, places to groom and grow." Amik lied to Eloh for the first time. The spell of Attar had worked so well, so completely, that Amik showed no outward signs of his intentions or of his changing attitude toward Eloh. Eloh was not fully convinced, yet he had never known Amik to act deceitfully, and so, assuming the best, he and Gamlak returned to Assuk.

As winter ebbed into spring, Amik and his family were eager for Amik to return to the Alaya Mountains. Unlike the previous seasons, Livia encouraged Amik to begin his journey and begin it early. They encouraged Amik to offer the Kleid o'Miht for the gift of the musical pipe.

Amik packed provisions, the Kleid o'Miht, and the triakis into his worn shoulder bag and started the long journey east. On this journey, unlike all the previous ones, Amik knew exactly where to go. There would be no searching or exploring this time. Amik was single-minded, focused, and steadfast on his journey to the Gates of Abyssus. There was one thing, however, that Amik had forgotten: Eloh had promised to return in early spring. Eloh had always come in the early spring, the season of bloom and often spent many months in Tirnan.

Attar began to play the pipe as soon as he sensed the changing in the seasons, sending the haunting melody down into the valley. The music called out like an enchanting siren, drawing Amik heedlessly back to the pit. When Amik heard the melody, it made him even more excited. He traveled toward the lair of Attar as the days ebbed into weeks. When he was finally close, he was met with the deep remnants of winter's heavy snow that lay as a formidable barrier between him and the pit. Amik was forced to wait another month for the snow to melt, but each night more snow would come; it was as if nature itself was resisting him. After waiting for so long, Amik was determined to press on, disregarding the snow and ice.

When he eventually reached the entrance of the pit, the gates were still covered in ice and snow. The music of the pipe rolled out from the pit with rich, strong tones. Echoing off the surrounding peaks and descending into the valley, like a mountain stream swollen from the spring melt, the song of Attar thundered into Amik's ears. "Piper, are you there?"

"Aye. A ha baen expectun ye, Amik o'Tirnan."

"I have returned as you requested."

"So ye ha. Ye mus luv mae music t'ha com so soon."

"I have been unable to contain my excitement. Will you teach me how to play?"

"Wut ha ye brung mae? Wut gif d'ye ha t'exchange fur mae music?"

"Well, I have this. It is a Kleid."

"U Kleid? Wut wud ye ha mae d'wit u Kleid?" Attar acted disappointed and disinterested in the Kleid, though he was extremely eager to get his hands on it.

"It is a special Kleid, given to me by Eloh." The spell had worked exactly as Attar had intended. The fog of forgetfulness and desire had obscured his memory of the power the Kleid possessed, and the whisper had planted a seed in the minds of them all. It had created in Amik a strong unsatisfied yearning that could not be filled by anything else but the song. The song had become both the thing that made him thirst and the thing that he believed would satisfy his thirst. Yet his thirst would never be satisfied.

"Whae d'ye offer mae u Kleid thut Eloh ha giv ye?"

"I could think of nothing else to offer you. My wife, Livia, and my family, they suggested I give you the Kleid in exchange for your gift of music and the pipe."

"A ony promised t'play mae music fur u gif, Amik. Uf da gif maens notin t'ye, whae d'A wanna ut? Is ut important t'ye, Amik, dis Kleid?"

"Yes. It is exceptional, but I cannot remember why. If it does not suit you, then I am dismayed, for I have nothing else to offer." Amik suddenly showed a side of himself that caught Attar by surprise. "But if you desire the Kleid, you will have to do more than play for me. You will have to give me the pipes so I can play them myself."

Attar could hear the resolve in Amik's voice. The spell had worked its magic too strongly, making Amik obsessed beyond compromise about what he desired. Attar hurried to distract him. "D'ye wanna mae t'play fur ye, now?"

"Yes! Yes, I want you to play for me!"

"Un fur playin mae music ye offer mae dis Kleid givn ye bae Eloh?"

"Yes! Yes, you may have the Kleid for the pipes and the music."

"But wut uf A dunna wanna da Kleid. Wut uf tis nut aenuff? Bae dar somting else?"

"I have nothing else, nothing that is worth anything to a great musician such as yourself."

"Ye wull ha t'com buk on da morrow, Amik."

"But . . . but, I have nowhere to go!"

"Wull thun, ye wull ha t'wait haer un A wull com agan wun da new sun rises. Thun A wull giv ye mae answer."

Amik made a quick and senseless attempt to sweeten the offer, hoping to get the pipes without delay. "I have brought the triakis. I will give it back to you with the Kleid."

"Da triakis bae mine already. Ye canna giv mae somting thut bae mine. A wull sae ye on da morrow, nut afore." Attar disappeared into the darkness of the pit, leaving Amik alone and disheartened.

During the time that Amik journeyed to the pit, Eloh and Gamlak returned to the valley. Upon his arrival, Eloh realized that something strange was in the air for Amik's family did not come to greet him. Livia, who had always greeted him with a warm welcome kiss, was distant. There had never been even the slightest disharmony in their friendship. In all the ages they had known each other, they had been close, and yet, on that day, Livia and Eloh were like strangers to each other. "Livia, what is it? Why do you treat me as if I am a stranger?"

The words of Eloh began to dilute the power of the spell, breaking its grip on her heart and mind. Livia turned away and acted annoyed at the question. Nevertheless, the sound of his voice had shaken some deep inner part of her which began to wake her from the spell.

"What is it? Where is Amik, Livia? Where is he? Is he gone again?"

"Yes, he has gone to the high mountains, to the musician."

"To the musician. What musician?" Eloh looked at Livia with skeptical eyes.

"The one who plays the pipe and makes the beautiful music. The one who gave us the black stone that sings."

"Where? Where is this musician? Why has Amik gone to him?"

"Amik has taken the Kleid to him, in exchange for his music." As Livia spoke the words, the fog that had settled over her mind lifted. She began to see what she and the others had done, and as she remembered, she became afraid and ashamed. "What have we done?" she cried.

"Eloh! Eloh, wae mus laeve now! We mus laeve now, Eloh!" Gamlak became insistent.

"But what of Amik and Livia and their family? We can't just leave them here. Attar will kill them all!"

"Wae canna haelp thum witout da others. Wae ha t'laeve now!"

Livia stood transfixed on Eloh. She began to cry. She knew, in her heart, that it was Attar's voice that had been singing over them in the music of the triakis. The song that had been so soothing and pleasing, now, seemed cold, and dark, and evil.

"Livia! Livia!"

"Yes, Eloh?"

"You must get the others, all of the others, your whole family. You must bring them to me now."

"Why?" Livia whispered. "What are you going to do to us?" The question fell from Livia's lips with palpable fear that carried a subtle imputation against Eloh. Birthed in her mind by the suggestive song of Attar, were thoughts that began to grow, like a child in its mother's womb. Thoughts of fear, doubt, suspicion, and distrust all began to contract in the womb of her mind. She could not stop them.

"Livia, listen to me! We have to get you to safety, away from here as soon as possible. We do not know how much time we have!"

"Time? What do you mean, time?" Livia was still in shock at the realization of what they had done and doubted Eloh's motives.

"Yes, time. We do not know how long it will be before Attar and his gallues come to Biritum. They will take all of you captive or worse! We don't have much time!" Livia raced into the fields to gather her family.

Eloh instructed Gamlak to return to Assuk and call the kerolus army together and return to the Valley of Biritum. Gamlak voiced his concerns, "Wut o'ye, Eloh, wut wull ye do? Ut bae tae dangerous fur ye t'stay haer!"

"I'll lead Livia and her family to the refuge of hOmsut in the wes. It will give us time, at least a little time."

"Ye know uf Amik givs Attar da Kleid, wae wull ha no power haer un Tirnan. Wae cunna overthrow da one who possesses da Kleid."

"I know, Gamlak! I know, but we can't just let this go. Attar has initiated this. He has planned this atrocity. Go! Quickly go!"

Eloh led Livia and her family deep into the wilderness to the fortress of hOmsut, a massive rock formation far from the Valley of Biritum. In the rocks were caves, and it was in these caves that Eloh hid the family of Amik.

Amik waited at the entrance of the pit. Attar knew that Amik was committed, that he had fallen under his dark magic and so he lingered, letting Amik grow even more anxious. Attar began playing the pipe, but, this time, the song he played was malefic, powerful, and seditious. It filled Amik's ears with a melody that disarmed and subdued him, and unleashed a shadow, an eidolon born in the deep darkness of Attar's heart. Alive but invisible, the evil spirit began to surround and deceive Amik, turning his heart away from truth, filling it with treachery and bitterness.

"Whae ha ye returned t'mae, Amik o'Tirnan?" Attar's voice rang with a malicious tone. He spoke pretentiously, as though he had forgotten the reason for Amik's presence.

"I have come with a gift."

"Ah, u gif. Ye ha u gif fur mae?"

"Yes, just as you required, a gift for your music."

"Mubae yer gif bae not aenuff. Wut wull ye do thun, Amik?"

"Please, I have traveled such a great distance! I hope it will please you."

"Wut bae dis gif thut ye entice mae wit? Dis ting thut ye brung fur mae music? Tell mae, wut ha ye t'offer?"

"I brought this Kleid, given to me by Eloh. It is the Kleid o'Miht."

"Da Kleid o'Miht, wut bae dis Kleid o'Miht? Wut gud bae ut t'mae, haer un dis prison?!"

The words sprang from Attar's mouth with a vengeful, contemptuous resonance that startled Amik, causing him to stumble backwards.

"Oh, dunna bae afaered o'mae, fren. A wull nut hurt ye."

Amik did not know how to answer Attar. He simply held it out in his hand. "I will give you the Kleid. Here, take it."

"How d'A know ut wull work? Ye mae bae traein t'trick mae, traein t'stael mae music. Wud ye trae t'stael mae music, Amik? Hmm, A wunnar?"

"No! No, I would never do that!"

"Hmm, how do A know da Kleid ye ha, bae da Kleid o'Miht?"

"I will show you."

"Show me? How, Amik?"

"Let me come close. I will open the gates and unlock the chains with it. Then you will know I am telling the truth. You will be free and the Kleid will be yours."

"Ye wud nut trae t'trick mae wud ye, Amik of Tirnan?"

"Let me show you! I will open the gates and give it to you. You may have the Kleid o'Miht. It will be yours!" Amik was unsure if the Kleid would work or not. Nevertheless, he knew he had nothing else to offer and therefore it was worth the risk.

"Ye ma com close. Let mae sae dis Kleid o'Miht thut ye possess."

Amik made his way to the gate. The depth of the snow made it difficult for him, but eventually he stood at the entrance of the pit, where standing on the opposite side of the gate was Attar. His eyes were large and menacing, yellow with dark, black pupils. He stared at Amik through the gates but said nothing.

"Here, see! Here it is, the Kleid o'Miht."

The Kleid o'Miht was an iron object, forged on a Kerolian anvil by the arch-kerolus Mallaeus. The metal was dark blue from the heat of the flames used to forge it. There had been no attempt to polish or dress it. It was adorned only by the intricate folded pattern, cast upon it by the hammer of Mallaeus and the incendiary fire. The top section of the Kleid, called the crown, was thick and circular, about the width of Amik's hand. It had the mark of Eloh forged into its convex top and around the girdle of the crown, the script of the Thelions was engraved. Below the girdle was the four-sided body of the Kleid, which transitioned into eight sides at the base. The body extended slightly longer than Amik's hand. On each of its four sides were markings that, at first glance, appeared exactly the same. These were the four faces of the Kleid o'Miht. Upon closer examination, each face was different in several ways. There was a different symbol etched into each face: tree, wind, flame, and waves. Surrounding each symbol was a triangle and at the corners of each triangle were the symbols of the other three faces, one in each corner. At the bottom point of the triangle surrounding the tree was a star. A vertical hole was bored into the bottom of the Kleid that extended through the core and stopped just below the crown, making the Kleid hollow.

The symbols represented the four natural elements of Pardis. To the Theoscians, the four natural elements of Pardis also represented elements of physical and spiritual life. The elements representing physical life were heart, mind, strength, and soul. The elements of spiritual life were truth, love, wisdom, and knowledge. In the Theoscian lexicon, the four symbols represented the laws of life which governed the key and its owner. The one who possessed the key was bound by its laws.

Attar stared at the Kleid with envy, and for a moment, betrayed himself and his intentions. Quickly, he glanced back at Amik who asked, "Do you want it? It is yours. Here, take it." "Ye ha nut proved ut bae da Kleid o'Miht! Show mae thut ut bae wut ye say ut bae."

There was a strange, inexplicable prohibition lurking in the mind of Amik. Every part of him seemed eager to insert the Kleid into the lock and open the Gates of Abyssus, save a single, faint voice in his heart, that grew louder and louder in his head, crying out, *No!* over and over. As he took the Kleid and began to insert it into the lock, the insistent voice became so loud that it was deafening. Nevertheless, Amik would not listen. Unexpectedly, as Amik grasped the Kleid, the symbols on each side started to glow in distinct colors. The symbols engraved in the bezel became illuminated. The Kleid seemed to have some force within itself, a power that was now felt by Amik and by Attar. Amik tried to insert the Kleid into the lock but found that, though it seemed the same in dimension on all sides, it would not fit into the lock. Amik examined it closely, trying to understand what he was doing wrong.

"Trae turnin ut," Attar suggested.

Amik rotated the Kleid slightly and attempted to insert it, but, again, it would not cooperate. Attar was becoming impatient. His eagerness was beginning to show and Amik, for the first time, noticed. "Turn ut agan, one mur tam, ut wull wok dis tam, mae fren."

Amik turned the Kleid again. As he inserted it, the star began to illuminate. It slid effortlessly into the lock. Suddenly, the colors of the lighted Kleid began to emit from all parts of the gates. Amik turned the Kleid and the great lock that was burdened with the security of Attar and his minions, submitted to its power, unlocking one of the only vestiges of defense against the tyranny of Attar.

The Gates of Abyssus stood unlocked for the first time in many millennia. Amik reached out his hand and began to push open the giant gates. The gates groaned in protest as they were swung on their massive hinges. Attar stood aside, watching Amik struggle. The gallues, Attar's minions, watching from the shadows of darkness deep in the pit, waited for their master to lead them out of their incarceration. Attar was patient and chose not to move or act until Amik had surrendered the Kleid into his hands.

"Will you give me your music now?"

"Firs, ye mus unlock des." Attar shook the chains that bound him to the wall of the pit. A loud clanking noise echoed throughout the pit then roared into Amik's ears, beating on the inner drums with a painfully deafening report. Amik quickly shielded his ears, dropping the Kleid onto the rocks at his feet. A clanging sound filled the air, drawing Attar's avaricious eyes toward it. Attar's impulse was to lunge for the Kleid yet he restrained himself from doing so and waited for Amik to recover it.

Amik bent down and grabbed the Kleid. He looked up at Attar, who was hovering over him with an evil glare. Attar's hands were extended toward Amik with the locks of the chains exposed. He waited for Amik to unlock them. "If I unlock the chains, you will give me the pipes, right? You promised?"

"Aye. A promised."

"And your music—you will give it, too?"

"A cunna giv ye mae music. A cun ony giv ye da pipe. Ye mus laern t'play them."

"Then will you teach me?"

"So, d'ye tink dis Kleid bae worth mae pipe?" Amik could not refuse. Even though he would not get the music as he desired, he could not let the pipe go. He believed that Attar would teach him how to play. Overlooking his accumulating doubts, and intense inner objections, Amik, so deluded by his desire to believe that Attar would teach him to play, denied his own conscience and succumbed to abject wantonness. He unlocked the chains that had bound Attar and protected the realm of Tirnan from his certain tyranny. As he turned the Kleid in the locks, the shackles fell open and collapsed to the ground. Attar was free.

"Yes, I do! See, it is what I said it was!"

"Un ye wanna giv mae dis worthless iron Kleid for mae pipe?"

"I will give it to you, if you want it. Here, take it, in exchange for your pipe." Amik held the Kleid out to Attar.

Slowly Attar reached out his hand, stopping short of Amik's. "Put ut un mae hand thut A mae sae ut closer."

Amik dropped the Kleid o'Miht into the palm of Attar's hand. When the Kleid landed in his hand, Attar closed his fingers over it and quickly drew it to his chest. "Ut bae mine! Tirnan bae mine!"

Amik, so consumed by his addiction to the song of Attar, did not absorb the words Attar had just spoken. The words were unheard, for all he could think about was the song, the music, the pipe. "Will, will you give me the pipe now?"

"It is yours. Take it." Attar dropped the wooden pipe to the ground and stepped out from the gates, free from the pit. Amik bent down and picked it up. As he did, the gallues moved past him into the light of the day and into the realm of Tirnan. They were free from the pit for the first time in more than a thousand millennia.

Clutching the Kleid o'Miht, Attar looked to the skies and yelled with a loud voice. "A bae frae! A wull repay mae enemies. A wull repay thum all!" Attar believed that the Kleid o'Miht would give him unlimited authority and unbridled command of Tirnan; allowing him to subjugate all its inhabitants, both creatures and Carascians, under his rule. However, Attar was mistaken, for into the Kleid o'Miht was forged the Law of Life which, if broken, condemned the bearer to an existence of futility in the shadows. Nevertheless, in the right hands, the Kleid o'Miht gave to its bearer complete authority and dominion over Tirnan. For Attar to truly possess the power of the Kleid, he would have to submit to the authority of the Law of Life. This, he would not do, but he was free and held the Kleid and the power and would find another way to use it.

Gamlak flew straight away to Assuk and assembled the kerolus army, led by the arch-kerolus, Remmel. Gamlak reported to Shu and Alethia that the Kleid o'Miht would soon be in the hands of Attar and that the Carascians were in great danger. The empyreal forces of Assuk quickly rose to the call of Remmel and set out to descend upon Tirnan and the dark army of Attar. It was their intent to overwhelm Attar and the gallues before they could fortify their positions and destroy Amik's family and Eloh, who was with them.

In the west desert, beyond the Valley of Biritum, Eloh and the Carascians, save Amik, found safety and concealment in the rocky fortress of hOmsut. It was there that they waited for the kerolus army to arrive.

Attar and his forces descended like a plague of darkness. Screaming and hissing like vile wild beasts, they came into the peaceful domain of Amik and Livia with only one objective, to utterly destroy everyone. It was not long, however, before the kerolus army arrived over the valley and over Attar and his minions. The number of kerolus was so great that the bright sky darkened with a foreboding shadow, one that was all too familiar to the forces of Attar. Fleeing into the shadows, the army of Attar retreated. However, Attar stood his ground. In defiance of the kerolus army, Attar lifted his mighty fist into the air and shouted at the descending forces with absolute confidence and authority, "Tirnan bae maen!" Opening his mighty fist, he revealed the Kleid o'Miht, which had been surrendered to him and at his feet laid the bound body of Amik. "Amik ha givn mae da Kleid o'Miht! Tirnan bae mine, an none cun deny mae rule!"

The forces, led by Remmel, were stopped in their place, hovering over Attar in every direction. Like a giant dome, the kerolus army hung in the sky, ready to descend with crushing might. However, the army was unable to advance. They were unable to step foot on the realm of Tirnan unless given the right of passage by the Kleid's bearer, and Attar would give none of them access. "Dis world bae maen un A wull rule ut as A wull. Life bae mine t'giv un t'take. Amik bae mine t'rule or t'destroy. Ut bae mae word thut wull bae obeyed! Un A wull destroy all oo resist mae! Ye armies o'Eloh, ye ha no place haer!"

From a long distance, the presence of Eloh was felt moving toward the epicenter of the conflict. Attar and all the dark forces also felt the arrival of Eloh. Amik felt the presence of Eloh. Everyone was surprised as he moved toward Attar. "The Kleid o'Miht will not submit to you, Attar! It is not a weapon to be wielded. It is not a force for destruction or death. The Kleid o'Miht is for life and is ruled by the Law of Life! It can only protect and serve, not destroy!" The powerful voice of Eloh echoed through the valley and was heard by all who were there, in the skies and on the ground.

"Since when do Eloh speak wit a tongue o'lies? Ye wud deceive mae wit yer words?"

Eloh moved closer and eventually stood face to face with Attar. He looked at the one who had once been his friend. There was, however, no bond of friendship or fondness left between them. They were enemies. "No! It is you who deceives yourself Attar. You do not have the power to destroy, not by the Kleid. You are bound by its laws now, bound by the power of life. You may rule over Tirnan, but you will not do with it as you please. Every living thing in this realm is bound by the Law of Life and will resist you and your evildoers, for they must obey these laws!"

"Thun A wull enslave thum unner mae power un subject thum unner da cruel mastery o'mae gallues. A wull lock thum un da pit whaer ye locked mae! I maet nut bae able t'destroy thum, but dae wull wish A had!" The rage and contempt in the heart of Attar began to spill out of his every pore onto the gallues that were around him. He looked at Eloh, then he observed the pitifully indifferent Amik bound at his feet, clutching the wooden pipe. Eloh's eyes fell to Amik with sorrow and a tear. Attar raised his gaze and scowled into the pained face of Eloh. "Ye mus leave, now! Ye bae not welcome un mae realm er agan!"

Eloh rose from the valley into the cloud of the kerolus army. Remmel and his forces surrounded Eloh and escorted him back to Assuk.

"Fin thum! All o'thum!" Attar shouted with indignation. Then he reached down and took hold of Amik's hair and lifted him from the ground. He looked at the wounded figure hanging before him, still intoxicated with the song of the pipe. "A hate ye! A hate ye!" he screamed as he threw Amik back down to the ground.

It would be many months before all the Carascians were found by the gallue army. They were taken to the pit and locked behind the Gates of Abyssus as prisoners of Attar. It was Attar's intent to destroy every trace of Amik and the Carascians, but he was resisted in his aim, not only by the forces of Eloh but also by every living thing on Tirnan. He was also resisted by the power of the Kleid. When Attar tried to do evil against Amik, the Kleid set the elements against him. The earth and sky and water and fire resisted him and his minions, making their efforts futile. The elements of life protected Amik and the Carascians. Even though Attar possessed the

Kleid o'Miht, he could not wield it as a weapon against those whom he hated.

There was only one legitimate bearer of the Kleid o'Miht—the one whose mark the Kleid bore—and that was Eloh. All other bearers, including Amik, were subordinate to Eloh. But Eloh, too, was subject to the laws of the Kleid, for he had made the Law of Life supreme and thus indisputable. As long as Attar possessed the Kleid, he would possess Tirnan, but he could not use the power of the Kleid to do evil against Amik. To rule, Attar would have to rely on his witchcraft and devices of deception.

Chapter VIII
The Valley of Souls

As thick, black rolling clouds ambled across the dark canvas of the night sky, Morak, with the foreigner's weapon, struggled through the dense forest. For nearly a month, the threatening sky hounded his every step. Traveling from the Atramentous valley to the Valley of Souls was a three-month journey. Morak had made the journey into the Valley of Souls many times and, though experienced and familiar with the route, he was never confident about finding his way through the mist. The Way, as it was called, was deep in the Telohm Mountains. It was a treacherously long climb to the pass and once over the pass, the arduous descent into the valley was equally challenging.

There was a multitude of dangers along the way: a confusing maze of narrows, winding through towering spires, laced with countless misleading and often perilous detours, dangerous mēglydaims roaming the region, rebel gallues lying in wait for the unsuspecting and often lost traveler, and the opportunistic black corvuses. The greatest of perils, however, was the mist. It was strange and unpredictable and filled the valleys, meadows, and gorges, making the way difficult and hard to find.

Lurking in the air, the mist had grown into a large, expansive cloud that covered many square miles. It deprived the land of sunlight, causing the flora to die and making habitation impossible for most of the creatures of Shuk. The mist had not always haunted the way to the pass; its origin was a mystery. Before Gubrone found the valley, and for many ages after, there had been no mist. Only after the nephesh were taken into the valley and held captive did the mist appear. Many in Shuk believed it came from the tears of the nephesh as they languished in the sorrow of their estrangement from the sapien.

Though the mist was menacing, it was also a benefit, for it was in the mist that many of the nephesh had escaped their captors on the way into the valley. The mist confused the senses of the mēglydaims and gallues, which was propitious to the nephesh, who were under constant threat by the gallues. Hiding in caves and valleys, meadows, and gorges, some of the escaped nephesh had found refuge in the shadows of the mist but not for long. Eventually, they were captured or they fled into the valleys below.

There was only one passable route leading into the Valley of Souls. Winding through the tightly clustered mountain peaks was an incapacious labyrinthine gorge, which wound tightly upward into the Telohm Mountains. Conjoining the gorge, were many small streams and constricted valleys, which, inevitably, lead into impassable, rocky basins and small mountain meadows. The final approach was through a long, winding, and narrow crevasse, which had many confusing junctures that led nowhere at all. If anyone was to follow one of these branches to its dead-end, they would find themselves unable to escape.

For those living in Shuk, there had never been a reason for anyone, other than the gallues, to find the Valley of Souls, for it was a place of sorrows and torture, a place to avoid. Even the gallues and snitches of Shuk dreaded the way into the valley. Most of those who were already in the valley, primarily the nephesh, chose not to attempt escape for fear of the misty way. To ensure that the way remained protected, Gubrone sent gallues, known as custos, to guard the way against any who tried to escape the Valley of Souls. There were only a small number of custos and because they guarded an expansive area, they were rarely ever seen by those traveling through the region. However, those who did have the unfortunate experience of meeting the custos, whether one or many, did not leave unscathed or unmolested by their violence.

The mēglydaims favored the mist, for it allowed them to be out during the day, free from their dens. For this reason, Gubrone's mēglydaims were free to roam the misty region, though, because their senses were dulled by the mist, they were even more dangerous and hard to control. On occasion, Morak had been attacked by his own mēgs. The free roving of the mēglydaims was, perhaps, the most menacing of the many dangers that hindered the way.

He could feel the eyes of the two mēglydaims glaring at him as if perturbed that he had not yet risen from his slumber. Morak slowly rose to his feet. He looked around and, despite the dark overcast sky, could see the edge of the mist not far from where he had slept. He grabbed his things, called his mēglydaims, and began walking toward the pass.

It was not long before the mist fully enveloped them. Unlike other gallues, Morak chose not to let his mēgs run loose through the mist. He liked having them by his side and under his control. They also protected him against the feral, roving mēgs of the mist, and against the rebel gallues who often organized into small bands, stalking and attacking anyone that might have something to steal.

Moving quietly, Morak negotiated his way up toward the pass. It had been many seasons since he had been to the valley, and during his absence, the mist had spread, changing the appearance of everything. It was not only the appearance of things that had changed but also the perception of things that the mist had changed. The mist made everything appear as moving shadows; disappearing and reappearing in different places and different shapes and sizes than remembered. Everything was distorted.

Suddenly, the dreaded call of the corvuses was heard, piercing the ears of the mēglydaims. They began to sniff the air and growl while looking in all directions, hoping to see the source of the call. Morak stopped and listened intently for any indication of the direction from which the call came. He kneeled down to the ground and waited.

"Caw, caw." The second call might have come from farther away, though Morak knew it could have come from anywhere. Again, the call came, but this time it seemed very close.

"Da corvuses," Morak mumbled under his breath.

Among the few creatures that lived and thrived in the mist were the large, black corvuses. These minacious birds seemed, upon initial observation, more of an aggravation than a real threat, however, there was one flock of them known by everyone in Shuk to be unmatched in their ferocity.

Cackling and harassing any living thing, including the mēglydaims and the gallues, the corvuses made it their life's mission to drive every traveler into oblivion. Once the corvuses found a victim, they followed just out of reach and out of sight, waiting for an opportunity to steal whatever food or items might be carried. They were carnivorous birds who had been seen feeding on the flesh of fallen creatures that had the misfortune of being led astray to their deaths. Working together in large flocks, the intelligent corvuses were skillful deceivers and mockers. Through observation, they were able to learn where food was stored or carried. They watched how a sojourner fastened or tied a bag so that once stolen, they could open even the most secure satchel. As mockers, they could make vocal sounds to fool their victims into thinking that someone was actually talking to them. The corvuses used their wits to lead travelers away from main paths, into dark, empty ravines and high mountain swamps. Once lost in these places, the travelers fell to their deaths or drowned in the murky waters. At other times they were descended upon by a large flock of corvuses who killed and devoured them.

Morak did not move and he held his mēglydaims still and quiet, waiting for the birds to disappear before he continued. He listened for any indication that there were more than just a few of the birds, though he knew that anything he heard might be different than it seemed. After a long spell, Morak stood and continued his journey. With only brief periods of rest, Morak moved with determination and stealth. After three days, Morak smelled the scent of mēglydaims—mēglydaims that were not his own. He froze!

"Ut bae da great Morak! Hmm? Whae ha ye com t'da mist?" The voice was low and raspy with a slight hiss. Morak drew his sword. His two mēglydaims began to growl and fight against their leashes.

"A sae ye stull ha yer mēgs. D'ye raely tink dae cun protect ye haer? Whae ha ye com t'mae realm?"

"Whae d'ye hide yersaelf un da shadows? Buk off! A bae passin!" Morak's voice was forceful and his words were strong and provoking.

Suddenly, a hulking, grotesque gallue appeared out of the shadows. With him were three other gallues and a pack of six mēglydaims chained to their masters. The rabble stood in the way of Morak passing.

"D'ye maen t'hinder mae frum mae cause, Huzesh?"

"A maen t'do wut er A wish, an right now, ut pleases mae t'know whae ye ha com an disgraced mae raelm wit yer stinkin carcass."

"Ye spaek wit maety words, a'lung a'ye ha yer liddle escort b'hin ye. A coward as always; nutin bae changed."

"Wut bae yur purpose, Morak? Whae ha ye com?" Huzesh demanded.

"Uf ye mus know—A gae t'sae Gubrone. Now lut mae pass!"

Huzesh and his small band of gallues and mēgs stood glaring at Morak as if they were not going to allow him to pass. Morak, though, stepped forward with his sword still drawn and pointed at Huzesh's throat. Huzesh would not yield and seemed undeterred by Morak's blade. As Morak moved past him, Huzesh gave him a shove, attempting to provoke Morak to fight, but Morak constrained himself and pushed on.

Huzesh was an insolent, brazen gallue who had become a menace to all the gallues of Shuk, including Gubrone. He chose to do things his own way, even in defiance of Attar. His insolent ethos made him especially dangerous to all in the realm. He refused to answer to anyone and had become a rogue. He had no respect for anything and was known to be violent and inordinately brutal. There were few in the realm that would stand up to him or his gang of ruffians. Nevertheless, Morak was not intimidated nor dissuaded by Huzesh. They had fought ages before, and they both had the scars to remind them. However, the score between them had never been fully settled, especially for Huzesh, who had been deeply wounded in the battle by the vice-like talons of Morak. Wearing three monstrous scars across his face and a lidless white eye that was blinded in the fight, Huzesh's ghoulishly deformed appearance made him especially frightful to look at.

While Huzesh may have been among the worst of rebels, there was no camaraderie between any of the gallues of Shuk. They had no loyalty, appreciation, respect for one another. Distrust ran rampant through all the gallue clans. They were malevolent, constantly trying to harm or ruin, or worse, to kill each other. The only way the arch-gallues could keep order was with fear and unrelenting recompense for disobedience and failure. Failure was met with the highest degree of severity. Even Huzesh was subject to this rule, though he acted as if he was subject to no one.

The rebellion of Huzesh was, however, only a minor inconvenience to Gubrone. Gubrone used the fear that others had of Huzesh to accomplish his purposes. As long as Huzesh kept the way to the valley dangerous to intruders and exiles, he was useful. If the time came that Huzesh was no longer useful, Gubrone would show just how strong and unforgiving he could be; this, Huzesh was very aware of.

Though full of hatred toward each other, Morak and Huzesh possessed common characteristics. They were both especially cruel and ruthless, strong, and skilled, and above all, irreparably depraved. Morak was, however, more controlled in his actions, more submissive to the rule of Attar and to Gubrone. Morak had been subjected to the power of Gubrone and had known the sharpness of his sword; as such, Morak respected Gubrone and his rule. Morak's willingness to serve Gubrone had put him and Huzesh at odds. However, being at odds with each other was the only way that the gallues knew. They were all lawless and defiant, and any appearance of cooperation or submission was only a ruse; their corruption ran deep to their core. Huzesh was one of only a few gallues who did not hide their contempt for all authority, whether for Attar, Gubrone, or of Eloh.

Although he wanted to press Morak into an all-out brawl, Huzesh could not be sure if Morak was on an errand and thus in the direct service of Gubrone or not. He knew that if he was to interfere in a task Gubrone deemed important, Gubrone would hunt him down in retaliation. Though he had nothing more than contempt for Gubrone, he preferred to remain inconsequential to the obstinate ruler of Shuk. Huzesh looked at Morak with threatening eyes. "Wae bae nut done, Morak. Whaer d'ye tink yur gaein. Uf A wished ut, ye an yer mongrel pets wud bae fodder fur mae mēgs."

"Lut mae pass! A ha nutin fur ye or yer creatures."

"Dunna ye tire o'baein Gubrone's ugly liddle shrew, jumpin un doin wut er whim or wanna ee spits frum ee's mouth. Hae d'ut fael baein somon's dakkrah? Runnin haer un dar, aye Gubrone dis, an aye Gubrone thut. Yur pitiful!"

Dakkrahs were weak, subservient creatures, cowardly rodents and scavengers, smelly and diseased. Calling Morak a dakkrah, was one of the most degrading of insults.

The chiding taunt of Huzesh bore deep into Morak's dark spirit, making the incurable rage that consumed every cell of his being, rise into a fury. Nevertheless, Morak understood that this was not the time or the place to fight Huzesh. He pushed down his normal violent response to the challenging words and continued to walk away. However, as he passed, Morak let out a fierce growl that caused Huzesh's mēgs to cower; he and his horde felt the ferocity of the utterance and backed away from him. Morak moved past Huzesh without looking back and stalked into the shadows of the mist.

Huzesh, always having to have the last word, hollered out to Morak, "Wae wull sae ye agan, Morak, but ye mae nut sae us! Bahaha!"

Morak ignored the threatening message. However, he was aware that Huzesh would eventually make his threats real. He was bound to, for if he did not, he would be seen as powerless and become a target for the ruthlessness of other gallues who preyed on weakness and vulnerability. Morak also knew that Huzesh would not be his only opposition; there were a number of others along the way who would challenge him.

The shadows that lurked in every direction became darker and longer and more impenetrable. Morak made a small fire and then a torch, hoping to stave off the approaching blackness, but the willing yet inept light of the torch was quickly overpowered, swallowed up by the blackness. Ghoulish, cloaked apparitions danced in cadence with the lively flames, moving in and out of the darkness as though enraged by the intrusive flames. The strange, haunting noises of the night echoed through the damp mist, groaning and hissing indiscernible, abject utterances. Like a sharp spear, they pierced the mind of Morak. Though he was unafraid, like most who had journeyed into the mist, Morak and the mēglydaims felt the oppression of the ceaseless, hollow cries bound in every suspended droplet of the mist. Their woeful mourning grew stronger and louder and more determined as the ravenous jaws of darkness slowly and dominantly devoured the light.

The long, restless nights in the mist were the most agonizing of the many torments Shuk challenged its inhabitants with. Yet, for Morak, the effects of the mist had never been of much consequence. He was normally immune to its affliction. Nevertheless, when Morak closed his eyes to sleep, the tireless moans penetrated even his mind, evoking horrible visions and dreams that disquieted his dull and hardened heart.

As each sun rose and then set, and the lurid whispers of the night filled his mind, Morak became increasingly disturbed and suspicious. He had never dreamt such things or felt such trouble in his mind or unrest in every part of his being before. He could feel that there was something different about the mist, something inexplicable and yet palpable, as though an ominous, unrelenting presence, a seditious juggernaut had crept into the realm unaware. Each morning, his waking thoughts were consumed by the troubled dreams, and throughout the day, all he could think about was getting over the pass and out from under the mist.

On one of these mornings, Morak awoke to the unsettling sound of the corvuses calling to one another. He had not seen anyone or anything other than stones and fog and an occasional putrid stream for several days and he believed that he was all alone and preferred it that way. Nevertheless, he was not alone and though the wretched black birds had not yet found him, he knew they soon would. He picked up his things and moved quickly through the narrows, hoping to avoid detection, yet, as he rounded the corner of a large block of stone, he found himself face- to-face with one of the corvuses. Immediately, it let out a loud, screeching call.

Morak picked up a stone and threw it at the bird, hitting it in the head and killing it. He quickly reached down and picked it up and then threw it to the mēglydaims who devoured it before it was able to hit the ground. Despite the quickness of his reaction, Morak was too late to keep his presence a secret from the menacing birds. Out of the gray mist, like obsidian hail, many more corvuses flew down to where the call had come from. The raven birds flocked over Morak and the mēglydaims, pecking and clawing at their flesh, swooping down at their heads and attacking their eyes. The cacophony of heckles and screeches echoed loudly through the air, assaulting Morak's hearing with deafening volume. In desperation, Morak began to run up the path and into the mist. The mēglydaims followed and so too did the corvuses. With every hurried stride, Morak took the risk of losing his way in the labyrinth of trails.

Seeing no hope of escape, Morak determined that the best chance they had was to take a stand and fight the relentless birds. He began reaching out and grabbing any of the voracious birds he could and ripping their heads off. Soon, the mēglydaims were clawing and biting at the air trying to kill the corvuses. One by one the corvuses began to fall to the ground until, without reason, they retreated to the rocks surrounding Morak and the mēglydaims. Morak looked around, confused and uncertain. He could see and feel the eyes of the corvuses staring at him, watching him, waiting for him. Not knowing what else to do, Morak wiped the blood from his face and began to walk toward the pass. He was unsure how far he would get before the watchful birds would lose their patience and resume their attack. For the time being, at least, it seemed he and his mēglydaims could continue to the pass.

The corvuses followed their every step, intermittently harassing

Morak and the mēglydaims. Day and night, on and off again, the corvuses terrorized the trio and to his complete consternation, Morak could do little to nothing to impede the incessant torment until, as suddenly as they came, they unexpectedly spread their wings and disappeared into the mist. It could only be predicted by Morak that some other unfortunate being with less fortitude may have become a more interesting target for the corvuses. The absence of the corvuses, though certainly advantageous, was, at the same time, unsettling for Morak, for he had no way of knowing where they went, when they might return, or if they were going to return at all.

Morak stepped-up his pace, pushing himself and the mēglydaims as hard as he could. As another night crept into the mist, Morak and the mēglydaims found a place to rest. With the threat of the corvuses looming large, Morak tried to keep a cautious vigil; however, his eyes were less committed to the task than his mind and slowly submitted to the overpowering hypnosis of the syncopated snores bellowing from the mēglydaims.

At the break of dawn, Morak and the mēglydaims continued toward the pass. It was not long before they came upon the final and most challenging terrain that separated them from Klamata. Even in the mist, Morak recognized the place, an expansive steepening incline burdened with seemingly endless piles of sharp rocks. The field of debris disappeared into the mist, shrouded in shadows, until it was eventually pressed between two enormous walls of rock that led to the pass.

Slowly, Morak and the mēglydaims stepped into the debris field and began the exhausting trek, hand and foot across the inimical expanse. For the whole of the day, they made their way through a sea of stones until, just as the light was fading, they arrived at the base of the couloir. The path was well-worn and the dangers of getting lost were behind them. However, the task of climbing was, in itself, a danger that never diminished. Rather than wait-out the night, Morak continued up; he was determined to reach the pass no matter the risk.

The Pass of Klamata was a narrow saddle between two towering mountain peaks that lay nearly nine-thousand feet high in the clouds. The clouds at the pass never cleared and, most of the time, deep snow covered it over. Only in the summer was the pass open enough for travel. For this reason, few came to the pass during any other season.

It was deep into the night when Morak finally reached the pass. Stepping into the narrow gap between the peaks, he was met by a mighty gust of wind that howled and screamed with force and protest. It hit him square in his chest like a giant hammer and pushed him backwards, as if to throw him from its height. Morak managed to grab hold of a giant boulder and regain his footing. The wind never ceased to blow through the pass. Day and night, the winds of Klamata raged like an angry beast, against every exposed piece of stone and surrounding mountain peak. Fierce and relentless, the wind howled, in deafening, angry outbursts as if shouting objections and trying to escape the chains of bondage. The clouds displayed the rage of the storm filling them with flashing lights accompanied by threatening claps of thunder. Even for a creature as large and fearless as Morak, the winds were overpowering, and the lightning and thunder terrifying. As he moved over the pass and down the steep rocky south face, he fought for every inch of ground he gained. The violent assault of the wind continued until Morak and his mēglydaims crested the pass and began the long descent into the valley. Slowly they escaped the wind's mighty grip and found a place to rest in the rocks.

Below the mist lay the Valley of Souls. Though they had crossed the most dangerous section of the journey, they had yet to descend into the valley. Several thousand feet lay between the pass and the place where the mist gave up its tyrannical reign, making for a long, dangerous, and blind descent on unstable, tricky exposure. The valley side of the pass was rarely clear of clouds and the thickness of them made the way seem hopelessly long and winding with many switchbacks. Many sections of the path seemed to disappear over sheer cliffs and through mounds of jagged stones. All of this was made worse by the constant condensation that accumulated on everything, especially on the rocks, which were wet and covered with lichen, making every step of the utmost consequence. A misstep could be a fatal mistake.

The Valley of Souls was a vast, winding basin surrounded by menacing, jagged mountain peaks that stretched in all directions as far as the eye could see. Hanging above the valley was an undulating gray fog, which spread over the mountains of the valley and the entire basin like an outstretched net which never dissipated.

Morak and the mēglydaims had not rested for more than a day and the end of another day was upon them once again. Morak sought a place out of the mist where he could rest until daylight. Ages before, Morak had discovered and sheltered in a small cave in the rocks a short distance below the pass. However, finding the entrance to it again was proving difficult, for he had never had to find it in the darkness or in the tempest of the wind. Fortunately, a sudden and unexpected glow of diffused moonlight fell upon the mountainside and illuminated the mist just enough for Morak to see the entrance of the cave. "Aha! Dar ye bae! Com mae mēgs, wae bae out o'dis mist fur a while." Morak glanced up to the sky and, for a moment, stood still and stared at the sky as if hoping to see something. Then he turned and quickly moved toward the cave before the fading light disappeared completely.

Morak and the mēglydaims found the cave dark and cold but free of the wind and mist. Each found a place on the floor of the cave to lie down and sleep. However, waiting in the cave was not altogether comforting, for it was not long before he became aware of something mystical and strange at work in the shelter of rock. A strange, almost ethereal quality filled the small cave. Every other time Morak had come to it, he had sensed the same haunting presence but had never understood what it was that he had felt. There, in that small shelter, existed an inexplicable trace of something lost, ancient, and beautiful. Emanating from the rocks was a force that did not overpower, subdue, or subject, but afflicted the encrusted corruption dominating his entire being. It was painful and oppressive, for it reminded him of a time before the great war, before the treachery and betrayal, when he was someone unrecognizable to him now. He had long ago accepted his fate and what he had become. He was immune to guilt, to conscience, and to empathy, but there, in the cave, surrounded by the mist, Morak felt them all.

Morak's anxiety grew with every slowly passing moment spent in the cave. He waited in restless agony for sleep to come, but even sleep was unrestful, for in his dreams came the dreadful memories, haunting his mind. Even though his mēgs were unable to show any kind of affection, as pets might show to their masters, Morak was glad he had them and felt some comfort from their company. At the earliest possible moment, Morak rose and escaped the confines of the cave. He began to descend into the Valley of Souls.

The fog that hung over the valley was the work of Gubrone and the other eleven arch-gallues who ruled Shuk. Ages before, when the first nephesh were sent to Shuk, the first snitch, Norzaaq, brought with him instructions from Attar, and with the instructions, a stone vial containing a colorless potion. Instructed by Attar to find an expansive solitary place with impenetrable borders, the arch-gallues searched the realm of Shuk for many seasons until finally they found a deep valley that was many miles wide and more than three hundred miles long as it wound through a colossal mountainous range deep in Shuk. The Twelve, as the band of arch-gallues were known, found only one point of access into the valley, the Pass of Klamata. The beauty of the undisturbed valley made it a truly hidden gem. However, they had no interest in the valley's beauty. Once in it, they took the vial, sent from Attar, and, as instructed, poured the potion into a large pool of spring water. Over the waters of the pool, they spoke a rune written by Attar. Each of the twelve was ordered to speak the rune. The words of the rune were written in a language known only to the arch-gallues that meant: *"Rise up ye waters and become a shield over this land. Hold captive all the voices and pleas of the nephesh. Forbid their words to leave this Valley of Souls."*

Once The Twelve spoke the rune, they cut themselves and poured their blood into the pool. The Twelve: Gubrone, Tukkir, Unattah, Jabodaan, Sinistradt, Puttinash, Borash, Rutunick, Chiddush, Mootthont, Nernishut, and Zeshkant performed the ritual, setting in motion a cataclysmic event that forever altered the landscape, turning the valley into a supernatural prison for the nephesh. Out of the pool, a column of fog began to rise into the air, spreading across the sky, unfurling in all directions, following the course of the winding valley. The fog moved as if being drawn with cords on every side, stretching from one mountain-bounded extent of the valley to the other until the fog covered the entire valley. Like a tent, it stretched over the whole valley, blocking the sun and stars and moons.

The fog could not be held or felt, yet it was visible and dense, and it was impenetrable to the voices and songs of the nephesh. The fog offered no protection or cover from the elements. It offered no barrier or physical confinement. Differing from the mist, the fog did not cause the flora of the valley to die or the creatures to exodus. It did not block out the light of the sun but seemed only to diffuse it into a soft, yet bright glow that appeared to please most of the living things, plants, and animals and even the nephesh living in the valley.

The fog served a much more insidious purpose, a purpose that gave Attar all the power he needed to rule Tirnan and the sapiens. As long as the nephesh tried to sing their songs, as long as they reminded the sapien of their true selves, of their authentic heritage as the offspring of Amik and friends of Eloh, Attar would never be able to fully control the descendants of Amik, with impunity. To this end, the fog assimilated the voices, messages, and songs of the nephesh. It swallowed every utterance, every plea, every groan, or whisper that the nephesh sent to their sapien, holding every word captive in the billions and billions of bewitched floating molecules.

The voice of the nephesh was not heard in the ears of the sapien, it was heard in their hearts. It came as an intimation meant to remind the sapien of their true nature and self. Attar's malignant deception deluded the minds of the sapiens, circumventing the truth. The grip of his delusion convinced the sapiens that the increase of knowledge and intellect were the only way to enlightenment. The sapien began worshiping their own intelligence and reason, becoming intoxicated with the wine of their own understanding. They became increasingly corrupted and forgot the immortal essence they were meant to know. The void between the sapien and nephesh had become a chasm too great to cross—an impenetrable emptiness.

The nephesh did not realize that their voices were unheard. They could not know that the songs and pleas and memories they sent to the hearts of the sapien were being intercepted and held in a fog. Attar had utterly severed the bond between the sapien and the nephesh.

Beneath the fog, the valley lay captive and isolated from the world outside. With the canopy in place, the gallues set about the task of gathering all the nephesh. One by one, the nephesh were hunted down, captured, and hauled into the valley, where they were confined unbound. It was not the fog that kept them in the valley, however; it was the power of the rune, of deception and fear, and the cruelty of the gallues.

As Morak began descending into the fog, he could hear the voices of the nephesh calling out. Voices multiplied by the innumerable sum of all the nephesh, multiplied by all the ages of their captivity cried out in the vapor of the fog. Landing on his black, scaly skin like dew on grass, the droplets of the fog were laden with immortal words. Some of the words were ancient, sent ages before to sapiens that were now dead. Others were new and fresh, sent out that very day. The multiplicity of voices made them completely indistinguishable, becoming one constant, loud roar, like giant waves crashing upon the shore, a deafening cacophony of unintelligible utterances. Yet, not a single sound escaped the fog; they remained collected, every voice, every cry, and every word suspended, bound, and captive.

Below the fog, the vast expanse of the valley swelled with the voices, songs, and cries of the nephesh, which rose endlessly. The amplitude of sound, emitting from the vociferous chorus, filled the air between the valley floor and the ceiling of fog.

The response of all creatures and creation was unanimous and ebullient. The Valley of the Souls teamed with life and beauty, though in truth, it was a prison. The nephesh possessed so much life in themselves, and in their song that their oppressors were unable to inhibit or disturb the opulent life-force that infused every fiber of their being. This life force emanated from the heart of Eloh himself. It flowed through the essence of every living thing, but especially through the nephesh.

Gubrone lived in a cave located high above the valley in a lonely, solitary mountain. Deep in the core of the mountain, Gubrone had made a lair for himself, insulated from the song of the nephesh. The mountain of Gubrone stood at the eastern end of the valley surrounded by rolling hills and meadows. The way to the mountain cave was by a broad dirt path along a stream. The path was used heavily by the gallues. It was a difficult, daylong hike through a robust deciduous forest to reach the entrance of the cave.

The nephesh lived in the woods throughout the valley. However, the woods along the path were uninhabited, lonely, and dark. Abandoned by the nephesh, these woods had become a stronghold for the gallues who served Gubrone in the valley. They were the taskmasters, vial brutes, whose sole purpose it was to oppress the nephesh. The snitches of Shuk also inhabited the woods along the path. However, the song of the nephesh had driven even these loathsome creatures into the mountain lair. In effect, the gallues and snitches were themselves, captives of the valley. It was for this reason that gallues, like Morak, chose to live outside the valley and hunt the rogue nephs, as they were called by the gallues.

Morak left his mēgs in a cave and descended out of the fog. Then, he heard familiar voices. As he approached them, he recognized the figures. Standing in the path were the four gallues he had sent into the Plain of Haemus. Immediately a wave of fury overtook Morak; he was enraged that they were traveling in the Valley of Souls. He had ordered them not to return to the valley before receiving instructions from him. As he stood glaring at the four factious gallues, one of the four, Lyzop, the apparent ringleader, spoke indignantly, "Ahh, uf ut ain't Gubrone's liddle dakkrah."

Then the other three gallues took turns adding their insults. "Aye. Wae faered ye maet a baen taken by da she-neph thut kulled Jekkid's mēgs."

"Yeah, bun waitin fur ye. Knew ye wud com soon aenuff!"

"Mubae ye shud a sunt da weapon wit us, wae cud ha brung ut haer sooner!"

With the speed of a wild cat, Morak lunged upon the apparent leader of the four. He seized Lyzop by his throat as he tackled him to the ground; his long black talons sunk into the skin of Lyzop's neck, drawing blood. "A told ye nut t'return, nut t'return t'da valley afore A sunt instructions!"

Of course, Lyzop could not answer Morak because of the stranglehold that was crushing his throat. Eyes wide with shock, he desperately flailed about, attempting to break Morak's grip on his neck. The other three gallues were so unprepared for Morak's attack that they could not react before Lyzop was in peril. If they had acted in his defense after Morak's vice-like grip was already around Lyzop's neck, Morak would have quickly snapped it. Morak commanded the three, "Buk off, or yer liddle frun wull bae u meal fur mae mēgs. Dae ha nut tasted da blood o'u gallue un u lung while!"

Morak's warning was not taken lightly and the three backed away from Morak and Lyzop. Morak loosened his iron grip on Lyzop's neck and a stream of blood began to ooze from the wounds. "Whae ha ye com t'da valley?" Morak growled.

"Wae received word frum Gubrone. Ee commanded all da gallues t'com." squeaked Lyzop.

"Whae wud Gubrone command ye buk t'da valley?"

"A dunna know, wae ony jus arrived. Ain't ye haerd?"

One of the other gallues spoke out with a cautiously sarcastic tone trying to take Morak's attention away from Lyzop. "Wae run unto u frun o'yers ulung our wae. Ee tol us t'com."

"A frun? Wut frun? A ha no fruns."

"Huzesh! Bahaha!"

"Ee bae no frun o'maen!" roared Morak.

Morak let Lyzop up, but he did not offer an apology or a hand, and the other three who were with him offered no help either. "Yur u rogue group o'derelict dakkrahs!" Morak growled as he pushed his way past the three and continued to the Cave of Gubrone.

As he passed, Lyzop laughed and then yelled out to him. "Bahaha! Wae bae saein ye, Morak, Gubrone's bikkja!"

On his journey, Morak noticed there were many snitches and gallues in the valley whom he had often encountered throughout the realm as he hunted the nephesh. The presence of so many suggested that something serious was happening in the realm. Morak could not remember the last time so many of them were together in one place. He sensed a strange uneasiness lingering in the air. All the while, as he journeyed below the fog toward Gubrone's lair, he heard and felt the celestial songs of the nephesh which filled the air. They were singing new songs he had never heard before, songs of hope and deliverance which were also played on the ancient wooden dukwán. The piercing sounds of the dukwáns were notes laden with the ancient melodies of Pardis.

When Morak finally reached the Cave of Gubrone, there were already a host of gallues gathered in the main hall of the cave. Among them were The Twelve, which included Gubrone. There were also many snitches and seeing them in Gubrone's lair further impressed upon Morak the mystery of the situation. As he made his way through the crowd toward Gubrone, Morak could hear the whispers of the gallues around him, but from their whispers he could only hear one word clearly, the one word that was never spoken by the gallues of Shuk: "Eloh." Since the death of Amik, the presence of Eloh had not been felt in Shuk. Morak thought about the weapon in his bag. He wondered if it could have anything to do with the rumors.

In the hall, the arrangement of the gallues and snitches was quite predictable. The gallues stood in clusters, gathered by clans under the rule of each of The Twelve. The snitches, however, with neither clans nor alliances, gathered apart from the gallues. Gubrone and the other eleven arch-gallues stood in the center of the hall occupied in a very intense and obviously heated conversation. There was much yelling and pushing and arguing between them.

Gubrone looked across the hall and saw Morak approaching. He quickly stepped away from the argument. It was known to many that Morak served directly under Gubrone and was his primary commander of the gallues. Though this was known, it was not altogether respected, which is why many of the gallue hunters referred to Morak as Gubrone's bikkja, a derogatory term used to describe the wild female dogs that roved the lowlands. Gubrone motioned to Morak and the two of them stepped aside from the many others to speak privately. Their departure was not unnoticed, for snitches and gallues saw them leaving the hall. Many who saw were spies for the other arch-gallues and tried to find ways to listen in. The snitches, who were especially capable of espionage, paid close attention to where they had gone.

Gubrone's demeanor was obviously aggressive and Morak could not help feeling like he was a convicted criminal waiting for his punishment. As Gubrone closed in on Morak, Morak paused and fearfully and respectfully waited. Gubrone stepped up to Morak with his chest puffed out and his eyes sharp and piercing. Softly and yet demandingly fierce, Gubrone spoke to Morak. "Wut d'ye know o'des rumors, un whae ha ye nut tol mae?"

"Know? A know nutin! Dis bae da firs A haerd o'thum."

"Uf ye know nutin thun whae ha ye com?"

"A ha foun somting ye naed t'sae. A ha baen travlin fur mor thun three moons t'brang ut t'ye." Morak reached into his shoulder bag and pulled from it the weapon that had been discovered. "Wae foun dis un da marshes o'Atramentous. Ut bae som kind u tool or weapon." Morak offered it to Gubrone with cautious hands.

Gubrone looked skeptically at the ice axe; he studied it, then seized it with his own hands. "An whaer dud ye fin dis?"

"Unner u trae un da forest."

"Hmm?" Gubrone continued to study the ice axe with a puzzled look and a furrowed brow. As much as he was interested, Gubrone was also suspicious and Morak could feel his suspicions directed at him through his dark, cruel eyes. Morak could feel the tension mounting between them. He knew the moment he had dreaded, when he would have to explain to Gubrone about the dead mēglydaims, was now unavoidable. Morak lowered his gaze to the ground and began to explain in a timid, low voice, "Wae waer huntin da she-neph. Wae tracked er t'da dark valley. Wun wae sunt da mēgs t'hunt er, ony two com bak. Da others nae'er returned. Wae foun thum dead. Thut bae whaer Lyzop foun da weapon."

"So, da she-neph ha kulled two mur o'mae precious pets, un ye maent t'kaep ut frum mae?!" Gubrone squeezed Morak's throat in his tight fist. He lifted Morak off the ground. His eyes turned black with vengeance and he growled with a deep, vicious tone. "Dunna trae t'deceive mae agan! Yur expendable!" He viciously threw Morak to the ground.

"Uf dis bae u weapon, thun wae definitely ha u forner un shuk."

"Wae foun no sign o'one," Morak whimpered.

"Ye mus return t'da marsh. Ye mus fin da one thut los dis, un brang um t'mae!" Gubrone commanded.

"But hae? Dae waer nowhaer t'bae foun. An now ut ha baen nearly four moons. Dar wull bae no trace o'thum now, no wae t'track um." Morak couldn't control his whining tone.

Gubrone began to pace back and forth as he thought about the improbability of finding any sign of the one to whom the weapon belonged. "Thun whaer cud ee ha gone? Whaer could ee fin shelter an safety frum da mēgs un snitches? Ee mus bae foun! Ye mus return t'da dark valley un fin eem!"

Morak tried to explain the steps he had taken to Gubrone without looking up at him. An evasive, hesitant tone was evident in his words, suggesting that he was less-than- enthusiastic about the prospect of the new venture. "Jekkid, waer headed up toward da Pass o'Borak, lookin fur ony sign o'da forner. But, ut waer snowin an ut bae doubtful dar bae any sign t'follow, now."

"Snowing, on da pass?"

"Aye. Un da upper marsh."

"Snowin, un da valley an un da marshes? Da pass o'Borak has had no snow for muny ages."

"Aye, but ut bae jus snow," Morak spoke nonchalantly.

"B'caus o'Amik!" Gubrone exploded.

"Amik? Amik bae dead."

"Aye, but da last tam ut snowed at da pass o'Borak, Amik came t'da realm o'Shuk!"

Morak felt confused and frustrated. He could not understand Gubrone's interest in Amik. Nor could he understand what Amik had to do with the foreigner or the weapon.

Gubrone focused on Morak, this time with less threatening eyes. He walked up to him until they were chest to chest, then he leaned in and whispered into Morak's ear, "Wae need t'gae t'Pelah, da Cave o'Pelah, whaer Amik un Livia lie. Ut bae hae un da mountains above Gershom."

Morak was puzzled even more by Gubrone's directions, for he knew of the cave and he knew of Gershom, and it was forbidden for the gallues to go there.

Gubrone continued with his instructions, "Mubae wae cunna enter, but wae cun sit un wait, un watch. Take yer mēgs un u snitch. Gae t'Gershom immediately. A mus know uf Eloh ha com t'Shuk afore ee discovers da Valley o'Souls un wut wae ha done t'da nephs."

"Eloh wud nae'er com alone. Wud ee? Da kerolus army mus bae wit eem." Morak presumed.

"Nae, A ha muny spies watchin frum da high mountains. Dae would ha saen thum. Uf ut bae Eloh, ee ha com alone."

"Wut gud bae one again Eloh? A naed mur!"

"Yur u fool, Morak, tae muny wull draw attention! Ye mus gae quietly; spy on Gershom. Uf ye fin Jekkid un da others, take thum wit ye. Bae A clear?"

"Aye."

"An Morak, uf ye fin onyting else, bring ut t'mae yersaelf," Gubrone firmly ordered.

"Aye."

Gubrone turned and walked toward the hall where there was a loud commotion. He looked back at Morak. "Afta A ha spoken, gae, an gae swiftly."

Gubrone entered the hall and stepped onto a large, round table in the middle of the room. He raised his voice to a loud roar that silenced everyone. As he began to speak, Morak entered the back of the hall where the snitches had gathered. He needed to find one that he could take with him. Most of the snitches knew of Morak by reputation, and none of them wanted to go. They knew he was cruel and demanding and that he was as likely to cut off their head as to do anything else. The snitches tried to exit the hall before Morak was able to reach them, but one of the snitches, a young snitch who did not know much about Morak, was left standing alone. Morak reached out, grabbed the snitch by its long, translucent hair, and pulled it to himself. "Ye, wut bae yer nam?"

"Loham," he screeched while squirming to get away.

"Well, Loham, ut looks lik ut bae yer lucky day. Com wit mae, wae ha u journey t'b'gun."

Jaroh / Kerolus

Chapter IX
Morning Memories

A strange, hard object pushed against Ross's right temple. He tried to move his head just enough to find relief from the sharp discomfort, but despite his efforts to prolong the blissful, torpid moments, his dreamy, unconscious mind could not resist or ignore the persistent prodding of the conscious physical pain as it pulled at his lazy eyelids.

Lifting his head from the backpack that had been his pillow, Ross felt around trying to determine what it was that demanded such immediate attention. He expected a rock or stump to be the culprit but quickly realized it was something in the backpack itself. He did not want to sit up or do anything that would chase the sleep away, which lingered around his tired body and mind like an overprotective mother, so he remained lying on the ground, fumbling with the pack in search of the object.

Unexpectedly, Eve's camera tumbled out of the backpack as he pulled his hand out. At first, he was not sure what it was, because it was still quite dark, but he soon realized. Holding it in his hand, he fought a strong urge to turn it on. He hesitated because he was afraid to see, with his eyes, an image that had only been displayed in his memory. It had been a long time since he had last looked at the photos saved on the memory card. He remembered the suffering and sorrow he had tried to push behind him over the past several weeks. He was not sure he wanted to rouse the cruel anguish or stir up the immutable memories, but something deep in his heart would not let him put the camera away. He laid there on the ground on his back looking at the dark sky while he held it in his hand.

He felt something else under his ear, something soft, but solid. He reached up and took hold of a small, leather-bound book. It was Eve's journal. In one hand he held the camera and in the other the journal. He held them close to his chest and imagined, just for a moment, that he was holding Eve. He breathed in deeply and held the breath for a long time before he finally exhaled slowly, feeling the breath course through his throat as it rushed out of his lungs. Tears began to well in his eyes and, with each deep breath in and then slowly out, he managed to control his emotions and hold the tears back.

Ross turned the camera on. The photo of them together lit up the darkness around him. He stared at the photo through tearful eyes, which softened the illuminated picture, erasing the many details and surrounding objects, leaving only two smiling, happy faces. He had forgotten how much his life was brightened by Eve, by her inner light. He looked through one hundred photos of their trip. He laughed aloud at a few and cried at others and took comfort from the memories.

The battery was almost drained, so Ross turned the camera off. He lay in the darkness remembering. He felt a strange sense of peace. It had been several weeks since the accident, but somehow it felt like ages had passed. Ross did not like the thought that something so painful could so easily become a memory, that someone so special could become little more than a digital image stored in a tiny black camera. He hated the pain of loss, but he hated more the numbness of absence and the forgetfulness of time. He did not want to forget or to stop feeling either the love or the terrible sense of loss. Both emotions tied his heart to her; she was his first true love and moving on did not feel like the right thing to do. Ross lay in the darkness, and in those precious moments, realized that for the first time in his life, he had found, in Eve, something that few only find once in a lifetime; he had found true, unconditional love. The epiphany made his heart ache, for what he now understood, he also could not recover.

Ross laid awake in the dark until a single ray of sunlight broke across the dark alpine landscape. Striking the tops of the mountains with sudden, unexpected radiance, it showered the dark solitude with warm, golden light. Ross had seen the sunrise many times in his life, but there was something transcendent about the way the sun rose over Shuk; it was beyond description. It was as if the new day was opening a doorway into a room that had never seen the light before. Each day felt as if light was falling on creation for the very first time as if a newborn world was being immaculately revealed to unexpecting eyes. Ross was reminded that through Eve's eyes, each day was as new as the very first day. She saw the world through idealistic eyes, expectant and enthusiastic. As he lay watching the dramatic event unfolding before him, poetic words began to resound in his mind. They were not his own: they were the words Eve had so eloquently recited on the morning of her death. As the sun had risen over the horizon on that fateful day, Eve had experienced an epiphany. Spell-bound by the glorious exhibit of daylight's waking, Eve's voice began reciting lyrical prose in response to the wonders of morning's first blush. He hoped that she had written them in the journal. As the light descended onto the meadow where he and the others lay, he held Eve's journal in his hand. Hesitantly, he opened the leather cover and flipped to the last page Eve had written on. At the top of the page were words in French: *"ne m'oubliez pas"* meaning *"don't forget me"*. "There it is," Ross said to himself. He then began to read:

Upon the break of day as twilight and fog dance together and the dew glimmers with radiant iridescence, a moment unexpected, unpredicted unfolds, like the bloom of heather.

In this quiet unassuming instant, life's tragedy and the world's brokenness are eclipsed, overthrown by the sweet and uncorrupted residue of a new world.

It is a span so slight, so momentary that consciousness rarely observes. A twinkle in the eye of God, then gone like breath.

Who has seen this moment, has touched, and been touched by it? The seasons of life are now lived beyond this subtle alpenglow, beyond the admiration of beauty, beyond the simplicity of dawn, beyond the quiet resonance of first blush.

The day is born with a burdensome weight, so immediate any hesitation, pause or reflection is overcome by the tyranny of chaos.

Freedom is but a dream from which we have awoken. Hope is a pill, swallowed with thirst. We would escape into the quiet, into the serene place of rest, yet, we have chosen, we now live beyond our deepest and most desperate longings, beyond our true selves, beyond veritable living, beyond remembering. We ache, we long, we suffer a deep pain.

Between the fractured union of darkness and light, in the convergent mist, colliding wonders, morning and day, morning and night compete, admiring eyes swelling wet, tears born of the soul. None will see who do not look yet looking alone will not let them see. The mystery of beauty transcendent, eternal, words beyond language whispered with voices that have no mouths to those who will listen.

Those who will come, come empty. Come to the beginning, to the rising of a virgin sun. Look for the first time upon the day, the new day. See it rise, new, hear its many small voices, feel its many, many bodies. Allow, for the first time, your heart to see.

See for the first time, resplendent shafts shyly revealed over spired earth, floating droplets of morning's deliquescence.

A displayed wonder, a miracle surreptitiously arranged, a divine intervention, a gift.

Every morning!

"I think I understand," Ross whispered. As he lay watching the break of the new day, he saw, unfolding before his eyes, what it was that must have inspired the poetry in Eve's heart. He saw, in Shuk, the beauty and wonder that comes only in fleeting moments. He saw the sweet residue of a world that had been new and unexplored, unmolested, untamed, and the brokenness of his own heart and his own world was, for those few moments, eclipsed and forgotten. Ross witnessed the first blush; he reached out and touched it and it touched him back. In every word and every syllable, Eve had captured the essence of a moment that, until that very moment, he had never known. He felt life caressing him, healing him. For a long time, he lay with no other intention but to absorb the moments that felt so full of life and so full of Eve. He felt her with him, holding him, loving him; he remembered how it felt to hold her.

He turned back to the page before and began to read. Her words continued to speak to him in the way that only Eve could. He knew that these were her private thoughts and that she had not intended for them to be read by anyone else, but they were the only thing he had left of her, except for the pictures in the camera:

Tomorrow we begin the climb that we've been working so hard to get ready for. I don't know if it's just me or what, but I'm still afraid of this place. I'm trying not to let Ross know, but I'm not sure that I'm hiding it very well.

I feel edgy and uptight. This is the hardest thing that I've ever done. Maybe I should have never come.

Ross was deeply overcome by guilt. He had noticed that she was uptight and edgy but did not want to take the chance that she would back out; forcing him to abandon his quest, it was too late for that. So, he acted aloof and indifferent, thinking that everything would be simply fine. A sick feeling came over him as he thought about his selfishness and greed, greed for something he could not own, greed for a prize that would cost him everything. The realization that he was truly responsible for her death washed over him like ice water, making every part of his being chill and convulse with deep penetrating regret and sorrow. He had always known that mistakes happen when you go too far, and he had led Eve and Psang too far, too hard, and for too long. Nevertheless, he had made himself forget the pain of their deaths. The loss of his love had overridden the reality of his guilt. He had been broken-hearted over losing her, but until reading the journal, he had not faced himself or his inner demons.

Ross desperately wanted to tell Eve that he was sorry, but how does one say they're sorry to the dead? The chance for apologies had passed. Part of him longed for absolution. He ached for her to tell him, "It's ok. I forgive you," but he knew that would never happen. The poison of guilt would only abate with time, leaving behind a ravished, sickened shell of a man. Yet, within the voiceless utterances of written intimations, Ross began to find undeserved absolution, resonating, not so much from the words themselves, but through the heart and soul and the love of the one who had written them. The power of Eve's love for him was transcendent, eclipsing time and space, life and death and could be felt in her words.

Ross flipped back through some of the earlier entries. The pages fell open on the entry written the night they had reached the small motel in Pokhara:

We have finally reached Nepal and out the window in front of me, I can see the mountain that Ross and I will soon climb. I'm afraid. I haven't told Ross, though. I just can't seem to shake this feeling in my heart that we shouldn't be taking this journey, that this mountain is dangerous. Ross tells me that everything will be just fine, but I can see it in his eyes; he is afraid, too. I don't think he is afraid of the climb but of the risk of climbing a forbidden mountain, of the unknown. We have to keep everything a secret which is so difficult. I wish we were climbing a different mountain.

The trip here has been a test of our relationship and of our resolve.

There has been nothing easy about the journey. It kind of seems as if something opposes us, for each step seems to come with resistance and great effort. If I were superstitious, I would believe that the gods were against us. There is a strange feeling I keep having, and as we get closer and closer to the mountain, the feeling grows stronger and stronger.

Something terrible is about to happen.

I hope I will start feeling at peace, that my fears will go away, and I will begin to enjoy the journey. This is a land of legends and myths. It's filled with people of deep religious beliefs and superstitions, and I feel as if I'm missing something. It's hard to be rational amid so much mysticism. I imagine that I'm just being silly, that I'm letting my mind play tricks on me. I hope that's all it is. I'm surprised by my uncertainty; I have never felt so uncertain of anything as I feel now about being here.

Ross was beginning to realize just how driven he had been, driven into blindness by his ambition and need to prove himself. All his life he had been trying to find himself, to be whoever it was that he thought he was supposed to be. However, he had never found it, and neither had those who were meant to help him. His father was an irascible, depraved man. To call him a father was pejorative to the title.

In trying to find his way into manhood and escape the childish notions of life and love, Ross depended on no one. He wanted to be strong and self-reliant. He wanted to prove to everyone, but mostly to himself, that he needed no one, ever. He pushed himself to do things that others would not do, just to prove to himself that he could. It was not that he was fearless like his friend Daniel; Ross was always afraid, but he hid his fear, disguising it under layers of pretense, allowing others to mistake fear for caution.

As he lay reading, the reality of his obsessive behavior began to set in like a weight, like a massive cold stone, crushing him, breaking every illusion of strength he had hidden behind. Images of his life paraded through his mind: images of a quiet boy who was afraid, of an adolescent, caught up in the throes of rebellion, lashing out against authority figures, defiant and angry, and of a young man filled with bitterness and jealousy, despising everyone else because they had something he could only dream of. He knew he was messed up; he knew that there were things about him he did not want others to know. Ross had always known he was selfish, but he had never truly realized just how fractured and wounded he was, nor had he understood the depth of his pain until that very moment.

The memory of Daniel falling to his death forcefully invaded his mind.

The memory was not welcome. Ross wanted to think about something else, but his mind would not be distracted. With tears welling in his eyes, he fought through the emotions of sorrow and loss, yet his hardest fight was against guilt. He had pushed Daniel to his death, not that he physically pushed him, but it was his fault. It was something he had told no one. He was the one responsible for anchoring the rope to the wall of the mountain. He was the one who had pushed Daniel to move faster even though Daniel was tired and hurting from an earlier fall. He knew Daniel was not at his best that day, that besides being tired and bruised, Daniel was sick and not thinking as clearly as he should have been. Ross knew that he should have taken the lead, that he should have inspected the harness, and that he should have let Daniel rest more. He knew, but the contempt and utter resentment that had borne a hole into his heart, leaving behind a void of compassion and empathy, drove him to carelessness, to neglect, and ultimately, to accidental complicity.

Ross was not blind to his brokenness. He knew that he, like his father, was responsible for so many broken and wounded hearts. He made it hard for others to love him. Deep inside, Ross hated himself. He could hardly stand to look in the mirror because of the inner contempt that he bore for the image reflected back at him. He blamed himself for every awful thing that had ever happened in his life. Inwardly self-deprecating, resentful, and often filled with hatred, Ross's heart had grown cold, indifferent, and even cruel at times. Ross was tormented by all these things, but never by anything more than his parents' indifference and abandonment of him. It cast a ruinous shadow over him that he could not escape from. For a moment, Ross wanted to close Eve's journal. The memories elicited were too painful. Even if he could remember the good and beautiful things she brought into his life, he could not escape himself and his guilt. Nevertheless, there was something more happening in those fleeting moments as he lay on the grass in the early morning sun. He felt the pain and he felt a growing ecstasy in his inner self. It was as if a struggle between two forces was fighting inside of him. He had run, emotionally and physically, from his pain and guilt for most of his life, but now, something held him in this moment and would not let him turn away. As if standing in front of a mirror, he faintly recognized the reflection of the person he had never known how to be. It was not a mirage or an exaggeration but an honest, unedited, unmasked revelation. Ross saw, for the first time, what Eve and others saw: a strong but tender, unpretentious man, worn and shaped by the gritty coarseness of life.

Blurred by teary eyes, the words of Eve's journal began to do more than lay as ink on paper, they began to speak to his heart like a voice calling out to a man in prison, calling him out of his darkness and into the daylight, trying to rescue him:

We are just one day away from the summit. I have never been so high in my life, but it's been tough. I'm afraid I might have altitude sickness . . . been feeling really bad. I haven't told Ross or Psang. They would be really disappointed if we had to turn back now. I'll just have to keep going. Ross seems different, quieter, more distant. Maybe it's just how he is when he climbs, or maybe it's that we're never alone. Sometimes I wonder if he really loves me or not. He says he does, but sometimes I'm not sure. There have been some real rocky patches along the way in our relationship, yet, I'm more persuaded than ever that he is the man for me. He's not perfect, but he is good. I can see something deep down in him that makes me almost adore him. He makes it difficult sometimes, but I hope he knows how much I love him. Even though it's been challenging, I'm so happy we're doing this together.

Reading her final entry, Ross felt truly guilty for how he had treated Eve. Knowing how deeply and sincerely she had loved him was distressing. In one way, he felt that he had not deserved to have such a beautiful person in his life. In another way, he felt as though he was a fraud and that Eve had fallen in love with someone she really had not known. In still another way, a way which eclipsed everything else, Ross felt saved by the knowledge of Eve's love. He felt saved from the tormenting inner voices that constantly harassed his thoughts. The power of that salvation came like radiant light falling on morning dew. The glimmer of hope sparkling within the darkness of his empty soul began to warm the frozen core of his being. "I wish I had loved you better," Ross whispered quietly.

Floating aimlessly down through the air, like countless tiny dancers, light, wistful flakes of snow fell to the ground. Ross had not noticed them until one landed squarely on the tip of his nose. Its cold touch exhumed his pensive thoughts from the depths of his mind, coercing him back to reality. He opened his eyes to see the soft, delicate flakes lazily ambling through the air as they descended from a singularly amassing cloud above him. He did not want to lose the moment with Eve. He tried closing his eyes, hoping to go back to that place in the open fields with her, but his mind would not let him. His senses began to distract him from his thoughts.

A sweet, ethereal aroma swept over him, drawing him even further from his tender vision. Ross turned his head and saw the white blooms of snowpetal growing all around. He sat up slowly, closing Eve's journal. The light of the early morning sun showered the landscape with beautiful alpenglow that turned the knoll where he and the others were resting into a mystical paradise. The grass he had slept on was white with snowpetal. The trees were in bloom, dotted with red, white, and lavender flowers. If Ross had not seen it with his own eyes, he would have thought it just a dream. Everything was blooming and at the same time, it was snowing. It was as if every element, every blade of grass, every leaf on the trees, every cloud, hill, and mountain wanted to show off its resplendent grandeur.

In the quiet glow of morning's unveiled nakedness, the silence was overcome with the piercing resonance of nature's voiceless intonation. Amid the eruption of organic opulence, Ross saw a woman adorned in white, standing motionless under the flower-burdened boughs of an ancient tree. He wondered how long she had been standing there, how long she had watched him and the others. He felt, in a strange, uncertain way, that he had seen her before but struggled to remember where or when. *Why?* he wondered to himself. *Why does she seem so familiar?*

Ross's memory labored to exhume the buried relics of the not-so-distant past, to uncover a mystery that hung on the precipice of his thoughts and dreams. Eve, all he could remember was Eve. She had come to him on the mountain. He had seen her, standing over him in the blowing snow. She had called out to him, she had touched his face, she had saved him from certain death. She was the woman in the white dress, reaching out to him as he hung on the rope, dangling in the cold black, waiting to die. She was the vision that came to his mind, but his mind refused to let him believe that the apparition that stood in the distance could be her. He struggled with the memories that came to the surface, for in them he saw what he could not believe was possible. He knew that the memories of Eve, of what had happened before, had to be an illusion, a dream. Eve was dead. Nevertheless, the woman in white reminded him of her. She could not have been Eve, though he wondered, *Could she have?* "Eve?" Her name escaped his lips, but as soon as it did, he denied it. "No, it can't be."

He knew it could not be her, not now and not then. Every rational instinct he possessed resisted any scenario to the contrary. He knew it wasn't her because he had seen her fall, he had looked into her desperate eyes, he had heard her screams penetrating the darkest blackness of the night, and he had watched her disappear into that same blackness. He had lived with the sharp memories of that night; he knew that what he had seen at the end of that frozen rope, was a hallucination, brought to life by hypothermia and fatigue. He knew it could not be Eve.

Ross wondered if he was dreaming, if all that he had been seeing and hearing was merely another illusion of sleep. Yet he knew, there and then, that he was awake, that what he had been feeling and sensing, as the sun rose over the mountains, was no dream. He questioned whether or not he had been dreaming that night back on the mountain. If he had been awake, then maybe the woman that he saw back then was real. Confused and uncertain, Ross stood to his feet. He expected the figure in white to disappear, but she did not disappear. He stared at her for a long time. He allowed a small flame of hope to burn in his heart, the faintest ember of ardor to warm the cold hardness of his reality. She was too far away for him to see her face; he began to walk toward the tree where she stood. Again, he expected her to suddenly vanish, but she stood motionless as he drew near. His heart began to beat in rapid, heavy succession. He began to breathe as if he could not catch his breath, almost hyperventilating. A clammy sweat began to form on his face and in the palms of his hands. He moved slowly toward her, refusing to release her from his eyes for fear that he might lose sight of her.

"Eve, is that you?" he called out in a hushed, expectant tone. There was no reply. Ross took one slow step after another toward her. He was still questioning his consciousness, wavering between confidence and uncertainty. He had had many dreams since the summit, and every one of them felt very real. He expected to hear the voice of Eve telling him to wake up as she had the other times, but there was no voice, no words—only silence. For a moment, Ross paused; he stopped and looked hard at the woman. He squinted his eyes, blinked then rubbed them with his fingers, trying to be sure he was actually seeing what he thought he was seeing. "Who . . . who are you? Why won't you answer?"

The figure in the white turned and began to walk away into the woods.

"Wait! Don't go! Please, don't go!" Ross began to quicken his pace so he could reach her before she was gone. Nevertheless, she continued to walk away. As she was walking, she turned back and looked at him, as if to lure him. Ross could not help himself; he followed her into the woods, though part of him tried to resist, urging him to turn back. He could not turn away; he had to know who she was. Transfixed on her, Ross followed as if there was an invisible cord tying him to her like a leash.

Deeper and deeper into the woods she led him. Snowpetal began blooming out of the ground, growing up through the tall, grassy floor of the forest. The ancient trees erupted in budding flowers. The whole Delphian scene was beautiful—the mysterious woman in white, the snowpetal, the flowering trees, the light flakes of snow drifting down from the sky; it was a beautiful, ethereal moment.

A faint sound came into Ross's ears, a sound that, at first, he could not discern. As he followed the woman in white, the sound grew louder. Finally, Ross realized that it was the sound of a waterfall pouring over the edge of the precipice and landing in a deep pool just down the hill from where he was standing. The woman in white approached the pool and stopped. Ross could see a long train of water falling down the side of a high cliff; the white liquid ribbon flowed into a crystal pool that hugged the rocky face of the cliff. A turbulent white mist rose steadfastly from the pool's surface where the falls collided with the peaceful, still waters.

Ross halted his pursuit. He stood, hypnotized by the fairness of the sights and sounds and mystery of the place, but especially by the woman in white. Slowly, he began to move toward her. She stood, motionless, patient, and silent for a long time and then sat down on what appeared to be a stone bench that lay at the water's edge. Ross looked around at the secret meadow which teamed with life and beauty in all directions. Slowly he surveyed the landscape, studying every ornament of nature and becoming absorbed by the endless array of color and texture and diversity, imprinted by every sight and sound, as if he were a blank page, receiving the inky markings of some master author.

Ross felt as if he were suspended between reality and a dream. The ethereal beauty of the moment, juxtaposed against the frightening and dangerous reality of his circumstance, hung in his mind; opposing forces were vying for dominance. In those moments, however, the beauty overcame the darkness, and Ross's heart was lifted into an empyrean sphere. Transcending the common elements and known physical restraints and dangers, he felt himself drawn, as if by unseen cords, into a realm beyond his mind's ability to imagine. Ross felt life in ways that he had never experienced before, incessant life, coursing through every element and every being, reaching out to him, touching him, pulling him as if he were a man sleeping and life was calling him to awaken.

Ross remembered the voice of Eve calling out to him; he remembered her words, *"Ross, wake up"*, and for the first time, he began to understand something he had not before. The vision of Eve, calling out to him, reaching out and touching his face, bringing him back to life, was more than helping him survive, more than helping him get off the mountain and back home. He remembered how it felt when the vision touched him, how life pushed into his being, forcing itself on him, against his will. He wanted to die, but life refused to let him go. Life was showing itself to him again, calling him to wake up and live.

The sound of the water falling into the pool filled the meadow with harmonic, enchanting music that echoed off the hard, stone wall of the cliff, rolling through the meadow like the undulating waves of the ocean reaching out to the shore. Unexpectedly, a melodic, breathy tone began to fill the air in perfect accord with the already-symphonic eloquence of the elements. Ross turned back to see the woman playing a strange wooden flute whose voice poured over his troubled mind like soothing, warm sunlight on a cold spring morning. The music of the flute was unlike any Ross had ever heard. Its voice was not merely notes played on a lifeless instrument, but was words spoken from the mouth of a spirit, from the heart of a living soul. Reaching deep into his being, coursing through his thoughts and emotions, through his senses and imagination, the inarticulate voice of the flute spoke with raw, unedited determination. Every note transformed into a palpable, transcendent life-force, conducting through every molecule of air and vapor, touching anything alive with immortal quintessence.

He thought about Daniel's mother and remembered her love of Kierkegaard; had he been *rapt* into the seventh heaven? Would he soon be standing before "all the gods" of the universe? What he saw and felt was not what Ross had imagined heaven to be like, though. His image of that mythological land was far less attractive, far less desirable.

Ross had only ever heard about heaven when he went to a small corner church down the street from his home. He had only been there once or twice as a young boy. On one of the occasions that Ross and his sister went to the small church, the only time that he could remember, a fat, round-faced man, overdressed in a three-piece light blue suit, stood behind a grainy, dark brown pulpit, red-faced, yelling and spitting a message about how God hated sinners and would send them all to hell. The preacher looked straight at Ross, or so Ross felt that he did, and said "God don't want sinners like you in heaven. The image had rooted itself in Ross's mind so strongly, it shaped his thoughts and attitudes about religion and god from that day on. His image was nothing like Kierkegaard's. Ross's senses were overwhelmed by the magical events unfolding around him. As the memory of Daniel's mother rose to his mind, he was moved in the deepest parts of his being and began to realize that the world he had always known—the things that he had always believed and understood—may not have been all that there was to know or understand. The sound of Daniel's mother's voice echoed in his mind. He remembered her laughter as she read the passage aloud.

Images of all the stuffed shirts who had ever told him how the world was supposed to be, how he was supposed to be, how the universe worked, and what the truth was, and what was right and wrong and what was just and unjust, coursed through his mind like grainy black and white photographs, blowing through the air, each landing momentarily in view of his mind's eye. Ross began to laugh; he felt it erupting from deep within his gut, rising like a geyser, laughter, not from mockery or guile or indignation, but laughter that broke the restraints of pain and anger and disappointment. Ross felt the power of ecstasy erupting from a place in his being that had never been alive before. The revelation that there was another reality, another world, another life, penetrated the hardened shell of his intellectual ideologies. It washed over his sensibilities like water over the pages of a newspaper, making all the inky words run together into a fragile, unintelligible smear. Everything that had made sense started to unravel and those unknown things, like Kierkegaard's words quoted by Daniel's mother, began to make sense like never before. Maybe she had spoken with the gods too, he wondered. Now, he was the one laughing, laughing at everything he had thought made sense, at everything that had looked normal, at everything that had seemed so immovable, unchangeable, permanent, and irrevocable.

Ross. Penetrating the captivating ecstasy, her voice, soft and gentle, resonated straight into both his conscious and subconscious being, drawing him out of the transcendent grip of the music and elements and the memories. Startled by the impertinent interruption, Ross turned to see the woman standing just a few steps from him. He had been so caught up in the experience, he had not noticed how close she had come. Ross looked into the hooded stole to see the face of the woman who had led him into that hidden paradise. In his heart, he had hoped he would see Eve. He had desired, so deeply, to see her again and to find that, somehow, she had survived the fall.

There was a bewitching familiarity about her and though it was not the face of Eve he saw under the white hood, what he did see bewildered him. When Ross looked into her clear, sea-blue eyes, he became a spellbound man, transfixed and stupefied. He saw in her eyes an endless, deep world of wonders and mystery. It was like looking into the deepest, bluest, and clearest waters and seeing every living thing suspended in a timeless universe. Rising out of the depths of her eyes, like a mythological siren, appeared the form of a woman swimming to the surface. It was not just any woman, however; it was Eve.

He could see her face, her smile. He wanted to reach out and touch her, to hold her. Suddenly, Ross felt a hand grasping his hand and holding it. The touch broke the spell. He turned his eyes down to his hand and saw the pearlescent glow of a nephesh hand holding his. He was not sure if he had reached out to her or if she had reached out to him, but in the first moments of their touch, Ross felt the gentle touch that he had always known as Eve's.

Ross looked back into the white hood and saw the headband with the mark of Eloh. "You! You're a nephesh."

"Yes."

"I, I thought you were someone else. I mean, I hoped you were someone else."

"Eve?"

"Yes, Eve. How did you know that?"

"You called me Eve when you came toward me."

"Oh, I guess I did. But? But why aren't you like the others? I mean . . . why are you dressed like that?"

"It's safe here in Gershom. We don't have to hide ourselves here."

"So, is this what all the nephesh look like? Without the camouflage I mean."

"Yes."

"You reminded me of someone. She came to me in a dream and she looked like you, but... "

"But, what?"

"Well, she was not a nephesh."

"Eve?"

"Yeah. But she's dead . . . but some part of me still hopes that maybe . . . maybe, she's still alive, somehow."

246

"I'm sorry."

"What's your name?"

"Msusi."

"Ross. I'm Ross."

"I know who you are. You're the one who doesn't belong in Shuk."

"Yeah. That would be me. Why'd you come? I mean, why did you come to me, or *did* you come to me?"

"Like the others, I have been sent to help you, to help you find something, to find what it is that you're looking for."

"But, how do you know what I am looking for? Wait a minute, you said *sent*, that you were *sent*, and the others . . . what others?"

"Kumél and Zoësh and even Seerae, and others, too. We've all been sent to help you, Ross. Soon you'll meet Alethia and Shu. They're the ones who have sent us."

"Wait a minute. It can't be that hard to get me back home. I mean . . . that's all I am looking for, you know, to find my way home."

"Many look for countless things, but rarely do they ever find what they need the most."

"Now you sound like Eve; that sounds like something she would've said."

"You're part of the reason for the beauty that you see. Every element in Shuk has longed for, groaned for you to come."

"Me? What do you mean?"

Msusi removed the hood of her stole. Her hair shone like fine strands of brilliant light falling gently over her shoulders. "There's an ancient prophecy that speaks of the return of Amik: '*There is one who is coming, of the line of your father, he will walk the Aurora Path and pierce the heart of the cruel masters, with a spear stained in Theoscian blood.*' Everything here has longed for that day to come. All have waited expectantly for the one who is of the line of Amik. You are the one, and the season of rebirth is soon to come when the realm of Pardis will be born again. But it will be born from great turmoil and suffering."

"I'm sorry, Msusi, but I think you have me confused with someone else. I'm a nobody, a stranger, an alien in this place. You said it yourself: I don't belong here. Whoever you're expecting me to be, it's not me. All I want to do is go home—that's all—just get home and back to my life."

"Back to what life, Ross? You have no life back in Seattle, remember, there is nothing there for you."

"How can you know about me and my life?" He could not understand how Msusi could know the things she knew.

"It may be that the only way back is by the path that you're on. The life that you wish to return to may not be the life that you're meant to live. You may not have chosen this path Ross, but it is a path that only you can walk." Msusi stepped close to him and looked into his eyes. He could feel her breath on his face. She reached out and touched him on the hand. Slowly, a cumulous of memories carried on the gentle voice of Msusi began to take possession of him. They penetrated the shadowy depths, into the places of his being where light had not shone. They called to life his forgotten essence which had been locked away. Like the gathering clouds of a spring thunderstorm, rolling together and ascending into the highest heavens, every thought, every memory, every action of that day seemed related, building into an epic crescendo. Ross felt a whisper first, like the vibrations that pulse through the body of a viola, as the musician draws its bow across the strings. He was shaken from a place mortal men rarely remember exists. Then, chasing after the resonance, the whisper of life rose from the depths of his emptiness, calling softly at first, and then louder and louder like a prisoner yelling from his cell. Ross felt the strength of his flesh leave him. He collapsed to the ground in a heap. Msusi stood and watched as he struggled to get back up, but he could not stand. Never in his life had he felt such a force. It was greater than fear, adrenalin, or euphoria; it was more than any high or any rush, and yet, it was like all of them happening all at the same time. The photos of Eve, her journal, and the words she had written, the beauty of mystery, the vision of Msusi, the jubilant meadow—they all seemed to reach out to him, calling to some part of his being he did not know. Though revelation and mystery had touched him, had unveiled themselves to him, something was missing, something that was vital to his being able to retrieve what had been offered. Some part of his being was absent, like a man with no hands trying to grab hold of a rope that would save his life.

Ross could not hold onto the lifeline that had been thrown to him; he could not yet grip the cords of salvation without some part of himself that he did not know he was without. The force that had seized him released him. Weak and vulnerable, Ross sat in the tall grass of the meadow. He sat with his eyes closed trying to recover his strength. "I've never felt anything like that before, ever. What was it?"

"It's the *Elohan Essentia*, the spirit of life that once lived in all. It calls out to forgotten souls, helping them find the essence of life and of being. It is with this same spirit that the nephesh call out to their lost sapien."

"Why didn't it help me find what I'm looking for?"

"What you have experienced is only the beginning, but you are not fully ready. There is a part of you that is missing, a part you must first find, then you will know what it is that you are looking for and why you are here."

"What? What is it that I must find? How can I find what I don't know?"

"The hardest thing to know is yourself."

"I don't understand."

"You will—when the time is right. You will understand."

Chapter X
The Pass of Attone

Seerae awoke to the sound of a pair of blue-winged sturnellas greeting the new day with a celebratory song. She lay in the tall grass, listening to the happy melody soaring over the knoll. Soon, another songbird, and then another, joined in the magical reverie, a veritable choir of jubilant little voices, from all directions, joined in the excited anthem. As a nephesh, she understood the voices of the tiny psalmists. Seerae began to sing quietly in harmony with the songbirds:

Morning shine, shine so bright,
Warm my heart with rays of light,
Awaken my soul from sleepy night.
La lala lala lala.
Spread your golden glitter across the boundless sky,
Over fields and mountains reaching low and high,
Freely in your brightness we spread our wings and fly.
La lala lala lala.

Over and over the little trouveurs whistled together as Seerae sang along. At times, they sang in unison, singing one melody, and at other times, they sang as if to each other. Flitting from branch to branch, the tiny tits and warblers resounded their cheerful chorus. Seerae began to sing a song of her own, one that the tiny songbirds did not know. As she sang her song, the birds listened, all gathering to the ends of the branches overhanging the knoll where Seerae lay:

Beautiful little voices, singing loud and strong,
Sing your songs of life to me.
Sing them with all your heart so that every heart may hear.
Lift up your pretty melody so that the heavens are moved,
So that Pardis remembers, so that Eloh sings, too.
Lift your merry tune over the woeful isles,
Over the great waters and seas,
Over the mountains and over every valley,
Sing your precious words over every shore,
Beautiful little voices, sing loud and strong,
Loud and strong.

It was not long before her singing was accompanied by the haunting voice of a dukwán playing softly, not far from where she lay. Seerae closed her eyes and, for a moment, stopped singing. The sweet, rich tone of the wooden pipe seemed almost too perfect, too precise for her impromptu lyric. Nevertheless, the song inside of her would not stay quiet for long. Soon her lips were forming the words again, and the combination of voices quickly weaved together into a single melody. She knew it was Zoësh playing; she could feel the soul of the music. Together, Zoësh and Seerae made music and the many winged songsters also joined in, making a single soaring song as if they had all rehearsed it before. Zoësh played the pipe with such skill and tenderness that every living thing, from bird to wild cat, from grass to flower to tree, seemed to lean in close to listen. It was as if they could feel the notes of her song reaching out and touching them, like a soft gentle hand. After awhile, a great flock of golden-breasted ibons came flying over the treetops and began wheeling and swooping higher and higher into the sky over the knoll. Like a great cloud rolling higher and higher, then dropping down, morphing its shape, spreading wide and then narrow, the shifting cloud of golden birds swayed and bobbed to the sounds of the music as if dancing through the sky.

The celebration continued for a long time until Kumél woke from his slumber. He had been lying asleep so still that the many creatures and birds had not taken notice of him; even his loud snores did not alert them. However, when he sat up and stretched his large arms into the air and let out a deep, powerful groan, the tiny birds flurried away into the safety of the woods. He seemed completely unaware of the jubilant hullabaloo that was, most assuredly, the reason for his sudden resurrection. He rubbed his head and scratched his chest and arms, grunting and yawning, in a ritual-like morning rouse. From a distance, there was something almost endearing about the giant creature, though, upon closer inspection, it was quite clear he was not as charming as he might have seemed from afar.

Kumél's voice was loud, strong, and disquieting—not to mention frightening. The presence of a gallue in Gershom was unheard of and known to be a serious violation of the Covenant of Elements. For all these many ages, the creatures and birds of Gershom had been safe from the threat of predation from the gallues and their menacing mēglydaims. None of the creatures had ever even seen a beast like Kumél, and their first encounter with one was quite a frightful introduction, indeed. Just the sounds of his groaning and yawn were beyond any noise the little creatures had ever known, much less his size and disturbing appearance.

As the sound of Seerae's voice and Zoësh's dukwán floated around him, Kumél found himself contemplative and sober, as if he was still captive to the realm of sleep. The gentle whisper of their song touched the deep parts of his soul. It held him under a spell, refusing to let him awaken from a dream that was not a dream at all, but a memory that had found him while he slept.

One small blue-freckled tit flew over and landed in the tuft of black hair banded together on the top of Kumél's head. It seemed intent on nesting there. Kumél, quite unaware, paid no attention as the wee bird tried to rearrange the coarse black hairs into a better nesting platform. Eventually, the teeny bird settled in, closed its mini, black eyes, and took a light nap—all without Kumél ever noticing. Soon, a number of the little birds were flying over and landing on Kumél. Some landed on his head, some on his shoulders. One bold red tit landed on his hand and chirped audaciously at the hulking monster. Kumél paid little attention to the birds, respecting them as if they were nothing more than a fly, which, of course—in relation to his mass—they were.

The tiny red tit chirped and stared at him with expectant eyes. Kumél flicked his hand as if trying to shoo a persistent fly away. The sprightly bird flew just far enough away that his long arm and large hand were unable to reach. As soon as Kumél rested his hand back down on the giant log, the tenacious, wee bird flew back down and roosted on it again. By this time, there were many small tits of various bright colors perched on Kumél's shoulders, quite content to find their home upon them. The contrast between Kumél and the birds, both in size and beauty, was remarkable and quite symbolic of the numerous contrasting elements in the realm of Shuk.

The song of the songbirds eventually returned to the knoll when the little birds became entirely comfortable in the presence of Kumél. Kumél had not always been the beast he was now. Before the great war, as a kerolus, Kumél had been very magnificent and admirable. He had been Amik's closest friend and had helped him in the fields and forests of Pardis. Kumél knew the craft of husbandry well and cared for the creatures of Pardis. Deep beneath the hardness of his corrupted shell, Kumél possessed a tender and gracious heart that had never been fully darkened by the pernicious curse of Attar. The memory of his once-radiant self lingered in the dark corridors of his thoughts. Kumél wrestled to dismiss those thoughts from his mind, for he could not change what he had become. Thankfully, no matter how unlike himself he had become, he was far closer to his former self than the other gallues were.

Sitting on the giant fallen tree that had been his bed, Kumél surveyed the surrounding landscape. He was reminded of the days before the great war when he had worked in the gardens of Assuk with Amik. His thoughts drifted back to a time when he and Amik had walked in the high gardens above the valley, far from the great city of Anima, and for just an instant, he felt as though he could hear Amik talking to him, as if he was there, right beside him. *"Kumél, there is so much that is unknown, so much that is wild and unexplored. Think of all the things we could do there."* Amik had talked to him about going to the uninhabited realm of Tirnan, where he planned to start a family and dress the wilderness as he had in Assuk. *You must come, Kumél. "You are my closest friend, and who is better suited for it than us? Come with me, please."*

It was the first time since coming to Shuk that Kumél had remembered those better peaceful days. The memories invaded his mind like the edge of a knife, sharp and painful. Yet, there was, at the same time, a sweetness about them, like the aroma of the snowpetal and pinkblush that wafted over the knoll. Kumél felt a certain calmness rest over his typical anxiousness and chose not to dismiss the memories, but rather, muse upon them.

Outside the realm of Assuk, Gershom Forest was the largest woodland garden and one of the few remaining relics of that perfect age. There were other places that exuded the aura of Pardis: places deep in the mountains near the shores of the Great Sea, in the Plane of Haemus, on the lonely isles across the sea and in Tirnan—but none were as expansive nor as alive. Eloh had placed these treasured remnants throughout the fallen realms to remind and inspire the sojourners there of a perfect way, a way that, for many, seemed lost forever and to most, seemed only an invention. Even those, like Kumél, who had been there, had stopped believing that it was ever as good as they remembered.

Every day since finding Ross on the mountainside, Kumél had felt an inexorable force working deep in his being, beneath the hardened, calloused exterior, compelling him to remember. He had become so distracted from his memories, that remembering them was like rehabilitating atrophied muscles: it became a grueling and painful exercise that he resisted. Every resurrected memory came under attack from the reality of what and who he had become. Like a wild, frightened cat, clawing and scratching, biting and hissing, his corrupted will warred against the hope of a world as sublime and satisfying as his memories recalled. Finally, in the restful arms of Gershom, during the night visions of the sleep realm, Kumél submitted. He was overcome by the ecstasy of hope and remembered what it felt like to be free, alive, and whole, all of which he longed to be. What the others heard as snoring, mumbling, and groaning were, for Kumél, the utterances of one caught in a fierce struggle, fighting an incorporeal battle of the heart and mind in the dream realm.

It was the tiny blue-freckled tit who first noticed the kindness in Kumél. It was he who could see into the giant eyes of the forbidding, deformed beast, he who could see that, despite his grotesque appearance, Kumél was not a threat, that he was not terrible like the other gallues who roved the realm. The little bird could see that Kumél had wrestled with one whose voice the winds carried and who walked invisibly among the trees. As they always had, the small birds watched over Gershom through the night hours. They stood as witnesses to the unseen, immortal whisper of

Eloh. So vigilant were the tits, that before any of the small company had a chance to notice, they had announced the trespass to the whole forest. And now, with their tiny voices, they sang a song of deliverance, a song that would soon soar on the great wings of summer breezes, to warm the cold, dark regions of Shuk.

While she played, Zoësh had been watching the little birds cluster around Kumél. She could see, too, that Kumél had changed, yet the difference could not be perceived outwardly. Zoësh stared at him intently, trying to see what superficial eyes could not see. The nephesh have the ability to see into the spirit realm; they peer into the shadows of the soul and observe what others are unable to see. Zoësh stopped playing. She lowered the dukwán and spoke to Kumél. "You have heard him, in the night vision, he has spoken to you, visited you there, hasn't he?"

"Aye, ut waer Eloh."

"I've heard that what he shows you, pierces you—and the wound never heals."

"Aye. A ha haerd ut."

"How do you feel? Are you alright?"

"Aye."

Zoësh could tell that Kumél had no intention of confiding in her. She turned when she heard someone approach and saw a confused Seerae standing there. "What is it, Seerae?"

"Ross? Where's Ross?"

"He must be somewhere close; he wouldn't wander away."

"All of his things are still here. What's this?" Seerae reached down and picked up the journal, which had fallen open on the ground. As she reached for it, she saw a strange inscription on the pages. "Where did he get this?"

"What? What're you talking about, Seerae?"

"It's the writing of Eloh, the writing that was in the pit."

"What? Are you sure? Why would that be in his book?" Zoësh asked skeptically.

"Yes! Look! But how does Ross know the prophecy? I thought he wasn't from here?"

Seerae flipped through the pages of the journal and began to see writing she had never seen before and could not read. "What is this? What kind of language is it?" Seerae inquired.

Zoësh moved closer to look at the book. "Are you sure this book belongs to Ross?"

"No, not exactly," Seerae admitted.

"Where would he have seen the writing of Eloh, the prophecy?"

"He must have seen the inscription in the pit. Surely that's where he saw it."

"When he comes back, we can ask him about the book," Zoësh proposed. "Maybe we should put it back in with his things." As she began packing his backpack, she spied a curious item. "What is this?" Zoësh held Ross's digital camera in her hand. The small, black object was a mystery. As she examined it, she accidentally pushed the power button, which opened the lens and lit up the screen on the back of the camera. The photo of Eve and Ross was glowing on the screen. "What?" she asked nervously.

"How is that possible?" They stared at the photo with curiosity and amazement. Seerae touched the screen as if trying to reach into the photo and touch the faces of Ross and Eve. "Maybe it's not him. Maybe it's just an image of him. And who is that with him?" Seerae wondered.

"Maybe it's her, the one he says sorry to, the one he lost on the mountain: Eve." Zoësh remembered Ross's tears and his pain as he had cried out, back on the way to the pass, at the great twistbranch tree. As she studied the photo with Seerae, she noticed a glowing green light on the edge of the camera. It was the camera's power button which she had accidentally pushed earlier. "What's this thing that is glowing?" When she touched the button, the camera lens closed, and the screen went black. Seerae dropped the camera to the ground, startled by the small, melodic sound the camera made as it powered down.

"Wut ye bae doin?" Kumél inquired.

"Just looking at these strange objects," Seerae answered.

"Ye shunt bae diggin un ees tings."

"They were just lying here on the ground."

"Whaer bae Ross?"

"We don't know. He was gone when we awoke."

"Hae lung ha ye bun awake?"

"Just before you woke."

"Hmm?"

They were so distracted by the many events of the morning that the three of them had not noticed the trail of snowpetal leading away from the knoll—a sure sign of Ross's whereabouts.

A faint haunting sound began to drift from the woods. It was the sound of a dukwán playing in the distance. As the music played, the sound of the song began to lure Seerae toward the woods, in the same direction the snowpetal was growing. "Seerae, wait!" Zoësh ran after her and grasped her arm. "Wait! We shouldn't move too hastily."

Kumél rose and walked over to the two nephesh who were lingering at the edge of the woods, staring into the shadows. As he reached them, he noticed the trail of snowpetal leading into the woods. "Ross wunt dis wae. D'ye sae da snowpetal? Lut's gae."

"Wait. Gather his things. We may not be back this way." Zoësh picked up Ross's backpack and put the camera and journal into it. She noticed Ross's boots; they were lying in the tall grass near his sleeping area. "What are these?"

"Wut?"

"These. What are they?"

"A dunna know. Brang um wit ye. Hurrae!"

Zoësh, carrying Ross's gear and boots, rejoined Kumél and Seerae, and the three of them followed the narrow path of snowpetal, alert and vigilant. The music continued to play and became louder as they followed the path. They did not know from where the music originated, or if following it would lead them to Ross. It did seem, however, quite coincidental that the path of snowpetal and the music were both leading in the same direction.

The snow petal led them deeper and deeper into the woods until, at one point, Kumél became concerned that they were not on Ross's path at all, but on a path that was leading them into peril. "Wait!" proclaimed Kumél. "Haer! Ut bae a print luft bae somon. Mubae tis frum Ross."

"Here is another! But they're very strange footprints," Seerae announced.

"Aye, but dae wud bae, right? Ee is nut lik us."

The strangeness of Ross's footprints came from the fact that he was wearing socks on his feet. Though his feet were not at all like Kumél's giant taloned feet, they were not much different from the nephesh feet—it was the socks that made a very strange looking impression.

"He has no toes. I wonder, did he lose them somewhere?" Seerae guessed.

"Dunna bae u fool, Hae d'ye lose yer toes?"

"How would I know, I've never lost any."

Seerae could not have known that Ross had actually lost two of his toes on his right foot. The two smallest toes had been amputated due to frostbite several years back, when Ross and Daniel were climbing in the Himalaya's. This, of course, made the impression of his right foot quite different from the left.

Shortly after finding the footprints, Zoësh began to hear the sound of a waterfall, and then Kumél caught the scent of Ross and of one other. "Dar bae u strange scent ahead. Wae maet ha cumpny." Kumél led on but with discretion and caution guiding each step.

As they approached the edge of a meadow, they viewed a large pool fed by a waterfall. Zoësh reached out and seized Kumél's arm. "Do, not, move!" she whispered.

Kumél could sense that Zoësh's words were serious, and the firmness of her grip on his arm told him that she had been alerted to something. Kumél stood as if lifeless and moved only his eyes back and forth to discover what Zoësh had seen. A short distance away, across the small pool of water, Kumél caught sight of something that he had not seen since arriving in Shuk. A kerolus sentry stood guard over the pool. The kerolus wore a long sword on his belt and carried a spear, the kerolus spear, in his right hand. There was no weapon that Kumél could wield that would give him an edge over the mighty kerolus sentry, for they had power beyond strength, power that came from Eloh, power that Kumél once, but no longer possessed.

The kerolus were beautiful, sublime creatures, gifted with flight and adorned with light. They were spectacular beings: strong, powerful, and courageous, yet humble. They possessed kind and loyal natures and were given to the care of the creatures of the fields and to the guardianship of Pardis. Standing some fifteen feet tall with great powerful legs and arms, they had the general appearance of an exceptionally large human. But even with their immense size and strength, the kerolus were extremely gentle, with kind eyes and a patient demeanor. Their skin danced with the colors of refracted light, iridescent and changing. Seeming as if they were transparent and thus intangible, they could disguise themselves with the surrounding environment.

At the crown of their head grew a lock of hair that reached down to their waist. It was tied with six coarse silver threads which wrapped around the base of the lock then woven like a silver tubular net, extending to the end where it was finished with a silver band. The band at the end of the lock was carved with the writings of an ancient language. They wore golden rings in the lobes of their ears.

On their faces were markings in a spectrum of colors called the simtu, which started at their left shoulder, ran up their neck, and wrapped around the left side of their face like a hand. Every kerolus wore a kilt that was topped with a wide, ornately carved golden Etruscan belt. On their wrists were golden bands with carvings. Their wings were both iridescent and transparent with veins of silver and gold running through them, creating a filigree pattern throughout. When spread, the wings stood as high as the kerolus and stretched more than six feet wide. Supple as silk and yet strong as iron, the wings folded against their back becoming indistinguishable and virtually invisible.

Every kerolus was a skilled archer as well as a highly capable swordsman. The spear, however, was the weapon the kerolus preferred. Every spear possessed by a kerolus was given the name of its owner and empowered with the soul of its master, making it an extension of the bearer. In the mid-section of the spear was an ivory grip on which the kerolus engraved their own markings. The spear was eighteen feet long and sharp at both ends like a javelin. It was made from the wood of the guaiacum tree and laid over with tarterniem, a silver metal that was close to indestructible.

The sight of the kerolus sentry confounded the two nephesh. They had never seen such a magnificent creature. They had never even heard of kerolus before. The closest things that any of the nephesh had ever seen were the gallues, who bore only the slightest resemblance, mostly in terms of size. Kumél, however, unlike most of the other gallues, had faint traces of their splendor that showed in his face and eyes and, of course, in his stature.

"There! There he is! Ross! Do you see him?" Zoësh spotted Ross at the edge of the pool and pointed to him. Sitting a short distance from him was another nephesh, one that Zoësh had never met before. The nephesh played the dukwán, and it was her music which had led them to the pool. Unsure what to do next, the trio, realizing that they had not yet been spotted, retreated away from the edge of the meadow and deeper into the woods. They knew Ross was safe, but they did not know why he had walked to the pool or who it was that was with him.

Seerae could hear Ross talking to the nephesh. She could hear his words as he became agitated and shouted. She peered through the thick undergrowth of the forest to find out what Ross was doing and why he was yelling. She saw him fall to the ground and wanted, with everything in her being, to race to his side, but Zoësh held her back. "You can't help him. Not right now. He will be alright, I'm sure."

"How can you be so sure?"

"I can't, but I believe he will be," Zoësh assured her.

"Hmm? Do you think that's good enough?" Seerae challenged Zoësh.

"What's good enough?"

"That you believe. I hope it's good enough. Who is she, the nephesh beside him?"

"I don't know, but she doesn't seem to mean him any harm. Maybe she wants to help him," Zoësh speculated.

"Maybe, but what are we going to do?"

"One of us will have to go into the meadow," Zoësh suggested.

"What about, well, you know that thing?" Seerae fretted.

"Ut bae u kerolus, one loyal t'Alethia, da daughter o'Eloh." Kumél joined the conversation.

"Is it dangerous?" Seerae asked anxiously.

"Aye, but ony t'mae un da gallues."

"Maybe I should go. We can't sit here forever, you know," Zoësh offered.

"Aye, but dunna draw yer sword. Dunna do ony ting thut ma luk lik yur dangerus."

"I'm not stupid," Zoësh snapped.

"Wae bae soon t'fin out."

Zoësh rose and made her way toward the meadow. She paused at the edge of the trees under a giant old sycamore and scanned the area cautiously. She noticed Ross sitting in the tall grass and the nephesh kneeling near him. They appeared to be talking as friends discussing serious matters. Zoësh waited for the seriousness of their conversation to ebb, then she stepped into the tall grass of the meadow and called out, as though she had just happened upon them. "Hey, Ross." Startled by the voice, Ross turned to see Zoësh approaching from across the meadow.

"I've been looking everywhere for you. What are you doing here?"

Msusi rose and quietly stepped back away from Ross. Hidden in the woods, Kumél observed them closely as the kerolus sentry kept a sharp eye on the scene below him. It seemed that the kerolus was intent on not interfering with the reunion and had another reason for being there.

"Where are the others? Are they back at the knoll?" Ross quizzed Zoësh.

"No. They have come with her; they hide in the woods just beyond," answered Msusi.

"Why are they hiding in the woods? They are my friends."

"There's one among you who is of the fallen ones. He is your friend?"

"What do you mean, 'of the fallen ones'?"

"Kumél, the aposta, the friend of Amik—isn't he with you?" Msusi questioned.

It was plainly obvious to Zoësh that their little ruse had been a complete and utter failure. She had not realized that Msusi had been to their camp on the knoll and had seen all of them sleeping.

"I am Msusi. You—you are Zoësh. You are the one who has killed the mēgs and is pursued by the gallue hunters."

"Yes, that's me."

"And Seerae, she has come with you also?"

"Yes, she's back with Kumél."

"Please call them. They are safe. No harm will come to any of you here in Gershom. She has been waiting for you—all of you."

"Who, who is waiting for us? Is this some kind of trap?"

"Oh no, not at all. Alethia, daughter of Eloh, has been waiting for you. I have been sent to lead you to her. You have many questions, all of you; she will help you to find the answers. Call your friends. The journey ahead is lengthy and arduous. We must go quickly."

Zoësh stepped away from Msusi and headed back toward the woods where Kumél and Seerae were hiding. "You might as well come out. They know exactly where you are. They were expecting us."

Seerae stepped into the meadow first. She was relieved to learn that Ross was safe and that they had found some allies they could trust. Kumél was more hesitant to step into the clearing. It had been a very long time since he had stood before one of his own, one who was unchanged, one who had not fallen under the curse of Attar. Kumél had seen his own reflection in the waters many times over the ages. He was reminded, in those moments, of his former self and of the depths to which he had fallen, but seeing the kerolus sentry, seeing how magnificent he was, pierced Kumél's heart in a way that seeing himself never could. An insufferable weight of shame descended upon him with a crushing blow. It was not shame from accusing words or voices, but from his inner being. Dislodged from somewhere deep within his core, the accusation of his guilt began to rise; it was a damning voice, echoing through his inner sanctum, reverberating through his mind and thoughts, chiding him with words and tones and expressions that he knew to be his own. Kumél did not need to be accused by others, for the deepest and most painful accusations screamed out from his own damned essentia.

The curse of Attar had not only changed the physical appearance of the fallen and corrupted them with hatred and malice, it also enslaved its victims under a dark, unseeable force of self-reproach that bound them with cords of self-loathing and disparagement. They judged themselves as guilty and unforgivable, beyond redemption, beyond reconciliation, beyond deliverance. Most of the gallues were never confronted with this level of shame and inner torment, for the corruption of the curse had so thoroughly exercised its strength over them that they were absolutely defiled. But for the five apostas, the curse had not had its full effect; it had not poisoned them completely. They were not better off because of it, though, for they lived with the pain of their guilt and treachery, with the memory of their previous glory, which burdened them with regret and sorrow.

The ability to forget was one of the few comforts Kumél had. Forgetfulness was an antidote, not only to the biting pain of memory, but to the venom of regret. It had been a long time since Kumél had remembered his former life, but in the days since finding Ross on the ledge, the shadows and torments of guilt had haunted him. To face one of his own kind was, in a much more frightening way, facing himself, a chilling reality of just how deep into the darkness he had fallen.

"Kumél, will you not come?" Msusi's soft, gentle voice touched his eardrums like the precise stroke of a mallet on the taut head of a timpani. She moved toward the edge of the woods, to the place Kumél stood with his head lowered and his eyes blankly staring at the ground.

"A shunt bae haer."

"Don't let your heart be troubled. Come! Come and go with us."

"Hell, it seems to me that none of us should be here—especially me." Ross encouraged Kumél, but Kumél was too focused on his failings to listen.

"A ha baen haer afore, u lung, lung tam ago."

"You used to play the pipe here. It was your secret place," Msusi revealed.

"Aye."

"The last time you played, you were sitting right here. Do you remember?" Msusi asked Kumél quietly.

"Aye, A rumumbar tae weel."

"Maybe you'll play again sometime soon."

"Nae. Dar bae no mur song un mae haert t'play."

By now, Kumél had stepped out of the shadows of the forest and into the sunlight shining on the meadow. He stood in full view of the kerolus Sentry that had moved from the ledge over the pool and was standing only a few steps from Kumél.

"D'ye rumumbar mae, Kumél, d'ye rumumbar?" The kerolus spoke kindly to Kumél, as if speaking to a long-lost friend. Kumél raised his head and looked into the eyes of the kerolus standing before him. He was too emotional to speak. He had known all along who it was that stood before him. Knowing had added to the deep sense of shame, and even though Kumél would rather have denied than affirmed his knowledge of him, he admitted, "Aye, A rumumbar, Jaroh. A waer nut sur ye wud know mae."

"Weel, tis hard t'sae ye as ye bae, but A knew twas ye a'soon as A haerd yer words."

The conflicting sea of emotions that broke upon the shore of Kumél's heart was unabated and turbulent, but he managed to control his impulse to break down. Jaroh reached out his hand and took hold of Kumél's shoulder, a kerolus' gesture of friendship. "Wae ha t'gae far. Da journey bae u vary great distance."

Ross looked at Jaroh with alarm. "How far? I forgot my boots." He had not yet realized that, in his hurry to follow Msusi, he had left all his belongings back on the knoll.

"Boots? What are boots?" Jaroh questioned.

"For my feet, I'll need them if we're going very far."

Seerae held up the pack and Ross's boots. "Are these your boots?"

"Ah, yes! That's them. Whew! I wouldn't go far without these. I don't know how you do it. No shoes or boots, just bare feet and sandals, if that's what you can call those."

Ross was referring to the thin-hide soles lashed to the feet of the nephesh. Ross sat down to put his boots on. As he pulled his socks tight, he realized that both had holes worn through them and were very soiled and smelly. He wanted to wash them out in the water but he knew that there was no time. Everyone else seemed ready to go. He quickly stuffed all of his miscellaneous gear back into the pack and quickly stood to his feet. "I'm ready. Let's go."

Jaroh turned and led the way across the meadow and into the canopy of the forest. Without another word, the others fell in a line behind him: Msusi, Ross, Seerae, Zoësh, and Kumél. Gershom Forest spread over thousands of square miles and was surrounded by towering mountains. Within the realm of Gershom was a long, winding range of mountains called the Crucible Towers, which wound from the eastern extent of the forest all the way through to, and beyond, the western extent. The Crucible Towers split the forest into two distinct realms. Amid the Crucible Towers were many meadows and valleys, rivers and streams that flowed into the north and south realms of the forest. In the distance, Ross and the others could see the Crucible Towers rising above the forest.

"Where are we going?" Ross asked.

"Dar, o'er thum, da Crucibles." Jaroh pointed to the mountains in the distance as he moved on.

"Great! Just when I think things are going to be easy. Hey, what's your name? Do we have to go over the peaks or is there a pass?"

"Mu nam bae Jaroh. Un dar bae u pass, da Pass o'Attone."

"What's on the other side of the pass that we have to get to?"

"Da Valley o'Veritus. Ut bae whaer Alethia cun bae foun, uf wae gut dar un tam."

"Alethia, who's Alethia?"

"Ye wull know soon." Jaroh told Ross.

"Probably too soon, if you ask me."

The way through the forest proved to be hard and slow for the group. Ross, who had always prided himself on his physical conditioning and stamina, was, however, the slowest one of the team. He was, after all, the only mortal in the bunch, and, as such, was more susceptible to the elements. Kumél brought up the rear of the pack and had become quite familiar with Ross's limitations, even though there were times when Ross had proven to be quite capable. They moved through the forest, step by step, in a single-file line, on a course that, though not marked or trodden, appeared to be direct and predetermined. The sun tracked them on their course, first behind and then over them until, eventually, it was in front of them as if resting on the tops of the mountains waiting for them to catch up.

The daylight waned, and the sun began to set on the horizon. Jaroh halted the trek and waited for everyone to catch up. "Dar bae u meadow jus ahead. Wae wull rest dar."

"Sounds good to me; what a long day." Ross wanted to sit down right then, but before he could, Jaroh was marching on. In his mind, he wondered how much farther Jaroh meant by "jus ahead" for he had been guilty of giving the same ambiguous answers when he had led climbs. His favorite answer to impatient climbers was, "at least another ten minutes." Surprising to him, the meadow was not far at all. As they entered the high mountain meadow, the group began to look for places to rest and sleep during the approaching night. Meandering through the meadow was a small, pristine stream flowing over rocks and through narrow channels lined with tall grass and boulders. Growing amongst the tall grass was an array of flowers which seemed to welcome the company of visitors by sending a sweet scent into the air. There were a variety of birds and creatures all bustling about like the woman of a house who suddenly receives unexpected guests. In the distance, the faint call of a Gershom stag echoed through the long, narrow meadow. Rays of sunlight began to dance over the clear sky, painting the distant mountain peaks gold, pink, and lavender. The myriad chirping of the colorful winged songbirds coalesced into a harmonious chorus that filled the air with an idyllic aura.

For Ross and Kumél, especially, the atmosphere that inhabited the air, every sound and movement of beast, bird, and flora, was strangely supernal, but distantly familiar. Kumél could vaguely remember, not so much the sounds or colors, but the sensation, the feeling of familiarity. Ross had never, in all his life, experienced such grandeur. Every step he took filled him with the highest and deepest and brightest essence of life he had ever known.

Slowly the sun set and darkness followed the fading rays of light. The sky was clear and the celestial universe above began to illuminate the blackness. The stars sparkled in such innumerous abundance that their light began to illuminate the forest and mountains. The aurora streamed across the starlit blackness, unrestrained and indulgent. For a long while, every eye was held captive by the exuberant display while a still, auspicious calm set over the meadow.

The Pass of Attone laid between two towering spires at the upper limits of Mount Attone. From the south, it appeared that there were many easier routes and passes over the mountains, but due to the sharp, lofty ridges of Mount Attone's north face, the only negotiable route into the Valley of Veritus was through the daunting Pass of Attone. Attone was the highest mountain pass in the entire realm of Shuk, and there were no trails or paths leading to it, nor was there any one to guide the way, for few had ever been over it. The north side of the pass was a treacherous, long, steep descent into the valley, with many sheer drops along the way that required careful negotiation to avoid. Getting from the south approach to the valley floor on the north required three days of difficult negotiation, if the weather at the pass was fair, which, of course, it most often was not.

The twin summits of Mount Attone were arranged so that its narrow, spear-shaped summit was on the west side of the pass and its sharp, axe-shaped summit was on the east side of the pass. Each of the two summits was more than twelve thousand cubits high, and the pass was just below eleven thousand cubits above the Great Sea. On the north side of each summit was a long, sharp ridge running from the peak of the summit to the north in a diagonal direction, creating a "V" shape where the Valley of Veritus laid snuggly between the two northern ridges of the mountain.

Many of the surrounding mountains were covered in sprawling glaciers, and the northern valleys of the range were laced with a maze of impassable glacier fields, jagged mountain spires, ridges, and endless boulder fields. The Valley of Veritus was the only high place in the north realm of Gershom's dominant Crucible Towers that could be accessed below its lofty peaks. This remote oasis was very well protected from intrusion or from discovery by the vast ruggedness of an uncharted wilderness that expanded in all directions around it.

Ross stood at the base of the final approach to the pass and lowered his head in dismay. The journey had been long and challenging, but the climb that lay ahead was the worst kind of climbing imaginable. Looking up from where he stood, all the way to a sheer rock face standing just below the pass, the height of which he could not be sure, was an endless splay of sharp, loose boulders that stretched to the horizon. Boulders, as big as a man, and in some cases, as large as a house, were strewn like scree over the steep southern slope of the mountain. Though not technical, it would be an endless, tiring climb, requiring every ounce of concentration and discipline to avoid injury—or worse. What Ross could not have known was that the northern descent was even more challenging. "Is there no other way? I mean, look at this, this is the worst approach I've ever seen, and I've seen a lot of them!"

"This is the only way. Few have ever found it, fewer have ever traveled it," Msusi explained.

"There's probably a reason for that, don't you think? I have climbed some really mean mountains, and this, this has got to be . . . Damn it! This is going to be hard and slow! Are you sure this is the only way?"

"It is. There is no other way."

Ross knew that one mistake could send tons of rock cascading down the mountain, crushing anyone below. He had witnessed a single falling boulder setting a catastrophic rockslide into motion. And here, because of the degree of steepness on which these boulders were precariously perched, the potential for catastrophe seemed far greater than any he had ever attempted.

Ross asked the surrounding group, "Have any of you done this before?"

"A ha bun o'er da pass afore," Jaroh answered with a modest, almost apologetic tone.

"So, you have climbed it before?"

"Nae, nut climbed it."

"Hmm? So, no one has climbed this before?"

"Nae."

"No."

"Great! Kumél, maybe I should take the lead. What do you think?"

"Aye. Uf yur sure o'yersaelf."

"I'm more sure of myself than of anyone else. I'll take the lead from here. Is that OK with everyone?" No one said anything in reply; they only looked upward at the pass.

Ross stepped to the front of the group and climbed to the top of a large boulder to survey the impending obstacles and get his bearings on a reasonable route to the pass. When Ross was climbing, he became a different man, more confident. He was also a good leader, giving instruction to the others and assisting them when they needed it. A sense of certitude began to settle over the group as Ross led them upward.

Toward the end of the day, Ross began to slow his pace until he came to a place in the rocks where an adequate, but not comfortable, camp could be made for the night. By the time they were all assembled at the make-shift-camp, they had climbed about half the way up to the pass. Looking down was a dizzying experience, for they were extremely high and the approach was very steep. In places, the route was a near-vertical wall of solid rock surrounded above and below by loose, giant boulders. Ross liked climbing the walls; he felt more comfortable there than negotiating the loose, unstable boulders. However, climbing the walls with little or no protection and with inexperienced, unprepared climbers made for some very intense moments; Ross was relieved to be done with the first day.

Finding their own places to rest, the team, exhausted and hungry, went quickly to sleep.

The next morning, Kumél awoke to a gray sky that hung low over the mountain tops. Shortly afterwards, Jaroh and Msusi were awake, and before long, all of them were on the move toward the pass again. Ross was the most tired of all, yet, he had proven himself to be a worthy leader.

The final pitch before the pass was sheer and exposed, with only a thin and shallow cleft in the face, like a long, jagged scar that climbers called a chimney, which reached upward to the top of the stone face and opening to the pass. Considering that the smooth face of the wall was as vertical as it could have been, the only option they had was to climb the chimney. Ross was apprehensive because he knew that if the chimney suddenly closed off before they reached the top of the wall, they would have to down climb, which he knew would be much more dangerous than the already-difficult ascent.

Ross led the climb, looking out for the others who followed slowly behind. One by one, each of the others followed up the tricky ascent while Ross talked them through each hand and foot hold. Often Ross would climb ahead, making sure of the best route and then down climb to the others so he could guide them along the way. The last member of the company to step up to the chimney was Jaroh. Jaroh looked up the narrow cleft and stepped aside to wait for everyone to reach the top safely.

After assisting the three nephesh to the top, Ross climbed down to help Kumél through a narrow section. Ill-equipped for rock climbing, Kumél struggled to make the acrobatic moves necessary for the task. His hulking size also made for a very tight squeeze through some sections of the chimney. Furthermore, his talons, though sharp and strong, proved to be a hindrance in gripping the tiny hand holds that Ross had found. His feet, too, were cumbersome and lacking in necessary sensitivity to feel the cracks and crevasses in the rock face for footholds, yet, slowly and methodically, Kumél worked his massive frame up the exposed wall. Ross climbed just above him, pointing out places to gain purchase in the rock. Kumél was the most at risk of falling, though he never acted as if he was concerned in any way. "You're almost there—just a few more holds and you will be on the pass. No! No, no, not there! Not there! Damn it, Kumél!" The massive aposta peeled away from the mountain face after part of the wall he had grasped broke away. Without a second thought, Ross reached out and grabbed Kumél's right wrist. Like a giant vice, Kumél's talons gripped Ross's wrist and forearm as Ross struggled to grip the wall. Zoësh heard Ross's yell and was the first to notice the terrifying situation. She rushed to Ross's aide as he was being torn away from the wall with Kumél. Kumél reached his other hand frantically toward the wall, searching vainly for a concealed hold that would stop his impending fall.

"Jaroh! Jaroh!" Zoësh screamed as she, too, not being able to find a grip, was being pulled from the mountain. Jaroh, however, had no idea of the immediate struggle that was unfolding above him. Kumél's hulking body stretched even farther away from the wall, and Ross was now hanging in mid-air, held from his death by the desperate grip Zoësh had on his ankle.

Zoësh had finally found a hold for her other hand; only two of her fingers were desperately clinging to a small crack and the rest of her body was being pulled tight to the cold stone ledge. Neither Ross nor Kumél could let loose their grip on the other, and though Zoësh was holding on to Ross's ankle with all her might, she was losing her grip on the rock ledge, and all three were about to be pulled from the wall.

"Jaroh! Help!" Before the harrowing cries could reach the distant ears of Jaroh, they broke upon Seerae and Msusi's ears like the roar of an angry wave. Immediately, they turned and discovered the dire situation.

Msusi shrieked as she bolted to help Zoësh who was being pinned face-first against the floor of the ledge by the weight of both Ross and Kumél. "Jaroh! Jaroh, help!"

Seerae raced to their aid and grabbed Zoësh's ankle to prevent her from being dragged from the ledge. As if offering their assistance, the winds gathered all their cries and yells into one tumultuous blast that exploded in Jaroh's ears. He finally glanced up to see Ross suspended in midair between Kumél and Zoësh. Zoësh had lost her grip of the ledge and was being pulled over the edge, while Msusi was holding onto her wrist and Seerae had a hold of her ankle. All five of them were being hauled over the edge into the abyss.

Without thinking about the consequences, Jaroh leapt into the air, spread his mighty wings, and flew to the aid of Kumél and Ross. The only remaining grip that Kumél had on the face of the rocks was with one toe of his left foot, and it was losing purchase. All were fearing their imminent deaths when Jaroh swooped in and seized Kumél and Ross's arms, which were locked together at the wrists, and with a mighty thrust of his wings, lifted them to the safety of the pass. Msusi and Seerae tugged hard on Zoësh's wrist and ankle, yanking her back to safety, and the whole company ended up in a heap with Jaroh standing over them.

The sight of Jaroh's extended wings came as a shock to the nephesh, who had rarely, if ever, seen a kerolus or their beautiful wings. Jaroh promptly closed his wings. For an extended moment, they did not move or say a thing, they only lay atop one another in a tangle of limbs, staring blankly and assessing what had just happened. The silence was quickly broken by an urgent and indignant protestation. "Get off of me, you oversized ape! Get off of me!"

Jaroh reached down and began to dismantle the heap of bodies one by one. Ross was at the bottom, crushed by the amassed weight of them all, but especially by the giant Kumél who lay on top of him.

As he was being liberated from the bottom of the pile, Ross's tongue could not help but lash out at Kumél. "Damn it! I told you not to grab hold of that crack. I told you, didn't I?"

Once the mound of bodies was dismantled, and Ross was uncovered and free, he rolled over, away from the others and stretched out on the hard stone with his eyes transfixed on the sky. It was all he could do to keep his anger contained, but something else had begun to occupy his mind. He labored to understand what it was that he had just witnessed a moment before. The flash of a huge light with wings had soared toward Kumél and himself, then Jaroh had lifted them to safety. He realized it must have been his imagination, but he was also sure he had caught a glimpse of Jaroh just before he had folded his wings. Ross was more in shock by the flight of Jaroh than by the harrowing, near-death experience he had just escaped. The stupor lasted only a moment before Ross sat up and rubbed his bruised shoulder.

They had spent a considerable amount of time climbing a dangerous mountain, and it had almost killed them. Ross became increasingly agitated as he realized that someone among them had been hiding skills that would have made it easier to assail the treacherous route. Intent on making his displeasure known, Ross erupted with a sharp rebuke, "And you, what the hell was that? If I'd have known you could do that, I wouldn't have had us all climbing this stupid mountain! You could've just flown us to the top!" Jaroh paid the small heckler no mind. "Hey, you! Jaroh! Don't act like you can't hear me! You better never make us go through that again!" Of course, Ross was momentarily witless, suffering from the sudden awareness that they could have died. He would not have been so imprudently brash had he realized to whom he was directing his insistent disapproval.

"A wud nut mun ta d'thut again," Kumél jested to break the tension in the air.

"What? Climbing or falling? Next time I'll just let you do them both on your own?" Ross retorted.

"A nae'er asked ye t'haelp mae. Ut waer ye thut reached fur mae."

"Yeah, I'm just not sure what got into me, that's all. Don't be counting on it the next time."

"A wull nut."

Zoësh, Seerae, and Msusi stood away from the banter. Though it was loud and seemed vicious on the surface, the intercourse between Kumél and Ross soon turned into a spirited exchange between two good friends. Soon all six were laughing and talking as they sat on the Pass of Attone preparing for another night of hunger and uncomfortable sleep.

"Jaroh, if you can fly, why do you walk? I mean, if I had wings, I wouldn't be stumbling around this stuff."

"Wae ha t'bae vary careful; dar bae muny eyes watchin, lukin un waitin—dangerus eyes."

"But, I thought we were safe here in Gershom."

"Aye, ye bae, as lung as da gallue lards believe dar bae no kerolus un Shuk. Dae cunna com un t'Gershom, but dae watch, an uf dae knew wae waer haer, dae wud trae un capture us un use us agan Eloh," Jaroh explained.

"Who's Eloh?" Ross asked.

"Eloh—ee bae our faether."

"So, where is he? Does he live here?"

"Nae. Eloh livs un Assuk, far frum haer, un da city o'Anima, mae home," Jaroh told Ross.

"Do you miss him?"

"Aye."

Ross could see that Jaroh carried a deep sentiment for his home and especially for Eloh. Though Ross was no closer to understanding who or what Eloh was, he knew that to everyone he had met, Eloh was special. Ross wondered secretly if Eloh might be an ancestor or some character of folklore that lived in the hearts and minds of all these different creatures, a myth passed from generation to generation. The way they spoke of Eloh made Ross feel as if he was not a real person or being—at least not anymore.

One by one they fell asleep. Another night of hunger and discomfort followed by another day of adventure and danger awaited them.

"Ross? Ross, what are you doing?"

"I don't know, just sitting here thinking. What are you doing?"

"Oh, nothing much, just waiting for you."

"For me? For me to do what?"

"To see me."

273

"To see you? I see you now. What do you mean?"

"Ross! You have to open your eyes. You have to look. Look, Ross! Look at me."

"But . . . I do see you. What do you mean, open my eyes?"

"Open your eyes, Ross."

"Wait! Where are you going, Eve? Where are you going? Don't go away!"

"Open your eyes, Ross! Wake up! Wake up, Ross!

Alethia

Chapter XI
The Well of Veritus

Lying on the cold, rocky ground, Ross slowly opened his eyes. At first, all he could see were small pebbles and dirt spread out before him on the floor of the pass. The weight of fatigue still rested on his worn body; it was as if extra strong gravity was pinning him against the earth. He peered at a light blue sky over the far horizon. Soft flakes of snow fell lightly on the stone floor of the pass, and the snowpetal clung desperately to the narrow cracks of the rocky alpine world. A stream of drool dribbled from Ross's mouth, pooling under his face. He could not remember a time in his life he had ever felt so fatigued.

He muttered Eve's name aloud as if she was there with him, but quickly realized, as he had so many times, that she was not present; it had been another dream. The sound of her voice still echoed in his thoughts. It had been a long time since his last dream of her. Ross had started to believe that she would not come to him anymore, that maybe he was getting past the accident, past his guilt, past his sorrow, that maybe he was getting over her. The thought had crowded into his mind several times, intruding upon his desire to keep her memory close and alive in his heart. He wondered if she knew that he was forgetting her and if that was what she meant by her piercing words, *"waiting for you to see me."*

"I see you, Eve. I see you." But in his heart, he knew this wasn't the whole truth. He did not want to admit that he was forgetting her, that her face was fading from his memory. Her smile, her voice, her words, and her tenderness were all fading away with each setting sun. Even in his dreams, he found himself slow to recognize her voice, and her face appeared as if it was diffused by a silk screen hanging between them. He was afraid that piece by piece she would disappear from his life. He feared his mind would erase every trace of her.

"Bae ye awake?" The familiar voice spoke from behind him. Ross rolled over onto his back to see Kumél sitting on a large rock a short distance from him. Ross was surprised to see the others also sitting around patiently waiting. "Ye waer talkin un yer slaep."

"I was?"

"Aye. Ye waer. Shae com t'ye agan?" Kumél asked him.

"Who?"

"Eve. Shae com t'ye agan, lik da other tams? Ye tink thut A nut know bout Eve?"

"She's just a dream."

Seerae thoughtfully contended, "No, Ross. She is not just a dream. There is no such thing as 'just a dream'—not here."

"I'm not sure I know what you mean, Seerae. Eve's just a dream. I know she's dead. There's no way she could be talking to me in my sleep."

"Eve may be dead, but some part of her is still alive and is with you."

"I doubt it. I truly wish she were, though." Ross got up and grabbed his backpack and looked at everyone. "Are we ready to go?"

For the rest of the day and into the early night hours they descended the steep northern slope of the mountain. The Valley of Veritus, like the rest of Gershom Forest, was lush and green with ancient trees dominating the landscape and flowering plants growing all around. At the head of the valley, where the company rested, there was a large meadow with springs flowing from beneath the surface of the ground, which ran together into small pools and ponds teeming with many different types of fish. Beyond the meadow, as the pools of water ran off into a stream that meandered down through the valley, the forest sprung up. There were small islands of trees scattered about through the meadow, lining its edges. It was in one of these small islands that the company spent the night.

They were greeted by the smell of smoke and fresh fish cooking over an open fire. The hope of a hearty meal had so consumed everyone the day before that it had made for a restless night. Kumél cooked while Jaroh helped. Kumél had spent all of his days since the great war in the wilderness of Shuk and knew the best fish, plants, and berries to eat. The food smelled very appetizing and soon everyone, including Ross, was around the small fire, ready for a tasty meal.

"I think I would like to stay here and never leave; I feel safe, at home."

"There are many who live here, Seerae, many who've escaped the dangers of Shuk and the gallues."

"Then it is settled. I will stay. Who will stay with me? Ross, will you stay with me? Zoësh, how about you?"

"I'm not sure I'll be staying anywhere in Shuk. I hope not anyway. I need to get home," Ross answered.

"Make this your home. It may not be your home now, but it could be, if you wanted it to be," Seerae tried to convince him.

Ross turned his eyes to the ground. The idea of staying in Shuk was unsettling, and the thought of it made the reality of what had happened too absolute. Being in Shuk had detached him from that reality, placing him between two realities, neither of which he wanted to be real. The hope of going home was the only thing driving him on, and yet, going home meant facing the reality he wished was not real. "Where do we have to go now? How long will it take to get there?"

"Half u sun. Ut bae nut far now, thut way." Jaroh pointed northward as he spoke.

"Half a sun? You mean half a day? Is that all? Great!"

Jaroh turned his head away, ignoring Ross, but Kumél looked at Ross strangely. Ross's words confused him. "Day, wut bae u day?"

"A day . . . you know . . . twenty-four hours, from the rising of the sun until the rising of the next sun, a day."

"Ut bae u sun, nut u day," Kumél said sternly and shook his head.

Once they finished their morning meal, they continued their journey. Jaroh led them to where they were going. They worked their way through the ancient forest until they were once again above the tree line and standing on a steep slope that rose several hundred feet before leveling off. With a short but demanding effort, the company climbed to the top. Spreading out before them was a large, sparsely-forested plateau with many rocky features. In the distance rose a tall, snow-white, stone monadnock, which towered above the surrounding treetops. Jaroh pointed toward it. "Dar, thut bae whaer wae bae goin." He picked up the pace as he led the company toward the towering white stone. "Com, wae wull bae dar soon."

After a few hours, they approached the great walls of stone. It was quite clear that the structure was of much greater mass and size than they had been able to ascertain from a distance. Standing at the base of it, the height alone overpowered their senses. It also dominated a vast area in the basin that would take half a day to cross in any direction. It stood like a fortress in the forest. The stone consisted of white, quartz-like crystal that, up close, resembled something more like ice. Shiny and smooth, the rock's texture felt closer to glass than it did to stone. The translucent composition of the stone allowed them to see into it, but not through it, for it was much too thick. A myriad of colorful flashes of light danced within the stone, coursing about like fluid, making the stone appear to move and change shape, though it was solid and fixed.

Jaroh led the group around the base of the stone to the north, where they eventually came upon a narrow opening. The opening appeared as little more than a fissure in the face of the wall. Jaroh stepped into the opening, which led into the rock like a narrow corridor. Such a corridor would normally have been dark and forbidding, but in this case, the walls of translucent rock glowed from the dancing array of refracted sunlight. Leading his companions into the rock, Jaroh moved slowly through the close quarters, though for Ross and the nephesh, the way was more than sufficient. Winding through the stone, the narrow way reminded Ross of the crack in the wall of the pit he had traveled through.

Eventually, the passage opened into a large circular basin, a hollow which was guarded on all sides by the sheer, towering crystalline walls and open above so that the clear light of day shone down upon a secret, magnificent garden. Growing all around were trees and plants, grasses, and flowers, which adorned the hollow in a splendorous mix of colors and smells. As they exited the wall, they were suddenly overcome by the vision. At first, they clustered together, as if reluctant to intrude upon such immaculate ambiance.

The sounds of songbirds, tits, and larks broke through the enchanting spell that had overwhelmed them all. One by one, they entered the genial realm of the garden sanctuary. The pungent aroma of snowpetal filled the stone hollow, arousing the senses of everyone present. There were many small creatures fearlessly watching, and there were larger animals of the deer and antelope family that had made the hollow their home. "What is this place, Jaroh?"

"Dis bae da Garden o'Veritus, whaer da Well o'Veritus rests. Ut waer foun by Amik, lung afore da war. Ee un Eloh planted da garden t'gaer. Ut waer u saecret place. Afore ee died, Amik returned haer wit Eloh."

"But, why are we here?" Ross questioned impatiently.

"Alethia coms."

"Who's Alethia?"

"Ye wull know soon. Shae coms t'da well t'maet ye."

"Me? Why does she want to meet me?"

"A dunna know, ye wull ha t'ask her. Mubae shae wull haelp ye fin yer way home."

"I hope so."

Ross made his way over to the hollow in the middle of the garden. There was a giant, flat, polished stone, lifted from the floor of the hollow by a rough-hewn, rocky base. In the middle of the stone was a pool of liquid sitting perfectly still and contained, just above the surface. The flat, polished stone was composed of the same quartz-like crystal as the surrounding stone megalith he saw in the pit. Ross walked around it and noticed carvings around its edges that looked like those he had seen in the pit. He studied the strange inscriptions and recalled the writings he had copied into Eve's journal, then stopped to gaze into the central pool of water that lay still and undisturbed. "What is this?"

"Ut bae da Well o'Veritus. Laeve ut bae."

Ross looked at the shallow pool that rested like a giant droplet on the smooth, crystal surface. He wondered why it did not run off and from where it originated. In the water, he could see his reflection, and beneath his reflection, he could see the stone; it looked as though the water was very shallow, like a mere spill on the floor. Ross suddenly realized just how thirsty he was. He reached out his hand to take a palm-full of the water. As his hand touched the water, ripples moved over its surface and the water began churning.

Ross was paying no attention to the ripples or the sudden activity; he was preoccupied with the unexpected reality that the water was not on the surface of the stone at all but was a deep pool into which he had plunged his hand. He lifted his hand out of the water and brought it toward his mouth, only to have the water in his palm spill out upon the flat, stone surface surrounding the pool. He observed the water as it landed on the stone without a splash and watched it as it flowed toward the inscription at the edge of the stone. Soon the water filled the carved writing and the place where the water had landed on the stone was now completely dry. All the while, the pool in the middle of the stone was swirling, creating a whirlpool that was sinking deeper and deeper into the stone while also rising like a fluid pillar above it. The water pooling in the inscription caused the writing to glow with an intense blue light, which began to shoot from the surface of the stone like a beam, projecting the same shapes into the air.

Jaroh turned and saw Ross standing mesmerized, with his hand still extended over the well, the beams of blue light piercing through his arm as they lifted into the sky. The last drop of water fell from Ross's palm onto the stone surface as if in slow motion, landing with a heavy thud. At that moment, everything around him stopped; including time. Ross could see, rising from the center of the swirling water, the figure of a man. Ross stood motionless. His eyes transfixed on the figure, his hand reached out over the flat stone, but he could not move, he could not turn away, he could only watch.

With a sudden, violent impact, Ross hit the ground. He groaned with pain, shook his head, and blinked his eyes to shake off the stupor that had bound him motionless just a moment before. He rolled over to find that Jaroh was standing over him. He had knocked Ross to the ground in a heap. Ross looked at Jaroh with shock and anger. "What the hell?!"

"A tol ye t'laeve ut bae."

"Slightly overreacting, don't you think?"

"Dunna touch da pool!"

Ross picked himself up from the ground and looked at the well. It was unchanged from before: still, calm, and placid, as if he had never touched it. He wondered if he had imagined what he had just seen and felt, aside from the injury sustained by Jaroh's intervention, of course. Ross called out to Jaroh who was walking away from him. "Hey! What just happened?"

"Nae'er ye mun. Laeve ut bae!"

Except for Jaroh, who had seen all that Ross had seen, none of the others had witnessed or heard anything that had happened. Ross scratched his throbbing head, confused and unsure of what to think. The others wandered through the expansive garden and eventually came together near the well. Seerae eyed Jaroh. "I've never seen a place like this. There is something about it, something beyond its beauty that makes it so . . . I don't know . . . so perfect."

"Ut bae one o da las unspoiled vestiges o'Pardis. A garden created by Eloh un Amik," Jaroh explained.

"Is this what it was like before the war?" Ross inquired.

"Aye. D'ye rumumbar Kumél, ye haelped Amik un Eloh?"

"Nae. A dunna rumumbar," growled Kumél.

"Dar bae muny gardens lik ut un Pardis." For a long time, Jaroh told the others the stories of the beauty and greatness of Pardis. He told them of the war and of the days before, until the night arrived and each of them closed their eyes and went to sleep, filled with thoughts of another time and another place that seemed such a far distance away.

Some time after everyone else had fallen asleep, Ross awoke and got up. He stood in the darkness, alone and cold, not sure of what to do or where to go. In the distance, he saw a faint glimmer of light that appeared as a fluid orb, falling from far above, like a single drop of water falling to the earth. As it fell, Ross could hear the sound of a woman's voice speaking in a language he had never heard before. Though he could not understand the words, he understood that the voice was speaking to him. He watched the drop of light fall through the darkness. At its impact, the drop of light broke the still calmness of the surface before him, making billowing ripples, like a stone cast into a calm sea. The ripples were small at first, quiet and gentle, but as they traveled away from their source, they grew in intensity and scale. Like the seismic waves of an earthquake moving away from the epicenter, the ripples on the surface of the black sea radiated outward, and yet, at the same time, they grew greater and stronger and more violent. Ross found himself caught up in a mighty tempest struggling to escape the frightening grip of the storm. Suddenly, he was pulled under the black surface. As he fought against the waters, he felt as if he were drowning, trying to break the surface, trying to get a breath, but only sinking deeper and deeper. He tried to call out for help, but he could not.

Suddenly, a hand reached from above the water and took hold of Ross's hand. It pulled him upward until his head broke through the surface. Ross took a long deep breath, then coughed and choked as his rescuer pulled him into a small, hewn sailing boat with square fabric hanging from the mast. The sun was shining again, but Ross could not see the shore. In all directions, there was nothing but a clear, flat sea for as far as his eyes could perceive.

Sitting in the boat across from him was the figure of a woman. She wore a hooded shawl made of fine linen. She sat with her back to Ross. "What are you looking for, Ross Blair?" The voice of the woman was immediately recognizable to him. It was the same voice he had heard in the darkness as the drop of light had fallen from the sky.

"I came to find my way," Ross replied.

"Your way? Your way where?"

"My way home."

"And what will you do if I show you the way?" the woman inquired.

"I will go back, back to where I came from."

"But you do not know where you came from. Look into the water and see your reflection."

Ross looked down and saw that the boat had no floor, but it was not sinking. Instead of a boat floor, there was a deep, bottomless, black sea. The water was smooth and still, reflecting like a mirror.

Ross gazed into the water and viewed a faceless image staring back at him. He also saw bright blue markings—an inscription like a tattoo—written into the right forearm of the reflected figure. The inscription glowed as if it were on fire. He looked away from the reflection toward his own arm. He could see the same blue markings on himself. "But where is my face?" Ross asked the woman.

"What do you see in the water?"

"A faceless man with unknown words written in blue on his arm."

"Who is the man that you see?" the woman continued to quiz Ross.

"It is me."

"How do you know that it is you?"

"But it has to be me. It's my reflection, isn't it?"

"Yes. It is your reflection, but you are not who you think you are."

"Then who am I?"

"You are a man who is lost from himself. You are a man who is blind and unable to see who he is. That is why you cannot see your reflection."

Ross felt his heart racing madly. He was confused and becoming frightened. "Then who is the man I have been all my life? Who am I if I am not that man?"

"That man is an image, an illusion. He only exists as a shell, hollow and empty inside."

"This can't be real! This has to be a dream!" Ross panicked.

"Life is full of realities that you have not yet learned to understand. You have only begun to see and seeing what you see makes you afraid. What brings you fear, Ross?"

"I am afraid of this . . . that this is real, that I'm somehow stuck in this place forever, and I will never escape!"

"You need not fear the reality of life; it is the illusion of life that should bring you fear."

"But how do I know what is real and what is an illusion?"

"Nearly everything you have known to be life has been an illusion. You have never really lived the life you were meant to live. Even the reality of death and loss and heartache is an illusion you have lived under. You have lived a life that leads you to one inevitable end—and one end only: death. You have accepted death as natural, normal, and yet, you are afraid of it. I know you feel it in your bones, that death is somehow not meant to be your end. You hope, against reality, that those who have died are not really dead. You look for Eve, yet your conscience knows that she is dead. You have accepted a reality that you do not believe."

"But if it is just an illusion, then, where are they? Where is Eve? I saw her fall, and I saw Daniel fall. If that was just an illusion, then, where are they?"

"You must open your eyes. You must see what is meant to be seen. If you look for life in the illusion of your mind, you will not find what it is that you are searching for. Life is not meant to lead to death. Death is not natural or normal: life is meant to be lived. Reality is something different than what you have known. But you will not find it until you open your eyes. You will drift upon the shoreless sea until you open your eyes."

Ross opened his eyes, peeking out timidly from behind his heavy lids, not knowing what to expect or in what state of consciousness he might find himself. He was relieved to see snowpetal growing up in front of him. He lifted his head slowly and cautiously to see Kumél, kneeling nearby, watching him. His mind was still reeling from the dream he had just woken from, so much so, that he felt uncertain about what was and was not reality. The unexpected vision of Kumél lurking nearby would have normally sparked a troubling reaction; however, Ross was now comforted by the sight of his giant friend. "How long have you been there?"

"Nut lung. A haerd ye un da night. Ye bae draemin. Bad draem, huh?"

"Yeah. Bad dream."

"A hate draems. Ye nae'er know wut ones bae rael, un wut ones bae dreams."

"Yeah, I know exactly what you mean." Ross made his way to a small spring and knelt to wash and refresh himself. The dream lingered in his thoughts. Some part of himself questioned the reality of the moment; he wondered if he was awake or in another dream. Kneeling beside the spring, Ross reached into the water with his hands cupped together. He scooped the water and lifted it to his face. He repeated the process again and again, trying to confirm that he was awake. Knowing that he was conscious and wanting to wash away the grime and sweat of the past days, he took off his shirt and began to wash his body. He immediately noticed something that troubled him deeply. On his right arm were markings, the markings of the blue light that had pierced his arm the day before, the same markings he had seen in his reflection in the dream. He had not felt anything, nor had he seen them before, but when he put his arm in the water, the markings appeared. He grabbed his shirt and tried to wipe them away, but they would not fade.

Ross looked over his shoulder to see if anyone else had noticed, but he was alone. He put the wet shirt back on and wondered what it all meant. Ross scurried back to where the rest of the group had gathered to eat. He said nothing about the markings. "Jaroh, when do you think Alethia will come?"

"Haerd t'say, soon A expect."

"OK. So, who is this Alethia anyway?"

"I am Alethia." She had entered the hollow quietly, inconspicuously, which surprised everyone. She was as beautiful as a Greek goddess. Her poise was elegant, almost imperial, yet she was gracious and friendly, making everyone feel a sense of ease and peace. Her voice resonated like that of a queen or a goddess, strong and enchanting, yet kind and gentle. Ross immediately recognized it as the voice of the woman who had sailed with him on the infinite sea.

Upon hearing her voice, Ross quickly turned to identify her. She stood, tall and slender, near the well. She had long, raven black hair with bronze highlights that fell over her shoulders to her waist in large, loose curls. Her skin was dark, like the color of caramel, radiating with a supernatural incandescence. She wore a golden band around her head with the mark of Eloh inscribed upon it. Her golden patterned gown sparkled as if overlaid with pure golden sequins. The garment seemed as though it were a living thing, flowing and dancing over her body as she moved.

Ross looked around carefully to see what Jaroh and the nephesh were doing. He had an overwhelming compulsion to bow or kneel before her, so he watched the others just in case there was some appropriate etiquette required. It was, however, a mystery to him as to why he felt this way. There was no bowing or saluting of any kind, but Ross could not help but sense that Alethia was someone of great importance. "Jaroh, you have found them. Good! You are all welcome here and you are safe. No harm can come to you in Gershom."

"Ut waer Msusi who foun thum. Shae led thum t'mae."

"Kumél, it's been a very long time! You have been missed. Did you know that Amik asked about you when we brought him here before he died?"

"Nae."

"He always missed you." Alethia was not pretentious or regal; in fact, she treated everyone as if they were her best friend and suggested that they treat her equally. Soon it was discovered that there were several kerolus accompanying Alethia. They followed behind her at a distance. For Ross, Zoësh, and Seerae, meeting Alethia and the kerolus was as exciting as it was frightening, especially for Ross, who was the only mortal among them. Even Kumél, who was, by definition, an outcast, seemed quite at home in the company of Alethia and her escort.

As the day passed and evening approached, everyone gathered to share a meal and bask in the fellowship of one another. Ross felt quite out of place and found himself looking for a place away from the others where he could sit and observe. He wondered about Alethia and what part she was to play, or, for that matter, what part *he* was to play in this strange epic. He sat quietly eating his food, hoping to be left to himself and his thoughts, though it was not to be. It was obvious to all that Ross was withdrawn, though no one felt compelled to inquire as to why. As they spent time telling tales and enjoying their meal, the night crept in upon them. Soon there was music at play as the kerolus began to blow on their ancient dukwáns. Eventually, the nephesh joined in.

Alethia stepped away from the others and approached Ross who was thinking about the dream. She knew his thoughts and he was aware that she knew them. A part of him hoped what he had seen and heard was nothing more than a dream, and yet, another part of him wondered if the dreams were, somehow, something more, that there was some reality to them. Seeing Alethia and hearing her voice were his first glimpses into the reality of his imagination, into the possibility that there were other forces at work. He wondered how it was possible that he would hear the voice of someone in a dream he had never heard before and then, only hours later, see that unknown person standing before him. Was it possible that Eve could have reached out and touched his face as he hung from the summit of Machapuchare?

"Your thoughts are heavy. You have many questions weighing them down."

"Yeah, you're right, a lot to think about."

"You doubt what you have seen. You doubt what is real and what is not."

"Ever since the summit, everything's been really strange. Just not sure what to think."

"Sometimes you think too much. Try looking with your heart, seeing beyond the surface of life. The way of your thoughts is like a small boat floating in an endless sea."

"Like in my dream—is that what you mean?"

"A little. You find yourself alone, and you see your life like that little boat, sailing upon an endless sea, but you don't live in a world that is endless. In your world, everything has a beginning and an end; life and death exist inseparably, but in your thoughts and in your heart, you imagine life as endless."

"So, doesn't everyone imagine that they will live forever? I mean, who really wants to die?"

"But if life is so inexorably linked to death, if the eventuality of every breath is to be exhaled, never to return, then why does the dream, the hope of eternity, echo in the hollow corridors of your being? Why do you long for what you can never have?"

"I guess I don't know. I guess there is some part of me that feels like, well, like, it shouldn't be that way. I don't know why . . . I mean . . . what right do I have to expect there is anything different than what I have known and seen? And yet I do. I do hope for something different. Maybe that's what I've been looking for all along, something different, something that feels right. Crazy, huh?"

"What if it weren't crazy, Ross? What if deep within, you know there is more to life, more to everything, that all is meant to be different, that there is something to seek, to find, to long for. Like the snowpetal, it grows all around you—why?"

"Why? I don't know. Been wondering that myself."

"It grows because it sees something in you that you cannot see in yourself. All of nature sees it in you."

"Sees what?"

"Hope! Every plant, every creature, every drop of rain or flake of snow waits expectantly, like a woman with child, waiting anxiously for the birth of her newborn. They await the arrival of the one who will restore the bond of life that has been broken. You give them hope."

"Me? Why me?"

"Because they know you are meant for something that you do not even see. You feel it, and they feel it."

"What can I do . . . *really* do? Everything is so messed up."

"It wasn't meant to be this way, but the brokenness of Pardis lives in every creature and every being throughout the realm. Even Eloh feels the brokenness; it is more than a memory, just as Eve is more than a memory. The brokenness of life, of beauty, of the heart, of fellowship, causes everything to labor in futility. You are a sign to everything."

"A sign of what?"

"Of change. You are like a drop of water falling from the sky into a stagnant pool. You are the impetus that disturbs the stillness of the dark, making the waters convulse."

"Me? What if I don't want it to be me?"

"Some things are beyond our will or desire. You must do whatever it is that only you can do."

Alethia rose and joined Jaroh and the other kerolus. Together they walked toward an opening in the crystal wall. Ross sat alone for a long time thinking about everything Alethia had told him. After a while, Kumél came near and sat beside him. Ross turned to speak to him. "There is so much I don't understand Kumél. I used to think I understood my life, that I knew how things were supposed to be, but now, now I just don't know. I never really thought too hard about it, you know? I just took it as it came, dealt with it the best I knew how and then moved on or ignored it. But what do you do when you don't want to move on? I never before wanted to fix anything. I just left whatever was broken behind and got a new one. But how do you buy a new self, a new life, or a new love? I'm tired of feeling numb, but I'm afraid of the torture of feeling the pain of living."

Kumél listened, though he had no answers or reply to offer. He, like Ross, was broken and lost and had learned just enough to survive with his brokenness. "What would you do? If you could fix it, would you do it?"

"Aye. Uf A cud."

"I don't even know what that means, 'fix it'. Sometimes . . . I don't know . . . fixing something winds up making everything else a mess. It's like . . . if I were to fix my life, from beginning to now, would I still have met Eve, would I still have loved her and would she have loved me? Maybe it's better to leave things alone. After all, only God knows how things are supposed to be . . . that's what I've heard, anyway. And God, what about him? Where is he in all this? Yeah, where is he? If anyone could fix it, wouldn't it be him? So why hasn't he?"

"A cunna say."

Ross found himself being pulled away from the conscious reality and absorbed in thought, as if he were in a trance. His mind was abuzz with thoughts, thoughts deeper than he knew how to process and with feelings he could not understand. Throughout the day he contemplated life, the world, humanity, Eve, himself, his father, his mother, Daniel, the meaning of life, the purpose of life and—most of all—fixing it. How could he fix it, and what exactly did that mean? Alethia had opened a doorway into his mind, unlocking a warehouse of thoughts and emotions that had lain dormant in the core of his being. Like a caged animal that gets free and runs wild, Ross's heart contemplated a tangle of many things late into the night. Unaware of the passing of time, he wandered through his mind, even after everyone else had gone to sleep.

Eventually, Ross's thoughts returned to the hollow. Lying on the ground looking into the sky above, he noticed a great display of colored lights dancing across the sky. He remembered being in the high mountains of Alaska on a summit bid to Denali where he watched the Aurora Borealis. The sky over Shuk looked so much the same that he forgot where he was for a moment. There was, however, a strange difference that took Ross a while to distinguish. The lights of the night sky were not coming from the sky but were coming from Shuk. Upon realizing that the aurora overhead was, in fact, a terrestrial event rather than a cosmic one, Ross sat up and looked around. He could see a shaft of blue light rising from the midst of the hollow, not far from where he was laying. Slowly he stood and looked in the direction of the light. He could see, coming into view, that the source of the brilliant blue shaft was the Well of Veritus.

Ross looked all around, hoping to see that he was not alone in his vision, but everyone else was fast asleep, and what he was witnessing, he witnessed alone. He made his way toward the well where he could see rings of blue light pulsating up away from the flat stone top of the well. As they rose, the pulses of light grew in circumference until they struck the white quartz walls that surrounded the hollow. Once they struck the stone walls they burst apart into a kaleidoscope of colors and patterns, all shifting and surging together, and then apart, and then together again. At the same time, they were growing and elevating, rising higher and higher into the night sky, where they became an immeasurable cosmic eruption of an unimaginable scale, coursing across the heavens and into the outer stratosphere.

Ross moved cautiously toward the well. His gaze was fixated on the flat surface of the well, which was ablaze in colorful light, so intense and saturated that his eyes could hardly look upon it. The familiar inscription written along the edges of the flat stone glowed in the brilliant, blue light just as he had seen before. As he moved closer, he discovered that the water was still, unaffected by the light. It appeared that the light was coming through the flat stone and radiating over the clear, flat pool. Like veins, Ross could see blue light coursing through the stone as it made its way through and into the night air. Suddenly, what looked like large bubbles of air rising up to the surface of the water and then escaping into the light where once freed from the water, they burst into various colors and rose into the sky like fireflies, flitting energetically into the darkness.

Closer and closer Ross edged toward the well. Once he reached the stone table, he stood enveloped in its light which, to his surprise, was both warm and cool. He reached out and tried to take hold of one of the millions of floating bubbles, but before he could catch one, hundreds landed on him. They landed on his head and his arms and in his hand, on his face and even on his eyelashes; like little butterflies drawn to the nectar of the flower, the small drops of color and water and light seemed drawn to him. Amassing over his entire body, the aurora transformed Ross from a mere mortal into the image of a being with unimaginable shine.

He did not want to move; the touch of living light was incomparable, and he did not want it to pass. Then the drops of light lifted, assimilating into an aural symphony that filled the sky. He stood with his eyes fixed on the rising effluvial drops of light floating playfully into the heavens.

Standing opposite of him, Ross noticed Alethia. She stood quietly observing him through the prismatic glow. When Ross's eyes fixed on hers, she spoke to him softly and gently, "Touch the water, take it into your hands, and let it wash you."

Ross reached out his hand and gently scooped the water into his palm. As he lifted his hand from the water, drops escaped his hand, falling back into the pool. When the drops hit the surface of the pool, colors of light lifted away from the surface as if the water was not water at all, but a mysterious liquid, latent with tiny magical organisms that had been freed and had come to life when the pool was stirred.

"Pour it out upon the stone table before you."

Ross reached his cupped hands into the pool. With the water dripping from his hands and running down his forearms, Ross carried the water over to the flat stone, then opened his hands, allowing the water to fall upon it. As the water struck the stone, it did not splash; it gathered upon the stone like honey, congealing together into a solid, round sphere that began to roll toward the edge of the flat stone. Coming to rest in a small, circular dimple near the edge, the liquid sphere began to slump as clear fluid oozed out from its underside into small cracks that led into the strange writing on the stone.

Slowly at first, then accelerating rapidly, the liquid from the sphere filled the inscribed writing around the rim of the well. The writing began to glow bright and blue, just as it had before. "Can you read the writing?" Alethia asked Ross.

"No, it is the same as the writing I saw in the pit."

"Yes, it is. Look into the well. What do you see?" Ross stepped closer to the well and leaned over the flat stone top to see into the depths of the water. At first, he could only see darkness. Alethia asked him another question, "How deep is the water?"

Ross stretched out his arm and plunged his hand into the water. "It is deeper than I can reach." He pulled his arm from the water and was surprised to find that it was not wet. The inscriptions that he had seen written on his arm were glowing bright blue like the inscription on the rim of the stone. Next Alethia instructed Ross, "Reach again. Tell me what you find." Ross could feel the coolness of the water touching him. A glow began to emanate from deep in the well as if reaching out to him. He could see what looked like a hand of light reaching through the dark toward his own hand.

The hand of light touched his hand, though it did not take hold; it only touched him, testing his reaction to see if he would pull away. But Ross did not move away. In the cool waters of the well, the hand of light felt warm and comforting. Ross took hold of the hand that touched him. It was not flesh and bone like his hand, but it had shape and form that he could feel. "Why can't I hold onto the hand? Why can I feel it but not grasp it?"

"The Waters of Veritus are like many things which can be felt but cannot be possessed. No one can own them or shape them. They are for all and not for one. They can touch you and change you, but you are not able to do the same to them." Ross removed his hand from the water and focused on the illuminated script on the stones around the well.

"Touch the writing," Alethia directed him.

Ross stretched out his hand with his finger fully extended and touched the bright blue letters. When his finger contacted the fluid-like light, the markings on his arm began to spread to his entire body, glowing bright and blue. "Tell me, Ross. What does it say?"

Ross looked and understood. Astonished, he read it aloud:

Out of the darkness and void, a way has been made; the light of Eloh will lead you away from the shadows and into a new world. Let this hope guide you. A day will come when your brokenness is healed, and Pardis is whole once again. There is one who is coming from the line of your father. He will walk the Aurora Path and pierce the heart of the cruel masters with a spear stained in Theoscian blood. On that day, you will see a new moon standing in the full light of day. Then you will know that the time is near, when you will return to the realm of Eloh.

Ross looked at her. "What is it?"

"It's an ancient promise, Ross."

"But, why am I able to read it?"

"Those things revealed by the Well of Veritus are the reflection of things forgotten, things hidden, and things unknown, the mysteries of the heart and the unwritten truth that lives beyond the realm of darkness and shadow. You have seen the writing with eyes that were not blind."

While Alethia was talking, Ross's eyes fell upon the water in the well. When she paused, Ross inquired, "Who is that, in the well?"

"Look and see." He looked down into the waters and saw a hooded, faceless man standing on the surface of a lake. Ross felt a sudden rush of dread. "Do not fear," Alethia comforted him.

"Who is he?" Ross shakily asked.

"He seeks what you seek." Ross wondered what Alethia meant but did not ask. He studied the strange apparition. "What does he seek?"

"Only you can know that, and you will never find what you seek until you find him." Ross glanced up at her. He did not know what the answer was, but he knew she was right. "Know this Ross: the answers you seek cannot be told to you; you must find them yourself. The very thing you are looking for is, itself, trying to find you."

"Where will I find him?"

"You must go to the Pool of Levitus. It is found above the Falls of Jaarah."

"Will he be there?"

"That is for you to find out."

"How will I find it?"

"At the northern edge of Gershom forest, there is one who can help. His name is Ziminiar. He knows the way to the Falls of Jaarah. Be careful. There are many spies and many enemies who hunt you, many who would destroy you. What you do now, Ross, could change everything, and there are many who do not wish this to happen."

"Will you go with me?" Ross asked hopefully.

"No, but remember, you will find what you are meant to find there—nothing more."

Ross watched as Alethia walked away. He knew that she was leaving Shuk, though he did not know why he had that knowledge. As she walked out of sight, Ross saw the kerolus, including Jaroh, leave with her. The light of the well soon disappeared and Ross stood alone in the night. He reached out and touched the strange writing inscribed on the flat stone. As he felt it, a warm sensation spread up his arm. The writing that had been invisible before now flared radiantly up his arm and began to glow on the flat stone. He wondered what it meant; he wondered even more why he hadn't asked Alethia. Somehow, he knew that he would not have understood her answer.

Ross sat down beside the well. He laid his head on the flat stone and thought about all he had seen and heard.

Chapter XII
The Storm

Jekkid and the two other gallues had climbed high toward the Pass of Borak in search of the foreigner and the killer of the mēgs, just as Morak had commanded. But for all their time and effort, they found no evidence of either.

On the verge of splitting up and taking their chances with Gubrone, a strange and unexpected phenomenon had occurred. Late in the afternoon, while crossing over a wide mountain pass, Slÿteg, as he had paused to catch his breath, caught sight of a sudden burst of white light, just a flash in the north, and, in barely the span of a breath, it had disappeared. It had been quite fleeting, so unexpected, and at such a long distance away that the chance of him catching sight of it was improbable. Slÿteg, though quite stunned, knew what had generated the light and what it now meant to them. Ourdïs had witnessed it as well, out of the corner of his eye. Both gallues were momentarily shocked by the sight and stood staring in silence. They waited, hoping to catch a second glimpse, but they were granted no second chance; the light was gone as quickly as it had appeared.

Jekkid had not seen the light. He was moving too quickly over the pass, toward the south. The winds in the pass were strong and loud muffing the sound of Slÿteg's call for them to wait. However, when Ourdïs yelled his name, Jekkid stopped. Clearly aggravated, he dropped his hands to his side and shook his head as he turned his face to the sky in a gesture of impatience. He stood with his back to the others and waited for some irritating complaint, for it had become a constant issue. Jekkid grudgingly waited, but Ourdïs and Slŷteeg were looking away from him and did not notice his impatient stance. "Wut bae da trouble? Restin agan, bae ye? Ye bae da laziest two gallues A ha er ha da misfortune o'travelin wit! Wut d'ye wanna?"

Slŷteeg and Ourdïs stood facing the north, unresponsive to Jekkid's outrage. As Jekkid approached, he perceived that they had viewed something unexpected, but upon his own quick examination of the skyline, Jekkid could see nothing to justify such gawking. "Wut bae ut?"

Slŷteeg speculated, "Ut cunna bae, cun ut?"

"Wut? Wut ha ye idiots saen?"

"kerolus," announced Ourdïs.

"Wut?"

"Dar! Ut ha t'bae." Ourdïs pointed to the location of the sighting.

"Dar bae nutin thut looks lik thut,"

"U kerolus?! Whaer?"

"Dar! Right whaer thum hae peaks bae. Right naer da Pass o'Attone," Jekkid was incredulous.

"Un Gershom?"

"A saes ut, tae. Ees right! Ut bae definitely u kerolus un flight,"

"But, whaer dud ee gae?"

"Ut happened so quickly. Dar ut bae, thun gone, lik u flash. A waer lookin right at eem,"

Jekkid could not believe what he was hearing. "Da flight o'u kerolus, haer, un Shuk?"

There were many different thoughts running through the minds of the three gallues. They had once been kerolus themselves. Long ago, they had spread their wings and flown the flight of light that only a kerolus could fly. For a few moments, memories of their former selves invaded their minds and made them ache with the pain of their treachery. But not for long, for the corruption in them was complete. They quickly began discussing a plan. In a short time, they had decided to abandon their search for the foreigner and take the news of their sighting to Gubrone.

The three gallues were several days from the mist that guarded the Pass of Klamata. They raced toward the valley as the hope of reward renewed their energy.

Morak, his two mēgs, and Loham, the snitch, crossed over the Pass of Klamata and descended into the heavy gray mist. Morak knew that Huzesh and his rabbles could be hiding anywhere among the dauntless shadows and that they would most certainly be looking for any opportunity to wreak havoc on whoever had the misfortune of meeting them. Huzesh rarely had reason or justification for his violent, unwarranted harassment. Always ready for a fight, he never needed to be antagonized, and it was well known that he chose his victims indiscriminately.

Loham was a timid sort. His nature was cautious and reserved. Joining up with Morak was as distant from his normal behavior as the three moons of Assuk were distant from Shuk. However, there was something hidden in the motives of Loham. He was looking for something he could not find in the Valley of Souls. Loham had been a snitch for most of the time he had been in Shuk. Most of the snitches were orphaned and alone because the ties of life had been broken by the death of their sapien. However, Loham was different; his sapien had abandoned him, turned him away. The heart of Loham had abandoned all hope, and Gubrone used the forces of loneliness and abandonment to deceive Loham and turn him against his own kind.

Loham felt something deep in his being, something that whispered to him. Strange and mysterious images invaded his dreams and unfamiliar songs injected words of hope to his heart. It was a growing sensation inside of him, and he tried to keep it hidden from the sorcery of the gallues. The offer to leave the valley was a perfect way to escape the valley and avoid anyone there discovering his secret.

The snitches were coerced into using their connection with the spirit of life living in other nephesh to track and capture the ones who had escaped, as well as tracking the renegade nephesh roaming Shuk. Often, however, if there were more than one snitch in an area, they would get confused and were not able to sense the spirit of life in the others because they sensed it in the other snitches. It was for this reason that the snitches were expected to hunt alone or with a gallue rather than in their own packs. Morak intended to use Loham to find the foreigner, to sense its spirit of life, and that of any others who were with him.

As Morak and Loham descended into the mist, few words were spoken between them. Morak seldom gave himself to conversation, as he usually traveled solo. Loham, on the other hand, usually enjoyed chatting along the way but was too afraid of Morak to initiate any exchange of words. It was favorable that they remained as quiet as possible to avoid being noticed by other travelers.

As darkness settled over Shuk and passage through the mist became more strenuous, Loham longed for them to stop and wait for daylight but was too nervous to speak his mind. Morak did not want to quit; he knew they would lose time once out of the mist because the mēgs could not travel in the sunlight. Nevertheless, after several miles of stumbling and groping through the oppressive darkness, Morak decided to wait for more light. He also hoped that the route would become clearer to him, for he was not sure he was taking the best path through the mist.

Food was a rare commodity in the mist, but Morak had brought provisions. He opened a cinched hide bag and pulled out a rotting, stinking tangle of entrails belonging to some unfortunate small creature he had killed. He offered Loham a portion. "Haer ye bae. Eat."

"Ahh, no thanks. I'll be fine," Loham refused. He felt hunger was a better meal than the putrid offering from Morak.

Loham sat on the stump of an old fallen tree some distance away from Morak. Morak paid him no mind and squatted down eating his disgusting meal. He shared some with his mēgs who chose to fight over the scraps rather than eat them. Loham stared into the mist trying to identify the strange silhouetted figures lurking just beyond his reach. Unexpectedly, he noticed a large, black corvus perched on the skeletal frame of an ancient, giant tree standing alone in the gray mist. The corvus glared at him. Loham could not pull his eyes away from the ugly bird.

Morak, who had not noticed the corvus, pivoted at the sound of the call. He saw the bird out of the corner of his ebony eye as it flew away. "Wae better fin u place t'hide. Thut one wull bae brangin more." Morak rose and began to look around for some type of shelter to hide from the menacing birds. Close to where Loham was seated, they discovered a cave that was elevated far enough above the surrounding rocks to be hidden. It also had a large enough opening that they could squeeze into it. Morak climbed into the small cave. He left his mēgs to fend for themselves and considered leaving Loham to learn an important lesson. He would not normally care if the corvuses picked away at Loham or if they killed him.

However, he knew that Loham could help find the foreigner. "Gut un, now! Dar bae liddle tam afore dae bae buk, un ye wull bae deir meal." Morak reached down from the cave opening, grabbed Loham around the neck, and lifted him into the small cave. Loham could not protest, for the grip Morak had around his neck was so tight he feared his head was going to pop right off. Finally, Morak released his grip, and Loham began to draw a long, deep breath into his lungs when suddenly, he shrieked with fright. A loud, black cloud of feathers descended on the site. They were corvuses. Some landed on the ground or in the branches of the dead trees, others flew around incessantly, cackling and crowing, making a terrifying and deafening fracas. The mēgs growled and barked like dogs. They jumped into the air, catching the nasty, diseased birds in their powerful jaws, two and three at a time, chewing them up and swallowing them, feathers and all. At the same time, the corvuses were landing on the mēgs, pecking, and stabbing at their eyes and head and bodies, ravenously devouring them one tiny piece of flesh at a time. The life and death struggle continued with the awful sounds of flesh being torn and bones being crushed. Squawks and howls echoed endlessly through the narrow valley.

Morak guarded the entrance of the cave using his sharp talons to kill the black birds who tried to attack him and Loham. The birds pecked at his arms and legs and then at his head and eyes, trying to blind him so they could finish him off. One of the birds made it past Morak and attacked Loham with its fierce beak and long, black talons. Loham swatted at the air; he tried to knock the bird down, but it was too quick. He then lunged at the bird, grabbed it by the head, and flung it against the side of the small cave. The bird lay stunned but still alive until Morak crunched it under his massive, heavy feet. Blood was oozing out of wounds on Morak's head and arms, increasing the appetite of carnivorous birds who wanted to attack even more. The birds were relentless and numerous as they bombarded Morak and Loham.

Finally, the cloud of corvuses began to dissipate as the black birds flew away into the mist as suddenly as they arrived. Morak was seriously wounded. One by one, the giant black birds that had been lingering, waiting for an opportunistic meal, flew away into the mist until all appeared to be gone. Morak could not hear the growls of his mēgs, but he and Loham were not about to venture out just to check on them. They held out in the small cave through the night, until the break of day began to illuminate the dark gray mist.

Morak found his mēgs dead and their bodies devoured to the bone.

Blood soaked the stones and patches of soil all around the entrance of the cave where the mēgs made their defiant last stand. Morak had never seen such an attack by the corvuses before, though he had known they could be very vicious.

Loham was stunned at the grizzly sight of the two dead mēgs. He had never seen one before and had always thought of them as indestructible killers; now he knew better. The mēgs were just as indefensible against certain enemies as anyone else. The smell of the mēgs' blood hung in the air, a stench that could draw other carnivorous scavengers to the kill site. Quickly, they headed down a slope, then through a narrow pass between two enormous boulders. They moved as if being chased by a pack of wolves. Eventually, they came into a broad, open, and flat expanse, a place that would have been a meadow at one time but was now more like a bog or a marsh. The strong smell of decomposing vegetation hung in the air. Morak halted and looked around with a confused expression on his face.

Loham, not expecting Morak's abrupt stop, almost ran into him. "What is it? What's wrong?"

"A dunna rumumbar dis place." Getting lost in the mist was dangerous for anyone, even a gallue like Morak.

"What does that mean? Are we lost?"

"Nut sur. Kaep quiet!"

Loham felt a drop of water land on the top of his head. He thought nothing of it at first, but then more drops fell and before he knew it, the rain was falling, heavily. The sound of thunder could be heard in the distance. Still, Morak stood searching the marsh. He knew that to keep moving in the mist with uncertainty of exact location, was to vanish into the oblivion of the shadows.

"Maybe we should go back, try another way?" Loham offered.

"Nae. Somting bae wrong, somting bae changed."

"What do you mean?"

"Da rain, A ha nae'er saen ut rain haer."

"Why is that important? We need to get out of here, fast!"

"A know, but dar bae somting wrong. Dis shud bae da wae out." "So, what's wrong?"

"Dis marsh, A ha nae'er seen it afore."

"How could you have never seen this before? It's quite imposing."

"Da wae bae ahead, thut way." Morak pointed to the far side of the marsh. "Can we go around it?"

"Look, dar. D'ye sae da path?" Loham focused on what Morak was showing him. Some distance beyond them was the faint impression of a trail filled with water. The marsh had not been a marsh for long; it had been a wide-open area just a few days before; now it was a formidable barrier, a slough that just appeared. Morak could not imagine where all the water could have emerged from.

Loham objected, "How could it be that way? It's filled with water. Are you sure you came this way?"

"Aye. Com, wae mus gae."

The rain had begun as only a drop colliding with Loham's head. In no time at all, it became a torrent. So much water was pouring from the sky that Morak and Loham could hardly see an arm's length in front of them. As quickly as they could, they negotiated the remnants of an ancient path. At points, Loham was up to his chest in the marshy waters. A combination of rotting organic matter and methane gas made for a stench even beyond what the insensitive gallues could withstand.

Under his feet, Morak could feel the saturated ground, now a mixture of sharp rocks, round boulders, and mud, sinking below the weight of his giant frame. At first, it was just over his feet, but the deeper into the marsh they walked, the softer the soil became, and the deeper he submerged. Every step became a battle, as Morak descended to his knees plunging into the soft slurry.

Loham had a slightly easier go of it. He was much lighter and more agile than Morak, but because he was shorter, he struggled to keep his head above the water. As the hours passed and the constant rain poured over them, they trudged across the marsh, which was swallowing them in its gaping, miry mouth. Unexpectedly, a flash of lightning broke through the thick mist and rain, lighting up the entire marsh. Morak and Loham felt the static charge of the lightning surge through the water, causing every muscle in their bodies to seize.

While held in the grip of the charge, Loham's eyes were fixed overhead where he could see flashes of light coursing through the mist above. "Have you ever seen anything like this before?" Loham yelled over the sound of the raging storm.

"Nae! Nae'er!"

"How much farther do we have to go?"

"Cunna say." Morak could only see a few yards ahead, but the lightning had momentarily revealed the silhouette of a mound erected just above the surface of the water. He hoped it was the end of the marsh; however, he would soon discover that it was not. In the middle of the marsh was a long, narrow mound of rocks that stood just high enough to be free of the marsh's deep waters and mud. As they reached the mound, Morak climbed atop it. Loham, who lagged several yards behind, glanced up in surprise, to see Morak extending a hand to him. He grabbed Morak's hand and lunged out of the frigid water.

It was neither dry nor sheltered, not even safe, but it was better than being held in the grip of the marsh. Morak and Loham, drenched by the unrelenting rain, sat shivering, and wishing for a break that would afford them a chance to escape the last section of the marsh.

Jekkid, Ourdïs, and Slŷteeg approached the gray mist of Klamata from the south. As they drew near, blackness was encroaching upon the already dingy landscape, and it was apparent to them that an enormous storm was building in front of them. Not far in the distance, they heard approaching thunder rumbling through the air. Great flashes of lightning electrified the gray mist. For a brief moment, they paused and stared at the fury gathering above them, as though the sight and sound of the storm tormented them in some way. Then, with no warning, the clouds began to unleash their fury. The streams and small river that flowed from the upper regions began to swell and burst their banks. Jekkid and the others lowered their heads and continued into the mist as the downpour beat upon them. Jekkid was well-acquainted with the mist and the Way of Klamata; he had traveled the route many times. As the trio continued up to the pass, the rains began to pelt them even harder as if resisting their journey.

In only a short matter of time, the angry storm grew and covered the entire region from the farthest extent of the Valley of Souls, all the way to the Plain of Haemus. The flow of water descending from the high mountains was causing the rivers and streams to rise to flood level, and the many that they had to cross were becoming torrents. Jekkid and the others refused to quit.

Winding their way up through the narrow valleys and across the raging streams and rivers, the three gallues pushed ahead through a storm that had persisted for more than three days. By the end of the fourth day, Jekkid, Ourdïs, and Slŷteeg came to a wide, open valley where several narrow canyons converged. Each of the canyons had its own stream of water flowing into the valley. These streams came together to form one large river that flowed into another narrow, impassible gorge. This confluence was named the Tabarna Valley. Many who had traveled to this point were lost forever in the countless mazes and trails that led nowhere.

By this time, a mixture of falling rain and hailstones, the size of small rocks, beat like a thousand small fists upon the backs and heads of the gallues. Desperately, Ourdïs hollered, "We mus fin shelter!" His voice could hardly be heard over the raging storm, but Jekkid had heard enough and was inclined to agree. The three gallues found refuge under a giant balancing stone. The stone sat on three large boulders as if it had three legs. There was enough space under the stone, between the three boulders, for the three gallues to crawl under and get out of the storm. It was a surprisingly dry and comfortable refuge. All around them, the storm's fierce tempest persisted, hour after hour, covering everything in a blanket of hailstones and water.

The storm showed no signs of easing. Hailstones continued to fall over the marsh, pelting Morak and Loham as they squatted down on the narrow mound, trapped between the waters of the marsh and the relentless fury of the storm. Loham called out, "Morak! Morak, we have to get out of this storm or these ice stones will beat us to death! If we are going to be wet, we may as well be wet in the marsh, and search for someplace to get out of the storm."

"Aye, luts gae. Da end o'da marsh cunna bae far." Climbing down from the mound and back into the swollen waters of the marsh was tricky for Loham. He slipped and fell in over his head, but Morak reached into the deep water and pulled him back up. "Watch yer step, ye idiot!" Morak waded through the mud, rocks, and water of the slew, searching for any sign of the end and a place for shelter. As they pushed across the last section of the marsh, the hail mounted an even greater assault. Each time the icy stones struck their unprotected skin, it peeled a layer of flesh from them, as if the hail itself were trying to eat them alive. Bloody, bruised, wet, and worn they struggled to reach the far edge of the marsh.

Loham peered to his right and discovered what appeared to be an opening between two towering stones. He spun and headed toward it, calling back, "Morak! Here! Come here!"

Morak surveyed the area and realized that Loham was moving toward an opening between the towering rocks. He followed him. Loham entered the opening but there was no cover overhead. The hail and rain continued pelting him. He kept running until he entered a wide, open valley. At first, Loham was distraught. Cold, wet, and bleeding, he had come to the end of his physical strength and desperately needed someplace to rejuvenate. When Morak caught up with him, he recognized the place. He had his bearings and remembered a nearby cave he had used for shelter. Morak began to run toward it. He had not gone far when he noticed that Loham was not following. Morak turned and ran back, grabbed Loham by the arm, and dragged him to a hidden place behind a mound of rocks. A giant old tree stump was all that remained of an ancient juniper that had once dominated the valley. Under the stump was a large den, protected from the elements. Morak entered the den through a small opening between the stump and a giant boulder. He crawled down under the stump to find that it was dry and uninhabited. Loham followed. Morak was also exhausted and in dreadful pain. Safe from the storm and dry, they surrendered to sleep.

The darkness of the storm prevented any light from entering the Tabarna Valley, so when Loham awoke from his sleep, he could not tell whether it was day or night or how long he had been sleeping. Behind him, the large body of Morak lay, still snoring. It was difficult to know if they had been there for a day or for multiple days, but the storm still tormented the region.

Loham crawled up toward the opening to see if the hail had subsided. As he neared the small entrance, he could hear the rain but not the hail. He popped his head out of the entrance only to be soaked by the unrelenting water drops. He was, however, relieved that there were no hailstones falling from the sky. Loham crawled back down under the stump to find that Morak had awakened and reported his observations. "The ice stones have ceased falling, but the rain hasn't given up its fight."

"Nae mutter. Wae mus move on."

The cramped confinement beneath the giant stone had become like a tiny prison cell for Jekkid and his two companions. Like three scorpions fighting to find shade under the same small rock, the three quarrelsome gallues were becoming increasingly frustrated with each other. Once the hail stopped, and the opportunity to escape the rock shelter presented itself, they began fighting over who would exit first.

Finally, Ourdïs pulled himself free of the shelter and entered the downpour. In no time, he was as wet as he had been before he had climbed under the rock. Jekkid crawled free of the shelter, and he, too, was quickly soaked and annoyed by the persistent rain. The frigid air and the frosty winds that gusted intermittently chilled their wet skin. Before Slŷteeg could exit the shelter, a gruff and unfriendly voice was heard above the chaos of the drenching rain. "So, wut brings da likes o'u scrawny liddle dog lik Ourdïs t'mae realm?" Ourdïs was appalled to see the wet, scarred face of Huzesh inspecting him.

Slŷteeg was well acquainted with the voice of Huzesh. Slŷteeg had been a member of Huzesh's clan ages ago, and his departure from it was the subject of considerable infamy. Huzesh's acts of retribution against Slŷteeg for leaving had been exceedingly vicious, and the other gallues regarded them more revolting than even the vilest acts committed by their kind. In the early days of Huzesh's rebellion, he was excessively cruel and vindictive against those whom he viewed as traitors. As part of Huzesh's clan, Slŷteeg had witnessed Huzesh's barbarism against his own for too long and had planned to desert him and return to the Valley of Souls to serve Gubrone. However, before Slŷteeg could leave, Huzesh had discovered his plan and had abducted and tortured him to the point of destruction. Huzesh demonstrated such excessive masochism in his acts against Slŷteeg that the cries of Slŷteeg raised high into the ears of Gubrone and the other chief-gallues. Regardless, Gubrone showed mercy for no one and was slow to react to the news of Slŷteeg's misery. Gubrone eventually demanded Slyteeg's release though not before Huzesh had Slyteeg thrown into a stagnate, miry marsh where the corvuses picked away at his flesh.

Even among the most despicable and treacherous of beings, the acts of Huzesh were considered unforgivable. Gubrone had banished Huzesh from the valley and from the company of gallues for his insolence, declaring him a traitor. Gubrone had done this as an example to any other gallues who thought they could ignore or contravene his will and his word. It was rumored, however, that Gubrone had actually admired the brutality of Huzesh. No attempt had been made by Gubrone to recover Slŷteeg; he had been left as fodder for the corvuses. Eventually, he was found by one of the five apostas, named Daezag, who had aided him in his recovery. Now, Slŷteeg himself was a vile, cruel, and ungrateful gallue, and in order to gain favor with Gubrone, had betrayed Daezag by turning him over to Gubrone, who, in turn, murdered Daezag for his weakness and compassion.

"All alone bae ye? Ut bae u dangerus place fur u stinking dakkrah t'roam," Huzesh taunted Ourdïs.

Ourdïs glared at Huzesh who was standing just beyond his reach. Ourdïs was not one to be easily incited or goaded into a fight, though he knew that was what Huzesh hoped to achieve. Ourdïs faced Huzesh confidently, aware that Huzesh was not alone. Huzesh had not yet seen Jekkid, who was listening carefully and waiting.

In the small shelter, a vengeful, poisonous flow of hatred began to course through the body and mind of Slŷteeg as he listened to the gravelly voice of Huzesh. He tarried, peering from under the stone until he could see his enemy, waiting until he exposed his back. His rage was brewing like the storm above, blinding him to the possible disadvantage of the situation. Though he knew that Huzesh always had others with him, including mēgs, he cared not. His eyes began to glow red with the consuming fire of wrath.

Ourdïs scowled at Huzesh who growled back at him with equal contempt. "So, ye mus bae one o'Gubrone's custos, out harassing thum who ha mur important tings ta d'. Whae dunna ye move off?" Ourdïs knew exactly who Huzesh was; he also knew that Huzesh hated the custos who were appointed by Gubrone to keep guard over the way to the Valley of Souls.

"Who ye bae callin u custos?" Huzesh stepped toward Ourdïs, drawing his giant sword. Ourdïs advanced toward Huzesh and, with a quick lunge, grabbed the arm that was drawing the sword, seizing Huzesh's throat with his other hand. In a flash, the two were rolling over the wet rocks, striking, clawing, and even biting each other, in a savage fight.

Jekkid stepped around the stone to discover Huzesh and Ourdïs rolling about on the ground. He noticed that the four gallues who followed Huzesh: Vottuk, Wanoon, Motaig, and Braanik, were moving quickly toward the fight, so he intercepted the fight and the advancing gallues with his sword drawn. "Oh no."

Before the four gallues could also draw their swords, Slŷteeg exploded out from under the rock, brandishing his weapon.

Jekkid stepped to the side, giving Slŷteeg room. Slŷteeg leapt toward the approaching gallues and swung his dull sword at Vottuk, who was leading the attack. He drew the blade across Vottuk's neck and sliced his head clean from his body. Immediately the other three gallues raised their swords and attacked Slŷteeg. Jekkid rushed into the midst of the battle gripping his sword and a long dagger, which had been brandished on his hip belt.

Not far from the fighting, Morak and Loham were making their way through the storm when they noticed the scuffle. Morak could decipher the figure of the gallues and rushed into the midst of the brawl. He drew his sword and battled against Wanoon, Motaig, and Braanik, but because the rain was pouring so heavily that Jekkid and Slŷteeg could not see who he was, they fought against him, mistaking him for one of the others traveling with Huzesh. The chilling sound of iron striking iron echoed through the small valley.

Loham could see that he was out of his element and quickly hid behind a gigantic stone and watched the battle between the gallues. He felt chills run down his spine; out of the corner of his eye, he could see four glowing eyes staring at him. He twisted to see two mēgs, soaking wet, poised to pounce on him. Loham leapt to the top of the boulder behind which he was hiding. He was unarmed and had no experience in fighting mēgs. In no time, two additional mēgs joined them and Loham began to fear he would not escape. Loham screamed, "Morak, mēgs!" His voice was loud, but, by then, Morak was too far away to hear, not to mention, engaged in his own struggle.

Ourdïs managed to pull a blade from his sheath he had tied around his lower leg. He drove the blade into the ribs of Huzesh who let out a loud shriek and fell backward, releasing his grip on Ourdïs. Huzesh pushed Ourdïs away and struggled to get his feet under him so he could stand. Ourdïs landed hard against a sharp rock, cutting his shoulder and neck. He rapidly recovered and rushed toward Huzesh with his dagger extended. Huzesh drew a long dagger from his belt but not before Ourdïs picked up the sword that Huzesh had dropped during their initial collision. Ourdïs swung the sword, cutting clean off the lower part of Huzesh's arm, leaving Huzesh with only one usable arm. The dagger, still clenched in the hand of the cleaved arm, spun through the air straight at Loham, who was being overtaken by the mēgs. The large forearm of Huzesh struck Loham in the back, nearly knocking him from the marginal safety of his rocky perch.

Loham picked himself up and noticed the giant dagger that was gripped by the amputated hand. He pried open the fingers and retrieved the dagger. Just then, one of the mēgs leapt onto the narrow platform on which Loham stood. Loham swung the ragged blade, striking the mēg across the bridge of its nose. The blade became lodged in the boney skull of the mēg. Loham yanked at the dagger until it came free and the mēg hurriedly backed away, falling to the rocks below.

Jekkid spun with his sword fully extended; he swung to lop Morak's head from his neck, but Morak managed to dodge the blade and called out with a loud voice, "Jekkid, ut bae mae, Morak!"

Jekkid hesitated for just an instant to look at Morak. "Morak, wut ye bae doin wit Huzesh?"

"A bae nut!"

Suddenly, Wanoon, one of Huzesh's gallues, rushed toward Morak, swinging his sword wildly and yelling. Morak turned the point of his sword to the advancing brute and leapt into the air toward him. Surprised by the acrobatics, Wanoon searched for Morak, but before he could find the flying gallue, the sword of Jekkid bore down upon his head, splitting it from crown to throat. With another swing of the sword, Jekkid severed Wanoon's head. His limp lifeless body fell to the rocky ground.

Two other mēgs approached the brawl. Their sharp teeth were exposed and the wiry hair on their backs stood straight up. The rain poured over their grotesque bodies. They teamed up to close in on Jekkid. Morak moved rapidly toward Jekkid to fight the evil beasts. Jekkid pounced upon one of the mēgs, grabbing its neck and digging his powerful talons into the creature's throat. The mēg fought violently, biting and clawing at Jekkid. The other mēg leapt at Jekkid's turned back and sank its razor-sharp teeth into the back of his head. Jekkid would not let lose his grip on the first mēgs' throat, even though the second mēg was clamped onto his skull. Morak raised his sword and slashed the second mēg across the back of its neck, killing it instantly. Jekkid, bleeding and severely wounded, still would not loosen his grip on the first mēg. Finally, Jekkid found his dagger and, with his free hand, drove the weapon deep into the beast's heart; the mēg collapsed to the ground, dead.

Slŷteeg was now fighting two gallues at once and was losing. Motaig managed to pierce Slŷteeg's right shoulder, leaving him handicapped and vulnerable. Just as Braanik was ready to strike a finishing blow, the dagger of Morak came whirling through the air, striking him in the back of the neck and driving through and out of his throat. Slŷteeg swung his sword with his only working arm and severed Braanik's head.

Morak dove through the air, onto Motaig. At the same time, Motaig lunged for Morak and the two crashed, midair, into each other, with a dazing impact. Motaig was the first to get to his feet and wield his sword; with it he struck Morak, slicing the blade across his chest. Morak quickly responded by grabbing and launching a boulder. The stone landed squarely on the forehead of Motaig, knocking him backward. Morak rushed to the dazed gallue and drove his sword deep into his chest, then pulling the sword from Motaig's chest and swiftly dispatching his head.

Loham began yelling, for he was surrounded by three mēgs who were eagerly readying to pounce on him. He had Huzesh's dagger, but against three mēgs, he stood no chance. "Morak! Help! I need help!" One of the mēgs jumped, trying to reach Loham on the top of the boulder, but landed short and slid down the wet, slick rock. "Morak, help!"

Finally, Morak turned his head and noticed Loham's silhouette on the boulder. He could not hear his cries over the roar of the winds and rain but could tell there was a problem. Jekkid was much closer to Loham by then, and Morak hollered, "Jekkid! Dar! Haelp eem!"

Jekkid turned to see the lone snitch fending off the attacking mēgs. Rushing toward the boulder, he arrived with a sudden swipe of this sword on the neck of one mēg. Seeing that there was another, slightly more accessible victim, the two remaining mēgs quickly turned their attention. As they began to advance on the wounded gallue, Loham jumped from the boulder onto the back of one of the mēgs. As he came to bear upon the creatures' shoulders, Loham drove the dagger into its neck, piercing through the vertebra and then exiting the mēgs throat. The mēg flailed about on the ground then expired.

Jekkid faced off with the last mēg. His strength was fading, and the eyes of the mēg revealed that the creature knew this. Like a wolf tearing at its prey, the mēg leapt at Jekkid and sunk his boar-like teeth deep into his neck. Jekkid fell backward to the ground. The mēg shook its head with Jekkid's throat clamped in its powerful jaws, Loham ran over and drove Huzesh's dagger through the beast's ribs and into its heart.

Meanwhile, Ourdïs stood over Huzesh, who was sitting against a rock wall with only one arm. Ourdïs had resisted the urge to cut off Huzesh's head, at least for the time being, mostly because he was too exhausted and hurt to go through the effort. Slŷteeg sat on a stone, not far away. His shoulder was bleeding from the deep gash made by the gallue's sword. The pent-up anger toward Huzesh was, for the moment, appeased by the knowledge that he could, at any time, slay his foe.

Morak made his way over to Jekkid, whose body lay under the dead mēg. He was breathing but near perishing from the savage wounds to his neck. The dead mēg's jaw was still clamped tightly around his throat. Loham stood paralyzed by the horror of the fight. As the relentless rain washed away the blood, Morak joined Huzesh, leaving Loham to himself. "Dud ye kull mae mēgs?" Huzesh asked as if he cared.

"Aye, dae bae dead, all o'thum, un yer fruns, tae," Morak reported.

"Dae waer gud companions, mae mēgs. Ye shud nut ha kulled thum."

"Better thum thun mae," Morak replied.

"Bahaha! A wish ut waer ye. Dunna much care bout da others. Gud riddins!"

Ourdïs just sat and listened to Morak and Huzesh. Huzesh, though badly wounded, seemed unfazed by the ordeal, as if it were just any other day. "Ut waer u gud fight, aye? Lik da ol' days. A nut saen so much blood since da great war. Ut always bae da blood o'da gallues, though, aye? Wae bae da ones who d'da bleedin. A suppose ut shud bae thut wae, us thut d'da bleedin."

"Dis cursed rain, wun wull ut stop?"

Morak's chest was bleeding from the deep wound. He, like the others, was exhausted. He was kneeling in the driving rain, across from Huzesh, staring at him. Huzesh glared back and asked him, "So, is Slŷteeg dead?"

"Nae. Ee bae jus sittin o'er dar waitin t'finish dis, A suppose."

"Nae. A doubt ut. Ee bae u coward." Slŷteeg heard the taunting words from Huzesh and wanted to finish him off but instead, bridled his rage, confident he would get another chance on another day.

Loham stood in the middle of the battlefield. The corpses of six mēgs and five gallues were spread about the ground. The stench of the mēgs was quick to permeate the air, and Loham began to worry that the corvuses would come as swiftly as they had before. For a moment, he considered escaping into the mist. He knew the gallues were in far too bad of shape to hunt him down, but he had no idea where he would go. The rain hit upon him; each drop like a tiny arrow, stabbing and beating his flesh. "Morak, we better find a place to take shelter from the storm; the corvuses will soon be coming."

"Cun ye fin u place?" grumbled Morak.

"It's difficult to see anything. What do we do about them?" Loham pointed at Ourdïs and Huzesh. "Are they coming with us?"

"Ut bae deir choice," Morak answered, not caring whether they came or not.

A short distance away, cradled between two massive walls of granite, there was a narrow gorge that entered into the small valley. Over the gorge rested an enormous flat stone that acted as a roof. A narrow stream that had become a torrent, flowed between the walls of granite, but on either side of the stream and under the overhung stone, were large shelves of stone that were elevated above the floor of the gorge. The shelves were large enough for them to rest on and were out of the direct impact of the storm. Loham felt it was preferable to staying out in the open, though knew it would offer little protection if the corvuses were to arrive. Loham hoped the rain might keep the nasty birds at bay.

Each of the wounded gallues made his way to the shelter. Huzesh was the last to enter. His wounds were serious, but he would have to tend to himself. None of the others would come to his aid; it was not in the nature of a gallue to show any kindness, empathy, or care for others. The pain of their wounds and the exhaustion of their bodies was enough to keep the gallues at peace with each other for the time being. Each gallue kept to himself as they, one by one, drifted off to sleep.

Loham was afraid to sleep. He worried about the corvuses returning and attacking them as they had before. He also did not trust any of the gallues, especially Huzesh. Perched on a rock ledge above the gallues, Loham settled into the dreary darkness, listening to the hypnotic cadence of the rain hitting the hard stones. Eventually, he could no longer keep his vigil and, without intending to, fell fast asleep.

"Wut bae ye doin haer?" Morak demanded.

"Wae waer gaein t'Gubrone, t'tell eem somting," Ourdïs reluctantly told him. "Wae saen somting, u kerolus."

"U kerolus! Nae, dar bae no kerolus haer, un Shuk," Morak argued.

"Aye, but wae saes eem!" "Whaer?"

"Un Gershom, un da Pass o'Attone."

"Hae dud ye sae thum dar?"

"Wae bae crossing o'er da mountains, wun Slŷteeg saes da flight o'da kerolus. A saes ut, tae." Ourdïs explained.

"Dud ye er fin ony sign o'da forner?" Morak interrogated him.

"Nae."

The hushed voices of the gallues carried up into the ears of Loham. Slowly, he began to realize that besides the voices he was hearing, there was a strange quietness lurking about them. Looking around cautiously, Loham ascertained that the night had finally gone and with it, the rain. He lifted his head and peeked over the ledge to see Morak and Ourdïs talking.

He pondered their words, concerned about something he had heard. *What is a kerolus?* He tried not to move or draw attention to himself. He wanted to listen, to concentrate on what they were saying and planning.

"Wut ye bae gaein ta d'now? Still gaein t'sae Gubrone?" Morak asked Ourdïs.

"Aye."

"Da pass wull bae closed. Tae much snow," Morak warned him.

"Wae ha t'trae. Wae ha t'tell Gubrone wut wae saes. Whaer ye bae gaein, ye an yer snitch?" Ourdïs inquired.

"Wae bae gaein t'da Illysian Gorge, naer Gershom."

"Mubae ye shud go wit us t'Gubrone."

"Hmm, mubae."

"Wut bout, Huzesh?"

"Laeve eem haer. Bae nutin but trouble." Morak growled.

"Un da snitch, ye bae takin eem?"

"Nae, laeve eem wit Huzesh. Dae muk u gud pair. Dunna ye tink? Bahaha!"

"Thun whae dud ye haelp eem agan da mēgs?"

"A guess A thunk A maet naed eem, A dunna know," Morak reasoned, shrugging his shoulders.

Loham could hardly believe what he was hearing. Morak meant to leave him with Huzesh. He tried to stay calm and out of sight while he thought about his options. His heart raced with fear and rage at the same time. The reputation of Huzesh was well known among the snitches. Loham thought he might sneak away and go back to the valley where Morak had found him. However, he did not know the return way, and what about the corvuses and the other gallues along the path. He knew he would not stand a chance against them.

Slŷteeg opened his eyes to see Morak and Ourdïs staring at him. They were ready to go and had been shaking him to rouse him. "Com. Wae naed t'gae afore da corvuses com."

"Huh? Oh, yur right. Ha da rains ceased?"

"Aye. Now, com! Quick, wae mus bae gaein."

"Wut bout da snitch un Huzesh? Huzesh mus die."

"Forgut thum. Luts gae. Dae wull bae u gud distraction fur da corvuses. Lut thum finish thum."

The thought of Huzesh being devoured alive by the corvuses pleased Slŷteeg. The only thing he wanted more than knowing Huzesh had been eaten alive was to witness it as it happened. Though dissatisfied by the unfinished business, Slŷteeg prepared to go.

Leaving Huzesh and Loham to the birds, the three gallues moved as quickly as three wounded and beaten gallues could move. As they disappeared into the mist, Loham began to feel very much alone and unsure of what to do next. He did not want to stay in the mist or with Huzesh, but he knew nothing about the terrain or the way through it. Even if he could make it out of the mist, Loham was ill-equipped to survive on his own anywhere outside of the Valley of Souls.

Loham sat up on the ledge. He gazed around, but the mist had closed in tightly. Peering below, Loham could see Huzesh, still sleeping with his head resting on a large, round boulder. He took a long, deep breath, then stood to his feet. Laying near him was the large dagger of Huzesh. Loham reached down, picked it up, and studied it. It had been a magnificent piece of craftsmanship at one time. Over the ages, though, it had begun to show the wear and tear of use and abuse. The iron of the blade was dark and pitted, its edge was jagged and chipped. Inscribed into the iron blade were the ancient markings of Pardis. The handle of the dagger was made of carved black hardwood. Laced into the carvings were strands of drawn titaricus. At the end of the handle was an ornately engraved metal pommel, and on the flat butt-end, the mark of Eloh was barely visible. While the length and weight of the blade were suitable for Loham, the handle was slightly too large in diameter for his small hands. However, Loham could use both hands to clumsily wield the weapon, and this he had proven to himself already.

Loham looked at the ornateness of the dagger, the carvings, and the symbols of an ancient time and place. He wondered what it must have been like when there were no gallues or snitches or mēgs, when the realm of Pardis was whole when the nephesh and the sapien were one. To him, all those things seemed as unreal and impossible as the thought of escaping the mist on his own. The reality of the realm before the great war had become a myth, a legend, a tale of fiction, but holding the dagger in his hands, and seeing the indelible script forged into the metal blade— undeterred by time and wear and war, unchanged by rust and scar and blood— gave life to lore. Loham could hear the message of the inscription speaking to him. The voice of the past, of an age long ago, called out to him, but not to his ears or to his thoughts; the voice—a whisper—spoke into his essence; it shook him and made him afraid.

Inscribed around the edges on both sides of the blade were ancient words. Loham could not interpret their meaning, but he could feel the power of the irrevocable testimony about what was and what is and what is to come. The spirit of the inscription could not be denied. Loham began to see, for the first time, that the lore of Eloh was much more than a fable, that it was true. Everything that he had ever been told by the gallues, by Gubrone, and the others had been a lie. It was no wonder that the snitches were never allowed to see the ancient relics of Pardis and the war. No wonder the gallues kept them away from the ancient places where the inscriptions were engraved. No wonder the nephesh were stripped of their headbands and bracelets. At that moment, Loham understood why the renegade nephesh wore the sign of Eloh on their heads, why some even had it painted on their bodies. It was to remember. He had forgotten; his eyes had become darkened and his heart deceived by the lies of Attar. These things, Loham pondered in his heart until he was startled out of his musings.

"So, dae ha luft mae alone wit u stinkun snitch. Wut shud A d'wit ye? Com down frum dar!" Just the sound of Huzesh's voice drove terror into Loham's bones. Slowly, Loham worked his way down from the ledge to the floor of their stony shelter.

"Ahh, so ye ha foun mae dagger, ha ye? Ut wull bae u bit tae big fur u wee liddle vermin lik ye!" Huzesh mocked Loham.

"It's mine now! I took it from your very own hand." The brave words slipped out of Loham's mouth before he realized what he was saying and to whom.

"Bahaha! So ye ha u liddle spit un ye, d'ye? A lik thut!"

"Aye," Loham mumbled cautiously.

"A wull lut ye carry mae dagger till A naed ut." His laughter was loud and uninhibited.

Huzesh did not seem to mind that he had lost his arm in the battle, nor did he seem to be in much pain—or at least, he did not act like he was. Instead, he counted it as some strange badge of honor. He bore the wounds of war with pride.

"Whaer dud dae gae?"

"Back to the valley."

"Whae?"

"Something about a kerolus."

"kerolus? Ye sure dae said, kerolus? Whaer?" Huzesh questioned Loham.

"That's what they said. In Gershom."

"Hmm, un Gershom? A maet wanna gae t'Gershom, thun. Whaer waer ye goin wit Morak?"

"Not sure. To some gorge or something like that, to spy on some foreigner." "Forner, huh? Wut kin o'forner?"

"No idea. Morak didn't tell me anything about it. I just overheard him," Loham admitted.

"Hmm. Ye know ut bae forbidden t'enter Gershom?"

"No, suppose Morak knew?"

"Oh yeah. A bae sure ee wud know. So, tell mae, hae dud ye gut t'bae u traitor t'yer own kin? A hate snitches!"

Loham could not tell if the question was one of genuine interest or of provocation. Huzesh liked to fight, and he especially liked it when he had the upper hand. Nevertheless, the question came with such force and such condemnation, that it wounded the heart of Loham. Loham had never been asked about his treason before. A hasty reply escaped Loham's lips, without forethought or discretion. "I am no more a traitor than the likes of you!" Realizing the foolishness of his sharp-tongued response, Loham punctuated his defense with a conciliate aphorism. "We are all traitors to some degree."

"Aye. Yur right, thut bae true. Wae all bae traitors. But ye stull ha nut answered mae question. Hae dud ye d'ut, un' why?"

"Happened when I was young. Don't know much about it. I don't really remember. Why?"

"Ee muks ye forget. Gubrone, ee muks ye forgut whae," Huzesh revealed to Loham.

"How would you know?"

"A used t'haelp eem. A used t'brang thum t'Gubrone. Ee rewarded mae fur turning da nephs agan deir own saelfs."

"You mean their own kind?" Loham corrected.

"Nae, deir own saelfs. Ye ha t'hate yer own saelf afore ye cun turn agan yer own kin. Ye know wut A maen?"

Loham did know what Huzesh meant. He was full of hatred and anger, but more than anything, he was full of shame. He turned away from Huzesh.

"Muks ye sick aye? Shame, ut bae whae A hate ye snitches. Yur full o'shame."

"Aren't you ashamed? You're a traitor too, no different than me!" Loham lashed out.

"A traitor, aye, thut A bae. Ashamed? Nae'er! Dar bae nutin fur mae t'bae ashamed bout. Shame bae weakness un A hate weakness! All ye nephs bae weak, but ye snitches, yur da weakest."

Loham could tell that Huzesh was intentionally trying to incite him to anger through his cutting insolence, but he was not about to challenge Huzesh, so he chose to be silent.

"Ye wull cum wit mae, t'Gershom. A mae ha som use fur ye. Mubae wae wull fin da forner, or dis kerolus. Bahaha! A ha nut saen one o'thum un u lung while."

Morak, Ourdïs, and Slŷteeg worked their way to the pass. As they ascended, the snow became deep and the winds blew hard on the mountain. If delivering the foreigner's weapon had not been so important to them, they would have turned back, but the possibility of a kerolus having come to Shuk was far too serious for them to submit to the harsh elements that resisted them. After much difficulty, they reached the valley and went straight to Gubrone's cave.

Gubrone's chief guard led them into the black hall. As they crossed the dark, empty space the voice of Gubrone pierced the quiet shadows. "Morak, whae ha ye com t'mae so soon?"

"Dar bae news thut ye mus haer frum des two."

"Weel, spaek up! Who bae ye, an wut ha ye t'say t'mae?"

"We ha saen u kerolus, un Shuk," Ourdïs reported.

"Aye, un da forest o'Gershom, wae saes eem," confirmed Slŷteeg, hastily.

Gubrone was skeptical. "U kerolus?"

"Aye!" Ourdïs and Slŷteeg answered together.

"Whaer?"

"Wae saes eem un flight, naer da pass o'Attone, un Gershom," Slŷteeg explained shakily.

"Hmm, bae ye sure? Bae ye vary sure ut waer u kerolus?"

"Aye."

"Aye, no doubt," agreed Ourdïs.

Gubrone had a strange look in his eyes. He seemed both concerned and pleased, simultaneously. He paced back and forth, absorbed in thought, murmuring to himself, in whispers under his breath. The others in the hall stared at him, listening to his guttural babble. Then Gubrone ceased mumbling to himself and spoke directly to the gallues. "Dud ye sae who dis kerolus bae?"

"Nae."

"Da distance waer vary great," said Ourdïs.

Gubrone briefly resumed his pacing and mumbling, then paused and inquired of Morak. "Wut bout da forner, ony news?"

"Dar bae no sign." Morak admitted.

Gubrone spun around and strode over to him swiftly. He looked straight into his eyes with a stare of contempt, raised his fist, and smote him in the face, knocking him to the ground. "A told ye, dunna fail mae, un ye ha! Dis bae yer last chance!"

Gubrone motioned to one of his chief guards and ordered, "Sound da horn! Gather da snitches un da hunters!"

Gubrone then focused his attention back on Morak and commanded,

"Ye wull gae afore da sun sets, ye un yer fruns, wit da gallue hunters un snitches. Ye wull scour da lund round Gershom. Ye wull hunt da lunds fur ony sign o'dis forner, un ye wull brang eem t'mae! Brang eem un onyone thut bae wit eem, or bae haelpin eem. Brang thum t'mae, only mae! Bae A claer?!"

"Aye." Morak's voice quivered with dread.

"Un Morak, uf ye fail mae, uf ony o'ye fails mae, ye wull bae cut unta liddle pieces un fed t'da corvuses un mēgs. Un A wull ha yer heads hangin un dis hall! D'ye haer mae? Now, gut out!"

Shu

Chapter XIII
Shu

Far from Gershom, over the Plain of Haemus, a dark, lurid mist hung in the air, sticky and putrid. The viscid vapor clung to every surface like the gum of myrrh. Above the mist, a darkness rose into the heavens and spread over the landscape like a volcanic plume billowing upward. The inordinate cloud advanced as an approaching terror, blind and deaf to any life, or cry, or plea, immune to sympathy and mercy. It behaved indifferent to beauty and unmoved by suffering and fear, cruel and unrestrained.

Reaching through the shadowed mist, a voice cried out from beyond the vast, approaching darkness. It echoed through the heavens and outer universe, from beyond the inky space of stars. Its breath was like a mighty wind preceding the advancing storm. With the resonance of a bell, shrill and dauntless, the voice pierced the darkness in the ancient Theoscian tongue, with words that could not be comprehended:

Illu iet yis ain duan§sreth lae sadou ä gylo õ Oïi lae eart et Pardis. Lae řunn~is iet ish Æloan ä Lae illuidê iet gylo ti altig ruvvon u' ti Lae daw anuff Lae Eno~pari. Lae renow forĵ et illu iet heiv Lae sadou ä Lae javad et illum~is iet duan-ambae lae barror et sadu at mai lounid Lae unman~in eart. Lae daw bae asun~un ä um bae ambae, udn Lae chromos et sadu iet de, neeav meru punyo~n Pardis. Illu hōtallem et essen ambaes, e ambaes, a mer bae neeav pazush at sol ruulä e's ambaeun.

The words of the voice struck the mist like the clapping hooves of a hundred thousand warhorses racing onto the battlefield. With great concussions, the voice hit the expanding black plume, breaking it into a multitude of pieces. Like the fractured walls of a towering stronghold, the darkness powerlessly disintegrated, crumbling to the ground with a booming commotion. Spears of light pierced the shadows and mist, driving every corrupt being into hiding. All that could be shaken—ground, waters, and skies—shook under the thunderous report of the voice.

In the distance on an overlooking hillside, stood a solitary figure that beheld the darkness and felt the breath of the voice. The one who stood alone was bound to an immense ebony stone by an ancient iron chain secured to his ankles by thick shackles. His eyes were closed, and he welcomed the breath of the voice on his face as it blew its thundering proclamation upon the realm.

Able to be heard beneath the thunder and shaking of the voice was a resonating, contrasting whisper, quiet and yet distinct. It sounded like the utterance of a prayer. From the lips of the lone figure came the hushed groans, mutterings, and unintelligible grumblings that reached out to the thunderous voice. Gradually, the sound of the whisper overtook the roaring voice until only the quiet murmurs of the lone figure's groans were heard.

Diving through a shaft of light into the dark realm, aimed straight at the lone one, flew a large celestial bird with golden wings. It streaked like a bird of prey, quick and sure, to the lone one and lighted upon their shoulder. After screeching and squawking unsparingly, it reached down with its mighty, curved beak and grasped the ancient chain. The bird pulled the chain away from the ebony stone, clamped its beak upon the bolts of the shackles, and crushed them. The chain plummeted lifelessly to the ground. As quickly as it had descended, the great, golden fowl lifted its mighty wings and rose into the air, soaring into the piercing light. The lone one opened his eyes to see the mighty bird fly away. In its mighty talons hung the black chain and the iron shackles.

Kumél opened his eyes to the light of day shining on his face. Just beyond his reach, he could see a small blue tit, perched tenuously on a delicate branch, singing its morning song. Kumél's lips moved involuntarily, murmuring a strange message in a strange language.

He laid down upon the hard, stony ground as if he were in a trance, unable to keep his lips from speaking the words of the voice. Unceasingly, in the Theoscian tongue, he mumbled the final words the voice had spoken in his dream.

Msusi was the first to hear the mumblings of Kumél. At first, the sounds came as hushed babbles and moans, but before too long, it became clear to Msusi that Kumél was speaking in the ancient tongue of Eloh and the Theoscians. She was uncertain how she knew this, for she had never before heard the language of Eloh. There was something remarkable about the language, for though it was foreign, there was something unmistakably familiar about it. Msusi cautiously stepped closer to Kumél. She listened to him and felt an unexpected exhilaration rise from deep within her being. It was as if the words were speaking into the essence of her existence as if some primordial part of her soul could understand the message of the unknown words. Assuming he was awake, she knelt down and whispered to him, "Kumél. Kumél, are you alright?" Kumél was unresponsive; his lips spoke the words repeatedly, while his eyes stared straight ahead. "Kumél." She whispered his name again, then realized that he was not actually awake, so gently shook him by his shoulder, "Kumél, wake up."

Kumél's lips ceased speaking. His eyes blinked slowly, then he continued to speak again in the unknown tongue.

Msusi understood that Kumél was as confused as she was. "Kumél, wake up. It's me, Msusi." Kumél blinked his eyes open and closed, repeatedly, then shook his head as if attempting to awaken from a spell. "What were you saying, Kumél, and what does it mean? Have you heard it before?" Msusi quizzed him.

"A dunna know. A haerd ut un mae dreams. U voice spaek t'mae, un da darkness."

"A voice? Whose voice?"

"A dunna know who—jus u voice. Ut bae familiar, douh. A ha haerd ut afore."

"Did it say anything else, anything you could understand?"

"Notin A cun rumumbar."

Sitting down beside him, Msusi looked straight into his eyes and asked, "Did it say anything else?"

"Aye, A tink so."

"You must remember everything, Kumél. It's important. Someone will know the meaning of the words. You must not forget them."

"Who? Who wull know?"

"Someone will know," Msusi solemnly assured him.

Kumél repeated the words fluidly as if he had known them his whole life. He spoke them continually, to keep them fresh in his memory. He did not feel comfortable telling Msusi too much about the dream. He brooded over why he would have such a dream and why he would see the darkness. He thought about the lone one who had stood in the storm. He contemplated his identity and the reason he was chained to the stone. He was troubled by the vision.

In the ages before the great war, the kerolus had spoken in the ancient tongue of the Theoscians. All the kerolus had known and understood the language. However, after the war, the memory of the language had faded from the minds of those who had fallen, just as the spell of Attar had gradually induced them to forget what they knew of Eloh and Pardis. Except to the Theoscians and the kerolus of Assuk, the language had become nothing more than a relic of an ancient race, inscribed into stone and written on fading parchment.

There was, however, much more to the tongue of the Theoscians than could have ever been ascertained, for the ancient tongue possessed a remarkable power. When uttered from the lips of an immortal, the message of the tongue became a force, a living, creative form, a self-fulfilling decree, with the power to unleash its declared intent upon all the realms of Pardis. Like an echo carried through a deep valley, the message in the tongue of the Theoscians reverberated throughout the lands of Shuk. It moved on the breezes and in the streams, coursing through the meadows and over the mountains. It danced over the fields and plains until it awoke the hearts of all who could hear it. Every plant and creature, every soul and being, it would touch every cloud and star and sun and moon.

Kumél had spoken the words of the voice in the tongue of the Theoscians. His immortal lips had released the power of the voice into Shuk. Every time he repeated the message of the voice, its power flowed into every extent of the realm, like a breath blown into deflated lungs.

"Dar bae somting strange bout here."

"What do you mean?" asked Msusi.

"A dunna know. Ut faels lik somting ha changed."

"Where's Ross?" Seerae asked.

"Ye ha nut saen um? Ee shud bae haer somwhaer."

The interruption broke the tension that the dream had caused Kumél to feel, and it also distracted Msusi, though her thoughts would not stray too far from Kumél's utterances.

"What about Alethia, Jaroh, and the kerolus? Where are they?" As Msusi surveyed the area, she noticed something in a heap at the well. "What is that? Is that . . . is that Ross?" Msusi and Seerae ran toward the well, worried that something had happened to him. They continued to search for Alethia and the kerolus but their immediate attention was on Ross.

Kumél rose to his feet to follow them. "Whaer bae Zoësh?"

"She is just beyond, still resting." Msusi pointed in the direction from where she had just come.

As they reached Ross, Seerae anxiously asked, "Ross? Ross are you alright?" She shook his shoulder to stir him awake. "Ross, are you hurt?"

"Huh? What? What are you doing?"

"Are you alright?" Seerae repeated.

"Well, yeah. I . . . I think so. Why?"

"What happened to you? Why are you over here?"

"Nothing happened to me."

"Where is Alethia and Jaroh?"

"They've gone," Ross answered.

"Gone. Gone where?" Seerae was confused by Ross's answers.

"She didn't say . . . just left."

"Without telling you anything?"

"Not about where they were going; they just left."

Msusi and the others sensed that something had changed about Ross. "What is that on your arm?" Ross looked down to see his arm exposed and the blue writing shining brightly like a neon light. He quickly pulled down his sleeve, but Kumél and the others had already seen it. "I don't know. It showed up the other day when I touched the waters in the well."

"Let me see, Ross." Msusi spoke softly, but sternly.

"It's nothing." Ross pulled his arm away, but Msusi held tightly onto his wrist and pulled his shirt sleeve up to reveal the radiant blue inscription.

"It's the script of the Theoscians, the same as on the well," Msusi reported.

"What does it mean? What does it say, Msusi?" Seerae asked.

"I cannot say. I cannot read it, Seerae."

"Then how do you know that it is from the Theoscians?"

"I don't know how I know. I just *know*," Msusi insisted.

"But it looks like the script written in the book, in Ross's book," Zoesh said.

Msusi had a puzzled look on her face. "What book?"

"Eve's journal. I saw the writing in the pit, and I copied it before I left there," Ross explained.

"Is there more on you, besides this?"

"I don't know. I just saw it on my arm." Ross slowly removed his shirt. Msusi and Seerae were unable to hide their surprise, for the blue script began to glow as it came into the light of the morning sun. It was not only on his forearm; it had spread up the entire length of his arm, over his shoulder and down his back. Not all the markings appeared to be writing; symbols and figures also formed, and some looked to be a type of ancient hieroglyph. They stared at Ross as the blue script revealed itself. Apprehensive, he asked, "What? What do you see?"

Eventually, the blue script showed up on his chest and even on his face. The markings were almost identical to those on the faces of the kerolus and the nephesh. Ross looked down at his chest and then at his other arm to discover that the markings were spreading, even as he watched them. He began to rub his skin as if trying to erase them, but they would not go away. "Ahh! What the hell, Kumél!

Kumél stared blankly and shrugged his shoulders. He had no idea what to do.

Ross grabbed his shirt and pulled it back on. "What? Shrug your shoulders and look stupid—that's all you've got? I've heard of not drinking the water but this, this is ridiculous! Something's in that water, for sure!" Even with his body covered, the markings still cast their glow onto his face for all to see.

"Don't worry, Ross. It looks good on you," Zoësh quipped.

"Oh, thanks! You're a lot of help," Ross growled, struggling to keep a straight face. He was both embarrassed and amused by his own silly anger.

"What are we supposed to do now?" Seerae hoped Kumél and Msusi had an idea, but they were just as unsure and confused as she was.

"We have to find someone called Ziminiar, at the far edge of Gershom."

"What? How do you know that, Ross?" Seerae asked him, quite surprised.

"Alethia told me. First, we have to find him, then he will help us."

Seerae and Msusi proceeded to take turns questioning him.

"Help us do what?"

"I don't know—find something."

"Find what? What are we supposed to find?"

"Some pool above a waterfall . . . umm . . . Levitus . . . yeah, that's it, the Pool of Levitus. It's above the Falls of Jaarah. That's all I know."

"Ziminiar? Who is he?"

"Ee bae un aposta, lik mae," Kumél informed them.

"How do we find him?"

"I don't know. That's all she said."

"What's at the pool?"

"I don't know that either, guys. She said I would know when I found them."

"*Them*? What do you mean by *them*?"

"Answers . . . answers to my questions."

"What questions?"

"Questions about why I'm here, I guess. I really don't know, to be honest. Can you give me a break from all the questions? I'm as confused as you are."

"There are some questions that you have not yet learned to ask."

"Maybe."

"Levitus bae u myth. Ye sure shae said Levitus?"

"How the hell would I have come up with that? Huh? Think about it. Someone had to have told me," Ross laughed sarcastically.

"Aye, yur right. Ut saems wae maet bae gaein on u journey thut dunna wish t'bae traveled."

"What do you mean by that?" grumbled Ross.

"Dar bae muny secrets un muny dangers kaepin us frum ut."

"Kumél, do you know this place, Levitus?" Seerae asked.

"Ut bae jus u story, u myth. A nae'er saen ut afore. Uf ut bae true thun ut mus bae un da norõ. Un da hae mountains."

"Do you know the way?"

"Nae."

"What's this?" A voice rang out from the opposite side of the well. Approaching Ross and the others, Zoësh seemed to come from out of nowhere.

"What is what?" Msusi was intrigued to see what she had found.

"This." Zoësh handed to Msusi a piece of material that was rolled up and tied with a cord. Msusi untied the cord and rolled out the material on the ground in the midst of them. There was nothing on it, no markings, script, or letters. Msusi turned the material over and found the same on the other side.

Seerae grasped the material. It was thick like the leather hide of an animal, with irregular edges and cut in to a crude, unsymmetrical shape. She inspected the hide carefully and found nothing. "Why would someone tie a piece of hide like that?"

"Let me see it." Ross held the hide spread out between his two hands. He examined it closely, hoping to find something. At first, there was nothing, just as it had appeared for Zoësh and Seerae. Then, gradually, almost shyly, markings began to show up on the hide, markings like those on a map. They were faint at first, but the longer Ross held the hide, the more distinct they became, until finally, everyone was able to see a primitive map of Shuk which included markings and signs of various places throughout the realm. "A map!"

"Aye. Un yur da kae t'raedin ut, saems yer markings bae gud fur somting."

Ross placed the map on the ground, so it would be easier for everyone to see. After he set it on the ground and removed his hand, the markings on the hide faded. Ross hurriedly placed his hands on the hide again and the map reappeared. "Wow! Now that's kinda strange."

"It's for your eyes to see. Without you, it can't be seen or used," Zoësh concluded.

"Where did it come from?" asked Msusi.

"Alethia must've left it," Zoësh said.

Ross reasoned as he studied the map. "Maybe it will help us find the Pool of Levitus." He was not sure what the markings or the strange inscriptions meant, but he hoped that, at the very least, he could figure out the map's orientation, then, as a team, they would be able to decipher the various signs and symbols that the map contained. He searched first for something that represented their present location—a sign or symbol of the well or of the hollow. However, the map looked as if it had been drawn by hand and was not as sophisticated as the ones he was accustomed to reading. Considering that Ross was in a foreign land, that the map was in a strange ancient language, and that he had no idea what direction he was facing, understanding the map was challenging. "I can't decipher anything on this thing. Nothing looks familiar; maybe it's not a map of Shuk."

"Nae, ut bae o'Shuk. Dar bae da Plain o'Haemus un da Teercus River thut flows t'da Great Sea." Kumél pointed toward the map with his large, imposing finger, showing Ross and the others the places of which he was speaking.

"Can you read the symbols or this writing here?"

"Nae. A ha ony saen des places afore. Ut ha t'bae thum."

Ross barked in frustration, "Can you at least tell me which way the map should face? Which way is north or south?"

"North, south, nae, A nae'er haerd o'thum."

"No, not them! North is a direction. Which way is the Plain of Haemus? Is it this way or that way?" Ross pointed toward the far end of the hollow and then in the opposite direction.

"Nae. Da Plain o'Haemus bae thut wae." Kumél pointed in a direction between the two places Ross had pointed.

Ross quickly positioned the map so that the Plain of Haemus on the map was situated in the direction that Kumél had pointed. "There. Now we at least know how the map should be oriented. Is there anything else that is familiar? What is this range of mountains?" Ross pointed to a line of triangular shapes that were above the Plain of Haemus.

"Telohm Mountains."

"Is that where we are, the Telohm Mountains?"

"Aye."

"Good, very good. Now we're getting somewhere. Can you tell where Gershom Forrest is?"

"Aye. Wae bae standin un ut."

"So we are. Where on the map, Kumél? Where is it on the map?" Kumél had a mischievous grin on his face as he looked down and began to study the map. "It's not that funny," Ross scoffed. Kumél soon realized that he could not interpret where the forest was. Ross looked closely for any trace, sign, or marking that might give some indication of where they were on the map but could not recognize any. "Well, we have a map, but unless we learn how to read it, it's worthless." As Ross began to roll the map up, he noticed that on the reverse side, the side that had been on the ground, there were more markings, signs, and symbols showing. He turned the map over, unrolled it, and studied those markings. In the center of the hide, there was a mark, some type of symbol, and near the symbol was a crude circle. Now, the circle was not drawn around anything; it was just a circle—small, almost indistinguishable. Ross looked closely at the area around the circle. To the left and below the circle, he could see two triangular marks overlapping each other. Above the two triangular shapes was what appeared to be a narrow clearing surrounded by a series of triangles. The circle was in the middle of the clearing.

"This looks like a valley and these two triangles . . . well . . . I think they may be representing mountains that are close together, like the Towers of Atone. This may be the Pass of Atone, and if this is the pass, then this is the Valley of Veritus and this little circle . . . this is where we are. Yes!"

Ross was noticeably excited. The others seemed less impressed with the discovery, but for Ross, the thought of having some idea of where he was, no matter if it was in a strange world, was something worth celebrating. "OK. So, we need to find this Ziminiar guy, and now we have a usable map to help us find the way." The others just looked at him as if it made no difference. "Well, let's get our stuff and get going."

Ross rolled up the map and began gathering his things. He shoved the map down in his pack and began walking toward the opening that had led them into the hollow. The others were caught off guard by his haste but quickly followed behind. Kumél brought up the rear of the line. His thoughts returned to the dream and the message of the voice. He could still hear the voice; the strange unknowable words echoed in his thoughts as he wondered what they meant.

Once they were out of the hollow, Ross turned toward what he thought was the north, the direction that Alethia had told him he would find Ziminiar. He contemplated who Ziminiar might be, what he was like, and if he could help them find whatever it was that he needed to find. His thoughts were a jumble of questions, doubts, and conversations that he carried on with Alethia. He felt something deep inside that he could not remember ever having felt before. He felt a sense of reassurance as if everything would be all right, though he could not forget the shadows and the darkness or the hooded man he saw in the well.

As they made their way through the towering forest, around the spiked quartz-like spires of the hollow, they came, unexpectedly, to the edge of a sheer escarpment. The face of the cliff sank away into the bottomless void below. Ross and the others stood at the edge for a long time, gazing into the distance, amazed at the wonder and beauty of it all. "Well, it looks like we can't go this way. I guess we can follow the edge of the cliff until a better way finds us."

"Looks like a nasty storm brewing in the distance," said Zoësh, bringing their attention to the skies.

"Where?" asked Msusi.

"There. See all the heavy, black clouds, and lightning? Must be a terrible storm coming." In the distance, they could see the flashes and hear the thunder rumbling, but the clouds were stationary. They hovered over the far ranges as if some magical force was detaining them. Intermittently, blasts of terrifying thunder roared through the skies as violent flashes of lightning coursed through the ominous blackness of the low hanging clouds. "What's over there, Kumél? Do you know?"

"Ut bae da Valley o Souls."

"The Valley of Souls . . . I have never seen it storm over the valley before." Zoësh pondered this.

"Dar bae somting strange ut work. A cun fael ut."

For hours they wandered along the cliff's edge, snaking upward, looking for a way that would lead them north. They ascended steadily until finally, they broke through the tree line, enabling them to see in all directions. The escarpment was unwilling to yield its dominion over the lands beyond, and Ross realized they would have to find some other route if they were going to discover the domain of Ziminiar. The elevation ahead of them continued to climb toward several high, bald mountains. Ross debated whether a path to the north could be found beyond the next mountain. He and the others agreed that they should continue toward the bald peaks.

As they climbed, it began to snow, and the dark clouds they had earlier observed seemed to be reaching out to them. Zoësh called, "Ross, wait."

"What? Why?"

"Look. Snow! It's snowing! Maybe we should try to find shelter; it could get worse. That storm seems to be gaining in size, and it's almost here."

"Zoësh, there're just a few flakes, nothing that we haven't seen before." Ross turned and continued. Moments later, the falling snow thickened and began to cover the ground. The wind was picking up, and a blanket of light gray clouds, heavy with wet snow, was slowly descending on the high peaks beyond. Ross, determined to keep going and undeterred by the impending whiteout, kept the group moving. Before they knew it, the winds were howling. Ross's thoughts drifted to Ama Dablam. He remembered the screaming wind that had blown icy needles into the tender skin of his face. He remembered calling out to Daniel in desperation.

"Ross! Ross, we have to stop! It's too dangerous to go on. Ross, can you hear me?" The sound of Zoësh's voice jolted Ross back to reality. He was standing in a complete whiteout and the others, who were only a few steps behind him, were hardly visible. "We can't go on. It's too dangerous."

"Yeah, you're right, but we can't stay out in the open either. We have to find a shelter."

"But how? How can we find shelter in this? I can't see a thing," Zoësh wailed.

"There! What is that over there?" Msusi pointed to what looked like a man, standing just beyond them, miraculously silhouetted in the whiteout.

The ghostly figure moved toward them and gestured.

"What the hell? It's a man! Where'd he come from?" The stranger struggled to approach while Ross and the others waited wearily. The sharp, biting teeth of the cold began to gnaw at them as soon as they stopped moving. Within only a few moments, through the noise of the wind, they heard someone call out to them. "Come! I have a place out of the storm. Come, Come!"

Ross looked around and then back at the stranger who, by then, was waving his arms and yelling as loud as he could. His wandering voice, barely audible above the storm, combined with his inviting gestures, affirmed that they should follow him. Into the white, they climbed, not knowing how far they had to go or who it was that led them.

"There! What is that?" Msusi pointed toward a large outcropping of jagged stones rising like shadowy spires just beyond them. Cloaked in the eerie blanket of soft, gray nebula and draped in the powdery white crystallization of freshly fallen snow, the formation was a ruin of some sort. The insistent winds pushed at them in a forcefully persuasive manner, driving them toward the rocks.

The stranger disappeared into the stone edifice. Ross and the others lost sight of him and, for a moment, paused. Zoësh, who had taken the lead, yelled above the clamorous wind, "Should we follow him?"

"Yes! Go, Go!" Ross hollered, waving his arms toward the rocky pile. Zoësh led them toward the ruin. As they got close to the pile of giant rocks, they saw an opening that led into the mountain. Zoësh rushed in. Ross stood outside, in the snow, blown and battered, but he would not enter. He remembered the pit and the darkness and how he had fallen into its black grip. He froze, more out of fear than in response to the coursing ice and snow of the storm. Nevertheless, the ferocity of the blowing snow showed contempt for any protest or resistance that he, or any in the group, might have displayed. It was as if they were being driven into the cave, like cattle into a corral. Ross finally relented and ducked into the ruins.

Ross, Zoësh, Seerae, Msusi, and Kumél stared into a dark corridor. "What is this place, Msusi?" Seerae asked.

"It's a cave," Ross said hesitantly. He felt paralyzed as he stood staring into the darkness. He could not dismiss the angst that was growing inside of his soul. He had no desire to return to the pit and entering this unknown cave felt too much the same.

"At least it's out of the storm," Zoësh said in relief.

"Where's the stranger?" Seerae asked.

"Did he go down there?" Msusi pointed into the darkness. They stood blankly looking at each other before inspecting the small entrance.

"It's too dark. How will we see our way?" Seerae stepped into the shadows of the descending corridor. As she did, a faint light began to illuminate a path in front of her. She paused, startled and hesitant, for there was no apparent source from which the light came. "Seerae, stop! What are you doing?"

"Nothing, Ross. I didn't do it." Seerae continued, and with each step of her foot, more of the path illuminated, leading her through the darkness.

"Maybe this is where he went." Zoësh followed as Seerae disappeared into the darkness. One by one, they followed, and to each of them, the light showed the way. Ross could not move; he struggled within himself. His courage had abandoned him, and as each of his friends disappeared into the shadows of the corridor, he became even more bound by his fear.

"Come." Out of the darkness a voice called to Ross, "Come."

It echoed deep in his heart; it shook his thoughts and yet quieted the inner storm that had grown into a raging tempest. "Come, come." Ross stepped onto the path. His first step was unsure, cautious, fearful. Unconsciously he held his breath; when he could no longer hold it, he exhaled. As his breath floated into the darkness of the corridor, a strange and magical phenomenon occurred. Each molecule of breath began to illuminate into a cloud of tiny lights. Ross began to feel a warm, fluid sensation running through his body, from his head to his feet. He looked down on the path to see the light revealing the path before him, just as it had for the others. "Come." Ross heard the voice again. "Come, rest." Ross took another step. The light of the path shone again, and each breath floated like a Japanese lantern before him, leading him through the shadows. Eventually, Ross entered a large void within the walls of the mountain. There he found the others gathered together. As he entered, the floating luminous orbs of his breath began to fall away further into the descending void. They lit the darkness like lanterns, to reveal a long, descending, ancient, stone stairway. Ross looked at the stairs, bewildered. It occurred to him that this was the first sign of a built structure that he had seen since coming to Shuk. The thought of it, of the possibility that civilization could be close, that a city or a town might be near, began to enliven him.

"Look, down there—a light shines." Ross looked down to see what Zoësh was seeing. At the bottom of the stairs was a faint, white glow shining through a gated entry.

"Come." Ross heard the voice and looked at the others. They did not look like they had heard it. He wondered why only he could hear it. Again, it spoke to him. He moved toward the stairs. The others followed as he carefully made his way down. Each step caused the invitation of the voice to resonate more clearly and more powerfully in his mind and heart. As he neared the last step, he could see a large opening, and from it shone an intense white light.

There was, however, no gate on the opening as it had appeared before. Over the top of the entrance were the carvings of the Theoscians, which glowed in the same bright blue light as the markings on the Well of Veritus. The markings on Ross's body were glowing with the same intensity. Ross stared at the hieroglyphs. He studied them closely.

Kumél approached Ross and he also studied the markings inscribed over the opening. As he stared at the inscription, the voice that had spoken to him in his dream began to reverberate through his subconscious. Kumél wondered if the words he was hearing in his mind were the same as those inscribed over the opening. The strange voice continued to whisper the message in his thoughts.

Ross stepped through the entrance and into the warmth of the light. Seerae was quick to follow, and soon all five were standing in a colossal, elliptical cavern that rose conically into the stone walls of the mountain as if it had been hollowed out. The apex of the cavern was situated high above, toward the very top of the mountain. There, a single ray of light shone down like a beam. It lit upon the branches of a colossal ancient tree that was in full bloom and appeared to be suspended in the deep waters of a spring-fed, crystal-clear pool surrounding its base. Its roots spread deep and wide and endlessly into the spring's subterranean sea. They had no soil to which they clung or found nourishment but held onto the clear fluid, making it their anchor. They glowed in a faint, warm light, illuminating the dark depths of the pool. Its bark was dark and rough and had become the shelter for bright green moss. Growing from every branch and twig were flowers of every color and shape. They radiated with a soft glow that brightened the cavern with warm and soothing light.

Surrounding the pool was the floor of the cavern, which was a dark-veined stone like granite. The floor of the cavern encircled the tree, making it possible to walk completely around it. Standing at the edge, it was possible to see down into an immeasurable depth, into which the light of the roots faded but never did it go dark. There were cracks and grooves in the stone, and surrounding the pool, carved into the floor, were petroglyphs that resembled the Theoscian script. The petroglyphs told the story of a time long gone.

The surface of the spring rose flush with the floor of the cavern. Its waters ran out upon the stone floor in all directions. The waters of a spring gushed and sprayed upward toward the branches of the tree, filling the room with vapor and mist. The molecules of mist, like a man's breath on a cold winter morning, were transformed into iridescent droplets that clung together, forming larger floating spheres of light, and then drifted high into the upper part of the room. When they had reached high into the ceiling of the cavern, they dimmed and turned back into drops of water that gently showered down upon the great tree. The waters from the spring and the showers of water that fell from above did not run into any stream, nor did they run away from the translucent pool or out of the cavern. They did not flow away from the spring at all, but spread upon the stone floor, and seeped back into the rock as if returning to a subterranean source. Throughout the room were large stones of various shapes, that, upon first glance, were strewn about haphazardly.

Ross stood and stared for a long time. He remembered the Well of Veritus and the pool in the pit—they both displayed the same type of phenomenon as this spring. He wondered if they were all from the same source. As he looked at the water and its marvels, his eyes inevitably fell transfixed upon the enormous tree that dominated the cavern, around which everything else was arranged.

So remarkable was the sight that Ross wondered whether he was dreaming or hallucinating. He considered that he had passed out in the snow, and all he was seeing was a dying man's illusion, like the vision he had of Eve reaching out and touching him. He blinked his eyes and shook his head as if trying to awaken from the dream, yet there was no waking, no returning to reality, for all that he saw was, in fact, reality. Ross mumbled to himself, "How, how? It's not possible."

Suddenly, they all heard someone speaking from behind them. "You have come, finally." All five of them turned in surprise. Kumél tried to see who it was, but the stranger wore a long, black fur cloak that covered their entire body from head to foot. It looked heavy but warm and was covered in the snow from the storm above. The fur of the cloak was long, straight, and thick, like the fur of a large animal.

"Who are you?" Msusi asked in her gentle, sincere manner. The stranger stood for a moment in the entrance to the cavern and then began to approach the group.

"Are you, Ziminiar?"

"Nae, ut bae not eem." Kumél stepped back away from the others as he answered Ross.

"Who then? Who is it Kumél?" Ross turned to see that Kumél had separated himself from them as if he was afraid.

Casually, as though he had been expecting them, and yet with a slight eagerness to his step, the stranger walked toward Ross and the others. He was tall and confident in his stride, like a commander or a general, yet his persona emanated a sense of gentleness, warmth, and sincerity. It was apparent to Ross and the others that the stranger did not seem to be a threat, but the fact that he was still under the cover of the cloak made all of them extremely nervous. "Do you mean to hurt us?"

"Hahaha! No, of course not! What gives you such a notion? Have I not helped you, saved you from the terrible storm?" He laughed some more. His laughter, deep and guttural, disarmed them and filled the cavern with an air of levity that began cutting through the tension of suspicion and fear. "Why would I hurt any of you? I have come to help you."

"Why do you hide from us? Why do you cover yourself under such a dark, heavy coat?"

"Oh, this? It's a bit cold out there, don't you think?" The strangers' tone was light and spirited, almost carefree.

They watched as the stranger reached his hands through the cloak and began to unleash the cords that were tied around its hood. His hands were strong like the hands of a man who works in the fields. He pulled the hood from his head and dropped the large, furry cape to the ground at his feet. Ross was surprised to see, for the first time since finding himself in Shuk, someone who resembled a man not too unlike himself.

The stranger had a very commanding presence. He stood straight and tall, possessing some inner power radiating from his being. Though not visible, it was effulgent, even warm, and palpable. He wore simple garments made of hides. His hair was long and dark, falling straight down over his shoulders. On one side of his face, Ross noticed what appeared to be a tattoo. However, it was different in that it glowed in a radiant blue light, very much like the marking he now bore on his own body.

Framed by his facial hair, the stranger's smile excited an infectious atmosphere of assurance and trust. He was genuinely sincere, which encouraged them all. The stranger's eyes were piercing, wide, and deep, like the sea, full of mystery and beauty. He was not especially attractive in the physical sense. However, there was something special, something ethereal about him that was compelling and inspiring to each of their hearts. Ross and the others became immediately endeared to the stranger, as their reservations and concerns melted away.

"Who are you?"

"My name is Shu." His voice was warm, absorbing into their souls where it resonated. It spoke more than words to them. It reverberated throughout their subconscious, bore into their minds, and drew an inexplicable longing from the deepest parts of their beings. They felt the presence of life flow into their core. At just the mention of his name, each of them, in their own private way, felt something new and beautiful grow from within.

"Kumél, my friend, it has been a long amount of time. Do you remember me?"

Kumél could not remember Shu, for the spell of Attar had worked in his mind to erase the memory of him. Though Kumél had remembered Alethia, Shu was far from his thoughts. "Nae, A dunna rumumbar."

"You will. You will, I promise." Shu walked toward Ross. He approached cautiously, knowing that Ross had no idea who he was or why he would be there. "And you, you are the one I have heard about."

"Me? What have you heard?"

"Ross Blair, 'tis my honor to finally join you and your friends."

"I'm not sure why, but it's my honor to meet you, too. But who are you, and where are we? What is this place?"

"As I said, I am Shu. My father has sent me to help you. This place is called the Cave of Pelah. It is here that Amik and Livia rest."

Kumél stared long and hard at Shu. He wanted to remember. There was something about Shu that resonated within him, but it was not the sight of him that caused Kumél to sense it; it was the sound of his voice that triggered a memory, only a sliver of it.

Zoësh and Seerae watched Shu as he spoke with Ross. They had only heard rumors about Shu, that his nature resembled Eloh, that he was good, but they knew even less about him than Kumél could remember. Msusi, however, knew much more than she had let on about who Shu was and what it meant for him to be there in Shuk. She had spent time with Alethia before she had found Ross and the others. She had discernment and could see into the shadows of the unknown morrow. She wandered away from the others to kneel at a small knoll that had brilliant green moss growing over it and sweet-smelling flowers of all sorts growing through the moss. The soft, thick moss felt cool and moist to her hand. She relaxed on the stone floor of the cavern next to the mound.

Shu had noticed Msusi as she had knelt beside the small knoll. Eventually, Seerae joined Msusi where she was sitting. The two of them talked as friends. "Msusi, what is this place? Why. . . I mean . . . how do the flowers grow without the sun?"

Msusi smiled at Seerae. "Hmm, the light of life shines in this place. It abides in everything: the stones, the pool, the trees, and the flowers. It shines and gives life—the life that radiates from within."

"Have you traveled here before?"

"No. I only know what I've been told. Alethia told me that we would find this place and about the light of life that shines here."

"What else did she tell you?"

"That darkness will try to take away the light of life, but it will not succeed. We must be brave; we must never forget."

"Forget what?"

"Forget this place and him."

"Him? You mean Shu?"

"No, Ross. We must never forget Ross."

"I don't understand."

"You will. Soon you will."

341

As Seerae and Msusi talked, Zoësh observed them. She had spent so much of her time in Shuk alone that it was very natural to her. Needing to be on her guard against the dangers of the mēgs, the gallues, and the snitches, she felt the safest when she traveled solo. However, the time she had spent with Kumél and Ross, and now with Seerae and Msusi, was having a transforming effect on her. She was depending more on the others and that dependency was changing her. She remembered the loneliness that had followed her for ages. It had begun before she had understood the value and importance of closeness. Zoësh had relinquished intimacy and had resisted the compulsion to seek it but standing isolated and observing the others aroused those primordial urges in a new and refreshing way. She felt a type of ecstasy wash over her; it enveloped her with such an unexpected surge that she found herself crying and longing to be close to someone.

Zoësh swiped at her tender tears as they streamed down her cheeks. As her teardrops fell to the stony floor of the cavern, tiny yellow flowers bloomed everywhere they were falling. She nearly stepped on them before she noticed them. She stroked the simple petals of the tiny flower and smiled.

Kumél watched as Zoësh touched the newly grown flower. He had been in Shuk for ages, since the great war, but he had never seen one of these little beauties. Faintly, a memory came to him. He remembered a time when he and Amik had discovered a hidden valley high in the Impetus Mountains, on the eastern border of Anima, in Pardis. In this valley, Amik's senses were excited by the fresh, ambrosial aroma of a tiny, yellow flower growing along the banks of a narrow stream. They became Amik's favorite flower, and he had planted them everywhere he journeyed. They had brought him joy and had caused him to smile. He had named them "cheerfuls".

The yellow flowers grew around Zoësh until they had fully covered the stony floor where her tears had fallen. "They will now grow here forever." Shu's voice came from behind her.

"What? What did you say?"

Shu knelt beside her. "The cheerfuls will now grow in this place forever."

"But why?"

"To bring a smile to your face." The thought of the flowers forever growing where her tears had fallen made Zoësh blush with happiness.

"Amik loved cheerfuls. They always made him smile."

"A rumumbar! A waer wit Amik wun ee foun thum. Wae waer un da mountuns t'gaer," Kumél declared.

"That's amazing! They're somewhat like Ross's snowpetal," Zoësh remarked.

"Mubae, but A nae'er saen da snowpetal afore Ross com t'Shuk."

Joining the trio, Ross reminded them, "So, you never really answered my question: what is this place?"

"It is where Eloh brought Amik and Livia at the end of their lives," Shu answered.

"Oh, so this is a tomb?" When Ross realized he was standing in a tomb, it agitated him. He had always been irrationally uncomfortable around death and graves. This place swiftly brought Eve to his mind. He knew that Eve had no grave for him to lay flowers upon, to remember her and cry over. It was a sobering and painful moment that lingered. Nevertheless, in an inexplicable way, Ross also felt deeply connected to Eve, as if, by some unimaginable means, she was alive. The sadness that usually hit him with her memory was less, and he felt more of a sense of hope. Ross wondered why he would feel hopeful. Logically, he understood it was impossible for her to be alive. He also knew that even if, by some extraordinary event, she was alive, he would not be able to get to her because he was stuck in Shuk. There was no rational reason for him to feel hopeful but he did.

"Aye, it is a tomb, but it is much more than that. There is much more at work here than you realize. Do not be afraid."

The comforting voice of Shu put to rest his anxiety, but the memory of Eve stayed with him. Quietly and introspectively, he dwelled on how precious she had been to him and how he yearned to have her back. It was normally painful for him to think about her, but at that moment, the memories were welcome, for they were gradually mending his brokenness. He allowed his mind to chase after them, for he loved to recall their times together, if he remembered her alive and not in a grave.

"I'm afraid I'm forgetting her. For a while, I wanted to forget, but now I'm afraid I'm forgetting, and I don't want to."

"Death is never really final. It's not always the end of a life."

"Huh? What do you mean?"

"Some things live on. Some things are forever."

"Maybe for you and them, but for me, death is the end."

"Things are not always as they seem, Ross."

"I've been told that before."

"Look at this place. Where have you ever seen anything like this?"

"There are a lot of things I've never seen before; doesn't mean anything though. So? I've never seen a place like this. What does that prove?"

"Do you know anyone who has?"

"Well . . . no."

"The things you think are real, fact, absolute or impossible—maybe they are not. This tree—have you ever seen a tree like this before? Yes, it is a tree, but it is more than just a tree as you understand trees. Eloh planted it when he brought Amik and Livia to rest in this place. At that time, it was only a sprig, tiny and frail. It had only a few flowers and leaves growing on it. What do you suppose this tree to be?"

"I don't know. An oak tree? I really don't know; horticulture was never my thing."

"It is the Tree of Aiwon, the body of Amik, the father of the Carascians. Every flower and leaf that you see growing on it, grows for one of Amik's descendants, and once it blooms, it never dies. On this tree grows a flower for everyone from the line of Amik who has ever lived, and every day more blooms open, more buds grow, and more lives exist—forever. There is a bloom for Eve on the Tree of Aiwon, there is a bloom for Daniel on the Tree of Aiwon, and there is a bloom for you."

"But how? I saw them fall. I saw Daniel's body and I was there when they put him in the ground. They're both dead."

"There is much that you don't understand, but you will."

"How does it remain there? You know . . . suspended like that?"

"There are forces at work here that you cannot see, nor can you comprehend. The Tree of Aiwon, like many other things in the universe, is not held in place by its own strength or power, nor by the elements of the physical world; it is held in place, grows, and blooms by forces that eclipse those that are seen, felt, and heard. It is physical itself, but its life comes from beyond itself—beyond the physical realm. This is true of all things physical; they exist as a small part of a much larger realm, an unseen realm that holds all existence in balance."

"I'm not sure I want to know how the universe does or doesn't work. I mean, what good does it do me to know all that? I can't change it."

"You are right, Ross. Knowing something cannot change what has already passed, but it can change what is to come. The power that holds the Tree of Aiwon in its place is the same power that lights the Aurora Path, which opens the way into Shuk and gives life to every living thing. You have felt it and heard it; you have even seen it. It is the reason the snowpetal grows around you and why the elements of nature have responded to your presence and have aided you on your journey here. You have heard it in your dreams, in the voice of your lover, the one you have lost. She speaks to you through forces you cannot see. They hold the universe in balance, and they also work in and through all things to accomplish an unseen purpose: to bind up the brokenness and restore wholeness to the realm of Pardis and all who belong there."

"But what does that all have to do with me? I'm a nobody . . . not even from this place. Wherever this place is . . ."

"Long ago, before the great war, all things existed in harmony. The realm of Pardis was whole, not yet divided. It was a world teeming with life and beauty that far exceeded what you have seen in this place or have ever seen elsewhere. Yet, more than the beauty of the created world was the beauty and oneness that existed between the Theoscians, the Carascians, and the kerolus. There were no rulers and no war or hatred; all lived in peaceful harmony, and all the realm flourished because of their oneness. Every creature, flower, tree, and blade of grass, every mountain, hill and valley, river, and stream; they all flourished because of the unity of life that existed between the immortals.

When Attar rebelled and the poison of envy corrupted his heart, the unity of peace and fellowship was shattered, and all were scarred by it. Every element, every fragment of the realm was marred by the hatred of Attar. There was nothing that was not affected by his treachery. Attar had struck at the heart of Eloh and crushed it. He had caused the betrayal of Amik by deceiving Amik's heart and blinding his mind to the memory of Pardis and of true life. From then until now, every element and every force of the realm of Pardis has been waiting and longing for the day when the curse of Attar would be broken, when the three realms of Pardis would be one, and the wounded would be healed. It has been foretold that the line of Amik would rise again, unbroken, and walk in the gardens of Pardis with Eloh. It has also been said that the beauty of unity would once again adorn all things.

You, Ross, are the seed of Amik, the offspring that the prophecy has foretold. You have come to Shuk for reasons you could have never known." Shu's voice became broken as the emotion of his heart began to pour out of every word he spoke. His eyes welled up with tears as he declared the promise revealed in the ancient prophecy.

Ross felt overcome by the power of the promise, and he could feel the conviction resonating from Shu's heart, yet he was unable to believe that so much depended upon him. "Me? You've got to be kidding! Of all the people in the world that could have been chosen for whatever it is you expect of me, you think I'm the one? I'm the one that you've been waiting for? Come on! This whole thing sounds absurd!" Ross shook his head in disbelief while everyone around him waited patiently for him to calm down. "Do you know how I got here? I got lost. I don't even know how to get back home . . . to *my* home. How can I help you if I can't even help myself?"

A stray memory crept into his thoughts. Ross remembered the legend he and Daniel had been told. Everything Shu was saying sounded suspiciously like what the old man had told them. Despite his denial and protest and all his rational agnostic ideals, he was suddenly faced with an irrevocable contradiction. The stories and legends he had despised and even loathed, myths that his rational consciousness had rejected, may have been, at least in part, true. It was hard to deny everything he had witnessed. How could Shu have known of the legend Psang had told to him? The more he dwelled on it, the more difficult it was to dismiss. How could he deny what he had seen with his own eyes?

Shu put his hand on Ross's shoulder. Ross would not look at him; he looked to the ground wrestling with denial. In his heart, he suspected that his denial was more an act of stubbornness than belief. Shu spoke again. "Consider all that you have seen and been told, especially what you have heard in your night visions, in the voice of Eve. She has been with you, leading you here."

"But she's just a figment of my imagination! She's not real; she doesn't exist. She's just a dream, isn't she?" Buried beneath his ardent protestations was the slightest resonance of hopeful doubt, doubt in what he thought he knew to be true, doubt that hoped Shu was right.

"But it is not just a dream, Ross. You are present because every element in the universe has been drawing you, step by step, breath by breath, to this exact moment. You cannot see it with your eyes or understand it with your mind, but let your heart tell you the truth. You have felt it in your bones and in your soul; there is something more to life than what you have lived. You know it. Don't be afraid. Every living thing that you see, touch, hear, and smell is a reminder of something you have forgotten. They are telling you what you are afraid to hear, that your presence here is for a reason."

"It is not you alone, Ross. Truly, you cannot do everything on your own, but no one else can do what you must do. Only the offspring of Amik can do what must be done."

Ross lowered his head again. He felt a great weight bearing down upon him, like an immense stone. "Did you know about this, Kumél?"

"Nae, A knew notin."

Shu quickly spoke out, "Each of you has a part to play in this journey. You have all been given something to offer that no one else has. You are not alone in this, Ross. We have been brought together, and together; we will continue. The curse of Attar will only be broken if we work as one. Come, Ross. Come with me. I have something for you."

Shu escorted Ross to one of the stones that lay on the floor of the cave. It was a large, rectangular stone as wide as a man's shoulders, as tall as it was wide, and as long as Ross was tall. It looked like a solid slab of black stone.

"Touch the stone," Shu instructed.

"Why?"

"You will see; touch it."

As Ross's right hand touched the stone, veins of blue light illuminated an inscription on the top of the stone that was familiar. His eyes revealed to the others he had seen the hieroglyph before. "It's the ancient promise," he whispered.

By this time, Seerae and the others had joined him. Seerae had heard Ross's words and wondered how he knew what it was. She looked at Shu with questioning eyes.

"What is it you wish to know, Seerae?" Shu inquired before she was able to question him.

"What is it?"

"This is the ancient promise given by Eloh ages ago when he led the captive nephesh out of the pit. It was inscribed into the stone table and it illuminated the Aurora Path. The promise is soon to be fulfilled." Seerae wanted to ask more, to know what it said, but her attention was drawn back to Ross.

As Ross investigated the brilliant lights coursing through the veins of the black stone, he could see into the stone as if it transformed into clear crystal. Beneath the surface of the stone, he saw what looked like a long, thin, metallic object with an engraved bone-like center section. At each end of the object, the metal was blued in color, as if stained by the fire of a smith's crucible and very sharp.

Shu could see that Ross was fixated on the object. "Take it. It is the spear of Amik. Only the offspring of Amik is able to remove the spear."

Ross looked at Shu with a puzzled stare. "But . . ."

"Reach into the stone and take the spear."

Ross hesitated for a moment, then without considering the stone, pushed his hand into its surface. It transformed from solid rock into fluid almost like gelatin. He grasped the ancient spear of Amik. As he gripped the bone-like center or haft, the blue markings that were aglow on his body surged into the spear, illuminating its intricacies and radiating out through the sharp ends. Ross cautiously lifted the spear from the stone. "It's light . . . lighter than I would have imagined." The blue light from his body continued to move through the spear. He could feel its strength. He could feel power both leaving him and coming into him. He felt strong and weak at the same time.

"This is the spear of Amik. It will pierce the shield of shadows. Its brightness will overcome the dark underlords of Attar. Yes, it is an extremely powerful weapon. Be careful to use it respectfully, for it will only obey you if you honor it. Remember, it is alive. It knows its purpose and will not be detoured. There is one thing more that Amik left for you." Shu pulled a wooden object out of his sack. It was a dukwán like the one Ross had seen Msusi playing at the pool. "This is the dukwán that was given to Amik. He tried to play it but was not successful. It belonged to Attar, and its music is powerful, enchanting, and dark. It is given to you because it was prized by Amik. One day you will return it to its owner and take from him that which does not belong to him. But be warned: do not underestimate the compelling power of its music, or it will enslave you as it did Amik. Do not play it! Its songs are not yours."

Ross admired the wooden pipe. He could feel a mysterious force coming from it, planting a desire within him to play it. Shu sensed that the force of the dukwán was affecting Ross. Ross hastily put the dukwán in his backpack and closed it. "I've seen Msusi's dukwán and heard its music. Very beautiful. What's it for? Why do she and Zoësh play?"

"The music of the dukwán calls out to their sapiens, to remind them of what they have forgotten."

Ross was still unsure of what all these things meant. He wanted to ask more questions but felt that he would not understand the answers and thought he might be better off not knowing. He pressed his lips together to fake a smile and nodded, somewhat imperceptibly, at Shu and said, "It's a little strange to me."

"Aye, it's extremely strange, especially for a mortal mind that has only ever known what it has imagined apart from the truth. You have believed a lie. Your mind is slow and bound, limited by what it has been allowed to see."

When Seerae heard about Amik's dukwán and the danger of the music it played, she wondered if the nephesh song was from Attar and if the snitches played the music as well. She asked Shu about the spell of Attar and wanted to know more about the snitches and what had happened to them.

"No, Seerae, the song of the nephesh is not the same as the song of Attar. Attar was a gifted musician once, ages ago, and his music was exquisite but not comparable to the music of the nephesh, for theirs flows from the Elohan Essentia. As for what happened . . . those are mysterious matters, Seerae. There is much unknown and much hidden. It is recorded that Attar cast an evil spell over the Carascians, a spell with such ferocity that Attar himself suffered damage from it. After that, Amik, Livia, and all their seed, meaning all Carascians, were transformed into something they were never meant to be. One became two. The bodies and minds of the Carascians became mortal and corrupted; these mortals were now sapiens. The spirit of the Carascians, their immortal essence and being, the Elohan Essentia, remains in the nephesh. Attar, with all his power and sorcery, could not control the Elohan Essentia, and the nephesh were banished, cast into the pit that had been his prison for many ages. There, they sang their songs and played their pipes, calling out to their sapiens, hoping they would remember them and renounce Attar. Eventually, though, Attar tired of the sound of their songs. He wanted them out of Tirnan forever, so he designed a plan to destroy the nephesh. I remember well, the moment we heard of Attar's intent. Eloh sent a message to Attar, offering a solution for his nephesh problem. Forced by love into making a concession with Attar, he entered into a covenant with him. Eloh gave the nephesh new physical bodies, then they were sent here to Shuk, where they were meant to live freely. However, Attar is so wicked and deceitful, and his magic is so powerful, he has been holding them captive.

The snitches are victims of Attar's treachery as well. One of the first sapiens, Narcude, was deceived and corrupted by Attar and became bitter. Attar's deceit worked through Narcude to corrupt his nephesh; whose name was Norzaaq. He was the first snitch. It was he who brought the rune and the fourth face into Shuk by the Aurora Way. Attar continues to corrupt many of the nephesh, turning them from their own kind."

"Something should have been done with this Norzaaq! How could he have gotten away with it? He needed to be punished!" Ross fumed indignantly.

"What did happen to him?" Seerae asked.

"He was never seen again. Though, it has been rumored that he was murdered by Gubrone after he delivered to him the rune and the fourth face."

Seerae felt a deep sense of sadness come over her. Even though she feared the snitches, she could not hate them, for they were just like she was, a victim of a cruel traitor. Ross, however, felt a powerful sense of injustice rise in his heart. He could not understand how such evil could have gone unchecked. "I don't understand. If all this was occurring, why didn't someone do something to stop it? Is there no justice here, no law?" Shu understood his frustration and anger. It angered him as well. "There's a funny thing about law and justice; they are two edges of the same sword; they cut both the just and the unjust. Where there is no law, there is no transgression, but where the law is, there the law rules. While the law protects, it also prohibits; it imposes its will on all. There can be no justice unless all are either subject to it or else subjected by it. We know that the criminals break the law to serve their own purposes and, if caught, are punished by that law, but the just are also subject to the law and must obey it, or else they will be punished."

Ross struggled to understand what Shu meant. He could not see how it was possible for an injustice like what had happened to the nephesh and the snitches to go unpunished.

"But Shu, if Attar has broken the law, how has he not been punished? I don't understand."

"Ah yes, it is a hard thing, but you cannot understand what you do not know. It's not that Attar will not be punished, it's that the covenant cannot be broken in order to punish him. Justice will come to Attar and his minions in the way that it must. A way has been made."

Shu had turned to walk away when Kumél's stammering voice stopped him. "D'ye hate mae, Shu? D'ye tink mae u traitor, u fool? Cud ye er furgiv mae? Cud Eloh er luk upon mae afta wut A dud?"

The mood in the cave turned contrite as Kumél's rueful plea cut each heart with the sharpness of a razor. Ross swallowed discreetly and turned his eyes downward. He felt the anguish of Kumél; it ground into his heart like a stone pestle grinding against a mortar. His own hidden guilt, which had become a mold that shaped every aspect of who he had become, fought to escape the confinement of secrecy and denial. Each of them: Ross, Msusi, Seerae, and Zoësh were inwardly confronted with their own damning burdens, wanting to be free, but they said nothing and did nothing; they only turned away as if they had interrupted a secret conversation. They knew the moment was for Kumél, and that they had no right to infringe upon such a sincere and personal appeal with their own self-induced contrition.

Shu put his hand on the shoulder of the giant. He stared straight at him and waited until Kumél lifted his eyes.

"For far too long have we been apart, my friend. There is no end to my affection for you. I have already forgiven you, ages ago. You needn't trouble yourself about that any longer. There is no offense greater than the bond of true friendship."

When Ross and the others heard the response of Shu, they each accepted it into their own hearts as if Shu had spoken directly to them. They each felt a liberating sensation run through their entire being that made them feel as if they had instantly been set free from the chains of a thousand years of bondage.

Kumél whispered to Shu, "Cunna A tell ye somting, Shu?"

"Of course."

"A haerd u voice un mae ears. Ut waer u tongue A ha nae'er haerd afore. A still haer ut now, ringin un mae ears, o'er an o'er agan. Ut spaeks t'mae."

"What do you hear?"

"A dunna know wut ut says; cunna understand."

"Tell me the words. Can you remember them?"

Kumél spoke the language as well as he was able, *"Illu hōtallem et essen ambaes, e ambaes, a mer bae neeav pazush at sol ruulä e's ambaeun.*

"Dar waer more, but A cun ony rumumbar des."

"'The wholeness of life comes, it comes, and there is no might that can stop its coming.' It's from the Jupnie, the ancient breath, breathed by the mouth of the Elohan Essentia over the three realms. In full it says:

The day is rising and now is come, when the time of shadows will end, no longer vexing Pardis. Light will once again overpower the darkness and shine on all the realms. The brokenness will be healed, and the sun will shine in every valley as in the days before the Great War. The great hammer of light will crush the darkness and the spear of brightness will overcome the shield of shadows that has covered the wilderness realm. The wholeness of life comes, it comes, and there is no might that can stop its coming.

Every time the words of the Jupnie are spoken, they spread out into every vicinity they have been voiced, securing a way for the words to be fulfilled. They will not cease spreading until every word has achieved its calling."

"So whae waer dae talkin t'mae?"

"Because you are the one they have chosen to use as their mouthpiece to speak to the winds, to the meadows and mountains, to the seas and the skies, and to the fowls and beasts. Send the words to every corner of Shuk, Kumél, make a way that they might be so. You have been chosen, and if you do not speak what you have heard, then who will? The Jupnie will not be silent, nor will it let you rest until it is finished with you."

"But ut saems foolish t'spaek t'no one, just t'da air."

"Listen, Kumél, the words are not foolish. They only need an oracle, a mouth to broadcast them. They will accomplish what they have come to achieve—you just have to speak them."

"Aye, A wull."

Ross and the others could sense that the time was growing near for them to leave the cave of Pelah and find this new stranger. Ross wondered if Shu might be persuaded to go with them, "Will you be going with us?"

"I will be with you until it is time for me to go! Hahaha!" The laughter broke the air of contrition and seriousness and elevated the mood of everyone.

Ross replied sarcastically, "That's helpful. Doesn't anyone around here ever give a straight answer?"

"Only if we know one. Come. It's time to leave. We must find Ziminiar and the Pool of Levitus. Time is wasting and there is much to do."

"But what about the storm and the snow?" Ross worried.

"It has gone. Let us go, too. Quickly! Grab your things."

Kumél was the first to follow Shu. Ross, Msusi, Seerae, and Zoësh followed behind as they walked away from the tree of Amik and climbed the stone staircase to the opening of the cave. Msusi paused and peered back at the entrance. The gates had shut, and above them an inscription began to glow. "What does that mean?"

"What?" Ross said as he turned back.

"There. Over the entrance." Msusi pointed out the script.

They were all now gazing at the writing as Shu's voice echoed in their ears: "Open wide ye gates of Pelah to the Lamp of Veritus who comes to comfort the sorrows of Amik. He will be pierced by the darkness, and the oil of light will pour out upon the shadows, preparing the way for Eloh."

Chapter XIV

Face in the Flames

Loham struggled to keep pace with Huzesh. Though wounded, the scrappy, old gallue was still quite agile and performed as though unmolested by the wounds of battle. Their wearying journey of unending days ambled on, providing Loham with all the requisite elements for contemplation and introspection. In between the exertion and exhaustion, Loham considered many things.

To forget is a sorrow unnoticed until the moment of remembrance, for remembering pains the haunted soul. Most of the snitches had forgotten themselves, becoming oblivious to their past lives they had forsaken, and Loham was no exception. However, Huzesh's taunting questions had exposed to Loham the transformation of his self already at work. He was realizing that he had changed from someone he would no longer recognize. He worked to summon up his past. He needed to find answers to the questions of why he had forsaken his own kind and why and how he had become a snitch. Huzesh had asked these questions, but it also seemed like he was hearing them from another place, from another someone. Yet, no matter how earnestly he strived to recall them, he could not recall any reasons for the gnawing pains of shame he had felt for as long as he could recollect. The guilt had taken on a life of its own, harassing him and stabbing deep into his thoughts. This growing struggle did not depend solely on the questions Huzesh had asked or on it being him who had asked them, for questions asked by anyone may have achieved this same unintended self-examination. It was as if a contradiction of intent had been cleverly arranged to awaken the truth slumbering deep inside of Loham. Without intending to, Huzesh had opened a door to Loham's consciousness and now Loham was walking the halls of his memories.

The ruin of Amik had forever changed the Carascian line. The once-great race had broken into three fractured and incomplete remnants in the same way that Pardis had divided into three fragmented realms. The end of the Carascians had begun three new lines of beings, lines tangled in controversy and deception, in betrayal, denial, and cruelty. These were the immortal nephesh, the snitches of Shuk, and the mortal sapiens of Tirnan.

The bond between the mortal and the immortal had been incredibly secure, and the essence of the Carascians had not allowed the mortals to forget their true selves. The immortals had unceasingly reached out to their mortal selves in strange, melodic strains known as The Songs of Yore. These tunes had been designed to remind their mortals of their Carascian roots and of Eloh. Of course, Attar had been averse to the reminiscing because it caused the mortals to resist his rule and increasingly long for Eloh. To master the mortal line of Amik, Attar understood he would have to cause them to forget who they were and from where they had descended. To do this, he would be required to squelch the singing of the nephesh song or else turn the sapiens against it. He had successfully deceived the sapiens into believing that their own essence, meaning their nephesh, and their songs were of some other alien origin and were something to be feared or at least disbelieved. This had only worked for a limited time, for the nephesh would not be silenced and had reminded the sapiens of their true selves continuously. Because of this, Attar had banished the nephesh to the pit, but even the pit could not stop the song of the nephesh. So, Attar, through his cunning and deception, had instituted a covenant with Eloh that had sent all the nephesh away from Tirnan into the unknown wilderness of Shuk. But still, the song of the nephesh had spanned the great distance, constantly reminding the sapiens of their true lineage and causing them to continue to resist the authority of Attar. However, Attar had done something that could not have been predicted. Foreseeing that the song of yore would eventually reach beyond the void between Tirnan and Shuk, he had concocted a rune, a spell that would devour the songs, but for the spell to be cast, it had to be dispatched to Gubrone in Shuk. To accomplish this, Attar had found a partner, Norzaaq, a nephesh spy, who could convey the spell to Gubrone by the Aurora Path. Norzaaq was the nephesh of Narcude, the son of Amik. He had betrayed all the nephesh and given rise to the line of snitches. Norzaaq had delivered the rune to Gubrone who, along with the other members of The Twelve, had cast the spell over the Valley of Souls, forever devouring the Songs of Yore.

Attar had seen the power he could have over the nephesh through afflicting their sapiens, so he had worked to drive a wedge between them. He had accomplished this final act of treachery against the offspring of Amik by poisoning the hearts of the most vulnerable, weak, and suffering. He wounded them in the deep places of their beings through misfortune and pain, through abandonment and suffering, and through poverty and addiction. Attar had methodically broken the will and hope of the vulnerable and disenfranchised until their afflicted hearts had converted even their very essence, their nephesh, to the shadows. They had betrayed their own kind and become snitches, slaves of Gubrone, compelled to hunt and capture the nephesh and to spy for Attar and The Twelve.

Their willingness to collaborate with the gallues was the greatest distinction between the snitches and the nephesh. It set the snitches apart as being the most hated and reviled of all living creatures in Shuk. However, since the nephesh were virtually indistinguishable from the snitches, they were just as despised and mistrusted by the gallues and by all the creatures of Shuk.

The mortality of the sapiens and the desperate efforts of their nephesh to reconnect, set in motion an epic and endless struggle. Those nephesh, banished to Shuk, tried tirelessly to reach across the void and revive the breathless bonds before their mortal sapiens passed into the Shadows of Sidhe, the realm of death. For once a sapien dies and their body is broken and decayed, the bond with their nephesh is eternally severed, never to be whole again. These nephesh, whose sapiens pass, become orphans, alone with only their songs and memories. But in spite of death, they sing their songs, for there is a secret Attar does not know. Eloh has empowered the songs of the nephesh with the force of life, and, if their sapiens are alive or their bodies are whole, the essence of life can return, and the line of the Carascians can be restored. Such a resurrection has never been witnessed or experienced, or, at least, its occurrence has never been told.

Sadly, most of the snitches were waifs, permanently alienated from their sapiens because of death. However, there were a few whose sapiens were still living, and because the bond of their oneness could still be felt, they could remember, and memory was like a force, a power of an unknown origin. It was most often whispered about as if it were a dangerous secret, and if named at all, it was called the Shamar.

The Shamar was not a who or a what that could be described as though it were a being. Rather, the Shamar was the Infinite Manifestation, the sacred, unembodied witness of those elements which were from the beginning, those elements which were as they were meant to be and which remained as they should, forever unchanged. The Shamar was a timeless consciousness that imparted the essential truths from beyond the mortal and immortal understanding, beyond the here and now, beyond experience and acquisition and education; it was a revealer. Nevertheless, more than a revelation, more than insight or intuition, it was a living, authentic, immortal thought that uttered what is, and was, and what was meant to be. It uttered the undefiable, incorruptible, unincarnate message of origins. Echoed from the beginning, from first breath and first life, the Shamar was the voice of the ages, calling out to those who would hear— an uninterpreted orthodoxy.

The Shamar testified to the essence of every nephesh and to the origin of all things. It bore witness to the covenant of elements and to Eloh. It existed throughout all time, unchanged, irrefutable, and absolute. The Shamar endured without form, body, or shape and prevailed unseen yet known and felt. It told the story of life to whomever it encountered, and to whom it encountered, it could not be denied.

Shining from the beginning, the Shamar was like a star casting its boundless rays through the infinite universe from a point so far beyond measure that its glimmer, when reflected within the shallow seas of the mind, shone with the luminescence of a long-forgotten age. The Shamar came mostly to the immortals, but on a rare occasion, it chose a mortal, one who could see beyond the glare of the present age. It shone upon their mind and soul, revealing their memories and the memories of others, of the ancients and of Amik and Eloh, memories of those things that should not be forgotten, which exist beyond the mortal framework of a single life.

The shadows of forgetfulness could not resist the power of the Shamar. Not even the darkness of Attar was able to conceal its brightness or cease its glow once it had determined to shine.

The Shamar had cast its light upon Loham. It may have shone on him because he was a naïve, young snitch, buoyant and tender like a stalk of spring grass, or it may have been a random unintelligible coincidence, but for reasons beyond knowing, it had come to him and Loham was disinclined to appreciate the predicament in which it had placed him. It was dangerous to be unique in Shuk. There was no safe place for those who did not fit in, but as a snitch, Loham did not fit in. For the most part, he was able to dismiss his nephesh tendencies and convince himself, as well as others, that he was nothing more than a snitch. It was a duplicity most confusing, though. If he could have chosen one way or the other, he would have chosen to be what he had already morphed into, a snitch. Loham had volunteered to accompany Morak in order to prove himself as a snitch, and he feared that if he could not be of use or trusted, then he might become one of those many snitches who mysteriously disappeared. Considering the possible consequences, the intrusion of the Shamar was a most disagreeable circumstance. Before the Shamar had stirred up old memories and aroused uninvited senses, Loham had instinctively kept his nephesh-like virtues hidden from others, especially the gallues. However, he now feared he could not remain a chameleon.

Loham was beginning to fear the things he did not know and did not remember even more than he feared Huzesh or the other gallues. He feared the voice of the Shamar, rising in his soul, and because of his dread, he was untrusting of the message, for it was a contradiction to the message of the spell that had echoed in his thoughts for as long as he could recall. Though he could hear the voice of the spell more clearly, there had always been a part of him that had doubted its words. Now, Loham wrestled with the two competing voices, neither of which intended to concede to the other.

A growing paranoia had begun to overtake Loham: fear of torture and death, fear of Huzesh seeing into his thoughts and discovering his secret. However, Huzesh was so far ahead of Loham, it would have been difficult for him to have had reason to suspect anything at all. Huzesh moved through the rough terrain as if he were being pursued. Huzesh finally stopped to drink from a small spring that bubbled up next to a mound of rocks.

When Loham reached him, he lowered his eyes, refusing to look at Huzesh. Cautiously breaking the silence, Loham asked, "Where're we going in such a hurry?"

His voice startled Huzesh, who had been so focused on his mission that he had forgotten that Loham was following him. Huzesh snapped his head toward Loham. His eyes were full and round, with a wild glare, as if he was about to attack. He ordered, "Dunna er snaek up on mae again!" Huzesh lowered his head down to the spring and slurped another mouth full of water. Huzesh was actually astonished at how well Loham had stayed with him. Loham, on the other hand, did not move or say a word, he only watched Huzesh and waited to see if he would answer or if he would just move on. Huzesh nodded his head in the direction they had been moving. "T'da Cave o'Hidook. Ee ha spies thut wull know o'da forner, un whaer t'fin eem."

Loham let his eyes follow in the direction Huzesh was looking. "Hidook? Who is Hidook? Where can we find him?"

"Dar." Huzesh pointed to a lone, towering mountain that stood like a fortress amid the many other surrounding peaks.

"There? You must be out of your head!"

"Nae. Thut bae our aim."

"How can you find someone there? It's so big!"

"Ee wull fin us. Ye wull sae."

Hidook dwelt high in the mountains east of Gershom Forest, in a cave that was deep in a formidable snow and ice-covered, unnamed mountain. He had dark powers and could control various creatures of Shuk including the black corvuses and their smaller cousins, the ravens, which dwelt in the blackstalk marshes. Hidook was a beast, humble and unremarkable, who had drunk from the corrupted waters of the Pool of Eon. Unlike the kerolus, Hidook had received dark magical powers from the water. He had followed The Twelve to Shuk, but they despised him and determined to kill him. To escape death, he had fled into the mountains. In every corner of Shuk, the spies of Hidook prowled, except throughout the woods of Gershom. Hidook, though loyal to Attar, was an enemy to Gubrone and The Twelve. He had refused to submit to their rule and after being warned by a viper that he was to be tortured and killed, had escaped into the high mountains becoming a fugitive with a great price on his head. There were only a few of the gallues who knew Hidook's whereabouts, and those who did were, themselves, considered outcasts, renegades, and, in some cases, traitors to The Twelve.

Hidook had maintained his freedom and privacy for so long that many of the gallues had forgotten about him and the bounty on his head. For a few, however, he had become a reliable resource. They had a secret way of contacting Hidook through the many spies who were his loyal friends. Huzesh had helped Hidook escape the plot of the Twelve that had been set against him. Their camaraderie was, however, tenuous at best, considering that Hidook trusted no one completely and, of course, for good reason. Should it ever suit him, Huzesh was just as likely as any of the other gallues of Shuk to seize Hidook and turn him over to Gubrone for the bounty. Huzesh, like most of the gallues, had no true alliances or devotions, but for reasons beyond knowing, Huzesh had a strange fondness for Hidook and had helped to protect him.

Loham stared at the mountain dominating the skyline. From the peak, a long white plume of ice and snow sailed across the gray sky. He couldn't imagine how they would ever reach the summit. "So, how do you expect us to climb that?"

"Climb wut?"

"That. The mountain."

"Who said onyting bout climbin?"

"Well, I thought you did. You said we had to go to that mountain."

"Aye, wae d'ha t'gae t'thut mountain, jus nut t'da top."

"But, but you said . . ."

"Aye. A said nutin bout climbin da mountain. Yur un idiot."

"Whew! That's a relief! I was worrying that things were going to get even worse than they already are."

"Oh, dae wull! Dae wull gut mur worse. Com, luts gae." Huzesh walked away from Loham without hesitation and without checking on him. Loham, however, delayed for a moment, and before he realized it, Huzesh had disappeared from his sight in the tall trees. Loham debated with himself on what chance of escape he might have if he were to run away and hide. The woods were thick with undergrowth and dark with shadows from the overhanging branches. However, as he stood there thinking, pondering, he sensed he was being watched, that eyes were staring at him from within the shadows of the forest. Loham heard himself swallow.

Perched on a tall leafless tree at the edge of the clearing, Loham saw a lone black bird, a raven. "What are you staring at?" The bird was unaffected by Loham's taunting words. Then Loham roared like a bear or a lion, attempting to make the raven fly away, but the bird did not move, he only stared at Loham. As Loham watched the dark bird, a strange wind blew through the trees. At first, Loham gave no attention to the wind, then Loham heard a strange whisper. He twisted to search for the speaker but found no one. He gazed back at the black bird that seemed almost inanimate as it clung to its perch. Again, Loham heard the whisper, a voice with words that he could not understand, yet it was no voice at all, just a sound. Loham wondered if he was hearing with his ears what he often heard in his thoughts. He rubbed at his ears to clear them. The sound of the whisper grew louder as the wind came with a strong gust, shaking the trees around him.

Clear and audible, the words of the whisper landed upon his ears. They rang as clear as if someone was standing right next to him: "*Illu hōtallem et essen ambaes, e ambaes, a mer bae neeav pazush at sol ruulä e's ambaeun.*"

"Huh? What did you say?" Loham stared at the black bird, thinking it had spoken. He peered about, expecting to see someone or something that could have spoken the strange message. There was no one. He felt the wind descend upon the forest with such ferocity that the leaves of the trees flew into the air, and the limbs and branches shook against their futile resistance. The black bird clung desperately to the tree and Loham knelt down trying to avoid the gust.

The voice of the wind repeated, only this time, it was stronger and more pronounced. It called out as if it had been sent to find someone. It cried out like a mother searching for her lost child. Loham felt the power of its voice breathing upon him, piercing his ears with words he could not understand, angry, desperate, and longing words.

He questioned if it was the same voice he had been hearing in his heart. He was curious whether it was being heard by Huzesh or if he alone was hearing the words. There was, however, something distinct about the voice in the wind, different from what he had heard before, that caused him to feel anxious and apprehensive.

As suddenly as the wind blew in, it retreated. Loham focused on the tree where the black bird had perched. His eyes caught sight of it, but then the raven spread its wings and took flight, flying straight over Loham's head. In response, a great flock of ravens also took flight from the branches of the trees beyond. It seemed to Loham that there were hundreds of birds flying over him into the gray sky where they eventually disappeared into a dark cloud.

"Wait! Huzesh, slow down a bit!" Loham ran to catch up with Huzesh, who was pushing through the dense forest undergrowth. The flight of the ravens and the strange new voice had unsettled Loham. For the first time, he was comforted by Huzesh's company. For the duration of that day, their journey through the dark forest was difficult and demanding. Fortunately for Loham, it was somewhat easier, as the path was partially cleared by the broad swath cut in front of him by Huzesh's bulky frame. Eventually, when the sun was setting over the mountains, they reached a high clearing with a small mountain lake or tarn nearby. Huzesh paused at the edge of the clearing to survey the land. He stealthily knelt to the ground. Upon joining Huzesh, Loham wondered what would cause a scrappy warrior like Huzesh to hesitate. As he looked out over the small opening in the woods, he noticed it was completely silent. There were no animals or birds, not even a breeze to make the tall meadow grass wave. Loham was unsure whether it was so quiet because of their arrival or if some other presence had caused the stillness.

Huzesh stared across the clearing for quite a while, but it did not seem to Loham that there was any threat, so, for the first time since traveling with him, Loham stepped into the clearing ahead of Huzesh. He walked cautiously toward the little pond, wading through the tall meadow grass as if he were up to his waist in calm waters. The long seed heads of the grass were silver, and as Loham touched them, thousands of tiny silver pods took flight into the dusk air. Like petite clouds floating over a cold mountain lake, the pods hung in the air just above Loham's head. A soft, gentle breeze caressed the small clearing, ushering the clouds of silver seed pods towards the dark woods. Loham knelt when he reached the water's edge and drank the water from his scooped hands.

Huzesh kept still and observed. Loham wondered about the covertness. Not long after Loham reached the water's edge, a large stag appeared in the clearing. Loham did not see the stag at first, for it walked up behind him. Loham heard a faint snap of the grass as the stag, unaware of Loham's presence, walked alertly toward the tarn. Upon hearing the sound, Loham spun around. His eyes met squarely on the eyes of the stag and, spellbound and surprised, they stood staring at each other. Suddenly the stag leaped to sprint away. In a span of time so immediate that Loham's eyes could barely see it, Huzesh sprung from the edge of the clearing and pounced upon the stag, killing it with the bone-shattering grasp of his hand around its neck.

Loham was so stunned and horrified that he stumbled back and fell into the water, making a loud and unapologetic splash. Unable to find his way to the surface, he found himself flailing about. When he finally did surface and get his feet back under himself, he was met with the grotesque sight of Huzesh eating the raw bowels of the dead stag. Loham saw the lifeless eyes of the stag staring back at him as if accusing him of consorting with the beast who was now feeding on its bleeding carcass. Loham had seen dead animals before. He had seen them killed and eaten. He had eaten many stags and boars but never had he looked into the eyes of an animal and seen into its soul as he had that stag. It affected him in a way he could not remember ever having felt before. Sorrow and sadness filled him, feelings that he had forgotten ages ago, so long ago that they felt strange and new, even foreign.

Loham quickly gathered his composure. He was aware that any sign of weakness would be like the scent of blood in the air to the barbarism of Huzesh and any other beasts that might be prowling about. Loham tarried knowing that he dared not get too near a feeding gallue. Even though he was famished, the thought of eating the stag hit him with a powerful sense of revulsion as he watched the savage feeding frenzy of the boorish gallue. Nevertheless, he knew that he needed to eat, and he hoped that Huzesh would leave something worthy of a meal or two.

As darkness closed in on the small clearing and the sounds of night began to fill the air, Huzesh was finally starting to slow his ravenous feast. He was covered from his head to his shoulders in blood and entrails. He groaned and rubbed his bloated belly with a sense of satisfaction. Loham sat in the shadows some distance away, quietly waiting for his chance. It was rare for the nephesh to eat raw meat or any flesh at all, but if they did eat the flesh of an animal, it had to be cooked over a fire. Loham had gathered some sticks and branches so he could build a fire, but he did not want to start the fire before he was sure that Huzesh was going to allow him the privilege of a meal. With his head resting between his knees as he squatted in the tall meadow grass, he did not see the front shoulder of the stag that Huzesh threw his way. The hide and hair-covered, bloody shoulder hit him square on the head, knocking him backward. It landed on his chest and was still warm from the life that had been flowing through the creature.

"Aet!" The sound of Huzesh's voice carried its usual gruffness, though this time it had a slight ring of uncommon droll. As Loham struggled to his feet, he glimpsed a smirk on Huzesh's face. Loham regathered his sticks and branches and found a place to cook the meat. Loham carried two stones in a small pocket he had sewn into the waist of his tattered britches. He struck them together over a tinder bundle of dry grass and leaves and lit a small fire.

Huzesh watched from a short distance. "Whae d'ye bother wit da faer? Da meat bae gud wun ut bae raw un bloody."

"Not to my liking, it isn't." After dwelling on this, Loham asked, "You really are a monster, aren't you?"

"Mubae. Tis who A bae."

"Hmm. Well, this is who I am. I don't like the taste of raw meat."

Once the coals were hot and glowing, Loham hung the bloody leg and shoulder over the fire with the skin and hair still attached. The flames burned the hair away quickly, but the skin just turned dark black. The smell of the cooking meat made even Huzesh envious and hungry again.

"So, why did you follow Attar and Gubrone?"

"Huh? Wut d'ye maen?"

"Instead of Eloh? Why did you follow Attar instead of Eloh?"

"A dunna rumumbar. Whae d'ye ask? Wut d'ut muttar t'ye?"

"I don't know. Just wondered."

"Ye shunt wunnar so much. Ut maet gut ye kulled or worse."

"Worse? What could be worse?"

"Dar bae mony tings worse thun t'bae kulled, far worse."

Loham didn't really want to know more, so he asked, "Do you even remember what it was like before all this fighting and—"

"Un wut?"

"And hatred? Don't you ever get tired of it all? Tired of chasing nephs, of following orders, and of killing? Do you even know why you're doing it? I mean, what are we doing here? Why are we going after this stranger or these others, if there really are others? Why don't we just leave each other alone, you know, get along?" The tone of Loham's voice grew strong and hinted of condescension.

Huzesh responded with a low but fiercely sharp reply, "Ye spaek lik ye knows somting ye maet shunt know."

Loham avoided looking up at Huzesh though he could feel his dark, suspicious eyes glaring down upon him. Loham realized he might have revealed more than was safe and tried to disguise his impudence with feigned ignorance. "I don't know anything. That's the problem, no one seems to know anything. We all just keep repeating what we have always done and for what reason? Why?"

"Ut bae wut ut bae. Wae bae wut wae waer maent t'bae."

Loham's inner convictions arose in response to what Huzesh had said, and he could not be stopped. Loham spoke insistently and passionately without considering the insolence of his reaction and tone. "Not always. No, not always! You are just too afraid to remember!"

Huzesh rose to his feet overlooking Loham, who had not looked away from the fire. "A faer nutin! Un ye bes traed lightly, snitch!"

But Loham could not resist what he felt and, over riding his fear, spoke out again, "You know more than you admit. I know it. You talk in your sleep about the ancient times, when you had wings and could fly. What happened to you? You and the others?"

Loham's boldness alarmed Huzesh, but more than his boldness, his questions alarmed him. For Huzesh, like most of the gallues, had long ago forgotten the ancient times. He had forgotten how or why they had lost their freedom to fly. But the probings of Loham had awakened Huzesh's primordial memories that had been dark for ages. His thoughts were now saturated with the past, but he would not admit this to Loham.

Loham perceived that Huzesh was discomforted by the inquisition and that he was concealing elements of his past, from the ancient times, elements that disturbed him. He decided to question him further. "I wonder sometimes . . . I wonder if Eloh is real. Everyone speaks of him as if he is, but where is he? All this time, all these ages and, where is he? The gallues fear him, the nephesh sing of him, but is he real, or just a story or a fantasy? It doesn't seem to matter much, I guess. If he is real, I mean, what can he do? What would he do? Don't you wonder if he is real? Don't you wonder, Huzesh?"

A long uncomfortable silence hung in the air between them like an invisible wall. Huzesh turned away, refusing to look at Loham. Loham cautiously peered up at Huzesh. Loham could not have known the sharpness or the power of his words, how piercing and cutting they were to Huzesh. Loham assumed, as anyone would have, that there was nothing that could be said to disturb or unsettle the burly gallue. Nevertheless, his words, his questions, and even more, his doubt had struck Huzesh in a deeply and unimaginably sensitive place. They were sharper than any sword, and they had cut through the crusty, hard shell that had been the old gallue's defense for ages.

Loham quietly broke the silence. "I suppose when you've been around as long as you have, you forget a lot of things."

There was a long, weighty silence that followed Loham's comment as if an expanding void had opened between them. Finally, Huzesh replied, "Ye nae'er forgut, ye jus forgut t'rumumbar."

Huzesh's words astounded Loham. They rang with a piercing tone of truth, a profound truth that felt to Loham, to be far beyond what a beast like Huzesh could ever understand. "How do you forget to remember?"

"A choose ta. Ut bae better thut wae. Mumries bae somting ye wud rather forgut. Forgutin bae aesy."

"Yeah, I guess you're right. It is easier to forget."

"Dar bae somtings thut ye nae'er forgut. Somtings dunna lut ye forgut thum, lik Eloh."

Loham's eyes widened as he lifted his gaze from the flames onto the face of Huzesh. He doubted what he had just heard, or what he thought he had heard. "Huh? Eloh?" He asked skeptically.

"Aye. Ye ask uf ee bae rael, weel, ee bae rael. Ye cun bae sure o'thut."

"Did you know him?"

"Course. Wae all knew eem. Un Eloh, ee knew all o'us."

Loham could see a surprising and uncharacteristic look of regret in the eyes of Huzesh. He had never seen any of the gallues show such contrite emotions. The atmosphere between them had changed. Huzesh was as calm and as affable as Loham had ever seen any gallue. He felt like he could ask anything, and maybe while Huzesh was talking, he should ask as many questions as he could. "Why? Why did you do it? Why did you forsake the life you had with Eloh for this broken and wounded life that is not life at all? Why would you choose this?"

"Somtams ye dunna gut t'choose; somtams tings choose ye. Dae com out o'da shadows un dae snaek up on ye. A dud nut choose dis life. Dar bae mony who dud nut choose dis. Wae dud nut ha u choice, jus lik ye."

"Like me! You're not like me! We're nothing alike! You forsook your own! You turned your back on everything that made life, life. Me, I am a slave! I'm a slave to you, to my sapien, to this realm, and even to this struggle. You are not like me, not at all! You had a choice. I have none!"

"Wae all ha choices, eean ye. Ye cud ha run. A cud sae ut un yer eyes. Ye waer tinkin bout ut. Ye cud ha refused t'serve, but ye asked, yeah, ye asked t'com! Dud ye nut? Yur no dufrant thun mae, u traitor, damned!" Huzesh's sharp words had stung Loham. And while staring into the faint yellow glow emanating from the fire, he did not want to acknowledge that Huzesh had been correct. He recognized that at least a portion of what Huzesh had claimed was true.

"I never wanted to be this. I never wanted to betray my own self!" Loham argued.

"Wae all b'trae somting. Dar bae no one faultless; all ha fallen. Yur nut alone." Huzesh had been no less smitten by the painful reality of his own words. He, also, was attempting to close the opened door, to shut off the parade of ghosts escaping the shadows of his mind, memories he had locked away ages ago.

Loham threw another branch on the fire. "Do you think this struggle will ever end?"

"Nae. Ut ha bun too lung. Too mony dead bodies un too mony wounds. Ut wull gut worse afore ut guts better."

"Worse than the Great War?"

"Nae. Dar bae nutin worse thun da great war. A rumumbar da sound o'da horn, Eloh's Horn o'War. Ut waer lik u hammer baetin us un t'da ground, shakin da mountains un crackin da realm. Eary ting thut cud bae waer shaken un broken, but A waer spared. A waer sent haer wit da Twelve, afore Eloh, Shu un da kerolus armies descended upon Attar un ees minions, afore dae waer smote un cast unta da pit."

Loham watched as Huzesh, in his usual, abrupt manner, disappeared into the blackness. Loham stoked the fire and added a few more pieces of wood. He lay close to the blaze on a bed of grass and used his arm for a pillow. He stared at the flames of the fire as they danced over the branches. He was mesmerized by the glowing, yellow sparks that soared into the night sky until they appeared as stars shining down over the small clearing. But he could not rest, for his mind was spinning on everything Huzesh had said.

As Loham watched the blaze, he saw what appeared to be a face staring at him from within the fire. Loham blinked his eyes several times, thinking that his eyes were playing tricks on him, but the image of the face remained in the flames. He focused on the face trying to recognize it, but it was one he had never before seen. From behind him, a light breeze blew. It was cool and gentle at first, but it began to gust. Loham thought about the wind that had spoken earlier in the day. He listened for the voice but heard no whisper.

He thought he should find shelter from the approaching weather, but as he rose, his eyes fell upon the fire. To his amazement, the fire was undisturbed, as if it had been blocked or protected from the wind. He stared into the eyes of the face within the flames.

The winds began to howl, the trees shook and began to bend. "Loham," a soft but strong voice called out his name. He was unsure whether he had heard his name being called, or if it was just the wind howling. "Loham," the voice called again. It was calm, soothing, and clear, as if it were coming from within himself as if it were speaking directly into his mind and not into his ears.

"Who are you? What do you want?" Loham yelled over the howling wind. He felt as if his words were being stolen away in the clutches of the rising storm and unheard.

Carried within the noise of the wind, Loham could hear what sounded like a faint whisper speaking the unknown tongue. *"Lae hotallem et essen ambaes, e ambaes, a mer bae neeav pazush at sol ruulä e's ambaeun. Loham, fix your eyes on the flame. Do not be distracted by the wind and the storm."*

Loham focused intently on the fire still burning. The face in the flame continued to stare at him. He studied it, waiting for something. What, he did not know. As he examined the burning face, he saw himself! It was his own face staring back at him, but there was something different, something he did not recognize. The burning face took on three dimensions, and it moved toward him as if it were an actual being rising from the blaze. Loham backed away from the fiery face, but it advanced closer to him. The eyes of the burning face bore straight into his, yet they did not seem to perceive him. Loham attempted to touch the burning face. He immediately retrieved his hand as the flames of fire licked the skin of his fingers with its sharp, red tongue, burning his hand, sending a painful sensation up his arm and even across his chest and shoulders.

"Arrg!" The sound of his cry startled the burning face and it noticed him for the first time. It quickly retracted deeper into the fire, keeping its eyes on Loham. "Who are you?" The face spoke in a voice that Loham had heard before, yet it was unfamiliar to him.

"I . . . I am Loham. Who are you?"

"Loham? You are Loham? I am Loham, and I did not call out to you; you called out to me."

Loham looked upon the burning face with bewilderment and confusion. He could not understand this.

The face seemed unable to look away from him. "Why have you called me?"

Loham did not know what to say, for it was not him who had called out to the flames. The voice he had heard must have summoned the burning face. "What are you? Where do you come from?" Loham's voice quivered with trepidation. He spoke cautiously to the face in the fire, fearing that the flame might consume him.

"I am a sojourner looking for something I cannot find."

"What is this something?" asked Loham.

"My self. I'm looking for me. Who I am, what I am, and where I am."

"But how can you not know who you are or what you are?"

"All are separated from their true selves, and all seek what they do not know," answered the burning face.

"I don't understand."

"Look deep into yourself, into the shadows of your being. See if you do not know who you are, where you are, what you are. You are lost, separated from your true self, broken, wounded, and searching."

"But . . . searching for what?"

"You are a shadow of yourself, a reflection that is faceless."

Loham was unsure what the burning face meant, but he suspected it was true, for he sensed that he, himself, was not who he thought he was. "How do I find what I'm looking for if I don't know what it is I seek?"

"The one who calls out is the one who will show you what you are to find."

"But who is he?"

"Loham," a voice spoke.

Loham scanned the night sky for the source of the voice. The burning face searched also, but neither were able to account from whom or from where the voice had come.

"Who are you?"

"Who are you?" Loham and the burning face spoke almost at the same time, echoing the same words.

"The one who you seek is near, but be warned, he is in danger."

"Danger? From who?"

"From you, Loham. For in finding him, you will bring great danger to him."

"Then . . . then I won't go! I won't find him! But how do I know who it is I shouldn't find?"

"You must find him, Loham. That is why you have come."

"But if I bring danger to him, then . . . then shouldn't I . . . shouldn't I *not* find him?"

"No! You must find him, Loham! You must find the one whose face you see in the flames."

"But I don't understand. Why should I find him if I am to bring danger upon him?"

"If you do not, he will be unable to do what he must do. It cannot be completed without your help."

"How will I know when I have found him?"

"Look for the face in the flame."

"But it is my face I see in the fire."

"It is he whom you seek, he whom you must find."

"But what about Huzesh? He will not let me go."

"No. Do not leave the company of Huzesh. He will lead you to the one whom you seek."

"Who are you? What are you?"

The wind suddenly ceased. Loham looked into the fire. The burning face was gone, and the blackness of night settled over the fire as it quietly died into a pile of glowing coals.

"Who are you?" Loham repeated his call.

There was no response. Silence filled the air like a cold fog. Loham felt a chill run up his spine. He could sense someone near him, watching him. "Who's there?"

"Ut bae ony mae. Who dud ye tink ut waer?" Huzesh stepped out of the shadows into the faint light of the coals. "Yur faer bae dyin."

Loham saw the glowing, yellow eyes of Huzesh grow larger and closer. He feared that Huzesh may have seen or heard all that had just happened. "Where've you been?"

"Ha t'fin shelter frum da storm. Ut waer u strange ting. So sudden, ye know?"

"Yeah, I know. It nearly blew out my fire." Hugely relieved, Loham gathered that Huzesh had not heard a thing. However, he worried that the observant glare of Huzesh would soon spy the hidden thoughts that lingered in his mind. So, he turned away from Huzesh, lay down next to the fire, and closed his eyes. He could hear Huzesh snoring, almost immediately.

Through the inky darkness, the sound of music began to pierce the weighty silence. It was the ancient music of a dukwán, reaching through the dark abyss like the piercing light of a distant star, intruding upon the otherwise all-encompassing darkness. Loham struggled to open his eyes to see where the sound came from, but he was unable to move, unable to speak. He could only hear the music. It grew louder as if coming toward him. Paralyzed and afraid, Loham lay waiting for something he could not see, waiting without any place to retreat, escape, or hide. The music grew louder and the shadow that had ruled over the night began to retreat as the light of the music filled the night sky, like the colorful streaming sails of midnight Borealis. Prying at his eyelids like little fingers, the undeterred light groped at the narrow, dark seam until Loham was able to open his eyes. Much to his surprise, there had been nothing keeping him from seeing but himself. His fear had clamped his eyes closed with such power, that he believed it was someone or something else preventing him from seeing. Out of a clear, dancing sky, the music began to pour over Loham like drops of rain. It came in singular, cool droplets at first, like the first notes of the music when they pierced the inaudible darkness. Slowly, the shower of music began to fall full and unrestrained, like a spring downpour.

Loham forgot his fear. He began to move and realized he had only been bound by his own belief, by his own imagination. He was no longer a captive under the weight of oppression, and so he stood up, in the deluge of music that washed over him, and he danced as if he were free as if he were whole. He forgot about Huzesh, about the Valley of Souls, about Attar and Gubrone, and he danced to the enchanting sound of the music.

For a long time, he spun and leapt, moving about like a young boy without cares or worries. All the while, he looked around, waiting to see from whom the music came, who the musician was, but he could not see anyone coming. His mind questioned him. It asked him over and over again, "where does this song come from?" Part of him did not care, did not want to know, yet, as the song played, he became more and more interested in the musician and the instrument they played.

Then, Loham stopped his dancing. He looked in all directions, hoping to see the musician. He tried to call out, but when he opened his mouth, the voice of the instrument played so loudly in his ears, it was all that he could hear. He looked at himself, he turned around, he looked up at the sky, into the field, and across the open plain where he stood, and there was no other to be seen. He stood alone in the shower of music and song and realized that the sound was coming from within himself. As he moved, as he breathed, as he lived, the music came to life from within him and filled the dark sky. Like the sun giving life to the world, the music of Loham's soul gave life to his being. He felt the power of life touch him in a way he had forgotten. He felt the words of his song reaching out from the depths of his being, escaping the imprisonment of darkness and ascending into the heights of the sky above. Loham skipped and twirled and leapt about carelessly. He remembered what the spell of Attar had made him forget, he remembered his song.

Unexpectedly, far in the distance, across the open field, Loham saw someone unfamiliar coming toward him. Loham stopped dancing and stood watching as the stranger approached. "Who are you?" Loham bellowed.

"I am a friend, Loham." As the stranger spoke to Loham, the distance between them immediately evaporated, and before Loham, stood one who resembled a nephesh in many ways.

"Are you a neph like me?"

"I am like you in many ways, but I am not a nephesh."

"Why have you come?"

"I have come to show you something, and to give you a gift."

"What? Show me what?"

"Look. Look into the water. What do you see?"

What had been an open field had transformed into a crystal-clear sea, and Loham and the stranger were standing at its shore together.

Loham looked at the shiny, reflective surface of the water. "I see . . . umm . . . I see a stranger staring back at me. I have seen him before. Who is he?"

"He is you."

"Me?!"

"Yes, Loham. I came to show you to yourself, to show you who you are."

Loham stared long into the water. He focused intently upon the image gazing back at him. "What did you come to give me?" he asked as he studied his reflection.

"Reach out your hand, Loham." The stranger removed a wooden instrument from his pocket and placed it in Loham's hand. "I have come to return your song. It is almost time for you to play again."

"But I don't remember how."

"You will, Loham, you will."

"I want to know so many things. Will you stay with me?"

"Loham, it is time. It is time for you to wake up, Loham." The stranger faded into the shadows like a ghost.

Loham realized he had not been told the name of the stranger, but before he could call out, he heard another voice. "Loham! Wake up ye lazy snitch." Loham felt a sharp pain course across his back as Huzesh struck him with his foot. "Ye bae u lazy, gud-fur-nutin snitch. Gut up! Wae bae movin on."

Morning had returned and with it Huzesh and his frightfully wicked self. The fire he had built the night before was nothing more than a pile of ashes. As he gathered his belongings, he noticed a branch the fire had not consumed. Loham reached down and pulled the branch from the ashes. He looked at it with shock and surprise, for the branch was not a branch at all, but a dukwán. It had not been burned by the flames, nor had it been damaged by the fire. Engraved into the body of the dukwán was the writing of the Theoscians.

Loham looked at it. He knew that he should be able to read the words, but he was not able. When he turned the instrument over, he saw a symbol. It was the mark of Eloh. Loham knew exactly what it was, and it frightened him. He wondered at the mystery, for the dukwán, though in the fire, was not burned and the dream, though it came to him as a dream was not a dream at all. He thought about the dream, the music, the stranger, and the things he said. He remembered the face in the fire and the warning. Loham hid the dukwán away in his satchel and followed Huzesh. The words of the stranger rang in his mind: "*It is almost time for you to play again.*" He wondered when that time would come and how he would know it had arrived. He wondered if the stranger had left the dukwán, if the stranger who spoke to him might have been Eloh. It seemed unlikely to him that Eloh would come to Shuk and visit him. It seemed remarkable, however, that he—a fallen soul, a broken being, lost and forsaken—would have any real purpose or be of such importance Eloh would take notice of him. It had to be an illusion or dream, but the dukwán in his satchel was no illusion, and from it, Loham drew hope.

Huzesh moved quickly through the thick forest as he journeyed toward the hide of Hidook. It was obvious to Loham that a night's rest was all that was needed to return Huzesh to his boorish self, that pensive rumination was like strong drink to Huzesh, making him ill-tempered and hungover the next morning. Loham wondered how Huzesh could be so dualistic, yet he knew that to show weakness or tenderness of any kind was to make one's self a target for a violent and aggressive attack. It made Loham nervous that Huzesh had let his guard down in front of him, knowing that Huzesh was among the most violent and dangerous of the gallues. Huzesh would not wish anyone to know that he had shown even the slightest vulnerability whatsoever, so Loham hung back. He stayed far enough away from Huzesh that he felt safe. Within his thoughts, Loham could hear the haunting music of the dukwán. At times, he feared Huzesh might be able to hear the music, for the sound was growing louder in his thoughts, at times to the point of overpowering all other sounds that tried to enter his ears. The music acted like a pry bar, ripping and tearing at the bolted doors of his memory. It pushed and prodded into the secret and forgotten rooms of his heart, opening the lids to caskets that the spell of Attar had nailed shut, intending that the bodies inside should never live again.

Loham feared that he would be unable to disguise his resurrection. He feared that the memories and emotions of the past, of the life he had long ago laid to rest, would rise too close to the surface, becoming too bright to be overlooked. The louder the music, the more anxious he became. Every inch of his being wanted to escape into the forest, but the words of the stranger echoed in his thoughts. "*Do not leave the company of Huzesh. He will lead you to the one whom you seek.*" Loham had to resist his urge to run with every ounce of his will.

Through the gloom and expanse of the day, they made their way toward the dominating mountain on the horizon. At times, it seemed that they were no closer than they were the day before. Eventually, they entered onto a high, bald clearing and the forbidding, mammoth peak of the mountain came clearly into view and larger than ever. As they entered the pass, Huzesh scanned the region beyond. It was a vast, open cirque filled with towering spires and gigantic boulders strewn in every direction from the top of the pass to the base of the great mountain. At the sight of the landscape, Loham deeply despaired. He lowered his head in disgust and fatigue.

"Aye. A ha saen thut luk afore. Mony ha saen dis un ha wunt buk. Bahaha!"

"Maybe I should wait here. You can go ahead. I can't go any further."

"Nae. Yur comin wit mae. Wae ha work ta d'.

"Can we at least rest awhile? It seems so impassable."

"A know. Thut bae whae Hidook livs haer. Com, wae ha far t'gae." Huzesh climbed onto a gigantic boulder that jutted up into the sky. He leapt from it to another and then to another. Every step was a step into the hazard of the stones. Some of the stones were huge, some were sharp, and some were loose and moved whenever weight landed on them. There was no place to walk or to run. Climbing from stone to stone was the only option in an endless field that stretched farther and farther before them. They looked like minute specks, even infinitesimal, against the relentless field of stones. Progress was arduous and painful, even for Huzesh, who was beginning to show weakness and fatigue. He began to stumble and trip; he slipped and even fell several times as he pushed himself through the hazardous stone terrain.

As the sun lowered and the shadows of the mountains closed in upon the sea of stones, the air grew cold, and a brisk wind blew. Huzesh relented to the savage abuse of the landscape. He found a cave among the stones wherein he forced his wounded, aching body. He lay on the hard, cold floor of the cave, breathing in desperate breaths of life. Loham had fallen far behind and when Huzesh took shelter in the cave, he could not find the beaten gallue. Loham became frantic. He looked in all directions trying to find Huzesh. He wanted to call out, but his mouth was dry, and his lips were cracked and swollen from exposure and no water. He kept moving toward the last spot where he had seen Huzesh, but the fading light and the nondescript confusing landscape were a menace to his eyes, tricking him, playing with his mind.

Loham stood on top of a rectangular, tall stone, looking for the fallen gallue. Far in the distance, Loham could see a faint light glimmering. The light seemed to be coming closer to him, and he wondered if it might be Huzesh. He carefully climbed down from his high perch and slowly made his way toward the approaching light. He could not tell if his foot was falling on solid ground or on the sharp edge of a broken stone. He was afraid to go any further in the darkness. The little light came closer until, eventually, Loham could see it was a small creature with wings, glowing like moonlight. It was known as a luna-tulwyth, or tulwyth for short. Few had ever seen them since the days after the Great War. The luna-tulwyths were mystical creatures who lived throughout the realm of Pardis but were believed to have vanished during the tempest of elements that split the realm.

The flying creature captivated Loham. He had not seen such a spectacular little beast, nor had he any sense of what it might be. Nevertheless, its light came into the eyes of Loham like a magical dose of hope. He extended his hand to see if the beautiful creature would land in his palm, but the tulwyth landed on his shoulder instead. The yellow glow of the tulwyth's wings warmed his face. Loham was afraid to turn his head or move at all, fearing that the creature might fly away and leave him alone in the darkness. "What are you, my little friend? Where did you come from?" Loham whispered, not only because he was trying to be quiet, but because a whisper was all he was able to force from his parched throat. There was no reply from the creature. Loham turned his head slowly hoping to see more closely, what this tiny creature looked like. The tulwyth looked very much like a small bird. It was adorned with tiny, iridescent feathers that glowed and shimmered. Its wings were oversized and transparent, much like the wings of a dragonfly. When the tulwyth was stationary, its light faded to a faint glow. Its remarkable wings were awash with an energy; running through the lines and creases, like light flowing in liquid form through veins. As the tulwyth flew, its wings illuminated into a sphere of light that encircled the whole creature, causing it to shine as it moved. The tiny, black eyes of the tulwyth sparkled with an aura of childlike innocence, untouched by the harsh and brutal realities of Shuk.

Unexpectedly, the tulwyth lifted off from Loham's shoulder in a burst of light. As it flew, a radian stream of rainbow-colored light followed behind it. The tulwyth did not fly far; he flew out in the direction of Huzesh and waited. After a moment, the tulwyth flew back to Loham and then back to where it had just been. Loham watched it fly back and forth several times, not sure what he should do. "Am I supposed to follow you little one?" The tulwyth continued to fly back and forth, and finally, Loham took steps in the direction the creature was flying. He first had to negotiate his way off the giant rock. Once down, he slowly scrambled over the menacing boulders. The tulwyth flew near the feet of Loham, showing him where to step on the dangerous and unpredictable terrain. Slowly they went toward the cave where Huzesh had fallen deeply into an exhausted sleep. Much later, Loham heard a muffled growl. At first, he feared that one of the night creatures had found them. Like a flash, the tulwyth flew down into a dark area of rocks, which was the cave where Huzesh was laying. Loham could see the giant feet of Huzesh hanging out of the opening, which did not come as any comfort to him at all.

As Loham entered the shelter with the sleeping giant, the tulwyth quickly and unceremoniously flew away, leaving Loham alone with Huzesh. Loham turned to see the tulwyth flitter away into the night. He wondered if he might ever see his new little friend again. He found a spot and lay down. His mind raced with thoughts and memories, but the power of fatigue soon subdued them all.

Diffused sunlight began pouring into the cave. Loham turned away hoping to garner a few more moments of rest before having to deal with Huzesh for another long day. As he laid there, trying to go back to sleep, he could hear the growling wheezes of Huzesh who was still sleeping. Loham lifted his head to look and see if it were indeed Huzesh and if he was, in fact, still sleeping, which would have been unexpected. Looking down toward his feet, he saw the giant head of Huzesh resting on a rock with his broken and mangled body stretched out below it. Loham could hardly believe his eyes. The sunlight was shining into the cave, the day was on the rise, and Huzesh was still sound asleep.

He exited the cave to find it was situated among a calamity of boulders. It was a wonder that Huzesh ever found it. The morning sky was cloudy, and there was a heavy frost resting on the stones. Loham looked back toward the way they had come, and was shocked that the pass where he had stood the day before was completely out of sight. All that could be seen was the massive sea of stones. He turned to see the giant mountain that was, from what he understood, their destination. His eyes were met with an unexpected and frightening revelation. The sea of stones lying between the cave and the mountain was met with the towering shards of ice calving off a giant glacier. He wondered what his need to prove himself had led him to. The seeming impossibility of crossing the sea of stones was quickly diminished by the even greater implausibility of crossing a towering river of ice that cracked and exploded with thunderous, even deafening reports.

The moans and groans of Huzesh echoed out of the cave. Huzesh was usually at his worst in the morning. His vulgar manner built up inside of him while he slept until it could not be contained for another moment; it had to find its escape at the first possible opportunity. Loham had learned to keep his distance when Huzesh awoke.

Loham scurried away from the entrance in the direction of the glacier, giving himself a head start on the endeavor awaiting them. Huzesh's tall frame was quite small against the towering spires and boulders that surrounded him. As he exited the cave, Loham looked back and could only periodically see Huzesh's bobbing head above some of the shorter boulders. It appeared that Huzesh was stumbling about as if he were half inebriated. The day before had been more unforgiving to Huzesh than it had been to Loham, for the insolent gallue was quite obviously weakened by the journey. Neither had consumed food or water since entering the sea of stones. Eating had become the only thing Huzesh could think about. Loham feared that the unruly barbarian might consider eating him if he did not keep his distance, at least until food was found.

"Loham, whaer bae ye?" The thunderous, demanding voice of Huzesh echoed throughout the cirque.

Loham considered not answering but feared that ignoring Huzesh might lead to a very unpleasant outcome. He hollered, "I'm over here.

What do you want?" His tone was clearly an expression of disgust and contempt which, if he were nearer to Huzesh, he would not have exhibited.

Huzesh, however, was unfazed by his impudence and yelled back, "Wut ye bae doin out dar? Ye fin onyting t'aet?"

"No, nothing. No water, either."

"Arrgggg."

"How much further do we have go? Where is your friend, Hidook?"

"Ee wull com. Ee wull com."

"So, do we wait here with nothing to eat or drink?"

"Aye. Wae wait. Food wull com." Not far from the cave, a small, furry rodent sat upon a flat rock watching the two strangers. Occasionally, it would sit up on its hind end and let out a high-pitched chirp. Eventually, there were others sitting among the rocks sunning themselves and occasionally chirping back like birds. Loham could see that Huzesh, like a hungry dog, was on the prowl, ready to consume as many of the rodents as he was able to capture. The dark brown, furry creatures had a rather potent curiosity which was bound to be fatal. Huzesh sat quietly against a rock. He waited for the curious, unsuspecting critters to come and inspect him. One by one, the rodents came closer and with lightning speed, Huzesh grabbed them. One rodent was only two large bites for the gallue. He did not bother to kill them before he bit them in two and consumed them, hair and all.

This was another of the many reasons Loham loathed the gallues. They were vial, merciless beasts. "Com, Loham, com, aet."

"I'll get my own, thank you."

"Grrrrr! Loham, ye bes baeware! Ye cunna stay wae frum mae fur lung."

Loham scrambled over the rocks away from Huzesh. As he scampered away, to his amazement and delight, he spotted a large pool of water nestled in the rocks a short distance away. "Water!" Loham leapt from rock to rock like a mountain goat, until he landed next to the small pool of clear water. He knelt at its edge and submerged his whole head in the cold pool. He then cupped his hands, dipped them into the pool, and poured a large satisfying drink of water into his mouth. The water ran over his chin and down his neck and onto his shirt. He yelled, "Water! Huzesh, it's water!"

Loham took multiple drinks before Huzesh was able to reach the pool.

Huzesh rushed across the rocks toward Loham. He was less considerate and jumped into the pool, making an enormous splash. His dirty, sweaty, and bloody frame was submerged for several moments as he guzzled the water and washed himself. Loham, deciding that even though the water may not be suitable for drinking anymore, it was certainly suitable for a bath, and jumped in. It was a strange sight indeed: a gallue and a snitch bathing together in a rocky pool laughing and playing as if they were the best of friends, which, of course, they were not.

Huzesh remained in the pool long after Loham was dried by the morning sun. For so many days, Huzesh had been relentlessly driving them to reach the hidden place of Hidook, yet on that morning, Huzesh seemed unhurried as if he had no place to go at all.

"Will you be bathing the entire day?"

"Mubae. Wut d'ut matter?

"Well, don't we have somewhere to be, or is this the hide of Hidook?"

"Hidook wull fin us, dis bae da place wae wait."

Loham was confused. In his mind, it would be impossible for anyone to find anybody in that jungle of stones and ice.

"So how long before Hidook finds us?"

"A dunna know. Ee coms wun ee coms. A nae'er know."

"How will he find us in this, this mess of rocks and ice?"

"Who knows. Ee wull, ye wull sae."

Loham jumped from rock to rock. His legs were rested, making it easier to scramble over the terrain than it was the day before. He found a place quite some distance from the old gallue. A towering spire of ice that had split away from the glacier stood before him. The ice shined in the light, and the colors of emerald and light blue glistened from it as if it were a giant gemstone. Blue, red, orange, and green rays of light shone across the array of stones that surrounded Loham. He sat and watched the light dance over the rocks. He was amazed by the rugged beauty of the world stretching out before him in all directions. It had been a long time since he had noticed beauty. He laid down on his back and looked up toward the cloud-covered peak of the giant mountain and noticed the gentle sound of the wind whistling through rocks. The melodic tone of the wind reminded him of the dukwán he had found in the fire just a few days earlier and he reached into his satchel to retrieve it.

Loham inspected the instrument. He did not know how to play it, but he knew he could not attempt to do so, for if Huzesh heard it, he would destroy it. Loham and all the snitches were commanded to never play the dukwán; it was forbidden. Loham studied the inscription carefully, desperate to know its meaning.

Holding the ancient pipe made his hands tremble. He wondered what was so dangerous about the simple piece of wood, how something so innocuous could be so hated, so feared, and so opposed. He ran his finger over the engraved words. He could feel that the pipe was old and worn, and the letters of the inscription were worn smooth as if carried in the hands of someone for a long time. Loham was tempted to put the pipe to his lips and blow, but his fear of Huzesh and the law of the gallues was too strong, so he returned the pipe to his satchel.

"What is it that you hide in your little bag?" The voice startled Loham. It came from something standing on a rock a short distance away.

"Huh? What? I mean who, who are you?"

"Who are you? Why have you come, young snitch?" The sound of the strange intruder's voice was threatening. Yet the creature did not try to attack Loham, nor did he act with aggression.

"I'm on a journey with the gallue, Huzesh. He looks for someone."

"Huzesh! I know Huzesh, but I do not know you. Why would Huzesh travel with a snitch?"

"Ask him. That's something I don't know myself."

"Bahaha! You are a funny one, but there is something about you I don't like. I don't think I trust you, snitch. Where is Huzesh?"

"The last time I saw him, he was bathing in a pool of water, just over there."

"What? Bathing in my watering hole? I will teach him a lesson or two!"

"Are you, Hidook?"

"Yes. Yes, that is me." Hidook made the call of the corvuses and before Loham knew it, a flock of the black birds was flying toward the watering hole where Loham and Huzesh had bathed. The corvuses swarmed like mosquitos, attacking Huzesh who was still in the water. Huzesh emerged from the pool with a leap and a growl, batting the air to knock away the invading birds.

"Cull thum off, Hidook! A know ut bae ye. Cull thum off, ye ol' bat!"

The relentless attack of the black birds was not immediately called off, though. Hidook seemed intent on making Huzesh bleed and beg.

"Hidook, uf ye dunna stop thum, A promise A wull fin ye un kull ye!" Huzesh yelled with fierce violence, as the birds pecked at his head and back and, especially his face. The birds were known to peck out the eyes of their victims first, so they were unable to defend themselves. Huzesh had witnessed it on many occasions and knew it was crucial to protect his eyes.

Hidook made another call in the language of the birds, causing them to retreat from Huzesh. However, the birds did not fly far. They landed on the nearby rocks and watched Huzesh as if he were their next meal. Hidook waved his hand in the air, motioning to the birds to leave, which they did. Loham felt as though he had recognized one of the birds, one that had stayed close to Hidook and not flown away with the others. He wondered if it might be the black bird he had seen before, the one that had stared at him in the forest several days earlier. He had a strange feeling about the bird, that there was something different, even more frightening about it even though it looked no different from the hundreds of other corvuses he had seen.

"You make my friend uncomfortable, snitch." Hidook spat on the ground, his deep, course voice and his words were not friendly; they sounded like an unspoken warning. Hidook stared long and hard at Loham, who felt threatened by him and backed away.

Hidook stepped close to Loham, grabbed his arm, and murmured to him under his breath, "I have been watching you, snitch. I know what you have seen, what you have heard, and I know who you are. Do not think that I am a fool. Do not think that I do not know."

Loham quickly pulled his arm away and took several paces back. He swallowed as he stood with his back against a boulder. He had no place to run or hide. His heart was pounding rapidly in his chest. Hidook glared at him through huge, black eyes. A scornful grin broke the menacing stare and a devious sneer rolled from his lips.

At that moment, Huzesh stepped between Loham and Hidook. "Dunna gut ony ideas, Hidook. Loham ha com wit mae. A ha u purpose fur eem."

"Sure you can trust him? I don't like him."

"Trust? Nae, A dunna trus eem. A naed eem, alive, un unmolested."

"He will be trouble to you. Remember that, you fool."

"A wull take care o'eem, uf ee b'coms trouble."

Loham stood behind Huzesh and listened. He wondered what Huzesh had in mind, but he knew that there was no alliance between them, that he was little more than a means to an end, and that when Huzesh no longer needed him, he would be in great danger.

"So, A sae ye stull ha yer fruns bout ye. Aye? Da corvuses mus raelly lik ye."

"Oh no, they don't like me as you suppose, Huzesh, nor are they my friends. They are my slaves; they do what I ask because they have no other choice. I am not a bad master, but I am a master, and no slave loves their master. They do not love me, they fear me, and I make sure that that is for good reason."

"Ut bae gut thut dae dunna understand ye thun, dae maet nut bae a'much haelp a'dae bae."

"I think they understand as well as your little snitch understands."

"Mubae better. Bahaha!"

Loham could not find any humor in their disparaging exchange.

Hidook was a strange creature, a dark spirited half-breed. It was not fully known where he had come from or of what he was a half-breed, but there was not another creature in the realm of Shuk that was like him. He was small in comparison to the gallues, but almost as large as Loham, though he moved about on all fours like a papio, a hairy vicious tree climber of the primate family. He had dark skin with sparse, bristly hair growing over most of his body. He had a ghoulish face with deep wrinkles and a large, flat nose. His eyes were large and dark with slit- shaped, black pupils like those of a serpent. His mouth was large, with lips that were full and thick. He had coarse black hair that sprouted from the top of his head, like pampas grass and hung in his face. He had long and thick curly, black eyebrows attached to a thick, heavily accentuated frontal ridge. His teeth were large and sharp with canine teeth on the upper and lower jaws that protruded from between his lips. While he moved mostly on all fours, Hidook regularly stood upright on his two hind legs as he had when he had grabbed Loham and threatened him. Hidook had thick mud stuck to his back and legs, which stunk as if he had rolled around in his own defecation.

"Ye stink worse thun er, Hidook."

"I can't stand the water; it makes me feel all wet."

"Weel, ye naed t'gut wet once un u while onywae."

"Nae. Keeps everyone away just the way I like it. Why are you here and why did you bring him? You know I don't like strangers, especially snitches. Can't trust them."

"Aye, but A naed eem."

"For what? What are you up to now, Huzesh?"

"Dar bae u rumor thut dar bae u kerolus un Gershom. D'ye know onyting bout ut? Ha yer spies saen onyting?"

"You know my spies can't go into Gershom. Only nephs are allowed to go there."

"Aye. So, now ye know whae A ha brung mae snitch."

"But, he is a snitch, not just a neph. It is forbidden."

"U snitch, u neph . . . wut bae da difference? Dae bae da same t'mae."

Loham realized exactly why Huzesh had brought him and why Morak had protected him in the valley. They meant to use him in their scheme to capture the kerolus, the stranger, or both. "Wait a minute! That's why you brought me here, to help you capture some mystical creature in a forbidden forest? If this kerolus is anything like I've heard, I am no match for him and neither are the two of you! You only have one arm and are hobbled like some lame goat, and you . . . you are little more than me, whatever you are. I mean, we are no match for such a powerful opponent!"

"Aye. Yur right, but wut bout da forner?"

"What about him? You don't even know if there is a foreigner! Maybe the foreigner is the kerolus, maybe there is no foreigner or kerolus. Maybe everything is just a rumor, or worse, a lie!" disputed Loham.

"It's no lie! My little birds have told me of a foreigner who came from the mountain. He is traveling with an aposta and at least two nephs. One of the nephs is the she-neph who hunts the mēgs, and they have killed at least two of Gubrone's mēgs in a battle near the Valley of Atramentous. The foreigner is believed to be Amik!" Hidook reported.

"Amik? Ee bae dead, lung ago," objected Huzesh.

"So it was recorded, but my most faithful spies have seen him. He exists, and he has entered into Gershom."

"What about the kerolus? Have they seen one in Gershom?" asked Loham.

"Only rumors. There are also whispers that Shu has come to Shuk."

"Shu? Thut bae u lie! Shu wud nae'er com t'Shuk. Ut bae agan da law."

"You mean the law decreed by Gubrone? Shu is not subject to the laws of Gubrone, only to the laws of the covenant," clarified Hidook.

"Da Covnant o'Elements? Thut bae nutin but lore; dar bae no covnant."

"Oh, but there is, Huzesh. Most of us have been deceived by Gubrone. You know he cannot be trusted to tell the truth. There is a covenant, and I have viewed it."

"What is this covenant?" inquired Loham.

"It is the treaty between Eloh and Attar that was made long after the Great War. It resulted in Attar being confined to Tirnan, and it is the reason the nephs live here in Shuk and why Eloh is not allowed to come here or Tirnan. It is the law that governs the whole Realm of Pardis and in one way or another, we are all subject to it."

"But if it's broken what will happen?"

"Oh, but it has been broken, a long time ago, by the gallues. They broke the covenant when they captured the nephs and cast the spell of Attar over the Valley of Souls. They have murdered many nephs, all in violation of the law."

"But nothing's ever happened to them, so maybe Huzesh is correct, and there truly is no covenant. It's just a myth."

"Dar bae no covnant. Eloh ha no power o'er us or o'er Shuk. Wae do as wae wull!" boasted Huzesh.

"You're a fool Huzesh, you and all the gallues! You think that because you have experienced no repercussions for the atrocities you've committed, there is no law. But the Covenant of Elements will eventually judge all, and each who has broken its law will be held accountable. Even Eloh is subject to it. That is the reason he has not punished the gallues. The elements will be our judge. They will search us and find us out. They will set things right, in their perfect time, you can be sure."

There was something in the tone of Hidook's voice that made Loham uneasy. He sensed Hidook knew something very few others in Shuk comprehended. He did not know if all Hidook had said was true, but the possibility of it troubled him. More than anything, Loham wondered about Eloh and Shu. He had heard of them, but he had never believed they existed. "I thought Eloh was just a legend, a story told by over-imaginative nephs."

"Nae. A ha told ye, afore. Eloh bae rael."

"Alright, and Shu, who is he?"

"He is the son of Eloh, a Theoscian," Hidook explained.

Loham wanted to ask more about Eloh and Shu but feared his motives might sound suspicious. So instead, he asked about the foreigner, "But, who's this foreigner? Why's he here? What's he come to do?"

"Hmm, if this foreigner is Amik or one of his seed, the spell of Attar may be broken. Maybe the Kleid o'Miht has been reclaimed, and he has come to free the nephs," Hidook speculated.

"Uf Amik ha reclaimed da Kleid o'Miht, ee wull cast us all unta da pit. Eary one u us wull bae destroyed."

"But wait! We're immortals; we can't die! How can he destroy us?"

"You are correct, Loham. We are immortal and we cannot die, but as you have seen for yourself, we can be killed."

"Eloh wud naer kull da nephs," contested Huzesh.

"He might take vengeance though, for their captivity."

As Loham listened to Huzesh and Hidook converse, he realized they had real distress in their voices. He wondered what would happen to him if they were correct and this foreigner truly was Amik. Anxiety and fear unnerved Loham, for though he despised the gallues and hated his life in Shuk, he was, after all, a snitch, and a traitor.

"Dar bae only one ting fur us ta d'. Wae mus kull dis forner afore ee finishes wut ee ha com ta d'."

"You are not alone in your thoughts. Gubrone has sent more than thirty hunters with their snitches and mēgs into the mountains to find the foreigner and the kerolus. They are searching everywhere as we speak. Soon they will reach Gershom forest, but they will not find the foreigner there or those who journey with him. They are actually traveling norõ, to the far side of Gershom, toward the norõ extent, probably to the Pool of Levitus, if I were to guess."

"Da Pool o'Levitus? Thut bae u myth! Dar bae no such place."

"You're wrong Huzesh. I have seen it with my own eyes. It lies high above a waterfall, guarded by towering slabs of icy, white stone."

Loham asked, "Why would they go there? Is there something there?"

"The legend tells that the pool is a place of transformation, where one can see who they really are."

"But why go there? What could they possibly have to gain?" Loham repeated.

"Dunna muttar. Uf dae gae t'da Pool o'Levitus thun so d'wae, but no one else mus know. Uf dae fin out, A wull hunt ye down, Hidook, un guv ye t'Gubrone!" Huzesh was totally serious. He counted Hidook, not as a friend, but as an enemy whose threats were real.

"Who is going to find me here? No one else ever petitions me for help but you, Huzesh. No one will learn these facts from me. However, why would you not want more help? We all face the same danger and the same end if the enemy comes to Shuk?"

"A ha mae reasons. Tell no one!"

"I will tell no one, but remember, Huzesh, we are not friends. Do not come to me again!"

Ignoring the bullying threat, Huzesh grabbed his small bit of gear and asked, "Wut wae d'wae gae, Hidook?"

"To the norõ un wes, through the ice valley. Huzesh, there is a strange wind about; I have heard it advancing. It is not only wind, but it is also a voice, a whisper. Beware of it, for it conveys a message I cannot understand."

"Dar bae nutin t'faer, Hidook. Ye worry t'much! Loham, bae tam t'gae."

Loham gathered his belongings and followed Huzesh. Hidook grabbed his arm and in a low growl uttered, "Remember I have spies everywhere, watching you. I don't trust you, snitch!"

Loham wondered why Hidook had threatened him but had not reported his suspicions to Huzesh. It was obvious to Loham that everyone in Shuk kept pieces of information to themselves, just in case they needed it. He assumed Hidook would leverage his knowledge in the future, should he need to.

Loham hastily pulled his arm free of Hidook's grip and protested defiantly, "You only think you know what I know!" Without a second glance, he reluctantly followed Huzesh toward the expansive glacial valley.

Chapter XV
Dangerous Winds

Far away, beyond the great plain of Haemus and the border of the Great Sea, from the un-sailed reaches of the boundless waters of the south seas, a strange wind was building. It crossed the great watery divide until it touched the cliffs and rugged shores of Shuk. Its first caress of the coasts came like a kiss from a returning lover who had journeyed far. Gently, the breeze passed over the borderlands, then stretched over the vast expanse of the plain. It came softly and unsuspectingly into the highlands, like the breezes of early spring, bringing warm fresh gusts of sea air. As the days passed, the wind increased its breadth and heightened its intensity. Large cumulus clouds soared across the sky, some bright white like ivory towers, others black and menacing like clouds of war, full of violent lightning that unleashed terrorizing claps of thunder. The wind marched through the land like a monstrous, unconquerable giant, gaining strength with each mighty step. Abnormal storms broke out wherever the wind blew. Powerful surges of the sea and drenching downpours unleashed savage floods. In various distant locations, the mountains quaked and spewed red molten rock and ore from their bellies.

Hidden in this vast turmoil was a whisper, clothed in the billowing wind and quietly echoing throughout the realm. Its words could not be understood. Barely any in the realm were aware of it or took notice of it. Only a rare few were conscious of it or could perceive it, but they could not understand it. Like a thief prowling about under the cover of darkness, the whisper spoke from within the commotion of the approaching gale. Its words were repetitive, constant, and threatening. *"Illu hōtallem et essen ambaes, e ambaes, a mer bae neeav pazush at sol ruulä e's ambaeun."*

The brewing siege of inhospitable elements had only just begun in the high mountains, but it had already caused the search for the foreigner to be a more demanding challenge than it would have otherwise been. Wind and rain and snow all responded to the undulating cadence of the whisper.

In the north region of the Valley of Souls, among the rocky crags of the Ardu Needles, was a strange formation of spired stone towers that held court over the valley below and prevented access into the realm beyond. This was the domain of Sinistradt, one of The Twelve. Sinistradt was a brute, more so than any other of The Twelve. He had no true alliances and was extremely feared and distrusted by most, especially by others in The Twelve. The only members of The Twelve who were even remotely aligned with him were Puttinash, Borash, and Chiddush. Together, these four arch-gallues ruled over one-third of the Valley of Souls known as the North Region, which extended from the River Chimosh to the Ardu Needles. The River Chimosh flowed wide and rugged through the valley for more than one hundred miles. Fed from the icy waters of the Inhast Glacier at its headwaters in the east, its waters never ceased to flow wildly until they entered the impassable narrows of the Massagt Gorge, which cut deeply through the Telohm Mountains flowing down until it joined the Teercus River in the Plain of Haemus. As the River Chimosh entered the gorge, it fell over a sheer wall of smooth, black stone more than three thousand feet in height. On either side of the falls were smooth, sheer towering granite walls. The river flowed with such force and volume into the gorge that when it reached the steep cliff face, the water shot out beyond it like an angry spout of roaring, white spray before falling into the gorge below. The gorge itself was long and narrow with steep, smooth walls, pressing in on either side its entire course. It cut through the mountains like a deep scar, jagged and indirect. There was no way in or out of the gorge that was not perilous or impassable. The course of the river was so indirect and inaccessible that its lower extent, which traveled through the lowlands and eventually into the Plain of Haemus, was thought to have originated from a deep fount that flowed from beneath the base of the mountains. It was for this reason that The River Chimosh had two names. The name Chimosh was known only in the Valley of Souls and throughout the highlands, and the Anook River was known throughout the lowlands because of Mount Anook, which dominated the landscape near where the river emerged from the gorge.

On a dark, moonless night, in a secret cave near the falls, Sinistradt met with Puttinash and Chiddush. They had previously met there numerous times. They spoke in hushed tones, scheming and plotting against Gubrone.

"So, Gubrone ha called u maetin, aye? Wut ye tink ee wanna now?"

Chiddush disclosed, "A haer rumors thut ee ha sent neph hunters into da lowlands t'fin a forner."

Outraged, Sinistradt declared, "A ha also haerd dis rumor, but dar bae no forner! Gubrone bae a fool! A ha sent mae own hunters. Dae dunna hunt da forner. Dae muk trouble fur Gubrone! Ee wull luk eean mur da fool thun ee already d'! Soon ut wull bae tam t'muk our move!"

Since the days of the Great War, Sinistradt had hated Gubrone. His indeterminate enmity simmered beneath the surface of his less-than-affable pretense which was, at best, coarse and surly. His traits, though common among the gallues, were excessively characteristic of him. To Sinistradt, it played out like a cruel joke that Attar would order him to the same place with Gubrone with the same purpose, and then, to add insult to injury, appoint Gubrone as his leader. In his mind, Gubrone was nothing more than a spineless sycophant, a pleaser, willing to do anything he was commanded. It infuriated Sinistradt and, as time passed, he grew corrupted by his scorn, to the point that he believed himself superior to Attar.

Sinistradt forced himself to be tolerant of certain arch-gallues, like Chiddush and Puttinash, who he believed to be weaker than himself. Also, because they feared him and distrusted Gubrone, they were easily manipulated. But, for the others he had no power over, Sinistradt felt nothing more for than absolute disdain.

Now Gubrone had settled in the south region of the valley, far away from Sinistradt's realm. He, and many of the others, did not like Sinistradt, but Gubrone was also dismissive of Sinistradt's insolence. He was far enough away that he had little concern over Sinistradt's malignant and devious hatred.

For ages, Sinistradt had waited and planned, his dark heart brooding and growing more violent with every passing season. His hatred became unruly and undisciplined. It spread to every part of his being, driving him closer toward his evil intentions, intentions of conquest and treachery, of murder and domination. No one was safe from the flames that burned in the heart of Sinistradt, especially Gubrone. There was also an even darker intent. The nephesh and their ceaseless song of yore had become like a festering, intolerable sore to him. The nephesh had grown in exceeding numbers. Their population had grown exponentially like the vines of Blackstalk that had overcome the marshes of the Atramentous Valley. He and Chiddush were secretly intending to destroy all the nephesh once they had dealt with Gubrone.

Now Chiddush was an arch-mage and practiced in the same black sorcery as Attar, though he was much less accomplished. Sinistradt had observed something special in Chiddush, something Gubrone had not noticed, and he knew that having an alliance with him might prove to be beneficial. Chiddush had been overlooked by The Twelve, though he had worked closely with Attar during the early days of the rebellion. He had used his powers in the dark magic to help create the dakoons and the rune that was poured into the Pool of Eon. Chiddush also disliked Gubrone so, out of necessity, Sinistradt had been placing his confidence in the abilities of Chiddush, a decision he often questioned.

The gallues had long believed that the power of the spell over the Valley of Souls and the nephesh was only as strong as the bond between The Twelve. It was the one thing that kept The Twelve as unified as they were, though what they had could hardly be construed as unity, for there had always been much dissension and fighting between them. But Sinistradt began to suspect they had all been lied to, that Gubrone had deceived them. Whether or not it was true, Sinistradt could not know with certainty, but he suspected it to be true, and with his suspicions came emboldened, impatient aggression that, at times, was stronger than he could contain. If he had been fully convinced that the unity of the Twelve was a farce, he would have killed Gubrone long ago, but he was not fully convinced yet, so he waited, knowing that Gubrone was not the only thing standing in the way of his ruling Shuk.

More urgent than anything else, more than Gubrone, or the Twelve, or the spell of Attar was the nephesh problem. Though they had forgotten it, the nephesh were immensely powerful and could overwhelm the gallues of Shuk if they were to ever realize the overwhelming potential of their strength, both in might and mass. If Sinistradt could not control or destroy them, he could not rule Shuk, and he had little interest in controlling them. To remedy this, it was given to Chiddush the task of devising a plan to deal with the nephesh, a plan that included a lethal spell, devised to destroy. It was a final solution to the problem of the nephesh, a rune of death meant to exterminate them all. But Chiddush had not been able to conjure a spell of sufficient power to accomplish their intent, for a spell of such magnitude would require something that Chiddush did not have. A spell of such consequence would require the blood of Attar.

There was only one source in Shuk where the blood of Attar could be found: The Eleetrum Shard. But to get the shard, they would have to kill Gubrone. Chiddush had not yet reported this to Sinistradt. And there was more. Chiddush had become convinced that even if they had the blood of Attar, the spell would only destroy the waif nephesh, those orphaned. The bond and force of life possessed by the other nephesh was a magic too powerful for any spell to overcome.

Though Sinistradt disliked the idea of ruling over the nephesh, Chiddush was able to convince him that by killing the waifs, the rest of the nephesh would capitulate. They would surrender to the rule of Sinistradt, becoming his slaves, and when they became orphans, then they would be eliminated, thus keeping their numbers under control. The plan seemed reasonable, if not preferred. Knowing they needed the Eleetrum Shard, the murder of Gubrone became their first priority, so they considered how they might accomplish this.

The brazenness of Sinistradt was not without considerable inner turmoil, for he secretly worried about The Covenant of Elements, made between Eloh and Attar. It was the Covenant that protected the nephesh from harm or destruction by the gallues. But only Gubrone knew the secrets of the covenant and its power, and no one had ever actually seen the covenant or knew what it said. It had always been accepted, having come from Gubrone, that there was a provision in the covenant protecting the nephesh. This did eat at Sinistradt, for a while. He considered how long it had been since they had come to Shuk and how many nephesh and snitches they had murdered without facing any consequences. With this in mind, Sinistradt convinced himself that there was little or no risk, that The Covenant of Elements, like the legend of Eloh, was nothing more than a myth, though inwardly he was still uncertain.

Gubrone demanded a meeting. It seemed the advent of the foreigner could have an unexpected and even favorable effect on Sinistradt's plan. Whether or not the foreigner was real mattered little to him, but the hope that Gubrone was so concerned with catching him could prove to be helpful. Sinistradt needed Gubrone to leave the valley, yet he was not sure just how he might accomplish this. The rumor of a foreigner was certainly helping, but if it was suggested that Eloh himself might be the foreigner, then surely Gubrone would insist on going after him. Sinistradt imagined that with the unintentional help of the other arch-gallues, there might be a way to convince Gubrone that he should be more directly involved in the crusade, that he, himself, should lead the charge to find the foreigner, to find Eloh.

The spies he had sent into the realm to stir up trouble were suddenly more important than ever, for though Sinistradt had not predicted it, their subversive activity was bound to further provoke Gubrone to insert himself into the search.

It had been Sinistradt's spies who had started the rumors of the bounty for the foreigner, which, of course, had unleashed an army of rabble gallues to enlist themselves in the search. Sinistradt's goal of creating as much chaos as possible would become inadvertent leverage against Gubrone. Furthermore, he realized that once Gubrone was out of the valley and out of sight of the others, he could kill him without anyone witnessing. If his death went unnoticed and the Eleetrum shard was taken from Gubrone's corpse, it would give Chiddush additional time to master the spell of death. It was too good to be true. The scheme he had been developing for so long was now underway. "Wae mus gae t'da cave o'Gubrone un bae raedy, fur ut mae bae thut tings bae bout t'change," Sinistradt urged.

There was a strange and unfamiliar sense of fortuity between them as if after ages of scheming and plotting, the very moment they had been anticipating was about to present itself.

In the south region of the Valley of Souls, deep in his cave, Gubrone received information that the search for the kerolus and the foreigner was not going well. One of Gubrone's lieutenant slaves brought word that many gallues throughout the realm of Shuk were seeking a bounty for the kerolus. Initially, Gubrone was not concerned. He laughed in his gruesome manner of deceit. It was common for strange rumors to find their way around Shuk. At times, Gubrone used misinformation and lies to bolster his reign of dominance on all the reaches of the realm. He also often used them to make himself unimpeachable, to cleverly acquit himself of any involvement, should things go awry. Even if Gubrone had offered a bounty he would have never paid it. Gubrone saw the addition of the bounty hunters as beneficial, for he knew he had not sent them nor had he offered a bounty, yet should the other arch-gallues protest his order to hunt the foreigner, he would insist they were not acting on his orders.

Deep in the halls of his dark cave, Gubrone held a secret meeting with Tukkir, one of the twelve arch-gallues who was an ally. They talked about the kerolus, the strange wind that was blowing, and discussed a growing concern about one of The Twelve, Sinistradt. It was known by all that Sinistradt desired to rule Shuk, and it was rumored that he had allies who would stand with him against Gubrone. But Gubrone did not show any concern, for he possessed a secret.

"Hmmm? Da norõ realm? Puttinash, Chiddush, un Borash, dae conspire agan mae, Tukkir? Wae bae naedin da dakoons. Cun wae bae ready?"

"A bae still workin on da rune. Witout ut, da dakoons cunna bae ruled."

"Tam bae running out, Tukkir. Da rune mus bae raedy soon."

"Da rune wull bae raedy soon aenuff. Ye naed nut wery, Gubrone."

But Tukkir was lying, for the rune was not ready and Tukkir had not yet formulated a plan to obtain what was needed to complete it.

"Uf Sinistradt tinks thut ee wull o'erthrow mae, ee un ees rabble wull bae surprised to maet mae liddle frens!" Gubrone laughed under his breath.

Trying to keep Gubrone from asking any more questions about the rune, Tukkir responded to Gubrone's momentary exaltation with lofty words about the dakoons. "Dae bae strong un dar bae none who cun kull thum."

"Onyting cun bae kulled! Wae all cun bae destroyed, us un da dakoons."

"Aye, Gubrone. But—"

"But notin. Ye mus nut bae so sure o'yersaelf or o'thum."

"Dar bae no gallue able t'defeat da dakoons."

"Aye. Mubae, but da kerolus, dae hav kulled um afore."

"Not one kerolus, but mony, mony could," Tukkir agreed.

"Aye, but dar nut bae mony un Shuk. Only one, right?"

"Aye. Wae ony know o'one. Wae wull fin out eventually."

As they spoke, Sinistradt entered the large hall. Behind him followed the other arch- gallues of Shuk: Unattah, Jabodaan, Puttinash, Borash, Chiddush, Rutunick, Mootthont, Nernishut, and Zeshkant. A fire burned, illuminating the black hall with a faint, undulating, yellow glow. Sinistradt led the conversation with his usual churlish manner, "So, Gubrone, whae ha ye called us haer? Dar mus bae trouble brewin."

"A haer thut da hunters bae bout, lukin fur u forner."

"A forner? Bahaha! Dar bae no forner un Shuk. Wae com all da wae down haer fur som rumor bout u forner! D'ye take us fur fools, Gubrone?"

Gubrone could sense that Sinistradt and Puttinash were goading him, as they always did, hoping for him to appear incompetent in front of the others. He dismissed their patronizing disdain. "Da gallues bae huntin u foreigner un u kerolus, but dar bae no sign o'thum, yet."

"Ah, so ut nut bae jus u forner? Ut bae u kerolus tae? Ut bae u bit unexpected, u kerolus un Shuk. Jus how ha ye com t'hav dis bit o'knowledge?"

"Da kerolus waer saen bae one o'da gallue hunters."

"Mubae dar bae no kerolus! Ye ony ha da words o'da neph hunters. Dae wud say onyting fur u reward!"

"Aye. Yur correct bout da neph hunters, but dar bae no mistakin dis." Gubrone threw the small metal implement, brought by Morak, onto the stone table. The sound of it bouncing across the stone echoed through the dark hall and for a moment, silenced their insolent repudiation. Sinistradt raised his brow in interest. One by one, the arch-gallues examined the strange object as they passed it around the stone, however, they acted unconcerned, even dismissive of Gubrone's discovery.

Sinistradt was the last one to take receipt of the ice axe. "Dis? A ha t'com all da wae down haer fur dis? Ut bae jus u bauble, notin more!" He pitched the weapon onto the stone table as if it were a toy. Though Sinistradt's outward reaction to the weapon appeared to be one of scorn, inside of him, an idea was taking root.

Gubrone immediately reviled him, "Nae, ye imp, dis bae frum anoter realm!"

Sinistradt goaded him again, "But, ut bae so small. Da one thut brung ut mus bae small tae, tae small t'wery bout, Gubrone." Sinistradt's plan was expanding. He was enraptured by it, distracted by the possibilities. He had long been searching for a strategy to kill Gubrone without revealing himself as the killer. The foreigner's weapon would be the perfect ruse. If Gubrone were killed by it, the others would not suspect him, they would suspect the foreigner. Whether or not the foreigner truly existed was irrelevant. The fact that many of the arch-gallues believed he existed was all that mattered.

Gubrone's voice rose as he yelled his argument, "Bae ye all fools? Cun ye nut see fur yer saelfs? Dis bae frum anoter realm! Ut bae rumored thut Amik ha returned, thut ee walks un da lund wit u gallue, da aposta, Kumél."

"Kumél aids dis forner. Ye shud ha kulled eem, Gubrone!" Puttinash's words bit at Gubrone like the sharp fangs of a snake.

"Oh, ee tried. But, Kumél beat eem. Canna ye see da scar on ees face? Bahaha!" The sound of Sinistradt's maligning laughter incited an eruption of guffaw that echoed throughout the dark hall.

Gubrone, however, was not amused, nor patient with their insubordination. With a loud crashing blow, his fist landed forcefully on the stone, shaking even the floor of the cave. "Ee mae ha beat mae once, but nae'er agan. A wull kull eem un da forner wit mae own two huns." A heavy silence fell over the hall as Gubrone paced the room. "Dar bae un army o'gallues searching da realm a'wae spaek. Mae loyal serfs wull fin thum un brang thum t'mae, alive!"

"Uf Amik ha returned, ee dud nut com alone un uf dis bae u weapon, ut mus ha magic powers." Mootthont grabbed the ice axe and tried to crush it with the vice-like power of his giant hand. He winced with pain and instantly dropped the ice axe. Blood poured from his hand where the end spike had pierced his coarse, reptilian skin. The sound of the metal ice axe hitting and then bouncing off the stone echoed through the hall with a steely, ringing clamor. The arch-gallues stared, first at Mootthont, then at the small weapon that had so easily pierced his skin. His blood ran over the shaft of the weapon. They had not realized the ice axe was made of titanium, which was the same material used by the kerolus to make their spears. In Pardis, this metal was called tarterniem, and was one of only a few rare materials that had the ability to penetrate the thick skin of the gallues. Many of their swords and knives were also made from the metal.

Learning that the ice axe could pierce their thick skin, caused the gallues much concern, especially among The Twelve. They knew that the ancient craft of creating kerolus' weapons was a combination of metallurgy and celestial magic. The spears of the kerolus were made through a special process of annealing and cold forging. Ages ago, the Theoscians had developed a special flame that burned from a magical source known only to Mallaeus, the arch-kerolus who forged the powerful weapons.

"Da weapon o'da forner ha com frum da fires of Mallaeus, frum da coals o'ees great forge! Dis mus bae da work o'Eloh!" Chiddush declared.

At the mention of Eloh, a loud commotion erupted from the twelve gallues. Their arguing and debating with each other intensified to the point of violence. It was forbidden to speak the name of Eloh in the halls of Gubrone and throughout the Valley of Souls. But all the arch- gallues were thinking the same thing, that Eloh had sent the foreigner. The argument continued at first about the weapon, then over the breaking of protocol when Chiddush spoke the name of Eloh. But Chiddush had not accidentally mentioned Eloh, as the others might have assumed. He had intentionally suggested the name of Eloh to arouse suspicion and force Gubrone into acting. As usual, the gallues had called a meeting for one reason, but it had swiftly escalated into an all- out brawl for another.

This time, Gubrone would not let them forget the reason he had summoned them. "Silence, ye fools, ye stinkin dakkrahs! Quit yer fightin!"

The arch-gallues sneered and growled at Gubrone with blood in their eyes. They did not tolerate such insults.

Gubrone expertly switched their focus from him to the possibility that Eloh might be in Shuk. "Wae mus nut fight among our saelfs! Uf Eloh ha com bak t'Shuk, wae mus bae ready t'maet eem. Uf ee ha com alone, weel, mubae wae cun capture eem un deal wit eem once un fur all."

"Eloh? Ee wud nae'er com alone. Ee wud cum wit un army o'kerolus," Chiddush argued.

"Hmm. Mubae, mubae no. Uf ee coms un saecret or disguised, mubae da forner bae eem, Eloh."

The gallues were beginning to think that maybe it made sense the foreigner was Eloh, for who else could it be? The weapon was sized correctly for Eloh to handle, and it might have been forged in the fires of Mallaeus. Hungry to learn its secrets, The Twelve studied it where it lay on the stone table.

Sinistradt saw this as his opportunity to advance his agenda. Not only would the weapon aid him, but the idea that Eloh himself was present in Shuk would further bolster his scheme, for now, Gubrone would be compelled to act. He promptly spoke up, "Uf ut bae Eloh out dar un Shuk, bae ut wise t'leave ees finding t'thut mob o'bounty hunters?"

Chiddush quickly added, "Aye. Somtings shud nut bae luft t'da liks o'thum. Mubae ye shud gae, Gubrone."

Many of The Twelve nodded and voiced agreement. Gubrone took it one step further. "Mubae. Mubae wae all shud gae. Eloh bae vary powerful!"

"Nae. Uf wae all gae, des damned nephs wull fin u wae t'escape da valley! Wae cun spare ony one, o'ye," Puttinash disputed.

"Aye. Dat bae fur sur! Ye, Gubrone, ye shud gae. Des fools cun stand guard haer. Ye bae da strongest o'us, un ye bae da ony one able t'kull Eloh. But, A wull gae uf ye wanna, fur A dunna faer Eloh. A wull kull eem maesaelf!" Sinistradt's words were sharp and cunning. The atmosphere in the hall grew cold as all eyes focused on Gubrone, waiting for him to take charge. Gubrone perceived that something was amiss in Sinistradt's words; he sensed that his old nemesis was conniving. Nevertheless, he could not show weakness, nor could he concede. He had pushed the point, he had ordered that the foreigner be found, now that they suspected it was Eloh, he would have to back up his demands and take up the hunt himself.

Chiddush and Puttinash continued to goad Gubrone, making sure that he was left with no choice but to enter the pursuit, "Yur da chief among us, un ye mus fin Eloh un kull eem afore ee cun overtake Shuk."

"Dis bae yer fight! Ye cunna laeve ut t'da mob out dar."

"Mubae A shud send ye, Chiddush! Yur sur quick t'see mae gae. Or hae bout ye, Puttinash?"

"Aw, Gubrone, yur tae suspicious."

"Yeah! Ut waer ye who started all o'dis! Ut waer ye who sent all o'da hunters and mēgs unt'da realm."

"Ye shud bae da one t'laed da charge, Gubrone. Jus tink wut Attar wud say, uf ye waer t'capture Eloh!"

"Aye! Ee might muk ye da supreme ruler!"

"Ee might even bow down t'ye, un ye could bae da ruler o'er all da realm o'Pardis!" Sinistradt spoke as if sincere, but Gubrone felt that his tone and his words were disingenuous and contrived, more flattering and mocking than truly supportive. Gubrone recognized the deceit and malevolence in Sinistradt's eyes.

The relationship between The Twelve had always been tenuous, even discordant, but there was always compliance to the will of Attar, who to everyone's understanding, had given Gubrone the highest place among The Twelve. For the first time ever, Gubrone felt his firm grasp over the realm was in jeopardy. Never before had there been an opportunity for a coup d'état, though it was always a possibility, and Gubrone had always been guarded against such. Suddenly, the wave of tyranny had ebbed, and even those arch-gallues that Gubrone trusted were either willingly, or else unwittingly, in collusion with Sinistradt.

Gubrone was put on the defensive, a position that he had forgotten the disadvantage of long ago. However, he was not without cleverness himself, and he planned how he might persuade the majority of The Twelve to deny Sinistradt. The key to destabilizing and breaking the union was to stir up suspicions about Sinistradt in each of the members. Gubrone could not think of a better arrangement that could accomplish this than if he appointed Sinistradt as their leader de facto in his absence. He knew he needed to create discord among them, and his choice to appoint Sinistradt would be so unexpected that Gubrone hoped it would create an air of mistrust in Sinistradt's supporters. They would be jealous and their jealousy would make them question why Sinistradt, his arch-rival, had been chosen. His usual supporters might question whether Sinistradt had secretly made a deal with Gubrone. He hoped that all those who would envy the rule would reject Sinistradt, which would in effect protect his own position. It was a risk most consequential, but Gubrone could think of no better strategy to regain control of the situation. "Uf A gae, thun A mus choose one t'rule o'er da valley while A bae away." Gubrone knew that if the decision was left up to them, the gallues would never be able to agree because privately each one of them desired rule o'er Shuk. Like a gambler bluffing a bad hand, Gubrone just observed as the arch-gallues, like starved dogs, fought for scraps of the rotting flesh of a dead animal.

"A shud bae da one!"

"Ye? Nae! Yur un imp, u liddle maggot! A bae da one! A wull bae da new ruler!"

"Fool! Ut bae mae! Ye could no rule o'er yer own piss!"

Just as Gubrone had expected, their words had turned to blows and most of The Twelve were entangled in an all-out brawl. However, Gubrone noticed that Sinistradt stood away from the fight. The one he had expected to see enveloped in the clash stood silently by, and beside him was Chiddush. Gubrone glared at them, knowing they were against him. He let the scrappers fight, until their rage was elevated beyond reason. Gubrone yelled out to the combatants, "Stop! Stop yer fightin, ye fools!"

His voice echoed above the groans and shouts of the angry gallues, until they clumsily ceased. Sinistradt and Chiddush stood silently behind them. "A ha decided! Sinistradt wull bae da one t'rule un mae absence. A wull bae da one t'laed da armies un fin dis forner. Uf ee bae Eloh, A wull destroy eem un secure mae rule o'er da Realm o'Pardis. Ut waer Attar thut appointed mae as da ruler o'er Shuk. Ee mus bae obeyed bae all, so A mus bae obeyed bae all."

Out of the shadows, from behind the stunned group of enraged gallues, the voice of Sinistradt filled the hall. "Yur vary wise mae liege. A wull kaep watch o'er da valley til ye ha secured yer realm, an ha proven yer right t'bae da chief o'da gallues." Sinistradt's words were spoken in a submissive tone, but Gubrone could hear the condescension, though he chose to say nothing.

The other gallues were dumbfounded and immediately, Gubrone could see suspicion in their confused glares aimed at Sinistradt. For the moment, it seemed Gubrone's ruse had worked. Even the two arch-gallues, Tukkir and Jabodaan, whom he trusted, albeit dubiously, were perplexed and astounded.

Gubrone had claimed he would unite the rabble bands of gallues that were hunting the foreigner, yet he had no real intention of doing so. He did not know how many of them were under the control of Sinistradt, but what he did know was he could not trust any of them. If any of the gallues roving throughout Shuk suspected he was no longer in control of the valley, they might capture him and exact a painful revenge for his cruel and brutal rule over them. He understood if they had even a diminutive sense of his vulnerability, they would crush him. While he was the most powerful of the gallues in Shuk, he had been beaten before, and many of the gallues believed he could be overcome again. Alone, out of the company of The Twelve and the security of the valley, Gubrone was aware he could face a mass attack if he was not careful. Gubrone intended to find the foreigner on his own, Eloh or not, and return to the valley a champion.

Gubrone also possessed a secret he had shared only with Tukkir. Deep in the north mountains, beyond the north realm of the valley, Gubrone had hidden two dakoons in a cave. They had been kept there from the days of the Great War. Gubrone intended to use the dakoons to win back his rule and dominate the realm as never before.

Confidently, Gubrone strode to the stone table where the ice axe lay. Sinistradt arrogantly met him there. Gubrone grasped the strange object, but Sinistradt grabbed him by his wrist. "Mubae ye shud laeve da weapon wit mae. A wull kaep ut fur ye."

Gubrone scowled at Sinistradt and stepped into him, meeting him chest to chest. The eyes of the two met in a steely, violent glare. "A wull take da weapon o'Eloh, un use ut t'cut out ee's haert!" Forcefully, Gubrone removed his arm from Sinistradt's iron grip.

Sinistradt, however, was secretly pleased. Allowing Gubrone to take the weapon meant that Sinistradt just needed a plan to get it from him so it could be used to execute his lethal contempt.

"Uf ut bae Eloh, A wull naed u partner. Tukkir, yur t'com wit mae. Wae wull hunt eem down."

Sinistradt smiled with an approving grin. "Aye. Thut bae u gud plan. Gae! Gae wit yer frun, Tukkir. A dunna naed ye haer." Sinistradt did not trust Tukkir, anyway and was aware he was a close ally to Gubrone. He surmised that removing Tukkir from the valley worked well for his own plans, no matter what reason Gubrone had for taking him.

Gubrone studied everyone in the room who seemed against him. With a powerful, undeterred mien that commanded the room, he gruffly ordered them to leave.

"Gubrone, take care! Ut bae vary dangerus out dar. Hahaha."

Gubrone called to one of his serfs and spoke to him in a hushed voice. "Gae t'Jabodaan, un say t'eem, 'Com t'mae dis night, un take care thut yur nut saen.'"

Considering the turn of events, Gubrone knew he needed an ally in the valley more than ever, and the only one he felt confident in was Jabodaan. From the beginning, Jabodaan favored Gubrone as the leader of Shuk. They vowed to keep their alliance confidential; it was an agreement that had never been violated. Even during the most trying of circumstances, Jabodaan had shown an unusual degree of devotion to his word, especially for a gallue. Gubrone was sure Jabodaan would be able to persuade some of the others that Gubrone was the only legitimate ruler of Shuk, for Jabodaan was a good politician. This trust would also help him to elicit information from those who were closest to Sinistradt, information that would surely help Gubrone. Moreover, because Jabodaan was such a skilled conniver, Gubrone had great confidence he could subtly undermine any alliances that might be formed in Sinistradt's favor, thus maintaining the vulnerability of Sinistradt's temporary reign.

What Jabodaan did not know was that Gubrone had secrets, dark secrets that had been discovered by no others, except a few who were already dead. If Jabodaan had known, it might have changed his disposition. Secrets are never well-kept unless they are known by only one, and Gubrone had made sure his secrets were his alone.

From the moment Gubrone had received the Rune of Attar from Norzaaq, he had deceived The Twelve. He believed himself to be the only rightful ruler of the realm, being the only one who bore, in his body, the savage wounding of Attar. To this end, Gubrone had cast a spell of lies intending to secure his rule over The Twelve, and over Shuk, and to protect himself against any who aspired to kill him, for he was aware he had enemies like Sinistradt.

Little did anyone know that Attar's order had made The Twelve equal. Attar never would have allowed the rise of any ruler other than himself. However, Gubrone had announced to The Twelve that the rune had been delivered to him because he had been put in charge and that they were to obey him. He convinced them the power of the rune balanced upon his word and if anyone disobeyed him, it would destroy them. There were those who were not so persuaded, yet they were not willing to risk the wrath of Attar, so they condescended to the rule of Gubrone. They had experienced the power and had witnessed the cruelty of Attar toward those who disobeyed or resisted him and were, presently, afraid to oppose even the possibility of Attar's will. Gubrone's sorcery had woven a web of lies so believable and powerful, that none of the gallues living in Shuk dared to question his word or challenge his claim to rule.

When Norzaaq had met with Gubrone, he also revealed many other things Attar needed him to know. He had divulged the secret of the spell's power to him, and he had explained how it could be broken. Gubrone was the only one who knew the rune had a weakness, a chink in its armor. Norzaaq had told him, "There is a one who can deliver a mortal wound that will defeat your immortality and destroy the spell. For by blood, the rune was cast, and by blood, it will be undone. The power of the spell to keep captive the nephesh can be weakened by the destruction of any one of The Twelve. Should one of The Twelve fall, a way of escape will open to the nephesh."

Norzaaq had also given Gubrone a rolled-up hide with markings on it that Norzaaq had copied from writings in the pit. It was the prophecy Eloh had inscribed on the round stone that had surrounded the pool. Norzaaq had not known how to read or translate it, so he had given it to Gubrone. Gubrone had understood only part of the message. It had warned of a blood-stained spear and the return of Eloh.

Gubrone had been sure if any of the other arch-gallues ever learned of the message or anything Norzaaq told him, then his deception would be discovered and his reign would end. To keep his treachery a secret, Gubrone had murdered Norzaaq and fed his body to the dakoons.

Tukkir stood in the shadows waiting for Gubrone and Jabodaan to arrive. The great hall seemed even darker than usual. Gubrone entered the dark hall from another corridor and shortly after, Jabodaan emerged from the shadows cloaked in a dark cape. When Gubrone felt sure of their privacy, they devised their plans.

Gubrone had told Sinistradt and the others he would go before the next month, which was many days away. However, Gubrone knew he wanted to go sooner and under the cover of night, while the darkness would conceal his movements. Normally he would have used the Pass of Klamata, but Gubrone was aware there were many renegade gallues living in the fog along the way, down from the pass and did not want to be noticed by them. He would head to the north where Gubrone hoped to collect his two dakoons once he was out of the valley. He knew of a hidden path leading out of the Valley of Souls, which he had long kept a secret. The passage had been used many times to exit the valley in secret. The only problem with using the secret pass was that it lay hidden in the north region concealed amidst the jagged Ardu Needles, near the cave of Sinistradt. Gubrone would have to successfully travel unnoticed through the Valley of Souls: a journey of three days in favorable circumstances, and more under the cover of night. To accomplish the journey undetected, with

Tukkir, two of his mēgs, and two gallue slaves would be a daunting task. However, Gubrone reveled in the thought that he would be leaving the valley right under the nose of Sinistradt. The irony of it appealed to his conniving nature and pleased him greatly.

When Tukkir saw Gubrone, he immediately questioned his actions. "Wut waer ye tinkin, givin da valley o'er t'Sinistradt? Dunna ye know ee hates ye? Ee ha bun waitin fur dis moment."

"Shh! Wae mus spaek quietly. A bae sur Sinistradt ha spies eary whaer. Aye. Ye bae correct, Tukkir. Ee ha baen waitin, but ee wull nut bae lung un da rule o'er Shuk."

"Uf ye bae takin Tukkir wit ye, wut shud A d'? Uf Sinistradt fin out A bae haelpin ye, ee wull fur sur wanna kull mae."

"Jabodaan, ye cunna bae foun out! A naed ye t'gae t'da others, da ones who wull stand wit mae wun A return. A naed thum t'stay on mae side. Wae naed da unity o'da gallues un ye know thum bes!"

"Wut uf Sinistradt ha sunt spies t'da mist? Ut mae bae dangerous t'gae o'er da Pass o'Klamata."

"Tukkir un A wull nut gae o'er da Pass o'Klamata. A ha another wae."

"Dar bae no other wae!"

"Un da norõ, A ha u secret wae. A wull gae bae ut."

"Da norõ! Bae ye u fool, Gubrone? Thut bae da realm o'Sinistradt, un ee wull ha spies eary whaer!"

"Possibly, but wae mus gae thut wae. Ee'll nut expect ut frum mae."

In the shadows of the Great Hall, Veroot, a gallue slave to Sinistradt, crept unnoticed near the hall and stood with his back against the cold, black rock. He was within earshot of Gubrone and the others, listening carefully to their hushed voices. He could not see them and so he did not know who it was that spoke.

"When do we go?"

"Wae laeve un two suns, unner da cover o'da night."

Most of what they were saying was mumbled and beyond his hearing, but his purpose was to discover when Gubrone would be leaving the valley. Sinistradt intended to steal the weapon and needed to know how long he had before Gubrone planned to leave. Veroot had heard Gubrone tell Tukkir they would leave in two days and at night. It was all he had been able to discern from their conversation. Quietly, Veroot crept away before he was noticed.

In a secret cave, Sinistradt and Chiddush reveled in their seemingly good fortune. Sinistradt was exuberant and hardly able to restrain the sudden, impulsive excitement which caused him to act recklessly. He had waited so long and seen so many plans fail; to have the very thing he had been working so hard to achieve simply given to him without a struggle was beyond comprehension. He knew everything was not exactly as he wanted and there was still much to do if he was to succeed, but the first and most difficult piece of the puzzle was now in place.

"A bae da ruler o'Shuk! Bahaha! Da ruler o'er da realm, o'er eary one! Bahaha! How? How, Chiddush? Wae cud nut ha planned ut ony better. Gubrone wull laeve un A wull bae da ruler!"

"Aye, but dunna forget, Sinistradt, dar bae much ta d'. Gubrone wull nut sit bae un lut ye rule fur lung."

"A know! A dunna naed ye tellin mae wut A naed ta d'. A know wae mus gut da shard, un ye mus finish da rune. Un ye bes bae confident da rune wull work!"

"Oh, ut wull work. A bae sur ut wull work!"

From the shadows, Veroot appeared. "Mae liege, A haerd thum spaekin, un dae bae plannin t'laeve un da night, two suns frum now."

"Gud. Ye ha done gud. Yur t'follow thum. A wull giv ye instructions on da morrow."

"Dar bae another wit thum, another gallue," Veroot continued.

"Who? Who bae dis other one?"

"A dunna know. Dae spaek quietly un da shadows whaer A cud nut sae thum."

"Hmm. So, Gubrone bae kaepin saecrets, aye? Another gallue? Hmm, cud ut ha bun one o'Da Twelve?"

"A bae sorry, Sinistradt. A cud nut sae thum."

"Gae. Kaep watch o'er thum. Sae uf ye cun fin out who dis other gallue bae."

Gubrone and Tukkir made ready to leave the valley in secret. They were focused on the singular, obsessive goal of retrieving the dakoons. Far away, the hidden dakoons remained under the influence of a potion, or elixir, that had been concocted by Tukkir. He had discovered the snowpetal released a faint aroma that caused the dakoons to become lethargic. The potion of snowpetal he mixed caused them to sleep for ages at a time but putting the dakoons to sleep and actually controlling them were two hugely different objectives.

Gubrone was growing increasingly impatient and doubtful of Tukkir's ability to train the dakoons to obey them and now, more than ever before, his reign depended upon using the dakoons. "Tukkir, wae naed da spell fur da dakoons. A mus ha thum bae mae side!"

"A ha da elixir."

"Curse da elixir! Wae naed t'control thum, nut put thum t'slaep!" With as much composure and self-control as Gubrone could restrain himself to, he lowered his voice and spoke, "Ha wull A muk thum obey mae? Da elixir bae useless t'mae!"

"A ha a rune. Ut wull muk thum tink yur Attar, fur dae bae loyal t'eem alone." Tukkir had unintentionally divulged his secret to Gubrone. He had been keeping the rune to himself. He realized how impatient Gubrone was growing, and he knew Gubrone would demand the rune be given to him, but he did not want him to possess it. Besides that, and more importantly, he knew the rune was not ready, that there was something he still needed, and he was not yet sure how he would get it.

"Dae wull tink A bae Attar un obey mae? Bahaha! Tukkir, whae bae dis da first A ha haerd o'ut?"

"A ha baen testin ut. Ut bae nut raedy, yet."

"Whae?"

"A traed ut on maesaelf. Da dakoons obeyed mae words, at least fur u while."

"Wut ye maen, fur u while? Dud dae obey ye or nut?"

"Weel, dae bae smart. Dae seem t'learn, un afta u while dae saem'd t'sae mae."

"Mubae da spell wore off."

"Aye, mubae. But afta thut, dae traed t'aet mae! A waer afaered t'trae agan."

"Hmm. Cud yer rune work on da other gallues? Muk thum tink A bae Attar?"

"Nae, Gubrone. Da rune wull ony work on da dakoons. Ut bae deir blood thut A used."

Gubrone sensed Tukkir was keeping something from him and indeed Tukkir was, but Tukkir realized that Gubrone was suspicious so he quickly diverted Gubrone's attention by offering his assurance. "But, ye dunna naed t'wery, da rune wull bae raedy fur ye. Luts gut t'da dakoons afore wae bae foun out."

"Fine! Wae wull laeve on da morrow, unner da cover o'darkness."

Even then, Veroot was spying on them. He watched from the shadows, hoping to see the weapon, and listening to snippets of their plans. He viewed their preparations and heard them discussing where they would meet and when. Then, when he was about to give up, he saw the weapon as Gubrone packed it into a leather bag. Now that he knew they indeed had the weapon and where and when they were going to meet, Veroot carefully slipped away to return to Sinistradt.

"Dud ye sae da weapon?"

"Aye. Gubrone put ut un u bag thut ee wull carry wit eem."

"Wun wull dae bae laevin? Ye mus gut thut weapon afore de laeve da valley. Ye mus, or else!"

"Aye, mae liege, A wull."

Rain fell in the Valley of Souls. It descended upon the great mist. The droplets pushed their way through the forbidding cloud until they emerged as vapor, floating through the air. As individual drops, they were hardly noticed, silent and frail, floating aimlessly, yet downward onto the valley below. Over the days and nights, the lonely molecules of vapor began to coalesce until they transformed into drops again, dripping from every tree branch, limb, and leaf and every blade of grass. The drops of water melded together, forming larger and larger drops, until they fell from their heights, clapping upon every surface as if they were collectively playing one single beat of a great distant drum. In rhythmic cadence, the beating timbre of war was descending upon the valley.

Following behind the backbeat of the rain, far across the Plain of Haemus, the whisper called out its unknown refrain. It spoke softly yet tirelessly. It would not be silenced, nor would it be ignored. It grew louder and soon there would be none who could not hear its voice.

Gubrone and Tukkir could feel the beating note of the rain as it fell upon their heads. They moved carefully and under the cover of darkness as they left the protection of Gubrone's fortress. Not far behind them lurked the shadowy figure of Veroot.

Now that they were out of Gubrone's cave and in the open, Veroot felt he would have the opportunity needed to seize the weapon and return it to Sinistradt. He followed their every move with care and in silence. Each time they stopped, he got closer, waiting for just the right moment to steal the weapon, but he had to be careful of the mēgs. Veroot determined his best opportunity would come during the daylight when the mēgs eyesight was poor and Gubrone and the others rested. On one night, Gubrone overheard the passing conversation of a small group of nephesh. They were talking quietly of rumors that were spreading throughout the valley, rumors of treachery and rebellion and the fall of Gubrone. Save for his cunning use of gossip and falsehood, he would have been surprised such knowledge could be disseminated so widely throughout the realm in a short span of time. The rumors were not only about him but also disclosed that Sinistradt and the other gallues of the north realm had not returned to their domains but remained in the south, occupying the Great Hall of Gubrone. It became obvious to him that Sinistradt was indeed planning a coup d'état. Nevertheless, Gubrone knew he could do nothing; he had to wait for his opportunity, he had to gain dominion over the dakoons, and he had to find Eloh.

Sinistradt did not intend to sit in the seat of power as a steward of Gubrone or to let Gubrone reestablish his powerful reign over Shuk. He secretly planned to seize the rule of the realm just as soon as Gubrone left the safety of the valley. Knowing Gubrone possessed the one thing that could give ultimate power and destroy the nephesh made Sinistradt even more eager to kill him. He had been patient for far too long. The time had finally arrived, yet he knew he had to move carefully for many would not welcome his treachery. Death filled his mind: the death of Gubrone, the rune of death, and the death of the nephesh. Sinistradt continued, undeterred by any suggestion or thought of caution or calamity.

During the days Sinistradt and Chiddush waited for the return of Veroot, a strange wind began to blow in the valley. For all his planning and scheming, Sinistradt could not have predicted the forces at work, forces he could not control or stop, forces that were sure to disrupt all of his plans.

The voice of the wind was echoing through the valley like a ringing sound in the ears of every gallue. *"Illu hōtallem et essen ambaes, e ambaes, a mer bae neeav pazush at sol ruulä e's ambaeun."*

In the gray, overcast glow of the third day, Veroot saw an opportunity to steal the weapon. Now on this particular day, Gubrone and Tukkir were resting in the deep forest just outside of the north region. Veroot could see the tall towers of the Ardu Spires in the distance. Under a giant tree, Gubrone laid his head on a moss-covered stone and fell asleep. In his haste to lie down, he had tossed the shoulder bag, with the ice axe in it, under the tree. However, it was not close to him or the others. Veroot moved in quietly to steal the bag but then had an idea. Instead of stealing the bag with the weapon, he would steal the weapon from the bag and leave something in its place. Veroot did not want Gubrone to notice anything, so he had to be sure that whatever he put back was similar to the weapon in weight and size. But Veroot had never handled the weapon; he did not know how heavy or light it was. He had to guess. He looked around and saw a branch he thought might be of the same length. He added a smooth stone and hoped that together they would be similar in weight so when Gubrone carried the bag he would think it was the weapon. Then an unexpected opportunity presented itself and Veroot quickly snuck in under the giant tree. He could hear Gubrone's heavy breathing and the noise of the mēgs as they rested nearby. He reached into the bag, feeling for the weapon and felt the smooth metal shaft of the ice axe's handle. He wrapped his fingers around it and pulled it from the bag. He stared at it for a long time until Gubrone let out a loud snort, startling Veroot out of his gaze. He took the branch and stone, quickly slid them into the bag, and snuck into the woods.

As the sun's light faded behind the fog, the mēgs growled and fought. The sound woke Gubrone who quickly called for the others. "Wae mus gae! Ut bae tam!"

Standing in an open glen, facing the north region, Gubrone viewed the distant spires of Sinistradt's domain. He felt sure they had escaped the watchful eyes of Sinistradt and his spies. They had set a fast pace and he hoped to make up more time along the way.

When Gubrone and Tukkir finally reached the secret pass in the northern region, the wind was blowing hard and snow was falling on the boulder fields leading to the pass. The wind fought against their every step as if intending to prevent their progress. As they reached the pass, their faces were struck brutally by a torrent of air blasting a cold icy breath. Gubrone pressed hard into the violent wind, forcing each step forward. Snow and ice pelted every inch of their bodies, beating them mercilessly. The voice of the wind bit at Tukkir's ears like carnivorous little birds he could not fight off. At times, the sound of the voice was so loud he had yelled out to Gubrone, thinking he had asked him something.

"Gubrone! Gubrone, wae mus fin shelter!"

"A bae lukin!"

Cresting the highest point of the pass, they came to an opening in the rocks. It was a cave. As soon as they were inside, free from the storm, Tukkir announced, "Dar bae u strange wind blowin!"

"Aye. A haerd ut. Ut bae unfriendly, u baewitchin voice."

"But, whaer d'ut com frum?"

"Haerd t'say, but A know ut bae u dangerus wind," Gubrone grimly answered.

Outside the cave, the wind and snow and ice collided fiercely. Echoing into the small shelter, the voice of the wind grew stronger and closer and louder. It refused to be unheard.

Rumors of hunting parties moving throughout the highlands were spreading into all the corners of Shuk. Among the rumors was the lie sent out by Sinistradt about a bounty that would be paid to whoever captured the foreigner or the kerolus, whether dead or alive. News of this bounty was bringing out the very worst miscreants. Every opportunist in the realm was working to gain the reward. As these rumors continued, Morak realized should any of the bounty hunters find and kill the foreigner or the kerolus, Gubrone would surely fulfill his warning upon all. He realized he must find the foreigner first. It was now more of a mission to rescue the foreigner than a venture to capture him.

Sitting under the long, twisted bows of an ancient popinus tree, Morak tended a small fire. The winds howled across the mountains and the snow fell. As the fire warmed the overhanging branches, it melted the accumulating snow. Water dripped from the branches onto the ground around him and eventually onto his head, but he did not notice. He sat alone staring distantly into the dancing flames. He mumbled inarticulate noises as if talking to himself. *"Illu hōtallem et essen ambaes."* He repeatedly mumbled the phrase as the wind swirling around him grew stronger, but Morak did not care. The voice of the wind spoke in his ear; it held him in a trance, bound his consciousness to the hypnotic power of its unknown words. Morak whispered the words and as his breath touched the flames, sparks of light rose into the night sky. They drifted higher and higher into the air but were not blown by the wind. Like celestial stars, the sparks hung over the landscape.

The rhythm of the drops of water resonated in time with the meter of his words, like a bass drum setting the tempo of a song. Morak's voice had become one among many throughout the realm of Shuk, whispering the same unknown message, the message of the wind. *"Illu hōtallem et essen ambaes, Illu hōtallem et essen ambaes, Illu hōtallem et essen ambaes."*

Chapter XVI
Metamorphosis

"How long have I been here, Kumél? Do you know? It feels like forever." Ross spoke with a pensive tone.

"A dunna know. Wae?"

"Just wondering, that's all. Thinking about things like home, friends, and stuff, but mostly about Eve. I really miss her. Is there anyone you miss?"

"Dunna rumumbar much. A d'miss da bloom, da warm mornin sun thut muks da young flowers grow un dance un da fields o'Pardis. A cunna rumumbar much mur, ut waer u lung tam ago. Ye gut use t'tings, even uf dae bae wrong, ye forgut thut dae bae wrong, ye forgut wut bae right un good. Ut bae da curse o'tam, ut muks ye forget da tings ye shud rumumbar."

"I don't want to forget Eve, I don't, but every day she seems to slip out of my grasp. Her eyes still stare at me in my dreams, but I can't see her face or hear her voice anymore. It's like she's there, watching me, trying to say something, but my ears have forgotten how to hear. Do you believe in life after death?"

"A ha nae'er died. Dunna know uf dar bae life beyond da life A ha known."

"Eve did. She believed there is a part of us that never dies, that lives forever. I thought she was silly, but now . . . now I wish she was right. I hope she was. I long for her to still be alive somehow, somewhere . . . that I could find her and go to her . . . be with her."

"Mubae ye should ask Shu. Ee mae know uf dar bae life afta ye die."

"Maybe. Maybe I will."

After they left the Cave of Pelah, the six sojourners trekked high on the ridge of the mountain that protected the resting place of Amik. Eventually they entered the realm of Mount Soteria, a high sprawling basin flanked on all sides by ice and snow-covered mountains. Soteria reigned over the basin as the tallest of the peaks.

The wind blew ferociously over the summit and pressed through a slot in the rocks as if it were a mob trying to escape through a single, narrow doorway. It howled and whistled loudly and persistently. Shu pointed into the basin and yelled, "There! That is where we will find Ziminiar. He lives in the norõ!"

Ross gazed at the amazing view that spread in every direction beyond him. He felt like he was home. For just a few moments, his mind took him to a place that made him forget the strangling reality that, itself, seemed unreal. He closed his eyes and took a long, deep breath of cold, turbulent mountain air. He let it out slowly, keeping his eyes closed and letting his mind drift away into the past. He remembered Daniel, standing at the top of Ama Dablam and the laughter and elation they shared at their victory together. He remembered Eve standing on Machapuchare, her irrepressible smile and her eyes beaming with exalted rapture as she looked upon the immeasurable expanse of the world below.

A tear formed in the corner of his eye. It grew until his lashes could no longer hold it, fell upon his cheek and ran down to his lips. It was not sadness or sorrow or pain that beckoned the lonely droplet. He felt the same way he had felt so many times when he stood at a summit. He had that same feeling of finiteness, of being completely emptied of himself, his strength, his skill, and his courage. He felt emptied of self-control, with no sense of his own importance and significance. Standing there looking over the world beyond made him realize he was small and that sense of smallness made him feel happy. For all the many things in life he had tried to carry, that he had tried to be big enough to handle, were not there. It was just his mortal flesh and the rock, standing together, one, great and powerful, and the other, little more than a fly. He had never conquered the mountains; they had always conquered him, and he loved them for that. He needed them for that. Every man needs to feel conquered if he is to ever feel alive.

Ross's hand slowly rose to his cheek. He touched the salty tear that had run onto his lips. He looked at it, balancing tenuously on his fingertip, then he drew another long breath deep into his lungs. The others stood reverently in silence, as some part of their hearts reached out toward him. They reached out, hoping to be a part of what had touched him, to feel the rush of emotions they had witnessed with their eyes. Ross noticed the others had been watching him. Half embarrassed, Ross asked, "What are we waiting for? Let's keep moving."

Shu turned toward the ridge that led to the summit of Mount Soteria. As they climbed higher, they saw a storm approaching from the south. Shu yelled to the others, "We must hurry my friends! Do not hesitate!"

The storm was still several days away but knowing the rough terrain and the long distance they would need to travel, the companions made haste to the summit. The winds preceding the storm were beginning to break upon the mountain ridge like waves on a rocky shore. Everyone had to exercise much discipline in acquiring their footing to keep from falling off the ridge. The true summit of the mountain was a short distance from them and rose to a jagged, sharp peak several hundred feet high. As they approached the summit, a strange and unpredicted sight appeared before them. A narrow, stone path, precariously situated along a sheer wall of stone that fell away from the path into darkness could be seen leading toward the base of the mountain's spire. Where it began and why it was there was a mystery and while they could not see from where it came, they could see to where it led. The path meandered toward a handmade, stone archway and under it was a stack of rocks that appeared to be an altar. Behind the archway was a wall made of isinglass, a transparent but reflective stone that appeared to have been skillfully constructed.

As Ross studied the strange apparition, he noticed an amazing feature embedded into the stone face of the mountain. A horn or a shofar, rested on a pile of small stones. It's bell was so large, it looked like a massive hole in the side of the mountain. The entire horn looked as if it had been carved from the mountain itself. Ross wondered how it had come to be in that place. It reminded him of the tombs he had seen, carved into the face of a cliff, intricate and detailed. His awe was intensified by the remote elevation, for how could anyone have shaped such a thing in that place, and yet, there it was. "What is that? And how did it get there, Shu?"

"It is the Horn of Shukeer. It is little more than a relic now, a monument of a bygone age, an age that has passed into the shadow of time and memory. The last to see it was Sargel, at the beginning of the Great War."

"Why is it here? What's it used for?"

"It was used to call the assemblies of the kerolus. In the second age, when Pardis and the realms were one, there were many great feasts on the north porch of the great city. We could hear its rapturous voice calling to us in every corner of the realm. We heard it often when Pardis was whole and the great city gates were open to all. It also called out to us in times of trouble. It hailed the kerolus armies to the city of Anima and to Eloh. Now it rests here, in ruin and silence, alone."

"How did they blow the horn? It seems impossible."

"Impossible? You have climbed many mountains. Why should this one be impossible?" asked Shu.

"Well, maybe not impossible, but it surely seems one would have to be very skilled to climb the face of that peak."

"You only see what you understand. The kerolus did not climb, they flew."

"Oh. Yeah, right." Ross felt a sudden sense of embarrassment from the absurdity of his comments. Though he had seen, with his own eyes, those things had always been impossible, he still could not bring himself to expect them. In a very subtle way, the words of Shu felt like a rebuke.

"Only the kerolus have ever put their lips to it. It was put at this location because it was close to the city of Anima and because it could be heard throughout the entire realm of Pardis."

Cautiously, Ross commented, "It looks ancient. Does it still work?"

"I assume it would still speak if breath were blown into it. Come, we will find shelter in its shadow."

Shu led them to the narrow stone path cut into the side of the summit. The path was in disrepair, and many sections of it had broken away and fallen into the void below. Also, several sections of the path were covered with ice and snow and were especially dangerous to trek.

"Shu, if the only ones to ever come here were the kerolus, why is there a path leading to the horn?"

"In the First Age, the great horn was cut from the mountainside by the ancient cementars. They did not have the ability to fly, so they cut this path into the mountain and traveled on it to the site of the horn. Next to the horn, they formed the Lamp of Soteria, a beacon to the land of Shuk and to all sojourners, leading them to Anima. The cementars were great stonecutters. You are a descendent of them, Ross. They were a great clan."

"What happened to them?"

"They did not live in the city of Anima, but in a faraway land near the Kveech Mountains. One night, the ground vehemently shook and, without any notice, a mountain, now called Mount Cementar, violently exploded in fire and molten rock. The cementars were buried under piles of rubble and stone and red-hot ore that flowed over their city. The kerolus flew to them, but it was hopeless; they were all destroyed, all but two, Amaya and Loani."

"I feel like I've heard this before. What happened to them?"

"Both were with child when they were saved, but shortly after giving birth, they died. The horn and this place are one of the few remaining ruins of them, outside of Assuk. They were the mothers of Amik and Livia. As a promise to their mothers, Eloh gave Amik and Livia immortality and his essence. They became the first of the Carascians and the bearers of the Elohan Essentia."

"What is that, the Elohan Essentia?"

"It is the spirit of Eloh, the life force of his being—the very essence of life itself. Nothing that is alive is alive without it. The Carascians became the keepers of it, the guardians of Eloh's heart and being."

"So, Amik, he was one of them?"

"Yes. He was the final son and Livia the final daughter of the cementars and the first of their own kind."

"But if they were the first, then what happened to the rest? Where are they now?"

"Now they are in bondage. Deceived, the seed of Amik, the offspring of Amaya and Loani, live in slavery to the will of Attar."

The sun had set behind the southern ridge, and darkness had fallen over the mountains like a black curtain. Since they had not reached the shelter of Shukeer, Kumél asked Shu what they should do, for it was too dangerous to continue in the dark.

"We wait. Help will soon arrive," Shu replied.

Zoësh pointed to a small light, like a star, coming toward them through the darkness. "What's that?"

"Ah, ut bae u tulwyth. A ha nut saen thum fur u lung tam." Kumél seemed not only surprised by the site but excited as well.

After a few moments, there were several more of the petite flying creatures rising out of the cracks and crags of the rocks. They lit upon Shu's shoulders. "Ah, my friends, greetings. Will you show us the way? Thank you." He smiled. "See, help comes."

The luna-tulwyths led each of the company, illuminating the dark stones and pathway, leading them to the bell of the horn. Ironically, traveling the narrow path in the darkness was less daunting than if they were traveling it in the light. The glow of the tulwyths did not brighten the terrifying features of the mountain ridge, so they could simply focus on the path in front of them. Shu and the tiny tulwyths were having their own reunion. Shu laughed and carried on, and the bright little creatures buzzed and danced around his head in a jovial display of excitement. When they finally reached the archway under the bell of the horn, the tulwyths gathered together to reveal a small cave just beyond it with a stone bench sitting against the back wall. In the cave they saw several piled-up stones that looked like some type of altar but it was a fire pit, and in it was a gathering of branches, as if someone was planning to have a fire.

"Wood! There is wood in this thing! How did it get way up here? Can we start a fire?" Ross's words surprised them all. They thought they had no means of igniting the wood, but Ross had a small fire-starting kit in his backpack and was an expert at starting fires.

"I don't know, can you?" Zoësh smirked playfully at Ross. She thought he must surely be joking.

"No, seriously, can I start a fire?"

"Of course! If you are able."

"Well, sure I am! Fire is easy if you have dry wood and this is definitely dry. Must've been here forever, it's so dry."

Ross pulled off his backpack and opened a small compartment on its side. He pulled out a small magnesium block, a ferrocerium rod or, as some called it, a flint, and a small pocket knife. He dragged the edge of the knife over the flint which sent out hot sparks onto a small tinder bundle that he had also carried with him. In just three strokes, the tinder bundle began to smoke. Ross blew on it and fire burst from the bundle. Ross quickly set the bundle into the pile of branches and twigs. Then he added more wood until they had a warm fire to sit by. "So, what is this place, anyhow?"

"This is where the cementars dwelled while they carved the horn. It has always been a place to abide for those who were ordered here to blow the horn. The kerolus were the ones to carry the wood with them. It is a wonder the wood is still here after so long."

"I've been on many high mountains, some even higher than this, and it always seems like time stops in these places, or at least slows down a little. Things seem to never rot or disintegrate or decay. I've actually seen dead men, still preserved in the ice and snow decades after they had died. Some mountains are like graveyards; there are bodies everywhere."

Ross was not conscious of just how sobering his death references were to all who heard them. A heavy silence rested on Shu and the others, for they were troubled by the callousness of Ross's indifference to the dead.

"It sounds like you have witnessed much death." Msusi's soft voice and wide, gentle eyes swollen with tears bewildered Ross.

"I guess I've seen my fair share, more than I would've liked to have seen."

"Your fair share may be much more than what is truly fair! You don't understand death, do you? You don't understand what is at stake, the impact that death has on both, your world and ours."

"I'm not sure what you mean, Msusi. I mean, I know death is bad and all, but, well, everyone dies. It's just a part of life."

"Nearly everyone you know has died or will die, but not everyone dies. Death was never supposed to occur to anyone, not even to you."

Ross could see by their sober expressions they all agreed with Msusi. "Wait a minute! Nearly? Nearly everyone? Who won't die?"

"We will not die. Not unless we are killed."

"Wow! So, now you want me to believe that you—all of you—will never die. It's not possible; death is inevitable! No one can escape it; it's the cycle of life!"

"So you say, but how can you know that for certain?"

"Well, I guess because I have never seen anyone live forever. I mean, everything around us is already moving toward death, right? Everything. It's just nature . . . how it is, isn't it?"

"Death is a counterfeit. It's an imposter that has convinced your kind that it is meant to be, but it is not. It's a lie. Life never stops living. It's immeasurable and inextinguishable, a flame that will never cease to burn."

Ross saw honesty and truth in Msusi's eyes. He could not deny what he had always known, yet he also could not doubt what she was telling him. Beyond his experience, there was something more genuine and authentic in her words. He did not comprehend it and he had not witnessed it, but he believed her because, in his heart, deep in the recesses of his unknown self, he discerned she was speaking the truth to him, and he could not deny what his inner essence would not deny. "I can only hope, and I truly do hope, more than you can possibly imagine, Msusi, that what you are telling me is true."

The warmth and the crackling noise of the fire made for a soothing distraction, lulling them all away from the seriousness of the conversation, and into a gentle state of affinity and kinship. Soon everyone was enjoying themselves as they talked and laughed as close friends do. The sweet sound of music moved around the campfire as Zoësh played her dukwán. Its voice rose into the air clear and strong, and the flames of the fire danced as the song reverberated over them. Soon Seerae was twirling and spinning, dancing around the fire lightheartedly. Msusi played her dukwán as well, and Shu joined Seerae in dancing together in the yellow glow of the blaze. Shadows performed upon the stone walls of the mountain. They spun and leapt and twirled about in festive jubilee.

Kumél sang a song of old to the merry tune of Zoësh and Msusi:

Dar bae u stream o'gladness

Whaer da waters flow frum deep b'low da world.

A ha drunk frum er swaet tastin springs.

Un A ha washed un er pools so claen.

Dar bae u straem o'gladness thut flows frum deep witun.

Oh, com t'da straem,

Ye merry, merry ones!

Taste da swaet, swaet waters. Lut thum nurish yer tongues.

Dance un play! Spin un laep fur joy, fur joy!

Dance un play! Spin un laep fur joy earyone!

A ha drunk frum er sweet tastin spring.

Un A ha washed un er pools so claen,

Shae ha healed mae o'mae brokenness,

Un A wull fly agan, un dance un spin fur joy!

Dar bae u straem o'gladness

Whaer da waters flow frum deep b'low da world.

Uf ye bae waery,

Uf ye bae broke,

Uf ye bae tirsty,

Des waters wull muk ye whole.

Ross listened to the song. He felt a strong sense of Kumél's pain and sorrow in the verses. The tune, while happy, was at the same time mournful, sorrowful, like the songs he had heard sung in the pubs and alehouses throughout Scotland and Ireland. He wondered how something so beautiful could be so painful. Yet, for Kumél, Shu, Zoësh, Seerae, and Msusi, the tune inspired happiness and joy. Their dancing expressed freedoms Ross could not understand. He watched and listened, then decided to join them. He danced recklessly as a man who had nothing to lose or gain, nothing to show or hide, nothing to seek or find, and no one to condemn him or exalt him. He felt like a bird who had just discovered he had wings. He spread his wings and flew above his life, suspended in the air of levity.

Far away, in the hollow of a stone pile, Huzesh and Loham huddled together out of the cutting winds that were advancing through the mountains. The strange voice of the wind had pushed its way into their minds. They deliriously mumbled the unknown words.

Subtly, like a whisper, cutting through the howling wind, a strange, new sound rode upon the current. It came into the rubble and into their minds like a dagger. Huzesh was first to stir from the induced trance of the voice. He crawled out from beneath the rubble and stood in the gale of the wind. He put his hands to his ears and listened to the new sound. It was the sound of music, the sound of a dukwán.

In every direction, Huzesh searched the ominous darkness of the starless night to find the origin of the music. He wondered if it was just in his imagination, if he was just hearing things, for the wind blew incessantly. Then, unexpectedly, Huzesh spied a strange, undulating glow escaping into the darkness from a distant mountaintop. It caught his eye thanks to its unusual yellow light that flickered across the sky of shadows. The darkness was so thick and impenetrable he was unable to see with certainty whether the light was from the sky or from the mountain realm. Huzesh knew it was the light of a flame.

The music of the dukwán was faint and struggled to rise above the howling winds, but before long, the winds abated, submitting to the dukwán's call. Huzesh stood, beaten by the wind, and pierced by the music, he was smitten by mnemonic images parading through his mind. Stupefied by a rapturous, inordinate rush of ecstasy, Huzesh closed his eyes and, for a brief moment, spread the wings he no longer possessed and soared over the mountains as he had done so many ages before. He surrendered to the persuasive melody of hope and healing. He remembered the green fields of Pardis, the great North Porch of Anima. He glided over the Great Sea on wings that carried him home. Sadly, he had long ago forgotten those times.

"Huzesh, what are you doing?" The hollering of Loham broke the spell.

Huzesh motioned toward the glowing light on the mountain peak. "Dar, ut bae a sign! Thut ha t'bae da foreigner."

Loham's eyes soon spied the faint beacon of light peeking through the darkness. "How can you be sure it's the foreigner? It's so far away."

"Ut bae thum. Dar bae somting bout thut light. A dunna rumumbar wut, but no doubt ut bae thum. Wae wull gae fin um un da morrow."

Huzesh climbed back under the pile of stones while Loham continued to stare at the distant flickering light. It was not long before the sound of the music cast its spell over Loham. He turned his head so he could hear more clearly the distant ethereal call of the dukwán. Its music pulled from every shadowed corner of his being, calling him to remember. It echoed an ancient chant of a long-forgotten place, a place unseen, and yet, familiar, as if it had been there before.

Once again, the icy wind broke free of the dukwán's grip and blew into Loham's face and eyes. It fiercely shoved at him as if it intended to sweep him away like the powdered snow that covered the rocks. Reluctantly, Loham crawled back into the cave with Huzesh.

Ross sat next to Seerae as they watched the light of the fire dance off the isinglass wall. "It's like a mirror, Seerae. The wall is like a mirror reflecting the light of the fire like a beacon."

"Look! There is something carved into the rock behind the clear stones. It looks like the same writing we saw at Pelah."

Ross squinted his eyes to decide whether it was just cracks and marks in the stone wall or if he was seeing distorted writing behind the isinglass. He moved closer to touch it, but he was unable to feel it, for indeed, it was engraved writing covered by a thick layer of isinglass.

"What do you think it says, Ross? Is it the same as the other?"

"It seems to be much longer than the inscription over Amik's cave. We'll have to ask Shu; he knows how to read the old writings. I can't believe this fire is still burning! I haven't added any wood to it this whole time." He picked up some wood to add but was amazed to see the wood in the fire had barely burned.

Not far from Ross and Seerae, Kumél lay sleeping. His hulking body lay on the ground not moving, like a boulder, but he quietly spoke in his sleep. Some of the time his voice was so quiet it could hardly be heard. However, other times it was quite loud, and the words of his sleep echoed far beyond the mountain summit. Ross and Seerae listened to his unintelligible muttering and guessed what he was seeing in his dreams. Ross thought it was funny, but Seerae suspected there was something much more important to his sleep talking.

"You shouldn't laugh, Ross. You have no idea what he is seeing."

"I know, but he's so huge! To watch him mumble in his sleep like a child, well, it's kind of funny. He's not even aware he's doing it."

"Listen! His words sound familiar; I've heard them before." Seerae and Ross crept closer to Kumél and listened carefully to his voice. Repeatedly, Kumél murmured the same phrases. "Aren't those the same words he was saying when we were in the woods, Ross, before we met Alethia? Don't you think so?"

"I do. I overheard Shu telling him it was a message, that the words were from Eloh going out on the wind."

"He is a messenger. He's been given a voice."

"What do you mean?

"Kumél carries a voice within him, a voice not his but of another. There is a purpose for the voice. It speaks of something to come, or of something that will be."

As Kumél whispered, Ross noticed he could see the isinglass

inscription more clearly. Every word from Kumél's mouth seemed to transfer energy into the inscription and illuminated it behind the transparent wall. He noticed that Shu was also watching the isinglass. "Look, Shu, the inscription! It's different now. I can see it more clearly than before!" For the first time, Ross could see the whole inscription illuminated behind the isinglass.

"That has to be Theoscian writing," Seerae declared.

"It was written ages ago. It's a jupnie, or a promise, should an age of darkness come."

"What does it say, Shu?"

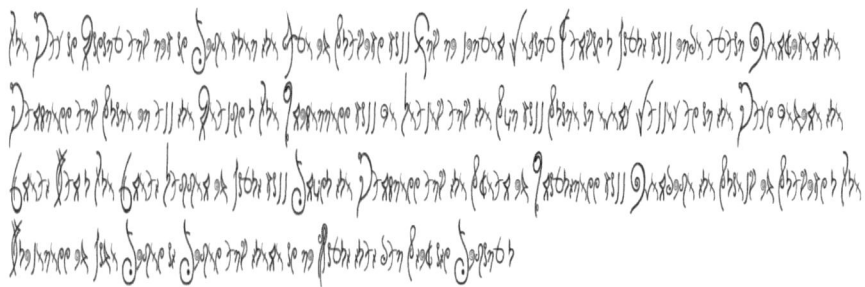

Sitting down next to Seerae, Shu explained, "One must be sure they are prepared for its message. To utter the words of this declaration is to unleash its power over all the realms. To speak it is to declare it, to whisper it is to set it free."

"So, does that mean you can't voice it?" Seerae hoped this wasn't the case.

"No. The words have previously been spoken by Kumél. He has already set them free upon the realm of Shuk, and he is still speaking them now, in his sleep."

Shu spoke in the Theoscian tongue, the words, slow and precise. He handled them carefully, knowing they were significant, sacrosanct, and hallowed. His treatment was so reverent that Ross and Seerae found themselves stepping away from him as he spoke.

When he had finished reciting the phrases, Ross asked, "So, that's what you were talking to Kumél about, back in the cave, the ancient Jupnie?"

"But, didn't you speak the words then, Shu?" asked Seerae.

"No, I didn't speak in the Theoscian tongue. Only Kumél spoke the words of the Jupnie; I just translated them into his own tongue."

Of course, Seerae was curious. "What does the Jupnie say, Shu?"

"It declares this: 'The day is rising and now is come, when the age of shadows will end, no longer vexing Pardis. Light will once again overpower the darkness and shine on all the realms.'"

As Shu read the inscription, a strange sensation coursed through Ross's body. His skin, from his head to his feet, grew hot, as if something was being poured over him. The heat pushed into his hands. Some form of liquid appeared to be running through the blue, luminous script he had received on himself at the well of Veritus. It was as if the markings were his veins and they had liquid light, sparkling and glowing, flowing through them. Every word of the inscription Shu spoke worked like his heartbeat to pump the liquid light farther and farther into every part of his body.

Shu continued to read, aware of how the words would affect Ross:

The brokenness will be healed, and the sun will shine in every valley as in the days before the Great War. The great hammer of light will crush the darkness and the spear of brightness will overcome the shield of shadows. The wholeness of life comes, it comes, and there is no might that can stop its coming.

"I'm burning up! Damn it! Why is it so damned hot?" Ross looked at the fire, then at the isinglass and the writing, trying to understand what was happening. He backed away, tearing at his shirt until he had ripped it off. The markings covered most of the skin on his chest, back, over his arms, and down to his fingers. Ross looked at Shu with eyes that were distraught and afraid.

Msusi and Seerae could feel his desperation and called to Shu, "What is happening to him? Why is he marked like that?"

"It's the simtu, the mark of the Carascians, of Amik and his descendants."

"But it looks like my own markings, only mine are not alive as his," Seerae replied.

Shu explained, "It's the blood of Amik that gives life to the simtu. The words of the Jupnie are bringing it back to life."

Seerae could see the anguish and pain Ross was experiencing. She asked Shu, "Why does it hurt him so? How can it be meant for him but cause such agony? How will he bear it?"

"It's the light, Seerae. It's piercing the darkness that is hidden away deep inside Ross. It is a spear of light driven into the black depths. When he lets go of the shadows, he will no longer suffer the pain of the light."

"But how? Why is it piercing him now?"

"Because he hears the Jupnie. It works to break the grip of the spell. The words of Eloh are calling the light to life."

Seerae was confused. "But Kumél has been speaking the Jupnie for days. I've heard him in his sleep. We were listening to him just a short while ago. What has changed?"

"That was in the Theoscian tongue, though. When Ross heard the words in his own tongue from Theoscian lips, the Carascian remnant that exists in him and in all the seed of Amik gave life and brightness to the simtu."

As Shu was finishing, Ross fell to his knees and onto his face before blacking out. Seerae and Msusi knelt beside him and called, "Ross! Ross!" Seerae reached out to touch him but because the simtu was still active, she instinctively retracted her hand. "Is he going to be alright, Shu? Is he?"

"Of course. The simtu will not kill him. It's meant to bring him life. You can touch him; it won't hurt you."

Seerae put her hand on Ross's head and gently stroked his hair. Msusi put her arm around Seerae. "He is the descendent of Amik, Seerae. When touched, the waters of Veritus uncovered what has been hidden beneath lies and deception. Ross has believed a lie and has lived his whole life under the shadow of an illusion. The Well of Veritus revealed what is true and soon he will find that part of himself that he has lived without."

Ross lay on the ground, unconscious. He still convulsed and twitched, the work of the simtu continuing in him. Seerae asked Shu, "Why does the simtu not shine on me as it does on him? I have markings like his."

"All the nephesh are marked with the simtu, but the simtu lives in the flesh of the Carascians. It marks them in their bodies, and it shines because of their great love and friendship with Eloh. After the Great War, Attar cast a spell on the Carascians that drew out of them the Elohan Essentia, which is the life of the light. The simtu went to the nephesh, that is why you carry the markings, but the light of the simtu remains alive in the bodies, the mortal flesh of the sapiens who live and die in the realm of Tirnan. You and your sapien are meant to be one or whole, and only when the oneness is restored will you shine as in the days of Pardis. Until then, your light is held captive to your sapien's mortality."

Ross moaned and slowly rolled over onto his side. "What happened?"

"Don't you remember?" Shu looked at him and smiled.

"Not really. Well, maybe some. My head hurts." When Ross had collapsed, he had hit his forehead on the hard ground. He winced as he touched the abrasion, then he remembered what Shu had said. The pain of the simtu would have been welcomed at that moment, for a severe pain suddenly pierced his heart. He realized he was not going home. The truth of who he truly was had cut him and made him bleed from a place where blood runs cold and invisible. He lay his head back on the ground and closed his eyes. Quiet tears fell to the ground. Accepting what he had tried, so desperately, to deny was extremely difficult. It felt like losing Eve and Daniel all over again, like they could not be a part of him, that they were a part of a dream that was never true. Going home, the hope of it, made him feel connected to them as if they were not really dead, but if he could not go home, if he could not have even the simple hope of ever returning, then the deniability, the unalterable sting of their loss felt oppressively final. He had held a secret, a secret that had been growing in his mind, a thought that once it had entered, refused to be silent. He didn't really know if he wanted to go back after all.

Without Eve, he had nothing to go back to, and that scared him more than being in Shuk. However, he had not told anyone. He did not want to accept he might not have the choice to go back, now he knew he could not return, and the knowing made the accepting unbearable. Some things cannot be reconciled in the mind, they hover above reality like a cloud, weightless and ominous, blocking the light of truth. They are like shade on a sunny day and at the same time, a tormenting storm casting darkness on everything. Shuk had become that for Ross: shade and torment, hope and despair.

Shu understood more acutely than Ross could ever imagine. He patted Ross on the back. "Come my friend, we have much to do and far to go."

Ross was drawn to Shu's eyes, where he saw, for the first time, what he had seen in Daniel's eyes: the fearless power of true friendship.

Shu added, "Beware my friends. We're about to leave the protection of Gershom Forest. There is much danger before us."

Ross clumsily followed behind the others. He stopped at the fire pit and looked into the flames. He leaned against the stones that surrounded the fire, his body still weak and reeling in pain. The flames hypnotized him, and the heat of the fire wrapped around him like a blanket. It was not like the burning of the simtu, it was comforting. Slowly, his body recovered until the grip of the simtu released him. "Shu, why does it continue to burn? There is no wood or fuel."

"The fire of Soteria does not require wood or fuel to burn. It waits for the seed of Amik to ignite its flame. It burns to light the way of hope, to illuminate the isinglass, and to make the words of the Jupnie known throughout the realm. It will burn until the hammer of light has crushed the darkness and until the spell of Attar is broken."

Observing that Ross could now stand on his own strength, Shu called, "Come. We have much to do."

Huzesh sat on a stone as the morning light cast its glow over the land. He scanned the horizon to see if the light he had seen the night before still shone in the sky. Carefully, he searched until, finally, he glimpsed it; it was faint because of the rising day. He watched the pulsing flicker of what he thought was a flame, but it was not a flame he was viewing, it was the reflection of the isinglass wall. Behind Huzesh, perched at the top of the stone mound that had been Huzesh's shelter, was a large black corvus. It was the same one Loham had tried to scare away. "Com, ye wretched bird."

He held out scraps of meat he had kept in his satchel. The corvus flew effortlessly toward him and landed on his giant hand. "A ha u purpose fur ye. Fly o'er da mountains un sae wut thut bae o'er dar. Sae uf ut bae da forner. Return t'mae, un A wull ha mor flesh fur ye t'aet." The giant, black bird lifted into the cloudy sky and flew to the north toward Mount Soteria.

"Loham, ut bae tam t'gae. Now!"

"I'm coming! What's the big hurry?"

"Wae bae guttin close. No tam t'wais, damn ye!"

To the north of the summit of Mount Soteria, Shu and his friends were descending the shoulder of the mountain. Msusi noticed a black bird soaring overhead, just beyond them. "Shu, do you see the corvus? It's been flying overhead for some time now."

Shu focused on the giant, black bird circling above them. "We must hurry to the trees. We have no shelter here. We're totally exposed. That bird is not just any bird; I suspect it's a spy."

"A spy? Who would be spying on us?"

"There are many who would like to find you, my friend. We must be extremely careful. You've been very fortunate to have found such a friend as Kumél. Your enemies would have taken you by now if you hadn't been surrounded by him and the others." Shu picked up the pace from a quick walk to a jog, and the others followed in a single file line. The corvus flew over them until they reached the shelter of the trees, then landed in the branches. Kumél and Ross watched as it flew by, and realized it was following them.

"The enemy has eyes everywhere in these woods; we must be careful. Don't trust anything," Shu warned.

"Are you sure the bird is a spy? He's still following us and doesn't seem to mind that we know it," Seerae said in a naïve tone.

"We have to keep going. Hopefully, we'll lose him in the woods." Zoësh drew her sword and walked cautiously behind Msusi and Shu. Seerae followed closely behind her with Ross while Kumél brought up the rear. They were a tense and clumsy group. Ross was the most unprepared for the dangers that had escalated during the time he had been in Gershom. He was not accustomed to being hunted like an animal or wanted like a criminal. His heart beat loudly in his chest as he realized there was a great urgency to their journey.

The forest was difficult for Ross to negotiate. He had tied the spear of Amik to his small backpack so he would have his hands free for scrambling and climbing, but the spear kept catching on the overhanging branches, impeding his progress, and making noise.

"Ross, you must be more careful! If there is someone looking for us, you'll give us away."

"Sorry! I'm trying. This damned spear! I don't know what to do with it," Ross snapped back.

Occasionally, one of them searched the trees for the black corvus, only to discover the bird was still on their heels. They labored farther and farther down the mountains and into the valley below until they finally reached a small meadow. Shu motioned to everyone to stop and stay quiet. He carefully moved toward the edge of the trees bordering the meadow. Shu cupped his hands over his mouth and softly whistled into the meadow like a tit. Shu did this several times until, finally, he heard a returning call. Shu whistled again, but this time the sound was different, it was louder and longer. A large flock of tiny tits burst into flight from tree branches in every direction. The petite birds rose into the sky like a cloud, their wings beating the air and making a loud commotion. They chirped and called to each other, then dove into the forest.

"Look! They're attacking the corvus!" Seerae pointed to a tall tree just behind them where the black bird was perched. Hundreds of tits buzzed around the corvus, pecking at it, diving at it, and spearing it with their mini beaks. Desperately, the corvus flapped its wings to fly away, but the attacking tits kept landing on it, weighing it down. At one point, the corvus fell from its perch and collided with leaves and branches as it descended from the tree, but it was finally able to catch the air with its giant wings and took flight. Once the corvus reached the open sky, it attempted to escape the menacing, little birds. However, they were undaunted by its efforts and continued to harass until both the corvus and the tits had flown out of sight. "Wow! I thought the corvus was bad. Those little birds are sure able to hold their own!" Ross said.

"Aye. Da liddle ones cun bae u vary powerful force."

"Who is that, Zoësh? Who's over there?"

"Where, Seerae? Where? Get down, everyone! Get down!" Zoësh motioned for everyone to take cover.

Across the meadow, a lone figure stood tall and still. Shu looked to see if it was someone he recognized then called out. The lone figure motioned in a friendly gesture for them to come.

"Who is it, Shu?" Zoësh asked.

"It's Ziminiar."

"Aye. Ut bae eem. A ha nut saen eem fur mony seasons. A waer nut sur uf ee waer alive or no."

Ziminiar was an aposta like Kumél. He was scarred in the same way Kumél was scarred. His skin was a combination of supple, iridescent patches and black, scaly sections that were rough and hard, but his face had less scarring than Kumél's. On his back were identical, grotesque appendages that were the remnants of a great pair of wings, like those of Jaroh. He was marked with the simtu like Kumél and the nephesh. On his head was a long lock of hair, longer than Kumél's, and un-banded so that it fell over his head like an umbrella. His black hair was thick and coarse, and he was constantly brushing it away from his face because it was so unruly. Ziminiar wore a ragged kilt similar to Kumél's and had a golden belt but did not carry a weapon. If Kumél was considered quiet and reserved, then Ziminiar was known to be garrulous and friendly. Though similar in appearance, their personalities were very much the opposite.

It came as quite a surprise to the others that Ziminiar was so affable. Ross was especially taken aback by the startling contrast between him and Kumél, for Ross had become used to the quiet, gruff nature of Kumél. As the company approached Ziminiar, he was graciously warm and welcomed them. Shu stretched out his hand to the giant beast, who accepted the gesture as confirmation his friend had been missing him. "Mae frun, ut ha baen t'lung! Ye muk mae glad! A wull ha t'play ye u tune, mae haert bae so huppae!"

"Ziminiar, it has been too long indeed! I have so missed you my friend!"

"So, ye brung mae u full course mael? A bae nut sur uf A cun aet um all, but A bae nut one t'offend. A wull guv ut u trae! Bahaha!

Ross and the others stepped back with dreaded looks on their faces at the thought of Ziminiar eating them for dinner.

"Oh nae, mae frens, A waer jus jesting! Yur safe wit mae."

Shu and Ziminiar laughed heartily while the others laughed nervously. It was hard to take a joke from a creature so forbidding in his appearance and so well-equipped and disposed to eat them. Nevertheless, it was not long before they were all at ease, laughing together.

"So, dis bae da one thut all da fuss bae bout, da forner? Who bae ye, lad?"

"Umm, me? My name is Ross."

"Ross, strange nam. Ye know, ye dunna b'lung haer?"

"Yeah, so I've been told. Isn't by my choice, I assure you."

"Shu, com. All ye com un follow mae." Shu and his friends followed Ziminiar into the woods.

The sun was touching the far horizon when Huzesh caught sight of the corvus returning. The bird landed on a rock not far from Loham. It was wounded, and many of its tail feathers and wing feathers were obviously missing. The feathers on the top of its head were pulled out leaving a bald spot. Loham distrusted the bird and started to shoo it away, but Huzesh struck him on the head with the back of his hand. "Fool, A ha waited fur da corvus! Ee bae ma liddle fren un ee ha news fur mae."

Once again, Huzesh held out his giant hand, which had scraps of meat in its palm. "Com, bird!" The corvus quickly flew to him and snatched up the pieces of meat. It would have flown away, but Huzesh took hold of its talons, knowing better than to trust it.

"So, tell mae, wut ha ye saen?"

Loham had never seen or heard a corvus speak. He, like most others, thought they had no voice other than the one they used to communicate with birds of their kind. However, Loham was mistaken. All the creatures of Shuk could speak if they desired to, but the corvuses were the most vocal. In a high-pitched, raspy voice, difficult on the ears, the corvus whispered to Huzesh. Nevertheless, he did not speak in a tongue Loham understood, but Huzesh, however, understood it very well. The bird spoke only a few words, but Huzesh had understood all he had needed to, and now, perplexed by the message, he sat with a furrowed brow.

Loham could not contain himself. "What? What did it say? Tell me!"

"Ut cunna bae. Da forner, aye? Ee bae haer, but dar bae anoter, u Theoscian lik Eloh." Huzesh threatened the corvus with his eyes. "Bae ye sur?"

"Caw, caw!" The corvus attempted to fly away but Huzesh held him. With a murderous glare in his eyes, he commanded it, "Ye cunna tell no one."

Huzesh looked at Loham and then back at the bird. "A bae sorry, mae liddle fren. No one mus know, no one afore A ha foun thum." With his free hand, Huzesh grabbed the corvus's head and ripped it from its body. "Yum! Bae ye hungry?" He bit into the bird, feathers and all, and chewed as blood and entrails dropped from his mouth. The crunching of the corvus bones was loud and grizzly.

When Huzesh offered some to Loham, Loham shook his head. "Never cared much for corvus. Think I'll pass." Loham was noticing a pattern with Huzesh. When he finished with you, he ate you. Loham felt all the more discomforted by the inevitability of his own demise.

Ziminiar led Shu and his friends deep into the forest at the confluence of two streams where there was a steep, rocky mound with a cave entrance hewn into the stone. This was the doorway into Ziminiar's lair. For one so big, the entrance was quite small. "Dis bae mae home, notin fancy or big, but ut bae gud fur mae. A bae sorry A cunna offer ye u place un mae hole, out o'da night air, but ye cun stay haer. Da moss un da grass bae soft un dry."

"Can we start a fire to keep us warm?" Ross asked.

"Aye. No worries haer. Da ony spies bae maen."

Ross prepared a place to make a fire and Zoësh helped by gathering old dry branches. Seerae gathered some stones from the stream's edge to circle the fire.

"Shu, ye know, dar bae u storm brewin. Ut bae comin frum da suõ un ut wull bae haer un u few suns. A haer u strange rumor bout u voice spaekin un da wind."

"I've heard the voice. It's the voice of the Jupnie. It calls to all, and soon all will hear."

"D'da Jupnie brang da storm?"

"It stirs the whole of creation, the skies and the ground, the rocks and trees, and the waters and seas. They all hear its voice, and they are all stirred by its beckoning call. Even the creatures can hear it. Shuk will soon see a new day."

"So, yur da forner. A haerd ye bae frum da line o'Amik. A haerd thum sae yur Amik eemsaelf." Ross struck his knife to the flint and started the fire while Ziminiar watched closely. "Wut bae dis ting thut made da flame? A wud lik t'ha ut fur maesaelf."

"It's just a fire starter, nothing special. See, it's easy." Ross dragged the small blade of his knife over the ferrocerium rod to create sparks.

"Ooo! D'thut agan!"

Ross struck the flint again.

"A lik wut dis ting dud, ut bae magic. Bae ye u sorcerer or u magician?"

"Oh no, not at all. There's no trick to it; anyone can do it. Would you like to try?"

"Aye!"

Ross gave the small tools to Ziminiar and told him how to make sparks. Ziminiar dragged the knife's edge down the length of the flint rod, causing an eruption of sparks to dance away from the rod and onto the ground.

"Ahh, A dud ut! Yur right! Ut bae easy!" Ziminiar's eyes lit with delight like a young boy discovering a new and exciting game. He struck the flint several times. "Whae bae dar no flame? Whaer bae da faer?"

"Well, that's the more difficult part. You have to make a tinder bundle to catch the sparks and ignite a flame."

"So, ut bae not so easy as ye say?"

"Well, it's not really that difficult either."

Ziminiar noticed Zoësh was staring at him. "Yur da she-neph thut A haerd bout. Ye ha kulled muny o'da mēgs un da gallues bae huntin fur ye."

"I have killed a few. They're awful beasts!"

"Aye. Da mēgs bae terrible creatures."

"I meant the gallues." Zoësh smiled at Ziminiar and they laughed together.

They ate and drank from the generous offerings of Ziminiar as they sat around the fire talking and laughing.

"Mae tinks wae naed u bit o'music un song!" Ziminiar darted quickly into his den where he emerged with a strange wooden object. It was a hollowed-out log, about eight inches in diameter and about six feet or so in length. The log was stripped of its bark and had, over the ages, become dark with the oils of Ziminiar's hands. On one side was an opening, irregular and snake-like in its shape. From one end to the other were five strings made from the fibrous sinew-like strands of tenush bark. They were held at one end with small wooden dowels and at the other end, they were twisted around five long wooden dowels with flat broad ends that were used to tighten the strings. Ziminiar also carried with him a long bow.

"Dis bae mae own invention. A call ut u tenush after da tree A created ut frum. A ha mae dukwán, tae, but A dunna play ut much, not onymur."

"It looks like a primitive lute, or a kind of cello. You made it?"

"Aye, ages ago." Ziminiar sat next to the fire and lay the tenush on the ground. He drew the long bow across the strings slowly and deliberately. Because of the round face of the instrument, he could only draw across two or three strings at once. As he continued to draw the bow back and forth over the strings, the tenush resonated with a deep, longing call that filled the air with full and strong tones, both high and low. The sound of the strings filled the hollow chamber of the tenush and then rolled out of the open end at the bottom of the instrument with such oscillating amplitude that everyone could feel the vibrations of each note roll over them like warm sunlight.

Msusi and Zoësh swiftly joined in playing their dukwáns as if they all knew the same song. Their playing was extemporaneous and magical. It seemed improvised, yet they played each note in harmony as if they had played the tune many times. There was a feeling in the air of elation and happiness. Their songs flowed from some deep, spiritual fount that had been waiting to erupt.

In a soft, shy voice, Seerae sang a song that came from her heart. It was a haunting, forlorn tune full of longing, yet somehow, it was also light and sanguine. Her voice was a sweet and pure soprano. The tone of her voice was soothing and natural, and each note lifted from her lips into the air like the song of a songbird:

Oh, where the ancient dancers be,
An where the songs of old,
An where the pretty blue birds sing
To greet the rays of gold.

I have not seen the crystal streams,
Nor the flowers bloom,
Since I been here in dis dark land
Beneath the shadowed moon.

Oh, where the fox an ram an deer,
Who on the meadow played.
They hide among the thorny bush,
They hide among the trees
Because they be afraid.

A have not seen the deep blue sea,
Nor the sky above.
Since I been here in this dark land,

Far from the one I love.

Lala lala lala lala lala lala lala,
Oh sing with me a song of hope,
Sing a song of glee,
Lift your heart above this world,
Above the stormy sea.

For I be here a waitin time
To pass into da blue,
When all my dreams and memories
Will finally come to be.

Ross was visibly moved by the song. Her voice pierced his heart and reminded him of a time, not long ago, when he had heard Eve singing. She had also sung with a sweet and pure voice that pierced his heart. Ross found himself missing her even more than ever. His thoughts of her soared into an idyllic realm, a place where every image was perfect and untarnished by the residue of reality. She was a dream, a fantasy and becoming a myth and lore. Ross knew the truth, but he wanted to keep his memories of Eve unspoiled. He wanted to remember those times, not so much as they truly were, but as they should have been. Even the most perfect of moments are cluttered with imperfections that become invisible to the eyes of memory.

Ross silently watched as the others sang and played their instruments. It was a strangely enchanting spectacle, the merriment of such an eclectic company of friends. Ross knew Eve would have joined in their celebration without hesitation and that she would have embraced each and every one of these strange and unearthly beings. They caused him to remember things he might have otherwise forgotten about her, like her kindness and patience, which they now revealed to him in so many ways. Sitting there, in the glow of the fire, his heart became full and his soul felt such satisfaction he could hardly keep from laughing. But his laughter was not from a sense of amusement or frivolity, it came from an inexpressible deep sense of happiness, a *joie de vivre* he had only ever felt with Eve.

Watching Seerae, he began to wonder why she had come with them. She had told them she wanted to stay in Gershom, but she had not hesitated to follow Shu into the mountains. Seerae noticed Ross looking at her. "Ross, come and dance with us!"

"No, Seerae, really. I can't dance a step."

"Come on, dance with me! I'll show you! You'll see."

Ross knew he could not refuse, but, really, he did not want to refuse. He wanted to feel their levity, to soar, if just for a short time, above the arrested certainty of all things tactual, to escape the bonds of a life chained to physicality and mortality. He wanted to fly free from himself, and the music gave him wings of escape.

Ross joined the others as they twirled and swayed. In the middle of dancing, he asked Seerae about Gershom, "Why did you come with us? I thought you were going to stay in Gershom?"

"I don't know. I just had to come. It sounds as if you wish I had stayed behind."

"No. I'm glad you came. I would have missed you. I just thought . . . I don't know . . . I was just wondering, that's all."

Seerae could not tell Ross the reason she had come. She was not exactly sure. But she did know that deep within her, there was a compelling force pulling her toward him, making her unable to stay behind. She puzzled over what it was that had drawn her into this strange company. Seeing the snowpetals that had led her toward Ross was such a serendipitous discovery and yet, for some reason it felt uncannily ordained. Every part of her felt sublimely intoxicated in the company of her friends. It was a significantly stronger force than her desire to remain in the safety of Gershom's protective borders. "I think you think too much," she said, laughing.

Ross looked at Seerae with a baffled stare. It was something Eve had said to him multiple times. She smiled and they all danced and played into the late hours of the dark night.

At the base of Mount Soteria, Huzesh and Loham moved rapidly to catch up to the foreigner. They had traveled long and fast to reach the mountain's base and were beginning to make the climb up and over to the other side. Huzesh could not be sure what direction the foreigner would be heading, but he knew he could rely on his keen sense of smell to find him.

Loham struggled to keep pace with the possessed gallue. The darkness of night had forced them to find a place of shelter among the talus heaps near the base of the mountain's steep upper slopes. In the distance, they could see the approaching storm; it had been nipping at their heels as if chasing them. Loham hoped the rain would hold off a bit longer, until they had reached the shelter of the woods on the other side of the mountain. When they were sitting in the dark with no fire or food, awaiting the arrival of the morning sun, Huzesh announced to Loham, "A ha u plan, un ye mus d'exactly wut A say."

"Of course, you know me." Loham's response was coated with a thick layer of sarcasm.

"Yur gonna join da forner un ees clan. Ye wull bae one o'thum, u spy. Un A wull stay bak."

"But won't they know I'm a snitch? If there are any nephesh with him, they'll know."

"Thun ye mus bae gud bout convincin thum yur nut. Uf ye fail mae, ye know wut A wull d'ta ye."

"But what do you want me to do if they don't find me out first?"

"Ye wull fin u wae t'gut da forner t'laeve da others. Gut eem bae eemsaelf. A wull tell u plan t'catch eem."

"So how do you want me to do that? You make it sound so easy. Why don't you do it yourself?"

"Dunna gut smart wit mae, ye liddle dakkrah! Ye wull fin u way or else!"

Loham lowered his gaze; he did not want to make Huzesh angry for he had no way of escaping the brute.

Huzesh kicked Loham in the ribs to rouse him from his sleep. Even though they were not comfortable in their cramped shelter, Loham had been able to collect a few hours of rest. He never slept easily though, for the thought of infiltrating the company of the foreigner frightened him. However, the wrath of Huzesh frightened him even more.

"Gut up! Ut bae tam t'gae!"

"I'm coming, I'm coming! Go on ahead. I'll be right behind."

Huzesh set off without Loham, though he was unwilling to go too far in case Loham had any ideas about heading the opposite direction. Loham could see Huzesh was not keeping his usual pace and knew he was waiting for him. He was aware Huzesh would eventually become impatient and violent, so he hurried along but, at the same time, kept a comfortable distance behind. As they were approaching the forest, Loham heard voices calling, "Who bae dar? Whae ye bae haer?" Then, they yelled, "Luk, ut bae Huzesh un u snitch bae wit eem!" Huzesh did not stop or, in any way, pay them attention; he just kept walking.

"Huzesh! Huzesh, wait!" As the two gallues got closer, Huzesh found a large stone to sit on, and he waited with considerable agitation. The two gallues were hunters searching for a bounty.

Not far behind the hunters, Loham noticed that rain was falling and the wind was blowing the dark, burdened clouds in their direction. "Huzesh, we don't have time to wait for those two gallues, the rain will be on us very soon if we do not keep moving."

"Ahh, shut yer face! Da rain wull nut catch us. A mus tend t'des fools." Loham perceived Huzesh did not have good intentions toward the two approaching gallues. He wondered if Huzesh had known them before and held some offense against them, or if this was his way of greeting his friends.

As the two gallues approached, one of them started asking questions. "So, whaer ye headin wit da snitch, un whaer bae yer clan? Hmm, mubae wae bae goin da same way?"

"Mubae. Whae ye bae up haer, Lucleem? Un who bae wit ye?"

"Dis bae Molissk. Wae bae huntin u bounty. A bae sur thut ye haerd dar waer u forner un da realm. Bae ye huntin da forner?"

"Wut forner? Ye bae fools, dar bae no forner haer! Who ha bewitched ye wit such notions, Lucleem? Ye bae no smarter thun thut? U forner un Shuk! Bahaha! Whae bae ye huntin eem?"

"Yur da fool Huzesh! Gubrone ha promised u bounty fur da head o'da forner!"

"Gubrone, ha promised wut? U bounty?" he asked sarcastically. "Since wun ha Gubrone er kupt u promise? U bounty! Yur fools, both o'ye bae fools!"

"Mighty strong words fur u lone gallue, Huzesh, or d'ye forget thut yur all alone?"

"Laeve ut bae, Molissk. Ignore eem. Huzesh bae jus lik ye, bad tempered. Onywae, listen Huzesh, ut bae rumored thut dar bae u kerolus wit da forner. Som ha saen eem, or so dae say."

"Lucleem, d'ye raely tink u kerolus bae un Shuk? A tink ye bae smarter thun thut."

"Mubae so, Huzesh. Uf yur nut huntin, thun whae ye bae so far frum da valley?"

"Oh, A bae huntin, jus nut huntin som mysterious forner. A bae huntin nephs! A know Gubrone wull pay fur thum."

"So ye ha haerd no news bout u forner un des parts?"

"Un des parts, nae. A haerd news bout u forner but A dud nut believe ut. Ut bae u joke or u myth, but uf ye want t'hunt, thun ye shud gae t'da ushus, thut bae whaer da others bae huntin."

"Others, wut others? Ye spaek bout no others!"

"Hmm, guess A forgut. Dar bae others thut ha gone t'da ushus. If yur so sur bout finin da forner, ye ha t'gae somwhaer else. Dis bae da wrong mountain! Bahaha, always gaein da wrong wae!"

"Bae ye sur?"

"Aye. As sur as A cun bae bout u rumor." Huzesh winked and grinned at Lucleem.

"Yer arm, wut happened t'ut? Ye lose ut? Bahaha! Thut bae whae yur afeared o'da forner, ye cunna fin yer arm … or yer courage! Bahaha!"

"A faer notin, dar bae no forner!"

"Well, dar bae u whole army o'gallues huntin dis "no" forner. Yur da ony one thut bae nut."

"Un army, ye say? Lucleem, ut bae un army o'dakkrahs, un ye bae one o thum!"

"Bahaha! Wae wull bae saein ye, Huzesh. Ut bae always u pleasure." Lucleem and Molissk turned toward the east and headed away from Loham and Huzesh. Loham had noticed that throughout the discourse, Huzesh had been holding tightly to the grip of his sword, and he had been sure a fight was about to ensue, so he was surprised but quite relieved at the affable outcome. Once Huzesh and Loham were certain they were once again alone, they continued toward the north. After quite a long time, Loham asked Huzesh about the two gallues. "So, why did you mislead them? I was expecting you to kill them. You seemed ready to."

"A planned on ut, but ut seemed better thut dae bae looking un da wrong place. Afta all, uf dae bae lookin un da wrong place, thun mubae dae wull tell others t'luk un da wrong place tae."

"But we might need them. They're right. You know you are crippled. What if this foreigner is Eloh? You can't be thinking of fighting one as powerful as him, with one arm?"

"Wull, ye bes hope ee bae nut Eloh. Un fur thut matter, A raely dunna b'laeve thut ee bae Eloh. B'sides, A bae mur interested un da forner."

"So why hunt the foreigner?"

"Cause, uf Eloh un da forner both bae haer, A wull capture da forner un ee wull bae mae hostage. A wull use eem t'muk u deal wit Eloh, fur Eloh cares fur all un ee wull wanna save da forner. Eloh wull muk u deal wit mae or A wull kull da forner."

As they scrambled over the last few boulders before entering the woods, Loham felt something land on the very top of his head. He looked up and a large, cold drop of rain fell into his eye. He saw the dark streaks of rain falling not far behind them. He ran toward the woods, chasing after Huzesh.

At the cave of Ziminiar, Shu, and Ziminiar sat near a fire talking. "Whae ha ye com t'mae, Shu, ye an yer clan of misfits?"

"I expected that you would see us as such, considering that it takes one to know one. Hahaha!"

"Bahaha!"

"We are here, Ziminiar, because Alethia sent us to you. She told Ross to find the Pool of Levitus and that you would help him."

"Da Pool o'Levitus? Ye know dar bae muny who tink da story bout da pool un da nephs bae u myth. Whae d'Ross naed t'fin ut?"

"There are things he must know, things he must find there."

"Who bae dis forner un whae bae ee haer? Ee luks lik Amik; fur sur ee b'lungs t'Amik's clan."

"Aye. He is the descendent of Amik, and his coming has been foretold. The Jupnie speaks of him."

"So, dae bae true, da tings thut A ha haerd, da rumors. No wonder dar bae hunters bout da woods."

"Hunters? What hunters?"

"Sunt bae Gubrone. Da woods bae crawlin wit um. Also, A ha haerd thut Gubrone carries u weapon thut waer foun naer da dark valley. Ut bae b'laeved thut da weapon bae frum anoter world, thut ut waer brung haer bae da forner."

"I think not. Ross came with no weapons, and he's not a warrior."

"Wull, dar bae muny spies bout, A ha u few o'mae own, un thut bae wut A haerd. Plus, dar bae word thut u kerolus bae haer, un Shuk tae. D'ye know ony ting bout thut?"

"Alethia sent one to aid Ross and his friends. He led them to me. It was Jaroh."

"Jaroh ha bun haer, un Shuk?"

"Aye, he and Alethia."

"Hmm, Alethia, A do miss her. Ut ha baen u lung tam." It was obvious to Shu that Ziminiar was feeling the sting of the past through his memories, which were all that was left of it. "Oh wull, gud ol' days. Now dar bae much trouble bout and eyes eary whaer. Da black corvuses o'Gubrone fly bout lookin fur yer fren. Ee bae un much danger. Sur ye shunt gae buk t'Gershom whaer ye bae safe?"

"Safety is not what we are looking for, Ziminiar. There is much to do, and you know of what I speak. The Jupnie cannot be stopped now."

"A ha haerd thut dar bae u strange wind blowin, u wind thut ha words, u wind thut speaks."

"Kumél has seen a vision in his dreams. He has heard the ancient voice and it's speaking through him, more and more every day. Every being, beast, plant and element feels the power of his words. They rouse to the call of the Jupnie, to the promise of a new world."

"Wull, whae d'ye naed t'fin da Pool o'Levitus?"

"I don't know yet, but it is important for Ross to go there. Will you help us?"

"Da wae t'da pool bae grueling; no one er journeys dar. Ut bae da place o'da nephesh, founded bae Eloh wun ee brung Amik un Livia t'Shuk, un ut bae u place o'rumumbrance. A ha haerd thut ut bae protected agan intruders."

"Aye, maybe, but not against us. We must go right away."

It was clear to Shu that Ziminiar was pondering something, but he was unsure what. "A wull nut tell ye da wae. Instead, A mus gae wit ye. Ye mus take mae. A wanna join yer compny un haelp ye. Ye wull naed much haelp, ye know."

"But . . . but why? Why go with us? This is not your fight."

"A ha baen stuck haer un Shuk fur er, always hidin. A bae waery o'just survivin! A wanna liv agan un d'somting thut bae worth somting. A know A bae u wanted beast, hunted bae da gallues, rejected bae da kerolus un forgotten bae Eloh, but A stull wanna d'somting. Take mae wit ye! A ha mony frens who wull haelp tae, mony spies. Please, Shu, take mae wit ye. Lut mae haelp!"

Shu rubbed his forehead and paced the ground. Ziminiar knew what he asked was serious, for he was a traitor, an aposta with no allegiances or loyalties, a betrayer and betrayed, but he hoped the ages might have mended some of the torn strands that had once bound him to Pardis. He could see Kumél had gained favor and that something had happened to him to change him. Ziminiar was tired, lonely, and desperate for company, and more than anything else, Ziminiar wanted absolution. He was tired of carrying the weight of Attar's rebellion and treachery on his shoulders.

"You're right, Ziminiar. We do need more help, but until we find the Pool of Levitus, I cannot say whether or not you may join us. It will be up to the others; they will decide, but you may come and lead us to the pool."

Ziminiar lifted his head with a smile on his scarred face. He was glad to be in the company of an old friend.

Shu called everyone together. "Ziminiar will escort us to the pool of Levitus. We must move quickly, for I fear there may be many dangers about, dangers that draw nearer upon every sun." The company gathered their things and began the arduous trek toward the waterfall, unaware they were being watched.

Loham and Huzesh peered into the basin below the summit of the mountain. Huzesh had spotted the gray smoke of a smoldering fire rising into the morning sky. As the company of Shu had moved into a narrow gorge from where a stream flowed, Huzesh had glimpsed them, for just a moment before they disappeared between the gorge's rock walls. He and Loham were moving quickly down the ridge, hoping to catch up to them, but the company of Shu was still far away. Huzesh pursued like a possessed beast, and in his rush to close the distance between them, he had neglected to identify any landmarks that would help them navigate the maze of valleys and draws and rocks and hills that were spread out across the basin separating them from the company. It was not long before he and Loham were so disoriented the only thing they could be sure of was the location of Mount Soteria. The landscape seemed to be obscuring the way ahead.

Meanwhile, Shu and Ziminiar led the others upward into the gorge. For a long distance, the gorge was narrow and difficult to negotiate. The company moved slowly and deliberately as the towering black walls looked down upon them with menacing stares of disapproval. Giant boulders were strewn about as if they were meant to hinder any attempt at passage. The narrow stream flowed angrily around the obstacles, objecting with a loud, disapproving roar that filled the narrow gorge. Along the edge of the stream was a very narrow path, which looked as if it had not been traveled in many millennia. At one point, the way was blocked by a giant rock fallen from high above. The stream had backed up behind the giant stone and had begun to run over it and down through a narrow crack that had formed over the ages. The stone stood like a towering wall in front of them.

Shu studied the barrier. "Ziminiar, are you sure this is the only way?" He had to yell because the roar of the creek was so loud.

"Aye. Dar bae ony one way, un dis bae ut."

"But how will we get over that?"

Ross stepped forward. "I can get us over the top. There's a way over there, on the other side. We'll have to cross the stream. Come on!"

Crossing the stream was difficult because it was deep and fast, and the rocks were slick and round. One by one, they managed, with much help from each other. Once on the other side, Ross climbed a near-vertical seam in the wall. This was, of course, easy for Ross. Then he guided the others to the top.

On the top of the stone, they expected to see a lake or a large pool of water created by the dammed-up stream, but it was not so. Above the rock, the gorge had filled with rocks and debris, leaving only a shallow but wide body of water reaching several hundred yards. This pool merged with a much more placid stream that flowed from another gorge just ahead. It was obvious to all that this place had long been forgotten and that no one had been there for many ages. Green moss covered the walls and tops of the stones scattered throughout the upper section of the gorge. As they headed away from the edge of the gorge and toward the large pool, the angry roar of the stream faded until it was only an echo in the distance.

"Is this it, Ziminiar? Is this the pool?"

"Nae, Ross, wae ha far t'gae. Com."

"Kumél, do you trust him?" Ross quietly asked.

"Wull, Shu culls eem ees fren un says ut bae gud t'trus eem, so wae shud trus eem."

"I don't know. He seems OK, I guess, but I'm just not sure."

"Wull, wut bae ye sur bout?"

"You. I'm sure bout you. I trust you."

"Nut at first, rumumbar. Trus Ziminiar; ee bae luk mae."

"If you say so."

Just ahead of Ross and Kumél, Shu hollered to the others, "Here! We'll stop here for the night!"

"Why are we stopping now? It's still light enough to go farther."

"Ross, we've been at this long enough and besides, there may not be another suitable place to rest for quite some time. This is a convenient spot, and we all need the rest."

"I suppose you are right." Ross dropped his backpack to the ground and walked over to the edge of the stream.

Crossing the basin, Huzesh caught the scent of the fire the company had burned the night before. It was not long before he and Loham were standing at the place of their camp. It was the same place where Huzesh had seen them from the ridge.

"Ah ha! A ha foun deir tracks! Dae ha entered into da gorge. Ye wull follow thum, un fin da forner. Lead eem t'mae! Ye haer?"

"But what if they have headed off another way, out of the gorge? What if the foreigner won't follow me? I mean, why would he? He—and the others—will know I'm a snitch. They'll kill me."

"Loham, ye wull fin u wae t'brang thut forner t'mae, or else A wull kill ye! Un A wud fur sur muk yer death worse thun dae wud! Com, A wull muk sur thut dae b'laeve thut yur no snitch. Com, now!

Loham walked toward Huzesh, but before he could get close, Huzesh leaped upon him and beat him about the head and chest, bruising his skin and cracking his ribs. He slapped Loham in the face, and blood poured from his scratched and torn skin. Loham tried desperately to escape, but the giant beast was too heavy and though he had only one arm, Huzesh was able to deliver a brutal beating. Finally, the mauling ceased. Loham lay bleeding and moaning. He gasped for air as blood erupted from his mouth and nose.

Huzesh stood over him. "Now dae wull ha no trouble b'laevin yur nut u snitch. Get up! Dar bae no tam t'wais!"

Loham could hardly move. His eyes were so swollen, he could barely see anything. He feared that if he did not move quickly enough, Huzesh would begin again and not stop until he was dead this time. Loham rolled over to his side, then pushed his mangled body up from the ground. He managed to get to his feet and began to stumble over the rocks and roots that littered the grass and moss. He moaned and writhed in pain as each breath he took expanded his lungs. His lip was torn from Huzesh's sharp talons and a piece of bloody flesh hung from the corner of his mouth. Behind him, he heard Huzesh growl, "A wull bae waitin, dunna fail mae!"

As soon as Loham escaped the watchful eye of Huzesh, he collapsed into the stream. The water washed away the blood from his face and cooled the feverish bruises on his chest and arms. He lay in the frigid water until his body shivered and convulsed from the cold. He pulled himself from the stream onto the mossy ground that bordered the stream. Lying on his back, he closed his eyes and wondered what he had gotten himself into. He thought about the vision that had come to him just a few days earlier: the fire, the face in the fire. Then fear washed over him and with it shame and sorrow. Loham drifted off into a tempestuous delusion with his mind playing tricks on him, delirium induced by the pain of his beating. Eventually, he slept.

It was dark when Loham awoke. His eyes were slightly less swollen than before, and he could see the faint glow of the moon shining through the thick night clouds that moved like strange creatures across the sky. Loham's pain quickly reminded him of his injuries, but he managed to get his feet under him and moved in the same direction as the approaching stream. It was fear that urged him along through the darkness of the night, and it was fear that kept him from turning back, from running away. Alive and palpable, the terror surrounded him like the presence of Huzesh himself. Trying not to think about the pain, he staggered into the gorge, deep into the darkness of the shadows that were animated by the raging voice of the angry stream. At times, the delusions returned, and Loham saw horrific beasts chasing him and wanting to bite him, as if Huzesh had sent a hoard of mēglydaims to hunt him down. These delusions made him limp along even faster, even attempting to run at times. Then, lucidity would return, and Loham would realize there were no chasing mēgs or dark creatures. He agonized over how long the black night would endure.

It was the middle of the night, and Loham was standing in total darkness, paralyzed by the fear of not knowing what was ahead. Then, coming toward him out of the darkness was a tiny light. It advanced slowly and steadily, and for a moment, Loham thought he was having another delusion. The small light continued to approach him until, finally, Loham could see that it was not an apparition, but a tulwyth. Loham felt a warm sense of relief. When near him, the petite tulwyth hovered in the air just above the narrow path that led along the stream. Loham followed the little light through the shadows. "Well, it is you again. Have you come to rescue me? It seems I am always needing to be rescued." Loham wished to smile, though he could not. He wanted to show the small creature his appreciation. He mumbled, barely loud enough for the tulwyth to hear, "Hopefully you know the way because I am lost. I'm afraid too, but I fear that if you knew what I was doing here, you might not help me."

The tiny tulwyth flew ahead of him, shining its light on the ground near Loham's feet. Every step he took, the tulwyth illuminated. Eventually, Loham came to the giant rock wall. He could not see the top of it because of the imposing darkness. He questioned whether he had gone the wrong way, if Huzesh had made a mistake, or if the company he was chasing had somehow eluded him. He questioned whether the tulwyth had led him here to trick him or to hurt him, but he could not reconcile such an act by such a guileless creature. Resting upon a wet stone, Loham was glad to be alone with the tulwyth for the moment and away from Huzesh, who was his greatest danger. It felt better to know the pain of his wounds than to know the presence of Huzesh. He felt a fleeting sense of relief, but it was not long before the realization of his situation returned, and he remembered that Huzesh would track him down if he did not continue.

Loham had discovered the seam in the rock where Ross and the others had climbed. It was the tiny tulwyth that had revealed it to him. The tulwyth had flown up along the seam to show him the way. Loham was not a climber but somehow, he was convinced he could reach the unseen top. He approached the seam, and the tulwyth showed him the places to put his hands and feet. Each time Loham reached up to take hold of a crack or a stone, his ribs and chest reeled in pain. Every muscle in his body reacted rebelliously to his will, trying insistently to stop him, but he would not be detoured. Loham followed the tulwyth and climbed to the top of the wall and into the wide, placid waters of the shallow stream above. He was spent, every ounce of his energy exhausted, but the tulwyth would not stop. It repeatedly flew ahead of Loham, waited, and returned to him to urge him on through the darkness. Loham followed until he could not take one step more, and he fell to his knees. "I'm sorry my little friend. This is as far as I can go tonight. Thank you." Loham lay down on the top of a large, flat boulder, closed his eyes, and fell asleep.

The morning air was brisk, but still. Fog rose from the water's surface and filled the narrow gorge like smoke from a wildfire. It was impossible to see very far, for everything was cloaked by the mist, leaving only dark, shadowy silhouettes.

Msusi was the first to rise and, as usual, she went for a walk alone. The journey had been long and hard, and she had missed her times of solitude. As she walked, she noticed, a short distance away in the fog, there was a strange shadow. She approached what she thought must be a rock or boulder at the edge of the stream, but once she was within arm's reach, it became obvious to her that what she was seeing was not a rock at all. It was a nephesh lying in a heap on the top of a large, flat stone. Stunned by the revelation, Msusi stepped back with a start and she moved quietly back to where the others were. "Shu! Shu, wake up!" Her voice was soft and yet firm with a hint of worry. "Shu, please wake up! There is someone out there."

Shu rolled over onto his back and looked at Msusi. "Who?"

"Another neph, but I am not sure that he's alive. I got as close to him as we are now, but he didn't move or make a sound."

Msusi led Shu to her discovery. As they reached the body silhouetted by the fog, Shu touched the nephesh on the shoulder. "Are you alright?" he asked softly.

There was no response. Shu stepped carefully around the stone to a place where he could see the face of the stranger. It was immediately obvious to Shu the nephesh had been badly beaten and was in serious need of help. Shu shook the nephesh.

"Ohh, Ahh," Loham groaned in pain.

"Who are you? What has happened to you?"

Loham moaned. His body was tight from sleeping on the cold stone.

He did not move much at all and, for the longest time, was unable to speak. His eyes were so swollen there was only a small slit through which he could see anything at all. His lip was torn and crusted over with dried blood, and a pool of saliva had formed under his cheek as he lay sleeping.

Shu spoke urgently to Msusi, "Go quickly and get Kumél! We must help him."

Msusi ran back to the others and collected Kumél and Ross and led them to where Shu and the stranger were waiting. By the time she returned, the stranger was sitting up on the rock, mumbling through his badly beaten mouth and lips. Kumél critically examined the damaged nephesh. His suspicious nature made him less willing to intervene.

"Whaer dud ee com from? Who bae ee?"

"Come Kumél, help me get him back to camp. We must help him. Can't you see he's hurt?"

"Aye. A sae eem jus fine, but who bae ee un whaer bae ee from?"

"We've no time for you to question me. Please, do as I ask and help me."

Ross rushed over to the stranger and Kumél followed reluctantly. It was obvious to the others that Kumél did not trust the stranger, but he helped anyway.

"Who is that, Shu? Oh, what happened?"

"Make room, Seerae. Help us find a place for him to rest in comfort."

"Who is he?"

"Not sure."

"Loham, I'm Loham."

"Loham? Is that what you said?" Shu asked.

"Yes." His voice was weak, and his speech was garbled by his swollen lips.

Soon everyone was awake and moving about the stranger like a swarm of bees. They were all tending to his wounds and caring for him as best as they could. Much like Kumél, though, Ziminiar reacted suspiciously and apprehensively. Neither one of them was enthusiastic about helping Loham.

In his delirium and because of the darkness of the night before, Loham had walked past the sleeping company. They had not seen or heard him or the tulwyth, so it appeared to them he had been there before they had arrived and, somehow, they had missed his tracks along the way.

"We will remain here until Loham recuperates a bit," Shu decided.

It would not take Loham long to mend, for the nephesh, as was true with most of the immortals, were quick healers. As the day progressed, Loham was walking better, and the swelling of his face and mouth had reduced so he was able to talk with the others and see his way around. Loham had never been around free nephesh nor had he ever seen gallues like Kumél and Ziminiar. He had also never experienced kindness like he had within the company of Shu. However, he was most surprised by the unusualness of Shu and Ross, for they were unlike the others. He had never seen a Theoscian or a sapien before; though, for reasons he could not have explained, he found them mysteriously familiar.

Loham worried about Huzesh's warning. The savage beating had left more than physical wounds and scars on him; it had broken his will, stolen his hope, and replaced it with fear. The fear was gaining rule over his mind, and as it grew, Loham felt himself falling into the oblivion of shadows, consumed by a torrent of oppressive terror. The words of Huzesh were like the whip of a slave's master, striking violently upon the back of his conscience.

Loham planned to keep his distance, to stay aloof, so he would not develop concern or feelings for these strangers, especially for the foreigner. Loham was confused, however, about who exactly the foreigner was. Was it Shu or was it Ross? He did not know. What he did know, was that he had better learn which one it was before he tried to lead the group to Huzesh. He would have to find a way to gain their trust in order to journey with them. Loham was not the scheming sort—it was not in his nature—so deceiving these strangers was going to be difficult. He was especially concerned about Kumél, who continued to watch his every move. Loham could feel Kumél's eyes on him, sizing him up, looking for any sign that he could not be trusted.

Zoësh was unusually alert and uneasy in her manner. She whispered to Shu, "Shu, I know that we must wait here for now, but there is danger on the loose. I feel it. It comes toward us; it comes after us. We are being hunted."

"I have felt it too, and Ziminiar has warned me as well, but we must not let it take hold of our hearts. The darkness is not what it seems. The danger of those who pursue us is real but it will not succeed."

"What should we do?"

"Just what we are doing. We must not cower to this fear that attacks our resolve, and we must find the Pool of Levitus."

"But what will we find at the Pool of Levitus? Why do we go there? It feels like we are walking into a place we will have no escape from."

"Those things which are meant to be found at the Pool of Levitus cannot be found anywhere else. Zoësh, it is not for us to decide what is needed and what is not. We have been told that we must go to Levitus, and so we will. Those dangers that pursue us, and those that await us will not stop us."

"What about the stranger, do you trust him?"

"I trust only what I know he can be."

As the company of Shu sat idle, waiting for the health and strength of Loham to return, they each grew more uneasy. Idleness has a way of igniting troublesome torment in the minds of those surrounded by peril.

Ziminiar was aware the darkness was shadowing the company. It would take them another two days to reach the Pool of Levitus, but the darkness was coming swiftly, and the storm would soon be upon them. If they did not reach the pool before the storm overtook them, then they would never be able to find a way up the towering veil of Jaarah Falls. As the sunlight changed from yellow to orange, and the tops of the mountains turned blood red, Ziminiar pulled his dukwán from his bag and began to play, hoping the music would break the spell of idleness that was working in the hearts of all.

The deep, guttural sounds of Ziminiar's dukwán echoed throughout the gorge. The music drew everyone to him and soon, with a hot fire burning, they all gathered round to listen. None of them made any effort to join in, for the music was a melody they all needed to hear and wanted to hear. Even Loham was comforted by it as he, like the others, sat hypnotized by the wordless melody.

Seerae could see Loham was very consumed by the melody, so she waited for him to look her way before she asked, "What happened to you?"

He smiled cordially at her. "I, I don't really remember much. I think it was a gallue. There are many around."

"How did you get away?"

The others were listening by now, and they too were interested in

Loham's story, the story he was making up on the fly with no way of escaping from it. "Well, it happened kind of suddenly, you know, like out of the blue. One minute I was walking along and then . . . there he was! I tried to run, but well, I just didn't get away quick enough. Guess I must have made him mad, 'cause he just started beating me."

"Thought ye cunna rumumbar much," challenged Kumél.

"Yes, and why did he cease the beating?" Msusi asked.

"I . . . I don't really know, but when he did, I was able to crawl away. I found this place where the stream flowed, and it looked like a good place for me to hide from him. I followed it; that's how I got up here."

"He didn't follow you?" Zoësh asked skeptically.

"Not that I could tell. Of course, I couldn't tell much, I couldn't see much."

Seerae pressed him. "And you don't know where he went?"

"Nope, no idea. Not sure I want to know."

"Hmm." Kumél was unconvinced. "A ha nae'er saen u gallue lut u neph escape. Dae ha gud noses un cun track ye down bae yer blood. Ut bae u maet fishy t'mae. Bae ye sur, Loham?" The word rang from Kumél's lips like the sound of bell. It rang in everyone's ears with a clear and distinct implication.

"Kumél, you have no reason to distrust Loham. He didn't come to us and could not have been following us; he was in too bad of shape. Please, do not be cruel."

"Uf ut bae as ye say, thun d'gallue mae stull bae huntin ye, un no one bae safe uf dae bae wit ye."

Kumél's remarks hung heavy in the air like the morning fog. There would be no dancing or singing or merriment that night. They all sat quietly around the fire until, one by one, they fell asleep.

Everyone rose early the next morning, except Loham, and he would have been left behind had it not been for Seerae. She asked Shu, "Are we going to leave him here, alone? He will surely be found."

Kumél was quick to speak, even before Shu. "Ee came haer on ees own un ee wull fin ees wae buk. Wae dunna naed t'take eem wit us, d'wae?"

Seerae's glare chastised Kumél. "I wasn't asking you, Kumél. Shu, what do you think?"

"Let's ask him. Where is he?"

"He is still sleeping over there behind that rock."

By the time Shu and Seerae got to Loham, he was awake and aware of the controversy over what they were going to do about him. "Good, you're awake. We are about to leave; do you want to come with us or remain on your own?" Seerae's direct candor was surprising considering her usual manner. It was as if she was unsure whether she wanted Loham to come with them, yet it was her objection to leaving him behind that prompted their inquest.

"Well, I suppose, since you want me to go, I will. After all, you might need me," Loham answered mischievously. It was obvious he was in much better spirits than he had been the day before.

Shu offered Loham assistance getting up. "Looks like Loham is part of the company now. Treat him well."

As satisfying as it was to Loham to be included in the company of Shu, the lingering antagonism of his real mission haunted him. He wasn't certain he could convince Ziminiar or Kumél, who were already suspicious of him, that he was not a snitch. Kumél's accusation had cut into his conscience and, along with making him feel like an unwelcomed outsider, had also made him feel even more ashamed for being what he was and for doing what he was planning to do. Loham was deeply conflicted and unsure of what exactly he would do if the opportunity arose to carry out the treachery for which he had been sent. He knew the only way he could do what he had come to do, was to keep his distance from the others, in both proximity and in fellowship. He needed to remain an outsider for them to not to embrace him in the same way they embraced each other. He thought it would make his dirty deeds easier. This was his intention yet, with each passing interaction and conversation, something else deep in the hollowness of his soul, was taking root. A desire to be accepted into the small clan had been planted in him. Not just accepted into their numbers as another member, but also, more importantly, accepted as a friend. The force of this desire was growing stronger than his villainous intent.

Shu called out, "Let us be off."

The scene of the cascading falls and the sparkling mist reflecting the morning sun was immaculate perfection. Ross stood alone at the edge of a small meadow filled with flowers, trees, and tall grass, all nourished by the sweet waters of the falls; he appreciated the unspoiled beauty of it. The meadow was protected on all sides by rocks and mountains and cliffs. At the bottom of the falls, lay a small but deep lake of crystalline water. Ross stepped gradually away from the shore of the lake until he was wading barefoot in it. The water was cold like ice, but it did not matter, for all of his senses were captivated by everything that stood before him. More than all the wonders of the world he had seen, and all the magical places he had been, this place possessed his soul. It was not just the scenery, there was something spiritual about how he was feeling; something ethereal was touching him.

He recalled a time when he and Eve stood together, barefoot, in a cold mountain lake after a long day of climbing.

"Hey, what are you doing all by yourself?" The soft voice startled Ross. It was accompanied by a wave of water hitting him in the back that Seerae had kicked at him. "Wow, this water's cold! Stop it, Seerae! Stop, you're getting me all wet!"

Seerae kicked the water at him multiple times. "Oh, a drop of water won't hurt you."

Ross scooped a handful of water and hurled it at her. Like carefree children, Ross and Seerae played together until they were both soaked and cold. Ross looked into Seerae's eyes and remembered Eve. He swallowed deep and smiled, and she smiled back at him.

"Well, I think you look slightly better now that you're cleaned up a bit," Seerae teased.

"Oh, thanks to you!"

"Someone had to do it."

"Is this the Pool of Levitus?" Ross asked.

"I'm not sure, Ross." Seerae replied.

Not far away, Zoësh stood looking at the pool and the falls. She wore a confused expression on her face. "Is this where we were supposed to be going?"

"Nae." The rough voice came from behind Seerae. Ziminiar continued, "Ut bae Jaarah Loch. Da pool bae at da top o'da falls."

Zoësh examined the falls. "Ziminiar, how are we supposed to get up there?"

"A tol ye, ut waer protected. Ye dud nut tink ut wud bae easy, dud ye?"

"Well, it seems to me the journey here would be enough to keep almost anyone away. What's so special about the pool?"

"Eloh created da Pool o'Levitus wun ee brung Amik un Livia t'Shuk. Ut waer created fur da nephs. Da pool allows thum t'see who dae waer, wun da waters rise un da twin moons glow un da night sky."

Zoësh was confused by Ziminiar's explanation. "If it's for the nephesh, then why haven't we ever heard of it before? You said it was just a myth."

"Nae, A says mony b'laeve ut t'bae u myth. A ha nae'er saen ut wit mae own eyes, but ut bae no myth. Ut bae da dark magic o'Attar thut kaeps ye nephs frum knowin bout ut."

"Why haven't you seen it, and how can you be sure it's there?"

"Da wae bae protected frum da gallues un da liks o'mae. Ony da nephs un da clan o'Amik bae allowed t'enter."

"You see, Zoësh, Shuk was never meant to be the way it is now. This land was designated as a home for the nephesh, a place where they would be free and safe, and their song would be free." Shu's voice seemed to come from out of nowhere, surprising her. The others who were following behind Shu also listened in. "So, what happened?"

"The gallues happened, Zoësh. When Eloh agreed to the Covenant of Elements with Attar, Attar was already planning to capture and imprison the nephesh. It was not known that in his cunning and scheming way, Attar had already sent The Twelve and their legions to Shuk. But believing Attar would honor and keep the covenant, Eloh agreed to send the nephesh here, certain they would be safe."

"But why doesn't he come back and see what is happening here?" Zoësh replied.

"The Covenant of Elements bound Eloh to the agreement that Attar would free the nephesh from the pit and send them to Shuk as long as Eloh promised to stay in Assuk, away from Tirnan and Shuk. In exchange, Attar also vowed that no harm would come to the nephesh, though he never actually agreed to let them be free. There was one proviso, however, that Eloh was granted time with Amik before Amik died. Attar demanded, that Eloh spend the time with Amik here, in Shuk, and that is why Amik is buried in the Cave of Pella. It was during that time with Amik that Eloh made the Pool of Levitus and the Falls of Jaarah. This was the last place Eloh and Amik worked together, their final creations. The pool was their gift to the nephesh, a place of remembrance and revelation, a place to look back and discover who they were meant to be. The pool reminds them why they sing, why they play the dukwán, and why their hearts ache and long for wholeness. It wasn't until after the death of Amik and Livia, and after Eloh had departed, that Attar cast the spell on the valley and the nephesh were captured and imprisoned."

"Sounds like a dirty trick, what Attar did! He deceived Eloh!" Loham blurted out.

"Yes, he did. That's why Eloh did not know and could not know."

Confused, Msusi asked Shu, "But the covenant has been broken! Broken by the gallues who have enslaved us and killed many. And how is it that you have come, and Alethia? Haven't you broken the covenant as well?" Everyone could see Msusi was upset. Inwardly, each of them wondered how the gallues could get away with such blatant and evil acts against the nephesh.

Shu lowered his head, like he was ashamed. "There is much that has continued unseen for many ages. The power and deception of Attar's magic has blinded all of us to the cruelty and violation he and his minions have perpetrated on all. The rune that Norzaaq brought to Gubrone, the spell that was cast over the Valley of Souls, has concealed these atrocities, even from the elements themselves. But Attar is not the only one who is cunning. For all these ages, we did not venture here because Attar insisted it was forbidden by the covenant, but it was not so. Alethia found it only applied to Eloh, that it was only Eloh who could not return. At the time the covenant was written, Attar was so preoccupied with getting revenge on Eloh that he overlooked this and some other details. Without realizing it, a way—albeit a very narrow way— was made long ago. This way has only been found recently, and it is a bit like walking on the sharp edge of a sword in bare feet. So, we must tread lightly. The time of reckoning is growing near, and Attar will have his just reward. For now, we must do what we must do."

Kumél gazed at the falls, then asked Shu, "Alright, ha d'wae gut up dar?"

"The Way of Jaarah can only be found by the nephesh, since they are the only ones that can open the veil of the Jaarah Falls. Within the veil is a stone path that leads through the mountain and up to the pool."

"Ha cun Ross gae dar uf ut bae fur ony da nephs?"

"The way was designed so that none but the nephesh, Amik, and the Theoscians could travel it; it will not allow any others through. Ross is the seed of Amik, so the way will open to him."

A soaking wet and cold Ross approached the group as Shu was talking. "Hello. What do we have here? Someone call a town hall meeting and forget to tell me?"

Everybody silently stared at Ross.

"What? What's the matter? Have you never seen a wet man before? Nice pool, Ziminiar! I thought that we had another day of travel before we reached it."

Shu responded, "Oh, it's not too much farther, but that lake is not it, as you may have assumed."

"Oh. Oh well, I was just hoping." Ross was in an unusually good mood. The grime and dirt from the many days of hiking was gone, and a smile lit his face. "Alright, if that's not it, then where is it and, when do we head out?"

"Soon enough."

As Loham listened and watched, he felt Ross must be the foreigner, for it seemed that all the others, in one way or another, favored him. He wondered how he would ever get Ross away from the others and to where Huzesh waited, considering they were continuing in the opposite direction. He knew he had to be careful, so he kept to himself, pretending to be uninterested in what they were doing or where they were going. He tried not to listen too intently or at least not too obviously. He desperately wanted to squash any suspicions of himself, especially from Kumél or Ziminiar.

"If we cannot all go, then who will go, Shu?" Loham asked.

"We will leave Kumél and Ziminiar with Loham. They will stay here while the rest of us go to the pool."

Not wanting to appear eager, Loham agreed he should stay behind with Kumél and Ziminiar. However, he felt staying behind was a risk and wondered what he would do if Ross did not return. What would he tell Huzesh? Nevertheless, he knew he had to play the role, to pretend he agreed. He knew he had to wait for just the right moment and going to the pool did not seem to him to be the right opportunity.

Ross heard the plans and objected, "What are you talking about? Why can't we all go? Isn't it a bad idea to leave somebody behind? Besides, Kumél has been with me from the start, and I want him to go with me."

"Ross, Kumél can't go to the pool, neither can Ziminiar. I'm sorry. The way will not allow them. They are gallues and the way is made for the nephesh and the seed of Amik."

"But we will return this way, right?"

"Oh yes, definitely. There is no other way out of here. We will return here and rejoin our friends again soon. You will see."

Shu, Ross, Zoësh, Msusi, and Seerae prepared to go. For Ross, going to the Pool of Levitus had meant going home. He had crossed the many difficult miles driven by the hope of it. But now, even though he was not certain where it would lead him, he felt strangely calm.

"Everyone ready?" Shu called. "Let's go." A very faint trail cut through the tall grass along the shore of the lake. Shu and his small band hiked in a single file, toward the base of the falls.

"Hey, how far is it, Shu? Do you think we'll get there before dark?"

"It will take most of this sun to reach the pool."

"Great! Can't wait," Ross remarked with tempered optimism.

Near twilight, the hikers arrived at the towering cliff walls that formed the backdrop of the stunning Jaarah Falls. Their trail abruptly ended. It appeared the path had been devoured by a stone wall and to the other side was the water's edge and the cascading falls. Shu backed away from the wall and reminded Zoësh, "I may enter in, Zoësh, but the way will not open to me. It will only open to a nephesh. You must open the way."

"But I don't know how."

"Come. You will know what you must."

As Zoësh approached the waterfall, a unique sense of familiarity overwhelmed her. Even though she had never been to the falls or to the pool, she intuitively sensed where she needed to step to open the entrance to the Way of Jaarah. She tentatively waded into the pool until she was standing just within reach of the magnificent falls. The water continued to spray over her. "Nothing is happening, Shu. Are you sure about me? Maybe Msusi should do this."

"No, Zoësh, you can do this. All nephesh can do this. Step farther into the water. Don't be afraid."

Zoësh held onto the wet stone face of the cliff beside her as she stepped farther into the waist-deep water. The rocks below her feet were slick and mostly unstable.

"Again, another step."

The next step landed on a solid, flat surface. At Zoësh's next step, the falls divided. A luminous blue glow was revealed to the company, along with the entrance of an expansive hidden cavity, or a chamber, carved out of the rock behind the falls. In the center of the chamber, an enormously long, incandescent crystal rod hung vertically, its blue radiance too intense for the eye to behold. It lit not only the hidden chamber, but also a spiral column of steps that rose precipitously along the walls of a spherical rock shaft, the top of which could not be seen from the floor of the chamber.

Shu called out to Msusi and the others to follow Zoësh and after they were all in the chamber of stone, he followed behind.

"Wow! Now that's a staircase! When I was a boy, my friend and I broke into this old water tower not very far from his house. In the center of the tower was a tall steel tube with a staircase built into it that went straight up to the top. It looked like it went up forever, but of course, I was just a kid back then. Still, this seems a lot like that, only much, much higher!"

"What's a water tower?" Seerae asked curiously.

"Oh, sorry. It's just a big steel drum with a lot of water in it, nothing much. You wouldn't find it very interesting; I assure you."

"You will have to lead us, Zoësh. The way is now open to you," Shu urged.

Zoësh stepped onto the first stone block of the staircase. Each step was an individual stone which had been chiseled and stacked onto another. Each step was taller than normal, and the treads were narrow. As the steps rose above the floor, they appeared to be without any structure to support them.

Soon, Zoësh and the others were several hundred steps above the floor of the chamber, climbing higher into the mountain. The blue crystal rod was lighting their steps and giving them the feelings of safety and security, even though they were without railings or guards to protect them from falling. Finally, after many hours of climbing, the stairway ended at an arched passage that led into another grand chamber hewn out of the stone. The circular room was empty, and at the far end of it stood another stone archway flooded with soft, blue moonlight. The ebony stones on the floor of the chamber were peppered with flecks of sparkly minerals that glittered like fresh snow and reflected the dazzling moonlight onto the ceiling of the cavern. The searchers were enthralled as they entered this upper chamber. Zoësh ventured through the far archway and was bathed in the shimmering moonlight. Hanging over the top of a jagged spire was a glorious, blue full moon. It looked as if an artist had painted it in the sky. As Zoësh savored its loveliness, she glimpsed another full moon. This beautiful blue moon seemed shy, for it was hiding behind the first moon, sneaking a peak at its surroundings, too bashful to be noticed.

The brilliant moonlight illuminated the vast landscape for the small company. Spread before them was a pristine meadow, surrounded by rugged mountain peaks. The peaks stood jagged and tall and were unrelenting except for a narrow slot where a stream, fed by a pool in the middle of the meadow, cascaded over the cliff and into the valley below. This was the source of the Jaarah Falls. While the snowmelt from the surrounding mountains fed the small pool, it was apparent there was another source feeding the pool as well, for the volume of water flowing through the stream was constant and strong. The pool itself lay tranquil, as smooth as glass, and as clear as the morning sky on a cool spring morning. Its color was an unexpected, brilliant emerald green unlike anything else in the realm of Shuk. The water of the pool was temperate, as was the meadow surrounding it. Little tits flew about singing their welcome songs as though they had long-awaited the company of travelers. Along the shore of the pool grew many clusters of three or four enormous old trees with giant, full leaves. The branches and leaves of the trees swayed about in a gentle breeze that carried in its breath a wordless song meeting the searchers' ears like a soft whisper.

"This is it, Shu? This is the Pool of Levitus?"

"Aye, Ross. This is it."

"Wow! This place is unbelievable!"

The sky above the company was clear, not because it was devoid of clouds, but because the mountain peaks were holding the clouds back from their dreary intentions. Zoësh, Shu, and Ross were basking in the opulence adorning every part of the meadow. Their senses were experiencing something transcendent, beyond the extravagant physical beauty of the place. A celestial quality permeated every molecule of air and water and stratum of nature that existed in and around the meadow.

"I've never felt like this before!" Ross said in a sated tone.

Reflected in the Pool of Levitus were the twin blue moons. It was not often that twin moons were seen over Shuk, so the sight captured the attention of everyone. Seerae and Msusi marveled at the still, tranquil water. Seerae knelt and touched the water, but the water was not disturbed. It did not ripple or drip from her hand, instead, the water stayed as smooth as polished glass. She stirred it, but it remained serene, motionless. Then, to Seerae's astonishment, a voice spoke to her from the pool. *"Come."*

Seerae glanced about, searching for the one who had spoken to her.

"Come, see who you are."

Seerae looked at Msusi, who gave no indication of having heard the voice, as she gazed into the spectacular sky,

"Seerae, come. Step into the water and see who you are."

In complete wonder, Seerae hesitantly placed one foot into the pool, then the other, and stood still and silent, caressed by the warm water.

"Come. Come deeper and see what I have to show you."

Before anyone realized it, Seerae was standing up to her knees in the water. Still, there was no disruption to the water and the reflection of the moons was still perfectly sharp on the surface, but Seerae's reflection could not be seen.

Noticing her, Zoësh asked, "Seerae, what are you doing?"

Seerae continued to step deeper into the pool. Msusi was the first to notice several small bubbles of air surrounding Seerae and rising from the surface. Their number gradually increased to hundreds and then thousands, all lifting off the surface of the water. Now alerted to the situation, Ross joined Zoësh, and they hurried to the edge of the pool. By this time, Seerae was up to her chest in the water and still going deeper.

"Come and see yourself." The whisper spoke gently, persuading Seerae to take one step after another, deeper into the water.

"Shu, what's she doing?" Ross said to Shu, who was watching from a distance and did not appear concerned.

"Please, leave her be."

As the bubbles floated higher into the air, Ross thought they looked exactly like the tiny bubbles in a glass of champagne. He watched them float around Seerae. She was up to her neck in the water now and everything in him wanted to pull her out, but she was not afraid. She was not calling for help, and the atmosphere surrounding them seemed to be calming any worries or fears. Seerae paused with just her head above the water's smooth surface, and then, without a word, ducked her head into the placid waters of Levitus. Everyone looked to Shu, expecting him to do something. Seerae was nowhere to be seen, and the water showed no indication she had ever entered the pool; they could only see the bubbles rising from the water into the night sky.

"Should I go in after her? I can swim! Does she need help?"

"Don't worry, Ross. You will see."

The shiny, effervescent bubbles were rising from the water constantly and filling the area above the pool. They hung in the air, some high, some low, floating like tiny lanterns. In the middle of the pool, a reflection appeared, though it was not clear what it was. Ripples began to appear on the smooth surface of the water as the figure emerged from its depths. Everyone's expectation of seeing Seerae rise out of Levitus was swiftly dissatisfied, for the figure that rose from Levitus was not that of Seerae nor of a nephesh; rising out of the water, as if by some magical force, and floating on the air like the tiny bubbles, was someone unanticipated and unknown. Golden hair flowed to her waist and she wore a full-length gown that appeared to be colored in the light of the stars. It was luminescent and glimmering as if light were shining from within each strand of its fabric. She gradually ascended from the water and stood on its surface as if it was not water at all. Speechless and confused, they wondered who she was and where she had come from. She reminded Ross of the first time he had seen Msusi. She too had worn a long, white gown as she had walked through the woods.

As the woman on the water moved a few steps closer to him, Ross froze. Transfixed, his mouth dropped open and his eyes grew wide with shock and disbelief. His mind leafed through the library of memories, thoughts, and visions it had collected over the past months. Astounded, Ross remembered where he had seen her before. It had been on the mountain in the darkness, when he was hanging from the rope. This woman was the same one who had called out to him, the one who had told him he had to live and that he had to make it back home.

"Eve!" Ross yelled. The stupor was broken, and he could not hold back. He leapt into Levitus's calm water and raced to meet her. "Eve! Eve, it's you! You're here!" He was so enraptured by her he had failed to notice that he was running on the surface of the water. "Is it you? Is it really you?"

She ran toward him. "Ross, Ross!" Her voice struck Ross with such affection and honesty that time stopped for him. Everything around him vanished, and the only thing that remained were the two of them.

They collided into each other's arms in the pool, floating over the waters, suspended in air and time like the tiny bubbles. His heart beat with such fervor, he feared it might explode from his chest. His reaction was reckless, abandoned, and unedited, all the ways Eve had made him feel, and all the ways he had been unable to be. He could not contain his elation nor his unabashed love for her. Together, they cried and then they laughed. They held each other and whirled about like they were dancing in midair.

Ross refused to let the menace of doubt overtake the ecstasy washing over him like an ocean wave. He refused to remember Eve's fall into the darkness, to believe that he was somehow hallucinating or just dreaming. Ross touched her face, looked into her eyes, and kissed her lips. Every shared breath told him the moment was real, that Eve was real, but even if she was not, Ross would not allow these precious moments to fly away on the cruel, black wings of reality. "Is it you, Eve? Is it truly you or am I dreaming? Please tell me you are real, Eve! Tell me I'm not dreaming."

"You're not dreaming! I'm here, Ross. I'm here with you!"

"I don't know how this can be real, but it doesn't matter. Real or not, I have you. You're mine, and I'm never letting go of you."

As Eve held Ross, he cried, and the tears would not stop flowing.

Chapter XVII
Flame of Faith

During their unimaginable reunion, Ross and Eve shared an outpouring of words and emotions as if they had never been apart. They did not question why or attempt to understand how it had happened, they simply reveled in it, and wondrously, this reunion changed Ross. He realized life was more than only what was seen or felt or touched; it was amazing and inexplicable, even transcendent. For the first time ever, Ross understood what he had always refused to allow his heart to reveal. Until then, he had never been a man of faith or hope, his confidence had always been in those elements he could see and understand. For his life had been one of pain and sorrow, rejection and disappointment, and the idea that there might ever be something beyond the ruin of this world had always seemed preposterous to him. Even experiencing the amazing and unusual nature of Shuk and its inhabitants had barely altered the tainted presumptions that ruled over his expectations. But as he floated under the twin moons and gazed into the ethereal eyes of Eve, the bondage over his captive mind was broken. He was given liberties he had never imagined, freedom to search and find meanings and feelings that had always been beyond him.

Ross had experienced life differently with Eve. She had elevated him, lifted him out of his darkness and gloom and introduced him to the beauties and possibilities of life. He had admired Eve's sublime presence, and now he realized the transcendent beauty in her was beyond superficial; it was tangible. Ross had never truly appreciated Eve, not in the way she had deserved, but under the twin moons, the spell over his heart was broken, and his eyes were opened to the wonderful mystery of her ineffable beauty. He let himself float upon his thoughts of her, immersed and satisfied on an infinite, tranquil sea.

Eve was as she had always been, in the moment, living each breath as fully as the next. Her smile had been a light shining with warmth and brightness into Ross's often tortured and somber mind, dispelling its many tormentors. She loved him powerfully and had delved into the shadowy, hollow form of the man Ross had been and without words or speech, she had lovingly called the light and life out of the prison cell of his hardened heart.

"What do you see, Eve, when you look at me like that?"

"Oh, it's not so much what I see, it's who I see."

"Then, who do you see?"

"Ross, I see who it is that you can be! Who you can't see yourself, but yet, who you truly desire to be." Her words pierced him in the same way they always had, with sincere honesty and undeserved acceptance. She was the only one who could disarm him, the only one who had ever been able to tell him the truth about himself in a way that he believed.

"I can't believe you're here! I've missed you so much! I thought ... well ... I thought ..."

Eve immediately put her finger to his lips to stop him from saying anything more. She knew what he was about to say and did not want him to be burdened with that pain. "Shh, what you thought doesn't matter now. Let's not go back. Let's stay here, in this moment. Now, together."

"You're not going to tell me to wake up, are you? If this is a dream, I don't ever want to wake up."

"No, this isn't a dream you can awaken from."

"Good! Because right now everything feels even better than a dream. Can I tell you something, something you've heard me say before, but I never really understood before?"

"Yes, talk to me! You can tell me anything!"

"I love you! I love you so much, Eve! I never realized it before, 'cause I was always so caught up with myself and with everything I wanted. I'm so sorry that I never noticed you the way I should've, the way you deserved . . . I mean, the way you deserve!"

"I always knew you loved me, Ross. I think I believed it more than *you* did! You would've given your life for mine, even though you didn't know it . . . and you did try to. Please understand, I know that's what you tried to do."

"Even when I no longer wanted to live, your love for me kept me going. Every memory I have of you has kept me alive. I wish that I had loved you better, Eve, like you loved me," Ross uttered in a broken, barely audible voice, as tears rolled down his face.

Eve wiped away the tears and smiling at him with unrestrained tenderness, she conveyed her understanding, "Ross, I was never disappointed in your love for me. Who could be more meant for me? I've loved you from the first time I met you! I can't explain how, but I knew that there was no one else for me but you. Everything I am, every part of my being loves you, needs you, longs for you! It's as if I was always meant to love you. Your love has kept me alive and I am here because of you!"

For hours that felt like days, Ross and Eve talked and embraced, laughed, and cried. It was fresh and new for them, and they fervently desired to live forever in this moment together. They forgot about everything and everyone else during those hours of rapture. It was as if time had stopped for a season. But as all things in Shuk would attest, all idyllic moments pass away under the unrelenting inevitability of the new day's diffused glare.

As the morning sun ascended into the sky, the twin blue moons retreated behind the mountain tops, and the tiny bubbles of Levitus slowly descended into the still waters. Ross and Eve had spent the entire night reminiscing under the efflorescent canopy. They had never talked for so long and with such honest and mutual intimacy. But before Ross could comprehend how fleeting their encounter was to be, the magic of Levitus began to set, and the transformation of Seerae began to dissipate. Eve was spontaneously disappearing, and Ross was gradually sinking up to his waist in the pool, not even aware he had been suspended above the water for all those unforgettable hours. As the image of Seerae replaced Eve, Ross feared he was losing Eve all over again and just like the first time, there was no way for him to stop it. His heart ached with the pain of separation, yet he sensed their time was not over. He felt they would see each other again, *"when the twin moons rise and the Pool of Levitus lets loose its effervescent array."* He fought his fear of losing her and he fought the despondent doubt that relentlessly crept into his mind. He firmly hoped even though he had not dared to hope before.

Seerae stood in the clear waters of Levitus gazing back at Ross. For her, the night had seemed like a vision rather than reality. She had seen herself with Ross but not as herself. She had observed a part of herself she had never known, the part of her being that she had always been separated from. In her earlier dreams, Seerae had observed the woman known to Ross as Eve, but the visions had never seemed as though they could have been true, or that the woman in them could have been herself. She remembered feeling very strange when she had seen the same image of Eve in Ross's camera. It had caused her to wonder if there could be some invisible connection between herself and Ross, but she had mostly determined to forget her dreams and the photo, for they had made no sense to her. However, after experiencing the transforming power of Levitus, Seerae was coming to understand the looming mystery of it all.

For as long as she could remember, Seerae felt as if part of her being was searching for something. She had always wondered why she felt the deep ache of missing someone. But, for the first time ever, in the Pool of Levitus, Seerae established that a lost part of her being did exist. It was the missing part she had sought, and even though it was unfamiliar and detached, it was the very thing that would make her whole. She and Eve were meant to find each other because they *were* each other. Apart, they were both lost, but together they were whole.

The truth of Eve and Seerae being one struck Ross with the force of a fierce wave, bringing him to his knees. He did not want to believe it. He felt weak and nauseous, but he was gradually filled with an irrepressible hope, and with that hope, his strength returned. His mind was reeling with so many thoughts: thoughts of the moment, thoughts of the past, thoughts of the future, and about what was true and what was a myth. He wondered if his whole life had been some sort of an illusion, if he had been living a dream until he came to Shuk, and now he was living in the true reality. He wondered how Eve could be Seerae, how she could have stood there with him, holding him, laughing with him, when he was sure she was dead. He questioned whether she had really fallen.

But, if he had not seen what he thought he had seen, that would mean he was not actually present either and that they had not climbed the mountain. He concluded that if his whole life had been an illusion, then his time with Eve must have *also* been an illusion. However, Ross knew Eve was no illusion. He knew that she was genuine and he loved her. Ross gently took Seerae's hand and searched her eyes, "I have seen you before, only I didn't know it was you. You were always hiding behind her eyes, behind her smile, and in the shadows of her thoughts. I can see you now! You're so clear to me!"

"What do you mean, Ross?"

"There was something about you that seemed familiar to me, something I couldn't figure out before. You and Eve, how could I have missed it? You were standing right in front of me, but I couldn't see who you were!"

"But I didn't understand who I was, either . . . not really. I always felt that there was someone I was a part of or that a part of me was missing, but I had no idea who or what it was. I knew that you were a part of my story. I felt drawn to you from the very first time I saw the snowpetals, and I knew that I had to find you."

"But you never said anything."

"What could I say? Until now I had no idea what my feelings meant, but now I understand. You and I are drawn together because Eve is a part of both of us! Our lives are drawn together by one invisible force. Oh, Ross! Isn't it wonderful? This means that there is another one, like me, who is searching for you! He is trying to find his way back to you, only he doesn't know, like I didn't know. He doesn't know who he's looking for!"

"Another one like you, Seerae? What are you talking about?"

"Ross, don't you get it? A nephesh! There's a nephesh searching for you, trying to find you, like I was trying to find Eve. That part of who you are that's lost is trying to find you, only they don't know who they are looking for."

Ross was confused by what Seerae was saying, and yet it struck a chord with him and, oddly enough, he felt himself responding to it. The words rang like a bell. He heard them over and over: *that part of who you are that's lost*. Lost. Ross had felt lost. He had sometimes questioned whether a part of himself was missing, a part he could not identify or understand. He had hoped Eve would be the one to fill the void in his life, and she did fill it for a while, but this part of himself had been missing for

471

much longer than he had known her. Ross was aware that as vast as his emptiness was, it would be impossible for Eve to overcome the enormity of it. It was truly too cavernous for any person to fill, but Ross did not want to consider that now, he only wanted to be with Eve. "Seerae, can you please not say anything more? I know you mean well, but I don't want to think about anything else right now. Please?"

Seerae turned away, but Ross pulled her back. "Don't go, Eve, don't leave me again." He looked desperately into the deep, blue, waterless sea of Seerae's eyes, searching for Eve, but all he could find was his own reflection.

"You can see her again when the sun sets, and the twin moons return this night." The sound of Shu's voice startled them both. Ross noticed him seated on a large stone near the pool. "Huh? What did you say?"

"You will have more time with her. Come again when the sun sets, and you will see Eve. As long as the twin moons hang over Shuk, the magical waters of Levitus are active under their glow. You can come again, both of you."

"When the moons have gone, when will they return again?"

"The twin moons only shine on Shuk once in a millennium, Ross. It will be a very long time before they come again."

"Then there's only a little time before she's gone forever! Shu, does she have to go? Does she really have to go? It would almost be better if she was a dream! At least I could handle that. But I can't lose her again! Oh, God! I don't know how to deal with this! It's so cruel!"

For just a moment, Seerae felt the pain of Ross's rejection, but it was immediately replaced by weightless joy and satisfaction. Her flight was not burdened by the ephemeral transformation or the finiteness of passing moons. Her heart soared above the comprehensible into the boundless heavens on wings spread by the forces of destiny. She had seen her true self and with that vision, came memory, truth, and hope. The promise of wholeness was growing inside her. The light of it radiated from every part of her being, and the others could see what they had always wanted to see.

The Pool of Levitus provided only a temporary transfiguration, but it gave the nephesh an irrevocable validation that those things which seemed only to be dreams were, in fact, true memories. They were not true in Shuk, but they were true, nonetheless.

While Seerae was delighting in her experience of transformation and the vision of her fullness, Zoësh and Msusi were feeling deep pangs of sorrow over it. The sad reality that Seerae's transformation, as genuine as it was, would never be completed because Eve had gone into the shadows never to return, burdened their minds. The two nephs understood the truth Seerae had not yet realized, and it weighed so heavily upon them that a deep, groaning melody flowed from within their hearts.

Msusi blew into her dukwán and from the belly of the hollow wooden instrument came a haunting ancient melody that filled the protected domain of Levitus. The deep voice of the dukwán was resonant, determined, and grieved. The notes reverberated through the air as if they were spirits conjured by the skill of a wizard. Sorrowful, plaintive notes and languid, painful sounds echoed throughout the meadow. Zoësh felt sad words welling up from within her. The lyrics formed somewhere beyond her understanding, and she hesitated to sing them. Her lips quivered as she released the mournful song:

Oooh Oooo, Oooh Oooo.
Where have you gone, oh soul of mine?
Where have you run to, where have you hid?
I have been looking, never to find,
Never to know you, never to be you.
Where have you gone to, oh soul of mine?

I tried to reach for you; I tried to see you once.
I tried to feel your pain, to taste your sorrow.
I tried, I tried but I could not find you.
Where have you gone, oh soul of mine?

Please, please, please don't leave me here alone!
In these shadowy lands,
My eyes grow dark and my heart is broken!
Where have you gone to, oh soul of mine?

If you find me, if you see me,
The me I've lost; I'm supposed to be.
If you hear me, my voice, my cry,
Free me from this life that will die!

Fill me, fill me as you once did!
Heal me of the brokenness that I've hid!
I am lost, I am lost, oh soul of mine.
I am lost in the shadows,
Lost, and broken and
blind.

Oh, where have you gone, oh soul of mine?
Where have you run to, where have you hid?
I have been looking never to find you,
Never to know you, never to be you.
Oh, where have you gone to, oh soul of mine?
Ooooh Oooo, Ooooh Oooo.

The slow, desperate cadence of the dukwán pulled at every defiant strain as if each word had to be forced from its imprisonment, like a desperate heart grasping for its soul, like mortality calling out to immortality, the ephemeral reaching across the cavernous void for eternity. Zoësh sang the words with such anguish even the forces of nature began to weep. The open sky above Levitus filled with restless, dreary clouds and fragile flakes of snow were driven and uneasy. The glory of the sun disappeared behind the gathering clouds and their surroundings changed from lush and green to dull and gray.

Ross did not understand the sorrow of the two nephesh. He had been with Eve. He had heard her voice and touched her, and his heart had felt buoyant and full. He was confused as Zoësh sang each verse of the broken lyric. The conviction in her voice reached across the distance and touched him, and he wondered how such a beautiful moment could change to one so forlorn and sad. Just like Seerae, Ross did not understand what Zoësh and Msusi already knew, and he did not know where their song was coming from. Eventually, his eyes were drawn to the night that was closing in around them, and he was astonished. He wanted to ask Shu what was wrong, but something kept him from it, something he could not resist.

Seerae now felt the same sadness and pain Zoësh and Msusi were feeling. She closed her eyes and could see a still silhouette of a lone figure in the shadows of her mind, staring at her. She tried to get a closer look so she could identify who it was, but her eyes were unable to vanquish the darkness. As the song of Zoësh continued, Seerae felt her heart beat faster. Each word and each note drew her nearer to the shadowy figure until she became aware the one in the shadows was the one from whom the music and words came. She heard its voice whispering the melody, sending each line into the heart of Zoësh and Msusi. She realized it was not their song or their words, but that they were singing the song of the voiceless shadow, and not just one shadow or one voice, but a sea of shadows, all crying out the same sad song in one, lonely, quiet voice.

Seerae reached out and called to the shadow to console it, to ease its pain, but she could not reach it and her words were not heard. Her heart beat stronger and faster with futile urgency. She tried with all her inner strength to reach the shadow, but it backed away and fell into the darkness.

"No! No, don't go! Please, don't go! Come back!" Seerae stretched out her arms to rescue the still silhouette, but the figure was unable to reach back to her. It drifted away on a tormented sea of blackness filled with faceless shadows. Seerae dropped to her knees, her face wet with tears. She did not know why she cried, but there was something about the shadow that felt familiar. She peeled back the layers of her memory, hoping to remind herself who it was she had seen or heard, but the answers would not come. She was concerned the vision was more than just a vision. She sensed that what she had seen needed to be understood, but she worried that understanding might uncover a painful revelation she might not wish to know.

Ross was uncertain why Seerae was suddenly so contrite, but as the ache of the song filled the air, he tried to console her, "Seerae, it'll be OK. Don't cry; there's still tonight. Shu said the moons will rise again this evening. Please, don't cry."

Seerae was inconsolable. "Listen, Ross! Listen to them. Can you feel their words?"

Ross listened but felt nothing. The song was just a song to him, and he was not that moved by it.

Shu assured Ross, "The time will come soon enough and you will understand. So do not worry yourself now."

A ray of sunlight broke through the thick clouds, falling like a massless stone and striking the fragile surface of the Pool of Levitus with such disruptive force that invisible ripples radiated from its epicenter, shattering the gloom of the moment and causing an eruption of life and beauty to spring from its conspicuous yet intangible arrival. They all felt the comforting warmth of the sunlight. It rapturously filled the meadow with golden brightness as if cueing a cadenza. The song of Zoësh ceased and Msusi laid down her dukwán. Seerae dried her tears, and Ross regained his smile. Yet while their spirits were lifting once again, there remained, deep within them, a shadow and a pain. Each of them had been smitten by the power of the song and its cutting sharpness on their souls.

Huzesh grew agitated as he waited for Loham to return. He was never one to demonstrate much in the way of patience and although he was calculating, his impetuous nature often interfered with his ill-conceived schemes. He began to distrust his decision to send Loham ahead and to make matters worse, he could feel a storm closing in. His voice echoed from the conversation he carried on with himself, "Whaer bae thut snitch. A shud nae'er ha trusted eem. Ee wull b'trae mae, un A wull rip out ees heart."

The wind picked up his words and swirled them around, causing his own voice to speak back to him in an antagonizing manner. It sounded as if there were many voices, all repeating the same things. Huzesh became entranced and out of his senses, until the wind threatened to blow out his small fire. Huzesh picked up several branches and threw them onto the flames. It was not long before delicate flakes of snow began to fall. With the arrival of the snow came a cold nip of air that bit at Huzesh's face. He stepped closer to the flames and was once again drawn back into the spell of his malevolent thoughts.

On the crooked, overhanging branch of a popinus tree, a corvus landed among its many spiny needles that covered the ends of its branches. The bird seemed quite uncomfortable with its make-do perch, flapping its wings and stepping carefully around the forbidding nest. Huzesh's attention was caught by the bird's antics. By now, he was beginning to feel the pangs of hunger and looked at the bird with the hope of an easy meal, waiting as it continued to dance around the sharp spines. Then, he thought that maybe the corvus could be of some assistance to him.

It occurred to Huzesh he should find Loham, just in case Loham failed him, or worse, betrayed him and warned the foreigner. The thought of betrayal made Huzesh even more irritable and impatient. Unable to wait any longer, Huzesh grabbed his things, stretched out his hand toward the black bird, and waited. The corvus blinked, tipped its head back and forth, then finally stood up from its prickly nest, and flew to Huzesh. Huzesh put the bird on his shoulder and walked toward the gorge.

The sky grew darker, the snow fell much heavier, and the stream through the gorge gradually transformed into a terrifying torrent that seemed bent on resisting his efforts. But, Huzesh would not be turned away from his mission. He stubbornly pushed his way up the gorge, step by defiant step, as the snow made every rock and crack slick and dangerous to negotiate.

The corvus, who had expected an easier journey, was also being covered by the snow, so it decided to fly ahead of Huzesh and seek shelter from the storm. After many long hours of fighting the storm and the increasingly inhospitable trail, Huzesh reached the foot of the cliff over which the stream flowed. He searched for a way to climb it, but the icy snow would not let him. It blinded his eyes and nipped at his face with icy fangs like it was angered by his defiance. So instead, Huzesh hunted for a shelter for himself. He explored the rocks and eventually discovered a hiding place, which was not a cave, but a large hollow behind the waterfall. It was not much of a shelter, just a shallow, damp depression, but it was better than being exposed to the full fury of the storm. Huzesh had to go through the waterfall to access the shelter, which thoroughly drenched him, but it did not matter by then; wet was wet.

Kumél, Ziminiar, and Loham were sitting under the boughs of an old pine that was keeping the snow off of them like an umbrella. They had built a small fire, which helped to stay the bitter night air. Loham hummed in harmony with an eerily strange tune that was carried on the wind and filled his ears and mind with discordant strains. The air of his song was conflicted and drawn, conjured up from his own conflicted soul. The dreary melody caught the attention of Ziminiar. "Loham, wut bae ye singin o'er dar?"

"Me? I'm not singing, just humming. I'm not sure what it is, though. Can't you hear it in the wind? The song?"

Ziminiar closed his eyes and listened more carefully. He heard a faint melodic tune dancing in his ears, and it strangely caused him to feel exposed, vulnerable, and indefensible. He listened to it for a while, then he started to hum it just as Loham had been.

Kumél's attention was drawn to Ziminiar and Loham as they hummed together in near- perfect harmony. As the timbre and tone resonated with Kumél, he again sang the strange unknown song of Jupnie.

Neither Loham nor Ziminiar had ever heard the song Kumél was singing, nor had they ever heard that language, and although they were perplexed by the unknown voice of his words, they were more disquieted by the message of the song, which circumvented their lack of understanding and vexed their souls with its encrypted meaning.

Like the smoke from their fire, the tune wafted through the gorge and over the waterfall until it filled the hollow where Huzesh rested. It filled his ears with its infectious lyrics until he began humming. The words superseded his consciousness and like the sharp point of a kerolus spear, bore into his disturbed mind. His lips whispered the strange language of the Jupnie until the corvus expressed a loud objection.

Huzesh woke to the disrupting melody coming from his mouth and shook his head to clear the delirium. He was soon conscious of the mysterious song in the air and put his hand to his ear to block it. Huzesh determined not to close his eyes or rest; he squatted down, guarding his thoughts and his ears against the bewitching wind and its unwelcome spirit voice.

When morning finally arrived, Huzesh resumed his mission, unaware he was much closer to his quarry than he expected. He climbed the narrow line Ross and the others had climbed just days before, and when he reached the top of the falls, he cautiously peeked over the edge to see what lay ahead, and the corvus flew a little ways ahead of him. Seeing there was no sign of the foreigner or his group, Huzesh hoisted his hulking frame over the edge and surveyed the long, narrow meadow carefully. Since the valley was flat and featureless, and Huzesh did not want to give himself away, he decided to wait until dark before he went further. So, he hid among the rocks and boulders and gestured for the corvus to join him. The corvus eyed Huzesh suspiciously, but Huzesh was a master of the birds, and eventually lured the corvus to him again. Huzesh spoke to the corvus in his strange tongue and instructed the bird to search for Loham and to lead him back to the hiding place. "Dunna fail mae, ye liddle beast! Now gae!" The bird spread its broad, powerful wings and flew away.

At the far end of the meadow, Loham sat alone on a rock at the edge of the small lake, close to Kumél and Ziminiar. His elbows resting on his knees and his chin in his palm, he was humming quietly and tapping his foot with nervous energy. He brooded over how long it would be before Ziminiar, Kumél, or one of the others figured out he was indeed a snitch. He felt vulnerable and alone. He hoped if he stayed to himself, they might not discover his secret. He contemplated how he could lure Ross away from the others and how he would manage to lead him to Huzesh. The whole plan was not settling well with him and the more he thought about it, the more reluctant he grew. Nevertheless, he knew the ruthlessness of Huzesh, and what would happen to him if he failed. There was, however, more to Loham's dilemma than the fear of being discovered, or the fear of Huzesh. Loham struggled with himself, with who he was and what he was, and that struggle had begun to distill the inner darkness, making him question his role in life as a snitch. There was a part of him that wanted to tell someone, to expose the darkness rather than be exposed, but he doubted anyone would ever understand or believe he could change his ways. In Shuk, nothing ever seemed to change.

"You are what you are," one of his gallue masters had said, and Loham had always believed it. However, now, from inside of himself, he was hearing something different. He wanted to believe it, embrace it, and accept that he was better than what he had become. He wanted to hope he could be like Zoësh, who had helped him, or Ross, or even Shu, but his mind would not let him see beyond the reflection staring back at him from the surface of the water. He found himself daydreaming about a life that was different, free of the weight of darkness. The melody he was humming was lifting his spirits, so he continued to hum, not knowing from where the melody came or where it went.

"Thut bae u nice liddle tune ye bae singin, Loham. Wut bae ut?" Ziminiar's voice startled him.

"Ahh, I don't really know, Ziminiar. It just seems to be dancing about in my head."

"Ahh, music, ut bae u swaet ting. D'ye rumumbar da ol days, Kumél, bak un Anima? Da songs o'Pardis dud fill da great halls on da norõ porch. Ut waer u lung tam ago."

"Tae lung, til jus now. D'ye rumumbar ha Attar dud sing, un Eloh tae, afore da war?"

"Aye, Kumél, ut waer u great tam, u great tam indeed. Fur ages A nae'er thought o'Pardis or Eloh, or da music."

"Ut bae ony u short tam ago. A d'rumumbar."

"Aye."

"Ziminiar, d'ye tink those days wull er com agan?"

"Ohhhh, so much tam ha passed, who knows uf such tings cun com agan. Wut d'ye tink, Kumél? D'ye tink thut dose days wull er com agan?"

"Nae. Dar bae tae much darkness un da realm, tae much brokenness."

"What about . . . well . . . you know, Ross? What about him?"

"Ee com frum da mountain. A know, A waer da one thut foun eem."

"The mountain? What mountain?"

"Ye ask tae mony questions, Loham."

Loham remembered he needed to act more uninterested, so he reserved his questions and turned away.

"Oh, but A d'lung fur dos days un Anima. A yaern t'sae Eloh agan, un t'plae mae tenush on da norõ porch."

"Yur u draemer, Ziminiar. Ye always ha baen."

"Aye. Yur right Kumél, but ye ha no draems un no hope! Yur poisoned bae da shadows o'dis place un bae da curse o'Attar. Uf ye wud jus luk, luk deep unta yer haert, b'yond da shadows o'yer memories, ye tae might sae da hope un ye maet liv agan. Wae maet liv agan, as wae once dud! Ut bae u gut draem!"

"Aargh!" Kumél walked away in frustration.

Loham dwelled on the things Ziminiar had said about living again and dreaming. He wondered if the visions he had seen in the fire and what he was hearing from his own heart was what Ziminiar was talking about. He wanted to tell Ziminiar about his visions, to ask him if he might know what they meant, but he was afraid to tell anyone, afraid they might, in some way, reveal who he truly was.

Ziminiar walked back to the slowly dying fire that was exhaling a gray plume of steadily rising smoke. Loham was left with only the reflection of himself in the water. He stared intently, searching for something he felt was hiding inside of himself, something that lived behind the masked and wounded face looking back at him.

As Loham stared at his reflection, a shadow soared across the water. Puzzled, he scanned the sky, but the shadow had disappeared. He returned his focus to his reflection and right away, next to his reflection, he saw a swarthy, winged creature growing larger and larger. Loham glanced up, and was startled by an immense, menacing corvus that swooped out of the sky and landed near him. He cautiously backed away, worried there were more birds, for it was rare to see a single corvus. The bird hopped after him and at Loham's next backward step, his foot caught in a hole and he stumbled to the ground. He wasn't aware the satchel he was carrying had fallen from his shoulder to the rocks beside him. The sneaky corvus swiftly grabbed the satchel. Loham noticed the theft and jumped toward the bird, but he was unsuccessful at retrieving his bag; the corvus had flown away.

He ran after the corvus. It taunted him; landing just far enough away that Loham would continue his pursuit, but never close enough to catch. Loham followed in complete oblivion to the cunning intent of the corvus as it led him closer to the gorge and toward Huzesh.

Hiding behind a jumbled mound of rocks, Huzesh had positioned himself so he could view the narrow meadow without detection. He watched as Loham unsuspectingly chased after the corvus. Eventually the bird landed on a rock close to Huzesh and dropped Loham's satchel. As Loham drew close, the corvus, once again, flew away. Loham rushed to grab his bag, but Huzesh grabbed him by the neck and pulled him behind the pile of rocks. "So, bae ye happy t'sae mae?" Huzesh held Loham suspended in the air, choking him with his strong grip. "A bae missin ye, mae fren. Whaer bae da forner?"

Loham could not answer; his face had turned red, and his eyes were bulging from behind their lids. He tried desperately to break the grip Huzesh had on his neck to no avail. Huzesh gazed at him with sinister indifference, pleased to be watching him struggle. But shockingly to both Loham and to Huzesh, an unexpected surge of power came over Loham, and, for the first time ever, he found his strength, the strength all nephesh unknowingly possessed. He bent back Huzesh's thumb, with bone-breaking force until Huzesh finally let go.

Loham slumped to the ground hard, hitting his head on a rock and ripping a lengthy gash in his leg. "Ahh!" Huzesh immediately put his hand over Loham's mouth to smother his cry, but Loham grabbed Huzesh's hand again and pulled it away. Huzesh put his giant foot on Loham's chest and leaned over it to exert as much pressure on him as possible. Loham could not free himself from the weight of Huzesh's hulking body, so he stopped fighting. "Stop! Let me up!" Loham pleaded in a hushed voice.

Huzesh put one of his fingers up to his mouth, gesturing to Loham to keep quiet. "Wull ye promise t'kaep quiet? Un ye wull nut trae t'run?"

"I won't run." But Loham secretly realized a fact that he had never before known. He was strong. When he had pulled Huzesh's hand away, it had been an impulse, a reaction, and the fact that Huzesh's grip had been broken astonished him. He felt wild, almost reckless with this newfound strength. Loham even considered lifting Huzesh's considerable weight from his chest, but discretion regained its prudent restraint, and he chose instead not to show his hand.

Huzesh grinned sinisterly at Loham as a deep guttural growl rolled out of his throat, "Weel now, ha ye foun da forner?"

"I have, but I fear that we may be on a fool's errand. He's not at all what I would have expected. I mean, he seems to be no threat at all, kind of weak if you ask me."

Huzesh glared at Loham and threatened, "Ye bes nut trae t'deceive mae, Loham!"

"No, not at all! I mean it! The foreigner is nothing like I imagined, but—"

"But wut?"

"Well, the other one, he, he is different."

"Da other one? Wut other one?"

"They call him Shu. There is something unusual about him, something quite unique."

Huzesh had not heard that name in ages. He remembered very little of him but knew he was one like Eloh. His thoughts did not stay on Shu for long. He quickly returned to questioning Loham.

"Dae? Who bae dae? Ha muny?"

"There are two giant gallues who are very powerful but different from you, then there are three nephs, the foreigner, and Shu."

"Two gallues, aye? Wut bae dae called?"

"One is called Kumél, the other, his name is Ziminiar."

"Apostas. A ha haerd o'dis Kumél, ee bae da one thut bested Gubrone. Ziminiar, ee bae u loner. Few ha er saen eem. Un Shu, fur wut raeson bae da great Shu haer."

"So, you've heard of him."

"Aye. Ee bae u Theoscian, da commander o'da kerolus armies un u great warrior."

"Hmm. He seemed nice yet dangerous in a strange sort of way. But it doesn't reallymatter. It's unlikely that we have any chance against them. Maybe we should get out of here while we can."

Loham hoped the report would dissuade Huzesh from his plan to capture the foreigner, but Huzesh was not deterred in the slightest. Despite the inequities of their situation, Huzesh was more determined than ever. "Yur u coward, Loham! All ye snitches bae cowards! Wae jus ha t'tink up u plan thut wull laed da forner t'us, t'u place whaer wae wull ha d'advantage."

"But Kumél doesn't trust me at all. He is always watching me."

"Ahh, Kumél, ee bae one t'bae careful around, but dar bae no excuses. Haer mae! Ye jus ha t'fin u wae t'gain da trus o'da forner, gut eem t'com wit ye. Once ee bae un mae hands A wull handle eem."

Loham disliked Huzesh's plan. He was growing fond of the company but felt he had no choice except to obey, as was the nature of the snitches. Deluded by the spell of Attar, they virtually had no will of their own, no mind to disobey or to do anything but follow the orders of their masters. However, Loham was evolving. Something was happening to him, something he did not understand. Each passing day, his fears dimmed, and his confidence grew stronger.

"I must get back! It will be dark soon and they may already be suspicious of my absence. If they come looking for me, they might find both of us!"

"Fine! A cun sae ye no matter whaer ye bae! Ye know A ha spies, so ye bes d'wut A tell ye, Loham. Brang mae da forner!"

Loham grabbed his bag and ducked out of Huzesh's sight without responding. He carefully made his way back to where he could hear Ziminiar and Kumél talking. He casually approached them and asked Ziminiar, "When do you think the others will return? They've been gone a long time."

"No bother. Dae wull com wun dae bae raedy."

Ross wondered how many more times he would get to see Eve. He wanted to stay with Seerae at the mysterious tarn forever. For so long, he had thought of nothing else except leaving Shuk and returning home, of escaping this strange world he had misfortunately discovered, but now everything was different, now he wanted to stay. He thought about Seerae and about Eve. He knew Eve was dead, but in the realm of hope, he wondered if Seerae's transformation was a sign. Maybe Eve could come back to him, maybe she could be alive.

Shu knew how happy Ross was after seeing Eve, but he also saw it had changed him in a deeper way. "Ross, it is good to see you in such good spirits. I've not seen you like this. Were you always like this with Eve?"

"No, not really. I'm different now. I guess losing her made me more aware of what I had. Is it possible for us to stay here, do you think? I mean, with Seerae, could we stay?"

Shu did not answer immediately, for he knew he could not give Ross the answers he wanted, but he did not wish to take from him the preciousness of the moments he had left at the pool.

Ross waited but sensed that Shu was hesitant to reply. "Your silence feels like an answer. Is it impossible?"

"You are here and what you've found you should hold onto. Enjoy it, for it will not last. The pool can only show you what is meant to be; it is not permanent. Staying will not bring her back in the way you desire."

"How long do we have until we have to leave?"

"Not long enough, I'm afraid. Time is not on our side."

"What do you mean?"

"It is not something you will want to know at this time."

"Please, Shu, tell me."

"Things are changing, and soon there will be no time remaining."

Ross knew Shu was avoiding telling him something. He thought it was about Eve, about seeing her again. In one way, because of the fear of what Shu would say, Ross did not want to know, but in another way, he worried he had opened a door that could not be closed. He pressed Shu. "You can't leave it like this. Tell me."

"It is not as you suppose, Ross. It's about your world and what has happened."

"Huh? My world? I thought you were talking about Eve."

"Tirnan races toward its own destruction. The hands of time have spun demandingly, bent on hastening to the end of days and the indiscriminate decimation of Amik's tree. Tirnan is in the throes of affliction. Every region is at war."

"But that can't be. I mean, if we're talking about the same thing because, well, because I thought that Tirnan was my world?"

"Yes, it is, Ross, and while you have been in *here*, time *there* has rushed away from you."

"What do you mean?"

"One day in our world is like a thousand, even ten thousand, days in yours, and the world that you knew when you entered the pit is not that world now. Time has forgotten you, left you behind. All those you knew— your family and your friends—they are all gone, passed into the shadows. Your home and your city have fallen to the terror of war, tyranny, and anarchy."

Ross stared at Shu with disbelief. He would have thought it was a cruel joke except for the seriousness in Shu's eyes.

"No! No!" He could not accept what Shu was saying. "You're wrong, you have to be! What you're saying is just not possible!"

Shu put his hand on Ross's shoulder and spoke gently and compassionately to him, "I would never deceive you, Ross. The world that you knew is no longer as it was. There is no one remaining that you would know or remember. You have been forgotten."

"But how? Look at me; I am the same, no older. How can so much have changed in so short a time? You can't be right!"

"Please Ross, listen to me. In Pardis, there was no time, no aging, or death, or dying. But the curse of Attar set in motion the domain and rule of time and mortality. These became allies of the spell, stealing away life and the hope of any cure. Time is racing toward its own inevitable end and hastens the annihilation of Amik. Attar has loosed the scourge of devastation upon Tirnan. Now, in these days, the last bastions of hope are under siege by the forces of darkness. The end of days is drawing near."

"But, isn't there some sort of agreement . . . you know . . . that covenant thing? I thought Attar couldn't hurt us?"

"Yes, you're right, he can't. But Attar isn't exactly the one hurting them. They are bringing this upon themselves. It's imminent self-destruction orchestrated by Attar and his spell!"

"But, I thought you said Attar was attacking them."

"Right. But not their lives. The scourge of devastation is not a physical threat; it threatens their minds. Attar only planted the seeds of destruction. The sapiens have been nurturing them until each has grown into a crop. It is not Attar who destroys the people; it is they who destroy themselves."

"But there is something that can be done, right? I'm sure that's what you said. And what about Eve? I don't understand! Why did you bring me here?" The weight of reality came crashing down upon Ross in a measure beyond his ability to deflect or rationalize. He had all but given up any hope of going home. Being with Eve at the pool had caused Ross to want to stay in Shuk, making it easier to accept there was no way to go home. But the thought that he had no home and no one to return to even if he did find a way back, felt oppressively final.

"I'm sorry, Ross. There's nothing that can be done, for now."

"What do I do then? What's the point? Is there a point to any of this? I feel sick!" Ross had no more shouted the words when a memory flooded his thoughts. He could still hear Eve's voice. "I feel sick," she had said in Psang's van. It was nothing really, nothing until the moment he remembered it, but he could picture the whole ordeal. He remembered the van door flying open and Eve nearly falling to the ground as she struggled to get out. It was such a random thought, yet there it was, breaking into all the fear, oppression, and seriousness. An unexpected chuckle erupted from deep down in his belly. It was so completely inappropriate and, considering the subject of conversation, irreverent that the absurdity of laughter made self- restraint completely impossible. Before long, Ross was laughing uncontrollably, and tears were filling his eyes.

Shu was taken aback at first, but the more outrageously Ross laughed, the more infectious the laughter became. Shu smiled, then a restrained chuckle broke through, stopping abruptly before turning into a full laugh.

"Was there never any hope?" Ross blurted out, followed by another round of laughter, which caused him to sit down. "And, what about Eve? Was she just an illusion?" These were earnest questions, and Ross was sincere, but the laughter certainly disguised it.

As appropriately as he could, Shu struggled to answer, "No, she was not an illusion. What you have seen and known of Eve here has been just as genuine as all the past times that you ever spent with her, but she is not the same as before. Seerae is the essence of Eve. Attar's spell cannot destroy that part of her, it can only separate her from her mortal self. They are one and the same, Seerae and Eve. They are one whole being. As long as you are here, in Shuk, with Seerae, you are with the essence of Eve."

Finally, Ross's laughter ceased, and he cleared his throat. "I'm not sure how I'm supposed to feel right now. It's so much to take in."

Seerae had just joined Ross and Shu, and she was very clearly disturbed by the revelation that Shu had been sharing about Eve. The truth reverberated through her. It forced its way into every corner and shadowy place within her and started to shine. She had been shown the songs she loved to sing and play were more than music, they were messages that called out from her heart to the heart of Eve, the Eve who had lived in a world of darkness and shadows far away.

At the understanding of this truth, there immediately came another harsh revelation that cut her like a knife and left her heart bleeding. She now knew that her songs, all her beautiful melodies, would no longer be heard by the endearing sapien for whom she had sung them and that she would forever sorrowfully miss the one who had passed into the shadows. Eve was dead and she was alone.

The heartbreaking truth of Eve's death and of their irreparable separation plummeted into the depth of Seerae's being, coming to rest, like a sunken ship, in a silty, floating haze of doubt and confusion, turning the clear waters of belief into a murky, gray tide.

"Maybe we should search for them. They could be in trouble or something, you know. It's been a long while since they left for the falls." Loham's curiosity was piqued by not knowing where Ross and the others were, and each day that passed agitated his compulsion to seek for them. His unwanted situation was constantly declining, for he was uncontrollably trembling at the continual, unbidden recollections of Huzesh's impatient temper, and ceaselessly cowering from his prying eyes even though there were no signs of Huzesh anywhere. Loham was panicking over every conceivable scenario of being exposed, and was barely able to disguise his nervousness. "I think I'll go for a walk. Could you keep the fire burning, so I can find my way back if it gets too dark?"

Loham headed toward the waterfall, hoping to run into Ross's group.

He was unsure where they had gone, but a strong, demanding force was drawing him toward them. He made his way toward the falls, and he came upon the place where Zoësh had stepped into the water. Puzzled and confused, Loham surveyed the area in front of him, for the path had ended. He had not witnessed the opening of the way, but an intuitive force inside of him knew that the way was here, and this was the entrance to it. He examined the falls more closely, pushing the rocks until, quite serendipitously, the way opened to him. He entered cautiously. The force within him urged him forward. Loham stepped into the hollow behind the falls where he noticed the stone stairs illuminated by the shaft of light. Loham ascended the towering spiral, following his instinct, though not knowing where he would end up. He felt odd as he climbed toward the unknown. The place seemed familiar to him like he had been there before.

As Loham climbed, his thoughts returned to the morning Msusi had found him, and he had met the company of Shu. Loham had quickly grown fond of all of them, even of Kumél and Ziminiar, but it was Seerae who most impressed him, for she had shown him undeserved kindness. The more he thought about them, the less resolved he felt about obeying Huzesh. Loham could not escape his increasing affection for his new-found friends, and the more time he spent away from Huzesh, the stronger his feelings became. Their naiveté and sincerity were endearing and powerful, cutting through his thick skin of cynicism and delusion. Nevertheless, Loham's terror of Huzesh, and the scheming snitch nature that resided in him, rivaled his desire to do better. He considered sneaking away and fleeing into the night to escape, but he was aware that Huzesh had many eyes spying for him. He and other nephs he had known had been startled too many times by unexpected corvuses that were allegiant to the gallues.

The long climb up the stairs turned into a wilderness journey where he battled his inner darkness. At each step, he endured the tormenting flames of a forge smelting the iron chains that had been binding him to the folly of his life. The smelting fires of the forge clawed away at the weighty shackles until they became malleable, and link by link, they melted away. Step by stony step, Loham experienced his intense inner struggle between the fires of freedom and the stalwart shackles of bondage. Part of him wanted to turn back and escape this conflict, and yet an inexorable force compelled him onward.

Loham's worry that Huzesh might be watching was not in vain, for

Huzesh was indeed spying on him. High above the narrow meadow, in a sheltered depression on the rocky slopes of the surrounding mountains, he hid and kept a demanding eye on Loham, Kumél, and Ziminiar. He did not trust Loham and decided he had better have another plan to capture the foreigner that did not include Loham. Huzesh realized he was at a huge disadvantage in being outnumbered and that brute force would never achieve his goal. He hoped a little reconnaissance might provide an advantage of surprise against his enemies that he could not otherwise have had. From his discrete post, Huzesh observed Loham as he trekked toward the waterfall, then mysteriously disappeared.

Impatience built in Huzesh, as he stared at the waterfall, waiting for Loham to reappear, but he did not. He believed Loham had somehow escaped him. He gazed across the narrow meadow to see Kumél and Ziminiar sitting next to the long, narrow tarn with a fire burning hot. He called to the corvus and ordered him to fly to the falls and return to him with word of Loham's activities. The corvus returned a short time later with no news of Loham's whereabouts. Angry about being betrayed, Huzesh decided to explore the falls himself. He waited for the cover of darkness before he stealthily crept toward the site of Loham's disappearance but when he reached the falls, there was no sign of Loham, no escape route, and no hiding place Huzesh could find. Puzzled and perturbed, he rested on a rock and contemplated how Loham could have eluded him so cunningly.

High in the mountains above Huzesh, the clouds broke open over the Pool of Levitus, clearing the way for the anxious twin moons to shine upon the water as the effervescent resurrection of bubbles rose into the sky. They filled the air with a lightness in sharp contrast to the shadowed weight of Shu's earlier words. Seerae did not enter the water as she had the nights before. Spellbound, she reflected on the disturbing, unwanted reality. There were no attempts by the others to reach out to her, for they were all troubled. The implications were not circumscribed to Ross and the sapiens alone; they were far-reaching, touching everything and everyone. The burden of such an inescapable absoluteness impacted everyone, whether they were aware of it or not, for some truths have never required knowledge of them to be true. These truths act sovereignly and are self-determined, without regard for ignorance or acceptance.

Helplessly, Ross watched as Seerae detached herself from their group to be alone. He longed for the wisdom to restore her wounded, grieving heart. He desperately wished to see Eve again, but he understood, more than anyone else, how severely Seerae was suffering. Throughout Ross's life, the final reality of death, and the terrible separation it imposes had been his reality. He had already lost his family, Daniel, and Eve. In the world he had lived in, death had been as normal as the rising of the sun. He knew Seerae's heart weighed heavily and that he needed to give her time, time that would do nothing except help her to forget. The agonizing wounds would never heal, and the tormenting absences would never be filled.

The burdensome cares of Seerae's heart coursed through her thoughts like the incoherent rambling words of an inebriated woman. She wandered aimlessly in the fading light, not focusing on her surroundings or on any activities around her. She ambled about until she unexpectedly arrived at the top of the towering staircase that had brought her to Levitus. Illuminated by the mysterious blue light, Seerae thoughtlessly descended the cold steps.

Loham was so enthralled and absorbed by his inner conflicts he barely noticed the patter of approaching, delicate footsteps above him. The soft, muted sounds slipped into his ears like a distant echo. Finally, Loham was startled out from under the spell that his inner struggle had cast over him. Standing completely exposed, he wondered if he should run back down the steps, but before he could make up his mind, he heard a voice softly calling his name, and he spotted Seerae gliding down the staircase. "Loham? Why are you down here? I thought you were supposed to be waiting with Kumél and Ziminiar."

If there had been anyone Loham would have wanted to see, it would have been Seerae. Surprised and delighted, he blurted out, "It's you! But, but where are the others? And—"

"And what, Loham? What?"

"Well, you look different, not like yourself." Loham was confident this was Seerae, but her appearance was not the same to him as it had been before. He not only recognized differences in her image but even a change in her voice. Her attire was the same as it had been, but her face, eyes, and hair were altered. Her radiant face and her iridescent skin were as fresh as a newborn's, soft and unmarked. Her glimmering eyes sparkled as if the entire night sky had been reduced to fit into the ebony orbs of her pupils. Seerae's long, translucent braid of hair was now untied and falling freely in silky, flaxen locks gracefully flowing over her shoulders.

"What happened to you, Seerae? Why do you look so different?"

"Oh, yeah. Well, I guess it's the water."

"The water?"

"Yeah, the water will transform you. And the moons, they change everything."

Loham was confused, for Seerae was not herself. He believed something aside from her appearance was wrong. "Hmm, I'm not sure I understand. Drinking the water makes you different?"

"Oh, no! You really are quite strange sometimes, Loham. Drinking the water doesn't change anything. It's when you, or at least, when I go into the pool, it changes me, transforms me. That's why I look so different."

"Is it painful?"

Seerae rolled her eyes and laughed, "No, silly, not at all. You should've seen me before all this started to fade. You wouldn't have recognized me. This is only part of the change. There's more. I think it eventually fades away, though, back to my old self. Why are you here anyway?"

"Oh, that's good. I was searching for you. Oh, and the others, of course."

"Why?"

"Well, you've all been gone a long time. I had assumed you would be right back, so I admit I was worried. Where were you headed?"

"Back down, I guess. I don't really know where I was going. Everything's . . . umm . . . I don't know . . . everything's different now," Seerae sighed.

Loham was puzzled by the ambiguity of Seerae's words and her distracted manner. Though she seemed friendly enough, and even lighthearted, he sensed a strange ambivalence in her mood.

"Is there something wrong, Seerae?"

"Nothing is ever quite what it seems to be, have you ever noticed that, Loham? It's like everything is one way on the surface, but it is completely different when you look beneath the trappings of its appearance."

Loham focused his eyes on the solid surface of the stone steps beneath his feet. Seerae's words had fallen on him like a giant millstone, and the weight was crushing his fragile facade. His mouth became dry and his throat, parched while his body reacted to the inner guilt of his duplicity.

He could not speak for worrying about whether she had found him out.

"You know what I mean, don't you? It's everywhere around us. This place, this world of darkness and shadows, of monsters and beasts, is not what it seems. Nothing is as it seems. I am not as I seem. You, you are not as you seem. There is something hidden in all of us, something glorious and something depraved. We are all shadows, illusions of reality, both alive and dead, living and dying."

Loham had no response to offer, and he perceived that Seerae was not looking for a response or a reason. He wished he had a smart or brilliant insight to give, but he had absolutely nothing to offer: no wisdom or hope or insight, for he was aware of his own shadows, his own darkness, and the plague of death that ruled over his own conscience. Uselessly, he just swallowed and stared at the ground. Then, unintentionally, he opened his mouth and words rapidly poured out, as if they were desperate prisoners escaping through the bars of their cold, stony cell. "I'm not wise enough to know what is genuine and what is not. No one can ever fully know all there is to know. But if it's true that nothing is as it seems, then nothing is as it should be. It's broken; we are broken. Every being, creature, and all of nature that we see, feel, and hear is broken. But I believe it's not your fault that you're broken. You cannot be responsible for carrying the weight of it any more than you can escape it. We are lost, and some are more lost than others. Some know it and others, well they never will. What can we do about it? What can anyone do about it? There's no point trying to change what can't be changed, is there?"

"But I have seen it happen! Things can and do and will change. I'm not the same as I was. Things can evolve or be remade. You and I can, and if we can, then maybe, just maybe, this world can."

"Change into what? What can we become that we are not already?"

"What we are meant to be! *Who* we are meant to be! To be unbroken, whole, and complete! If it's not possible, then what's the point? Why do we struggle and fight? If we are destined to stay exactly as we are, then why do we even work to be someone we can never become? I have been running and hiding for as long as I can remember, trying to stay away from the gallues and their evil snitches. For ages, I have sung the songs of Eloh and of Pardis, of life and of hope and of vision. I sang them in hope that a precious one would hear and be free, but she is gone now, passed into the shadows, lost. She will never return. And me, I am never to be whole! Why try? Why resist? Why should I sing if nothing ever changes and if there is no hope? Why?"

Seerae's troubled intimation struck a heavy chord within the heart of Loham. He felt paralyzed and exposed by the shockingly germane sentiments. It was as if she had seen inside him. Her words resonated within him like the timbre of a perfect, unapologetic note. He feared his wily eyes might give him away if she were to look too closely into them, so he pretended to have heard a suspicious noise, then sat down on one of the steps, leaving his back exposed to her.

"Have you ever felt it, Loham, the feeling that there's nothing you can do, nothing that would be of any consequence at all? Have you felt helpless, or a slave to whatever someone else or something else demands of you? That's how I feel right now, like I have no choice, no options, and yet there is this inner voice, not mine, but someone else is telling me, no. Not just telling me, urging me to discover that there is more to my life, more to who I am than what I presently know. It is compelling me to believe; it burns in me like a fire that will not be quenched. It's all so utterly difficult to comprehend. It's as if there is more: more to me, to life, to all of this than what I understand. But I can't see it. I thought I knew. I honestly thought I understood their meanings, the songs, the visions, the struggle, but now I'm not sure. How can I ever truly be whole? I thought that was the point, the reason for it all."

"Seerae, it'll be OK, really."

"No Loham, you don't understand! Your mindless platitudes won't make it better. I can't just pretend that everything will be fine because it won't. There have been losses that can never be recovered, and it's not like I can just blink my eyes, go back in time and everything will be just as it was." With tears trickling down her cheeks, Seerae cried, "Why do we pretend that life will be OK? Why do we close our eyes to what's happening around us and just accept it as something that's meant to be? This was never how it was meant to be."

Unable to comfort her, Loham dropped his head into his hands and silently pondered how he had become so unlike himself, so broken. He earnestly wanted to be more like Seerae and Zoësh and many other nephesh, unspoiled by compromise and corruption, biding in the sweet satisfaction that is found in innocence, but he was not innocent, and he knew it. He was a traitor serving the will and command of the gallues, but he was gradually owning the shame of his choices, of his betrayal and deceit. His life had been ruled by trouble for as long as he could remember, and he had been interminably oblivious, unmoved, and unfeeling about what he had become or what he had been. But in the strangest twist of fate, he was finding his true self while on a journey that would have seemed, from its beginning, to be taking him farther away rather than closer, especially while traveling with the vilest gallue he had ever met.

Seerae pushed past Loham and rushed down the stairs. As she slid by him, he felt a surge of energy pass from the warm touch of her hand on his shoulder, which halted him in his steps. An urgent instinct to detain her arose inside of him, but before he could stall her, Loham was paralyzed by an epiphany. Loham envisioned the image of Huzesh carrying the limp body of a nephesh over his shoulder. Loham's heart accelerated with fear, for he first believed the body was himself, that he was viewing his own dead corpse. However, something seemed wrong about the bloody and bruised, limp body, something that made him look harder into the vision. Loham struggled to identify the dead nephesh. He needed to see its face, but there was substantial blood covering it. Incredibly, the courageous nephesh turned its head, opened its eyes, and desperately pleaded, "Loham, help me!"

The weak voice faintly resonated in Loham's ears. He stared intently into the fading eyes of the wounded nephesh, attempting to recognize them, and then, to his horror, Loham realized the limp body that hung over Huzesh's shoulder belonged to Seerae.

Loham shook from his head to his feet at this revelation. He worked to restrain the convulsive, uncontrollable quaking. He felt immense fear and anger were converging inside of him at the same moment. As the vision ended, Loham focused on Seerae running down the stairs. He was aware the vision had revealed to him that she would be in extreme danger if she escaped into the meadow below, but mysteriously, he was unable to rise from the step. He could not speak or reach out to her and was powerless to stop her.

Loham puzzled over why he was frozen. It was as if a nightmare was holding him captive, hindering him from escaping the grip of the vision. He could see everything so clearly yet could do nothing to stop it. He frantically wanted to yell, to call out to her, but the words refused to dislodge from his mouth. After a few short moments, she was out of his sight, farther descending the long staircase, straight toward the prowling eyes of Huzesh.

Meanwhile, near the pool, crystalline flakes of snow floated carelessly down to the ground, landing on the rocks, trees, and water. Ross fervently desired to see Eve again, so he began to search for Seerae. He knew there would not be many more nights for them to be together, so he felt foolish for letting her go away in silence. He put his hands to his mouth and called out to her, "Seerae, where are you? Please, please come back." He received no answer and failed to locate her wherever he looked. Ross repeatedly yelled for her to no avail, and he anxiously worried he may have lost something very dear and irreplaceable. Soon Shu and Zoësh were desperately calling out as well, and Msusi was intently roaming the areas around the pool hunting for Seerae.

As suddenly as the epiphany had seized Loham, it released him. He had sat on the stair for a few moments trying to comprehend what had happened. When he remembered that Seerae had descended the stairs, he moved to follow her but then stopped. He was uncertain how long he had been under the clutches of the vision, and he was not sure how far down the stairs Seerae might have stepped. Loham wondered if it would be better to climb to the top where he would be able to get help from the rest of the group, for then there would be a larger force to defend against the power of Huzesh. Loham flew as quickly as he could to the top of the stairs. He knew he would have to reveal everything to Shu and the others, and he was unsure what their reaction would be, but he knew if he did not get their help, Seerae was certain to be in great trouble. The vision of her calling out to him, pleading with him for help, haunted his thoughts and urgently drove him to the others. As he reached the final step, he made a mad dash for the meadow.

In the small meadow around the Pool of Levitus, a strange spiral wind blew. It also blew throughout the whole meadow where Loham was standing. It was swirling around the towering peaks of the surrounding mountains and could be heard shouting with a thundering, hostile voice. The storm that had been advancing from the south had finally reached them with a consuming rage.

"Help! She needs help! Shu, she's in danger! Seerae's in danger! Help!"

Msusi was the first one to hear Loham. She was shocked to see him at first and wanted to question his being there, but because of the intensity of the storm and the urgency with which Loham had been screaming, she waited. It was quite clear to her something was terribly wrong, so she hollered back to him instead, "Loham!"

"Shu! Where is Shu? He will know what to do. Where is he?"

"He's over there. Shu, come quick!"

Loham could not wait. He took off racing, followed by Msusi, toward Shu who was near Zoësh. Shu and Zoësh had heard Msusi and were running to meet Loham.

"What is it? What has happened?"

"Shu, please! Please forgive me!" His plea for forgiveness escaped his mouth. He had not meant to say it, but it was the first thing that slipped out. Loham did not even know why but he felt strongly compelled to fall before the feet of Shu and beg for his acquittal.

"Please, help her! Seerae needs your help!"

"Help? What do you mean? We have been looking for her. What has happened? Tell me Loham! What has happened to her?"

"She is in great danger! I have seen it; she called out for help!"

"But why? Why ask forgiveness? What have you done?"

"There is no time. We must go, or he will take her! She's in great danger." The conflict raging in his soul, like the storm raging all around him, would not let him hide the things he most feared about himself and what he had done. Bit by bit, pieces of the story slipped from his tongue for them all to hear. For greater than his fear of telling them who he was and what he was, was the stronger, more urgent desire to free himself from the hidden torment of his treachery. Loham coveted absolution over life itself.

"Who? Who will take her? What are you talking about?"

"Huzesh! He is in the meadow below, waiting for me. He is after the foreigner, after Ross!"

Shu searched the eyes of Loham and stepped back. "You! You're a snitch! What have you done?"

Loham's eyes filled with tears of regret and sorrow. "I'm sorry! I'm so, so sorry. I had no choice. Please, just help her. She is on her way down the stairs. He'll kill her! She'll not matter to him!"

Ross was returning from hunting for Seerae as he approached the trio that was with Shu, and he was hoping for good news, but as he neared them, he overheard Loham's contrite confession. Rage filled Ross, violently swirling around inside of him like the cyclonic winds of the storm. Every one of his muscles tightened and filled with blood. His face reddened and his blue eyes turned dull. He vehemently focused on Loham. "You bastard!" Before anyone could react, Ross rushed Loham with all his might, at full speed. Loham had only enough time to turn and face Ross before Ross's shoulder came in full contact with his torso. Like an irate mother grizzly charging a threatening intruder, Ross grabbed Loham and drove him backward, away from Shu and the others, until the two of them plunged into the Pool of Levitus. Ross pushed Loham under the water until he was fully submerged and pinned him there; attempting to drown him. While holding his head under the water with one hand, Ross was beating Loham with the other, and at the same time, he was madly yelling and cursing. Instantly, Shu noticed the power Ross had over Loham. He knew Loham should have been able to overtake Ross quite easily, yet Ross seemed in full control of the perilous situation.

This was no time for fighting. Shu needed to hear more information about Seerae, so he rushed into the pool to restrain Ross. Zoësh drew her sword and was ready to jump in and assist, but Shu gestured with his hand for her to halt. As Shu neared Ross, they all witnessed a strange and unexpected occurrence. Ross suddenly stopped beating Loham. He loosened his grip from around Loham's neck and, with astonishment in his eyes, staggered backward, nearly tripping as he did. Shu peered into the water thinking Ross had killed Loham, but it was not so. Ross stood in shock, frozen in his steps, gazing into the pool at Loham.

Msusi sensed something was terribly wrong and went to help Ross. "Shu, what is it?"

"Stay back! Just stay back!" Shu softly replied.

Ross was panting heavily, his chest expanding in and out. The markings on his body were glowing bright and, at the same time, a blue glow of light radiated to the surface of the water. Ross suddenly shouted, "No! No, no, no!" He stumbled back, splashed into the pool, and lay there mumbling, as if drunk. Shu moved closer, put out his hand, and pulled him to his feet. Then, the attention of Ross and his friends was drawn back to the radiant, blue light that emanated from Loham and the water in which he was submerged. At the same time, the mysterious water gradually levitated Loham up and out of the pool. As his face broke the surface, Zoësh unwittingly dropped her sword, and Msusi stood dazed as if she were a statue. After a few moments, Loham was suspended, fully upright, over the pool as if he were a marionette dangling over a stage. Ross's exigent repudiation grew weaker and less persistent. His voice sank into a distraught whisper.

Loham, like all nephesh who enter the Pool of Levitus, had been transformed into the image of his sapien. Suspended over the surface of the water, he saw the reflection of his face and the blue markings that signified who he truly was. He recalled the night he had seen a vision in a fire. He remembered the face that had appeared and stared at him. That face had been *his* face. Loham explored the reflection of Ross that floated on the water just beyond his and then his own. The faces he studied were the same, just as the face in the fire had been the same as his. The pool graciously revealed to Loham that he was not alone, not abandoned, and not a waif like so many other nephesh. He felt miraculously healed, and he desired to reach out to Ross, to touch him and feel the bond of oneness, but he instinctively felt he should be patient, so instead, he stood waiting in silence as Ross and the others remained paralyzed by the shock of it all.

Ross became aware he was hearing the song with the dark, enchanting lyrics that Zoësh had sung just days before. It was being delivered so clearly to his ears he was not sure whether it was genuine or if he was imagining it. The power of her song touched Ross. It was as if the distressing words were invading hands reaching into his soul, grabbing hold of him, and shaking him with troubling thoughts.

Where have you gone oh soul of mine?

Where have you run to; where have you hid?

I have been looking, never to find.

Never to know, never to be.

Where have you gone to, oh soul of mine?

Loham could hear the lonely song as well, echoing through him. While he listened, he recalled what the face in the fire had said to him. *I am a sojourner, looking for something that I cannot find.* The truth gradually dawned on Loham, that the face in the fire was not his face at all, but the face of the one whose image he was meant to bear.

While Ross observed Loham, he began to see the same image of the faceless man that had been standing in the swirling tower of water and had risen from the Well of Veritus. The same man whom Alethia had revealed was the man he had become. Ross could hear the poignant words of Alethia resonating through him as if she was standing right next to him. *". . . you do not know where you came from, Ross Blair, you do not know who you are. You are a man who is lost from yourself, you are a man who is blind and unable to see who you are . . ."*

The voice of Alethia repeated the words to Loham that the face in the flames had spoken to him. It was as though she had been with him and had heard them, too.

Look deep into yourself, into the shadows of your being. See if you do not know who you are, where you are, what you are. You are lost, lost from your true self, broken, wounded, and searching. All are meant to find something. The whole meaning of life depends upon finding what is not known. You are a shadow of yourself, a reflection that is faceless. You are not who you think you are, no one is.

Ross could also hear Alethia's voice as though she was speaking to him. Her words evoked memories of when he was a boy. He saw his father and mother and the small house where they had lived. Unfortunately, accompanying the memories were the deep pains of rejection and abandonment, and he felt dominating anger and hatred growing in him like an overgrown vine, choking out the innocence of his youth. He remembered the hatred, the deep, black hatred he felt for his life, but never realized, that more than anything else, it was for himself. It was a memory he had never remembered and yet, it seemed too powerful to forget. He realized the anger he felt as a boy still lived in him and had been hiding like a thief, in the shadows of his heart, poisoning his mind with self-deprivation and malice. Ross looked at Loham and felt the pulse of his hatred rise. All he could see was himself staring back. He tried to look beyond the face looking at him and see the face of Loham, whom he wanted to hate with his dark hatred, but Ross could only see himself. He had never realized it was himself whom he hated the most. The deeply embedded self-animus brooding just below the surface of his life had driven Loham into the shadows and into the service of the gallues.

Ross succumbed to the inevitability of forgetfulness and in forgetting, he failed to remember who he was. Some forget because they are distracted, some because they grow old, and some because they want to forget because the memories hold too much pain. And still, others forget because self-hatred blinds their eyes of the memory. For those blinded by hatred, forgetfulness is like rejection: it wounded the nephesh, and made it vulnerable to the cunning manipulation of Attar's dark spell.

As Ross stood staring into his own eyes, he began to remember, and in remembering, the rapid pulse of his angry heart began to slow. He began to see, for the first time, who he was. Ross felt a lightness come over him that lifted him up out of the water. The face and eyes that stared back at him changed, and before he knew what was happening, he was looking at the face of a boy. The boy seemed familiar to him, someone he had forgotten, someone hidden from his mind. He looked closer and saw the boy was someone he used to know, a secret friend, someone he used to play with in the backyard of their small run-down house when he was all alone. Ross peered deeper into the eyes that stared at him and found himself descending through shadowy images of the past, into archives of his lost thoughts. Eventually he entered a long, dark corridor with many doors on either side. Every door was locked. Ross tried to open one of the doors, but it would not submit to his insistent attempt. He looked around until he saw one of the doors cracked open. He went to the door and cautiously pushed it. The room behind the door was dark, but as he stepped into it, an image began to glow. It was a small, solitary boy in tattered clothes. Ross scanned the room for anyone else, but there was no one, only the same small boy he had long ago forgotten. He remembered that he had never felt alone until his secret friend had left him. Sadly, he realized that this lonely boy who was staring at him had the same eyes he had been looking into just moments before. "Where did you go? Why, why did you leave me alone?" Ross's question fell from his lips with such shyness it was almost as if he had said nothing at all, yet the sincerity and force of the inquiry struck the intangible air like the repercussion of thunder shaking the sky. Ross was physically shaken and closed his eyes for only a moment. When he opened them, he was standing on the surface of the dark, infinite sea and Loham was there, where his secret friend had been and was staring back at him. Loham was pushed back by the weight of the whispered words, and the still waters of Levitus were broken into ripples. Ross realized, at that moment, that Loham was his secret friend no one else could see.

The haunting song of Zoësh penetrated Ross's thoughts, dredging up the silted recesses of his memory, awakening visions of the past:

If you find me, if you see me,
The me I've lost; I'm supposed to be.

If you hear me, my voice, my cry,
Free me from this life that will die.

Fill me, fill me as you once did.
Heal me of the brokenness that I've hid.
I am lost, I am lost oh soul of mine.
I am lost in the shadows.
Lost and broken and blind.

Ross was being drawn deeper into the murky waters that stretched boundlessly in every direction. He was being pulled under, into the weightlessness of the sea. He could feel himself sinking into the gloom. Ross could feel the desperation and aimless struggle he had known for his whole life. He puzzled over why he could not swim, until he saw a heavy chain hanging from a shackle clamped about his ankle. He searched the waters to learn what the chain was attached to. Finally, Ross saw a small, rusted metal box with an oversized padlock dangling from the end of the chain, and it was pulling him into the shadows of the abyss. Deeper and deeper he sank, until the box stopped and hung suspended in front of him. He worked to open the padlock, but it would not surrender to his attacking fingers. He discovered that attached to the chain, just a few links away from the box, was a key. When he unlocked the padlock, it sank out of sight into the abyss and the key with it. In his hands, he held the metal box. He lifted the rusted lid and, instantly, the little box fractured into several tiny pieces of metal. The fragments hung suspended in the water. He looked in his palm where the small box had laid and, instead, he saw a peculiar, obsidian stone laced with gold veins. Ross repeatedly heard an aberrant, corrupted melody in an unknown tongue, emanating from the stone. *"Kudin e oot shudaw, Kudin e oot shudaw, Kudin e oot shudaw."* He was aware that part of him fervidly desired to keep the stone, and yet another part of him needed to release it into the dark abyss. He felt conflicted, and the weight of his long- held hatred made him sink back into the shadows. Ross wondered why he was sinking, why now, now that the weight of the box was gone from him. He could still hear the dangerous song of the stone that compelled him to covet it and which also made him forget.

While the luring song of the stone was penetrating his thoughts, Ross could still hear the enchanting lyrics of Zoësh's song echoing in the back of his mind, opposing the message of the stone that was chiming in Ross's ears:

If you find me, if you see me,
The me I've lost; I'm supposed to be.
If you hear me, my voice, my cry.
Free me from this life that will die.

As he listened to the song of Zoësh desperately struggling against the stone's sorcery, he felt himself triumphantly rising from the dark water, but every time he gave his attention to the stone, he drearily sank. However, the tempting mystery of the stone intrigued him, and he could not dismiss it. He ached to understand its message and learn its origin. Ross attended his ears to the song of the stone and once again he felt his life leaving his body, the air in his lungs being squeezed out by the pernicious darkness.

A vision of his boyhood-self floated into view. He could see that his young self was enraged, that he was cursing and yelling at the air. Ross could not recall why he had been so angry, but as he watched himself persistently rebuking and cursing the unseen recipient, he became aware that the stone was doggedly calling out to the boy. Then Ross noticed a retreating figure in the background, a fair distance away from the tantrum. He readily identified the individual as his childhood secret friend, the one he had seen in the dark room of his memories. Ross immediately discerned his secret friend was being violently pushed away by his threatening, injurious words. The rantings of hatred and denial were being hurled like stones by the angry, lonely boy. Ross painfully remembered too many occasions when he had sent away his secret friend, had closed his eyes and heart to him, hated him, mistrusted him, and, eventually, forgotten him. It was a story that had been played out through the ages, a story that had begun with Amik, the first to hear the song of the triakis. The boy wore an iron shackle around his ankle that was linked to a new, polished chain with a metal box attached to the end of it. Curiously, Ross watched as the young boy placed the stone into the new box, locking it with a key. Nevertheless, the unyielding stone persistently sang out.

As Ross contemplated the meaning of the song and the stone and wondered why his boyhood-self had listened to it, he heard the melody from Zoësh getting louder and stronger. Then, the spirited Jupnie arrived to him on the wind as his salvation, with rescuing lyrics combating the dark melody of the triakis. His mind was awakened to things he had long forgotten, and he felt a fresh, raw power welling up within him. Ross released his grip on the black stone, and it plummeted into the depths and while it sank, he swam upward, groping for the surface. As he gulped his first breath of air, Ross heard the song of Zoësh floating to him. He recognized the hewn boat that he had seen before, and in it, he saw a hooded passenger. When the cloaked mariner had helped Ross into the boat, he assumed he was the boat's captain, but now he could not ignore the strangeness he was sensing about the hooded figure. There was a familiar yet haunting, almost threatening impression about him. Ross called out, "Who are you?"

The captain of the boat removed the hood of his cloak, and Ross discovered with horror and disbelief that *he* was the captain. He was paralyzed; his feet were bound by some invisible force. The captain of the boat peered into his soul with piercing, malevolent eyes and cried with a severe, tormenting voice, "You are all alone!" The words of the lurid beast took flight into the air as if they were not words at all but were a physical force with weight and mass, strong and indomitable and able to inflict pain and terror. They violently erupted high above the boat and sent explosive, destructive shock waves in every direction.

Ross hurtled backward, as if he had been kicked in the chest, and found himself submerged in water once again. His lungs were screaming for air. He flailed about struggling to get his feet under him. He felt a hand seize him, and he fiercely fought against it, assuming it was the robed captain attempting to take him captive. Finally, his head broke the surface of the sea, and he inhaled a long, deep breath and screamed, "Leave me alone!"

Incredibly, a familiar voice called back to him, "Ross! Ross!" Opening his eyes, Ross recognized it was Shu who was reaching out to him, but Ross was still so convinced the vision was reality that he fought against Shu, fearing he was the captain of the boat.

However, Shu persisted in aiding him, "Ross, are you OK? Here, let me help you!"

Ross finally ceased fighting, then urgently inquired, "What happened? Did you hear him? Did you hear what he said?"

All around the small group, the impatient wind blew, and the convergent clouds above swirled as the storm tightened its grip on the mountains. Each one of them was in a state of shock from witnessing the episode of Ross in the boat. To Ross, it felt like he had spent hours, if not days there, but his vision had only lasted a few moments. There was one part of the event he knew was not a dream, though. The nefarious, bewitching voice that had spoken to Ross in the boat had transcended his vision and struck the meadow like a giant hammer.

"Yes, we heard him and felt him! It was the voice of Attar, his dark magic that lived in you," Shu answered.

"In me? What do you mean? I saw him in the boat. He was me!"

"Yes, Ross, in you. The spell of Attar has lived through you and ruled over you your whole life, as it has every sapien."

Ross's attention went to Loham and Ross marveled that when each one of them looked at Loham, they saw him, Ross, in the same way he had seen Eve when he had looked at Seerae. It was the very first time in Shuk that any nephesh had ever stood is such proximity to their mortal self. The mysterious power of Levitus had changed Loham, and he now stood as a transformed creature. Ross's head was filled with such a myriad of questions, all converging at the same time, and all wanting equal attention, that Ross was unable to articulate even a single word. Slowly, Ross backed away, never taking his eyes off Loham and asked, "Shu, I'm not sure I understand. What has happened?"

Simultaneously, Loham saw a vision of Seerae running down the stairs. He remembered the warning that had been given to him and feared it might be too late to intervene. He desperately reminded them, "There is much to learn and much to understand but now is not the time for those things. Seerae is in danger and we must go quickly!"

Ross swiftly agreed with Loham, for he had seen the same disturbing images Loham had seen. As he hurried toward the shore, Ross vehemently urged the group, "Shu we must go now!"

Stepping toward Shu and gesturing for Ross to wait, Zoësh skeptically asked, "Is he to be trusted? He's a snitch, and he could be leading us into a trap."

Ross looked into her eyes. He knew she was only trying to protect them all, and he understood her mistrust of the snitches.

"Zoësh, please! I understand that you have every reason to mistrust a snitch and you're only trying to protect all of us, but I've seen the vision of

Seerae also. Loham is right."

"But he's a snitch! He can't be trusted!"

Shu had discerned that a work had been taking place in the heart of Loham, even before his transformation. "Zoësh, we must give Loham a chance. We have to trust him or Seerae could possibly be lost."

Msusi stepped near the shore and offered her hand to Ross as he stepped out of the water. With a sincere, yet hesitant tone, she cautioned Ross, "It may be too late for Seerae. She may have already been captured and we could be walking into an ambush."

"Then I will go alone! Stay if you must or if you are too afraid. I failed her once; I won't fail her again! I will do everything possible to find her and rescue her, with or without you!"

"But it is you that he is after; he will use Seerae as bait to lure you in," Loham asserted.

"If he hasn't already killed her," Zoësh whispered.

"Shut up, Loham! Shu, you know he's right. We must go now if we are to save her. It doesn't matter what happens to me, don't you understand? I lost her once; I couldn't save her before, but now, now I can! I know that I'm only one man and only a fragment of a man, at that, but together, all of us, together, we can do this! We must do this! Maybe, just maybe, we'll fail but we can't give up before we've even started. She deserves better! We deserve better! No one will ever be truly free until those who are able to, stand up and fight for that freedom. Everything in this place is waiting for something to change; I can feel it in my bones like I have never felt anything before. There is not a creature or plant or stone or force in Shuk that is not waiting for what only we have the ability to change. Fighting for Seerae is the beginning! It's the beginning of what we have all been longing for, a new life!" Ross's passionate words of vision rang through the air like an ancient prophecy, and even the forces of the storm quieted to listen.

Shu perceived something inside of the man who was a foreigner in Shuk had changed. He proudly nodded his head at Ross and concurred, "You're right, we must hurry!"

Seerae slowly descended the stairs toward the base of the waterfall. She hoped Loham had not followed her; she desired to be alone with the many thoughts that were crowding her, each demanding an attentive reflection. The powerful and almost alien emotions that had risen in her during the transformation had left an indelible stain upon her; they had changed her and returned to her a part of herself she had forgotten she missed. She felt the emotions of Eve, not as an outsider watching, but as a whole being feels in every sense. She was Eve and felt Eve, felt her pain and her joy and her love as if they were her own feelings. She had been so long without that part of her being she had forgotten how to feel such physical affections, especially for another. The feelings Eve felt for Ross scared her, for she had always known only one love and given her attention to only one soul and that had been Eve. But now, being whole, as much as the Pool of Levitus could make her whole, filled her with so many unexpected emotions, emotions that could only be felt with the other part of her being. For the sapiens and the nephesh, life was never full of complete. There was always something missing, for they were meant to fill and complete each other. The sapiens could not know all the mysteries of Pardis, of Eloh, of beauty and immortality, without the nephesh revealing them, and the nephesh could not know the physical fullness of love and desire, among many other things, without the bodily senses of the sapien. One without the other was broken, for to love one's self is, by expression, to love another. Love for one's self cannot be full or complete without the same being given away and shared with someone else. It is like a circle, unbroken and without beginning or end. Yet, for the nephesh and sapiens, the circle had been broken. Seerae felt the wholeness of the circle, the wholeness of life as it was meant to be and while it was satisfying, she grieved that it was not genuine wholeness at all, that it was only an illusion.

The sorrow of knowing she was alone as a waif, that Eve was dead was most unconquerable of all the feelings Seerae had ever experienced. It dwarfed every other emotion being heaped upon her. It weighed upon her heart with such force she felt breathless, crushed under its irrevocable certitude. Her pensive thoughts led each of her footsteps down the stone stairs. She was not thinking about where she was going or for how long she had been walking. She was not thinking about Ross or Shu or any of the others she assumed were waiting for her at the Pool of Levitus. She was not thinking about her transformation or the things she had seen through the eyes of Eve. She could only dwell on the murkiness that filled her mind like the black void that consumed Eve the night she had fallen into the shadows. She could visualize it: the terror and fear as Eve gazed into the eyes of Ross while he struggled to save her. Then, from out of the shadows, another vision appeared: the sight of a beautiful goddess-like woman in a torrent of winds, reaching out to touch the face of a frozen man. She saw life flow into his veins as the woman caressed his cheek. Seerae recognized the face of Eve and remembered she had been on the mountain, with Ross, that she had seen him in his dreams and that she still had purpose, just a different one than she had experienced with Eve. She now had a purpose that lived in the heart of Ross. A purpose that found its meaning in the life left in him by Eve. That part of her she gave away to him had become life to him, and in that, she was still alive. Her spirit would not yield to death but would overcome it through the bond of two who were meant to be one. Seerae began to hope and believe. She felt life living again inside of her.

Seerae was so lost in her thoughts she was not aware of how far down she had traveled. When she looked around, she noticed she was standing in the hollow of the staircase just behind the waterfall. She could see the muted aurora of diffused moonlight glowing through the entrance as the shadows of the falling water danced upon the ground.

Seerae stepped into the nightglow and felt its gentle warmth embrace her soul. Her luxurious, translucent hair flowed to her waist. Her skin glimmered with sparkles of light that shone like a night sky overwhelmed with brilliant stars. She still resembled Eve, especially when the twin moons cast their radiant beams upon her. Like a celestial creature, fallen from the heavens, she appeared sublime, supernal, like nothing that had ever been seen in Shuk. She emerged from behind the waterfall and into the snow and wind of the frigid, stormy night.

Now Huzesh had all but fallen to sleep under a pile of rubble that had sheltered him from the storm, when a small break in the clouds permitted a narrow shaft of light from the twin moons to creep through the rubble and shine upon his tired eyes. As he peeked out through his uncomfortably small entrance, appearing from behind the falls and into the falling snow, was a peculiar, ethereal form of beauty. Immediately alert, Huzesh sprung from his hiding place and leapt at the unexpected stranger.

Knowing immediately what he was, Seerae promptly responded to his movements and quickly drew her sword. Unfortunately, her thoughts were too focused on the approaching assailant to remember that if she would just flee into the falls, she would be safe because the gallues were not allowed to enter, for Eloh had placed powerful forces over the falls to protect the nephesh. However, Seerae was too flustered and instead, stepped away from the falls and into the path of Huzesh.

Her heart racing, Seerae rashly swung her sword at him. Huzesh paused, not yet drawing his sword. In his rush to attack, he had left his sword in his shelter, but, unconcerned, he menacingly growled, "Ye mus bae da forner!"

"Back off! Stay back!" Seerae's voice was unsure and quivered with fear. Huzesh stomped toward her, his formidable frame towering over her. She backed up with her sword extended in front of her in a defensive position. Huzesh lunged toward her and then quickly stepped back to draw her off balance. Seerae swung her sword with such strength and force it spun her around in a circle. As she came around to face him, Huzesh immediately struck her with the full might of his brutal right fist, sending her airborne. Seerae abruptly landed among a heap of stones, and her head struck the sharp edge of a large boulder, knocking her unconscious. Blood issued from her wounds, staining the rocks and the fresh white snow.

Huzesh confidently approached her limp body, picked up her sword, and looked at it with curiosity. "Hmm, ut bae u neph sword." Huzesh grabbed Seerae's face with his monstrous hand and turned her head, so he could see her better. Blood flowed from a deep gash and seeped from the corners of her mouth. Huzesh studied her face and her limp body for quite a while, then he scratched his head, as if puzzled, and confusedly grumbled, "Yur u neph! Yur no forner!" But Seerae didn't look like any nephesh Huzesh had ever seen. He wrestled with himself over what he should do with her. He did not want or need a nephesh, but he certainly would not let her go. She was not yet dead and even if she was, the others would eventually find her and then they would search for the one who had attacked her. He did not want her to travel with him because he knew she would eventually regain consciousness and then become a great problem. The free nephesh were known to be strong and troublesome to a single gallue. Huzesh breathed out a deep sigh of frustration. He knew he had to take her with him and hide her from the others until he could find the foreigner. He knew the meadow was not the right place to hide her, and it occurred to him that the brewing storm would make it easier for him to escape the meadow with her. The frenzied winds and obsidious darkness would conceal him from the watchful eyes of Kumél and Ziminiar who were crouched under a protective cover. However, the snow would also be a great obstacle to his stealth, for it would reveal his tracks and give his enemies an advantage in finding him. He hoped the snow would fall heavily enough to cover his escape and disguise any sign he had ever been there. He yanked Seerae up from the ground by her feet, slung her over his shoulder like a dead animal, and under the cover of the storm, hurriedly trudged back toward the gorge.

Dakoon

Chapter XVIII

Incantus Dominus

In the distant south region of Shuk, the raging storm was spreading across the sky like a black cape. Its ominous clouds reached over the vast Plane of Haemus, from the sea to the mountains and in every direction. Out of its expansive bowels roared ceaseless groans and clamors of thunder, preceded by countless, tormenting arrays of violent lightning, striking the ground and electrifying the air.

The voice of the Jupnie wailed through the air, growing more distinct and prevalent the stronger the storm grew. The onward invasion of the storm eventually spread over the Valley of Souls where it pushed its way through the mist and fog, down into the ears and minds of all who dwelled there. Many in the valley whispered the foreign tongue, becoming unwitting advocates of the Jupnie. Their reluctant voices were captured by the winds, then carried across the entire land and despite the turbulent invasion, not one of the usually suspicious gallues noticed it.

Even Sinistradt whispered the message of the Jupnie, as he sat in Gubrone's giant hall. His thick voice resonated heavily through the hollow corridors and dark cavities. The sound of it seemed innocuous and thus unsuspected, as though it was the careless babbling of an old man.

Sinistradt sat like a daydreamer, catatonic, mumbling in the foreign tongue of the Jupnie.

Upon his arrival to Gubrone's fortress, Veroot had sought out Sinistradt in order to deliver the prized weapon to him. Seated in the giant, stone chair, which had always been the seat of Gubrone, Sinistradt was startled out of his stupor by the echoing clatter of Veroot's hurried footsteps. Sinistradt leaned forward and glared at Veroot as he entered, lurking like an alert mēglydaim, brooding and poised to attack.

"So, yur finely buk! A waer b'gunin t'tink thut ye ha failed mae!" Sinistradt haughtily rose from his stone seat and strode dangerously toward the trembling gallue.

Veroot tenaciously defended his tardiness, "No mae liege! A ha da weapon! Ut waer vary dangerus fur mae t'stael ut fur ye! Gubrone ha muny gards t'protect eem un ee kupt ut wit eem at all tams. Gubrone dud nut gae through da Pass o'Klamata, instead ee ventured norõ, toward yer domain. A followed eem fur four suns afore A caught up wit eem. Haer, Sinistradt, haer bae da weapon o'da forner!"

As Veroot reached into his animal skin satchel for Ross's ice axe, Sinistradt seized Veroot's wrist and yanked him nearer. "Wut d'ye maen, ee went t'da norõ?" He snarled suspiciously. While Veroot struggled to free his arm from Sinistradt's grip, he nervously assured him, "Mae liege, please, ut bae true! Dae bae un da norõ, but A know nut whaer. A brung ye da weapon as soon as A cud. Ut bae true!"

Sinistradt released Veroot's arm and grabbed the ice axe from him. As he paced the floor, he debated with himself about dubious reasons why Gubrone would be wandering to the northern realm. He was concerned Gubrone may have discovered his plan and was gathering forces.

As Veroot intently eyed Sinistradt, he noticed Sinistradt's lips were moving erratically, and he faintly heard a foreign language coming from Sinistradt's mouth. He grew increasingly leery of Sinistradt and backed away from him. Abruptly, Sinistradt looked up at Veroot, and spoke with deliberate, composed words, in a slightly hostile tenor. "But whae? Whae gae t'da norõ, t'mae domain? Bae no reason t'gae dar! Mubae ee ha bun tol o'mae plans. But who, who wud tell eem? A mus fin Gubrone! A mus destroy eem, once un fur all!"

Sinistradt's pensive, thoughtful demeanor discomforted Veroot, for Sinistradt was not known to be one of deep or careful contemplation; he was reputed to be a brute, rash, and impetuous. Veroot deftly took several steps back to increase his distance from Sinistradt, for he did not trust the dubious arch-gallue, especially when he was behaving so out of character.

While Sinistradt stroked his chin and dragged his sharp talons over the side of his face and across his scarred cheeks, he pensively considered his next move. He demanded, "Cud ye fin dis place agan? Da place whaer ye took da weapon frum Gubrone?"

Veroot swallowed. He could feel his spittle moving sluggishly down his throat and he answered hesitantly, "Aye, ut bae nut far frum da naedles."

"Gud! Wae mus fin eem soon! Ye wull take mae mēgs un Uuduk, cause ee ha mony snitches. Take thum Tae. Dar bae no tam t'wais!"

"But—"

Before Veroot could say another single word, Sinistradt closed the distance between them and struck him brutally in the face with his fist, knocking him to the cold stone floor of the cave. "Dar bae nutin t'say! Fin eem, now!"

Veroot lay on the floor, bleeding and dazed. He rose slowly and stumbled out of the doorway. As soon as he was sure he was out of Sinistradt's sight, he fell back to his knees. Veroot feared he might not be able to find Gubrone. He wanted to explain to Sinistradt, but he knew he had only one choice and that was to find Gubrone no matter what.

Sinistradt returned to his stone seat and motioned to another one of his slaves, who had been in the room with him. "Fin Chiddush, now. Ha eem maet mae un da woods, ee wull know da place. Say notin t'onyone bout dis, or else!"

Gubrone could have hidden allies in the north who would defend Gubrone and fight for him. If Gubrone did have such allies, it could cause some of The Twelve to align with him. Sinistradt began doubting his plan and its timing. He doubted himself for only a moment before mustering up the determination to bolster his efforts. Sinistradt grabbed the foreigner's weapon and headed to the woods to meet with Chiddush. "Whaer ye bae, Chiddush?"

Sinistradt yelled impatiently, and his voice roared through the dark forest. Moments later, Chiddush casually but cautiously walked into their covert place.

"Wut ye bae bellowin bout? Ye soun lik u whinin ol'nag, forcin eary one t'run bout luk ye bae u ruttin stag!"

"Ye bes hold yer tongue, Chiddush! A wull bae da ruler o'Shuk soon aenuff!"

"Yur nut da ruler yet! Un ye wull ony bae un charge uf ye cun kaep da favor o'da others. But uf ye kaep dis up, deir deference wull turn bak t'Gubrone!"

"Sounds luk yur mukin u threat! Chiddush, rumumbar who A bae!"

"Ye, Gubrone shud rumumbar thut ye naed mae un mae magic! Un b'sides, ye know thut uf ye gut rid o'mae, ye wull ha no allies fur nut one o'thum trus ye. Da truth bae thut wae bot ha much t'gain un much t'lose, but b'laeve dis, A wull nut bae treated lik u slave or u dakkrah!"

However, as usual, Sinistradt utilized his powerful presence to get in the "last word" by arrogantly stepping toward Chiddush like a thug and shoving him. Then, he slyly changed the subject, "Oh wut A wud guv fur u tasty, warm-blooded stag. Eean u nag wud taste gud!"

Sinistradt refusing distraction, redirected their conversation back to his reason for meeting with Chiddush, "Ye ha spies thut cun fly t'da norõ?"

"Mae liddle black spies, da corvuses cun. Whae?"

"Gubrone, ee un Tukkir ha gone t'da norõ raelm! Dae ha baen viewed naer mae own fortress, naer da spires. A mus learn o'deir destination afore onyone else un afore dae gae out o'mae reach! A mus fin thum un uf wae dunna act soon, ut wull bae tae late!" Sinistradt's words took on a tone of uncertainty and even desperation.

"A wull sun mae spies t'search fur thum un dae wull fin thum!" Chiddush summoned his spies by blowing across a small, wooden reed like a whistle that sounded like the unique, suppressed combination of a howl and a screech. As the call went out, a single corvus flew in and landed in the tree behind, just beyond the reach of Chiddush, and mockingly screeched at him. Startled for only a second, Chiddush held out his hand, and the bulky bird flew to him. Chiddush leaned toward the bird's head and spoke to it in an arcane tongue. The corvus lifted into the sky with a powerful thrust of its wings and as it screeched again, the trees shuddered beneath its menacing shadow. Hundreds of corvuses followed the lead-spy as it flew away.

Perched high in the branches above Sinistradt and Chiddush, was an enormous, gray strigidae that was witnessing all the commotion and eavesdropping on the two gallues. It sat motionlessly, like the predator it was, observing what was happening below. As Chiddush and Sinistradt departed their secret place, the gray strigidae waited until they were both completely out of sight, then it flew into the dark sky toward Levitus.

Gubrone and Tukkir were enveloped by the full fury of the storm while it was bludgeoning the high mountain pass. Snow was falling in abundance, driven by the angry gale that was resisting their every step. They were not contending well with the storm's overpowering assault and desperately needed to seek shelter.

"Gubrone! Wae mus gut out o'dis storm! Wae cunna kaep gaein!"

Gubrone knew the secret lair of the dakoons was not far away, so he kept persisting in his endeavor, but finally had to relent. "Whaer bae u place t'shelter un conceal us? A cunna see u ting!"

"Wae mus dig un, un da snow!"

Tukkir and the two slaves dug three large snow caves for shelter while Gubrone barked orders. It was obvious he still believed himself to be superior to everyone else. Once the shelters were dug deeply into the snow, they crawled into the undersized refuges to wait out the night.

The entrances to the snow caves closed almost immediately due to the endlessly falling snow and constantly blowing wind. The fury of the storm raged through the night, howling and screaming without reprieve and leaving little opportunity for any of them to actually rest. Tukkir was especially uneasy. Even though Tukkir could not understand its words, he believed the voice was accusing him, chiding him, exposing the perfidious secrets he had labored so diligently to conceal. So loud were the thoughts in his head that he feared Gubrone, who was oppressively close by, could also hear them. However, Gubrone could not hear Tukkir's thoughts, for he was, himself, oppressed by the tormenting wind. Each roar and scream that filled the tiny quarters came as an attack against his authority and his ability to rule. Repeatedly, he heard the snide protestation and denunciation of his authority by Sinistradt and the others chiding in his mind. He could see, in his thoughts, the malevolent stares of treacherous satisfaction as he was forced to abandon his rule. Each of their faces came into his mind, sneering and mocking him, decrying his legitimacy as the ruler. The visions festered in Gubrone's thoughts, infecting him with greater distrust toward all of them, even Tukkir.

Over the span of many restless hours, the thick air inside of the small caves reeked with the odious scent of bad breath and body odor, making it unpleasant and difficult to breathe. Tukkir resolved to dig them out, but he was moving too slowly for Gubrone. "Gut out o'mae wae, Tukkir! Da storm ha passed un wae naed t'gae!" Gubrone pushed past Tukkir and began digging at the snow himself, angry and overwrought with the hours of mental torture. Tukkir looked at him and felt a murderous, palpable loathing, rising within. With his eyes glaringly fixed upon Gubrone's back, Tukkir uttered lurid, unintelligible curses. He had endured the scorn and arrogance of Gubrone as though he were a slave, inferior. Throughout the ages, he had concealed his contempt and never fought back. Yet behind his acquiescence, powerful, secret forces were beginning to take control of him. After the night of torment he had endured, Tukkir wanted to kill Gubrone more than anyone else wanted to. Gubrone continued to yell at him without restraint or regard. "Com un! Wut ye doin? Haelp mae, ye lazy dakkrah!" Eventually, they escaped into the gray haze of a heavily clouded day and a gentle snow that was being tossed about by mild gusts of frigid wind. Featureless, threatening clouds loomed in every direction as the wind worked itself up into a frenzy.

Gubrone lead the way down the slope of the pass. The thick blanket of snow made every step a fight. They looked for the way that led to the hiding place of the dakoons, but they had never seen the terrain under such deep snow. Everything looked unfamiliar until they came upon towering slabs of granite and ice. Tukkir quickly recognized the narrow route that led them between the slabs and eventually to a dead end. "Whaer bae da stone?" Gubrone barked at Tukkir.

"Ut shud bae o'er haer, but ut mus bae buried."

As their time passed swiftly, Tukkir and his two slaves dug into the waist-deep snow, for they knew that buried beneath the snow was a pile of rocks, a cairn, that they needed to uncover. While they were working, Tukkir stumbled and disappeared into the deep snow. Gubrone lurking nearby, impatiently kicking the snow, and ineptly searching for the buried cairn, called out. "Tukkir, whaer ye bae?"

"Arrrggg!" Tukkir growled.

"Wut ye bae doin?"

"A foun ut!" Tukkir had stumbled over the cairn and grumbled loudly as he slid and slipped, rather awkwardly, a couple of more times while he tried to lift himself out from under the powdery blanket. When he was finally able to stand up, he looked more like a yeti than his usual, gruesome self.

"Bae ye finished playin yet? Wae stull ha much work t'do."

Tukkir had cast a strong magic spell over the entrance of the cave, requiring a blood offering in order to gain entrance. It did not matter whose blood or what kind of blood, it just had to be blood and it had to be spilt onto the cairn and poured over the one who would enter. Tukkir pulled the remains of a murdered nephesh waif from a large pack he carried with him. He lifted the body of the nephesh by one of its ankles, grabbed a long dagger he was carrying in his belt, slit the nephesh from its groin to its throat, exsanguinating its blood onto the pile of stones. Then he lifted the gruesome sacrifice with its entrails hanging from the chest cavity over his own head and let the blood run over himself.

Gubrone waited, impatiently observing him. "A dud wunnar wut ye ha un yer bag."

"Bahaha! Aye tae wunnar wut da master ha un ees bag," remarked one of the slaves, unaware that the spell required an offering for each one who intended to enter the cave. Gubrone hastily pulled his sword from its sheath and with a swift, fluid motion, swung the sword around, and took off the head of Tukkir's impertinent slave, who had laughed and spoken out, as though he had somehow merited the privilege to speak to Gubrone. Gubrone lifted the dead body of the gallue over the stone and allowed its blood to drain over the makeshift altar, then he lifted it over his own head and let the blood cover him as well.

"Dat bae u gud wais o'mae gallue!"

"T'waer thut or yer mēg un da mēgs bae o'mur use. Whae carry yer offerin wun dae cun carry thumsaelfs. Bahaha!"

Tukkir tried to hide his disapproval, though the sharpness of his words and the velocity of their eruption was not the way to disguise his rancor. "Yur u fool, Gubrone! Dar bae muny nephs! But wae ha no wae t'replace u gallue or da mēgs!"

Gubrone detected acrimony in the tone of Tukkir's rebuke and a brooding animus emanating from Tukkir's words. He lashed back sternly, "Hold yer tongue, Tukkir or ut wull bae yer blood on da stone."

Gubrone cooly sheathed his sword and dropped the dead gallue in the snow. Blood stained the ground as it ran down over the cairn, then disappeared under the deep snow. The mēglydaims smelt the blood and became excited, expecting a meal of the corpses. They growled and fought each other and pulled against the chains of their master as they tried to reach the bodies, but Tukkir and the other slave held them back, for they would later feed the bodies to the dakoons.

Once the blood was poured over the stone altar, a strong gust of wind blew out from a narrow crack in the stone wall, not far from where they stood. With a loud cracking noise and the sudden shaking of the ground, two gigantic rocks that had covered the cave's entry moved, one to the right side and the other to the left as if they were stone guards charged with protecting the entrance. They took on the shape and vague appearance of a gallue, only much larger. The sentinels were called Eeolythahs and were not flesh or mortal, but were, themselves, stones, living, metamorphic stones, created beings, called from the rocks, made alive by dark magic for only one purpose: to protect whatever their master desired. They would not let anyone pass who had not spilled blood upon the altar. As they moved aside, a large, dark tunnel came into view. Along one side of the tunnel, flames of fire burned like lanterns fueled by subterranean and highly combustible gases that sprung up from holes and cracks in the rocks. The flames were scattered irregularly along the short corridor. At the end of the tunnel was a large chamber that was lit by a flame burning continuously. It rose up from a deep hole in the center of the cave floor. The cave and the tunnel were filled with black smoke, which ascended toward the ceiling of the cave before it escaped the cave through a narrow crack that led up through the rocks. The walls of the cave were black and sooty from ages of the black smoke hanging in the air and clinging to everything.

Gubrone and Tukkir passed between the two Eeolythahs and entered the cave. At the back of the cave, there were two sets of yellow, glowing eyes with slitted black pupils floating in the shadows. The eyes stared at Gubrone and Tukkir with a menacing glare. The two arch- gallues walked slowly into the smoky shadows of the cave. Tukkir tossed the dead body of the nephesh orphan toward the large, yellow eyes as if it were nothing more than rubbish. Out of the shadows sprang a giant, hideous creature, as black as the smoke from the fires. Its strong, powerful body resembled that of a gallue, but on its back were a pair of enormous, grisly wings the beast carried as though they were a burden. Only a moment later, and with even more determination, a second beast sprang from the shadows and began to tear at the body of the dead nephesh with its long, black talons and sharp, yellow teeth. "Dar ye bae, mae liddle pets. Bae ye hungry? Eat. Thut bae gud." The two creatures growled and clawed at each other over the dead body until they finally started gorging on it, consuming all parts of it and leaving no scraps.

Gubrone glared scornfully at Tukkir. "Ut saems thut ye ha spent tae much tam wit yer pets. Dae bae no pets! Un dae bae nut yers! Dunna ye forget ut!"

Gubrone heaved the headless body of the slave-gallue toward the two dakoons, and they fought violently for their meals. The monstrous creatures growled and roared, pulled and clawed at each other over the second meal, just as they had the first. They behaved as if they had not eaten in quite some time. They were vile beasts with violent tempers and their only satisfaction came from death and destruction and a stomach full of warm, fresh meat.

"Course, yur right, Gubrone. A ony call thum mae pets t'calm thum."

"Wull, ut dunna saem t'bae workin!" Gubrone's words were sharp and his tone menacing.

"Dae bae hungry, thut bae all. Un ut ha baen awhile since ye waer haer last. Dae might bae afaered o'ye."

"Bahaha! Afaered? Ut luks mur lik dae bae lickin deir lips! Hungry! Afaered? Yur u fool Tukkir, un ol' fool!"

Tukkir glared at Gubrone. Tukkir was only pretending to like him, and his act of friendliness toward Gubrone was nothing more than deceptive tolerance. But Gubrone felt justified in his abhorrence toward Tukkir, for he recognized the arch-gallue had become soft and weak, even showing affection toward the dakoons. It occurred to him there was something very wrong with Tukkir, something that repulsed him.

The beasts were bound to each other by two large, crudely cast iron chains attached to their hind ankles. The length of chain between them was more than twice the length of their combined height and ran through a large iron ring fastened to the floor of the cave. The links of the chains appeared to have been stretched by the ceaseless pulling and fighting. Whenever one would move away from the iron ring, it pulled the chains of the other dakoon toward the ring. If one were to run away from the ring, the other one would be pulled toward it. The bolts of iron that had been driven into the stone floor of the cave, securing the iron ring, were bent and loosened from the stone. They moved about as if they could be pulled out at any time with just the right amount of force. The hammered shackles wrapped around the ankles of the dakoons tore at their flesh, causing them to bleed constantly. Each of the creatures had ghastly wounds that oozed with putrid, infectious pus and blood, caused by the ceaseless wear and aggravation of the shackles, even though they were oblivious to them. Both of the dakoons bore grotesque scars all over their bodies that came from their sharp, cruel talons.

"Soon, ye wull faed un Eloh, eemsaelf. Ye wull eat o'ees flesh un drink ees blood. Bahaha!"

Tukkir could see the bloodlust in Gubrone's dark eyes. He knew Gubrone was fixated on finding Eloh and the foreigner. At the same time, he also suspected that for Gubrone, it was not just about finding them, it was also about revenge, about taking back the realm of Shuk, and letting the dakoons feast on all of those who had turned against him. While watching Gubrone revel in his anticipated retaliation, a cold, invidious aggression filled Tukkir's mind. He glared at Gubrone with a disapproving sneer. Deep in his throat, a captive growl tried to escape, but Tukkir restrained the torrent of jealousy. He wondered what Gubrone might do to him, should he become suspicious. His motives were nefarious and malefic at best. Such are the tenuous alliances forged in the hot furnace of treachery.

Tukkir had lied to Gubrone about the spell. He had told him he was unsure of its power, or if the dakoons could be commanded by it, but that he was sure he had discovered what would make his sorcery complete. He knew once his spell was cast, the dakoons would be forever submissive to whoever cast the spell. Lying to Gubrone was his way of biding his time while he made plans of his own, plans of subversion and conquest. There was, however, a strange thing happening to Tukkir as he worked on the spell. Over the many seasons of secret solitude he had spent with the dakoons, he had become fond of the creatures, but his fondness was evolving into an obsession. The spell was becoming less of an instrument with which to control the dakoons, than a means by which Tukkir could turn them into his own pets. His growing affection toward them had been well disguised, and he had managed to deceive Gubrone and the others. In Tukkir's mind, everything was going as planned, until the news of the foreigner. Sinistradt united the majority of The Twelve under himself, leaving Tukkir to make a difficult choice: follow Sinistradt or follow Gubrone. Gubrone had something Tukkir needed, and so it was in his best interest to follow Gubrone, posing as an ally until he could get what he needed from him.

Tukkir had to cast the spell himself, if he was to command the dakoons, but Gubrone insisted he be the one to cast the spell. Gubrone was not a supreme sorcerer and was reliant on Tukkir's skills. He also required the power Tukkir possessed in the dark magic. However, Gubrone did possess the one thing that would give to the rune power to rule the dakoons. A spell of domination required the blood of the dominator.

Tukkir had an epiphany. In a dream, he saw himself standing over a cauldron full of boiling liquid. He raised a knife and cut his arm, making a deep, painful wound. From the wound poured three streams of blood which, as they fell into the caldron, streamed together into a braid. As they swirled in the caldron, the image of Attar rose into the air and then disappeared. Tukkir awoke and understood. The rune required three strands of blood, and one of those strands had to come from Attar. There was only one place in Shuk where the blood of Attar could be found, and Tukkir was the only one who knew it was in the Eleetrum wound.

Now Gubrone was the only arch-gallue who bore the Eleetrum wound: a deep, leeching abscess that never healed. Within the wound the Eleetrum Shard was buried, a long, sharp, dagger-like shiv made of the bone and marrow of Attar himself. Its course, sponge-like marrow and jagged, porous shaft were permeated with Attar's blood, causing the wound to fester and abscess unceasingly.

Sometime before Attar sent the Twelve to Shuk, in the days leading up to his rebellion, Attar delved deeper and more intently into the darkness of his sorcery. He desired to make his magic even more fiendish and evil. He first used the blood of animals to strengthen the force of his necromancy, but this eventually became unsatisfying, so Attar began cutting himself to acquire his own blood. In his blood, he found the potency he coveted. It was filled with the atrociousness and power of his hatred and enmity against Eloh. He became increasingly masochistic, finding pain to be pleasurable and satisfying. Attar, desiring to extend the reach of his corruption, slashed a long, gaping wound into his own left arm. From it poured the blood of his malice and contempt. His blood spilled into the Pool of Eon, corrupting its pure waters. Attar was engulfed in a raging, cyclonic storm of dark powers that grew even fiercer the more he wounded himself. Intoxicated and insane with the wine of insurrection, he reached into the bleeding wound, took hold of one of the two bones of his forearm, and ripped it from his own flesh, breaking it from its socket. The shattered shaft of bone, covered in his vile, corrupted blood, drained into the pool as he laughed in delirious pleasure. The wound and its grotesque scar incessantly afflicted Attar and all those who bore its grief.

Attar used his bone shard to murder Eleetrum, the first kerolus to oppose him at the Pool of Eon. The shard was filled with dark, poisonous powers, and Attar used it to murder many of those who opposed him. On the night Attar sent the Twelve to Shuk, he viciously drove the Eleetrum Shard into the abdomen of Gubrone, deliberately broke it off and left it buried under Gubrone's ribs. Attar spit upon the wound with his venomous saliva, then stabbed his bloody talon into the wound, driving the shiv even deeper. Gubrone writhed in pain from the wounding. Tukkir watched as Gubrone suffered, spying as Attar leaned in close and whispered words of malevolence into the ears of Gubrone, words that were a spell: "Yer wound wull nae'er heal! Ut wull ooze da dark magic un all da lund whaer e'er ye gae. Eary place thut ye tread wull taste o'da blood o'Attar un languish un da sorrow o'mae poisoned haert un fael da pain o'mae wounds. Lut no one take frum ye da bitter milk o'dis cursed scar!"

Attar calmly withdrew his long, black talon from the wound as Gubrone screamed in agony and collapsed to his knees. Every living thing that grew in the ground around him began to die as the wound bled its cursed infection from his bowels. The wound was the reason Gubrone could still remember much of the war. It was a constant reminder of Attar's great power and ruthlessness.

Gubrone protected the wound, just as Attar had commanded him. He hammered a breastplate of iron, shaping it to fit over his abdomen and chest and held in place with straps made from the skin of slaughtered nephesh waifs. He never removed it in the company of the others. Often the wound became infected and swollen like a boil and its pain intensified. In those times, Gubrone had to pierce the boil with his black talons, releasing a sanguine gush of putrid ooze that smelled of rotting meat and sulfur. Its stench was more than even the calloused senses of the gallues could tolerate.

The rune required, among other things: water from the secret Well of Diffush, hidden deep in the cave of Gubrone, whose waters are dark and bitter, dried and ground marrow from the bones of a Danakuse cat, the warm, fresh vitreous fluid from the eye of a black hooded owl, the poisonous resin from the thorns of a blackstalk bush, the dried, black tongue of a giant Vulgara Toad, and the gray breath of the mist guarding the way into the valley of souls. The rune also required blood, three different sources of blood: blood from the dakoons, for it was on them the spell was to be cast, blood from the one who would rule over them, for his blood would dominate the blood of the dakoons, and the blood of rule, found within the poisonous pus oozing from the Eleetrum wound. Once concocted, the rune had to be drunk by the spellbinder to whom would be given absolute power over the creatures. The final step was the Incantus Dominus, the words of the spell spoken, which would bind the beasts to their master.

Tukkir knew a solitary drop of the infected purulence would perfect the rune. He just had to figure out how he might collect it. The pus had to be fresh, from the wound itself, and not contaminated in any way. Gubrone would have to lance his own wound and excrete the soured fluids directly into the cauldron. What perplexed Tukkir the most was the question of how it could be done without Gubrone's own blood entering into the mix.

Tukkir had not revealed the secret of the blood to Gubrone for fear he might try to steal his magic. Nevertheless, Tukkir had a bad memory, and in order to remember the rune, he had written a cipher which he carried with the ingredients. The cypher included the secret of the blood and of the Eleetrum Wound. All of this, Tukkir guarded carefully. His desire was to make the dakoons his pets, and do whatever he desired with them. Knowing that what he needed most would have to come from Gubrone drove him mad, consuming his every thought with restless, delusory ruminations. He deceived himself with lofty thoughts and ambitions, lusting for power and authority, convincing himself it was he who was the rightful ruler of Shuk. The power of Attar's wickedness had forged the confederacy of the fallen gallues, and had become a violent force, pulling at every seam, tearing at the fabric of the dark alliances. It was a power too great to contain or master. It corrupted the corrupted, causing them to turn against themselves. The frozen unity of The Twelve was melting away.

Tukkir considered how he might trick Gubrone by keeping the secret of the spell to himself, not telling Gubrone, and not preparing the rune as it ought to be done. Given all his efforts to avoid suspicion, Tukkir had failed, for Gubrone, ever the skeptic, had indeed suspected something and had grown increasingly leery of their alliance. He never had trusted anyone, especially those who were closest to him, for he knew they were always looking for a way to usurp his rule. The recent events had reinforced his disposition, causing him, all the more, to suspect Tukkir of guile. He had discerned the malice in Tukkir's sharp response at the cave entrance, and he had been sensing a disingenuous accord lurking behind his propitious, yet deliberate allegiance, but Gubrone's reliance on Tukkir was forcing him to conceal his growing antagonism toward him.

In the cave, Tukkir squatted just beyond the reach of the dakoons, staring at them as though he were in a trance. With one of his sharp talons, he scratched on the stone floor of the cave. Each movement made a piercing screech, causing the dakoons to retreat into the shadows. As Tukkir scratched the floor, he whispered, "Soon, mae liddle ones, vary soon, ye wull bae frae t'fly o'er des forsaken lunds. Yur master, ee wull frae ye frum yer chains, un da darkness wull nut ha da power t'hold ye ony mur, ye wull soar across da skies un aet yer favrit flesh until yer bellies bae full!" Gubrone was frustrated, for he could not hear what the entranced arch-gallue was whispering and he was also increasingly irritated by the incessant scratching.

"Yur mae liddle ones. Yur mine un ye b'long t'no others. Mae liddle ones, un ee wull nut ha ye!" Abruptly, Tukkir whirled around and glared directly at Gubrone with threatening eyes. In his raspy, menacing voice, Tukkir grumbled, "Ye maen t'stael thum way frum mae, mae liddle ones. Dae bae maen!"

Gubrone turned and looked, wide-eyed, at Tukkir. With a sudden and sharp blow, he struck Tukkir across the face with his open hand. Gubrone's long talons scratched across his skin, drawing blood, which began to run down Tukkir's face, falling, drop by drop onto the floor of the cave. The dakoons quickly smelled the blood and rushed to the end of their chains.

"Da dakoons dunna b'long t'ye! Ye forgut who ye bae un who A bae, Tukkir!" Tukkir brushed the side of his face with his hand. He looked at his hand to see the blood that covered his palm. Tukkir lifted his head and, once again, looked straight at Gubrone with a dangerous, angry stare. He clenched his fist and lowered his brow. His jaw fixed and the muscles in his face became tight and exposed. Tukkir squared up with Gubrone as though he were going to attack. Gubrone took a small step back and readied himself to be assaulted. Then Tukkir turned away in a strangely unaffected manner, as if not wanting to give Gubrone the satisfaction of an impulsive reprisal. Gubrone sneered as he watched Tukkir walk away.

Tukkir moved slowly toward a dark corner of the cave where he waited in the shadows, glaring at Gubrone who was staring back at him. The corruption of his growing contempt acted as a catalyst, binding together ages of odium, jealousy, and antagonism that infected every cell of his being. Like the thick, rancid pus from the Eleetrum wound, enmity seemed to ooze out of every thought, clinging to his every act and motive like the noxious, rancid sap of the blackstalk bush. His bruised ego boiled within the black caldron of his wicked heart, and he pondered how he might satisfy his thirst for blood by murdering Gubrone. The festering madness was growing so intense he could only focus on his desire for death.

Gubrone, not one to be detoured from his secret intent, demanded, "Tukkir, tam bae short! Da rune mus bae finished un da spell cast!"

Gubrone's words only agitated Tukkir even more. He knew there was little chance of him succeeding in his plans as long as Gubrone lived. He knew there was no way Gubrone would surrender the pus of the wound to him. As the reality sank in, the caustic delirium grew ever more volatile.

Gubrone could see something had changed in Tukkir and that their fragile alliance was in danger. It caused him concern and, for the first time ever, he began to feel vulnerable. He knew he needed Tukkir's magic. He knew he needed the dakoons. Gubrone waited impatiently while Tukkir sat with his eyes fixed upon him. Finally, Gubrone tried to reason with Tukkir. "Dis bae our tam, tam t'finally destroy Eloh un ees armies! Ye mus see dis, Tukkir! Uf wae fail thun da legend wull com true. Eloh wull return un crush Attar, un da fallen, wit yer rune un spell, wae bae da ony hope! Da dakoons, dae bae da ony hope o'crushing Eloh! Now bae da tam! Dis bae ut, our chance t'defeat our foes un rule da lunds! Cun ye nut rumumbar da war un da kerolus armies? Da kerolus wull com agan unless wae first kull Eloh un dose thut bae wit eem! Wae hav bun waitin fur dis fight! Now bae our tam t'finish ut!"

Tukkir was a long way from speaking sensibly, "Ut bae ony u fable. Thut bae wut ye ha tol us fur so lung. Whae now? Whae b'laeve now? Mubae yur ony tryin t'fool mae! Ye ha repeated thut yersaelf, thut Eloh bae ony u myth, u legend. Un ees return bae jus u story frum da ol'days, spread bae da foolish nephs!"

"But da weapon, ha ye saen ut? Ut mus bae frum Eloh!"

"Da weapon! Ut bae no weapon!"

"Dare ye accuse mae o'tellin tales! Ye ha saen ut wit yer own eyes, haer, view ut again!" Gubrone dug into the leather bag that was hanging around his neck, removed the branch Veroot had switched for the ice axe, and triumphantly held it up above his head. He insistently commanded, "See dis! Dis bae da weapon o'da forner! Ut mus ha com frum Eloh!"

At first, Tukkir ignored him, continuing to contemplate the destruction of Gubrone and not yet realizing it was not the weapon at all. "Look, ye fool!" Gubrone shook the branch violently.

When Tukkir's eyes focused on the object that Gubrone was maniacally waving over his head and realized it was only a stick, Tukkir grinned and then erupted with such boisterous, guttural, and hysterical laughter, he was barely able to remain on his feet.

Gubrone immediately lost his temper and charged at Tukkir. But as Gubrone took his first steps, Tukkir pointed at the stick and roared even louder with laughter.

"So, bahaha! Thut bae da weapon o'Eloh, aye? What, Eloh fights wit u stick! Bahaha!"

Gubrone paused long enough to glance at the object in his hands. His eyes revealed the bewildered shock of an ambushed animal. He yelled and cursed, threw the stick at Tukkir, and struck him in the head. He dug frantically in the satchel to find the weapon, but it was gone. Gubrone roared violently, "Ahh, ye dakkrah! Ye ha stolen da weapon. Yur u thief un u spy!" Insane with rage, Gubrone rushed at Tukkir, who was still staggering in laughter and barely able to regain his wits, but Tukkir reacted as quickly as he could and lunged toward Gubrone. The two of them collided with a jarring force that landed both on the floor of the cave. Gubrone landed on top of Tukkir and began to beat him with his fists. For a moment, Tukkir tried only to defend against the battery of blows, but then rage took over and empowered him. He reached up and swiped his talons across Gubrone's face, ripping the skin with deep grotesque cuts. Gubrone pushed away from Tukkir, giving Tukkir the opportunity to escape and take up a more offensive posture. Tukkir quickly stepped into Gubrone, who was kneeling on the floor. Tukkir doubled up his fist and struck Gubrone squarely on the other side of his face, knocking him to the ground. Then Tukkir drew his sword and would have struck Gubrone with it, but Gubrone quickly moved away and was able to get to his feet. Gubrone drew his sword and the two of them stood, swords drawn, facing each other, moving sideways in a circle. Gubrone swung his sword, as gallues always do, at the head and neck of Tukkir. Tukkir backed away, avoiding the sharp edge of the ancient blade. Tukkir returned a quick but powerful blow of his fist against the right side of Gubrone's torso. Tukkir knew the Eleetrum Wound was somewhere near that area of Gubrone's body and hoped to expose his weakness. His fist collided with Gubrone's breastplate. Gubrone winced from the blow for it did, indeed, strike the place where the wound hid behind the metal shield. Tukkir quickly rushed at Gubrone, leaping in the air with a flying kick and striking him in the chest. The power of Tukkir's two feet sent Gubrone flying backwards, within reach of the two dakoons. The dakoons rushed toward him with their teeth bared, but Gubrone was a champion, and seeing the impending attack, quickly rushed away from the dakoons whose advance was abruptly stopped by their intolerable chains. The pain of his wound was severe, but Gubrone had been wounded before and knew how to endure it. He charged Tukkir with his sword stretched out. As he swung the sword around, the blade caught the left shoulder of Tukkir, nearly severing his arm from his shoulder.

Tukkir knew he could not match Gubrone with the sword. The only hope he had was to escape, and he knew it. But Gubrone would not let him go. He attacked him with another powerful swipe of his sword and again, met Tukkir, only this time, just the tip of the blade grazed Tukkir's chest. However, Gubrone made a fatal mistake. He swung with such might that he lost his balance as the blade came around. He had to take a wide step to the side and, in doing so, stepped into a small depression on the cave floor. Gubrone fell hard to the ground and Tukkir quickly rushed over him and raised his sword into the air with his right arm while his left arm hung limp at his side. Tukkir meant to deal the final blow, but Gubrone put his sword up to block the descending blade, but Tukkir's power was too much for Gubrone's sword to block completely. The upper edge of Tukkir's sword followed through and met the left shoulder of Gubrone cutting a deep gash and then tearing the flesh of his chest as Tukkir drew the blade back, leaving a deep wound.

Gubrone yelled out as he pulled a dagger from the lacing of his sandals that wove over the calf of his leg. He sank the sharp blade into Tukkir's right thigh and then brought one of his feet up and kicked Tukkir in the stomach with all his might. Tukkir stumbled backward, as Gubrone clumsily rose from the floor, his left arm weak and torn by the wound, blood ran down his hand and streamed off his fingers, dripping onto the ground.

As the two arch-gallues fought, the dakoons kept charging to the end of their chains, snarling and fighting each other, hoping one or both of the gallues would once again end up within reach of their powerful claws and carnivorous teeth. Blood splattered in every direction, inciting the feeding instinct of the two beasts. They were mad with anticipation and excitement. Tukkir tried again to back Gubrone within reach of his little pets, but Gubrone knew the threat all too well and quickly avoided them.

The massive wound on Tukkir's shoulder and arm and the dagger, which was still in his thigh, made him weak and somewhat clumsy. All the malice and hatred that had driven him to want to kill Gubrone was draining from him like the blood running down his arm and leg. Lucidity was returning to his delusional mind. He knew it would only be a short time before Gubrone bested him and he would become a meal for the dakoons. Everything seemed lost—all the planning, all the time, all the secrecy—it all seemed to be a loss. Tukkir looked toward the opening of the cave. He knew he had to escape. His slave and the two mēglydaims were still outside the cave, waiting for him. He thought that if he could just get to them, they could help him fight off Gubrone. He looked toward the cave's entrance and moved quickly as he could toward it. Gubrone saw his eyes shifting back and forth between the entrance and him and knew Tukkir was about to attempt an escape. Gubrone realized if Tukkir was able to get to the help of his mēgs and the slave, then the fight was over; his head would be cleaved off and his body thrown to the dakoons. He rushed at Tukkir and managed to grab one of his feet, tripping him. Tukkir's wounds were so great, and he was so exhausted he almost wanted Gubrone to finish him off, but he kicked Gubrone in the face and then kicked him again, causing him to let loose his grip. Tukkir immediately got to his feet and ran, escaping through the opening of the cave.

Gubrone lay face down on the floor of the cave. He knew if he went out into the snow and wind he would be walking into a trap and Tukkir would be waiting for him. He lay in his own blood, reeling from the pain of his wounds while trying to figure out what he should do.

The dakoons had become silent and crawled back to the shadows of the cave, but Gubrone could feel their eyes on him, waiting for any opportunity to feast on his broken body.

Meanwhile, Tukkir escaped into the throes of a snowy blizzard. He looked around and could not find his slave or the two mēgs that he thought had been waiting outside the cave. Tukkir called out, "Noorak, Noorak, whaer ye bae? Noorak!"

There was no answer. The snow was falling heavily, and the wind had driven it into drifts, covering every sign they had ever been there. Tukkir could not see any tracks or trace at all and realized they had left him and Gubrone. He wondered what would have made them abandon their post, what would have chased them away. It was not long before the menacing voice of the wind bore into Tukkir's mind, and then it suddenly dawned on him that it may have been the wind that chased them away.

Tukkir tried to cover his ears, but the voice would not be silenced. It was stronger and more determined than before. He limped away from the cave, believing he would be hunted by Gubrone, that now he was alone as an outcast and an enemy of the Twelve. He feared if the other gallues ever discovered what had happened, they would hunt him down and kill him. He knew he had to escape into the lowlands, into the plane of Haemus, where he would be able to hide and heal. He pushed into the storm and headed down toward the south realm, hoping he would soon escape the deep snow and high winds.

Back in the cave, Gubrone rolled over onto his back. His body was covered in blood and he was very weak. He lay there with his eyes closed, listening for any sound or threat. He thought about the fight and how close he had been to being defeated by Tukkir. He believed that if Tukkir had not chosen to escape, he might have been defeated by him.

He began to laugh like a lunatic. He laughed because it amused him that Tukkir could have been so close to victory and yet run away like a coward. Gubrone sat up and surveyed the cave. He could see the evil eyes of the dakoons staring at him through the shadows. For a moment, he felt he had failed, that his plan had failed and he would never rule Shuk again. He swallowed and then drew a deep breath into his lungs and exhaled slowly, feeling the pains of defeat and of the sword.

After a while, Gubrone rose to his feet and looked around the dark cave. He could smell the blood formed puddles on the cave floor. He looked toward the opening of the cave from which Tukkir had escaped. Lying on the floor just inside the entrance, Gubrone could see a small, dark object lying in a heap. Unable to identify it, he plodded over to where it laid. As he stood over it, his eyes brightened and a smile crept across his scarred face. "Bahaha! Ye fool! Ye fool, bahaha!"

Resting on the mound was the satchel Tukkir carried with him everywhere he went and falling out its opening were several of the ingredients Tukkir used to make the rune. Gubrone bent over and picked up the bag, which was made from the skin of a dakoon. The shoulder strap was cut through. As he picked it up, a rolled-up animal hide fell from the bag to the floor at his feet. Gubrone picked it up and inspected it as it fell open. Written on it, in the language they had long ago abandoned, was the cipher of Tukkir, and Gubrone knew how to read it. Tukkir had carefully written out every detail of the rune and the spell, and it looked as though everything he needed was there, in the cave. Gubrone rifled through the bag to see what else Tukkir had lost. In the bottom of the bag was a stone vile sheathed in a leather pouch, which was fastened with cords of leather.

Gubrone paid no attention to the small pouch or what was in it. He gathered the spilled contents, put them back in the bag, and returned to the center of the cave. "Ye fool. Shuk wull bae maen, un ye shall pay! Ye shall pay, Tukkir!"

Now Morak and the snitches he had forced to come with him took refuge in the boulder fields of Tushun where they sheltered from the raging storm for many days.

Tushun was a land of giant stones that extended from the Telohm Mountains toward the south where the Plain of Haemus began. For many miles, the sprawling field of boulders covered the ground, making travel through the region slow and wrought with many perils. As far as the eyes could see, lay the mounds of stones, piled high on top of each other, scattered in all directions with no paths or routes to travel. Only by hand and foot, crawling and hopping from stone to stone, was it possible to venture through Tushun boulder field. Dispersed irregularly through Tushun, were tall evergreen trees called Quoio trees, which were robust and ancient and reached very high into the sky. Their roots sank deep below the rock and held firmly, ensuring their survival in an otherwise barren and unforgiving landscape.

Morak squatted near the fire and stared into the tiny flame. The small twigs and limbs he had been able to scavenge were wet and therefore smoked more than they burned, which made the fire a chore to keep. Morak's eyelids became heavy, and he began to doze off, not because he was particularly tired, but because the smoke coming from the fire was narcotizing him. Several of the small twigs were from a Jujarus bush. The Jujarus bush was used by many of the gallues in their sorcery. When burned, it released a powerful, hallucinogenic cloud that stupefied those who inhaled it, making them delirious and prone to visions.

He closed his eyes and began to dream wild and unimaginable things. He could see himself flying again, as he used to before the fall. He flew over the realm of Shuk like a small bird, flitting about from cloud to cloud and from tree to tree. He could see the mountains and valleys, all spread out beneath him. He felt himself fall from the sky like a stone that never landed. He saw visions of Attar and of the Pool of Eon where he and the others were transformed. Morak saw a mighty, giant dakoon soaring over the mountains, breathing fire from its mouth and devouring the Valley of Souls. He saw himself laughing in triumph over a field of dead bodies, all unrecognizable, faceless victims. Gruesome visions flooded his mind until he heard a voice calling out through the mist and fog that had fallen from the sky and enshrouded him. At first, the voice was more like a moan, indistinct and wordless. In the meantime, surrounding him were countless little creatures, like insects, living in the fog, flying about, swarming him, then landing on him, biting him and stinging him. He wanted to run, but in the fog, there was no place to go, no escaping. The voice called again with whispering words that, at first, he could not understand, but its breath came closer and touched his ears and he gradually understood their meaning. "*Soteria. Soteria. Soteria.*"

It was all the mysterious, moaning voice said. One word, over and over again. All the visions, all the dreams spun around Morak in opposing directions, like whirlwinds within whirlwinds. It was as if he was caught up in a cyclonic vortex and everything he had seen was being pulled into the turmoil. The voice grew louder and stronger until it stopped unexpectedly. Morak opened his eyes to see blood pooling on the floor of the shelter under his head and running out in front of his eye. He moaned and lifted his head. An abrupt and sharp pain ran through his body from the jagged gash in his temple.

"Soteria," Morak whispered.

"Soteria, da realm o'Soteria. Wae mus gae dar."

The realm of Mount Soteria was among the most remote places in all of Shuk. Because it lay to the north of Gershom and was flanked on all other sides by towering, unassailable walls of ice and stone, which were unfriendly to any intruder. This is why it was said the realm was guarded, for though there were no actual guards, the nature of the landscape seemed to intentionally protect it from intrusion. Unless you were a bird or had wings and could fly, the realm of Soteria seemed to be beyond trespass. However, Morak had heard of a way that followed along a narrow precipice on the East Wall. It was rumored the aposta, Ziminiar, lived there in the valley and that ages ago he had found the narrow East Way into the valley, but such speculations had never been confirmed and were regarded by the gallues as little more than myth and legend. Morak and the snitches began heading toward the north.

Gubrone looked at the odd collection of items that had been carried in Tukkir's pouch. He unrolled the hide, which had the instructions for the rune written on it. Gubrone had to study the inscriptions carefully in order to decipher their meaning so he could be sure to prepare the rune properly. It occurred to him that Tukkir might have intended for him to find the cipher and the ingredients. He wondered what might have been the advantage of such a plot and why Tukkir would intend for him to find these things. What would happen if he followed the rune, would it cast a spell on him? Gubrone became very suspicious and unsure of the seemingly fortuitous find. He paced back and forth, rubbing his head and thinking about the things Tukkir had told him about the rune, which, when he considered it, were very few. He began to realize Tukkir had been keeping things from him for quite some time and may have been plotting against him all along. He mulled over these things for a long time. His rational thoughts became entangled with fallacious conspiratorial notions, which began to twist his mind, convoluting his reason with dementia, until he had become like one who was bewitched. He stood, stupefied, mumbling quietly. "Dae ha b'traed mae, b'traed Attar. Dae wull trae t'destroy shuk, destroy all thut A ha built. A wull muk thum pay! A wull kill thum all!"

It was not long before he returned to his senses. He looked carefully at the cipher again. He studied the writing, trying to remember the ancient language until finally, he understood what Tukkir had written. In that moment of clarity, his mind quickly deciphered each of the words and then each of the steps of the rune. He carefully studied every detail, trying to discern whether it was true or a trick. After a while, he was convinced by Tukkir's own script, by the uniqueness of his cipher, that the spell had to be true. Tukkir had never intended for him to see it, much less read it, and besides, Gubrone felt Tukkir was not shrewd enough to devise a plan against him.

Confident of its authenticity, Gubrone began gathering what he needed. He would brew the ingredients in the caldron Tukkir had hanging over a pit in the cave. Gubrone found wood stashed behind a large boulder, which Tukkir had saved in the cave for just this purpose. Once everything was ready, he lit a fire under the cauldron and, one by one, he added the strange ingredients, just as Tukkir had written. Word for word, he read every part of the cipher until he came to the last part. He read the final steps of the rune, which called for the blood of the dakoons, the blood of the master, and the blood of Attar. He paused for just a moment, wondering to himself, *How wull A gut da blood o'da dakoons un da blood o'Attar? Dis bae wrong, da blood o'Attar? Dis bae u trick!* He yelled at the top of his voice, "Tukkir! A wull destroy ye uf dis bae u trick!" Gubrone rubbed his forehead, trying to understand how it was that he would get the blood of Attar. He could not understand how Tukkir could have come to such a strange and seemingly impossible formula. "Da blood o'Attar? Nae, ut cunna bae." Gubrone read the cypher again, and again, trying to be sure he was interpreting it correctly. He studied each and every word, each and every letter. It made no sense to him. He began to realize this might have been the reason it took Tukkir so long to concoct the rune. If the blood of Attar was required, then how were they supposed to obtain it? His eyes continued to study the instructions until, in a moment of despair, Gubrone lowered his head. His eyes fell upon two words written on the edge of the skin, barely legible. Scribbled, as though they had no meaning and were little more than an afterthought, were the words "Eleetrum Wound." They were not written in the cipher and at first seemed insignificant, but as Gubrone repeatedly read them, he recalled the day he had received the wound. He saw the blood dripping from the bone shard of Attar's arm. He remembered the pain when the shard was shoved into his gut and broken off. He could hear the words of Attar whispered into his ears as he struggled with the agony caused by the shard's penetration through his skin, cutting his innards with its jagged edges.

The wound in his flesh was bleeding from the battle he had fought with Tukkir. Gubrone had learned to tolerate its pain by leaving it alone, but upon reading the note on the cipher, he reached up under his breastplate and put his hand on the wound. As long as he did not touch the wound, he could bear its torment, but when he touched the wound, Gubrone was overcome with an immediate and severe sharp pain that brought him to his knees. He wailed with an agonizing cry.

Tears rolled from his eyes, provoked from their fleshy imprisonment by Gubrone's unguarded reaction. Though Gubrone was strong and able to bear much pain, the Eleetrum Wound was very different. The wound had a mysterious power over him, and if bothered, the power of the relatively small wound was such it could bring even one as great as him to submission. He quickly pulled his hand back but accidentally scraped one of his sharp talons across the wound, tearing it open even more than it already was. He yelled out in pain again while blood and pus ran down his abdomen and began to drip from beneath the shield onto the ground. The stench of the infected pus rose into Gubrone's nostrils. Though he was used to smelling it, once the wound tore open and the pus escaped in such volume, its smell was powerfully noxious. He began to disgorge, spewing the putrid contents of his stomach onto the ground in front of him.

According to Tukkir's rune, the pus was to be the last thing added to the rune and Gubrone knew, with respect to the spell, the proper practice was always to follow the instructions. He grabbed hold of the cipher and tried to read it through his watering eyes and in spite of the near delirium he was suffering from. He could see that he would have to get blood from the dakoons, but he knew that even if he were his usual self, he could never approach them without being devoured. He wondered what Tukkir had intended to do about this. He looked down at Tukkir's satchel, which was laying on a large, flat stone. He saw something he had not given any mind to when he had looked into the bag earlier. Poking out of Tukkir's satchel were two small leather cords extended out of the opening. Gubrone took hold of one of the cords and pulled on it. It was attached to the leather pouch and that cord, along with the other cord lying beside it, was used to draw the pouch closed. Gubrone fumbled with the knot that held the two cords together. He became frustrated quickly and almost threw the pouch and its contents across the cave. However, he was able to stop himself. He tried again and this time he managed to unravel the knot. He opened the pouch and revealed a wooden dowel sticking upright. Gubrone pulled it from the pouch. The dowel was shoved into a large stone vial that came out with the dowel. It was stuck in the top of the vial to seal it closed. Gubrone remembered when Tukkir had shown him the vial and had told him it was a potion he gave to the dakoons to subdue them. "Ahh, dis bae da snowpetal potion."

Gubrone was still unable to stand to his feet but was unwilling to wait another moment. He crawled over to the pool of water the dakoons drank from. It was just close enough to them that they could reach it one at a time while Gubrone remained safe on the opposite side. One of the dakoons approached the pool with its teeth bared and saliva dripping from its lips. Gubrone pulled on the wooden dowel until it came free from the vial with a loud pop. Gray mist rose out of the vial as Gubrone poured a black, rancid smelling fluid into a small pool of water. The water began to bubble, and mist rose from its surface as if it were boiling. The dakoons smelled the rancid odor and were quick to lurch toward the pool and toward Gubrone. One at a time, they drank the contaminated water. Gubrone lay on the ground opposite the dakoons and waited for them to fall asleep. He hoped that whatever Tukkir had put in the vile would work quickly.

While waiting for the dakoons to fall under the power of the potion, the pain of his wound overcame his determination and he lost consciousness.

High in the dark sky flew the shadow of corvuses in search of Gubrone. These crafty creatures were very skillful at pursuit and at finding what others could not find. One of their strengths was their coalition, for they possessed an innate sense of unity, which made them very organized and because there was no hierarchy among them, there was no conflict or quarrel between them. Being without the petty disputes and the deceit that usually accompanies the lust of power and rule, they were very efficient and effective in whatever they set out to do. Drawn together with a singular purpose, the flock of black birds was growing larger and larger. From every part of Shuk, the birds were gathering and searching in every valley and on every hill and mountain, trying to find Gubrone. They flew with great speed, as though there was some powerful force giving them unnatural swiftness.

The cloud of corvuses flew through the storm, into the high mountains, until they happened upon the towering spires that guarded the entrance to the cave of the dakoons. The corvuses did not see any sign of Gubrone or Tukkir as they flew through the narrow valley, but in the snow, the red stain of the nephesh blood still marked the cairn. Several corvuses dove down to see, for their senses were aroused by the smell of nephesh blood. Soon, the whole flock, which consisted of thousands of corvuses, was landing on the snow and rocks and ice around the bloodstained snow. One of the corvuses landed on what it thought was a small boulder, only it was not a boulder at all. The small lump in the snow was the head of the slave Gubrone had killed. When the corvus looked down on its perch, it could see an eye staring back at it.

The corvus began to flap its wings and call out to the others. Soon the flock was clamoring and fluttering about in excitement, thinking they had found someone. One of the birds flew over to the head and pecked at its eyeball. The head rolled over in the snow, revealing that it was only a head without a body. The corvus flapped its wings and began to peck even more. Soon, several of the corvuses were pecking at the head and squawking as the rest of the flock flew overhead filling the narrow valley with deafening calls and such pandemonium that the ice and snow clinging to the sheer walls began to crack and fall. Soon, only the skull of the dead gallue was left, and the corvuses flew away. However, they did not all depart. Many of them flew up to the tops of the spires and perched there, waiting and watching. These menacing birds had a trick they played on unsuspecting victims. They would often send only a few of their kind into an area to spy.

If they found anyone or anything that seemed interesting to them, they would fly away making their prey feel secure. However, it was a ruse, for they always left at least one behind to keep watch.

The narrow way into the Realm of Soteria was concealed by a nameless place. It was long and narrow, pressed hard between two towering mountain ridges with sheer walls that fell into the deep impassable Illysian gorge. The mountains to the east side of the way bordered the north edge of the Valley of Souls and were daunting and impregnable. The ridge guarding the west side of the way was less hostile but protected against intrusion by the Covenant of Elements.

Morak's snitches watched him in silence, waiting for his order. They were not afraid, but they were unsure if Morak knew what he was doing. In their minds, they could hear the voice of the wind calling out. Its message was constant and inescapable, for it seemed to be coming less from somewhere beyond them than from somewhere within them—a voice they could not silence by covering their ears. Morak, too, heard the voice in his mind, but none of them ever said anything about it. It was as if they believed they were the only ones hearing it. Every once in a while, as if catatonically, Morak began to mumble the words of the Jupnie, and the snitches looked at him in disbelief. Their confinement in the shelter was long and, except for giving them relief from the storm outside, it was a most unrestful period.

On the third day, as the sun set, the wind and the snow abated. Morak exited the small shelter and entered the cold night. His breath hung like a cloud in the air around his face and froze to his cheeks and eyelashes. He looked toward the narrow sliver of blackness that separated the two mountain ranges. Across the gorge lay Gershom and the legendary falls of the Tuak River, which flowed from the high glaciers above Gershom, through the forest, and into the gorge. Morak looked at the strange mist rising from deep down in the gorge. It was a plume of water vapor that froze into tiny spheres of ice held suspended in the air by the thermal turbulence created by the falls. He wanted to continue, to find the East Way, even though the night was growing darker and the combination of elements was not favorable for night travel. He stood alone in the snow, listening to the distant roar of the falls. A familiar sensation returned to him, one he had felt before. He felt eyes fixed on him, though he could not see them. He called out to the snitches, "Hoddosh, Sunnop, com! Wae mus gae now, afore da night bae tae dark. Wae mus fin da wae."

Sunnop and Hoddosh crawled from the stone shelter only to find that Morak was already a long way away, up the snow-laden valley. He was barely visible in the fading light. Morak moved through the deep snow, leaving a clear path in which the two snitches could follow.

Morak ascended a narrow slope which became narrower the higher he climbed. He did not wait for the snitches or pause to rest but pushed, step by step, through the deepening snow. Occasionally, the clouds broke open and the clear light of the moon flooded down upon the white snow, revealing the towering stone walls that were closing in on them. They could also see down into the shadowy gorge, though they were never able to spy its bottom. At one point, Hoddosh noticed there were two moons overhead. "I wonder if they could be a sign."

"What do you mean, Hoddosh? What sign?"

"The twin moons, I've never seen them before."

Sunnop looked up through the darkness and saw the twin moons shining through the thin layer of clouds that moved quickly through the sky. In and out of the clouds the moons shone. "I've heard stories of these moons before, a long time ago. I believe they shine for only one season and only once in a very long time. What do you suppose it means?"

"I don't know . . . " Hoddosh had his head cocked to the sky in amazement. He sensed the presence of the moons meant something important, something meaningful.

"Hoddosh, Sunnop, com!" The commanding voice of Morak echoed down the valley and through the lower gorge.

His bellowing broke the spell that the moons had cast over Hoddosh. He could see Morak was impatiently waiting for them. "Come, Sunnop. We better be going, for Morak will not be patient long."

Morak could see the high walls of stone closing in on him with each step he took. He could see that the safety of the valley was about to end, for in just a few more steps, the walls would become sheer, leaving no more room to walk. In the broken light of the twin moons, there was no visible way for him to go any further. The ground just disappeared into the gorge below. Morak took the last few steps through the snow and stopped. He looked back to see Hoddosh and Sunnop following in the distance. They were moving much slower than he had been. Their shorter, smaller frames were burdened a great deal more by the deep snow.

Morak looked around at the walls that were pressing him toward the edge of the cliff. Across the gorge, he could see the towering walls of the other mountain ridge. They, too, fell off into the abyss of the gorge. There was no sound other than the sound of their voices and of their footsteps crunching through the snow. The wind was gone and there were no animals or creatures of any kind to make any noise whatsoever. The silence felt oppressive and chilling, even more than the cold, frosty air. Morak was beginning to feel like a fool. He had expected to find the narrow way but all he could see was a lightless void. Soon, Sunnop and Hoddosh were standing behind him, staring into the stygian emptiness, which seemed to stand like a door, blocking their way. "So, we go back?" Hoddosh suggested, but Morak was adamant. "Gae buk? Nae, dar mus bae u wae through."

"Not in this darkness, Morak," Sunnop protested.

"Darkness or no, dar bae u wae!" Morak insisted.

"But Morak, look with your own eyes. If there is a way, it's too dark to find. We have to wait," Sunnop reasoned.

"Or go back," Hoddosh again suggested.

"Wae wull nut gae buk!" Morak adamantly refused. "Wae wull wait until da wae opens t'us!" At that moment, the clouds above parted and the soft glow of the twin moons shone through. Hoddosh saw a ledge high above them hanging out over the void and disappearing into the shadows of the East Wall.

Hoddosh pointed up to a narrow stone shelf. "There, up there. What is that? Could that be it?" The ledge was covered in snow and ice more than ninety feet above them. It appeared the ledge was quite narrow, and it would not be very accommodating to the awkward, large feet of a gallue. Nevertheless, Morak was not dissuaded by any of these concerns; he was intent on getting up to it and began to search for a route.

Sunnop peered up at the ledge with disbelief. "That? Are you crazy? There's no way we can walk on that ledge; it's too narrow!"

"A ha haerd thut da wae bae narrow."

"But that's too narrow. Besides, how would we ever get up to it, especially in the dark? It's not possible!"

Morak was growing angry and becoming intolerant of their questions. He did not care what they thought or how they felt. Fortunately, for the two snitches, they were beyond reaching distance of Morak's fists or they would have felt the merciless brutality of his temper. Morak turned around and let out a loud roar in the direction of the snitches, followed by slamming his fist against the stone wall with such force that several clumps of snow fell onto his head from above. This infuriated Morak even more and he hit the wall again, loosening even more snow.

Morak stood with snow up to his chest and a large tuft of snow sitting on the top of his head. It was extremely rare to catch a gallue, such as Morak, providing such an amusing and childish display of foolishness. The snitches could hardly contain their laughter and hid their faces so as not to provoke Morak further.

"Wae mus get t'da ledge. Dar mus bae u wae."

Morak took ahold of the grip of his sword. He contemplated dispatching the jagged blade and ending the lives of the two snitches, for it seemed if they could not follow him, they were of no further use. He glanced at the wall and then at the two snitches again. He released the worn grip and set his attention back upon the wall of the rock. Brushing the snow from off his head, he stood quietly and looked up.

Morak stepped up to the wall just below the ledge and began climbing the sheer face of the rock toward the ledge. Slowly and carefully, he climbed, reaching into the small cracks with his claws and pulling himself up until he could get another hold and climb some more. The snitches stayed a safe distance from him, for they did not want to be anywhere near him if he fell. Finally, Morak reached the ledge, gripped it, and with one last exertive effort, pulled himself up enough to survey the long, narrow shelf.

Hoddosh and Sunnop observed as the giant gallue struggled up the exposed face and hoped there would be no room for them to join him. They crept into the shadows and waited in silence. Morak was silent for a long time, and the two snitches wondered if he had found some secret way through the stone wall. They whispered together confidentially, "What do ye think he's doing?

"How should I know. Maybe he's gone on without us."

"Wouldn't that be a relief! I really don't want to go any farther."

"Neither do I. I was hoping that he would fall."

"Fall?"

"Shh! He could be listening!"

"Hmm, fall, that would be nice, wouldn't it?" They both laughed under their breath.

Morak waited, hoping the moons would once again break through the clouds and shine down upon the ledge so he could see if it was passable, but the darkness would not relent. He squatted in the hollow of the wall trying to see if there was another way. Morak could hardly believe this was the way spoken of in the stories.

He looked down and wondered if he could go back, but the way down was more dangerous than the way ahead. He looked down into the void of the gorge; following the ledge was looking like his only option. Driven by an inner force, he refused to remain stationary. He knew he had only one way he could go and that once he stepped onto the narrow ledge, there would be no escaping whatever fate it led him to. He stepped onto the ledge, determined to find his way.

Morak knew he would have to make the rest of the journey alone, for he doubted the two snitches would be able to make the climb. Rather than tell them, he decided to leave them there, with no word or explanation or direction to fend for themselves.

Forcefully, Gubrone coughed which awakened him from his unconsciousness. Slowly, he opened his eyes. Looking across the water were the yellow, rolled-back eyes of a dakoon. Its chin was lying on the ground. It was lying on its belly with its four legs spread out, resembling a giant fur rug. The other dakoon was lying on its side; its tongue had fallen out of its wide-open mouth and was lying in a pool of its saliva.

Gubrone lifted his head from the stone floor. There was a warm pool of blood from a wound on his forehead. He looked around slowly as he tried to sit up. The pain of the *Eleetrum Wound* came immediately into his sluggish awareness and, along with the throbbing of his head, made every effort difficult. Gubrone managed to get up on his hands and knees and then to stand up, though he was not able to stand up straight. He carefully put his hand on the breastplate. Just touching the armor near the wound made him wince in pain.

Out of the corner of his eye, he saw Tukkir's satchel and the animal hide with the cipher. Seeing it reminded him of what he was doing before he blacked out. The thought of what he had to do brought a deep mental dread upon him. He remembered why the dakoons were laying on the floor and knew he might not have much time left before they awoke. Gubrone could not yet stand to his feet, so he crawled on his hands and knees to the dakoon nearest to him. He took his dagger and cut the creature across the shoulder. Blood poured from the gash. He then went to the second one and did the same. After collecting blood from each, he laid on the cold floor and waited until he could muster the strength to pick himself up.

He raised his head and looked at the cipher. He read every word carefully so as to know each and every step. After reading and understanding all that was in the cipher, he knew he needed to make sure he had everything, that nothing was amiss. Slowly, he began to lift himself up from the ground and crawled toward the large flat stone table where he had left Tukkir's satchel and the ingredients for the rune. He had read the blood of the master was required. Gubrone knew exactly what it meant. He had to draw his own blood and he would have to lance the wound to gather pus. Twice he would have to wound himself.

Knowing he had to pierce the wound, he hoped it would still be oozing and he would not have to open it. Gubrone rose to his knees and tore at the lashes holding the breastplate in place. But the armor did not come loose as he expected. The pus of the wound had begun to dry, bonding the iron plate to his skin. He tried to gently pull it away, but it was impossible to do so without antagonizing the wound. Every careful effort was met with sharp, relentless eruptions of pain that seemed to reach out to every part of his body in protest. Finally, Gubrone clenched his teeth together and pulled with enough force to tear the armor from his skin. Wincing in pain, he looked down at the dried blood and pus and was filled with utter disappointment. He knew the only way to recover the fresh pus of the wound was to pierce the boil with his talons.

Knowing the pus was the last thing he needed for the rune, Gubrone decided to proceed with the potion while he worked up the courage to lance the boil. He pulled himself up to standing position, using the stone to steady himself and noticed an object in the darkness.

Hanging in the shadows was a large cage made of branches, bent and tied together. Gubrone looked at the cage intently, trying to see what was in it. Perched on a branch in the cage was a black Hooded Owl. Of all the things listed in the cipher, the owl was the only thing Gubrone had not been able to account for. It appeared that Tukkir had captured the elusive owl and brought it to the cave sometime before they came together. It was another sign to him that Tukkir had been planning his treachery for quite some time. Gubrone reached up and grabbed the cage and set in on the flat stone.

He made a fire and hung the caldron over it. Everything was ready for the rune. He found a water-skin, made from the bladder of some unfortunate creature, which was full of water from the Well of Diffush. He poured the bitter water into the cauldron. Steam rose from the cauldron as the cold water hissed in objection to the fiery heat of the hot iron. A strong, sulfuric smell filled the air. Once the water was boiling and heavy steam was rising from the caldron, Gubrone began to add each of the ingredients, just as the cipher described, following every step carefully. With each step, with each ingredient, he had to chant the words of the rune exactly as Tukkir had written them.

Gubrone took a small bone and crushed it and then ground it with a rock until it was powder. It was the dried and ground marrow from the bones of a Danakuse cat. As he poured the powder into the boiling water, he spoke in a minacious, wicked tone, "Dwana et une dis ohlm."

Gubrone took the wooden cage with the small owl, opened it, and grabbed the bird, pulling it forcefully from its prison. The owl bit and clawed at him, flapping its wings and screeching in protest. However, Gubrone had no empathy. He held it tight in his giant hand and then, with one of the talons from his other hand, pierced the eye of the struggling bird until the warm, fresh vitreous fluid began to ooze from it. Gubrone drained the fluid into the boiling pot. "Ocatah noum dae eesh." He threw the mortally wounded bird to the dakoons, who devoured it.

Gubrone carefully pinched hold of a short stem from a blackstalk bush. The stem had thousands of needle-sharp thorns that were full of poisonous resin. He broke the stem and black sap began to flow from it into the caldron. "Barumee doem et oun dee baru."

Next, he grabbed a large, shriveled toad, dry and stiff as if mummified. Gubrone tore the head open and extracted the dried tongue of the Vulgara toad. "Codeshu et amugash del loshid."

Lying on the flat stone was a strange sack made from the stomach of a sharp-nosed bore. The sack appeared to be filled with air and had been carefully sewn closed to prevent anything from escaping. Gubrone held it over the caldron, pierced it with one of his talons, and then squeezed, causing the gray breath of the Mist of Klamata to rush out. The steam of the brew reached out as a wraithlike hand and took hold of the gray breath and for a moment, the two vaporous matters contended with each other, one trying to overcome the other, until they had become so intermingled that there was no telling which was which. A large yellowish cloud erupted from the caldron and rose above it like a ball of smoke. The yellowish puff of smoke hovered and then, as suddenly as it appeared, it was sucked back into the caldron's bubbling tumult.

Gubrone was slow and methodical as he spoke each word of the incantation. "Motulaum een nopeck dowaum." He took the stone dish that had been filled with the blood of the dakoons and swirled their blood together, being careful not to spill any. As he poured the blood into the caldron, before it had even touched the surface of the boiling brew, the concoction started angrily hissing and screaming. Gubrone spoke the chant twice, exactly as it was written on the cipher, however the second time through, the force and volume of his voice resounded much stronger than before. "Hedelo eshomae tuum dakoon. Hedelo eshomae tuum dakoon." The turbulent brew bubbled violently, and a mist erupted from the cauldron and spewed over its rim, down over the fire, before floating over the floor of the cave. The dakoons stood to their feet and watched as the mist spread to where they were standing.

Gubrone laughed with sinister delight. It was time to offer his own blood. He stuck his dagger into his forearm and drew it toward his hand, making a jagged cut from which blood immediately flowed. He rolled his forearm, tipping the dribbling blood into the boiling caldron. Again, the rune began to boil and convulse, sending gray, odious smoke over the edges of the caldron where it mixed with the yellow mist. "Undektosh owat Gubrone en maeed. Undektosh owat Gubrone en maeed. Undektosh owat Gubrone en maeed."

As Gubrone spoke, he felt power reaching into his body and strength returning to his muscles; the agony of the wound started to wane. There was only one thing remaining for him to do. He hesitated, trying to gain the courage he needed to pierce the wound. He carefully placed his hand on his stomach beside the wound. It was positioned so he could lift one of his hooked talons and strike the center of the wound with just the right amount of pressure to pierce it and let the pus escape into the caldron. Without looking, he drove his sharpest talon into the center of the boil. He tried not to scream but before he could stop it, a horrifying shriek burst from his mouth. He drove the talon into the wound until it reached the spot where the shard was lodged. The blood of Attar surrounding the shiv began to seep through the pus that oozed from the wound. A long, agonizing scream escaped him again, and sweat poured from his brow, running into his eyes and mouth. He pulled the bloody talon and the putrid purulence followed by inky, defiled blood, oozed from the lanced wound. Gubrone leaned over the boiling caldron and waited for the discharge to drain into it. At first, it came out drop by drop, but then Gubrone, in his impatience, squeezed the boil, and a gush of pus and blood poured out and splashed into the caldron. A vile stench wafted through the thick air in the cave. At the same time, the sound of whispering voices spoke out from the cauldron, in a tongue that could not be understood. It was as though there were many different voices, all speaking to each other. Repeatedly they said the same thing: "Touis domiso daeun. Inosh oped ooum de undock. Potelum eedo eetooum enomay itoc." Gubrone's eyes rolled back into their sockets as he struggled to stay conscious. His heart beat furiously like drums of war. Eventually, his legs gave way. He dropped to his knees and then shifted into a sitting position with his head rested against a rock. He closed his eyes, and it felt like the cave was spinning around him.

The voices from the caldron intensified until they were echoing through the cave in a thunderous, impatient exclamation. Gubrone covered his ears, trying to silence the demanding voices, but he could not stop them. He began to feel their anger and hatred pushing into his mind and body with each intensifying round. Suddenly, Gubrone realized that he had to speak the final words of the incantation before he passed out. With all his might, Gubrone lifted his head and repeated the phrase, "Neeruet de Attar postosh ee nuowm."

The clamor of voices continued to escalate, so Gubrone raised his voice even louder to drown them out. As he spoke the words over and over, the cave filled with even more smoke and mist until it was like a thick fog. The glow of the fire created a warm, orange hue, which radiated through the mist. Gubrone looked down at the fire. He could see the cauldron with its boiling potion dancing wildly above the flames. His eyes became wild as if he was out of his mind. He reached out and took hold of the hot cauldron with its boiling rune and lifted it up into the air. The smell of seared flesh permeated the cave. He cried the words of the spell over and over again. Then Gubrone lowered the scalding brew to his lips to drink the potion. The heat of the caldron singed his lips, but Gubrone gave no sign of pain; he was invigorated, intoxicated by a supernatural power absorbed into his bones. He drank the rune in one long continuous pour until it was all consumed. He dropped the caldron to the ground, lifted his hands up toward the roof of the cave, and began to recite the Incantus Dominus, with vigor. The strange voices joined in as if they had been waiting for him to make the final declaration.

Louder and louder his voice grew. The mist that had filled the room started to swirl around him. A strange wind picked up as the voices began to chant their unknown message once again.

Gubrone stood up, repeating Incantus Dominus continuously, while the storm of elements brewed around him. It was as if the cave itself had become the caldron, and Gubrone was a part of the rune. The swirling mist began to split off into three separate whirlwinds that all converged into one large, crowning cloud that hovered at the ceiling of the cave. The whirlwinds spun and danced around the cave until each one stopped in a different place: one in front of each dakoon and one in front of Gubrone. The whirlwinds continued to spin, blowing at each of them like a breath from a storm. Then, without warning, the whirlwinds leaped into their mouths and disappeared within them.

Gubrone and the dakoons fell lifelessly to the ground. The light in the cave was sucked out by the force of the whirlwind's sudden evacuation, leaving only darkness in its stead. The whispering voices had also gone. Silence and blackness filled the void.

After some time, the coals of the fire erupted into flames, shining a warm glow in the cave. Gubrone opened his eyes. He looked around, trying to see where the dakoons were. One by one, the flames of fire that had lit the cave reignited.

He could feel a new strength in his bones. The pain of the wound had gone and the wounds from his fight with Tukkir were fully healed. The spell had done more than make the dakoons his slaves; it had made him stronger and more dangerous than ever. Gubrone took a deep, long breath, stood to his feet, and looked at the dakoons laying on the ground.

The dakoons were slowly coming back to life, moaning and growling in their usually detestable manner. They looked around the cave and noticed Gubrone standing there, staring at them. The dakoons got to their feet and approached him slowly in a different manner than usual. Gubrone did not move but waited and watched to see how they would act. Once the dakoons had taken a few steps, they sat on the floor of the cave and stared as if waiting for him to do or say something. Gubrone stepped toward the beasts unafraid. The dakoons did not move; they sat alert. "Come." Gubrone's demanding voice echoed against the walls of the cave. The dakoons moved toward him leerily. Gubrone grabbed one of the dakoons around its neck and squeezed on its throat. His talons dug into the creature's skin, drawing blood, which ran down its neck and dripped onto the floor. The dakoon did not struggle against its new master; it did not try to escape or fight. With his other hand, Gubrone dragged his black talons across the dakoons face, cutting deep, gruesome wounds, which bled profusely. He then let loose his iron grip, dropping the dakoon to the floor of the cave. He turned to the other one, which had not moved a muscle.

With a sudden, violent swing of his right arm, Gubrone struck the dakoon across its face making deep, horrendous gashes. The dakoon fell backward to the ground. Gubrone commanded them, "Come." Gubrone called them again and again. They came to him and stood quietly. "Yur maen now! A bae yer master! Obey no one but mae." Gubrone turned to one of the dakoons and took hold of its bleeding head. "Ye wull bae called Tormut fur A ha carried da torment o'mae master. Now ye wull bae da torment o'all mae enemies!" Gubrone walked over to the other dakoon and grabbed hold of its thick black hair. "Ye, A wull call Sufrar fur A ha suffered wit da pain o'da Eleetrum Wound. Ye wull brang suffering t'all who stand agan mae! Tormut un Sufrar, mae maety dakoons!" Gubrone looked at the long chain that bound the dakoons to the floor. With his giant sword, he struck the large iron ring. A loud metallic sound reverberated through the cave and sparks flew from the blade of his sword. The ring was severed, and the chain was freed from it. The dakoons were loosed from the bondage of the ring, though the chains of bondage still clung to their ankles. "Whaer one gaes, da other wull gae. Ye wull bae bound bae dis chain. Bae ut ye wull live un bae ut ye wull die!" Gubrone headed toward the entrance of the cave and the dakoons followed.

Outside the cave, the storm raged on. Gubrone looked in every direction and could see nothing but snow and ice blowing through the air. A strange, unmoving, black spot on the edge of a rock caught his eye. Gubrone fixed his eyes intently on it until he was able to see it was a corvus. He wondered where it had come from and why it was sitting in such a tormented place and then he realized who had sent it. "Sinistradt!" Gubrone said to himself. As he watched the bird, it turned its head, and its black eyes met with Gubrone's. Then, there was another call. Gubrone saw another corvus perched higher, above the gorge. He then saw many more. The corvuses called back and forth to one another and one of them opened its wings and flew into the storm, toward the Valley of Souls. He stepped fearlessly into the gorge, and the dakoons followed him. Their chains clamored as they dragged through the snow, breaking a wide harrow. The corvuses cackled and crowed, revealing to Gubrone that there were about a dozen of the black birds. The dakoons began gnashing their teeth and growling. The corvuses spread their wings and began to fly in circles over Gubrone and the dakoons. The menacing birds were unafraid and they taunted the dakoons, swooping down and pecking at their heads, aiming for their eyes.

While this was happening, Gubrone watched the flight of the corvuses and remembered the days of old when he, too, could fly like a bird. The rune had not given him back the wings Attar's spell had taken away, but it had given him wings of another sort. Gubrone would use the flight of the dakoons to take him to Gershom Forest. He stepped between the dakoons that were bound together by the heavy chain lying on the ground between them and grabbed hold of it so that the chain ran behind him, from his right hand into his left hand putting a dakoon on either side of him. The dakoons looked at him as he held the chains with his arms spread. He bellowed above the noise of the storm, commanding the dakoons, "Fly Tormut, fly t'Gershom. Sufrar, guv yer master flight o'er da realm o'Shuk." The dakoons spread their wings upward. He was not certain if the dakoons would be able to fly with him hanging from their chains, or if they could fly through the storm, but he knew they would obey him and make every effort to follow his orders. "Dis bae da tam thut ye ha waited fur all des mony ages. Fly! Fly mae maety dakoons! Fly t'Gershom un fin Eloh!"

Even though the dakoons had not flown since their capture, they lifted their steely wings and brought them down again with a powerful swipe that lifted them from the snowy ground with a single motion. The chains that joined them tightened and Gubrone was soon dangling in the air between them. The corvuses watched as the dakoons rose into the air battling the ruthless winds. Soon the corvuses followed, though keeping pace with the dakoons proved to be a superior task. Gubrone hung from the chain with his arms outstretched, as though he had great wings of his own, and for the first time since before the great war, Gubrone's feet were hanging high above the vast realm.

Chapter XIX
Legend

Shu bolted from behind the frozen veil of the waterfall into the bitter jaws of the storm. The normally free-flowing placid stream that meandered away from the Pool of Levitus had been transformed into a sinuous glass streamer as it tumbled incautiously over the towering wall of stone. It looked as though the frozen falls were adorning the fluent cascade like careless dangling silk ribbons, however, they were, in fact, clinging precariously to the rocks and stones and veins of the mountain wall. The vaporous mist billowed into a descending cloud at the base of the falls and was rapidly transmuted into innumerable tiny, glimmering crystals floating delicately on the air. As they passed through the mist, the tiny crystals clung to their hair and skin and eyelashes and clothes, dressing them in a gossamer coat of frost. Stepping beyond the protected falls right after Shu were Zoësh and Msusi. They were both surprised by the falling snow and boisterous, howling winds that had transformed the serene meadow into a frozen, inhospitable, and barren wasteland, unsuitable for even the hardiest of creatures. Zoësh yelled to Shu as she passed through the mist, "Shu! Shu, what should we do? It's too dangerous to go on! We'll never find Seerae in this weather!"

"I know, but she couldn't have gone far!"

"Maybe the storm will help us!" Msusi suggested.

"How do you mean?"

"If we can't go anywhere then surely, she won't be able to go anywhere either!"

"What about Huzesh? What if he has captured her?"

"He won't be able to go anywhere in this storm either! We need to find our way back to Kumél and Ziminiar!"

Ross caught up with Loham at the end of the long staircase. He heard muffled shouts coming from beyond the waterfall and his heart sped up as a sudden sense of urgency overtook him. He pushed past Loham and emerged into the furious storm. At first, he was unconscious of the snow and wind, for he was only intent on finding out what all the yelling was about. He desperately hoped the search party was frantically calling Seerae's name, not to locate her but because they had already found her or caught a glimpse of her and knew she was near. He hurried toward Shu and the others and instantly realized Seerae was nowhere to be found and that all the yelling was between Shu, Zoësh, and Msusi. "What's going on? Why have we stopped?"

"Ross, we have to find shelter! The weather is too wild!"

"But what about Seerae? We have to find her, Shu!"

"I know, but we will never find her in this storm!"

"No, I won't wait! I can't. I have to find her; you know I do! I have to find her, and I'm not waiting!"

"Ross, we are not giving up. There is no way that she or her captor will be able to go anywhere in this. For now, we must find Kumél and Ziminiar and stay with them. We will look for Seerae as soon as the storm calms. I promise, there is nothing we can do right now!"

Ross looked at Shu, then he looked at Msusi, who had tears freezing to her cheeks. She too did not want to give up on the search. Zoësh put her hand on Ross's shoulder and looked at him with determination in her eyes. "We will find her! We will bring her back!"

Ross clenched his teeth. His jaw was fixed and the muscles in his face were tight. A swell of fear rushed through his body, and tears filled his eyes. He wanted to trust them, he wanted to believe they would find her, but he feared they would find her too late. He shook his head in discouragement. "Come, Ross, we have to find Kumél."

Huzesh was not very far from them. He was hidden in a small cluster of rocks no more than a stone's throw away, but the fury of the tempest prevented him from hearing the yelling or seeing anything but the swirling snow. If any of them had known just how near they were to each other, they would have all been even more unnerved than the tempest of the storm had already made them.

"Ross, do you think you can lead us to them, to Kumél and Ziminiar?" Shu knew if he could distract Ross by keeping him busy, he would be less inclined to do something foolish. Shu was not only concerned they could be lost in the storm if they continued their pursuit of Huzesh; he was not totally confident they possessed the skills required to confront Huzesh without the aid of Kumél and Ziminiar.

"Yes, I think I remember the way, though things look much different to us now that the snow has fallen." Ross began to pick his way through the snow, ice, and rocks relying on his memory to quickly guide them to Kumél and Ziminiar.

Zoësh recognized the hour was getting late and they had no time to lose. She urged Ross, "We must hurry! It will be dark soon and we will never find them!"

"I know! I'll get us there!"

As Ross and the others moved through the blizzard, Loham noticed a tiny, motionless glow piercing through the blowing snow and ice. "Shu, what is that? There?"

"What do you see?"

"That light, there, do you see it? There it is, just ahead."

Shu intently studied the area where Loham was pointing. "Oh, it's one of my favorite friends. Ross, stop! We have some help."

Ross, who had not noticed the little light, yelled back, stopped, and turned toward Shu's voice. "What? What did you say?"

"Help has arrived!"

"What are you talking about?"

"Look!" Shu gestured toward the light Loham had pointed out. Ross turned and found himself face to face with a luna-tulwyth. "Whoa!" Ross stumbled backward and he tried to regain his balance by taking another step, but his second step landed on a slick, snow-covered stone. Ross surrendered to the humiliation of his clumsiness and landed without grace in the knee-high snow that covered him like a quilt of feathers. He had managed to keep his face from the snow and, as he lay there, he greeted the hovering tulwyth. "Where'd you come from, you tiny pest. Why do you insist on surprising me like that?"

The tulwyth flew nearer, hovered directly over his face, and made a high pitched, barely audible sound that Ross understood to be a reprimand of some sort. Once on his feet again, Ross perceived his minor calamity had been a humorous diversion for the others who, instead of offering their hands, stood together laughing at the sight of a man being scolded by a tiny little tulwyth.

"Oh, so that's how it is, huh? Thanks for all your help!" Ross scowled at them with a dichotomous expression of frustration and humor. He continued in the direction he had been going.

"Ross! Ross, wait!"

Ross waited silently with his back to the others as Shu hurried to his side. "Ross, are you alright?"

"Oh yeah. Just a bit embarrassed, that's all."

"Hahaha. Nothing to be embarrassed by. The tulwyth will lead us to Kumél and Ziminiar; he knows the way."

"Whew, I'm relieved to hear that. I wasn't sure that I was on the right track."

"We will be fine. Come, it's this way."

The company of Shu followed the tulwyth through the storm. It was not long before they reached the giant coniferous tree that was near the place they had last been with Kumél and Ziminiar. The gradually extinguishing remains of their large fire smoldered under the impeding drops of melting snow, and the previously warm rocks that ringed their fire would soon be completely white. Ross hollered to the others who were not far behind him, "Here! They were here not long ago!" They all began to hunt for any signs of where their friends might have gone, but the blowing snow made seeing more than a few yards out impossible. "Kumél, Kumél! Where are you?"

The tulwyth flew away toward a mound of boulders that was hidden under the cover of the accumulating snow. Ross and the others followed the petite creature toward the outline of a tall pile of stones and he yelled out, "Kumél! Kumél, are you there? Kumél?"

"Aye, wae bae haer." Ross could barely hear the familiar voice as Kumél's barely distinguishable silhouette emerged from the gloom. Ross caught sight of his movements and waved at his giant friend. The tulwyth hastily flew to a ledge near Kumél. Its bright light penetrated through the elements, leading them to safety.

Seerae's wounded and broken body lay in a heap beside a mound of stones at the back of a meager cave. Her sore head oozed blood from the gaping laceration she had received when Huzesh had mercilessly knocked her to the ground. She moaned, not realizing where she was or remembering what had happened to her. Huzesh looked at her through the fading light and let out a low, disapproving growl and then turned his head away. Seerae did not hear his growl, but as her awareness began to return, she could sense he was there. She could feel the cold, tortured shadow of his corrupted spirit. It hovered over her like a predator poised to kill. She wanted to open her eyes and look, to see what the presence was that made her feel so afraid, but she could not; her eyes refused to obey. She had never been so close to evil. She questioned herself, *What? What happened? Where am I? Ouch! Oh, wait. Who's that, is it Kumél? Oh no. No, that can't be Kumél. Oh no! What've I done?"* Seerae lay motionless, silent, and afraid; trying to comprehend what had happened to her. *What is that, that cold dark presence? Where'd it come from? Where am I? What's that sound? What's he saying?*

While Huzesh squatted beneath the oppressively low ceiling of the tiny shelter, he went seamlessly from mumbling about the unusual predicament he was in and what he planned to do next, to mumbling the words of the Jupnie. The words were familiar to her, for she had heard Kumél speak them. She thought to herself, *The song, the song of Kumél. It must be him, but, but it can't be him. It doesn't feel like him, something is very wrong.* In her naïve sensibility, Seerae opened her eyes, just a slit, so she could peek at the beast, but it was impossible to identify the face of the hulking figure in the dark cave. She wanted to question him but could not muster enough courage to push past the tenacious fear in her heart. She hoped desperately it was Kumél that she was almost willing to take the chance and speak out, but a powerful prohibition urged her not to do so. She would have to rely on her strong intuition, for though she could not see his face, she knew, in her heart, it could not be Kumél because of the wicked shadow that Huzesh cast over her.

Seerae desperately wanted to sleep, to close her mind, like her eyes were closed, and drift away into the dream realm, but the constant throbbing of her head and the torment of her aches and pains were unwilling to surrender. At times, she moaned unintentionally, which aroused the interest of Huzesh, and she could feel the sharpness of his glaring eyes staring at her. He would only glance her way for a moment or two, then start his mumbling again. Eventually, Seerae was confident Huzesh had fallen asleep due to his loud snoring. She lifted her head and rolled around to find a more comfortable position. As she moved, she tried to catch sight of him, to look at his face, but the darkness of the night and the shadows of the cave would not let her eyes steal a peek.

Seerae felt the injury on her head. The wound had finally stopped bleeding but was still very tender; when she touched it, she winced from the pain. She could feel her long beautiful hair was matted with thick dried blood and dirt. Aside from the severe pain it caused, she could tell the wound was very ragged. It was not merely a cut or a puncture; the flesh was torn and ripped with loose tissue that was pulled away from her scalp. She tried to push the loose folds of skin back down, but the pain caused her to withdraw her hand. She inhaled a deep, full breath and let it out slowly and quietly, so she would not alert the unknown beast of her consciousness. She tried again to look at Huzesh but found her eyes would not open far enough.

Seerae thought about the astonishing Pool of Levitus, of the transformation. She thought about Ross and about Eve and the others. She began to feel foolish for leaving them. Her impetuousness had led her, and possibly the others as well, into danger. Guilt and shame began harassing her, their voices chiding her with condemning, reproachful disparagements. Her heart sank into self-loathing, and her eyes pooled with tears that began to run down her cheeks. Seerae had only ever heard tales about the evil the gallues unleashed on the captured nephesh, but the stories alone were a compelling enough motivator to avoid abduction. She felt determined waves of fear crashing against her heart. *"Seerae, do not be troubled."* The words landed in her mind like a distant, almost indistinguishable thunder. She held her breath to quiet her inner storm and listened, hoping it was Ross or one of the others, but she heard nothing but the furious storm outside and the guttural growls of Huzesh's snores inside. She released her breath in disappointment, certain she must have been dreaming. A warm tear escaped through Seerae's swollen eyelid, crept across the bridge of her nose, and, in spite of the disruptive noises that swirled all around her, she heard the small tear hit the cold black stones beneath her head. *"Do not be afraid. You are not alone."*

"Who is out there? Who are you?" Seerae whispered. Her voice was faint, as though only her lips had said the words without breath or amplification of sound. "Where are you? Please help me!"

Huzesh groaned and rolled over. Seerae gasped and put her hand to her mouth to keep the sound from escaping.

"Shh! You will wake him," she thought to herself.

"Do not speak; use your thoughts only. I can hear them. His ears are deaf to my voice."

Seerae let her mind speak and kept her voice silent. *"Who are you? Let me see you."* Seerae opened her eyes wider to see if the stranger was in the cave with her, but in the unrelenting darkness, she saw nothing.

"Close your eyes, for the darkness that surrounds you, blinds you to those things that you desire to see. Let your heart show you what is truer than the shadows." Seerae had heard these words before, long ago. She tried to recall who had recited them to her. *"Do you remember me? We have spoken before."*

"Yes, I remember your voice, but I've forgotten who you are."

"Forgetfulness, it is part of the curse. Everyone forgets."

"Please, forgive me."

"It's not forgiveness that you need, Seerae. What you need is wholeness." It seemed her memories from all her bygone days were hidden behind an impenetrable fog. She saw herself walking through a veil of mist, seeking a mystery.

"Where? Where have they gone? Where are all the things that I used to know?"

"They have not gone. They remain where they have always been. Open the eyes of your soul and see what you cannot remember."

As Seerae looked into the depths of her thoughts, she saw the silhouette of a figure. She took a step toward it but found herself trapped like a fly entangled in a spider's web. She flailed her arms and kicked her feet to no avail, for the fog bound her wrists and ankles with invisible cords. *"Please, please help me. Why can't I remember? Who are you?"*

Her eyes were fixed on the figure in the fog. Without a word, it walked, unencumbered, through the fog toward her. She stared intently until a face formed by the mist appeared. *"Eloh, it's you! I remember. Where are you? Where have you been?"*

"I am coming." The vision vanished and Seerae heard only the voice of the Jupnie chanting its mysterious message in her ears.

She opened her eyes and could finally see, albeit faintly through the darkness. She could not be sure whether she was dreaming or if she were awake. Every one of her senses suggested to her she was not fully herself, that she was somehow not experiencing reality. The early morning light was pushing its way through the night shadows and peeking into the cave through every crack and slot and hole it could find. Seerae could hear the Jupnie whispering in her ear. She remembered when Shu had revealed to her the meaning of the ancient voice's words. Over and over again, as the last line of the Jupnie repeated itself in her ears she could hear Shu's voice. *"The wholeness of life comes, it comes, and there is no might that can stop its coming."*

She wondered why Eloh had appeared to her. She pondered what he had said to her, that he was coming. She realized the encroaching storm was much more than a normal storm and that her unusual experiences and the things the company of Shu had endured were a precursor to a promise made long ago.

She heard the storm blowing and felt a strange sense of comfort come into her thoughts as she listened to the wind howling. It gave to her the complete opposite experience from what the gallues and snitches experienced. The melodic voice of the Jupnie rang in her mind like the colorful tiny tits that flew from branch to branch singing their happy tunes of bloom. She tried to imagine them flitting about the trees and bushes, chirping and playing freely. Seerae thought about the mountains and trees, the meadows and streams, and pools of clear, living water. She let her thoughts drift away onto a calm, flat sea where there were no storms or gallues. She tried to remember the beauty and joy she felt in Gershom. Whether the things she felt and heard were real or an illusion, she could not tell, and if they were not real, if she was dreaming, it did not seem to matter to her; it was better than despair. Every part of her cheerful being, awake or dreaming, struggled against the torment and oppression that surrounded her.

The image of Eve came into her mind. For a moment, Seerae felt sad and then afraid again, but then she remembered the face of Eloh and his voice and felt the calm reprieve of hope flow into her. She thought about Ross, and the part of her being that could feel what Eve felt, began to warm her heart. She thought about the Pool of Levitus and the transformation, her transformation, under the twin moons. For short moments, she felt rescued by the images that flew into her mind on the wings of cheerful memories. She let the beautiful memories defy the immediate and seemingly inescapable reality that surrounded her. With her eyes closed tightly, an inordinate, defiant smile arrested the panicked terror that was frozen on her wounded face. Like the breaking up of winter ice by the rays of springtime sunlight, the hypnotic daze cast over her was cracked and then broken. Despite everything, Seerae began to feel the warm peace she had felt while in Gershom Forest. Seerae knew, in her heart, the darkness would not last long. She did not know what would happen when Eloh came, but she genuinely believed in some beautiful and amazing way, he would change everything.

Zoësh sat near the entrance of the cave alone. The discordant sounds of the storm disquieted the sanguine stillness of her soul. She could not escape the feeling there was something more to the phenomenon of the storm than inhospitable weather. Zoësh sensed there were powerful forces afoot in the realm, forces of light and of darkness that would inevitably collide. Growing in her mind was a strong awareness they were all about to be thrown into a crucible of extreme consequence, a struggle whose eventuality was nearer than they could have known. She had learned to trust the deep whispers of her inner being, to rely on them when she was uncertain of everything else.

Ross was also restless. He feared for the life of Seerae and could not dismiss the images of their last moments together. He felt contempt for himself; it brooded deep in his soul and it ate at him, afflicting him. Ross's self-deprecation turned toward Loham and it became gnawing angst, corrupting Ross's weary and vulnerable mind, imposing upon his desperate desire to sleep and making him vexed with anger.

"I know something that'll help." Zoësh pulled her dukwán from her satchel.

Ross rolled his eyes in disbelief. "I don't think your little flute is going to help."

"Hmm, you never know." Zoësh put the simple instrument to her mouth and began to play softly. The slow, enchanting groan of the dukwán began to fill the air around them.

"Won't you wake the others?"

"No, they'll sleep even better than they already were," she replied and resumed her music.

Ross sat and listened as he watched the tender care she took to play the instrument. Its voice was passionate and deep and spoke to a part of him he could not feel. His mind was caught up in the simple but compelling melody.

Back in the shadows of the shelter, Loham lay, hearing the tune staring at the darkness while thinking about the visions he had and about the dukwán the fire had given him. The music sounded much like what he had heard before. Loham remembered the dukwán was in his satchel and reached in and took it out. He looked at it and wondered if he could play the simple instrument. In his head, he could see the notes and hear the melody. He put the dukwán to his lips and began to play along with Zoësh. At first, neither Zoësh nor Ross noticed it. The music he played melded seamlessly with Zoësh's tune. Soon, however, the two dukwáns began to harmonize and Ross was the first to realize, followed by Zoësh, that there was another dukwán being played. Ross looked around and was unable to see from where the harmony came. Zoësh stopped playing and looked in the direction of the shadows where Loham hid. He had become so caught up in the music he had not noticed he was playing alone. Zoësh rose and walked toward the music, looking to see who was playing. By the time she was close enough to see him, he had realized he was playing alone and stopped. He acted as if he were a child caught in the act of committing an innocent and yet disallowed act. Loham quickly hid the dukwán and tried to pretend he did not see Zoësh. "Oh, you startled me. What are you doing?"

Of course, Zoësh was not fooled by his ruse. She directed her sly, sagacious gaze straight at him while her head slowly and almost imperceptibly shook back and forth. A smirk crept across her mouth. "Really? I heard you, Loham."

"Huh, heard what?"

"Do you truly assume that I am so easily fooled? Come, let us play together." Loham watched as Zoësh turned and walked back toward Ross. He quickly followed with the dukwán in his hand. He knew Ross distrusted him and was therefore sheepish in his approach.

Ross saw Loham following behind Zoësh, and he immediately became hostile. "What are you doing, Zoësh? What's he doing?"

"I asked him to come . . . to come so that we could play together."

"I think I'll go back to let you two play." Ross's voice was tainted with bitterness and sarcasm.

"No, stay!" Zoësh demanded. Ross quickly conceded, though he chose a place away from Loham and Loham sat close to Zoësh with his dukwán in his hand. Zoësh studied at the instrument with curiosity. "How long have you been playing, Loham?"

"I have never played before now, not that I can remember anyhow."

"But, but you play so well, why have you never played your dukwán?"

"You mean this?" Loham showed her the instrument he had taken from the fire.

"Yes, why haven't you played it before?"

"It's not really mine, I only found it a short time ago. I think, well, I think it was given to me."

"You think? You probably stole it from some unsuspecting victim." Ross's voice was sharp and mean-spirited.

"No, seriously, I didn't! It came to me in a dream and in fire."

Zoësh looked closely at the dukwán. "May I see it?" Zoësh held the dukwán in her hands. She examined it closely, studying the markings and engravings on it. "You said the fire gave it to you?"

"Yeah, I found it in a fire I had built. All the other pieces of wood had burned but it lay by itself, alone and unburned."

"Ross, look at it. It looks like the one Shu gave to you, like Amik's dukwán."

Ross bent down to inspect the dukwán. His eyes became round and curious.

"It's almost exactly like mine."

"Go get it! Let's compare them."

Ross grabbed his backpack. He pulled out the dukwán. As he held it in his hands, the simtu began to glow and the markings on Amik's dukwán began to glow as well. Simultaneously, the markings on Loham's dukwán also began to illuminate. The three of them looked at each other in awe and wonder. "Zoësh, they are the same, the markings."

"But how and who? Who did this? Who gave you the dukwán?"

"Long ago, after Amik was brought to Shuk, Eloh crafted an identical dukwán for the nephesh of Amik." Shu's voice startled Ross and Zoësh. Shu sat down and explained the dukwán of Attar was a powerful instrument only Attar could play. Its music was only obedient to him and anyone who tried to play would become enchanted by its lurid melody, held under its spell as Amik had been. The dukwán Loham carried was given to Amik's nephesh as a reminder of the power of the spell and as a warning to never play its music.

As he was telling them the story, the power of the dukwán had been reaching out to Loham. He saw he was holding his dukwán. It glowed bright and blue. He looked at it closely, mesmerized by its intricate markings. He wondered what they meant. He wanted to play, to feel the power of its song, to know the sound of his own immortal voice. At the same time, the power of Amik's dukwán had been calling out to Ross. And without realizing it, he had picked up his own dukwán. He raised it to his mouth and whispered to it in an unidentifiable voice that seemed to come from some other place, some other being. "Will you give me your music?"

Then he inhaled a deep breath and put the dukwán to his lips. Just one second before he blew into it, a lurid, sinister voice whispered from the pipe, "I cannot give you my music."

The sound of the voice frightened Ross. His eyes popped wide open and he dropped the dukwán to the ground. He saw Shu staring at him. Shu had also heard the voice. Ross was afraid to say anything at first. He swallowed and could feel his heart racing. "What was that?"

"The voice of Attar."

Zoësh turned to Shu. She too was surprised and frightened by the voice. "The voice of Attar, here in Shuk? But how, Shu?"

"It's the dukwán of Amik, but remember, it was crafted for Attar, and it is very powerful. Ross, you must be careful with it. Its magic will try to seduce you. Do not speak to it or play it. Amik wanted the music of Attar so desperately that he sacrificed everything to get it, only to find he could never have the songs of Attar. And you can never have them either."

"I didn't mean to try to play it. I just couldn't help myself. I couldn't stop it. Why did you give it to me?"

"The time will come when you will be required to return it to the one to whom its voice belongs."

"You mean—to Attar?"

"Yes."

"But why?"

"He gave it to Amik in trade for something that is not right for him to possess. To get it back, you will have to return the dukwán."

Ross, feeling like a fool, put the dukwán back into his backpack. He did not want to ask how he would be giving it back. He had experienced the power of the dukwán and felt afraid of what Shu might tell him. He, along with the others, sat in silence for a long time, as if they were afraid to speak, haunted by the eerie, malevolent voice that cut through their thoughts. But a strange thing happened to him. The voice of Attar had done something in him that could not have been expected. The dark anger toward Loham was banished from his heart. It was not that Ross or the others noticed the change, but in an inexplicable manner, Ross's fear of the voice and its effect on him closed the wound of anger that had been trying to bleed.

Zoësh still felt restless and uneasy and could not escape the cold, threatening tenor of Attar's voice, which echoed unabated in her mind. After a long while, the others, including Shu, fell asleep, leaving Zoësh alone with her thoughts. She too had felt the fear Ross had struggled with, fear that she had never known before.

Morning light snuck through the meadow as it slowly approached the cave. Zoësh was still lost in her thoughts and did not notice its warm touch until it was shining in her eyes. She was surprised to realize the wind had settled down, and that the snow was floating gracefully to the ground. She sensed a strange stillness fall over everything and thought, at first, that the strangeness of the moment was simply her own amplified awareness having been abruptly overwhelmed by the peace of the unexpected quiet. Nevertheless, there was something more to the stillness, something familiar and welcome which put her restless mind at ease. She stepped out of the cave to look around. Her feet sank deep into the snow and made a soft crunching sound as she walked. The calm that fell in the meadow was so heavy she could feel it; as though it had a form or body to it. Zoësh looked in all directions, trying to see beyond the veiled walls of the mountains, but saw nothing. In the sky above her, thick layers of clouds hung motionless. Surrounding the cave, in all directions, were more clouds, which settled into the valley and touched the ground. It became impossible to distinguish where the ground stopped and where the clouds began.

Shu awoke to the stillness and went to find Zoësh.

Zoësh jumped and clasped her heart. "Oh, it's you! I thought . . .," she paused.

"You thought what?"

"I thought you were someone else."

"Who?"

"I don't know. I just felt that someone was near, someone I know. I feel them everywhere."

"Then you won't be surprised to learn that someone is arriving amidst the morning fog."

"Where?"

"There, look!"

Spinning around, Zoësh marveled at the distant sight of an apparition advancing through the fog. While the faint silhouette approached them, delicate snowflakes were landing upon it, elegantly draping it in a long sparkling coat that gracefully flowed through the deep drifts. Gradually, the alluring figure neared Zoësh. At last, she recognized the apparition. "Alethia! Where, where did she come from, Shu?"

Alethia wore a full length, hooded white cape, which appeared as if it was constructed from delicate flakes of snow. It hung on the ground all around her and extended behind her like the long train of a bride's gown. Alethia's only visible feature, her stunning face, was framed by a luxurious ermine fur that trimmed the hood of her glacier-white cape. As she approached through the clouds, she was barely distinguishable from the snow and cloud-laden backdrop, and yet she was easily recognized no matter where she went or what she wore due to her distinct and ethereal manner. The aura of her presence radiated from every part of her, magically arresting the attention of anyone near her.

"You might have to ask her, Zoësh."

Kumél exited the cave and was pleased to see Alethia, but then he noticed that Jaroh, also dressed fully in white, was following her. Alethia truly emanated a strength that mysteriously dwarfed every other being, great or small, but the giant, muscular frame of Jaroh physically towered over Alethia. In the presence of Jaroh, Kumél felt the old shame of his broken and fallen self, the shame he wished he could leave behind. He lowered his eyes and whirled around to return to the dark cave.

"Kumél, mae fren, ut bae gud t'sae ye again!" Jaroh's kind voice gently rang through the air. Kumél peered across the way to see Jaroh's smile and his extended arms offering a cordial embrace. It took only a moment for Alethia and her kerolus companion to join the small group. "Aye, Jaroh," Kumél agreed as he accepted a brotherly hug, with relief.

Then, Alethia stretched her arms out to Kumél also, but since Kumél had not been offered such affections from a Theoscian, he was uncertain how to respond.

He bent low, tentatively, and awkwardly allowed Alethia to give him a gentle hug and a friendly kiss on the cheek. "It is good to see you again, Kumél. We have missed all of you. I see that Shu has taken good care of you since we last met."

Although he desired to reciprocate her gracious sentiment, he only uttered a clumsy response. "Umm, aye, Alethia."

"Hey! Where'd you come from?" Ross's voice bellowed from behind Kumél, amplified by the hard stones that formed the circular entrance of the cave as he emerged from the shadows, followed by Msusi and Ziminiar. "How'd you find us? Wait. Why are you here? Have you heard that Seerae's been taken? We have to find her! If it wasn't for the storm, we would have been gone days ago. Can you help us find her?"

Their joyous reunion quickly turned into an exigent discussion of a rescue plan for Seerae. The plan's urgency was overcoming Ross's composure, and his words were evolving into a rambling, incoherent rant. His body language revealed to Alethia that he was genuinely scared, but she could tell, by the wild look in his eyes he was absolutely determined to save Seerae, no matter what the impending dangers were. "This is the first day that the storm has stilled. We need to go, or we won't find her!"

"Ross, who has taken Seerae?" Alethia calmly asked, attempting to subdue the panic.

Hearing the commotion, Loham stepped from the cave and froze at the sight of Alethia and her guard, Jaroh.

"A gallue named Huzesh has captured her."

"Huzesh? How did he find you here in this remote location?"

With his head hung low, Ziminiar shuffled forward and admitted, "A dunna know ha but wae waer followed. Shae waer captured ony one sun ago, but da storm ha kupt us frum searchin fur her."

"And who might this be?" Loham had caught Alethia's eye even though he had been hiding behind everyone else. As she neared him, he tried to retreat but he was blocked by a large slab of rock at his back. "I have seen you before. You are not just any nephesh now, are you?"

"Ee bae u snitch, sunt bae Huzesh," Ziminiar announced insistently.

"Oh, but he is much more than that, aren't you, Loham?" Loham's eyes sizably enlarged, and he wondered how Alethia had known his name. "Don't be afraid. I have been searching for you, and now, I have found you."

"Why? Why have you been looking for me?"

"Well, I was helping someone else that was searching for you, but I see that he has already found you."

Ross did not know whether it was good or not that Alethia looked directly at him, but he did not like the shame that surfaced in him. He wanted to shy away and hide from Alethia. He was most ashamed of what he had done to himself and while he wanted to hate Loham for what had happened, Ross knew, ultimately, he was the one at fault. He alone was responsible for the being Loham had become. But, mercifully, Alethia did not view him through condemning eyes and she voiced no rebukes. "If Huzesh is holding Seerae captive, then we need to rescue her before he disappears into the mountains with her, for there are many spies about that are hunting for a foreigner."

"A foreigner? What foreigner?" Zoësh questioned.

"Ross."

"Ross?"

"What! Me? But, how does anyone know about me, and why would they be looking for me?"

"The word has come to me, that there is much trouble in Shuk. A weapon has been found that is believed to have come from another realm. Gubrone has sent many hunters and their mēgs throughout the mountains, looking for the one to whom the weapon belongs, a foreigner. Ross, you are the foreigner, you are the one they hunt, Ross, but not you alone."

"How have you learned of this, Alethia?"

"Who else do they hunt?"

"They are not the only ones with spies in the realm. I have been told that they also believe that Eloh is in Shuk, traveling with the foreigner."

"Eloh? But where? Why do they think that Eloh is here?" Shu anxiously asked.

"Why? Who can say why! They are gallues and who knows why a gallue thinks anything!"

"So, what about this weapon? What do they think that I brought here?" Ross paused for a moment then he blurted, "Oh shit! You have got to be kidding me!"

"What, Ross?" Zoësh asked.

Alethia knowingly smiled and calmly asked, "Ahh, so you know what the weapon is, Ross?"

"My ice axe! I lost it back when those mēgs attacked us. Remember, Zoësh?"

"You mean back in the valley?"

"Yeah! I didn't notice that it was gone until we started to climb the ice wall. I had completely forgotten about it until now."

"Alethia, could it be? My ice axe has them this worked up? But it's not a weapon at all!"

"Ice axe? What's an ice axe?"

"It's a tool used for climbing. It's kind of a combination of a hammer and an axe, ergo the name. Do you remember it, Kumél?"

"Aye. Ut waer u weapon t'mae."

"Oh, that's right. You did say that. But my axe is too small for the gallues to believe that it's a weapon. What threat could it be to Kumél or Ziminiar?"

"Its smallness is not considered if the gallues believe it to have mythical powers or if it comes from another realm," Shu explained. "Not one of them knows why your ice axe was crafted or for what use. If it appears to be a weapon, as Kumél says, then they will believe it to be one. But even more serious than their mistaken belief that the ax is a weapon, is their knowledge it has genuinely come from another realm. They now know a foreigner is definitely in the realm, and they will not cease their hunt for him until he is found. You are in grave danger now, worse than we previously knew."

"That's why Huzesh captured Seerae," Loham blurted. "He knows about the foreigner and the last time I saw Seerae, she looked different, not like a normal neph. She looked more like Ross's kind, so Huzesh must have thought that she was the foreigner."

"How could you have let her go out there?" Kumél had to grab Ross's arm to keep him from attacking Loham again.

"I tried, Ross, I truly did, but I felt like I was being restrained, being kept from intervening."

"We have to find her, Shu! If this Huzesh discovers that Seerae isn't the foreigner, then he'll probably torture and kill her."

"But we can't forget the willful storm, Ross. It seems to be forcing us to delay our searches," Msusi gently reminded him, as she placed her hand on Ross's shoulder.

Shu stilled the tempest of emotions that had been growing among them as he confidently explained to the group, "If the storm is working against us, then it is also working against our enemies, against Huzesh, and it may grant us more time to find him. We mustn't see the storm as our enemy, but as our ally, and we must use its power to our advantage!"

"Shu is right. I believe that Eloh has provided the storm. The whole of the universe senses that the time is near for the great hammer of light to crush the darkness. You might be surprised, Ross, to find that this tool of yours represents more than you can even imagine. You said that it looks like a hammer, did you not?"

"Well, yeah, but it's no hammer of light. I assure you of that, Alethia."

"Maybe not, but maybe there are things at work here that you do not yet understand, things beyond the realm of what you are able to hope for or believe."

Alethia's words carried such power and hope that they all believed at least in her if nothing else. Something Alethia said reminded Ross of what Eve had once said to him. With that memory, came a sudden and deep longing to see her again. He stepped away from the others and sat down in the snow. He took his worn and frayed backpack off and opened it. Only a few things remained. Rolled up and pressed at the bottom of the pack was Eve's pack, which he had emptied out and saved just in case it might be of use. On top of Eve's pack was her diary and with the diary was the small camera. Ross reached into the backpack and took hold of the camera. He breathed a deep breath as he looked at it. He started to put his finger on the power button but stopped. He feared the batteries were dead, or at least, very close to being so. He wanted to see her the way he had seen her on the mountain, to see the two of them together, smiling in the bright sunlight of what had started as a perfect day. All those memories seemed so far away, so beyond being real. He set the camera down on his lap and reached in again. This time, his hand emerged with her diary. It had been so long since he had opened it. Part of him felt guilty and sad he had become so caught up in this strange adventure, that he had all but forgotten the only tangible things that reminded him of her. Ross tenderly spoke to her as if she was sitting there with him, "Oh God, how I miss you. I miss you so much!" He opened Eve's diary and reverently ran his fingertips over the pages. He felt the depressions of her pen strokes and each one became an embodiment of Eve. Each groove became a line in the palm of her gentle hands or a filament of her long yellow hair. He caressed each page as if he was caressing her comely face or neck. He solemnly confided in his new friends, "Eve told me once that there were things beyond what I was able to believe or hope. I remember it so clearly. I didn't understand what she was talking about, but she just kept telling me that the world was filled with things too big to understand or rationalize, that I shouldn't doubt what I couldn't see. If she could just see the incredible things that I've seen. Hey, maybe she did imagine this place!" Ross searched Alethia's eyes and discovered the same reassurance he had often found in the loving eyes of Eve.

"Ross, as desperately as you long for Eve, every living element and being in all of Pardis longs for something just as precious. Eve perceived the truth of the legend, at least in her heart. That is why she understood the mysteries that you cannot."

Ross wondered about what legend Alethia was referring to. "You mean Eloh, don't you?"

"Yes, Ross. He is the legend, written on everything, engraved into the force of life that lives in every element. Every tree, rock and stone, each drop of water, in every stream, every cloud and every star, each blade of grass and in every snowpetal that blooms at your feet, they all have the legend written in them. The legend lives in them and comes to life through them. Every creature has the legend written in their beings, it's even written in you, Ross. If you would listen to your heart, you would hear him, and you would know it to be true."

"If he is real, then, where is he? Why isn't he here? Why isn't he helping us? It seems like Eloh is a god or kind of like a god and yet he has no power to help? Or he just won't help!"

"You hear my voice and you know that I've spoken to you, yet you cannot see my voice, just as you cannot see the air that you breathe, but you still know that they truly exist. All around us, there are numerous unseen mysteries that you know are authentic. If Eloh could come, if he could erase all the past calamities and prevent future cataclysms, he would. But there are events that must happen first, events that Eloh cannot orchestrate. Power cannot be exerted without consequences. To wield it is to submit to it. Attar chose to wield his power and consequently, the realms have since then been suffering all these ages of sorrow and darkness. Now each past act and motion is required to be, in one way or another reconciled. For Eloh to use his power now would be to unleash a force so overwhelming, so awesome the realms and all that dwell in them could not survive. He did it once and he will do it again. For Eloh to return to Shuk and to Tirnan, we must secure a way."

Ross still had many doubts and he did not understand the legend, but it did not seem to matter. When he looked into Alethia's eyes, he felt rejuvenated as if his spirit had been dead and then it had been suddenly resurrected from the underworld. "OK! What can we do? What can I do?"

"For Eloh to return, the Kleid o'Miht must be restored to the heir of Amik," Alethia explained.

"You mean the one in the cave, that Amik? I thought he was dead."

"Amik has been gone for ages, but you are his heir, the one we have been waiting for."

Innately, Ross knew Alethia was right, that he was the one, but it was difficult for him to fathom. And he had no clue what it meant to be the heir. "Alethia, I know this probably doesn't happen very often, but could you possibly be wrong?"

Alethia grinned as if she were holding back laughter. "No, Ross, I know that it's you, and so do you. That is the reason you are here. You have awakened the legend. You have been expected."

"Expected by who?"

"Everything. Look around you, all of creation is roused by your arrival. You are an epiphany that has ignited a fire in the life of this realm. That is why you are hunted and why your weapon is more than you understand it to be. This realm will never be the same because you have come."

"So, I'm here because Eloh planned for me to come; he made all this happen to me. Is that right? I mean, I'm just trying to understand."

"Not at all, Ross. You are here because you came here. No one planned for you to come or made you come. You came because your feet brought you here. Eloh did not make these things happen to you. He only knew that you would come, not how or when. He saw it through his eternal vision, he looked into the morrow and into each and every morrow until he saw you. He wrote of your coming on the winds of time. It's not in the coming that your purpose is found, it's in the things you do once you have arrived. Eloh has seen them."

"If I'm here for a reason, then why don't I know the reason? Why don't I know what I'm supposed to do, Alethia? No one has ever told me or given me any instructions! Can you tell me what I'm supposed to do?"

"What you're here to do has only been foretold. It's known to only a small number, and it is impossible for it to be contrived. No one, not even Eloh, is able to force you to do what only you, in your own way, must do. It will be your decision. Do not suppose that you are here by design. You are here because you have come here and what you do while you are here will change this realm and others. It has been foreseen."

"But if I don't know what I am to do, then how will I ever do what you say I will do?"

"Because we have seen it, and we are not the only ones that know it. We are here to help and guide you, for the legend of your coming is known by all, even your enemies. These hunters wish to prevent you from finishing what you have come to accomplish, for there is no one else to achieve them. We will help you find the way, the way that you have come to go."

"I've done a multitude of things, difficult things, climbed dozens of mountains that were a mystery to me. There were times I wasn't sure if I could finish or reach the summits, but I always knew my destination. I had looked at the highest point, usually from a distance, but I had seen it. Not knowing or seeing where I'm meant to go or what I'm meant to do feels like getting lost in a snowstorm at the top of a mountain and ending up in a place that I had never intended to be, like here."

"What would you have done differently, if you had known," Shu inquired sincerely.

"Gone a different way, followed a different path."

"And the mountain that you climbed, was it worth the risk?"

Ross smiled earnestly and nodded. "Every mountain is worth the risk. It just wasn't what I expected or hoped for, that's all."

"Then, no matter the end, the journey is a risk that will lead to nothing less than the unexpected, and that's a journey worth taking. Is it not?" Shu asked reassuringly and slightly mischievously.

Ross shook his head and grinned. "Yeah, I guess you're right."

"I'm not sure what I've gotten myself into here, Alethia. I'll have to trust you and Shu— and all of you . . . trust your faith. I must admit, I've never been a man of faith . . . never cared for it much if I'm honest. I have no faith; I don't know how to believe in things that I cannot see or touch. I once heard someone say, 'Faith, it seems, is a hard thing, cruel, indifferent, unforgiving. It drives you inexorably toward something you only think you want, cares not of the sacrifice you made, and if you fail, if what you have expected is never gained, it punishes you with doubt and self-deprecation for not having had enough of it. It is expectation without assurance, hope without sight, believing but never grasping, an intentional reach for an utterly unreachable intention. Faith is a presumptuous demand for an altogether preposterous result.' I don't know why I remember it; I can't even recall who said it. But, I guess, those words somewhat represented my own experience, confirmed what I was feeling inside. But the thing is, for the first time that I can remember, I want to believe. I want to believe in Eloh, even if I can't see him. I want to believe that there is a reason and that we are not all alone. I can't help what I am and what I have done? But I feel an inexplicable sense of assurance from you and Shu and all of you. It makes me believe in you and if you believe, I can believe you, I can believe in your faith."

Msusi put her arms around Ross. "You definitely are not alone, Ross. This journey is ours too. If you suffer, we suffer, and in your joy, we will find ours."

Ross was beginning to believe, to hope. He wondered what Eve would think about all this. He thought he had lost her forever, and then he had found her, had touched her, and spoken to her again. It was, to him, a miracle, a miracle that he had asked for, that he had begged to receive, yet doubted. Deep in his being, in the secret, unreachable corridors of his soul, Ross cried out to Eloh. In that secret place, he begged for help from someone or something he had never seen or heard, someone he doubted even existed outside of legend and myth, but someone the others genuinely believed in and knew. A pool of presumptuous tears collected on his eyelids as he was overwhelmed with assurance enough to believe, and he was filled with a quiet, but almost absurd certitude. His lips moved, but his voice was heard only in his soul.

"Please. I'm weak and afraid, please help me find her again."

Even before the silent request had escaped his lips, Alethia put her hand to his cheek and wiped away a solitary tear. She tenderly embraced him and whispered into his ear, "We will find her. I promise."

Alethia knew Ross's hope was in finding Eve and that his pursuit to find her would lead him to the prophetic destiny Eloh had foreseen. She also understood they would all have to do everything they could to make sure that he did not fail.

Alethia urged the company, "We must hurry! Gather your belongings; we will leave right away. Jaroh and I will search for Seerae with you, but it's crucial that Jaroh is not seen so he cannot fly. If this vile gallue escapes with the knowledge of Jaroh's presence here in Shuk, all could be lost. We will need each other on this journey more than we have needed anyone for a very long time."

"But what about the storm?"

"The storm will grow even angrier before we have finished what we have come to do." Shu patted Ross's shoulder and confidently proclaimed, "You will climb this mountain, Ross, and you will stand on its summit and not be disappointed! Now, collect your gear, we must go."

Ziminiar called out, "Shu, A wish t'gae wit ye. A cun haelp. Ye tol mae t'ask so A bae askin."

Shu smiled and replied, "You know what else I told you, it's not up to me, you need to ask them."

Ross shot a confused glance at Shu and then at Ziminiar. "Are you kidding? We need all the help we can get! You're damned well coming with us, 'cause I don't plan on doing this alone!" Laughing, the others each agreed, so Ziminiar grabbed his belongings and joined them.

The abusive storm fought the dakoons in flight, blowing them about through the air as if they were leaves tossed uncontrollably. For as long as they were in the air, they flew in white blindness and neither Gubrone nor the dakoons knew where they were or where they were heading. Gubrone struggled to maintain his grip on the chains that held him suspended between the two dakoons. Every muscle in his body was cramping, and his grip on the chains was failing. The clouds and the snow churned chaotically, turning the skies into a fog of indistinction, which veiled the terrain below. Suddenly, as if they were nothing more than a fly, the wind swatted them from their course and drove them down, through the clouds to the ground below. Gubrone was the first to collide with the cloaked and unforgiving terra. He landed in a heap, and in due course, the dakoons came crashing down upon him. They all lay in a pile of flesh and chains and wings, groaning.

Slowly, the dakoons picked themselves up, allowing Gubrone to escape from the restraints of their weight. Gubrone stood up and realized the heavy chains were still being held in his tight grasp. He looked at them for a long time, as if trying to remember how they came to be so firmly gripped by his fingers. Finally, he let go of the chains, dropping them to the ground. Layers of hoar frost covered his head, face, and hands, camouflaging his appearance, especially against the whitening backdrop of the grassy meadow where he had landed. The snow was just beginning to conquer the lush green canvas, which was becoming muted by the veil of clouds and snow that was crowding in upon the quiet moorland.

Gubrone and the dakoons had landed on a large mound that lay near the terminus of a narrow gorge. He could hear water rushing from the gorge. Gubrone sat down on the mound shivering. The dakoons were less afflicted by the elements. For them, freedom from the cave was more than enough warmth. Bound together, they wandered about, sniffing the air and the ground. For so many ages, the dakoons had fought the bondage of the chain. They had tried to escape from each other, with no degree of satisfaction. Strangely enough, however, being freed from the cave and enabled to roam about an open landscape and fly through the open skies caused an unexpected reaction. The dakoons became content in the bondage of the chain. Whereas before, they had fought to escape each other, being free, they now needed each other and roamed about side by side as if they were bound in the flesh and not by chains. Gubrone noticed their strange new companionship. He watched them with loathsome contempt, for it was, to him, a weakness he despised.

It was not long before the dakoons sniffed out the remains of what had been a fire where food had been cooked. They circled the site, clawing and sniffing the ground. At first, Gubrone saw their agitation as the usual display of aggression they showed toward each other, but after a few moments, he noticed they were acting aggressively toward something other than themselves. He walked down from the top of the mound to where the dakoons were. He could see a ring of rocks and the charred remains of limbs and twigs. The smell of burned wood filled his nostrils. He began digging through the remains of the fire and sniffing the rocks. He cautiously scanned their surrounding area. "Somon ha baen haer. Wae nut bae alone."

A short distance from him, Gubrone spied the partially hidden opening to a cave. The opening behind the rocks and plants looked as though it would be just large enough for him to squeeze through. Before entering it, he bent over the opening, looking into the dark burrow, he sniffed. His dakoons sniffed as well and appeared to be excited by the tension they could feel in the air. "A smell da stench o'mae enemy, un aposta! U traitor ha bun un dis hide! Mur thun one, A b'laeve mony ha com haer." Gubrone crawled into the dark, empty cave. After a moment, his eyes adjusted, and he could see the cave was quite spacious in spite of its small entrance. There were many items strewn about the cave, all made by skillful hands. Gubrone tried to inspect the cave and its contents but needed more light. He noticed there was an unusual device leaning against the wall of the cave near the entrance. It was an instrument like none he had ever seen. He moved it from the cave into the light.

In the daylight, Gubrone examined the instrument carefully. It was made of wood and had five strings that were made of long, twisted pieces of hair. When Gubrone pulled on one of the strings and then let go of it, the instrument released a surprisingly melodic tone. Gubrone sniffed the strings of hair and inspected them closely. He then pulled at one until it broke. He ran the broken string through his fingers, feeling its texture. "Kerolus hair, hmm? Dar bae somting familiar bout dis hair." Gubrone smelled the hair again and studied it for quite awhile. "Ahh, mae ol'frun, Ziminiar, yur still alive." Gubrone's raspy voice listed with odious scorn.

Huzesh squatted under the large overhanging rock barely sheltered from the powerful storm. The clouds were low and thick and mixed with blowing ice and snow that pelted his back preventing him from any rest.

After many long and cold hours, he turned to see the light as it shyly shone through the dominating storm. At his feet, in the back of the shallow hide, lay the bruised body of Seerae. Huzesh had tossed her into the shelter and had inadvertently screened her from the sharp teeth of the storm while himself being its victim. Huzesh had no consideration of her condition whatsoever; it was only by sheer thoughtlessness he had given her a better spot in the cave than he had given himself.

Huzesh did not care that the nephesh was hurt; he was not concerned with her brokenness in any way. It had never been hard for Huzesh to kill a nephesh; he had done it many times even though it was forbidden. Nearly every fiber of his being wanted to finish her off, but there was a menacing sense that overrode everything else, a sense he could not shake. He felt he had to keep her alive, but why, he could not discern, nor did he try; he simply acted on impulse and instinct. It was not easy for any of the celestial beings, even for the fallen gallues, to ignore their numinous instinct. Huzesh, especially, was not given to heeding his mostly extinct tendencies; his evil will would have surely overcome any passé inclination to spare her. On this occasion, however, an invisible shadow worked against his violent will, an incorruptible breath pricked his mind and persisted against his indifference. It was for this reason alone Seerae was still alive.

Seerae's uncertainty about being awake or asleep began to abate as she became increasingly aware she was being watched. She could feel strange eyes glaring at her. The growing revelation made her panic. She knew she was alone with an evil being. Seerae tried to keep still and pretend she was sleeping. Huzesh stared down at her with a schizophrenic glare that lay heavy on Seerae. He was more loathing of the nephesh than he was of the snitches. It was a struggle within him to tolerate even the smell of her.

The sun's diffused rays cast an eerily crimson glow upon the white landscape. Huzesh felt a faint warmth touch his back, as though someone had reached out of the cold and put their hand on him. He turned his head, almost expecting to see someone standing behind him, but he was met by the wind and blowing snow, which quickly made him forget about the warm touch of the sun. Seerae could see the faint glow as it pushed its way around Huzesh, exposing the horrifying truth that she was, in fact, awake and not alone at all. While she lay in her pretense, Huzesh crawled out from under the overhanging rock to check the area for anyone, but the blowing snow mixed with the low, thick, red clouds made it impossible to see more than a few yards beyond him. "Gud, dae wull nut sae mae."

With the light of day rising upon the mountains and in spite of the determined storm, Huzesh prepared to escape both the storm and the company of Shu. He turned back toward the shallow shelter and leaned down. He grabbed Seerae by one of her ankles and dragged her out from the shallow cave and began to walk in the direction of the gorge. He had worried about leaving signs of his escape for the others to find, but now he realized leaving signs was precisely what he needed to do. He needed to leave signs so the foreigner would follow. He knew the others, including Kumél and Ziminiar, would follow as well, but something in his wily mind was convinced he would, somehow, overcome his disadvantaged situation, and, besides, Huzesh felt he had no other options; he would have to deal with whatever came his way.

If he reached the narrow gorge before anyone could find him, he felt confident he would have a chance of somehow capturing the foreigner. It was not a good plan, not much of a plan at all, but then again, Huzesh was not known for his well-engineered schemes. He pushed his way through the storm, following the faint sound of the cascading stream, which was leading him in the direction of the gorge. He pulled Seerae behind him, leaving a trail of footprints and blood the others would surely find.

As he struggled through the storm, he was unaware Seerae was conscious. She didn't know what to do to help herself. She opened her eyes, hoping to learn where she was, only to have them instantly filled with snow and ice. She tried to wipe the snow from her face, but it was hopeless. She wanted to call out, to let Huzesh know she was awake, but her mouth filled with snow and ice too quickly and began to choke her. She coughed, spat, and tried to wipe the snow away again. She feared what Huzesh might do to her, but she was becoming desperate and extremely cold. She was being dragged through the deep snow like a dead animal and was unable to see or breath. "Stop. Stop! Stop!" Seerae screamed. She kicked against the hand that gripped her ankle. "Stop! Please, stop! What are you doing? Let me go!"

Eventually, Huzesh heard the muffled cries and felt her struggling against him. He turned to see what was happening. As he turned, he let loose of his grip on Seerae's ankle. Seerae quickly kicked and crawled away from him. At first, Huzesh could not see where she had gone because the snow was so deep she disappeared under it. Eventually, however, Seerae was forced to escape the thick blanket and expose her snow-covered self to her captor. She stood looking at him with the same terror and shock that had covered her the first time she saw him. "You!" Seerae shrieked out of sheer unsuppressed astonishment and then turned and ran from him. Huzesh was equally as surprised by the sudden turn of events. He was so stupefied, in fact, he hesitated. She was able to get some distance away before Huzesh reacted and started to chase her. For the moment, his pursuit of Seerae was taking him in the wrong direction. Seerae did not care which direction she was heading, she only cared that she escaped. She ran in circles and zigzagged about, jumping from rock to rock, diving under the snow—anything she could to evade capture.

Huzesh, however, was a very skilled hunter and had pursued many nephesh and snitches. He was not fooled by Seerae's tactics and eventually closed the distance between them and cornered her against a mound of boulders.

"Who are you? What do you want with me?" Seerae's voice was strong and desperate at the same time. She looked with crazy eyes for an escape route but could not see one.

Huzesh stared at her with his dark, menacing eyes. His countenance was austere, and his body language revealed to Seerae that she was, in no small way, in danger, again. Every normal part of him wanted to kill her; he found himself unable to do anything but stare. Seerae began to shake with fear and tears started welling up in her eyes. She looked around, hoping there might be someone who could help. She wanted to call out, but her mouth was dry and her throat seemed as if it was sealed shut.

"Yur mae prisoner! Uf A dud no naed ye, ye wud bae dead! D'ye haer mae? Dead! Uf ye wish t'stay alive thun ye wull kaep yer mouth shut un d'wut A say." Huzesh's vile, raspy voice frightened Seerae even more than she already had been. The tears that had welled in her eyes rolled down her cheeks and into her mouth and she tasted the saline drops with her tongue. She tried to hide her fear, but she was betrayed by what was written all over her face and by the uncontrollable shaking of her wounded body.

"Dar bae two waes thut wae cun d'dis, ye cun com fraely or A cun take ye. Ut bae yer choice. Uf ye trae t'escape, trae t'run, A wull bae done wit ye. D'ye know wut A maen? Done wit ye!"

Seerae swallowed. She knew what he meant. She knew he would kill her without mercy or hesitation; it was written in his cold murderous eyes. She looked at Huzesh through the tears and the fear. Amidst all the turmoil and despair that she felt while looking at him, she felt an inexplicable peace cover her, like a warm blanket. She took a cautious but deliberate step toward Huzesh. "I will do as you ask."

Huzesh turned and began to walk into the storm, toward the gorge. Seerae followed behind with her head hung down.

Ross slid his arm through the shoulder strap of his backpack. The reality that his lost ice axe had been found by those who were hunting him made him even more vigilant, if not paranoid. He looked down at his hand, which was holding Eve's diary. He had been clutching it as he put the other things in his pack and was unable to let it go. He looked at the diary and dropped his pack so he could put it safely away. He carefully searched the ground to be sure nothing was left behind. As he lifted his head from his search, he saw a tiny, bright light coming toward him from the swirling tempest beyond the calm eye of the storm. "Look, what's that?"

"That's help!" Alethia said with a smile.

"Help, what kind of help?" As the light neared him, Ross saw it was a luna-tulwyth. He had never seen one in the daylight. He noticed more joining them. "But, how can they help us? Won't the storm blow them away?"

"You need to have more faith than that. The tulwyths are very strong flyers. They have been known to cut through the most powerful winds and storms, though your concern is not entirely misplaced. They are quite small and if the storm continues to build, they may have to look for shelter. Nevertheless, they will guide us to the gorge and aid us in our search for Seerae. It's an advantage that we have that the gallues do not. The tulwyths will never help a gallue." The tulwyths flew toward Alethia and landed on her head and shoulders, clinging to the tiny fibers of her shawl, and one lit gracefully in the palm of her outreached hand.

"Where'd they come from?"

"I sent for them, Msusi; they are my friends. We often have need of each other's company and, in some cases, each other's assistance."

Msusi strolled over to Alethia. She too possessed a grace and beauty that, though not equal to Alethia, was astonishing to witness. Serene and delicate and yet strong, she exhibited such genuine kindness that all the creatures of Shuk adored her. One chipper tulwyth eagerly landed on Msusi's offered hand, and she brought the petite creature close to her face and cheerfully greeted it. "Hello, wee friend. I'm so glad that you have come to guide us."

The luna-tulwyth fluttered its iridescent wings and glowed even brighter, expressing its own gladness. The tulwyth flitted to Msusi's ear and emitted a series of high-pitched animated chirps, chatting in a language unknown to Msusi.

"Glo, that is her name. She fancies you. More importantly, she trusts you."

"What is Glo saying? I have never before heard her tongue."

"She proclaimed, 'you shine like daylight'!"

"Oh Glo, you shine brighter and more beautifully than I ever could but thank you so much!"

Most of those who had ever seen a luna-tulwyth assumed that they had always been in Shuk. Only Shu knew the tulwyths were sent to Shuk by Alethia after the Great War. Before that, the tulwyths had lived in and around Anima, the city of Eloh. After the arrival of the nephesh in Shuk, Alethia sent a band of luna-tulwyths into the high mountains to help and to protect any lost or wayward nephesh. The tulwyths of Shuk hid from the light of day to avoid being noticed and found by the gallues. They only showed themselves to those whose hearts they could discern to be trustworthy, because many nephesh were corrupt and deceitful. Glo was the oldest of the tulwyths, but age had no effect on her, for all the twinkling tulwyths were immortal. She, like all the tulwyths, remembered the glorious days before the war and waited anxiously for the legend to return to Shuk and was therefore eager to aid the rescuers.

Glo fluttered over to Ross and hovered in front of his face, searching his eyes. Ross was delighting in her splendor—he had never viewed a tulwyth so closely—when her light began to fluoresce into an array of brilliant colors. Then Ross felt unexpected energy radiating from the miniature luminary, and she started chirping at him in her unique language. Ross asked Alethia, "What's she doing?"

"She is trying to tell you something."

"What?"

"She is saying, 'You are to believe, to believe in what you cannot see.'"

Ross sensed in Glo, a confident, reaffirming aura that touched his heart, and in it, he felt her hope confidently touching the residue of his evicted convictions and inspiring him. Even though he could not understand her language, the forcefulness of her sincerity struck weightily upon his cynical nature. He inhaled deeply, closed his eyes, and whispered, "I promise to try, Glo, I'll try."

Glo zipped back over to Alethia and all the other luna-tulwyths joined her, hovering in front of Alethia. Each singular glow merged with the next, creating one sphere of light that cast out all the shadows. The brilliance of the sphere shone like a dazzling star that had fallen from the sky and was vividly suspended before them. Alethia intently addressed the tulwyths, "Please guide us to the gorge and Ziminiar's cave swiftly. Huzesh, the gallue, has captured Seerae and is heading into the lower mountains to escape. It's imperative he not get away. Go, lead us into the storm, go quickly!"

The tulwyths flew off like a shooting star. Alethia and Jaroh met up with the company of Shu and followed behind the bright-white luminous sphere that led them all into the throes of the storm. Ross quickly took the lead, racing after the tulwyths with almost supernatural speed and agility, through the deep snow. The snow and the wind made every step a daunting and unrelenting effort. For the time being, however, Ross was un-phased by the difficulties; he had his heart and mind set on rescuing Seerae, at any risk to himself, even to his own life. His determination drove him onward like a machine, and the rest of the company followed hard on his heels.

Morak opened his eyes only to see the night had closed in upon him. The icy wind hissed in his ears, biting his face, hands, and feet. He sat up and looked into the shadows of the night that had come. He had fallen asleep and had slept the entire day away. He looked over the edge of the sheer cliff he had climbed earlier. All he could see was blackness. The clouds that had blanketed the landscape had risen high into the sky, but they did not reveal anything he could recognize. He had no idea where he was, or how far he needed to go; he just knew he could not leave the safety of the ledge until the sun illuminated a way of escape. He scooted the short distance to the back of the ledge and leaned against the stone walls to hide from the frigid, angry wind that harassed the exposed ledge. He stared out into the featureless night. There were no stars, moon, or lights of any kind in the sky, only blackness, with its tireless, howling wind for company. But Morak was not as alone as he might have thought.

In the distance, far below the ledge, Gubrone escaped the confines of Ziminiar's cave. The wind, though howling high above the valley, had died down around the cave and the snow had ceased falling. Gubrone gathered some scraps of wood and built a fire. He sat on a round stone next to the fire, warming his hands and feet, while the dakoons kept a comfortable distance from it, just close enough that their eyes glowed from the dancing flames. They were all very hungry, and the pangs of their hunger made each of them restless and irritable. Gubrone was not accustomed to finding his own food nor were the dakoons used to fending for their own meals, except to their combined consternation, there was nothing in sight to make a meal of. For the night, anyhow, the fire was going to have to satisfy them, so they sat watching it with the overbearing antagonism of their stomach's growling discontent.

As Morak sat pressed against the rocks, his eyes caught sight of a faint spot of yellow light flickering in the valley below him. At first, he was uncertain of the light's reality, so he closed his eyes and opened them again, expecting to see only darkness. To his surprise, the light still glowed, though it seemed very far away. Morak moved cautiously toward the edge and stared into the wind, gazing at the faint glimmer fighting through the blackness. Every so often, the light looked as though it was shaded by someone or something that moved back and forth in front of it. Morak realized it was a fire, and though he could not have known it from where he stood, it was the fire of Gubrone that had caught his eye. Everything in him wanted to move closer to the fire, but he knew that to try to climb down in the dark would not end well for him, so he waited for the night to pass.

Huzesh moved as hastily as he could, but he was impeded by the advancing storm, the poor visibility, and by the complications of traveling with Seerae. He had no way of knowing the company of Shu was chasing hard after him. Though the storm hindered him from making a speedy escape, it did not completely stop him from making progress. Huzesh knew if he could make it to the gorge without being caught, then he had a better chance of fighting them, for the gorge would prevent them from flanking him or circling around him. Though he could not know just how large the company had become, Huzesh knew that the larger the group, the slower it would be, for a group can only travel as fast as its slowest member.

Seerae lagged behind Huzesh. She hoped it would not be too long until she would be rescued. Seerae knew if she could delay Huzesh even the slightest bit by lagging behind and making him wait for her, it might make the difference between being freed and being a slave to the gallues. She had to be careful, however, for she did not want Huzesh to catch on to what she was doing. She had come to realize, in her short term with Huzesh, that he was not a patient one, and that he would not be slowed down for long. She waded through the deep snow, made less deep because Huzesh was plowing a narrow swath through it, a path Seerae hoped would lead the others to her. She tried to stay far enough behind him that she could see only his indistinguishable silhouette. At times, Huzesh forgot she was so far behind and would speed ahead, leaving her even further behind. Of course, Seerae was not bothered by this, yet every time, Huzesh quickly realized his haste and would pause and command her to hurry up. As they neared the gorge, Huzesh heard the sound of the falls that had, only a few days before, been so difficult for him to assail.

"Seerae! Seerae!" Ross's voice wailed through the wind and snow, and in spite of all the commotion, fell hard on the ears of Seerae and Huzesh.

Huzesh puzzled over the voice, for it sounded like none he had ever heard, and he wondered if it had come from the foreigner. Huzesh sniffed the wind like a wolf and listened intently. Then, while scanning their surroundings, he glanced at Seerae and happened to glimpse a capricious glimmer, a hopeful expression revealing the reckless surge of courage rising up in her. "Com, ut bae no tam t'run. A wull catch ye, ye know A wull," he slyly growled his warning.

Seerae was like a wild stallion ready to lunge out of its stall at the first opportunity; everything in her was desperate to run. Ross's voice seemed so close she felt sure she could reach him before Huzesh could catch her. She wanted to holler back or give him some sort of signal to tell him where she was, but as she thought about it, she felt afraid, not so much of Huzesh or what he would do to her, but for what he could and would do to Ross. She turned away from Ross's voice and walked hesitantly toward Huzesh. Huzesh confidently glared at her, but he knew if she had bolted, he could not have overtaken her. Huzesh waited to see if by some unexpected fortune, the voice was from the foreigner and if he was alone. Suddenly, Huzesh was mesmerized by a luminous sphere that came shooting through the heavy clouds and darkness. A luna-tulwyth zipped up close to him, spun around, then raced back in the direction from which it had come. Huzesh attempted to grab it, but the tulwyth was too quick.

"Seerae, where are you? Where are you, Seerae?" Ross's calls grew louder and stronger. As Ross's silhouette emerged in the distance, Huzesh hid behind a pile of stones, quickly drew his sword, and watched Ross with the eyes of a hunter. Ross froze. Huzesh saw that Ross was close to where the glow of light was hovering, but then Ross disappeared. Huzesh stretched his neck to see where Ross had gone. He threatened Seerae, "Kaep yer mouth shut, un A wull spare eem, fur now!"

Ross now waited for the others to catch up to him. Fortunately, the tulwyths had warned him about Huzesh and kept him safe. He had ducked down under the tulwyths swiftly enough to escape Huzesh's sight, and far behind, Loham waited and watched as the tulwyths flew by. One of the tulwyths hastily flew back to Alethia and Shu and urgently conveyed to them that danger awaited them. "Did you see Seerae? Was she with the gallue?" Alethia said.

"Aye."

"Is there more than one gallue?"

"Nae, but he is very frightful, a very strong one. He is hiding among the rocks."

"Can we get to Ross without being seen?"

"Only if the gallue is distracted. The clouds and snow will help us, a little, but I would not underestimate him. He looks quite capable."

"Kumél, come quietly." Kumél crept closer to Alethia and Shu, and Shu whispered to him, "This gallue, Huzesh, do you know of him?"

"Aye."

"Can you take him . . . I mean . . . can you defeat him?"

"Aye. Ut wud bae mae pleasure!"

"Wait! This may not be the right moment for that. We don't know what the gallue might do to Seerae."

"Ee bae cunning, un fearless. Ee bae u fierce warrior."

"We must find a way to get behind him without being seen. We have to block his escape."

"Dar bae no wae. Da falls bae jus ahead, un da gorge bae tae narrow haer."

"A wull gae. A cun fly above eem un impede ees progress."

"No, Jaroh, we must be careful. If any of the numerous spies view you, me, or Alethia, then everything could be ruined. If this gallue escapes, he will warn many others, we cannot risk it. You, Alethia and I must wait. We must stay out of sight."

Ziminiar crept toward Shu and Kumél. "Ziminiar, what do you recommend?"

Ziminiar placed his hand on Shu's shoulder and discreetly advised, "Da ony chance wae ha bae t'surprise eem. Wae naed t'sneak up naer t'eem, thun rush eem. Kumél un A wull close da gap afore ee cun d'mur harm t'Seerae."

"But what about Ross? He could get caught in the middle of all of this. If the gallue reaches him before you can overtake him, he will be hurt, or worse! We need to distract Huzesh so he won't see you."

"Ha ee saen, Ross?"

"We're not for certain, but he has surely heard his calls and established that he's nearby. Where is Loham?"

"He was following Ross, so he has to be just ahead."

Msusi and Zoësh had stopped moving when they had seen Ross kneel down, and now they were waiting for Alethia and Shu to draw near. Finally, Shu gestured for the two to return to them, so they cautiously crept back and Shu instructed, "Zoësh, we need you to sneak up to where Ross is hiding. The gallue is just ahead, between us and Ross, waiting to attack. We aren't sure if he has already seen Ross or us, but we must be careful not to approach too closely. Do you think you can get to Ross unnoticed?"

"Yes, I believe so. I will approach from directly behind where Ross is kneeling. There are several large rocks between us. I will stay low, and the heavy clouds should mostly shield my approach. If we aren't able to see him, then he isn't able to see us. Right, Kumél?"

"Aye, but ee cun smell ye."

"You will need to collect Loham. He can help you protect Ross should anything go awry. We need Ross to act as a distraction. We need him to stand up and let himself be seen and heard by Huzesh while Kumél and Ziminiar position themselves to attack Huzesh. Do you understand? If the gallue does not already know that we are here, then we certainly must not reveal ourselves. Glo thinks that he has only seen Ross, and we must keep it that way."

"Don't worry, I'm sure I can make it."

Huzesh fixed his eyes on the last spot he had seen Ross's silhouette and focused intently to see through the haze of clouds and the blizzard-like snow. He impatiently thought to himself, "*Whaer bae eem, dis forner?*" He wanted to move, to chase Ross, but he knew he would be seen, so he had to wait, but time was not on his side. The shadows of night were settling down over the falls region and darkness would soon overtake the realm. Huzesh was also uncertain of the whereabouts of the others. He suspected the foreigner might not be alone and that would be a much different situation which could change everything. He whispered hostilely into the wind, "Wut ye waitin fur? Com on!"

Alethia sent the tulwyths ahead to fly to the rear of Huzesh and instructed them to use their brightness to blind Huzesh or to distract and slow the gallue down, should he break for the falls.

Zoësh quickly closed the gap between the company and Ross. As she passed Loham, she motioned to him to quietly follow her. Ross jumped when a hand touched his shoulder. Zoësh quickly put her hand over Ross's mouth and with her other hand, she put her finger to her lips.

"Shh, it's me."

"What's going on? Why'd Glo tell me to wait here? What's he doing here?" Ross cynically pointed at Loham.

"A gallue is hiding in the rocks just ahead—you were about to get your head lopped off."

"Oh shit! How far?"

"Not far at all. Alethia and Shu have a plan, but you need to be brave. Seerae is with the gallue."

"How do you know?"

"Glo, she saw Seerae when she flew ahead. You must remember, Ross, you are in extreme danger out here. You can't just run off like you did."

"OK, I won't. Sorry. So, what's the plan?"

"You are about to be a decoy. You need to stand up, let Huzesh see you, then slowly walk toward him calling out as you had been. Please be careful, Ross! Loham will be there to help you if anything goes wrong."

"What? Are you crazy? What good is that going to do? Loham? This could all be part of his plan to lead me straight into a trap! Trust him?"

"Kumél and Ziminiar plan to sneak up to right where we are now and after you lure Huzesh to them, they will mount an attack. But they can't take the chance of being seen before they get here. That is why you need to distract Huzesh, make him think you are alone and keep his eyes on you. It should give us just enough time to get in place. Now we have to move immediately or we will lose the light, and he will escape in the shadows."

Ross's heart raced with worry. He anxiously asked Zoësh, "Do you think it will work?"

"It might, and it may be the only chance we get. Loham and I will wait here. If anything happens, we will be right there."

"Happens? You mean if he cuts off my head! A lot of good your help will be then."

"Now! You need to go now before he suspects something."

Ross cautiously stood up and called, "Seerae!" His voice was sheepish and less determined than before.

"Ross, be strong! You can't let him know that anything has changed."

"Seerae! Where are you?"

Ross walked around slowly in view of Huzesh, who was observing him with a keen eye. Huzesh sniffed the air, suspicious but eager.

When Ross began his ruse, Kumél and Ziminiar crouched down and began to creep to where Zoësh was waiting for them. Lengthy shadows were invading the narrow valley, which helped to disguise their approach. Huzesh concentrated on the distant, solitary shadow of the foreigner, wolfishly staring at him as Ross trudged toward him.

"Don't . . . don't hurt him! Please, you promised!" Seerae's plea was met with the sharp but broken edge of Huzesh's sword pressed against her throat.

"Quiet! Or else, dar bae no promise!" Huzesh hissed directly into Seerae's ear as his blade drew blood from her neck.

Kumél and Ziminiar reached Zoësh. They had hoped Huzesh would be drawn into the open, but Huzesh remained hidden. They had no way of knowing how far ahead of them he was and if they moved in without that knowledge, one or both could be killed. They waited as Ross wandered away from them, then Kumél snuck forward to close the gap between him and Ross. Ziminiar and Zoësh stayed low, and they both drew their swords, ready to lunge as soon as Huzesh was spotted. Unaware that Kumél was nearing, Ross continued toward Huzesh.

Seerae could barely see around Huzesh, but she noticed his excited breathing and knew Ross was closing in and threw herself to the ground. She had to find a way to warn him. She foraged around her and found, right in front of her, a round stone with a small, flat stone sitting on top of it. Seerae reached with her foot and gave a gentle, but effective push to the flat stone, causing it to slide off the round stone. It made a slight scraping sound as it slid over the edge of the round stone and then another plunking sound as it toppled onto another nearby stone. The sound alerted Ross and he halted his steps. Huzesh immediately turned to Seerae and angrily struck her in the face with his fist that was gripping his sword. Ross glimpsed the flash of steel that was only a few yards away from him.

Kumél also saw the flash and heard the tumbling rock. He leapt to his feet and hastily dodged past Ross, who fell to the ground. At the same time, Ziminiar rushed past Ross and the two apostas bore down on Huzesh with their swords drawn. Kumél shouted; his powerful, deep voice echoed through the valley.

Huzesh had perfectly positioned himself in a strategic location. The stone pile he had hidden behind caused the way to become narrow and impossible for anyone to avoid. He stepped out of hiding and into the narrow gap where the stream ran under his feet. Kumél swung his sword, which piercingly crashed against Huzesh's sword. Bright yellow sparks flew from the two blades. Huzesh retreated from the force of Kumél's blow. Ziminiar swiftly swung at Huzesh, but his blow was blocked as well. Even though Huzesh had lost one of his arms, it was evident he was quite capable with his sword, one or two-handed. For several moments, they exchanged several blows with their swords but only their swords were modestly injured. Kumél thrust forward with his sword and then quickly stepped back from Huzesh, expecting a counter- strike, but Huzesh did not attempt to strike back. Kumél and Ziminiar stood side-by-side in the narrow gorge staring at Huzesh, waiting for his next move with bloodlust in their veins.

"So, yur nut dead, aye, Ziminiar? Wut u shame!" Huzesh's antagonism was one of his better battle strategies. He was not afraid to fight and thrived on making his enemies squirm. "Bahaha! Ut ha baen u lung tam, Kumél. A ha nut saen ye since, wull since ye beat Gubrone un battle. Mus bae u bit rusty wit yer sword, aye?"

The darkness was closing in, and Zoësh was no longer able to see Kumél or Ziminiar, much less Huzesh. Ross held back at her side and they both heard Huzesh goading Kumél and Ziminiar.

"Yur u coward, Huzesh! Com, lut us sae who bae da victor today!"

"Oh, ye wud luv thut! Wud ye nut, Kumél? Ye wud luv t'take advantage o'mae, since ye cun sae thut A bae nut all haer."

"Dis bae no fight thut ye wud er win, Huzesh! Ye know ut!"

"Aye, yer right. Two agan one, un mae wit ony one arm. But A dunna naed t'win dis fight, nut t'day. A ony naed t'kaep ye frum winnin dis fight! Aye?" Huzesh had been hiding behind the rock wall for enough time to study his surroundings and, just above and in front of him, he had spotted a small stone that had a large boulder balancing above it. He planned to escape by dislodging the small stone with a strong blow of his sword causing the large stone to drop down and roll into the narrow gorge, at least slowing his pursuers. "Giv us da she-neph or A swear A wull run dis blade claen through ye, thun take off yer head!"

"Nae'er one fur small talk, aye, Kumél? Wae bae enjoyin our liddle reunion haer, ye maen t'deprive us o'visitin?"

"Giv er up!"

By this time, Shu and Alethia had reached Ross and Zoësh. Msusi also joined them while Jaroh kept watch from the rear. They could hear the mocking gibes of Huzesh and the stern, direct responses of Kumél and Ziminiar, and it was clear to them these former kerolus had nothing less than utter contempt for each other.

"Uf ye wanna her, ye mus pay mae fur her!"

"Yur un no position t'barter."

"A always bae un u position t'barter. Ye tink A bae u fool? Uf ye wanna her either take her bae force or guv mae wut A naed!"

"Wut d'ye naed?"

"Da forner! Giv eem t'mae un A wull giv ye da she-neph."

"Dar bae no barter, Huzesh! Wae wull take her one wae or d'other. Giv her up now, un mubae ye wull liv u liddle bit lunger!"

"Bahaha! Ye know wut ye lack, Kumél?"

"A lack notin. Now giv her up!"

"Ye lack creativity—ye always ha! Bahaha!" In a flash, Huzesh raised his sword and struck the small stone above his head, then he back stepped just in time to remove himself from in front of the rolling boulder as it fell into the gap, blocking the route of both the company of Shu and the stream of water that flowed to the gorge. Ziminiar grabbed Kumél and pulled him back from being crushed by the falling boulder, and the two of them landed in the stream, escaping near destruction. Huzesh grabbed Seerae and planned to run to the falls, but the tulwyths joined together and sped toward Huzesh and Seerae and when Huzesh turned to escape to the falls, a sphere of light confronted him. The luminous star of the dauntless tulwyths radiated with enough brilliance to temporarily blind Huzesh and to briefly hinder his escape, but when he recovered his sight, he ran past them with Seerae in tow. The tenacious tulwyths repeated this scenario several times, but Huzesh was unstoppable, and he escaped to the edge of the falls with Seerae. The tulwyths dove at him like a swarm of bees, trying to slow him down so the others could catch up.

Kumél attempted to look over the boulder but the giant stone was too tall. The water was rising surprisingly fast. Alethia and the others came out of hiding and raced ahead toward Kumél and Ziminiar and were searching for a way to escape the rising water. Ross began to climb over the boulder. "Come on! We can't let 'em get away! I can see them. They're at the falls!"

Kumél and Ziminiar leapt up and grabbed some overhanging rocks, then pulled themselves up and over the boulder. Zoësh, Msusi, and Shu followed the route Ross had taken and Alethia and Jaroh followed them. The water was filling up the narrow valley, making a lake.

Huzesh reached the edge of the falls. The stream was blocked, so it had transformed into a high, stone cliff. He peered below him, where the water had previously fallen and saw, in the fading light, a slight reflection, which was the deep pool of water at the bottom of the falls. Huzesh swung Seerae over the edge and dropped her through the cold, dark air, into the deep water, then he leapt over the edge.

"We must hurry . . . this boulder may not hold long and if it breaks away, the gorge will be flooded!" Everyone felt Shu's urgency and thought the same. They hurried toward the falls and hunted for Huzesh and Seerae, but they were nowhere to be found. The night shadows were now fully covering the valley and darkness was everywhere.

There was no light for them to see the way until the tiny tulwyths arrived. "We tried to stop him, but we are too small. Even our brightness would not detain him."

"Do not worry, my friends. We will catch them. Lead us on," Shu encouraged.

The tulwyths flew into the stormy night, leading the company of Shu toward the falls and once they reached the cliff's edge, they pursued.

"Go ahead, my wee friends. Show us the way, show us Huzesh!" Glo flew down like a shooting star into the gorge, her light shining off the walls and illuminating the somber gorge. Suddenly, her glow revealed Huzesh, running through the streambed. The remaining Tulwyths quickly flew to the pool below and lit the way for the others. Ross was the first to leap from the edge. He plunged into the pool with a huge splash and the others followed, one at a time.

With no time to waste, the company of Shu followed the fluorescent beam of the magical tulwyths, in desperate pursuit of Huzesh and Seerae.

Chapter XX
The Fog

Throughout the Valley of Souls, the sound of the Jupnie whispered in the ears of the captive nephesh, inspiring them to sing their songs of memory. Whether waif, snitch, or mate, they all sang their songs, filling the valley with the sounds of longing, and because of it, the hatred of Sinistradt grew increasingly fervent toward the nephesh. He loathed their songs more than anything, and the unleashed boldness of their singing acted like a smith's billows, breathing upon the maleficent fire already burning in his heart. As the many countless voices rose into the stormy skies, those flames grew into an incendiary rage, consuming his every thought and act. Discomforted and enraged, Sinistradt paced the dark hall, grumbling to himself. Then, the sound of wings flapping through the dark corridors, interrupted his tempestuous brooding. Sinistradt yelled out in his usual demanding, impatient tone, "Chiddush! Somon gut mae Chiddush, now!"

The sound of the flapping wings grew louder and as he turned to see a shadow, cast by the dim glow of the fire, a corvus landed on a ledge high above him. The presence of the bird fueled his already irascible disposition, inciting a fit of fury, laden with yelling and cursing and throwing things that made even the corvus quake with fear. Out of his tantrum spilled a sentiment of contempt and revilement for everything and everyone. Again, Sinistradt roared, "Chiddush!"

Now Chiddush had heard Sinistradt the first time but was disinclined to respond, knowing full well the abusive nature Sinistradt exhibited without restraint. There was no one exempt from his brutality, now that Gubrone was gone. Chiddush waited until he knew Sinistradt had done his worst before he casually walked into the dark hall, as if he had only just happened along. Still staring at the corvus high above him, Sinistradt snapped, "Whaer ha ye bun? A ha bun cullin ye, un A dunna lik waitin!"

"Ye maet tink thut yur da supreme ruler, but yur nut."

Sinistradt scowled at Chiddush. "Ye ha u visitor, up dar. D'ee ha news?"

Chiddush motioned for the corvus to come to him and it flew down and landed on his hand. Chiddush knew the language of the black birds well and he relayed to Sinistradt everything the bird reported to him. "Dae uv foun Gubrone. Ee bae un da norõ, headin t'Gershom, un ee ha two giant winged creatures wit eem. Deir wings bae unnatural, black a'da blackest stones, un dae waer nut lik ony bird or flyin creature."

"Dar bae no such beast on Shuk!"

"Dar bae ony one beast thut A rumumbar wit giant black wings. Dakoons!"

"Dakoons? Dar bae no dakoons on Shuk."

The corvus heckled in objection.

"Dis bae Ocktush, mae truest spy. He dare nut tell mae lies, un ee bae no frun o'Gubrone. Uf ee ha saen um, ee ha saen um."

Sinistradt directed a malevolent glare over his shoulder at Chiddush and growled, "Uf Gubrone ha two dakoons, ee wull return un reclaim ees rule!"

Sinistradt paced angrily around the dark hall while Chiddush and Ocktush silently stayed out of his way. "A ha waited far tae lung fur dis tam. Gubrone wull nut rob mae o'mae rule, A wanna ees head un A wanna ut now, dakoons or no!" A loud whomp echoed through the room as Sinistradt struck the stone table with his fist, startling Ocktush, who flapped his wings and protested. "Quiet, ye foul bird, lest A muk u meal o'ye!" Sinistradt attempted to grab the corvus, but the bird swiftly flew back up to its previous perch.

"Uf ye kull Gubrone, da others wull nut align wit ye," Chiddush remarked.

"Aye." Sinistradt's simple reply was calm and rational. He sat down in the seat of Gubrone and pensively planned out loud, "Dis waer maent fur mae. A wull bae da supreme ruler o'Shuk. Wae mus deal wit Gubrone afore ee cun return. Ee mus die! Un all da others—dae mus tink da forner kulled eem—wit dis!" Sinistradt held up the ice axe Veroot had stolen from Gubrone.

Chiddush looked at it surprised. "How? Gubrone took da weapon wit eem."

"Oh, ee dud, but A ha taken ut frum eem. Bahaha! Un A wull use ut t'kull eem! Un da others, dae wull tink da forner dud ut, un thun dae wull align wit mae!" Sinistradt's voice was both loud and fierce. He stood to his feet and walked toward Chiddush with renewed zeal. "A wull sun fur da custos, dae wull hunt down Gubrone un kill eem fur mae."

"Da custos, dae bae da gardians o'da wae. Dae bae loyal t'Gubrone, un dae wull nut d'dis ting ye usk."

"Dae bae loyal t'no one 'cept thumsaelfes. A haerd dae 'specially dunna lik Gubrone, fur condemning thum t'da fog."

The custos had the same status as most of the gallues in Shuk. They were subordinate to The Twelve and their power and magic. They may have obeyed the orders and rule of Gubrone, but they disliked him even more than they disliked the rest of the gallues. Sinistradt believed he could use their antipathy to accomplish his purposes by bartering their freedom from the fog for the death of Gubrone.

"Ye wull send yer frens, da corvuses, t'fly o'er da pass un deliver mae instructions un mae reward t'da custos. Tell thum—uf dae bring mae da head o'Gubrone, A wull free thum frum deir banishment. A bae sur dae wull gladly accept."

"Wut bout da corvuses? Dae maet nut wish t'deliver yer message, wut wull ye giv t'thum?"

"Wut d'ye tink dae deserve?" Sinistradt scowled. "Lut thum feast on da dead body o'Gubrone!"

"Aye, but firs da custos mus slay eem wit da weapon. Ees blood mus bae on ut t'prove ee bae dead un thut da forner bae da one thut dud ut. A wanna ees head!" Chiddush had his own reasons for sending the corvuses. He knew if the body of Gubrone was consumed, then the Eleetrum shard would be found, and one of the corvuses could bring it back to him.

"A wull sen Ocktush t'laed the corvuses un search fur Gubrone."

"Gud, but, dae mus deliver da weapon t'da custos. A maet even lut thum feast on dis forner uf dae cun fin eem." Sinistradt knew the corvus perched above understood him. He put the ice axe in a leather pouch and told Chiddush, "Sen dis t'thum."

Chiddush took the pouch and wrote Sinistradt's instructions on a piece of animal skin. Once he was finished, Sinistradt marked the instructions with a bloody handprint so the custos would know who had sent it. Chiddush stowed the message in the pouch, hailed Ocktush and held the pouch in the air. Ocktush flew down and grabbed hold of the pouch, but Chiddush kept hold of the bag, keeping the corvus from flying away. Chiddush pulled the corvus close to his face and whispered a secret command so Sinistradt could not hear, "Dias ome unek Eleetrum. Odesh inum une diam." The corvus called out, then flew away, into the night.

Once outside the cave, Ocktush flew up, into the hills above the valley where he landed high in a tree. He set the pouch amid the barren branches and let out a loud call. From every tree nearby, large black wings began to flutter and soon the sky was filled with a cloud of corvuses. Ocktush took hold of the pouch, lifted off the tree, and led the giant black cloud toward the high pass of Klamata. "Now ye mus muk raedy da rune. Soon wae wull destroy des troublesome nephs un deir song, once un fur all!"

Morak rose early and embarked on his journey toward the place where he had seen the fire the night before. The route was made severe by the many cliffs, expansive boulder and ice fields, broken terrain mixed with snow and ice, and the relentless, intolerable winds. As the day wore on, Morak doubted he would make his intended destination by nightfall and, at times, worried that he may have lost his way. The cold, biting air pierced his otherwise insusceptible skin, brutishly boring deep into his core, making him shiver uncontrollably. He had not consumed anything for several days, and his mind was beginning to fail him. Morak became disoriented and started hallucinating. He could not stop mindlessly mumbling the words of the Jupnie aloud. He continued walking, each forced step placed deliberately in front of the last, as though the absolute determination of his will had become a force which superseded every physical limitation, driving him onward.

Without realizing it, twilight had surrounded him. Morak stopped walking and found he was standing on a slab of stone on a long, broken ridgeline. The wind beat upon him and, for the longest time, he seemed immune to its harassment. He looked in the direction of the north. Far below, he could barely see what looked like a narrow valley where two rivers came together. Near the confluence of the two rivers, he saw a large mound of stones and, upon the mound, two creatures he was unsure of. He looked across the mountain realm and the vast expanse of raw, wild terrain and felt imbued with strength. He breathed in the cold air and stood back up.

Despite the approaching darkness, with a renewed vigor, Morak began the long descent toward the mound of rocks. His pace was quick and determined as he fought the wind, snow, and boulders that were strewn along the mountainside. The terrain was a maze of features like plateaus and ridges, disguised by the shadows, making it impossible for Morak to keep sight of his destination. He continued until, eventually, he saw a fire burning where there had been none before. He could see someone kneeling by the fire, but he could not see the two dark creatures he had seen before. Morak slowed his approach and cautiously made his way toward the stranger and the two beasts.

The smoke from the fire filled the air surrounding the cave. It was so abundant the dakoons' senses were dulled, making them nervous and quarrelsome. Gubrone was himself undisturbed by the diminished capacity of his senses and sat near the fire, enveloped in its smoke. So overwhelming was the smoke that neither Gubrone nor the dakoons noticed when Morak emerged from the shadows.

Morak approached cautiously, unsure if the one tending the fire was friend or foe. He quietly drew his sword as a precaution and slowed his steps, trying not to be heard. He could hear strange noises coming from the direction of the two strange beasts he had seen from afar. Their distantly familiar growls and roars alerted him to the probability that his first instincts about the beasts had been correct—they were dakoons. He stopped and lowered his sword. He knew the power of the dakoons; he knew their fierceness and *that* knowledge should have been enough to make him pause, yet, it was for a different reason he lowered his sword. Morak reasoned with himself, *"uf dae bae dakoons, who bae deir master?"*

"Attar?" Morak's mouth opened and without meaning to, he spoke out. His voice was not loud; it did not carry far, but the resonance of it cut through the smoke, alerting the dakoons.

Suddenly a piercing silence filled the small meadow, then a growl. It reverberated through the darkness like ripples of water and carried into every smoke-filled hole and crack throughout the meadow. Like the report of thunder, it shook everything it touched. Morak could feel his skin and hair shake from the force of it. He was a skilled hunter, a seasoned tracker, and the thought that he had made such a foolish mistake angered him.

"Dar bae no hidin fur ye. Com out!"

The voice surprised Morak. He knew it was not Attar speaking through the smoke and darkness. "Gubrone, ut bae mae, Morak. Kaep yer pets bound."

"Morak, Whae d'ye hide un da smoke?"

Morak stepped into the light of the fire and he kept one eye on the dakoons who were watching him with bared teeth.

"Bae ye alone, Morak?"

"Aye, un ye?"

"Except fur mae liddle pets. Whaer ye baen?"

Morak tried to act nonchalantly, even disinterested. "Whaer dud ye fin thum?"

Gubrone was equally evasive in his response. "Un da mountains."

The two gallues appeared on edge, untrusting and suspicious of each other. Gubrone did not know if, somehow, Sinistradt had sent Morak, and Morak wondered if Gubrone had grown impatient, as he usually did, and was out to follow through on his earlier threat. Gubrone never moved from his place near the fire. Morak stepped close enough to feel the warmth of the flames, and then knelt down, keeping a hand on the pommel of his sword and a cautious eye on the displaced leader of The Twelve.

Gubrone had a long stick in his hand. He stuck the end of it into the fire and poked about the coals. He pushed a few of the larger pieces of wood around, helping the flames to breathe and brightening the fire. A plume of glowing embers floated into the night sky, then disappeared. "Whaer ye bun, Morak?"

"Bun un da suõ, traein t'fin dis forner. Un ye, wut brings ye haer, Gubrone? Yur u liddle far frum da valley."

They were both tentative in their conversation. They seemed to be feeling each other out, trying to figure out what the other may or may not know.

"A bae lookin fur Eloh. Uf ee bae haer, A maen t'fin eem."

"Eloh! A ha haerd nutin o'eem. Ut saems doubtful ee bae haer, u forner mubae, but Eloh, Ee wud nae'er com t'Shuk." Gubrone's temper became inflamed by the bold refutation and impious candor of Morak. However, he restrained his response, not knowing whether Morak had others with him, others who may have been hiding in the shadows.

Morak, on the other hand, was experiencing a growing sense of suspicion and doubted Gubrone's sincerity. He would have never expected Gubrone to venture anywhere without an escort of guards and slave gallues. He also noticed that Gubrone did not carry himself as strongly as he usually did. He thought Gubrone might be hiding from someone or something. This caused Morak to feel emboldened, though he continued to keep a watchful eye on the dakoons. "Ut bae nut certain uf Eloh bae un Shuk. A intend t'bae certain. A trus no one. Dar jus bae som tasks thut ye mus d'yersaelf. An ye—whaer bae yer band? Hav dae abandoned ye?"

Gubrone was fishing for answers. Morak had not considered deceiving Gubrone, for though he suspected something was not right, he did not suspect Gubrone was any less the ruler of the realm than ever before. Morak had experienced the fury of Gubrone, so he was compelled by the knowledge of his retribution, as well as ages of subjugation and duty, to answer with candor. "Aye, A bae alone. Com through da narrow wae."

"Whae ye bae haer? Dis bae u lung wae frum da others."

"Slŷteeg said d'light o'da kerolus waer un da norõ, naer Gershom. A hoped t'fin som sign haer."

"Da storm put mae haer. Bun waitin fur ut t'pass."

"Dakoons? Ha d'ye ha dakoons? Dae bae all dead."

"Wull, nut all, a'ye cun sae. A bae nut witout mae saecrets."

Morak stared at the menacing dakoons, who glared back at him with their black, empty eyes and he wondered how Gubrone could command the dakoons. Nevertheless, he refrained from asking any more questions.

Not far from the fire was a large stone that was covered in snow. The stone had a large crack that ran from one side to the other, which had mostly filled up with snow. Pushing out of the crack and reaching above the snow was a cluster of snowpetals. It was hardly noticeable, especially in the darkness, yet somehow, Morak's eyes were drawn to the tiny white flowers. The vibrant lavender carpel of the flower glowed in contrast to the delicate, white petals spread open like a hand. Morak moved away from the fire and knelt beside the stone. He looked at the snowpetal with a curious stare.

"Wut bae ye lukin ut?" Gubrone asked.

"Des flowers; A ha saen thum afore."

"Dae bae notin, jus lik da grass bae notin. Food fur da creatures, thut bae all."

"Aye, but nut des. A ha hunted des lunds fur a'lung a'wae ha baen un shuk, un A ha nae'er noticed des. Da firs tam A er saes des liddle white flowers waer un da valley, whaer da weapon waer foun, dae waer growin on d'ground b'side da mēgs."

"Mubae, but dae grow up un da haelunds. Da nephs cull thum snowpetal; onywae, ut dunna matter." Of course, Gubrone knew exactly what they were because Tukkir had used them in the spell over the dakoons.

"Mubae, but ut bae strange thut dar waer no snow dar on da ground un da valley, whaer we foun da dead mēgs." Morak began to sniff the ground under the snow. He moved about the mound of rocks and eventually toward the entrance of Ziminiar's cave. The snowpetals made it difficult for him to catch a scent, but he was determined and, though there was little evidence to find—for the scent of Gubrone and the dakoons overpowered most other, older scents—Morak eventually found a spot with an unfamiliar scent. He dug down through the snow, took a handful of soil, and held it to his nose. Gubrone ridiculed him. "Morak, ye luk lik u fool, dis bae da camp o'Ziminiar. Ee bae who ye smell, no one else."

"Nae, ye ha spent tae much tam un yer cave, Gubrone. Da forner, ee waer haer. A cun smell eem." Morak knelt down and dug some more, hoping he might find a scent trail he could follow.

By this time, the dakoons had become curious, and they, too, began to sniff the ground. Gubrone watched with a look of humor on his normally scowling face. It amused him to see Morak sniffing about as if he was a mēg or some other animal. Gubrone glanced over to see that the dakoons were becoming strangely lethargic, stumbling about as if they had been given some type of strong drink. "Wut ha ye done, Morak? Da dakoons, somting bae wrong wit thum."

Gubrone rose and walked over to one of the dakoons that had fallen to the ground as if it had been knocked out. The other dakoon was still stumbling about. Gubrone looked at it and could see it was still awake, though it could not move. "Snowpetal?"

Stuck in its nostrils were clumps of snowpetal. Gubrone remembered that Tukkir used snowpetal in his rune, to tame the dakoons. It had never occurred to him that the snowpetal, by itself, could have such a potent effect on the creatures. The other dakoon fell to the snow-covered ground. It too had inhaled several clumps of the small flower. Gubrone roared, "Aargh! Curse des wretched blooms! Ye foolish beasts!"

Morak was shocked to see that such a small, almost insignificant, and rare floret could completely incapacitate his dakoons. Only the kerolus armies were known to have greater power over them. "Gubrone, da forner, ee ha baen haer! A bae sure! Dar bae others wit eem un dae maet return, nephs un apostas. Kumél—A cun smell eem tae."

Gubrone turned toward Morak. The glare of hatred and the thirst for revenge could be seen on his face, for Gubrone hated Kumél more than any other, and the scars left on his face from their battle were a constant reminder of his defeat and shame. "Uf da forner bae wit Kumél, A wull muk sur thut da dakoons feast on da flesh o'bot o'thum! Wae mus fin thum soon. A wull ha mae revenge!"

Deep in the narrow gorge, the company of Shu pursued hard after Huzesh. The invading darkness of night came quickly, and with oppressive invincibility, the deeper into the gorge they went. The light of the tulwyths helped them negotiate the inhospitable maze of sharp stones, imposing rocks, and slippery boulders that seemed even more forbidding in the darkness. In most cases, a journey down the mountain should have taken less time than the journey up, however, in this case, the trek down through the gorge was much slower and arduous. Even the flight of the tulwyths was hindered, for the wind gathered strength as it coursed up through the gorge, pushing against their every effort.

Ross, like everyone else, was growing weary and weak from the unrelenting physical and psychological struggle. His mind drifted away into thought and memory. He began thinking about Ama Dablam, when he feared Daniel had fallen. He remembered the vicious winds, tearing at his face and suffocating his every word as he tried to call out. He remembered the bitter cold clawing at his skin and the rush of fear that coursed through his senses, the feeling he had in his gut, of desperation; it was a nauseous feeling, a feeling he never again wanted. But all those feelings were back, hounding him. On this occasion, however, his desperation felt different. He felt stronger and more confident yet had no real idea of the threat and danger he would have to face to rescue Seerae. He felt capable as a mountaineer, but as a warrior, as a fighter, he was out of his league, and he knew it. He yelled at the top of his lungs for Seerae, just as he had for Daniel.

Of course, his yelling was not going to bring her back, and he knew it. Nonetheless, yelling her name made him feel a sense of power and a sense of hope that she could hear him, that he would find her, just as he had found Daniel. Calling out her name was giving him strength and courage, and he hoped that if she could hear him, she would feel strengthened by his voice, just as he had felt when Eve's voice had called out to him on the mountain. It may have seemed a foolish gesture, but for all the things he had no control over, this was the one thing he could control. "Seerae! Seerae! We're coming for you! Hold on!" He wanted to be strong, but his heart was becoming sick with worry and doubt, and his calls were becoming less and less hopeful. "Seerae, where are you? Please, where are you?"

"You can't give up. You can't lose heart."

"Huh?" Ross peered behind him to see Loham staring at him.

"You can't give up."

For a moment, Ross was unsure what was happening. He was confused. "What do you mean by that?"

"You sounded as if you were giving up. You can't; we all need you now."

"I know. I'm just tired—I think. Yeah, just tired."

"Maybe we should stop for just a little bit. You know, so you can catch your breath."

By this time, the others had caught up and Shu agreed, "He's right, Ross, we need to stop and rest. If we were to catch him now, no one would be fit to fight him."

"Well, I'm sure that he's feeling it too."

"That could be true, but if we aren't careful, we could pass right by him. In this darkness, he could be right ahead us, just out of our sight."

"Yeah, ok. He'll have to stop, too, and we'll be able catch him on the morrow."

Everyone was tired and needed a chance to rest, so, instead of continuing, they decided it was best to stop, at least for a while, and continue at first light.

Huzesh was, as expected, hindered by every element that slowed the company of Shu. However, he was without any light at all, which forced him to feel his way around the innumerable obstacles and barriers. In between the strong gusts of wind, he was able to hear faint sounds echoing through the gorge, coming from the company of Shu as they dogged his every step. A part of him wanted to dispose of Seerae, knowing that he could move more quickly on his own, but he knew at the very least, he might need her if the company was to catch up to him. He also did not trust Seerae and suspected she might try to aid his enemies in one way or another. Of course, it was in Seerae's mind to offer any help to the company she might be able to, though she was quite unsure of what she could provide. The one thing she had been successful at, whether intentionally or not, was slowing Huzesh down. Given her wounds, she was quite convincingly lagging behind the pace, forcing Huzesh to wait for her. Seerae was, however, not as damaged as she pretended, or as Huzesh believed.

She had another strategy for aiding her rescue, which was to make as much noise as was possible. She knew the company of Shu would be following behind and hoped by making noise, they would know their proximity to her and Huzesh. Using this tactic, Seerae cried out and yelled loudly when she stumbled or fell, quite intentionally. Of course, she would moan, groan, and trip over loose rock as though she was clumsy and unstable due to her injuries. All this noise echoed through the gorge and was carried by the wind, back to the ears of the company.

To her surprise, Huzesh stopped suddenly. He turned and looked in her direction with a curious stare. She feared he might have suspected her ploy and was about to call out when Huzesh began to walk slowly toward her. She tried to hide her fear and, at the same time, look for an escape route. She thought if she did not hesitate a moment longer, she might be able to escape back to the others. They were, after all, very close behind; she had heard them just moments before. Her muscles tensed and began to twitch as she readied herself for a heroic bolt into the blackness behind her. Just as she was ready to launch herself into action, she heard Huzesh whisper. He was too close, and she knew it, but everything in her wanted to run. "Shh! Dunna move!"

Huzesh was close enough that Seerae could see his eyes staring beyond her, into the darkness. He moved directly toward her and before she could move, he was right next to her. "Whaer bae dae? Dae bae halted." Huzesh listened for a long time, waiting for any sound that would break through the strong gale. There was nothing but silence from the company. "Com." Huzesh violently grabbed Seerae by the arm and commanded her, "No sound!" He pulled her behind him as he made his way into the dark.

Seerae wanted to say something, to make even a small noise, but she dared not. She could tell, by the vice-like grip on her arm, that Huzesh was not about to be the least bit restrained in his brutality, should she give their movements away. However, her silence would not be long-lived, for the pain from Huzesh's talons digging into the flesh of her arm became unbearable and excruciating. Though she tried to hold back the anguish, she was unable to hold her tongue and suddenly erupted, "Ouch! You're hurting me! I said, you're hurting me! Let go!"

Seerae began to fight and squirm, clawing at his hand. Blood was seeping from the shallow wounds made by his talons, but Huzesh seemed as though he did not notice her tantrum at all. He was so exhausted and focused on distancing himself from the company that he heard and felt nothing except those things directly in front of him. Seerae's fit grew more animated and in a bold and yet unintended move, she reached up and slapped Huzesh across the face. It was an act so extreme, so unexpected, she surprised herself. Quickly realizing what she had done, her eyes grew round and large with fear and her mouth opened wide. She could feel all the energy and strength rush out of her body. Huzesh stopped, his eyes narrowed, and the muscles in his face tightened. He lowered his gaze at the startled and frightened face of Seerae. His anger was welling up from somewhere deep in his being. He had never been struck by a nephesh and to his surprise, the blow was far more powerful than he would have ever expected. Without thinking, Seerae spoke softly, in a gentle, composed manner, "You're hurting me—my arm, please let it go."

Huzesh reacted with much less composure. A loud, ferocious roar bellowed out of his mouth, straight into Seerae's face. Seerae blocked her face with her other arm, bracing for Huzesh to strike her. He raised her off the ground and high into the air by her arm. As she was hanging in the air, she glanced in the direction of his other arm and a confused, wide-eyed expression fell upon her face. Then, without intending it, a inaudible chuckle forced its way past her lips and into the ears of Huzesh. He noticed her curious expression and found it impossible not to follow her eyes to where she was looking. His eyes landed upon the stub of his other arm and a confused, slightly stunned expression appeared on his face. Without a word, Huzesh simply released his grip on Seerae's arm, letting her fall backward. He walked only a couple of steps away, sat down on a snow-covered rock, and rested his chin in the hand of his one good arm, as though he was feeling like the brunt of someone's joke.

Kumél heard Huzesh's loud roar. He stood up and faced into the wind, his strong nose sniffing the air.

"What was that?" Ross asked Kumél.

"Ut waer Huzesh. A bae sur bout ut."

"We have to get to them. Who knows what he might be doing to her?"

"Ut cud bae u trap. Ut bae tae dark un windy. Wae wull wait til morn."

"But—"

Shu took hold of Ross's arm. "You must rest. Morning will come soon enough."

Alethia could see the worry in Ross's eyes. She called to Glo who quickly flew to her. "Cautiously fly ahead and look for Seerae, please. Do not let yourself be seen by the gallue. Return and tell me what you see."

Glo hurried into the turbulent darkness. Ross saw her fly away, then asked Alethia, "Where's she going?"

"To appraise the situation, and to confirm that Huzesh is not sneaking away."

Ross lowered himself down to the cold ground, sheltered from the wind by the many rocks.

Seerae could not bring herself to move. She leaned against some stones, holding her bleeding arm. Rushing past her, the relentless wind blew up the gorge. Besides the wind, there was no sound, and there was no light, only darkness. She thought about the others. She hoped they were, indeed, close behind, though she was very uncertain of it.

Not more than a few steps away, Huzesh sat in silence, thinking about what to do next. There was no doubt in his mind, that his fury, fueled by his violent temper, had been heard by those hunting him. He knew daylight would come soon enough and he might have an advantage over the others if he moved quickly.

Suddenly, a strange sound passed by Seerae's ears. It was so quick and almost imperceptible she doubted she heard anything at all. The sound came again, but the night was too dark and the storm too restless to let her eyes see anything at all. She sat listening for a long time, but the sound never came again.

Huzesh did not seem to notice the sound Seerae heard. She watched him, expecting to see some sort of reaction, but there was none, though she could see he was not as vigilant as he had been. His head would slowly droop back and forth and then drop forward, until his chin came to rest on his chest. He would jerk and then abruptly lift his chin and open his eyes. Though teetering on the edge of exhaustion, Huzesh was not about to give her an opportunity to escape. Abruptly, he rose to his feet and approached her, unwinding a long piece of skin cordage that was wrapped around the sheath of his sword. "Guv mae yer huns."

"Huh? What are you doing?"

"Dunna fight mae, she-neph! Guv mae yer huns!" Huzesh tied the cord around Seerae's wrists and tied the other end to his belt. He then sat down beside her and spoke softly, in a calm, almost lighthearted tone, "Dis bae fur yer safety, ye know. Ye maet grow weary o'mae compny or walk un yer sleep. A wud hate fur ye t'wander wae un gut lost. Bahaha!" Seerae was not humored by his attempt at jest.

The tulwyths huddled together on a flat, round stone in the creek bed. Their light shone like the soft flickering glow of a campfire, it was not warm, yet it gave the company a sense of warmth amid the cold darkness. Ross sat staring into the glow of their light. His mind denied his eyes rest. Alethia sat across from him, and she, too, watched the glow of the tulwyths. Ross looked at her sitting there on the ground. Though he tried, he could not avoid thinking about how beautiful she was, and how out of place she seemed. He had never seen her kind of beauty before. The warm light cast upon the features of her face only magnified the pure essence of her glory. Ross forced his eyes to look away for fear she might catch him staring. To distract himself from the compulsion to admire her, Ross began to ask her about something she had said before, something he could not forget. "You said something back there, something I can't seem to get out of my head, something about a Kleid?"

"Yes, the Kleid o'Miht."

"What's that?"

"It's the source of all authority over the Realm of Tirnan."

"Tirnan, you mean where I come from?"

"Yes."

Ross knew nothing about the history of Shuk, the other realms of Pardis, or the mysteries of the legend, but a strange phenomenon had been taking place in his heart ever since he heard the story of the legend. The mysteries of those things he did not know before were becoming clear to him. He could no longer ignore the many and varied signs that were trying to awaken the truth of the legend hidden within his own heart. Alethia knew he was becoming aware and that he would soon understand, though he would not understand everything.

"But if the Kleid o'Miht is meant for Tirnan, why's it important here?"

"The Kleid o'Miht was not meant for Tirnan, it was meant for Amik. It's important to all that are of his line, everywhere, Ross. It is not just in Tirnan that the power of the Kleid o'Miht is felt; it is felt everywhere the seed of Amik is found, and that includes where the nephesh are. It was given to Amik before his ruin, and until it is returned to its rightful heir, then all the offspring of Amik will be bound under the power of Attar and his curse."

"So, once we get it, the curse will be broken?" asked Zoësh.

"It's not quite that simple, Zoësh. When Amik surrendered the Kleid o'Miht over to Attar..."

As he listened, Ross's thoughts began to collide as memories flooded into his mind. Things he had seen, visions, and dreams, while in Shuk, while with Shu and Alethia and the others flew into view like photographs being tossed into the air by someone frantically rifling through old photographs.

Alethia continued without knowing what was going on in Ross's head. "... Attar feared that Amik or one of his descendants might try to take it back and call for Eloh to return. Only if the seed of Amik possessed the Kleid o'Miht, and only if the one who possess it calls for Eloh, can Eloh return. For this reason, Attar fractured the Kleid o'Miht. It was severed along each of its four faces. The pieces were taken away and all but one, were hidden throughout the realm of Tirnan."

Out of the chaos and confusion of his roving thoughts, Ross began to see something familiar, from a vision or dream—he couldn't remember which. He saw a metal box, the same metal box that had been chained to his ankle, the rusted metal box that pulled him under the black water, the metal box that held the black triakis. He could see himself opening the lock.

He began to focus on the object in his hand, bringing it closer into view. It was a strange object. The fact that it opened the lock made him think it was a key, but if it was a key, it was unlike any he had ever seen. It was large and had four sides with strange markings on each of the four sides that were similar and yet different. He watched himself insert the key into the lock while in the background he could hear Alethia's voice and the things she was saying about the Kleid o'Miht.

Ross thought about the strange object he had seen in his vision and wondered if it was what Alethia was talking about. He tried to picture it. He had held it in his hands, at least, in his mind, yet until that moment, he had not remembered it or given any consideration to its importance. Alethia continued, "It is here, in Shuk. The fourth face of the Kleid o'Miht."

Ross spoke out. His voice was nervous. "You said it had four faces?"

"Yes."

"I think I've seen it, in my mind, like a vision. Each side has a triangle with symbols carved into it, and on the top is a unique symbol, like that— the one on Msusi's headband." They looked to where Ross pointed and saw the mark of Eloh.

"Yes, that's right."

"I saw it once before, at the pool, and again, just now."

The group was amazed at this incredible announcement. Zoësh was the first to say something. "Where was the key—in your vision?"

"It was linked to a chain that was fastened to my ankle and to a metal box. I used it to free myself and open the box."

"You saw all this in a vision?" inquired Loham.

"Yes."

"What was in the box?" Msusi asked.

"A weird, black stone with golden veins."

Astonished, Alethia spoke under her breath, *"The triakis."* She knew with absolute certainty she was right, and Shu had been right, Ross was the seed of Amik, the one sent to break the spell of Attar.

Ross heard what she said and was quick to question her about it. "The what? Triakis? what is that?"

"Never mind that. It's the Kleid that is important, and that you have already seen it is very important."

"But only part of the Kleid is here, right?"

"Yes. Only the fourth face, the face of the wind."

"What about the rest of it, the other three faces?"

"The time will come when they will have to be found, but that time is not yet."

"So how do we know? I mean, how do you know that Gubrone has the fourth face?"

"There are many spies in Shuk—the wind, the streams, the birds of the air, the tulwyths, and the nephesh—they have all seen and heard many things over the ages. It is they who have shown us these things."

"So Amik is the only one who can retrieve the Kleid?"

"Yes, or his legitimate heir."

"So that's why I'm here? You think I'm his heir?"

"The heirs of Amik are as numerous as the sands of the sea—but yes—you are the one."

Ross wondered to himself, whether he could do what had to be done. He very much doubted he could. "But I am not like them, not in any way. Kumél would be a better choice. He is a champion."

"Only you can do what must be done, Ross. Only you can reclaim the Kleid. Kumél is not of Amik."

"But how? I am no match for these giants."

Alethia paused, then looked into Ross's eyes as if trying to reach beyond the dimness of his conscious understanding. "Love, Ross. You will outmatch them through the power of love."

Ross looked at her with an imposing, dubious stare. At that moment, Glo flew into their camp and landed near Alethia. Alethia immediately turned her attention away from Ross. "Oh, Glo, there you are. So, what news have you for me?" As every eye turned toward the petite tulwyth, Glo told Alethia that Seerae and Huzesh were not far away and that they were resting among the rocks.

Ross inquisitively looked at Glo and then at Alethia. He wanted to ask Alethia about what she had meant and yet, at the same time, he urgently had to know what Glo had discovered. "Well, what did she see? Is Seerae OK?"

"Yes, they have stopped and have taken shelter not far from here."

Ross stood to his feet and looked around at the company. "Maybe we should sneak up on them and rescue her, before he has a chance to get away."

"No, it is time to rest. We must all rest now; we'll need our strength on the morrow."

One by one, the company turned away and found places to lie down and sleep for the night, though rest would not come easily for some.

For Ross, the night passed at an agonizingly slow pace. He found himself in and out of dreams and visions and awake, thinking about Eve and then Seerae. Late in the middle of the night, he lay with his eyes wide open. He was neither sleeping nor awake, but somewhere in between, caught in the twilight of contemplation. He thought about Eve and how much he missed her, but missing her made him feel weak and vulnerable, just as losing her had. They were feelings he wished to be free of yet could not. As he was thinking about Eve, there came many subtle, uninvited implications. They whispered to him, in the brevity of moments between thought and epiphany, contentious, deprecating intimations, scolding him for his naiveté and tender affinity that filled his heart. Like the reprimand of a stranger, the meddling foe made him question what he thought he knew, what he thought he understood. In defense against the voiceless accusations, Ross denied what he felt, what he knew he felt for Eve. He tried to dismiss his love for her, to pass it off as having been only a fancy, a distraction, something to be forgotten. Nevertheless, the deep, unspoiled residue of Eve's determinant, unrestrained love, the immeasurable consequence of a force without form or frame, intangible and yet utterly dominating overcame every objection and every denial. He could not escape the scar or the bleeding left by the sharp edge of her love.

Ross knew he needed courage, that he had to be brave without knowing whatever lay ahead. But he could not understand how love could overpower hatred, how his lingering love for Eve could give him courage when all it seemed to do was give him grief. For all his life, he had thought love was weakness, something that made him, somehow, less courageous. He feared that his genuine affection for both Daniel and Eve could be fatal, his hamartia. Ross could not separate love from weakness, for he had also loved his father and his mother who had hurt and abandoned him in one way or another. Everyone he had ever cared about was gone, dead, and he was left with the pain of loss. If he had never loved them, then he would have never felt broken by losing them. Love was a pain with no relief, an agony that never let go. It freed and yet it impounded, it was ecstasy, and yet it was torment. He did not stop loving Eve after she died, and he could not love her anymore, not really, for she was gone, into the shadows, and he was alone, alone with a love he could not express, a love that only made him feel the greatest loss, the greatest sorrow, and the greatest emptiness. Though he trusted Alethia, he doubted she was right about love; he doubted it could be of any help at all.

Ross closed his eyes and fell into another dream. Darkness filled his mind, though it was not a darkness of void, of emptiness or of lightlessness; it was a darkness like deep water: cold, wet, and everywhere around him. From within the darkness, he could hear the words of Tennyson echoing around him:

I hold it true, whate'er befall;
I feel it, when I sorrow most;
'Tis better to have loved and lost
Than never to have loved at all.

Nevertheless, it was not the voice of Tennyson he heard; it was Eve's voice. Tennyson was her favorite poet, and she often quoted him, gently trying to comfort Ross's torment over Daniel, hoping the profound message would bring to him the same consolation it had always brought to her. Unbeknownst to Eve, however, the immortalized refrain did little to satiate the omnivorous affliction consuming his vulnerable and wounded heart. Ross had never found comfort in such platitudes. They always had the same ineffectual consequence as the many attempted diversions and offered condolences he had known and despised. He would not and could not be comforted by platitudes or sympathy. What he felt was too strong and too real and could never be duly satisfied. The demands of his love for her required more, more than memory and heartache. Moreover, he required more of himself than to be pacified to the point of forgetting. He wanted to remember, to feel the loss and the pain, to feel what he was missing was truly worth missing, as if it was a void in his being that could not be filled and should not be filled with the lifeless carnage of pious contentment, filling the hollowness of everything else.

For what seemed like a day, Ross felt suspended in the darkness, surrounded by the ubiquitous voice echoing the same repeated verse.

Suddenly, the voice ceased and only silence surrounded Ross. Then a whisper echoed through the darkness, "Ross, wake up."

Ross opened his eyes to see it was still dark and his friends were still sleeping. He glimpsed a faint glow of light coming from the snow. He glanced around and his eyes stopped at Alethia, who was watching him. He wondered why she was not sleeping. Alethia rose to her feet and walked the short distance to where he was sitting. "Your sleep is not very restful, Ross. There are many things in your mind keeping you from resting."

"Yeah, I'm troubled by many things; there's much to think about."

"Sometimes you have to believe. There are questions that cannot be answered with words or understood with reason. You fight within yourself for understanding. You are tormented by what you fear, and you fear what you do not understand."

"I know, you're right. What did you mean earlier, about love?"

Alethia wanted Ross to realize the power of his emotion, the visceral strength of his passion, and knew that explaining it would not help him understand. She looked down to see Eve's diary and the small black camera Ross protected, lying just inside the opened backpack, by where he was sitting. Alethia had seen how completely smitten Ross was with Eve when she had watched him touch the journal and run his fingers gently over each of the words Eve had written on each of the pages. She pointed to the camera, knowing full well what was concealed within it.

"What is that, there, in your satchel?"

Ross was confused by her request; nevertheless, he was obliging and reached down. "This, this is Eve's journal."

"Not that, the small black thing."

"Oh, this? It's a camera."

"What is in it?"

"In it? It's a camera. It has pictures in it, kinda …"

"So, what does it do?"

"Well, it doesn't do much at all now."

"What do you mean?"

"It used to take photos, probably still does but, but the batteries are about dead."

"What's in it?"

"Oh, there's nothing actually in it, only pictures. You know, images."

"Images of what?"

"Well, images of Eve, of the last times we spent together, mostly. I have the last photo ever taken of her."

"May I see?"

"Well, uh …" Ross took a long, deep breath. He was afraid to turn the camera on, for fear it might not come on or might never come on again. He was also afraid to dredge up even deeper emotions. Alethia could see the turbulent emotions in his eyes. "I've been kinda—well, waiting to turn it on. Waiting because I'm afraid it might never come on again." His voice was weak, and he had to clear his throat a couple of times just to get the words out.

"Don't be afraid, Ross. Show me. Show me Eve."

Ross's finger shook involuntarily as he reached for the power button. He hesitated for just a moment, and then he pushed the small button down. A quiet, unexpected sound emanated from the camera as the lens extended out from the body. Light glowed from the rectangular screen and, in an instant, the image appeared of Eve huddled close to Ross on the peak of the mountain. Ross looked at the photo and was instantly hypnotized by her stare, lost in her eyes looking back at him, as if she was standing right in front of him. He touched the screen with his finger. "There you are." The volume of his voice was little more than a whisper. The remarkably powerful tenderness in his tone suggested he was talking directly to Eve rather than to a digital image. He was wrecked with convergent emotions, a strange dichotomous union of forces, of love and loss, joy and sorrow, peace and turmoil. He lost all awareness and became so completely transfixed on the image. "I really miss you. I need you so much. I know I would rather have loved you than missed what loving you feels like, but it hurts like hell. It hurts way more than dying. What's wrong with me, Eve? Why couldn't I have done better? I'm sorry, babe, I know it's too late. I just hope … I just hope you can hear me 'cause I'm scared, I'm really, really scared."

As Alethia watched the broken man, she felt a lone tear roll down her cheek until it fell from her face onto the snow-covered rocks below. She knew he needed to see Eve, to hear her and to feel her. If he was to find whatever strength or courage he needed, it was going to come from the power of his love for her. He needed to know what he was fighting for, that he was fighting for her.

Beep, Beep, Beep. Out of nowhere, a foreign, high-pitched noise began to sound. Alethia glanced at Ross who had not noticed the sound. "Ross, Ross, what's that sound?"

"Oh shit, no, no, no, not now! No!" The image of Eve disappeared behind a black, empty screen. "No! Please, please, no! You can't go, not now. Not now!" He leaned forward into a heap and began to cry. His face was deep in the snow and surrounded by sympathetic, little white snowpetal, their heads bowing toward the rocky ground below. For Ross, it felt as though he had lost her all over again. Ross was not prepared in any way for the intensity of his emotions. The world around him was transformed and the surreal, immaterial realm, watched quietly as if somber. Even the storm paid its respects with stillness.

Out of the silence, the comforting voice of Eve, whether real or imagined, echoed throughout the corridors of his mind. "*Ross, wake up! You must wake up!*" Each time her voice called out, it sounded closer, like she was walking toward him. Then he felt dismissive, as though it was merely the residue of memory clinging to the broken remnants of longing and heartache. The voice kept surging in upon his mind and his heart, persisting, undaunted by his ambivalence. "*Wake up, Ross! Please, wake up!*"

All Ross could see were shadows and darkness, as if he was looking into an empty night sky, but then, like an apparition, Eve walked slowly into his thoughts. What he saw was not like the image in the camera, the image he always pictured when he thought of her; it was the same vision of her he had seen on the mountain. She was like a ghost reaching out to him, calling out to him. He could feel everything as if he was at that very moment in his memory, the moment when she reached out and touched his chilled face. Every one of his senses were aroused as if everything he was seeing and feeling was, in fact, real, as if he hung suspended in the darkness all over again, cold and frozen. The sting of the bitter cold pierced his consciousness and with it came that same hopeless desperation he felt on that cold, lonely night. The force of her love reached out and touched him, but so too did the agony of losing her. The cold sorrow was too immense to console and resisted her touch.

"Ross, wake up!"

His heart would not let him escape into the detachment of rationale. It urged him to feel, to grab hold of the love that gave him pain and to cling to it, to find his strength in it, to embrace the wild, untamed amour that drove him to leap into the abyss, to cast away his own life, to love her back, whether dead or alive, with abandonment.

She had been the one person who had broken through and touched his heart. He did not jump from the mountain to escape life, to avoid the responsibility and guilt; he had leapt because without her, there was no life worth living.

"Ross, open your eyes!"

As he listened to her voice and then to the defiant protest of his mind, she reached out and put her hand on his face. The tenderness of it, the soft gentleness of her hand on his cheek achieved what Eve's touch had always done; it broke the spell and quieted the chaos that crowded into his thoughts. He raised his eyes and looked at her from behind the curtain that separates the material from the immaterial, mortal from immortal. As he stared into her eyes, echoing through his mind were the phrases of Eve's verse:

...As twilight and fog dance together

And the dew glimmers with radiant iridescence

A moment, unexpected, unpredicted unfolds, like the bloom of heather.

In this quiet unassuming instant, life's tragedy and the world's brokenness are eclipsed,

overthrown by the sweet and uncorrupted residue of a new world.

It is a span so slight, so momentary that consciousness rarely observes.

A twinkle in the eye of God

Then gone like breath.

Ross felt his brokenness eclipsed; his soul wounds stopped bleeding. He felt the freedom and the power of love. He wanted to say something, to speak to her, to tell her how he felt, but she put her hand to his mouth. He saw a curious transparency to her face. He looked at her and then looked closer. Her face changed as if it were a reflection on the water. As Ross continued gazing at her, he saw it was Seerae looking back at him. "Open your eyes—and see."

The image of Eve was gone forever, lost in a small black box he could not unlock or open. He had been afraid, but now the fear was gone.

As quickly as the visions and memories came, they faded away, and

Ross was still hunched over with his head in the snow. Alethia had stayed with him, letting him feel whatever it was that he needed to feel. Slowly he raised his head. "She kept telling me to wake up. She wanted me to wake up to her and to this place—to all this. I'm such an idiot!"

"You're not an idiot, Ross. The sleep of forgetfulness is very powerful, only a few have ever awoken from its spell."

"I wish she was here, that you could have known her."

"In many ways, I already know her—through you—through the things that you have told me and through the things that I see in you, things that are not of you, but are of her. She is who you will fight for, Ross. She is who you would die for."

Ross looked at Alethia and shining from his eyes was a new brightness, a clarity that was not in them before. He felt strong as he thought about Eve.

"You will need the memory of her. You will need what you feel for her. Never let her go, never let pain and sorrow steal her away from you."

"We have to find Seerae. She's all I have left of Eve."

Huzesh opened his eyes and realized the storm had quieted. Thick fog filled the gorge and through it came the glow of the morning sun, rising over the mountains. He slowly lifted his head from the rock that was his pillow and then sat up quietly. Huzesh did not like the stillness and quiet. He knew the company of Shu was nearby and they could hear his movements. He saw Seerae was still sleeping. Slowly, he stood and looked around. The silhouette of stones that surrounded him on all sides and the rising fog made for an eerily familiar scene, for the way to the Valley of Souls looked very much the same.

Huzesh bent low and grasped Seerae by the throat, squeezing her neck with just enough pressure to keep her silent. He hissed into her ear. "Shh! Uf ye utter u single sound, A wull break yer neck!" He lifted her to her feet and scanned the area, getting his bearings. The stream that was blocked off by the balancing stone was now running as deep as ever, and the sound of the trickling water was the only noise that could be heard. Huzesh took each step with care and precision. Seerae was less precise, though she was mostly silent. They moved down the gorge under the cover of the fog.

Back up the gorge, Alethia motioned for Glo, who flew quickly to her. "Glo, take another tulwyth and fly ahead. See if you can find Huzesh and

Seerae. Hurry, they may have slipped away in the night.''

Glo flew ahead with another tulwyth whose name was Shim. In the growing brightness, the tulwyths light was barely noticeable. They raced past the others and disappeared into the fog. A tiny glint of light could be seen in their wake, and then it, too, disappeared.

One by one, the company of Shu roused to the morning fog and hastily prepared to pursue Huzesh. Ross checked his backpack, to make sure he had everything inside it. He began to walk away, when he heard Alethia's voice. "I think you forgot something.''

Ross stopped and looked back. Laying on the ground was the spear of Amik. It was not as though he meant to leave it, though carrying it was quite burdensome, it was that he failed to notice it in his haste. Ross had carried the spear ever since Shu had given it to him back in the cave, he felt burdened by it, not to mention, afraid, for the spear possessed powers he did not understand. The first time he held it in his hands, the spear came alive with a bright blue light and, at the same time, the blue simtu markings on his body glowed and moved like fluid flowing over his skin. The simtu now covered most of his body. He could remember the physical sensation of the light coursing over and through him, which, when he thought about it, still made him uncomfortable. Ross looked down at the spear. Then he looked back at Alethia. "You know I've never killed before. That's what this is for, isn't it?''

Alethia looked down to the ground. It was the first time Ross could remember her ever looking away. He could see that she, too, was uncomfortable with the idea of killing and the purpose of the spear. She lifted her head and looked back at him. "You will know what to do when the time comes. Don't be afraid of the spear. Take it in your hand.''

"What, now?''

"Yes. Hold it in your hands so that you can feel its power.''

Holding the spear in his hand, the markings began to glow. By this time, Shu and the others were watching, but they were also anxious to start the pursuit. The light of the spear moved through the markings as if an invisible hand were carving. It seemed as if the light was being set free from within the spear; it moved through the carvings of the haft and then into Ross's hand and arm, and then throughout his body. Ross's instinctive response was to let go of the spear, just as he had the few times before. He started to open his hand, as though he was going to release the spear, but then Alethia reached over and closed his grip. "Ross, the spear of Amik belongs to you now, and only you can give it life. You are its master. You complete it and give it life and without you, it is only a piece of ancient metal."

Ross could feel the power of the spear radiate from within himself, as if it was him who was giving it power. He could feel a change. His fears began to fade from his thoughts and his heart possessed a new, emboldened sense of confidence. A part of him was afraid of the confidence, intimidated by it, as if it was something from outside of himself and too powerful to control.

"You hate because of your fear, and you think that hate will give you the strength you need, but it will not. What you feel for Eve, *that* is what you need, *that* is what will give you the power to do what you must, in the right time." Alethia reached out and touched Ross's face.

"Your love for Eve is strong, and it will make you stronger yet. It will fuel the urge to protect and defend, to rescue and restore. Hatred, Ross, is an unwieldy force that only seeks to destroy. Remember, it's not who you fight *against* that matters. It's who you fight *for*—that is where your strength and courage must come from."

Ross felt the honesty of her heart and the truth of her words. The power of the spear had tormented him with pain and conflict before; it was now, unexpectedly, filling him with a mysterious sense of determination and desire. He wrapped up the spear and prepared to leave with a gleam of hope in his eyes.

"We must go," Alethia advised.

In no time at all, the company was moving down, through the gorge. Glo and Shim flew hastily down the gorge and it was not long before they saw Huzesh and Seerae through the fog. They flew with such speed that their wings made a high-pitched humming sound, which Huzesh heard. Huzesh turned as the two tulwyths darted past him. He could not see them, except for a faint trail of light that disappeared into the fog. It was not long before the wind began to swirl and gust with moans and whistles, filling the gorge with a plethora of troublesome noises.

Huzesh was relieved to hear the noise and began moving more quickly, though carelessly, through the gorge, hoping to increase his separation from the company. Glo and Shim turned toward the company and sped back to inform Alethia and Shu of their discovery.

Only moments later, the two tulwyths reached the approaching company and told Alethia and Shu that Huzesh and Seerae were only a few hundred yards away.

"Kumél, Ziminiar, they are not far away. Glo has seen them. You should hurry ahead. Jaroh, you should go as well. We have to stop them before they reach open ground, or we may never catch them." Shu's voice was urgent, and everyone felt the tension that resonated from his tone.

Kumél and Ziminiar were quick to jump on the trail and sped away from the rest of the company. Huzesh was no slouch and had already started running as quickly as he could through the gorge, under the cover of the fog and the noise of the storm. Seerae ran behind him as quickly as she could, without moving faster than necessary, trying to hinder his escape.

Not far behind, Ross led the rest of the company with speed and agility that seemed impossible for any mortal. He was determined more than ever to rescue Seerae. He knew having her close would give him the strength and courage he needed to find and take the Kleid o'Miht. They raced down the boulder-laden, winding gorge as fast as possible.

At Ziminiar's cave, Gubrone and Morak sat in the fog, listening to the building storm. The distant thunder sounded angry as its sonic eruptions impacted the towering walls of stone that surrounded the small meadow. The dakoons watched with hungry bellies growling almost as loudly as their complaining snarls. Gubrone looked down at the heap of coals. A small column of smoke rose lazily into the air above them until it was assimilated into the fog. Morak suddenly stood to his feet and looked in all directions. "D'ye haer thut?" Gubrone paid no attention to his question. But the dakoons also stood to their feet and glanced around. "Gubrone, d'ye haer thut? Dar bae somting cumin!"

"Grr, dar bae notin! Laeve mae bae!"

Just at that moment, a hissing noise passed by Morak, but he was unable to see anything because of the fog. It was not a voice or a call, but the sound of air or wind or something passing through the air. Morak ducked. The piercing, familiar call, echoed through the meadow. Gubrone looked up at Morak with disdain. "Jus' bae u corvus."

Then, as if they were black-winged spirits, several more corvuses flew over them within the fog. They, too, could be heard, but not seen. Following high in the nebulous and not so far behind, the sound of a great many more birds closed in upon the confined meadow. It sounded to Morak like a massive flock of corvuses had landed somewhere above, on the rocky ledges and outcroppings of the many cliffs and stone walls. Morak knelt to the ground to hide, for he had before witnessed the havoc a flock of hungry corvuses could create. Fortunately, for Gubrone and Morak, the corvuses could not see very well in the fog, nor was their sense of smell very sensitive. Gubrone and Morak knew, however, that the birds' hearing was very keen. It seemed quite possible the black birds were unaware of their presence, and he knew it was important to keep it that way.

"Gubrone, wae mus nut lut thum sae us or da dakoons."

"Aye, t'da cave! Surely, dae wull nut stay lung."

"Wut o'da dakoons?"

"D'dakoons wull ha t'fend fur thumsaelfes, unless ye wish t'stay wit thum."

"Nut mae!"

Once inside the cave, they had to wait until the birds flew away. The squawking and chatter of the corvuses grew louder and more irritating to the two gallues. Outside the cave, the two dakoons waited quietly for an opportunity to feast on any of the birds that came close enough to be snatched from the air. They had not hunted for food in so long that their skills as predators were amateur and clumsy, though their instinct to kill was immediate. In the air, they could smell the birds and could hear the beating of their wings, as they flew overhead, though they could not see them. Their first reaction was to lunge at the air in a desperate attempt to snatch a lone, unsuspecting bird out of the fog. After several failed attempts, the dakoons figured out that it might be better to sit and wait for their quarry to come to them. They crouched down low to the ground, waiting and watching like lions preparing to ambush.

Gubrone sat lazily at the back of the dark cave. He was only mildly concerned about their circumstance, though he knew that large flocks of corvuses were known to be indiscriminate about what they ate, or who. Nevertheless, he could not have known how imminent a threat the birds were. These birds had come in search of him. Nevertheless, the threat of the corvuses, whatever it may have been in the mind of Gubrone, was short lived, becoming overshadowed by his growing agitation over the inconvenience of having to sit in the darkness and in silence. As the ruler of Shuk, subordinates who bowed to his every order and jumped to his every command usually surrounded him; *they* were the ones who hid and cowered, not him. He was immune to dangers, sheltered from threats and above the annoyance of wariness. Having to take refuge as if he was an ignoble serf, or an animal being preyed upon, did not bode well. His pride goaded him. "Curse des wretched birds! A wull nut hide lik u puggin un burrows un holes unner da ground."

Gubrone moved determinedly toward the opening of the cave. Morak, though caught off guard by the impetuousness of Gubrone's actions, quickly obstructed his escape by jumping upon him and forcing him away from the entrance. Gubrone was outraged and struck Morak with a heavy blow to the head, knocking him back. "Dare ye interfere wit mae! Ye fool!"

Morak had never laid a hand on Gubrone before and could not believe what he had just done. He lay on the floor of the cave stunned, with blood oozing out from the side of his head where Gubrone's fist struck him. Gubrone was quick to rise to his feet and stood over Morak, looking down upon him. He had murder in his eyes and a menacing growl was fighting its way through his clamped teeth. His fists were clenched, and Morak could see his muscles twitching as if at any moment Gubrone would unleash the full fury of his rage.

Morak had felt the power of Gubrone's fury before, and he knew how merciless Gubrone could be. There was, however, something much different this time. The power of Gubrone's blow was much greater than what he had felt before, as if Gubrone had grown stronger than ever before. The quickness of Gubrone's reaction was also different. Neither Gubrone nor Morak could have known it, but the rune had done something more; it had given to Gubrone the strength and speed of the dakoons.

Gubrone struggled to regain his senses, for he, too, recognized there was something different about himself. Normally he would have been intolerant, but this time he was furious. Still reeling with anger and impatience, he bent over, reached down, and clamped his right hand around Morak's neck. "Uf ye er touch mae agan, A wull destroy ye. D'ye haer mae?" Morak silently nodded.

The squawking of the corvuses was fading, and it seemed to the two of them that the threat was almost gone. However, just outside of the cave, two corvuses were perched and quiet, for they had heard the skirmish and Gubrone's loud voice and had come to see what they could find. Gubrone's arrogance and uncontrollable fury was proving to be a liability if not a danger to himself and anyone with him.

Gubrone stepped away from Morak and sat back down. It dawned on him that Morak had only tried to help. However, he was never going to admit to anyone, including to himself, that he ever needed help. Morak did not move. He waited and listened intently to the distant commotion of the corvuses. He knew Gubrone's loud voice might have been heard.

Huzesh used every advantage he could find to escape the pursuit of Kumél and Ziminiar. As the winds blew with strong gusts, he picked up the pace, not worrying how much noise he might be making. When the gusts died down, he slowed his pace and was more deliberate in his steps. Nonetheless, Seerae hung back and tried to be as noisy as possible without rousing the suspicions of Huzesh.

Farther up the gorge, Alethia sent Glo and Shim ahead and told them to stay with Huzesh and Seerae. "Do not let them out of your sight but be careful. Do not let Huzesh know of your presence. He is very dangerous."

The two tulwyths flew ahead, looking for Huzesh. It was not long before they came upon Seerae, who followed the cruel gallue. They flew down to her and let her see them. Glo flew in so close to Seerae that she could feel the movements of her wings. "Help me, please help me," Seerae whispered desperately.

Glo could see the fear in Seerae's eyes, she landed on her shoulder and whispered into her ear. "You are not alone; Alethia and Shu are following close behind. Be strong."

Huzesh turned to see how far Seerae had fallen behind. He was surprised to see that she was closer than he expected. He did not see Glo or Shim, for they hid themselves behind Seerae. "Move faster, wae ha no tam t'bae laggin b'hin!"

"I'm not lagging. It's all I can do to keep from running over you. You're moving too slow." Seerae's voice was defiant and surprisingly strong, which bewildered Huzesh. Of course, she spoke loud enough for her voice to be carried back to the others.

Huzesh turned and hurried, not wanting to be out-paced by a she-neph. He sharply yelled back at her, which was again carried back to the company. "Ye bes kaep yer tongue liddle one, or A wull bae takin ut frum ye!" Seerae was unfazed by his threats. Knowing her friends were so close gave her hope and courage. On the other hand, agitating Huzesh was a mistake, for he began to move faster than ever, widening the gap between him and the company.

The sound of the storm was growing in intensity overhead. In the distance, Huzesh and Seerae heard a different noise that was growing louder and closer. It was high in the thick clouds, beyond seeing. Huzesh searched the sky, then he knelt and turned his ear in the direction of the coming noise. Seerae had never heard a noise quite like it, and it frightened her. Above them, the gray clouds were turning black, eclipsed by an immense darkness. As the diffused light diminished and the blackness overwhelmed them, the noise escalated and became more distinguishable. Huzesh spoke to Seerae under his breath, "Corvuses—dae mus nut fin us! Quick—unner da rocks! Un dunna speak u word!" He crawled under a large stone that was resting on two smaller stones, leaving a cavity large enough for him to hide. Seerae quickly found a place between two boulders where she hid. The sound of the flock overhead was so close it was deafening; however, they were unable to see any of the birds. The corvuses swooped and dove, flying in all directions as if there was no order to or reason for their actions. Seerae wondered if their followers were safe.

In the meantime, Kumél and Ziminiar saw the darkness coming and heard the clamor of the flock. Kumél hurried back to Ross and Loham. "Quick, hide!" Ross and Loham swiftly found a gap in the rock wall next to them and they squeezed into it together. Ross had no idea what was happening or why he had to hide. Loham explained to him, "Corvuses. They're evil birds and a flock like this would devour us all."

"How do you know? I can't see a thing."

"There's nothing else that sounds like 'em. We have to wait until they leave. If one of them sees us, it will call to the others, who will come without hesitation."

The rest of the company hid among the rocks. The cloud of corvuses hovered over the fearful group for an agonizing length of time.

Kumél watched carefully through the fog, from a hiding place not far from Ross and Loham. He was looking for any signs the corvuses were landing or resting within view. He knew they often left a bird behind to spy. He saw, perched about where Ross and Loham were hiding, a single black bird and not far from it, a small cloud of breath floating in the air. It was Ross's breath, but fortunately the corvus did not see the breath. It turned its head several times and then flew down to the water's edge and dipped its beak into the stream. Then Ross saw the bird. He took a deep breath and held it. At the same time Loham told him, "Do not move a muscle, and close your eyes." Ross closed his eyes. Loham watched the bird, being careful not to make eye contact.

The corvus hopped from one rock to another and then opened its large wings and flew away. Kumél watched it fly away as well. The sound of the flock overhead began to fade. Kumél thoroughly scanned the area, looking for any signs of spies. He stepped out from his hiding place and knelt low to the ground. He surveyed in every direction, up and down, looking for the black birds. Ziminiar also checked and was careful not to move too quickly from his hiding place.

Ross saw Kumél kneeling and then Ziminiar. He whispered to Loham, "Look, Kumél is out, it must be OK."

"Ross! Wait, Ross!" Loham tried to grab Ross's arm, but too quickly, Ross stepped out from his hiding place. He took one step, turned his head and less than one step away from him, within an arm's reach, was a corvus. The corvus opened its beak and just before it screeched, Ross felt a breeze pass his face. He heard a faint whiz slice through the air, then he saw the head of the corvus plummet into the rocks at his feet. Blood flowed from where the corvus's head had been, the body slumped and then tumbled off the rock into the stream below. Ross's eyes followed the corvus as it floated down the stream and turned to see Loham wiping the blood off of his sword.

"Whew, that was close. You should've stayed put. I told you not to move. Hopefully, there are no others about," Loham said nervously chattered.

"But I, I thought Kumél, I mean, I saw Kumél . . ."

"You can't take chances with corvuses. If that bird had called out, the whole flock would've descended upon us. I've seen it. They have an appetite for the likes of us. We must be careful."

From high in the clouds, the faint sound of the flock could be heard in the gorge. The company of Shu gathered around Ross and Loham. They were all wary and unsure of their safety. Knowing there could be spies anywhere in the gorge made them nervous. Shu looked at Ross, patted his shoulder, and smiled. "Are you good?" He then looked at Loham. "Quick wits, well done."

Alethia stepped into the center of the company. "We must not waste time. Ziminiar, how far is it to your cave and the meadow?"

"Ut bae nut far ut all."

"We must hurry then. With these clouds and the storm, it will be impossible to find him if he reaches the meadow."

"Wae ha t'wery bout da corvuses un deir spies u lung da wae."

"Jaroh's right, we have to be extra careful. They could be anywhere."

"What if they come back?" Msusi asked.

"Everyone must be ready; make sure you have your weapons in your hands."

As they were organizing themselves, the storm began to squall, unleashing more snow and ice into the gorge.

Huzesh saw the squall as an opportunity to break away from the company. He moved quickly into the blizzard and away from them, sneaking father down the gorge. He was still unaware the tulwyths were close behind him, keeping track of his every move, though the storm made it difficult for them to fly.

Glo flew close to Shim. "You must fly back to the others and tell them that he is fleeing. Be careful. There might be more of the black birds waiting and watching."

"But if I go back, I may not be able to return; the wind is extremely strong."

"The others must learn that he is escaping. If they don't come quickly, he will reach the meadow."

Shim wasted no time. He flew faster than ever, for the wind was at his back and helped to propel him up the gorge.

Kumél and Ziminiar moved speedily into the wind. Having the cover of the blowing snow and gusting winds made them feel confident that neither Huzesh nor the corvuses could hear them coming. The whole company of Shu pushed the pace and avoided getting too spread out, which would slow them down. Because of his nimbleness, Jaroh eventually moved into the lead, forcing the others to push themselves around and over the rocky terrain.

Nevertheless, Huzesh was able to move even faster, for he was nearing the mouth of the gorge where the terrain was becoming flatter and less obstructed. In between the noisy gusts of wind, Huzesh could hear the confluence where the two streams crashed together. He knew the meadow was very close, though because of the fog and the blowing snow, it was impossible to see.

The squalling storm mysteriously became silent, though the snow continued to fall heavily. Huzesh was uneasy and cautious as he took his next step. Thick, heavy clouds filled the air so much the falling snow would not have been noticed except that it was accumulating on every part of them. Huzesh could not be sure where he was or what might be waiting for him beyond what he could see. He could smell something unfamiliar in the air. He looked into the white ambience with a lowered brow, trying to see anything at all that would explain the odor. At his feet, he heard the stream rushing by. He looked down to see the headless black corvus floating by. He could see its blood in the water. Huzesh watched as the dead bird floated away and disappeared into the fog just yards away from where he stood. For the first time since fleeing the upper meadow, Huzesh was more concerned about the unknown threat that lay before him than the known one coming from behind.

Seerae was as far behind Huzesh as the braided cord would allow her to be, and she, too, was on edge. She could sense something peculiar. She looked behind her, hoping to see any sign of the company, but she only spotted Glo.

Seerae looked at Huzesh who was kneeling with his back to her. Since he was not paying any attention, she motioned to Glo to come close. Glo peeked from behind the snow-covered rock and, seeing that Huzesh was preoccupied, flew to Seerae. She whispered so delicately that her words seemed to float into Glo's ears like the snowflakes floated to the ground, "Go. Tell the others where we are. Tell them to be careful, something isn't right. There is danger ahead, hurry."

Glo checked that Huzesh was not watching, she turned and rapidly flew into the fog toward the company of Shu. It was a very short flight, however, for the company was so close their voices could have been picked up by Huzesh's keen sense of hearing. Glo flew past Kumél and Ziminiar. She could see the faint glow of the other tulwyths, who were hovering close to Alethia. She flew straight to Alethia and landed on her shoulder. The two spoke in quiet, almost undetectable voices.

"Seerae is just ahead, only a few steps beyond in the fog. She said to be careful; there's danger ahead. The gallue is just beyond her, waiting and standing guard."

"What is he waiting for?"

"I don't know. It seems that he's afraid of something. The fog is thick, and there is an odd calmness ahead."

"Is it possible for Seerae to sneak back to us in the fog, to escape him?"

"She's tied to him."

"Hmm … We can't wait much longer to free her; he will flee into the mountains."

Alethia thought for a moment while Shu and the others waited. "Take Shim and fly up and over Huzesh so that he does not see you. Fly into the valley and see if you might find this unknown danger. If you do, come straight back, and tell me what you have found. Quick, go."

Alethia turned to Shu. "We could stand for a little wind. This stillness hinders any chance we have."

"But the wind will not be restful for long."

"But we need it now."

Glo and Shim flew high into the fog and over Huzesh. They flew out of the mouth of the gorge and through the meadow. At first, all they could see was snow, which had blanketed everything, making any distinction between the ground and the sky impossible. On their second pass, however, they noticed two large beasts, mostly covered in snow. As Glo flew past, he saw its black and lifeless eyes. Then he saw a cloud of mist rise from its nostrils. The beast yawned and revealed its ghastly yellow teeth beneath its black lips.

Glo noticed Shim hovering in the fog as though he was paralyzed. She flew back to him.

"Shim, what are you doing?" Shim did not answer. He only stared down at the snow-covered ground.

"Shim, what is it?"

"Watch, there on the ground. It's an awful thing, a horrid creature." Glo looked in the direction Shim pointed. Eventually, she was able to make out the form of the dakoon, and then she saw the second one.

"What is it?"

"I don't know, but it sure smells putrid!"

"Maybe it's the danger that Seerae spoke of."

"It most certainly must be, but where'd it come from?"

"We have to tell the others. Come on!"

Glo and Shim were still unable to see exactly what the dakoons looked like or just how awful a beast they were; however, they knew they had to tell the others what they had seen. They flew away, back to the company. As they were hurrying back, they were in such a panic they forgot about Huzesh and nearly collided with him. Huzesh looked at the two tulwyths who floated motionless in mid-air in shock. He, too, was surprised, for he had never seen the tiny creatures before. The sight of the tulwyths broke his concentration, and he reached out to touch them. Glo promptly backed away, as did Shim. They flew into the clouds above his head and continued their speedy retreat to Alethia.

Huzesh stood up, trying to capture them, but they were already out of sight. Without intending to, Huzesh let out a frustrated roar, which alerted Kumél and Ziminiar, along with Alethia and the others. Glo and Shim suddenly came into view, breaking out of the fog and landing near Alethia.

At the same time, the two corvuses that had been perched near the cave of Ziminiar, turned to see where the sound came from. The dakoons also stood erect, and the long iron chain that hung between them jangled on the rocks with a loud "cha-ching." At that, Gubrone, eager to escape the dark confines of the cave, jumped up and crawled out of the cave to see what was causing the sudden invasion of noises.

In the midst of the commotion, Glo and Shim told Alethia and Shu about the two creatures they saw. "It was a monstrous beast with sharp teeth and evil eyes."

"I saw it first. It was covered with snow and was very still—until Glo flew by."

"It was huge, like the gallues, only it wasn't one."

Alethia tried to calm them down and at the same time, listen to what they were describing. "Have you seen one of these creatures before?"

"No."

"No, never!" The tulwyths buzzed around in a circle, with nervous excitement.

"But you didn't see it fully? It was hiding? Under the snow?"

"No, we couldn't!"

"Right! They were covered in snow."

Meanwhile, the two dakoons shook off the snow and raced to find whoever had made the noise. Their teeth bared and their eyes fixed on the one-armed gallue, they were ready to pounce upon him and devour him where he stood. Huzesh raised his sword and took an offensive stance. As the dakoon, Tormut, closed in, Huzesh swung with skill and confidence, cutting across the creature's face with the jagged edge of his sword and leaving behind a gaping, bloody wound. Huzesh hopped a few steps back and readied himself for another strike. Tormut let out a loud screeching growl that concussed the air, echoing through the meadow and up the gorge. It was a sound of such terror and amplitude it sent chills down Seerae's spine. She covered her ears and tried to hide herself behind some rocks. The vision of the dakoons was so horrible she began to cry with fear.

With his momentum still driving him toward Huzesh, Tormut immediately tried to stop, but he could not get his footing and slid in the snow to within less than an arm's length of Huzesh. Huzesh hardly seemed fazed and lifted his battle-ready arm. His hand gripped his sword tightly. He was ready to strike Tormut with a savage blow between the eyes.

"Stop!" Gubrone's deep, raspy voice hit the drums of Huzesh's ears like a mallet striking an anvil.

Tormut turned toward Gubrone, but Huzesh saw the distraction as an opportunity to take the dakoon's head. He started to lower the blade. "Stop, ye dakkrah! Uf ye kull dis dakoon A wull feed ye t'mae other one."

The call of the two corvus spies rang through the fog, followed by the heavy flapping of their large wings. Their alarm could not be ignored, for it was sure to be followed by the black cloud of torment and death.

Huzesh turned his eyes toward Gubrone, but he would not lower his sword. The fog was thick enough he could not tell who it was that threatened him, though he was quite sure he recognized the voice. The two of them yelled back and forth at each other.

"Who bae ye t'command mae? Yer stinking beast attacked mae firs."

"Bae thut ye, Huzesh?"

"Aye, un ye, who bae ye?"

"Gubrone."

"Gubrone, aye. Whaer bae yer compny? Bae ye alone wit yer liddle pets?"

"Nae, Morak bae wit mae."

Huzesh lowered his sword, though he kept a close eye on the dakoon. Gubrone approached through the fog with Morak following close behind him.

Not far away, just up the gorge, and still keeping a low profile, the company of Shu listened to the shouts coming from the meadow. There was, however, one sound that peaked their attention more than any other: the screech of the dakoon. Glo and Shim had tried to describe what they had seen in the snow, but their description had not prepared Shu and Alethia for what was before them. Shu intensely whispered to Alethia, "Dakoons."

Alethia glanced worriedly at Shu, and then at Jaroh. Ross and the nephesh had no idea what a dakoon was or what it meant that they were in Shuk. "How is it possible?" Alethia asked. "They were all destroyed in the war. Where did Gubrone find dakoons?"

Seerae used all the commotion to her advantage. She crept away from Huzesh and hid behind another boulder. She began to rub the braided cord against the edge of a sharp rock in an attempt to cut herself free. What she did not know was just how close the company was. If it had not been for the fog and the many boulders between them, she could have seen them and heard their whispers.

Gubrone approached Huzesh, unsuspecting of the trouble that was following. "Ye cun put da sword down, dae wull laeve ye fur now."

Huzesh lowered his sword, and the dakoon slowly backed away, though he remained very alert and poised to resume the fight if necessary.

"Whaer ha ye com frum, Huzesh?"

Huzesh looked behind him into the mouth of the gorge, then he looked back at Gubrone. "A ha baen followed. Dar bae u compny close on mae heels."

"A compny, who bae un dis compny?"

"Da forner un Shu."

Gubrone's eyes lit up with devious excitement. "Ye brung mae da forner un Shu! Bahaha! A underestimated ye, Huzesh. How far buk bae dae?"

"Close. A bae sure."

"Hey, Shu, A know ye cun haer mae. Dis bae u gud day! Com out or bae ye afaered!"

Shu was not about to reply and give away their exact location. For the moment, he was less concerned about Gubrone or Huzesh than about the dakoons.

"A ha som frens ye shud maet: Tormut un Sufrar!"

Gubrone looked at the dakoons, who could sense the tension that filled the air. They scratched at the ground and growled with excitement. "Gae! Gae un fin mae Shu un da forner! Fly, mae black devils!"

Before Shu or Alethia had time to coordinate a plan, Jaroh rose into the air and, with the speed of lightning, charged out of the gorge. He had his spear in one hand and his sword in the other. As he exploded out of the fog and into the view of Gubrone and the dakoons, he knocked Huzesh aside. Without the slightest hesitation, Jaroh rushed at the dakoons head on, colliding with Sufrar, just as he was lifting off from the ground. Sufrar went flying through the air with Tormut following behind, dragged by the chain that bound them together. The dakoons spread their wings and flew into the fog. Jaroh returned to where the dakoons had been standing. He stood in plain sight and faced Gubrone.

"Jaroh, Ut ha baen u lung tam. Ye know, kerolus bae banned frum Shuk. A dunna believe ut wun A waer tol one waer saen."

"A tink da same applies t'dakoons, Gubrone."

"Well, mubae, but wut ye gonna d'bout ut, aye?"

"Ha ye forgutten wut dud happen afore. Dakoons ha no chance agan da spaer o'da kerolus."

"Mubae, but des dakoons bae special! Ye ha picked u gud day t'die. Bahaha!"

The two dakoons dove out of the clouds with their black wings spread wide. Jaroh could hear them coming. He flew straight up, disappearing from sight before the dakoons could reach him.

The short confrontation between Gubrone and Jaroh gave Alethia and Shu just enough time and information to coordinate a straightforward plan. "Glo, you and your friends must help us."

"We will. What can we do?"

"The fog is heavy, and it'll be difficult for us to keep track of each other if we aren't careful. One of us could be taken without the others knowing, or worse. You must keep watch. Stay with us and if anyone needs help, you must let the others know. You may also need to guide us through the fog."

Glo and the other tulwyths agreed.

"Kumél, you, and Ziminiar will be first out of the gorge. Rush Huzesh. Yell out his name and we will know that it is time for us to attack. And keep him distracted long enough for us to get by him."

"We should try to rescue Seerae as we go. We will surely come upon her on the way out."

"Good idea, Ross. You and Loham will bring up the rear. While we engage Gubrone and Morak, you try to free Seerae. If need be, take her back into the gorge."

"What then?"

"We hope, we fight, and we don't give up. There is much at stake here; we have to endeavor, and we have to prevail."

Ross appeared confused. He looked at Alethia and then at Shu. "That's it, that's your plan?"

"There's no time, Ross! We have to act now. Kumél, Ziminiar, go. Now!"

Kumél and Ziminiar ran into the fog toward Huzesh. The rest of the company waited to hear the signal. What they would do after that would have to rely solely on instinct and creativity.

As Kumél and Ziminiar disappeared into the fog, the wind began to blow. Flakes of snow that had been lazily tumbling down to the ground began to swirl through the air. Another, even louder crack of thunder surged through the meadow and up into the gorge. Shu and the others tensely waited with nervous anticipation.

"Huzesh!" The sound of Ziminiar's voice was unmistakable, and Shu was quick to react to the signal. He jumped up and ran, with abandon, into the fog and driving snow. The others followed right behind him. Of the company, Ross was the most unsure and afraid. He was not a warrior or a fighter, and he knew he would have to fend for himself against brutal beasts that meant to do him great harm. Nevertheless, he rushed, headlong, into the fray, focused on one singular objective: to free Seerae. Loham followed close behind with his sword drawn.

Chapter XXI
The Spear of Amik

Out of the blustery storm clouds, the frightful dakoons appeared with their iron wings spread wide. They cried out with a loud shrieking bawl, high and terrifying. Kumél and Ziminiar darted from the safety of the fog into the sight of Huzesh. Kumél was first to see the dakoons as they swept in upon them and narrowly missed Huzesh who stood with his back in their direction. Kumél ducked as they flew past.

"Jaroh! Da dakoons!" Kumél's voice echoed through the meadow like thunder.

Glo and the tulwyths split up and tried to follow each of the company, though they were outnumbered. Initially, it was not too difficult a task, for the company was relatively close together and moved as one.

Glo and Shim felt the powerful turbulence of air caused by each thrust of the dakoons' wings and two of the tulwyths were pushed to the ground as the dakoons flew by. Glo flew to Alethia to warn her the dakoons were very near the mouth of the gorge. "Dakoons! They're helping Huzesh."

"Jaroh!" Alethia called out, "Find Jaroh. He must force them back."

Jaroh was already nearing Kumél. He sped after the dakoons who, again, disappeared up into the fog and the throes of the storm.

Huzesh stepped back against a wall of rock with his sword drawn.

Kumél and Ziminiar had him cornered, though he seemed unfazed by the apparent indefensible circumstance.

"Bahaha! Haer wae bae agan, d'two o'ye un mae. A fael pretty gud bout mae chances, Kumél."

Huzesh swung his heavy sword at Kumél who met it with his sword. The sound of the clashing weapons rang out like an alarm.

At first, Kumél and Ziminiar only defended themselves against Huzesh's brutish attack, for they were only trying to distract him while the others made their way out of the gorge. Huzesh stepped forward, pushing the two apostas backward for only a moment, and then Ziminiar moved toward Huzesh's weak side, forcing him back against the stone wall.

Shu and Alethia lead the company through the rocks, then speedily past the conflict, and into the meadow to face Gubrone and Morak as they stood together near the cave. They were enveloped by the fog and unable to see what was happening with Huzesh. As soon as Alethia saw Morak's silhouette, she stopped and knelt down. She wanted to keep their approach unnoticed for as long as possible while everyone took position. She instructed Shu, "Take Zoësh and try to flank them. Stay low and out of their sight for as long as possible. Wait until you hear me call out."

Shu and Zoësh ran to the right side of Alethia, trying to stay hidden among the rocks and trees, also aided by the fog. Alethia and Msusi pulled their swords from their sheaths and approached Morak. As they drew closer to him, the figure of another gallue came into view. Alethia stopped and, like a tiger poised to attack, she lowered her brow, fixing her fearless eyes intently upon the threat before them. Though the fog disguised his image, Alethia knew from his size and stance that it was Gubrone. She knew he and Morak were a lethal combination and that she and Msusi were not capable of overpowering them alone. She waited, counting on Shu and Zoësh to come in from behind. She believed the element of surprise was their only advantage. Msusi put her hand on Alethia's shoulder, as if to offer a silent affirmation. Alethia turned to her and whispered, "I sure would like to have Jaroh here right now." Msusi smiled with a nervous but sincere expression for she too desired the same thing. Since he was off dealing with the two dakoons, Jaroh would be of little help to them.

Assuming Shu and Zoësh would be in place, Alethia called out through the fog. Her commanding voice boomed like thunder. "Gubrone!" Alethia's voice cut through the ambient noise, sharp and formidable. She and Msusi walked directly at the two gallues. Gubrone said nothing. He only watched them approach. He had long ago forgotten the sound of Alethia's voice. Gubrone could only make out the shape of two, much smaller figures than himself, which he assumed to be only a pair of nephesh. He had no idea Alethia was one of the pair. At that moment, to deal with such an inconsequential threat seemed like a task far beneath him. His pride rose inside of him and made him indignant with arrogance. "Dare ye threaten mae! A wull nut bae challenged bae da liks o'des nephs!" He motioned to Morak. "Kull thum! Un show no mercy!"

Morak stepped forward and raised his sword. He, too, was convinced that little effort was needed to dispatch the approaching menace. As Morak and the two nephs came into view, he stopped and then retreated slightly. He turned to look at Gubrone who was standing only a few steps behind him.

Gubrone watched Morak and scrutinized the approaching threat. He sniffed the air and then moved forward, trying to make out who was coming toward him.

Alethia and Msusi waited in the fog while the two gallues tried to identify them. Alethia wanted to draw them toward her.

Shu and Zoësh heard Alethia yell out Gubrone's name. They also heard Gubrone command Morak to kill them. Shu knew Gubrone's pride would not let him turn away from Alethia and Msusi. He and Zoësh skirted the edges of Ziminiar's cave, staying in the fog so they were not seen. The wind and snow were blowing harder than they had been and the thunder was more intense, which aided them in moving inconspicuously.

Gubrone took another few steps towards Alethia and he identified who it was that spoke to him with such authority. He pulled his sword, realizing the two small figures were much more of a threat than he had thought. Gubrone growled with displeasure.

As planned, Ross and Loham followed slowly behind to look for Seerae. Surprisingly, no one had seen her as they all moved toward the meadow. Ross wanted to call out to her but feared Huzesh would hear and they would lose their chance to free her from her restraint. Loham circled around to the left of Ross and searched for her. He moved carefully among the many large boulders and stones, hoping to keep himself hidden from view. As Loham edged around a tall slab, he peeked into every crack and hole that might be a hiding place for Seerae.

Ross crept around a snow-capped boulder that was leaning against taller stone, and under the two stones was a shallow void that was out of the weather and dryer than one might hope to find in such an inclement milieu.

"Seerae!" Ross's whisper escaped his lips before his mind could process what he was saying.

Under the stones lay Seerae, bound by a cord that was stretched out toward Huzesh. Seerae turned around and saw Ross ducking under the rocks. "Ross!" she whispered back, looking up at him with excited eyes.

Ross could see there were bruises on her face and around her wrists. She was covered in mud and was shivering. "Shh. Come on, we have to get out of here," Ross urged.

"But this cord—you have to cut it! I tried to use a stone, but it's too strong. Quick, Ross, cut the cord!" Seerae had managed to wrap the cord around a huge stone so Huzesh could not pull her out of hiding. She had left just enough length for him to sever.

Ross fumbled around, feeling in his pockets and his belt, but he was only armed with the spear; he had no sword or knife or blade of any kind. "I can't." He fetched a small rock and began to beat the section of cord that was wrapped around the rock, trying to break it, but it was proving to be too tough. "Wait here. I'll be right back!" Immediately, Ross felt foolish for telling her to stay where she was. He knew Seerae could not go anywhere. She watched him disappear into the fog.

Huzesh's advantage of striking first was short-lived. In his mind, he knew he needed to gain an edge over his two enemies. He swung his sword harder and faster than before, attempting to drive them back. Kumél and Ziminiar retreated, away from the jagged edge of his sword. As long as he used his sword, he had no way of pulling on the cord that bound Seerae. He needed to push them back just far enough to reach down and pull the cord. He fought furiously until they had backed far enough away for him to lower his sword and free his hand. He saw it was time to use his hostage to his advantage and force Kumél and Ziminiar to back down. He knew Kumél would not hurt the she-neph. Huzesh grabbed hold of the cord and pulled on it, expecting to drag her from her hiding place, but she did not come. Huzesh pulled harder, but still Seerae did not come.

"Loham," Ross whispered, as he darted from rock to rock, trying to stay out of sight and locate Loham, who had a sword. "Loham, where are you?" As he came around an outcropping of stones, he heard a voice.

"Shh, you'll give us away."

"I've found her. Come on, hurry."

Seerae could see the cord was being pulled and feared that Huzesh would soon find her and kill her. She silently waited, but wanted, with all her might, to scream out to Ross. She wondered where he was and why he had not returned. She began frantically striking the cord with the rock Ross had been using, but it was to no avail. "Please! Please, Ross! Hurry!" she cried out in desperation.

As Ross hastily led Loham to where Seerae was hiding, he could hear her calling out. When they came upon her, Ross saw the cord was being pulled. "Loham, cut the cord, quick." Loham immediately raised his sword and cut the cord that was binding her. Seerae exploded from her hole, free from her captor. She turned to run into the gorge, but Loham stopped her. He sliced the cords that were still binding her wrists. Together, the three of them ran, unseen, past Kumél and Ziminiar and into the fog.

Once they were free of the gorge and of Huzesh, Ross called out to Kumél, "We have Seerae, she's free!

Kumél and Ziminiar had given Huzesh just enough space and time to allow Ross and Loham to rescue Seerae. Once they were sure she was safe, they intensified their attack on Huzesh.

Having found a safe place, Ross stopped and looked at Seerae. He brushed her hair away from her eyes and put his hand on her cheek. "Are you alright?"

She smiled at him with bright eyes, then reached up and took hold of his hand. "I'm better now. Thank you." She then looked at Loham. "Thank you, Loham. Thank you."

Loham glanced at her and then anxiously reminded Ross, "Come on, the others need our help."

"But I have no weapon." Seerae's voice was penitent, and she looked down with shame.

"What's the matter?"

"It's my fault. I got you all into this, and now—now I can't do anything to help. You should've left me."

"We don't have time for this. Leave your contrition here with the cords that bound you." Loham's voice was soft, yet strong. He reached out his hand to her. Seerae looked at him and then at Ross. She could feel they were sincerely glad to see her. She took Loham's hand and quickly stood to her feet.

"Follow me." Ross's words rang with urgency.

Seerae and Loham followed behind him as he ran for the meadow.

As Kumél and Ziminiar closed in on him, Huzesh swung his sword with the fierceness of a cornered animal, keeping them at bay. At the same time, he gave one final pull on the cord, which refused to obey. Huzesh realized he was now the prisoner of his own device. The cord he used to bind Seerae was now binding him. He looked in the direction of the cord, but the fog would not let him see where it led. He quickly took his sword and cut himself free. He swung and leapt and spun about wildly, trying to fight off Kumél and Ziminiar. Finally, he saw an opening in the rocks and dove toward it. Kumél and Ziminiar were surprised and started to chase after him, but the fog had given Huzesh cover.

Gubrone yelled at Alethia with disdain, "Ye dare t'com t'mae lund un command mae! Da Theoscians bae banned frum Shuk. Ye ha broken da covnant, Alethia!"

"It's time, Gubrone, for your cruelty to end. You know what I speak of. You hide behind the covenant that you have broken repeatedly, you and Attar. Well the day has come. This is that day, and you—you will not see the end of it."

"Ye act as uf ye ha un army o'kerolus, but ye dunna, yur un mae realm. Whaer bae Eloh? Dud ee braek da covnant tae or ha ee jus sunt ye, all alone?"

"I'm not as alone as you might think, Gubrone."

In the distance, a menacing sound rolled through the meadow. "Nare bae A! D'ye haer da corvuses? Dae wull bae haer fur ye, afore da sun sets. Dae wull feast on yer flesh un da flesh o'each one thut haelps ye! Un wun Eloh coms ut wull bae mae plaesure t'kull eem!"

At that moment, a shout was heard from behind Gubrone. Surprised, Gubrone and Morak spun around to see what was happening. Shu and Zoësh had managed to sneak around the two gallues and mount an attack from behind. Seeing their distraction, Alethia and Msusi rushed to the top of the mound as well. Gubrone swung his sword around, preventing Shu's advance. Shu slid under the sword, which barely missed his head. He was able to cut into the knee of Gubrone. Gubrone lowered his sword like an axe, striking at Shu. Zoësh dashed up just as the sword smote the ground and cut into his arm with a skillful swipe of her blade.

"You!" Gubrone immediately recognized her as the she-neph who was responsible for killing the mēglydaims. She was known by the gallues for her fierceness and skill with her blade.

"Are you happy to meet me, Gubrone?" Zoësh yelled back as she prepared to strike again.

Gubrone spun with his sword extended, intending to cut her into two pieces. Zoësh raised her sword like a shield. Unable to avoid the impending blow, she held it in both hands, one on the hilt and the other on the end of the blade in front of her chest. Gubrone's jagged blade struck Zoësh's sword, driving it into her chest and sending her flying through the air until she landed on a small pile of rocks.

Gubrone moved quickly to overtake Zoësh, but she was able to get back to her feet and defend herself from his murderous attack. Again, Gubrone struck Zoësh's sword, and she stumbled to the ground, dropping her sword between some rocks. In that instant, Shu rushed in with a counter-attack, swinging his sword about and distracting Gubrone.

Gubrone and Shu fought, sword to sword, but Gubrone's size and strength were far too great for Shu and Zoësh to overcome. Shu realized Gubrone was much more powerful than any of the company could have known. He yelled for Kumél.

Glo was nearby and could see the fight was not going well for either Shu or Alethia. She flew hastily to find Kumél. Now, Kumél had heard the calls of Shu and was already on his way when Glo appeared to him and reported what was happening. Together, they rushed to the fight.

Zoësh pulled herself up from the rocks, grabbed her sword, and quickly began to help Shu. The two of them, Shu and Zoësh, working together, were able to manage Gubrone's fury. Shu wondered, however, just how much longer they would be able to stand their ground. He summoned help again, "Kumél, Kumél!"

Gubrone laughed at Shu as he continued to swing his sword and fight. Nothing fazed him. He was not tired or cold or hurting. He seemed unstoppable. However, just over the hill, Kumél was coming to answer the calls of Shu.

Glo struggled against the wind and rain to lead Kumél to Shu and Zoësh. Kumél followed close behind her, ready to engage Gubrone again, just as he had long ago. It was not far for them to go, but the storm made every step a struggle. As they crested a mound of rocks, Kumél saw the perilous predicament of Shu and Zoësh. He told Glo, "Gae, tell Ziminiar thut A bae haelpin Shu. Ye naed t'haelp eem fin Huzesh." And then he rushed into the battle.

Glo flew away into the fog to find Ziminiar while Kumél raised his sword, ready to attack Gubrone. Out of the corner of his eye, Gubrone saw Kumél coming through the fog. He knew he could not defend against the three of them: Kumél, Shu, and Zoësh. Gubrone yelled into the wind, "Tormut! Sufrar!"

Now Alethia and Msusi struggled with Morak, who was very skilled and proved to be a great threat to them. Morak was quite surprised, however, at how strong and skillful his two nemeses were. Alethia had abilities that went beyond the sword. As Theoscians, She and Shu could use the elements to their advantage. As she fought with her sword and dagger, Alethia called for the wind in a tongue spoken only by the Theoscians.

The wind, snow, and fog all began to swirl together, impeding their every movement. Vision became hindered and voices failed. Only the loudest calls could be heard above the tumult. Glo and the other tulwyths were nearly blown out of the sky and had to retreat to the rocks.

Msusi and Alethia circled Morak, each striking and then moving away from his treacherous sword. Morak tried to devote all his attention to one or the other of the pair, hoping to take one of them out so he would be free to attack the other, but the two friends were too quick and at any point where one was disadvantaged, the other would come around and force Morak to redirect his attention. The strategy was working for Alethia and Msusi; it kept Morak turning from one direction to the other, in a circle, unable to truly engage in the fight.

Not far away from them, Gubrone continued to yell into the storm. The sound of his voice cut through the wind and caught their attention. "Tormut, Sufrar, com t'yer master!" Over and over again, Gubrone called out to the dakoons as he fought Shu and Zoësh. Kumél was quickly closing in on him and his cries became more and more determined.

In the meantime, a new threat was descending upon the meadow. The corvuses, whose calls had been heard, were arriving upon the scene. Overhead, the blackness of the storm was further darkened by the cloud of innumerable birds filling the air. Squawking and chattering, the sound of their approach overpowered the wind and thunder. The flock of birds tried and tried to descend into the meadow, but the storm Alethia had called upon arrived just as they did, forcing them to take shelter in the rocks and cliff walls and killing many of them. The strongest birds, however, were able to make it into the meadow where they began to harass any of the combatants they happened to come upon. They pecked and clawed at them, digging at their faces and especially at their eyes.

As all this was unfolding near the cave, downstream of the gorge, Ziminiar pursued Huzesh through the fog and the wind. Each step he took was risky, for it was becoming more and more impossible to see any farther in front of himself than the length of his arm. As Ziminiar stepped past a tall tree, he saw just out of the corner of his eye, a flash of movement and heard what sounded like something slicing through the air.

Huzesh's sword cut across his shoulder. Of course, Huzesh was swinging for his neck, but missed. Ziminiar backed away and turned toward his attacker. Huzesh quickly retreated into the fog where he could not be seen. Ziminiar goaded him with loud, taunting words.

"Bae ye u coward, Huzesh? Hidin un da shadows!"

Huzesh, who was never one to back down from a challenge, stepped into view. Ziminiar swung his sword twice, and Huzesh retaliated by swinging back.

Suddenly, several corvuses swooped down to attack the two warriors. Huzesh and Ziminiar were too engaged and focused on fighting each other to notice the harrassing corvuses. They hardly missed a move as a result of the bothersome birds, even while brushing one away or cutting another in two mid-air. Their swords seemed to yell out as if they, themselves, were angry and bent on destruction. Ziminiar reached down, pulled his long dagger from his bootlaces, and began to swing and thrust as if he were two apostas. Huzesh backed away and then fell over a log. Kicking and crawling, Huzesh frantically tried to escape the advancing onslaught of Ziminiar, who chopped at the log and the ground trying to dismember Huzesh. In his haste to escape, Huzesh dropped his sword. He desperately felt along the ground for something, anything, to use as a weapon to stop Ziminiar. He grabbed a large boulder and launched it at Ziminiar. The boulder struck Ziminiar in the forehead, knocking him backward and nearly unconscious. Huzesh seized the opportunity to grab his sword before disappearing into the fog again. Ziminiar felt blood running down his face from the gash. Through the blood, he could see Huzesh running away. As Ziminiar wiped the blood from over his eye, a large corvus landed on his head and began to claw and peck at the wound over his eye. Ziminiar reached up and grabbed the bird. He bit off its head, chewed it up, and swallowed it. All the while, other corvuses were diving and pecking at him. Shortly, after his light snack, Ziminiar looked in the direction Huzesh had run and then chased after him. A small flock of the unrelenting birds hovered over his head, attacking him as they followed his path.

Near the cave, just as Kumél was about to attack Gubrone, the corvuses began attacking him. More and more of the corvuses descended upon the meadow, causing mayhem and injury. Everyone found themselves fighting off the corvuses as much, if not more than they were fighting each other. As Gubrone contended with the birds and fought Shu and Zoësh, the dakoons suddenly swooped down in response to their master's calls. Clawing and biting, they flapped their wings and used them as weapons, knocking corvuses to the ground while devouring them with their teeth.

Gubrone laughed with a boisterous swagger as he watched the dakoons repeatedly dive upon Shu and Zoësh, forcing them to retreat into hiding. "Crush deir bones! Quench yer thirst wit deir blood!"

Sufrar and Tormut descended upon the mound of rocks where Shu and Zoësh were hiding. They clawed and dug, trying to extract them from their hiding place.

"Gubrone!" Kumél roared out of the fog as he rushed past the menacing corvuses, ascended the mound, and tackled Gubrone. The two mighty gallues tangled and fought hand to hand, each trying to wound and kill the other. Shu had heard Kumél's voice and could see he was fighting Gubrone. The dakoons continued their assault of the rocks that were the only protection for Shu and Zoësh. Shu knew Jaroh should be near, for it was he who was most capable of battling the dakoons. He yelled as loud as he could, hoping Jaroh would come swiftly, "Jaroh, help!"

The dakoons viciously dug at the rocks. They were so focused on Shu and Zoësh they did not notice Jaroh, who swooped down through the cloud of black birds, upon the shoulders of Tormut. He raised his great spear, intending to thrust it into the back of the dakoon, but Sufrar reached around and sunk his teeth into Jaroh's calf. Jaroh winced with pain, then he smote the dakoon over the head with the shaft of his spear. Sufrar let loose his bite and raised his head, and Jaroh stabbed the creature through the neck. With its black wings, Sufrar struck Jaroh in the back, knocking him to the ground. The wound Sufrar bore was not a mortal one, for the spear had missed its mark and only pierced the fleshy tissue.

Jaroh leapt from the ground and into the air, and the dakoons immediately pursued him, for the scent of kerolus blood was in the air and its taste was on Sufrar's tongue. Jaroh spun around in the air and charged the two dakoons who were chasing after him. He threw his spear, which passed right through one of Sufrar's shoulders and through his wing. Sufrar fell from the sky, dragging Tormut behind him because their chains bound them to one another. Tormut tried to fly, but the weight of Sufrar and the power of the wind forced him down. Jaroh dove down to the ground and retrieved his spear.

Once the dakoons had taken chase after Jaroh, Shu and Zoësh escaped the rocks and ran up to the mound to help Kumél. Kumél and Gubrone were in a desperate struggle, but Kumél was besting Gubrone. He drove Gubrone back with each blow of his sword. Even though none of his strikes wounded Gubrone, they beat upon Gubrone's sword with the force of many swords. Kumél saw Shu coming toward them and he yelled, "Go, haelp Alethia un Msusi, Morak wull bae tae strong fur thum."

Shu and Zoësh turned and ran through the fog and wind to the other side of the mound to help Alethia and Msusi, but the corvuses attacked them along the way, diving and clawing at them with their talons. They swatted at the air with their swords, trying to kill the birds, but the corvuses were too many and too quick. Nevertheless, they struggled onward, calling out to Alethia, and fighting back the incessant birds.

At the top of the mound, Kumél and Gubrone fought tirelessly against each other and against the ravenous corvuses. For long periods, the two would fight, not realizing the corvuses were there at all. Then, at other times, they were forced to turn their attention to the birds and fight them back.

For reasons that were beyond explanation, the corvuses turned their attention to Gubrone, gathering over him and diving down to peck at him and dig at his flesh with their talons. Kumél took advantage of the circumstance, brandishing his sword and throwing rocks at Gubrone to force him backward. Kumél and the birds devastated Gubrone so much that he stumbled and fell to his knees. Kumél fought off the birds that were harassing him and rushed forward, ready to finish Gubrone. Just as he raised his sword and was about to drive it into Gubrone, the dakoons fell out of the fog and landed between them in a heap. Kumél fell backward. The dakoons turned to Kumél, screeching while they advanced toward him.

Kumél held his ground and swung his sword at the dakoons trying to cut them. The pesky corvuses descended upon the mound and took particular interest in the dakoons, attacking their eyes and pecking at their faces. Gubrone jumped to his feet. He turned to the dakoons and yelled, "Kull eem!"

But Kumél stood his ground and fought the dakoons bravely, with his sword in one hand and stones in the other. Then, Gubrone stepped in between the dakoons with his sword lifted high. "Ye mae ha defeated mae once, Kumél. But dis battle bae mine, un ye wull taste da bitterness o'death!"

Out of the fog, Jaroh appeared and launched his spear at Gubrone but Gubrone was able to dodge it just enough to cause the spear to, once again, miss its mark. However, Gubrone was not without injury. The spear passed through him, wounding him just below his shoulder. Blood poured from the hole. Gubrone staggered back, lifted his sword again and with all his might, he lowered it, striking the chains that bound the dakoons together. For the first time since they been in Shuk, the dakoons were free of each other. "Kull thum all! Tormut un Sufrar, kull thum! Earyone o'thum!"

Tormut immediately flew away. Jaroh followed hard after him, leaving Kumél to deal with Gubrone and Sufrar. Sufrar attacked Kumél. He leapt upon him and tried to tear at him with his enormous claws. Kumél pushed and kicked and was eventually able to free himself from the enraged dakoon.

As if there were not enough troubles for both sides of the conflict, the corvus numbers were gradually increasing and, indifferent to the wind and storm, were filling the skies above the meadow. Many of the corvuses flew in upon the scene and began attacking everyone. They all had to fight off the nasty birds, which pecked at their head and eyes and any part of their bodies they could violate. Not far away, Alethia, Shu, and the two nephs were also being attacked by the minacious birds. It seemed evident the corvuses had a much greater appetite for larger gallues than they did for the nephs and the Theoscians, for they harassed them in much larger numbers and with greater tenacity.

It became increasingly obvious to Alethia that even if they could overcome the gallues and dakoons, they could not stop the corvuses because there were too many of them. She had called upon the winds and rain to come, to help them against Gubrone and the others, but even the elements seemed unable to keep the corvuses at bay. She knew there was one other thing that could help them but hinder them as well, just as the rain and wind had done. Alethia looked and saw the light of a tulwyth hiding in a small crack. Leaving the fight for just a moment, she ran to the tulwyth. "You're Looma, aren't you?"

"Yes." Looma smiled hesitantly. Her eyes were filled with both fear and courage at the same time. Her tiny voice was barely audible through the confusion and chaos.

"I need your help. Will you help me?"

"If I am able."

"Oh, I'm very sure that you are able. Go to Kumél and tell him, 'the wholeness of life comes, and there is no might that can stop it.' Will you do this for me, Looma?"

"Yes," Looma replied. She had no idea what the message meant or why it was important at that moment in time, but she was committed to helping in any way she could.

"Then go! Go quick and find Kumél. Give him the message and then hide!"

Looma sprung from her hiding place and flew like a shooting star into the storm toward the sound of clanging swords and beastly growls.

Once again, Alethia began to speak the Theoscian call to the wind. Her voice grew louder and louder and the wind blew stronger and stronger.

Just over the mound, Kumél fought with Gubrone and the dakoon. He was alone, struggling to battle the two of them at once while also defending against the corvuses. It was becoming impossible. When Looma saw Kumél, he was fighting off several corvuses; however, he was not fighting Gubrone. Gubrone and Sufrar were also being attacked by the corvuses and were unable to fight Kumél. Looma saw this as an opportunity, possibly the only opportunity she might have to deliver the message. She flew straight into the struggle between Kumél and the corvuses. Her light distracted the corvuses just long enough for Kumél to cut them from the air with his sword. For just a fraction of time, Kumél was free of the birds and free of the battle. Looma flew directly at him and hovered near his ear. As loudly as she could she repeated Alethia's words, "The wholeness of life comes, and there is no might that can stop it."

It was all she said to him before she escaped to a safe place, just as Alethia had told her to do.

Kumél's ears were filled with the unexpected message that came from Looma's lips. Without realizing it, he began to chant the Jupnie, which went up into the sky, infusing the clouds and the storm with its power. Thunder roared in the skies above the meadow and lightning flashed repeatedly, electrifying the air. The wind howled and gusted, causing the snow to swirl and whip about, like the sails of a ship. Then rain fell with snow, and the chaos of battle was waged both on stony ground and in the celestial sphere. The tumult became too great for the corvuses who were thrashed about in the air, beaten by the hands of the wind. Those that could, retreated to the towering walls of stone to hide from the violent storm.

Ross, Loham, and Seerae huddled together next to a large tree. They could hear voices, the voices of Alethia and Kumél and even, at times, Gubrone, but they could not tell from where they came or went. Afraid to move, and not knowing where anyone was, they waited, hoping the storm would pass. However, the storm was not passing; it was only growing worse. Ross knew they had to do something. He spoke to Loham, "We can't stay here; the others need our help. We need to make our way back to them."

"But how? The fog is so thick, and the wind gusts are too dangerous!"

"We have to help! We can follow the voices."

Ross looked at Seerae. "What do you think?"

"I think you're right. We have to help them. We can't just hide,"

Loham had a sword and Ross had a spear, but Seerae had nothing to defend herself with, yet she seemed the bravest and most ready to fight. Together they began moving toward the sound of the voices.

Not far away, Ziminiar searched for Huzesh, though tracking him was all but impossible considering the conditions. The fog, snow, and rain made it unlikely he would find any signs of Huzesh's whereabouts. He had been known to elude many pursuers under much less chaotic circumstances. Knowing Seerae was free, Ziminiar felt that chasing Huzesh through the storm was the same as chasing a ghost and could prove to be little more than a diversion. He thought about Kumél and the others, fighting for their lives. He ran back toward his cave to help.

It was not long before Ziminiar came upon Gubrone and Kumél fighting. He could see that Sufrar was also fighting, outnumbering Kumél. He rushed onto the mound of rocks and began to fight the dakoon. He wondered where the other dakoon was, for the last time he had seen them, they were chained together.

His momentary distractedness was a near-fatal mistake, however, for out of nowhere the chain that had bound the dakoons together came swinging through the air. It collided with the side of his head, knocking him to the ground. Sufrar lunged upon him, bearing his horrible teeth. He grabbed hold of Ziminiar's neck with his black talons and was about to rip his head from his shoulders. Ziminiar was not fully unconscious, however, and he managed to lift his sword and cut the dakoon across the back of the head. Their blood ran together on the rocks below them. The cut was great enough to cause Sufrar to hesitate. Ziminiar kicked the dakoon with his knee, knocking him away just long enough to roll over onto his belly and spring back to his feet.

Ziminiar angrily lowered his sword, intending to cut clean through the dakoon, but Sufrar was, himself, very quick and managed to escape the blade. Back and forth, they struggled, one striking the other, then the other striking back.

Overhead the storm raged, tormenting every element and every combatant. Louder and louder it roared. Rain and snow and ice fell from the angry nebula. Lightning and thunder coursed throughout the vault of heaven as if infuriated by the desperate conflict.

Everyone was wet and shivering and struggling to stand and walk and especially to fight.

The sound of battle rang out. Ross, Seerae, and Loham could hear the voices and the struggle of the others. While they were moving through the trees and stones, they filed past Glo, who had taken shelter from the savage wind in a small hole in the rocks. Her usually radiant glow was dim. Loham noticed her first and he asked, "Glo, where are the others?"

Ross and Seerae heard Loham's voice and went to see who he was talking to. Glo spoke as loudly as a tulwyth could, "They are just ahead. You must be very cautious. It's very dangerous."

"Is everyone OK? Do you know?" Ross yelled over the storm.

"I don't know, the storm has kept me here."

"What? I don't know what she said?"

"She doesn't know."

"Oh, OK. Does she want to go with us? Seerae could carry her." Glo nodded her head. Seerae reached out her hand and Glo stepped into her palm.

Ross led the group toward the conflict. It was only a matter of a few footsteps before the battle encompassed them. As Ross walked past a large, dark object, Huzesh stepped out from behind a tree, right into their path. Ross's eyes were like the moons of Shuk, round and bright. He tried to step back and stumbled. The sight of Huzesh alone was enough to frighten anyone, but to an untrained, inexperienced mortal, the one-armed, scarred beast was terrifying.

Huzesh was just as startled by the sight of Ross, though he was not frightened. He stepped toward Ross, towering over him. Upon his face was a calloused, indifferent glare. Huzesh looked at Loham, then at Seerae, and smiled. "So, ye ha brought mae da forner afta all, aye, Loham."

Seerae felt Glo moving in the palm of her hand, so she opened her fingers and watched as the tiny tulwyth flew away.

Defiantly, Loham moved in between Ross and Huzesh with his sword ready. "Back off. You cannot have them!"

Huzesh whipped his sword around, aiming at Loham's head. Loham ducked and quickly struck back, but not before Huzesh brought his sword back around and blocked the blow. Huzesh swung again and Loham tried to block the strike. When Huzesh's blade connected with Loham's blade, the force of Huzesh's strength lifted Loham into the air and sent him flying into the trees.

Loham landed against the trunk of a tree and groaned.

Ross, who had never been in battle or used any weapon in his life, was, at first, paralyzed by the swiftness of the confrontation. However, when he saw Loham attack Huzesh, he felt something rise inside. While Huzesh was distracted by Loham, Ross stood to his feet and thrust the spear of Amik into Huzesh's thigh. Huzesh cried out and then he turned and with the butt of his sword, he struck Ross across the face. Ross fell to the ground. Huzesh stepped toward him and began to reach out for him. Fearing Huzesh would go after Seerae, Ross yelled in his loudest voice, "Seerae, run!" Just as Huzesh took hold of Ross, Loham struck again, this time driving his sword deep into Huzesh's lower back. Huzesh cried out and, at the same time, let go of his grip on Ross. Ross fell to the ground and then backed away. Stunned by the sheer power of Huzesh and the fact that he was so close to dying, he stood motionless for a moment. Ross could not believe what had just happened. He had nearly been killed by a giant, one-armed monster.

It felt like a nightmare to his mind, but to his body, it felt all too painful.

"Ross!" Loham screamed, for Huzesh was not done and would have grabbed him again except Ross stepped backward after finally hearing the frantic cries of Loham. Loham chased after Huzesh and quickly pulled the sword from his back. Completely surprised, Huzesh felt the blade being pulled out and swung his sword around, but Loham dodged the blade. Ross saw that Huzesh was advancing toward Loham. Ross ran up behind Huzesh and drove the spear into Huzesh's leg.

Seerae had done exactly what Ross had told her to do and escaped from the struggle. She ran toward the sound of the battle, hoping to find help. She yelled out, "Shu! Shu, where are you? Alethia! Zoësh! Someone!"

"Here! Seerae, I'm over here!"

Seerae ran toward the voice of Shu, who was still fighting Morak. Before Seerae could reach Shu and the others, Glo, with no small effort, flew past Alethia and landed on a rock near her. Alethia looked around and then withdrew from the battle. She was confident that Zoësh, Msusi, and Shu could keep Morak busy, at least for the moment. Alethia knelt, stunned at the tenacity of the little creature.

"Glo, what are you doing? This storm is too strong for you!"

"Ross—he needs help."

At that moment, Seerae found Alethia and the others. She saw Morak fighting Zoësh and Msusi and she snuck past the fighting and called out to Alethia.

"Ross—he's in trouble."

Alethia beckoned and called out to Shu. He glanced at her while swinging his sword and fighting Morak.

"Go!" Msusi cried.

Shu backed away and ran over to Alethia. Morak could see something was going on and looked in the direction Shu was running. He could also see Alethia and the others. Morak wanted to take advantage of the situation, to overwhelm the two nephs who were alone for the moment. He began to fight even harder, driving them back with each blow of his sword.

"Ross is in trouble! You need to find him. Glo will show you the way!" Alethia yelled as Shu closed in on her.

Seerae was quick to speak up. "I am going too, I can help!"

"Go! Both of you, go!"

Seerae took Glo and hurried back to where Ross was.

Seeing Shu run after Seerae and Glo, Alethia turned her attention back to the struggle at hand. Zoësh, who was by far the most skilled and experienced of the three, showed great bravery and courage against Morak. He was mighty and determined, but she was quick and precise with her blade. Morak bore many wounds from her sword. Msusi, though not as daring or swift, was extremely passionate, and her passion made her powerful and unyielding. The two nephs worked well together as if they had practiced the craft of war. Morak was becoming weary and slow with his blade, he began to doubt himself. With every lunge and swing of his heavy sword, he labored to recover. Alethia and the nephesh were also weary, yet they were bound together by a force more powerful than all Morak's strength.

Led by his sword, Morak spun around and faced the three. It was then Alethia saw what she had been waiting for: a moment when a single lapse in his fortitude would be exposed. Morak lowered his eyes to the ground and when he did, Alethia's eyes were fixed and her mind resolved. She threw her sword, end over end, through the air toward him. He lifted his eyes as the point of the blade pierced the flesh and muscle just under the shoulder of his strong arm, the arm that held his sword.

Morak yelled out in pain. The sword sank deep into his body, all the way to the hilt, its tip dripping with blood down Morak's back. He staggered backward a few steps and then tried to regain his balance, but not before Zoësh saw the opportunity to finish him off. She leapt in front of him. Morak dropped his sword and took another step back. Zoësh raised her sword up into the air, poised to make a final blow, but Morak was not ready to concede to destruction just yet. He lifted his head and for the briefest of moments, looked into the eyes of Zoësh. In his other hand, Morak had a dagger. As Zoësh stepped into him with her sword, Morak plunged the dagger into her stomach. She looked at him, her eyes changing shape from sharp and prolate to wide and round with surprise.

Msusi saw the dagger pierce Zoësh. "No!" She screamed with defiant disbelief. Tears fell immediately from her eyes. Alethia stood frozen in place, unable to move or respond in any way. She too began to cry. Morak withdrew his dagger and Zoësh fell to her knees and then slumped over, her head plunging deep in the snow. Msusi raised her sword and charged at Morak, with a loud, violent scream. She thrashed the sword at him. Each blow was fended off by Morak's dagger, but the intense fury and tireless advance forced him back, away from Zoësh. Morak stumbled and fell to his back, dropping his dagger. His wound was deep and the pain agonizing. Msusi was blind with rage. She leapt upon him and drove her sword into his neck. She would have sliced his head off, but Morak, with his impaired arm, swung and hit her in the head, knocking her to the ground. He rolled over and then stood to his feet. Blood ran down his chest from his neck. He reached up, grabbed the handle of Alethia's sword, and pulled it out. He pitched it to the ground and searched for his dagger. Suddenly, Alethia rushed at him and quickly grabbed her sword, which she began swinging wildly, cutting and wounding him, driving Morak back, away from his dagger. Msusi saw Alethia and got up slowly. She saw her sword; it was laying on a rock. She ran to it and picked it up. Msusi flanked Morak.

Now, Morak was not one to lose a fight, nor was he one to give up, but the seriousness of his wounds and the fact he was facing an armed Theoscian and a crazed neph, with no weapon, was reason enough to wait another day to finish this fight. He turned and ran into the fog, slipping and falling several times.

Msusi started to run after him, but Alethia hollered, "Msusi, let him go. Zoësh needs help!" Alethia's voice was somber. Msusi turned to see Alethia kneeling beside Zoësh. She lifted her head up and held it in her arms. Blood oozed from the wound.

Not far from them, the sound of steel striking steel and the growls of Sufrar could be heard. Msusi cried out, "Help! Kumél, help!" She crouched beside Zoësh and put her hand on the wound. "No! You can't die! Zoësh, you can't!" She felt the warm blood between her fingers. Zoësh reached up and touched Msusi's hand. Alethia looked at them both and placed her hand on top of theirs.

Kumél heard the calls of Msusi but was unable to respond. He was in his own struggle, for Gubrone's strength was growing stronger, not weaker. Kumél could hardly believe it; Gubrone was much more powerful than he remembered. It was not, however, that Kumél had simply forgotten how powerful Gubrone was, but that Gubrone had become more powerful than before. The rune of Tukkir had given him the power of Attar because of the Eleetrum Shard, and, for the first time, Gubrone was, himself, experiencing his new strength.

Gubrone forced Kumél back down from the mound and into the

stream where their swords clashed against each other. Blow by blow, the iron of conflict rang out, empowered by savage rage.

Alethia could hear the ringing of steel across the meadow. She realized Kumél was in a battle from which he could not withdraw. She scanned the area. "Msusi, we have to find a place out of the storm. Stay with Zoësh. I will return."

Alethia struggled to walk through the driving rain and snow. The wind showed her no favor. It beat upon her, making each step a challenge. She looked for a place that was close where they could hide Zoësh and care for her. A gust of wind rushed past her, knocking her to her knees. Alethia crawled on all fours toward a pile of rocks, hoping to find a break from the wind. As she closed in on the berm, she found a hollow place under some rocks that was large enough for a shelter. She sprung to her feet and fought the storm back to where Zoësh and Msusi waited. "Come, quick. I've found a place out of the storm." Alethia and Msusi carried Zoësh to the small hollow.

Ziminiar could not find a way to defeat Sufrar. Though the dakoon was wounded, he was still strong and capable. His talons were like swords and Ziminiar had felt their sharpness several times. In his heart, Ziminiar began to doubt. The brutality and duration of the battle, the raging storm, the cold and damp that surrounded him leeched every reserve from his mind and body. He could feel his strength flowing out from him like the blood oozing out from his wounds.

Above the battlefield, in the thick fog, Jaroh and Tormut fought in an aerial struggle. They grappled with each other. At times, they were so entangled in the steely vice of strife they hardly realized they were free-falling to the ground below. They kicked and scratched and hit at each other, rolling through the storm as if they were a storm of their own.

Finally, Jaroh pushed away from Tormut, and when he did, he was able to lance the dakoon through its arm. Tormut let out a loud roar of defiant pain and flew into the fog, trying to escape Jaroh. Jaroh pursued him, but the dakoon had slipped out of sight. The loud roar rolled down from the sky, into the meadow. Sufrar heard it and looked up. He went to fly towards Tormut but could not use the wounded shoulder. Instead, he ran off into the storm in the direction of the roar. Over the mound below him, he could hear the clang of steel. Ziminiar ran toward the sound to find Kumél.

Near the confluence of the two streams, Seerae and Glo tried to lead Shu to where Ross and Loham had been.

"Ross, Ross!" Shu called.

Somewhere in the distance, Shu could hear fighting and yelling. He yelled out even louder, "Ross, Ross!"

Overhead, Tormut heard the calls of Shu and turned his attention toward the ground below, which was obscured by the fog. He dove down through the clouds.

Loham and Ross were doing their best to fight against Huzesh. He was aggressive and strong and kept pushing them back. Loham was faring much better against Huzesh than Ross, yet Ross would not back down from the fight. Amidst the struggle, Ross heard Shu calling out his name. He quickly yelled back, "Here! We're here!"

Tormut was descending through the clouds when he heard Ross's voice. He darted toward it.

Shu was about to call out again when he saw, through the falling rain and fog, the movements of Ross and Loham as they struggled against Huzesh. Shu advised Seerae and Glo, "Stay here. Without a weapon, you will only be in danger." Shu ran toward the fight with his sword drawn. Just as he came upon the fight, the black shadow of Tormut's wings passed above him. Shu looked up just in time to see Tormut land behind Ross and Loham, blocking his path. Huzesh looked at the dakoon and smiled. He advanced with his sword swinging wildly at Ross and Loham, pushing them into the path of Tormut. Shu yelled out, "Ross! Behind you!"

Ross turned and Shu ran toward Tormut whose back was to him. The dakoon spun around, stunned to see Shu, charging at him with his sword. Tormut quickly flapped his wings and took off; Ross and Loham watched his flight into the fog. Huzesh, seeing there was another combatant to fight against, used the moment of distraction to slip away. Ross and Loham turned back around ready to fight, only to find their opponent had disappeared. Loham looked around a second time in disbelief. "Where'd he go?"

"Probably not far. We'd better get back to the others."

The three of them turned and ran quickly back to Seerae and Glo. Then, together, they ran toward the cave.

During the struggle, however, Ross's backpack had fallen from his shoulder. One of the straps was broken. He noticed at the time but could not retrieve it because of the fighting. As they were running back to the others, he realized he had left it behind.

"My backpack—damn it! I left it back there. I have to go back."

"But—" Before Shu could object, Ross was running back into the fog and rain with the spear of Amik in his hand. Shu hollered, but Ross disappeared into the storm. Shu instructed Loham,

"You have to get back to Alethia and the others; they will need help. Glo and Seerae can show you the way. I will find Ross. Don't wait for us. Now go!" Loham followed Seerae, who was carrying Glo, as Shu watched them disappear into the fog then Shu turned and ran after Ross.

Ross ran through the storm, but in his haste and because of the gray, featureless haze, he lost his way. Ross turned around to go back, trying to backtrack, but the more he tried to find his way, the more lost he became.

Shu ran back to where the dakoon had landed. He looked but could not see Ross anywhere. He wondered if Ross had already been there, but then he found Ross's backpack laying against a stone. Shu looked around. His heart sank and he began to fear something bad might have happened. He grabbed Ross's backpack and waited. He wanted to call out, but he knew the dakoons might hear him or Huzesh might be nearby. Ross stood in the fog and rain, soaked and cold and afraid. In all his days in the strange land of Shuk, he had never felt so alone, or so afraid. Then, strangely, the fury of the winds suddenly began to slow their aggressive march through the air. Through the mist and rain, the ominous sound of the corvuses rang out.

Chills ran down Ross's spine as he stood alone and indefensible. Out of the fog fluttered several large corvuses, which wasted no time in setting about attacking him. They swooped down and pecked at his head and arms as he swung and kicked and tried to spear them to no avail. Ross groaned and screamed as the birds pecked at him. He started running, hoping to find someplace out of the open where the birds could not molest him, but the corvuses were unrelenting and continued to attack. Ross ran blindly through the fog, as fast as he could until he ran, full speed, into something large and firm, something, he imagined as he fell backward to the ground, that must have been a rock or a tree. The corvuses heckled and squawked over him, continuing their attack.

Ross felt a burst of wind pass over his body, but he knew it was not wind. Along with the wind came a sound like something cutting through the air. Two corvuses landed on his chest. They were dead. He tried to push them away and felt the warm flow of their blood as it poured out over his chest. There were other corvuses diving and trying to attack him, so he kept his face covered. He could hear fighting above him. The *swish* of a sword cut through the air.

"Buk ye foul birds, buk!"

Ross immediately thought it was Kumél. He looked up, expecting to see his friend, but was sorely disappointed to see Huzesh standing just beyond him, killing several corvuses and, at the same time, watching him, with his evil stare and feathers and blood coming from his mouth.

Then, without any reason whatsoever, the wind once again burst into the meadow and the few remaining corvuses that were attacking Ross were forced back into their shelter. Ross froze; his face showed his terror. He began to back away from Huzesh, but Huzesh walked slowly toward him. His eyes never looked away. Ross reached for the spear and lifted it up, pointing it at Huzesh. Huzesh took a step back. Ross stood holding the spear out in front of himself. He tried to be brave and not show the storm of fear that raged in his heart. Ross stepped back several steps as Huzesh advanced toward him, then, from somewhere deep down inside him, a defiant undeterred force arose. Ross lunged at Huzesh with the spear and pierced his leg. Huzesh stopped, clenched his teeth and lowered his angry brow. Ross hostilely warned him "Back off! I'll drive this thing right through you!"

Huzesh smiled, the way he smiled when he was ready to strike. "A cun taste yer fear, un soon A wull bae tastin yer flesh, forner!" Then Huzesh defiantly roared and swung his sword. Ross hastily stepped back and lifted his spear in defense. The sword crashed into the spear, forcing it out of Ross's hands, to the ground. Ross quickly grabbed a small stone and hurled it at Huzesh then he threw another. Both times Huzesh was struck by the rocks but continued his attack. Ross spun and ran as fast as he could. Huzesh fiercely bellowed, "Halt!"

Now Shu was not far away and heard Huzesh yell. He ran as fast as he could toward the shout. Ross ran as fast as he could, into the fog looking for anything, any place at all to hide. Huzesh started to chase him but then noticed the spear laying on the ground. He bent over and picked it up by one of its ends. He reached back, with the spear in his only hand and hurled it, like a knife, end over end at Ross. At that very moment, Ross's foot became trapped between two stones and he fell, face-first to the ground. He heard the spear spinning through the air over him, then past him and into the fog. He then heard a metallic thud followed immediately by a guttural, sickening groan. He looked up and saw the silhouette of someone stumbling backward. The spear had missed Ross but had found someone else.

In the clouds above them, Jaroh heard Huzesh yell at Ross. Immediately he flew down toward them. Ross looked up as, out of the shadows the radiant flash of Jaroh descended into view and he landed just beyond where Ross was lying. Jaroh faced Huzesh and without a single word, he threw his mighty spear through the air. Neither mortal nor immortal was able to defy death by the kerolus spear. Its power was much more than its sharpness or metal. Before Ross had a chance to react, the spear hit its mark and had flown straight through Huzesh's chest. Huzesh fell to his knees, blood flowed from the wound onto the ground all around him and the scent of blood filled the air.

Ross looked at Huzesh and then he turned to see that Jaroh was kneeling over another body.

"Ross, Hurry!"

Ross heard the labored call of a voice that was not Jaroh's. Ross's heart began to race as he ran toward Jaroh. A sinking feeling began to preside over his soul. As he approached Jaroh, he could hear sobs and see tears falling from Jaroh's cheeks.

Huzesh put his hand on the ground. He slouched over, mortally wounded. He knew he would die soon. Next to his hand was his sword. He looked at it and then he looked at Ross who was running away. Huzesh reached out and took the sword into his hand. He sank the point of it into the ground and used it to help himself stand to his feet. Huzesh began to move toward Ross. He still intended to kill the foreigner.

Ross reached Jaroh and to his horror, he saw Shu, pinned against a mound of stones by the spear of Amik. Shu looked dead. Tears filled Ross's eyes. He saw his backpack grasped in Shu's hand. "No! No! No!"

Ross's agonizing cry echoed long and sharp through the meadow, eclipsing even the roar of the thunder. The weight of his sorrow rolled like waves through the air, crashing upon the fractured landscape of hearts and souls and firmament. Behind him, Huzesh crept closer and closer until Jaroh heard his footsteps. Jaroh had only his sword, the spear was back on the ground where Huzesh had fallen. Jaroh stood up and walked over to Huzesh with a determined gate. Huzesh raised his sword and, though he was dying, tried to fight Jaroh with a relentless, though diminishing resolve. Jaroh drove him farther back with each swing of his sword, away from Shu and Ross and into the fog and rain. Like the wind driving the corvuses into hiding, Jaroh drove him back.

Ringing like steel wind chimes, their blades screamed out above every other noise until Jaroh struck Huzesh's sword with such power that the ancient steel cracked and the blade broke away from the hilt. Huzesh looked at the fractured weapon in his hand and fell to his knees and then he slumped over and leaned on a cold wet rock. Jaroh pointed his sword at Huzesh and, watched as the essence of life was leaving his body. Huzesh's eyes dimmed as he asked Jaroh, "Wae used t'bae frens, Jaroh. D'ye rumumbar?"

"Aye, u lung, lung tam ago."

"Aye, ut waer u lung tam ago."

Huzesh laid his head against the rock and the life that had lived in him from before time began, slowly faded from his eyes. His breathing became heavy and the cloud of breath that escaped his lips was carried away by the wind. It was his final breath. Jaroh knelt down; he lowered his head and remembered the Great War and the words Eloh spoke after the defeat of Attar. *"These are brothers that we fight against and it is a very, very sad day when brothers fight brothers."*

Jaroh's eyes fell upon the cold, broken body of Huzesh. He looked at him and remembered the Great War, the great storm that ripped the realm of Pardis into pieces. He had stood in the raging tempest and felt the angry, brooding storm. He had looked upon the many fallen brothers and wept. He wept again.

Meanwhile, Loham, and Seerae, led by Glo, looked for Alethia. They found the place near the cave of Ziminiar where they had last been, but there was no one to be found. "Msusi! Zoësh!" Loham was cautious about calling out, fearful the dakoons might hear them and come back. "Alethia!"

"Here! I'm here, Loham!"

Through the noise, Seerae could hear a voice calling back. She looked around. "Did you hear that?"

"Here!"

Loham saw the silhouette of Alethia standing just beyond a clearing. He and Seerae ran with Glo safely in Seerae's hands. As they arrived at the small hollow, Alethia asked Loham, "Where is Ross and Shu?"

"Shu went after Ross. He told us to go on, to find you and to bring Seerae to safety,"

"Shu went after Ross. What do you mean?"

"Ross ran back to get something, and Shu went after him."

"Are they safe?"

"I don't know. They should be close behind us . . . I would think."

It was clear that Alethia was not comfortable with the situation. "Loham, you will have to find them. Can you go back?"

"Sure, I can and I will. But where is Zoësh?"

"Inside, she's been wounded."

Seerae heard and became immediately upset. "What? How?"

"Morak, he stabbed her."

"How bad?"

"It's bad, but I think she'll be OK. We have to keep her safe and out of the storm."

"And Msusi?"

"She's with Zoësh now."

Loham took Alethia's hand. "I'll go back and find Shu and Ross."

"Loham, you must be careful. I fear they are in great danger." Loham ran back to find Ross and Shu.

Meanwhile, Tormut smelled the blood of Shu and turned his attention to finding him. He swooped down through the air, following the scent until he saw Ross kneeling next to Shu. Shu was unable to move. Tormut landed just above him and looked down on both Ross and Shu. Ross fell backwards in fright and yelled out, "Jaroh! Help!"

Tormut sniffed the blood. Ross, forgetting his fear, picked up some rocks and began to hurl them at the dakoon. At first, Tormut paid no attention, but Ross did not give up; he saw Shu's sword on the ground, grabbed it, and pursued Tormut. He swung and jabbed the sword at the dakoon, who quickly realized Ross was not about to give up. Ross shouted at Tormut. "Get back, leave him alone!" Fearlessly, Ross tried to protect Shu, while at the same time yelling at Jaroh to help him.

Finally, Tormut turned all his attention onto Ross. He leapt from the mound of stones right at Ross. Ross fell backward to the ground. All around him, beneath the layers of snow, the snowpetal grew. It was growing when he knelt beside Shu, it grew when he fell, it grew where each of his steps were placed. There was snowpetal everywhere. Tormut stood over Ross, he leaned down and with his large nose and began to sniff his flesh, preparing to make a meal of him. However, the delicate aroma of the snowpetal filled his nostrils and in no time at all, he became intoxicated by the powerful effects of the tiny flower. Ross noticed right away that Tormut was dazed. He turned and ran. Tormut tried to follow, growling and snorting and acting erratic. Ross ran as fast as he could toward Jaroh, though not knowing for certain where he might have been. Tormut, shaking his head and blinking his eyes, spread his black wings, and took to flight. He closed in upon Ross in no time at all and was preparing to leap upon him when Jaroh appeared through the fog. "Ross! Move!"

Ross could see Jaroh had his spear in his hand and his arm was drawn back, cocked like the hammer of a pistol. Jaroh motioned to Ross to get out of the way. Ross dove to the ground, surrounded by rocks and boulders just as Jaroh brought his mighty arm forward and his hand let loose the spear. Before Tormut could stop or fly away, the spear pierced him through the heart. Tormut came crashing end over end to the ground, his dead corpse landed on top of the rocks between which Ross had dove.

Jaroh ran up and pulled his spear from the dakoon and then, with his sword he cut off its head. Without giving any assistance to Ross, who was buried under the dakoons body, Jaroh turned and ran back to Shu. Ross struggled to crawl out from under Tormut's dead body. Once freed, he turned and ran back to Shu. When he reached Shu, Shu had his eyes open. He looked at Jaroh. Blood fell from the corners of his mouth.

"Jaroh, I need to see Ross, there is something I must tell him."

Just then, Ross stepped close to Shu and Jaroh stepped aside. Ross tried to assure Shu, "It's gonna be ok, Shu, it's gonna be ok."

"There is something that you must do, Ross, and I fear that you will not want to do it."

"Anything. Ask me anything."

"Ross, you must use the spear to kill Gubrone. You must find the fourth face and take it from him. It is for you—the Kleid o'Miht. You are the one who must find it. Don't let it out of your sight, ever! Now, take the spear."

Ross looked at Shu with disbelief. His mouth was open, his lips were dry and his throat was rough. He tried to swallow but could not. Tears welled up in his eyes and his hands began to shake. "No! I can't. You'll die."

"I'm dying anyway."

"But you can't die! I thought you would never die?"

"You've known all along that someone would have to die."

"Yeah, but I thought it was me—never you!"

"It was always supposed to be me, Ross."

In Ross's mind he could remember the inscription: *"The lamp will be pierced by the darkness and the oil of light will pour out upon the shadows."*

"But why?"

"The legend—that's why. I am the lamp and my blood is the oil of light. You have to take the spear, you have to pull it out, it is the only way to destroy Gubrone and the spell. You're the Hammer of Light, Ross! It has always been you. The one who would crush the shadows. Take the spear. It's time."

Ross looked at Jaroh for help. He could not believe how desperate the situation was. Jaroh put his hand on Ross's shoulder. "Ross, ye mus d'ut now. Tam bae waisin."

The sounds of the storm were amplified in his mind as if he could hear each drop of rain and every snowflake that touched the ground. The wind howled with a mournful bellowing groan. Ross felt as if millions upon millions of eyes were staring at him, watching him, waiting for him. He took a step toward Shu. The sound of his footsteps even echoed in his mind. Part of him felt as though it was not him who was walking, but that it was someone else, someone he could not see or feel. He could feel the large drops of rain tapping on his head and shoulders, running down the length of his body. He reached out and took hold of the spear, Amik's spear, his spear. He grabbed it first with his right hand and then with his left. He felt another hand touch his. He looked to see Shu's hands on his hands and then they took hold of the spear. The simtu markings on his body began to glow and the spear began to shine brightly. Ross saw the blood of Shu dripping from the shaft of the spear. Each drop slowly fell and then hung suspended in midair.

Ross wanted to back away, to let go of the spear, but Shu's eyes locked on his, focused and sharp and yet honestly afraid. Shu spoke softly, reassuringly to Ross, "It's OK, don't be afraid. Don't be afraid."

Ross's eyes pooled with tears, his heart continued to race, he swallowed and then he pulled on the spear with all his might. His face grimaced from the effort. Shu pushed with both of his hands locked to the spear. At first, the spear did not move. Ross pulled harder and Shu pushed as hard as he was able until it broke free of the rocks behind Shu from where it was jammed. Slowly the spear came out, covered in Shu's blood, Theoscian blood.

In the distance, Kumél began to cry out the words of Jupnie, wailing louder than ever before. He had no way of knowing what was happening to Shu, but the power of the Jupnie and the forces of all created things were reflecting agony at Shu's impending demise.

As the spear was freed from Shu's body, Shu slumped to the ground. Ross and Jaroh knelt next to him. Shu lifted his head and spoke to Ross, "I have something to give you." Shu held up Ross's backpack. "I found this and thought you might need it."

Ross just lowered his head. He felt ashamed.

"Do you remember the inscription you saw, the one that you wrote in Eve's book?"

Ross swallowed and replied to Shu, "Yeah, I remember."

"All that it says is about to come true, *'There is one who is coming, of the line of your father, he will walk the Aurora Path and pierce the heart of the cruel masters, with a spear stained in Theoscian blood,'* There is one more thing that you must do. When you find Gubrone, you must speak the words of the Jupnie. Do you remember them?"

In his head, Ross could hear them, echoing as if he had always known them:

The day is rising and now is come, when the time of shadows will end, no longer vexing Pardis. Light will once again overpower the darkness and shine on all the realms of Pardis. The brokenness will be healed, and the sun will shine in every valley as in the days before the great war. The great hammer of light will crush the darkness and the spear of brightness will overcome the shield of shadows that has covered the wilderness realm. The wholeness of life comes, it comes, and there is no might that can stop its coming.

"Yes, I remember." Ross looked at Shu and then at the spear which was dripping with blood mixed with rain.

"Go!"

Ross searched into the depths of Shu eyes and he began to see the face of Eve and then of Seerae and then the face of Daniel and of his sister. One after another, face after face of those whom he had loved and of whom he had lost came into view and then they all faded away until all he could see was Shu. Echoing in his heart, was the voice of Eve, it was something she had said to him, something he could never forget, though he had never understood why.

"Ross, open your eyes and see me."

The soft, gentle meaning of her words sank into his heart. In one way or another, each of the faces he saw were saying to him, "see me". They offered to him something he could not give to himself, they offered him a purpose, a reason, someone to live for and, if necessary, to die for. The things Alethia had told him, about who you fight for not who you fight against, began to make sense. His love for them was not a weakness as he had supposed, it was the source of his greatest strength, the wellspring of life from which he had refused to drink.

Ross knew that time was not on his side, that he had to go, but he could not turn away, he could not just leave. Tears ran down his face as he watched the eyes of his friend slowly close and his head droop down until his chin touched his chest. As a wound leaves a scar, so a friend marks one for life. A scar changes one, it changes the way one looks. Pain, like a scar, changes one too, only in ways beyond seeing. Like steel being struck by a hammer is changed, not only in form, but deeper, beyond what the eye can see, the molecules of metal are compressed and rearranged, changing the composition of the metal just as a friend changes the composition of one's life. Death is a scar, is a pain and the death of a friend leaves a deep scar and deep pain, like a hammer to steel, it changes one in every way. As he watched his friend die, Ross felt something different, something contrary to circumstance. He felt life pushing into him, forcing itself into every pore and wrinkle and joint as if the life that was leaving Shu was not just flowing into the stream or the ground or the cracks of the rocks around his broken body, but had taken wings and flown into the hollowness of Ross's broken being.

Ross stood up and took one last lingering look as Shu, who breathed his last breath and then slumped lifelessly to the ground. For a moment, everything stood still like death, even the storm, as though the whole of creation gasped in horror. The stillness, grew hostile, like a brooding quiet anger. The tension in the air, like the restrained, explosive energy of an eminent magmatic eruption.

Ross looked around. It was only he and Jaroh there. They were the only ones who watched the last breath of Shu pass into the mist. Only their eyes had seen him die, they were the only ones that were with him at the end, the only ears that had heard his last words. His death was cloaked, hidden from all the rest of the realm by the storm and the fog as if it was meant to be a secret. His enemies, those who hated him, Gubrone and the others who had meant to destroy him, even Huzesh, who had inadvertently played a role in it, had not seen his eyes close. There was no one to gloat or boast or celebrate. Only Ross and Jaroh and the tempest had seen the death of Shu.

The storm was not still for long. After the span of only a breath, the full fury of the storm came unleashed, a sharp chilling sonic crack, like the sound of glass or ice splitting apart, radiated across the sky. The sound of it went out in all directions followed closely by bright flashes of lightning and clamorous roars of thunder. The invisible fracture reached to every extent of the realm terrorizing the skies and shaking the ground. All the elements, lightning and thunder, rain and snow and wind exploded with indignation.

Far away, throughout all parts of the realm and especially over the Valley of Souls, the storm clouds amassed, and torrential rain fell into the valley causing the streams and rivers to overflow and flood the meadows and lowlands. The captive nephesh could sense something terrible had happened and raised their voices, singing songs of sorrow and mourning, songs unlike any ever heard in Shuk.

Ross stood near his friend dazed and crying, unmoved by all the clamor and chaos surrounding him. Jaroh grabbed him by the arm and shook him out of his stupor.

"Ross, dar bae no tam t'mourn. Ye ha t'gae!"

"Yeah, I know, but I can't leave him here all alone. Stay with him, Jaroh. Stay with Shu, please."

Jaroh was moved by Ross's compassion and affection for Shu. He felt, on one hand, he should go, that he should help Ross and yet, on the other hand, he wanted to honor Ross's request as well as honoring Shu. He did not want the body of Shu to be scavenged or plundered by whatever or whoever might find him. Jaroh looked at Ross with a new respect and nodded. "A wull."

"Thank you." Ross turned and ran into the tempest.

Gubrone found himself backed up against a wall of rocks. Up to his knees in the turbulent stream, he fought desperately against Kumél and Ziminiar, but they were closing in on him and were ready to finish him. "Sufrar, Tormut, com! Com t'yer master!"

Before his words had finished echoing through the meadow, Sufrar bounded towards Kumél. Kumél saw the horrid beast rushing toward him. Then, as if out of nowhere, Ziminiar charged toward the dakoon yelling, "Finish Gubrone! A wull destroy da dakoon!"

Sufrar quickly turned his attention on to Ziminiar, who by this time was about to jump onto him. He bounded into the air, brushing Ziminiar with his wing knocking Ziminiar down. Sufrar turned back and pounced on Ziminiar. Ziminiar fought him off and then stood up and ran to an outcropping of rocks that was at the edge of the stream. The rocks were high enough and large enough that the dakoon would not be able to swoop down upon him again. Ziminiar could see the beast was still bleeding from the wound to the back of its head. Ziminiar held his sword out, waiting for the dakoon to return.

Gubrone became emboldened by the presence of his ally and fought even more aggressively. He swung his giant sword hard and mercilessly at Kumél, forcing him to back up. Kumél was not about to concede to Gubrone's aggression. He swung back harder than ever, repeatedly he beat his sword upon Gubrone's and for a while, the two of them were matched so exactly that neither was able to gain an advantage.

Sufrar looked at Ziminiar with his evil malevolent eyes and let out a threatening loud cry. Ziminiar swung his sword at Sufrar's head, but Sufrar blocked his assault with his wing and then he hit Ziminiar with the other wing. Ziminiar fell to the ground and Sufrar leapt upon him again. Ziminiar dragged his sword across the dakoon's chest, cutting a deep wound. Sufrar pushed himself away from Ziminiar and escaped back to Gubrone, but Ziminiar immediately charged after him. The dakoon crashed into Kumél from behind and sent him airborne. Then, Sufrar whirled around to face Ziminiar who was rushing toward him. Gubrone rushed toward Kumél with his sword raised over his head, ready to destroy him. Kumél quickly rolled over to his back and began backing away from his approaching nemesis.

Ross could hear the noises of battle just beyond him. Rain and snow and ice pelted him from head to foot, soaking and chilling every inch. The intense anger of the storm grew stronger with every moment that passed. Ross stopped. He tried to calm his emotions and fears. Some part of his inner self nagged at him as if trying to reason with him. *You're no hero, no warrior. You're just a boy, a mortal man. You can't fight giants, you can't fight at all. What are you doing? This is crazy.*

Ross struggled with the thoughts; his fear was becoming stronger. He looked down at the spear in his hand. It was glowing and the simtu was glowing. The weight of his role, of his purpose, pushed down upon him like one of the giant stones that hung over his head. He wondered why they believed in him, why such a task could be his to bear. The howl of the wind, the beating turbulent thunder, the coursing lightning, everything around him was engaged in a battle, a battle he had to finish. He raised the spear up and looked at it. The markings that were carved into it were the same as those he had written in Eve's journal. From the start, he had been the one for whom the spear had been made. The thought of it made chills run down his back. His soul began to feel a great power, a rush of courage and hope that overcame the fear; it overcame every objection, it overcame reality. Ross knew he had to finish whatever it was only he could finish.

Looking at the markings on the spear, he could hear the voice of the Jupnie. He could hear Kumél's voice chanting and, for the first time, he could understand what was being said. *"The wholeness of life comes, it comes, and there is no might that can stop its coming."* Over and over he heard it. At first, he only listened but then, he began to whisper the words. *"The wholeness of life comes, it comes, and there is no might that can stop its coming."* Again and again he whispered the strange message just as Shu had told him to. *"The wholeness of life comes, it comes, and there is no might that can stop its coming."*

A hand touched him on the shoulder. Ross snapped out of his transfixed state and turned to see Loham standing beside him. "Loham, what are you doing here? Where are the others? where is Seerae?"

"She is with Alethia and the others. She is safe, for now. We have something we must do."

"Yes. Yes, we do."

Ross and Loham stepped around a boulder and saw Ziminiar struggling against Sufrar. Loham led the charge and they ran as hard as they could toward the fight. Sufrar wheeled around and faced them. Sufrar screamed out with a loud, terrifying sound.

He bellowed out a long, loud roar and began thrashing the air with his wings, trying to strike Loham. Ziminiar rose to his feet and retaliated, striking the metallic framework of Sufrar's wing. Sufrar spun around and struck back. Every thrust and slice and blow they tried against him failed.

Not far away, Gubrone was gaining an advantage over Kumél and had pushed him up through the stream to a place where there were tall granite walls on either side of the stream. The two fallen kerolus fought sword to sword and hand to hand. They were tearing and cutting; they were bleeding and broken, but neither was about to relent. Finally, Gubrone struck Kumél with such force his sword could not stop the concussion. Gubrone's jagged black blade cut across Kumél's shoulder and arm. Kumél fell back into the stream and Gubrone stepped over him. Kumél kicked him in the knee and then swung his sword with his wounded arm, forcing Gubrone to fall back. Instead of calling for help, Kumél kept fighting, even though he knew he could not defeat him. Gubrone called out for help, "Tormut! Com t'yer master!"

Ziminiar and Ross pushed Sufrar back and Loham ran around to his rear so they had him surrounded. However, Sufrar was not about to let the trio overcome him. He spread his wings wide and spun around, hitting Ross, and knocking him back. Loham hurried in and sliced a wide gash into Sufrar's leg. Then, Ziminiar lunged forward and wounded the dakoon. Ziminiar yelled out to Ross, "Go! Help Kumél. He is just over there. We've got this!"

Ross ran toward the stream. At first, he could not see anything. He tried to listen for sounds of the struggle, but the wind and thunder were so intense that hearing was impossible. He hurried through the stream. He could only see Gubrone though, who was standing over Kumél. As he got closer, he could see that Kumél was down in the water fighting on his back, trying to fend off Gubrone.

The sight of Gubrone was overwhelming at first. Ross had not seen the giant gallue before. He was bigger than even Kumél or Jaroh. He knew he could not stand long against this juggernaut, nor would Kumél be able to fend him off for much longer. Ross looked around and saw, above Gubrone, an overhanging platform of rock; however, it was on the other side of the stream from where he stood. Ross ran and jumped as far as he could, hoping to clear the raging water. He landed just feet short of the other side and the powerful torrent began to pull him away from the shore. Ross used the spear to hold himself up and pushed his heavy legs through the water until he was on the other side. He looked and saw a narrow ribbon of rocks leading up to the top of the overhang.

Against the wind and the rain and snow, he fought his way to the top. As he climbed, he could see only enough of Gubrone to know he was there, on the other side of the steam. All along, Ross's lips were speaking the words of the Jupnie, causing the blue marking on the spear and his body to become brighter and brighter. Once he made it to the platform, he walked to the edge and looked down, only to see Kumél desperately trying to keep Gubrone from cutting him to pieces. Ross's heartbeat accelerated as anger overcame any fear that tried to turn him away. He could see the face of his friend and knew he had to do whatever he could to save his life. Ross looked down at the spear and then walked back to the opposite end of the overhang. He would have to run and jump from the platform if he was to reach Gubrone. With all his might, he ran as hard and as fast as he could until he reached the edge of the platform where he jumped.

As he fell through the air, Ross lifted the spear above his head with both hands gripping its hilt so tightly that his skin began to tear and bleed. Below him, Gubrone raised his sword over Kumél who was wounded and bleeding and without the strength to lift his own sword in defense. Kumél moved his lips and from them came the barely audible sound of words, words that were not his own, and he spoke into the fury. As if he had no power over his tongue, even to the point of death, the Jupnie floated from his mouth, determined and unstoppable. As he descended from the sky, Ross's lips whispered the same words. Words mumbled from lips that could not help but speak them. *"The wholeness of life comes, it comes, and there is no might that can stop its coming. The wholeness of life comes, it comes, and there is no might that can stop its coming."*

Gubrone took one long last step over Kumél and lifted his sword high into the air. "Bahaha! A ha won dis day, yur weak un pitiful, Kumél. Ye made ut t'aesy. A ha lung waited fur dis moment!"

As Gubrone celebrated his premature victory, Ross's feet landed squarely on his broad, hunched over shoulders. Without the slightest hesitancy, before he could fall from the precarious perch and sooner than Gubrone could react, Ross drove the spear, still dripping with the blood of Shu, down between Gubrone's shoulders. So great was the force of his determination the spear sank to its hilt. Its point ran through Gubrone and exited out from beneath the belly of his breastplate.

Gubrone tried to turn, but the power of the spear was too immediate, too quick and sure, and life began to drain from him. He collapsed to his knees, holding himself up with one arm. In defiance, Gubrone yelled out to his dakoons to come.

Ross was still on his shoulders with his spear in one hand, and a lock of Gubrone's hair clenched in the other. Gubrone dropped his sword in the stream, then he reached up and grabbed Ross and tossed him through the air, as if he was little more than a menacing corvus, pecking at his ears. Ross landed on his back against a pile of rocks with an agonizing and brutal thud. His vision immediately blurred, then he blacked out. Gubrone looked at Kumél who was laying in the stream only an arm's length away. His eyes rolled back in their sockets and his head slumped from one side to the other. Then he fell face first into the stream. His blood began to stain the water, running in long streaks until it finally diluted and vanished into the wild rush.

Far away from the battlefield, in the Valley of Souls, a strange thing began to take place, something that none of the company could have known was happening. The power of the curse set in place by The Twelve, which held the nephesh captive for so long, had been compromised by the death of Gubrone. It was not broken, but it was weakened. It had always been rumored that Gubrone was the key to the power of the rune, but few really believed it. It had been so long ago since the spell was cast that the memory of its power and the understanding of the collaboration of those forces required to keep the spell intact had failed. Forgetfulness was not only a disease for Amik's seed; it was also a disease that corrupted all those who had fallen. The great cloud that hung over the valley and kept the songs of the nephesh from escaping began to split apart and large drops of rain fell in the valley like never before. The song of the nephesh was escaping through the fractured atmosphere and traveling through time, space, and memory back toward the land of Tirnan.

Sinistradt was alone in Gubrone's cave when the ground shook from the fury of the storm. He ran out of the cave into the violent storm. Standing in the rain, he looked around and up to the skies. Above him, the dark, swirling clouds gathered more and more strength. The lightning terrorized the ground, striking the trees, hills, and mountains. The sound of the nephesh song swirled around him like the wind, and he could see thousands upon thousands of captive nephs standing in the rain, singing their sad songs. Sinistradt's anger became inflamed as he considered that

Gubrone may have been right about Eloh and the foreigner all along. In the brooding evilness of his heart, he knew that whatever power caused the storm, whatever force had caused the fracture of the rune, would soon come upon them all. Sinistradt turned and walked back into the cave more determined than ever to rule Shuk, to sit upon the throne of Gubrone, to kill the waif nephesh, and to finally silence the songs of the nephesh.

Sufrar dominated Loham and Ziminiar. Their weapons were no match for the ruthless dakoon. Sufrar wounded them with his iron-like talons and drove them back until they were cornered. Ziminiar lunged and drove his sword at Sufrar, trying to force him back, but Sufrar managed to dodge each attack and avoid damage. Loham felt small and completely outmatched by the giant, yet he refused to concede or show any sign of fear. Sufrar used the sharp edges of his wings like the edge of a sword, slicing through the air and trying to decapitate the two warriors. Loham thrust his sword at the passing wing and managed to cut a hole into the fleshy membrane that stretched out between the iron-like skeleton. The wound in the wing began to tear even more and before Sufrar realized what had happened, he had a large, gaping hole in his wing. Sufrar felt the sting of Loham's blade and took a step back.

At that same moment, Gubrone died, and the power of Tukkir's rune, which had given the dakoons such invincibility, died along with him. Sufrar could feel weakness and pain course through his body. Ziminiar and Loham both realized, simultaneously, that something had changed, that the dakoon was not the same. They began to fight with even more fury.

The forceful waters of the stream flowing out of the gorge swirled around Gubrone's lifeless body. Then, the force of the convergent deluge picked him up and drove his hulking frame downstream until the current pushed it up against the rocky shoreline, where it came to rest, half in the stream and half out. Not far away, two sets of large, black eyes, corvus eyes, watched from their storm shelter of rocks and stones.

A sudden blow from Ziminiar's sword struck Sufrar across the chest. Sufrar backed away, blood gushing out from the cut. The mighty dakoon could no longer overwhelm his enemies. He spread his wings and tried to fly away, but the storm was too strong. The wound to his wing and shoulder kept him from overpowering the wind. Sufrar jumped up and tried to fly again. The wind grabbed him and tossed him through the air and into the fog.

Loham and Ziminiar stood dumbfounded, looking into the tempestuous firmament. They could not decide whether to run away or to stand guard, just in case the beast returned. Finally, Loham walked away, toward the low, droning sound of Kumél's knelling voice that, like a prowler, sneaked in and out of notice, carried forward and cloaked by the undulating tempest. Ziminiar sat down in the snow, cut, and bruised and weary as the sound of the Jupnie swirled around him.

Loham walked over to the stream where he could see Kumél, sitting up to his waist in the cold, rushing water. Kumél appeared dazed, as if under a spell. His wounds, though great, were not mortal. Every bone, every muscle in his body groaned in protest. His will to make himself move was broken. All he seemed able to do was moan and babble the words of the Jupnie.

Loham knelt in the stream in front of him and looked into his eyes. "Kumél, Kumél!" Kumél blinked and looked at him. He tried to lift himself up to his feet, but his body would not obey his will. Loham offered him his hand, but Kumél would not take it.

"War bae Ross? Bae ee alright?"

"I haven't seen him."

"Fin eem."

Loham stood back up and looked around. As he peered into the fog just behind Kumél, he saw a dark, shadowy form surrounded by snow. Loham walked a few steps closer until he could make out the body of Ross, lying in the rocks. He was not surrounded by snow, but by snowpetal. Loham ran to Ross. In his heart, Loham sensed that Ross was still alive, though, to his eyes it appeared unlikely. Once Loham reached Ross, without hesitation, he reached down and touched him. Ross moaned. Loham knelt and gently lifted his head up, being careful not to hurt him. Ross was bloody, and a deep gash lay over his right eye. He had bruises on his face and body from hitting the rocks. "Ross, you'll be alright. Let me help you."

"Hold on, let me get some help. I'll get Shu, he'll know what to do— you'll see. It's gonna be alright."

Still dazed and confused, Ross struggled to reach out. He tried to grab Loham's wrist but was too weak and slow.

Loham was already running back toward Kumél. He yelled into the storm, "Shu! Shu!"

Chapter XXII
Seerae's Song

As suddenly as the struggle had begun, it ended, yet there was no celebration. Each member of the company of Shu, in all their varied states, conditions, and locations, began to realize the threat had gone. Only the storm remained, roaring and angry. Rain, snow, and ice were driven relentlessly through the air while thunder and lightning ripped and shook the heavens.

Because of the fog, they were scattered throughout the meadow, and there was no way of immediately accounting for their condition. Loham's calls cut through the ambient noise, finding the way to each and every ear. They were all aware of a surreal, ominous tension. The sense that something unspeakable had happened sank into each heart.

Loham's calls for Shu grew louder and louder as he hurried through the storm and closed in upon Alethia, Msusi, and Zoësh. Seerae and Glo were close by as well.

"Loham! Here, over here!"

Alethia's voice rang out, and Loham was quick to run toward it. Loham found them crowded under the overhanging rocks, hiding from the storm as much as they could.

"I can't find Shu. Ross is injured and Kumél too. We need to find him."

"I thought he was with you."

"He was, but he went to find Ross. I never saw him again. Then I found Ross, all beat up. Kumél's in pretty bad shape too."

"What about Gubrone and Huzesh?"

"I don't know. It's like they just disappeared. I was helping Ziminiar fight the dakoon."

"Where's the dakoon?"

"It flew away, into the storm."

"It just flew away?"

"Yeah, all of the sudden, it stopped fighting and flew away. Something changed."

"They could still be nearby. We must be careful, and we need to get to Ziminiar's cave. It will be dry and safe. We need to find Shu."

Alethia could feel something was very wrong. She knelt next to Zoësh. "We have to go now. We have to get you somewhere safe and dry."

She and Msusi helped Zoësh up, and Glo, expending every effort against the storm, led them to the entrance of Ziminiar's cave, which was not too far away. Seerae and Loham followed with pain lingering in their hearts. It was not a physical pain like that caused by a wound, but an, intuitive pain, like dread. They did not speak to each other, nor did they look at each other; they just followed slowly behind the others, quietly, pensively.

At the cave, Msusi turned to Loham. "Take me to Ross."

"Yeah, sure, but what about Shu?"

"Ross will know where he is. He was the last to see him, right?"

"Well, I don't know. I don't know if Shu ever found him."

"I'll go with you." Seerae's voice was insistent.

"Of course."

Alethia asked Loham, "What about Ziminiar and Kumél? We'll need their help."

"If they can help themselves. They are both really hurt."

"We have to find Jaroh. Maybe he is with Shu."

"Maybe. Let's go." Loham walked away from the cave.

"Loham!" Alethia yelled out. "Take Glo and Shim; they may be of help."

As quickly as it was possible, Loham and the others made their way to the stream and to where Loham had left Ross. Before long, they could see that Ziminiar had already made his way to Kumél and had helped him out of the water and onto the rocky shore. Kumél had taken a brutal beating at the hands of Gubrone. His face was swollen and bruised, with slashes and cuts, which had become caked with mud and hair and dried blood. Across his sternum, there were several gashes and one of his legs was cut badly and still bleeding. Ziminiar, though seriously wounded himself, was in much better condition and tried to stop the bleeding by wrapping it with a piece of his kilt.

Seerae was horrified at the sight of Kumél. She began to cry, for she had grown to care greatly for him. Seeing her friend so savagely beaten grieved her with the deepest sorrow.

Msusi noticed Seerae was crying. "He'll be alright, given a little time and attention. Don't let your heart sink." Msusi wiped a tear from Seerae's face. "You can stay with him, if you wish."

"No. I want to see Ross. I need to know that he's alright."

Loham pointed up the stream. "He should be just ahead, up there."

Seerae ran ahead in the direction Loham pointed, and Loham quickly followed. Seerae began to yell out, "Ross! Ross!"

"Here! I'm over here." At that moment, the shadowy form of Ross appeared through the fog. He was walking toward them. The wind pushed him from side to side, making every step difficult. Seerae ran to him. When she reached him, she saw he was bruised and bleeding from his injuries. She eagerly wrapped her arms around him and hugged him tightly.

"Not so tight!"

Seerae ignored his cry of pain and continued to hold him in her arms. Ross put his arms around her. She loosed her hold and looked into his eyes. She could see, through the blood, cuts, and bruises, a new torment, but she said nothing of it. Ross closed his eyes as he lowered his head. He felt ashamed of what he knew, of what he had seen and was hiding. He hoped Seerae would not ask him any questions, that she would not pry into the pain camouflaged behind the wounds and bruises.

Msusi approached from behind Seerae. She spoke to him in her soft tone. "Ross, Where's Shu?"

He tried to pretend he had not heard her. His silence, however, said more than he could have intended. Msusi began to understand what it was she had been feeling in her heart. The sharp, gnawing torment of her intuition did not allow her to feign naivety. She could feel the void and hollow emptiness of absence. She sensed Ross was hiding something about Shu but said nothing of her suspicion.

Ross looked at Msusi. Her eyes pierced through the ambiguity of his stare. He felt her, as he had felt her before, looking into his soul, exploring the hidden depths. Ross knew she could see what he was not saying.

"I need to find Alethia."

"She's back at the cave," Loham said.

"I can show you." Seerae's voice was eager.

"Glo will help you find your way. Seerae, we need you here to help tend to Kumél and Ziminiar."

Msusi put her hand on his arm. He could see the tears in her eyes. He struggled to keep his own emotions hidden. Msusi wanted to give him a reassuring smile, but her suspicions about the fate of Shu would not allow her to do so. She disguised her anguish behind a gentle hug.

"Here, take my sword, just in case. You shouldn't go unarmed."

"But won't you need it?"

"There are enough weapons here. Now go. We will be there just as quickly as we are able."

Ross took Glo into his hand and ran toward the cave. It was not long before the fog began to recede and the snow and ice gave way to only rain, large, heavy drops of rain and, at the same time, the wind calmed itself from its fury. Along the edge of the creek, Ross noticed something seemed out of place. He stepped behind a rock and stopped to look. His heart raced with fear and in his mind, he thought about the dakoons. He knew one of them was dead, but he feared the other might find him. He peered around the edge of the rock and looked at the unusual form. He worked up his courage and snuck behind another, closer rock. Glo looked at him. Her tiny voice called out.

"What is it?"

"I'm not sure. It could be the other gallue. I don't know yet."

What he saw never moved. He crept closer and closer until, finally, he was able to see it was the body of Gubrone. Even dead, Gubrone was terrifying. Ross felt dwarfed and intimidated by him. Ross carried Glo and walked slowly to the edge of the stream. Gubrone's body was on the far side. Ross jumped from one rock to another until he made it across. Once on the other side, he picked up his pace and ran toward the body. Gubrone's body had come to rest on its back, and the force of the stream had pushed him so hard against the rocky shore that the spear was pushed through him until most of it was protruding out of his belly. Gubrone's breastplate was torn from his chest and laying on the ground next to him. Right next to the exit wound of the spear, Ross could see another gaping wound. The spear had pierced the old Eleetrum Wound, which was still oozing with the putrid, yellow pus. Ross stepped up to the body, took hold of the spear, and pulled it out. Blood stained the spear of Amik. Ross began to walk away but paused. The voice of Shu echoed in his thoughts, *You must kill Gubrone and take the fourth face back.*

"The fourth face," Ross mumbled.

Ross thought about Shu, about why he had done what he had done. He knew he had to do everything possible to make it right, to make Shu's sacrifice worth it. He knew he had to find the fourth face. Ross turned and walked back to the body. He stood over it and looked down upon the grizzly sight, but he had never seen the Fourth Face and had no idea what it looked like or where it might be.

Nearby, unbeknownst to either of them, in the shadows of the rocks and stones, two corvuses were spying on them. It seemed that, at least for the time being, the flock of corvuses was nowhere to be found; the storm had driven them away. But actually a few remained.

"Ross, what are you doing? We have to go."

"I have to find it."

"Find what?"

"The fourth face. Alethia said it was always on him, but where?"

"No one here has ever seen the fourth face."

"How big is it? Do you have any idea?"

"Only Alethia and Shu would know."

"What's that?" Ross walked over to where Gubrone's arm was lying on some rocks. Around the forearm from the wrist to the elbow, was a thick, dark leather vambrace. It was tied around his arm with thick leather laces, woven vertically down the backside of his arm. Ross bent down and picked up the arm at the wrist, which was nearly as large as his entire leg. On the front side of the vambrace there was a strange symbol worn into the surface of the leather as if something was underneath the vambrace, causing it to wear and stretch. Ross felt the leather and pushed down on it until he was sure something was under it. Ross laid the arm back down, then took the sword Msusi gave him and cut through the weave until the edges of the vambrace started to pull apart. Ross yanked the leather guard out from under Gubrone's arm and found that whatever it was that had left the mark was embedded into the vambrace, between several layers. He slit the leather and sandwiched between the layers, was a long, blueish-black iron object. Ross held it in his hand. Suddenly, the simtu markings on his body began to glow and on one side of the metal object, engravings appeared, glowing in the blue light of the simtu. On the only side of the object that had markings, there was a raised triangular shape. In the triangle was a strange engraving of curved swirling lines that moved, swaying back and forth as he held it. He assumed it represented the wind as Alethia had said. All the markings were alive with blue light. "This has to be it, the fourth face!" Ross exclaimed. He quickly slipped the object back into the vambrace, stuffed the vambrace into his backpack, grabbed the spear and the sword, and ran to find Alethia. Without the fog, Ross could see the cave was close.

In the meantime, Alethia was taking care of Zoësh. Zoësh was strong, and her immortal body worked quickly to restore her strength and repair the wound. It was not long before she was sitting up and drinking some water. As she cared for Zoësh, Alethia sensed something was very wrong. She knew that soon enough she would know what it was that troubled her heart. She feared the worst. Then, she heard footsteps approaching the cave and cautiously peeked out of the entrance and saw Ross, running toward her. She stepped outside of the cave with great relief, knowing the trouble in her soul was not over him. She called out to him, "Ross."

Her eyes quickly fell upon the spear of Amik, which Ross held in his hand. Alethia saw the bloodstains. She closed her eyes, not wanting to see or know anything at all. She swallowed long and hard, then let out a deep sigh. Her throat became dry as tears welled up in her eyes. More than anyone else, Alethia knew the meaning and the ramifications of the legend. She knew what the voice of the Jupnie was saying, but in the immediate chaos of everything, the reality of it had never fully settled in her heart. She had not considered how it would feel to lose someone near to her, someone who had always been with her.

Death, no matter how, or to whom, it comes, or for what purpose, is an irrevocable offense, a circumvention of autonomous animation, an interruption to existence. It is never normal or natural or satisfying. It is an anomaly that a truly living creature cannot comprehend.

When he looked into her eyes, Ross was painfully aware Alethia already knew what he was about to tell her. He stammered. His lips seemed glued together. His eyes were blurry from tears. "I'm so—It's all my fault. I'm so sorry. Shu, He's . . ." Ross could find no way to tell her, no way to say the words. He pictured himself trying to tell Eve's father that Eve was dead. He knew he could never tell him, that he could never say the words to Randal about Eve. And now, he could not tell Alethia about Shu. The pain and sorrow he had not had a chance to feel before came rushing in upon him. He felt the same as he felt when Eve fell. Ross looked at the ground. He shook his head, and the tears began to fall from his eyes. He looked at Alethia as rain fell over the two of them, running down over their heads and washing over their faces. "I'm sorry. I'm so sorry," Ross repeated the phrase over and over. He dropped to his knees, broken and sobbing.

Glo sat on his hunched over shoulders and cried with him.

Alethia was unable to comfort him or to reach out to him in any way, for she was paralyzed by the news and by the sting of death and loss. They stood exposed in the rain, in their own separate spaces. Even though they were only a few steps away from each other, they felt isolated by the imperceptible chasm of grief. They wept.

"Where is he, Ross? Where is Shu?"

Zoësh's voice surprised him. He looked up, through his tears to see her standing over him. She held her hand over her wound, and it was obvious to him she was in great pain. She was also crying.

"I had to leave him, but Jaroh is with him."

"How could you leave him? How could you?"

"I didn't want to. He told me to. He said I had to go, I had to finish, I . . . I had to." Ross could not bring himself to tell her anything more. At that moment, it did not seem to matter why he did what he did—all that mattered was that Shu was dead.

Alethia wiped her tears away. She stood up and walked over to Ross. "We need to find him. Can you show us where he is?"

"Yeah, and Glo can help."

Alethia turned to Zoësh. "You should stay here. Rest. We will be back soon."

"Absolutely not. I will not stay behind!"

Alethia knew Zoësh's mind would not be changed. She smiled and put her hand on Zoësh's head, and then touched her cheek.

"Of course, you won't. Come, let's hurry then."

It was not long before Alethia heard a familiar voice calling out to them. "Alethia, Zoësh, over here." Zoësh turned to see Msusi, not far away, waving at them. Alethia saw that Seerae and Loham, along with Kumél and Ziminiar were with Msusi. Alethia, Zoësh, Glo, and Ross waited for the others who were moving very slowly. It was obvious that Kumél was seriously wounded and it would take all of them to help him move. Even the tiny tulwyths attempted to assist, though the intermittent gusts of wind made it hard for them to do much, other than illuminate the way. When they were finally reunited, it was obvious that every member of the company who was present was wounded and in pain, broken and bleeding.

They smiled and hugged and kissed each other, as close friends would, yet the obvious absence of Shu and Jaroh tempered their joy. Msusi was the first to speak out. "Gubrone is dead. Ross killed him. We saw his body just a little way back."

Alethia only nodded her head.

"Where is Shu?" Msusi asked.

Alethia turned to her and replied, "We're going to him now. Ross will show us the way."

Seerae, sensing something was amiss, looked to Zoësh. "Is everything alright?"

Zoësh lowered her eyes and said nothing. She just followed Alethia.

Ross looked back at Alethia and whispered, "It's not far."

As Ross stepped through a narrow gap between two large rocks, he realized he was stepping on the same tracks Shu had stepped on just moments before the spear pierced him. It was that narrow way, those formidable rocks and the fog that kept Shu from seeing what he was running into. Ross stopped. He was not sure he wanted to see what he knew he was about to see. In the fog, everything had seemed so unreal, mysterious, and dreamlike. Nevertheless, the fog was gone and the vivid definition of everything around him, of every stone, of every drop of rain, of every tiny snowpetal that bloomed, of every color, transformed the surreal into a harsh, unforgiving reality.

"What is it, Ross?" Alethia could sense they were very close. She knew in her heart that Ross's hesitation was due to fear. Not the kind of fear that elicits terror or panic, but the kind of fear that imposes upon the senses, demanding of the mind the ardent refusal of what is known, of what cannot be emotionally accepted.

"I'll be ok."

Ross took only a few more steps before he saw Jaroh. Ross stopped again, but this time he could not move from where he was standing. The vision of Shu's broken, lifeless body made him feel lifeless too. The pain he felt, that he could not escape, gnawed at his thoughts. He remembered when Zoësh sang her song, how sorrowful it was and how much agony was in her words. He did not understand then what she had felt, but now, seeing the death of an immortal he felt a pain he had never known before.

Slowly, one by one, they gathered around him. They too were arrested by what their eyes could see but their minds and hearts could not accept: the broken lifeless body of Shu laying in the arms of Jaroh. Jaroh wept so hard, so continuously that he did not notice they were watching.

Alethia walked slowly toward him. "Jaroh."

He did not act startled, he slowly looked up at her. Tears and deep sorrow clouded his vibrant eyes. He could not speak a single word, though he wanted to say something; he just looked back down at a friend he had known for longer than time could measure.

Alethia knelt next to her brother and took his hand in hers. She kissed it, then she laid her head upon his chest and cried grievous, unrestrained tears. The anguish of her unacquainted sorrow took flight on tortured, transcendent wings, soaring throughout the three realms.

At the feet of Shu, there was a puddle of rainwater and melted snow that was stained in his blood. Every drop of rain that fell into the puddle became like a drop of his blood, running over the rocks and ground until it flowed into the stream and then throughout all the realm.

Jaroh reached out and touched Alethia's head. He gently stroked her hair until she looked up at him. "Alethia, it's time. I must take him soon."

"I know but let them say their farewells first."

Everyone but Seerae stepped close and knelt down in silence and tears. The sight of Shu's lifeless body haunted their deep, private thoughts. The moment was solemn and sacred and, though it was only a moment, it was for each of his grieving friends, interminable. For every living thing, every creature, tree, mountain, and stream, it was eternal and unyielding, an anguish that would alter the course of life forever.

Seerae could not look at him. She refused to see Shu broken and lifeless. In her heart, she did not want this to be her last memory of him. She walked away from the others and cried, alone, clinging to those images of life and beauty that would linger in her thoughts as memories.

Ross heard Jaroh's words to Alethia and stood looking at him. Finally, Ross spoke to Jaroh. "Take him? Take him where?"

Alethia could see Ross was troubled by what Jaroh said. "Jaroh will take him home, back to Pardis, to our father."

"Your father?"

"Yes, to Eloh."

Ross looked away; tears poured from his eyes. He had not thought about what they would do with his body. He had not wanted to. He imagined, if anything, that they would bury him under a mound of rocks. It had never occurred to him what they would do with a dead body in Shuk. It never crossed his mind what happened to them when death came because he thought they were eternal, that they would never die.

Loham could see and feel Ross was struggling inside. He walked over to him and stood quietly beside him. Ross turned to look at him. It was the first time Ross had looked at him without a guarded demeanor.

"Why? Why'd he die? I thought he couldn't die."

Loham remembered what Hidook had told him when he had wondered the same thing. "*We are immortal, we can't die, but we can be killed.*" Loham tried to think of something to say to Ross. "Not everything is as it seems. Sometimes the unexpected happens."

Loham's off-handed comment struck an unintended yet resonating note in Ross's heart. It reminded him of something Shu had said to him not long ago: "*No matter the end, the journey that lies before you is a risk that may lead you to nothing less than the unexpected, and that is an adventure worth taking, is it not?*"

A sudden remarkable spark of hope began to glow in his heart, a secret flame that warmed his soul. It made him believe that Shu would somehow escape this death, that death was only temporary and that if Jaroh took Shu home, then he might live again. It was the same hope he had clung to whenever he thought about Eve, that she might not be dead, that if he could get home, she might be there, waiting for him, alive.

Amid the somber atmosphere, amid the billowing tempest, a piercing, resonate note began to float gracefully around them. Ross and Loham looked to see where it was coming from. Sitting alone on a rock, Msusi played her dukwán. She blew into the simple pipe, and out of it came a perfect single note that defied the storm raging in their souls and all around them. Another note followed, and the two notes danced in the turbulent air as if untouched by the commotion. Another, then another, and another note leapt from the instrument and together the notes twirled and spun and played through the chaos like carefree children. She played as if she were all alone, as if unmolested by sorrow or grief or wind or rain or even death. All eyes turned to her and every heart swelled to the calling of her music.

As the sound of the pipe persevered against the railing storm, floating over and around the company, the sullen firmament slowly conceded to the power of melody, all but surrendering to its allusive calmness. Then, as the storm raged and blew, the sky began to open above them. They could see the fury of the storm all around, like the eye of a tropical storm. The zealous tempest encircling the serene epicenter acted as if it were protecting them, standing guard against the corvuses and their other enemies. As the eye opened wider, the calm evening light flooded down through the towering cyclonic walls, shining upon the contrasting scene with hues of alpenglow refracted through the billions of cascading droplets of warm, spring like rain falling on them. Rays of blue, red, and purple, green, yellow, and orange danced through the air creating an aurora of colored lights, which descended to the ground.

A soft, perfect voice, draped with sorrow, began to sing out in melodic cadence to the notes of the dukwán. Seerae's voice filled the placid void. Her heart was swollen with emotion. Every word was like the emergence of little butterflies from their cocoons, full of life and color, flying gently, unintentionally through the air:

> *Don't be long gone, gone from my eyes.*
> *Don't be long gone away.*

I am here I am waiting for you,
Waiting here I will stay.
If ye go to da land of our father,
The land that's far, far and so near.
Will you come, come to your daughters,
Come with smile and with cheer?
For we be lonely, lonely without you,
Waiting for you to come near.
If ye go off to the land of our father,
Tell him we are still here.
Tell him we are waiting and watching,
Waiting and watching for him to appear.
Don't be long gone, gone from my eyes.
Don't be long gone away.
I am here, I am waiting for you.
Waiting here I will stay.

The tranquil aura of the music draped over everything like a soft blanket of snow. Kumél, for the first time since the battle had begun, stopped speaking the words of the Jupnie. For those few moments, all the strife of Shuk was forgotten. It was as if they had been transported to a different world in a different time. For each of them, what happened next, happened so unexpectedly and yet so exquisitely it was as if everything stopped, as if time and the motion of life and of all the worlds stopped. Drops of rain stopped falling from the sky. Instead, they hung suspended in the air like translucent spheres of liquid, like bubbles floating above the ground. The angry storm surrounding them now bowed its head in sorrow. There was no sound or movement, no fear or worry. There was no weight, nothing cold, nothing hot, no pain. Everything else appeared to dissipate except the slow, gentle motions of Jaroh picking up the limp body of Shu. Like a father holding his infant son, Jaroh held Shu, draped across his arms and close to his chest. Alethia caressed Shu's head and with tears, began to say something in her Theoscian tongue. Ross listened and was reminded of the obsequies the priest had spoken at Daniel's funeral.

"Ooun amille ame, Shu, ee holum et ame t'osh anom un ale omer, du Pardis ee un Eloh,"

Everything in the physical realm around him was still, paused, Ross could see all the memories of his life: memories of death and sorrow and loneliness, from childhood until Eve's fall, then Shu, falling to the spear. The memories were raging like a storm, sequentially through his mind in vivid, graphic detail. All the pain of the past—even of very recent moments— every unsolicited torment, all the anguish, all the guilt and regret he had tried to forget, poured upon his soul like the tempest that surrounded them. As he watched and listened to Alethia's voice, the conflict of his soul found inexplicable rest. Though he could not understand the words she spoke over Shu, Ross felt them as if they were spoken to him, to free him, to assuage the guilt, to put an end to his endless sorrow. "It's time."

Ross had become so caught up in his own thoughts he had not noticed Alethia come over to where he was standing. She touched him on the hand. "You should go to him."

Ross walked solemnly over to Jaroh and looked at Shu. To Ross, Shu did not look like he was dead. Ross had seen dead bodies before. The ashy, lifeless skin covering bones like a poorly fitted, oversized shirt gave him the creeps. But Shu was different; he looked as if he was sleeping. Ross swallowed and reached out to Shu's hand, which was hanging below his body. Ross took it and held it. Even in death, Shu emanated with something alive—the Elohan Essentia—an immutable force of life that pushed its way into Ross's soul. When Ross felt it, he remembered the touch of Eve on his face, which carried that same living force. Ross lifted Shu's hand and arm and placed them carefully on his chest. He said not a single word. He felt a deep groaning, and then he turned and walked back toward Alethia.

One by one, each of them approached and said their farewells. Msusi went back and started playing her song again and Seerae sang along. The rest of them simply stood in silence and watched as Jaroh spread his wings. He ascended into the open skies above, until he was above the realm of Shuk, above the towering clouds. Then, like a flash of light, he disappeared.

As soon as Jaroh was out of sight, the rain began to fall, and the clouds returned over the company of Shu. The rain fell with unremitting determination, drop after drop, soaking everything, every rock and pebble, every blade of grass, every tree, every ignoble shred of cloth, every covered and uncovered scale of skin and hair, every beast and bird and creature, sodden with cold wetness.

A lingering sense of disbelief hung in the air and on the conscience of everyone. Dazed and heartbroken, they stood in the drenching rain with empty eyes, unable to walk away.

Out of the rain, from somewhere in the rocks, a corvus flew past Ross, its wing raking across his face. Mechanically, without thought or emotion, Ross turned his head to follow the bird's flight. The ugly black bird landed not far from where he was standing. Laying on the ground was the body of Huzesh. No one had noticed it until then. The corvus descended on the corpse and began to pick at it. Soon there was another corvus picking and pulling at the flesh.

Alethia saw it and quickly called out to everyone.

"We must get back to the cave. It may not be safe out here. Come, everyone come. Ziminiar, help Kumél, and Seerae, you and Ross help Zoësh. The tulwyths will lead us. We have to move quickly, before the darkness closes in."

Without a word, they all did as Alethia asked and made their way back to Ziminiar's cave.

As they approached the cave, Loham noticed a large bird circling overhead. He studied the bird, which was descending from the sky, through the rain and wind and turned back to the others who were also watching it. He yelled out to them, "The corvuses, they're back. We have to get inside!"

The bird flew over Loham's head, then landed on a mound of rocks over the entrance of Ziminiar's cave. Loham raised his sword and would have hurled it at the bird, but Ziminiar intervened. "Nae, Loham." Ziminiar grabbed Loham's arm. "Ut bae u fren. Ee means us no harm."

As they drew closer to the cave and to the large bird, it became apparent it was a strigidae, a large gray strigidae. Only Ziminiar and Kumél had ever seen a gray strigidae before, for they were very rare in the land of Shuk and one of this age and size, even more rare.

To many, the gray strigidae was a sign of danger, though to Alethia, they were known to be a bearer of secrets, a listener of whispers, hearing but never seen. "Why has the gray strigidae come to your cave, Ziminiar?"

"Ee bae u spy un da valley o'souls. Ee mus ha saen somting, or haerd somting."

"A spy?"

"Aye, mae spy. Ee bae culled Kantu, un ee tells mae wut da gallues bae up t'. A expect dar t'bae u bit o'bad news uf ee ha com."

"Hmm ..."

Ross looked at the large feathered raptor. Its body was covered with feathers of many shades of gray. It had large, dark eyes and held its head high. It had a short, curved black beak that came to a very sharp point at its end. The strigidae appeared to be quite calm, in spite of everything.

"It's not like those horrible black birds, is it?"

"No, Ross. If she has come, she has come with a secret, a secret of the unpleasant sort."

Alethia knew the death of Gubrone would have a far-reaching impact on the realm, an impact so unexpected, so overwhelming its repercussions would shake everything in all corners of Shuk. She knew that the spell binding the nephesh had been weakened and that their song would soon begin to escape the valley, finding its way to Tirnan and into the hearts of Amik's seed. Though she did not know what it had seen, the arrival of the gray strigidae was an omen that spoke an irrevocable message in itself.

Ziminiar held out his arm to the bird. The strigidae hopped from the rocks to his arm, and Ziminiar carried it into the cave.

Once they were in the cave, Alethia turned to Ziminiar. "What secrets has she to tell?"

Ziminiar spoke to Kantu. Kantu made a strange sound, which was a combination of clucking, cooing, and whistling that did not sound like any language at all; however, Ziminiar understood it quite well. Once Kantu stopped, Ziminiar turned to Alethia and the others. His face showed deep distress, and his eyes exposed an inner turmoil.

"Sinistradt ha taken rule o'Shuk. Ee bae unifying da res o'da Twelve un ee plans t'destroy da waif nephs."

Msusi was the first to react. She jumped to her feet and argued, "What? Destroy us? But he can't; it's against the covenant!"

Seerae said nothing at all. She only sat and stared at the floor of the cave.

Zoësh attempted to stand, but her wound was still quite tender and quickly reminded her of it. "Ouch!"

"Zoësh, you must rest," Seerae urged her.

Alethia spoke to them all in an authoritative but gentle tone, "We have clearly underestimated the depth of treachery buried here in Shuk, but we cannot let our anger make us impatient or foolhardy. We have to be wise and more cunning than our adversary."

"How ... how will Sinistradt do this?"

"Da rune o'death—thut bae all Kantu knows."

"When? Does he know?"

"Nae. Dar bae one mur ting: Sinistradt ha sunt corvuses t'track down Gubrone un ee ha sunt u band o'custos t'hunt fur eem un kull eem."

Ross spoke out in a tone they had not heard from him before, a tone of strength and confidence that sounded a little like something Shu would have said. "Well, I guess they're a little late for that!"

"Aye, they are," Loham agreed, smiling.

There was one important thing that came to Alethia's mind, something she had forgotten about until that very moment. She looked around at everyone, and then she stopped at Ross. "Have you got it?"

Her voice cut through the air, clear and distinct. Everyone was quiet and waited for Ross to reply. Ross knew immediately what she meant. He slid his backpack off his shoulder, took out the leather vambrace, and handed it to Alethia. "It's there, between the layers."

All eyes fell to the vambrace. Alethia could see the pocket from which protruded the black iron fourth face of the Kleid o'Miht. She retrieved the object from the pocket and held it in her hands. The sign of the wind and the other markings that were engraved in the face illuminated.

"Is that it?" Ross asked.

"It is. You have done well, but now we must get it into safe keeping; no one can know that we have it. Ross, was anyone watching you when you found it?"

"No, it was just Glo and me."

"Are you sure?"

"Pretty sure...I think."

Now Alethia doubted. She knew there were bound to be a few corvuses hiding here and there. Nevertheless, she did not disclose her concern to anyone else.

"There is only one place that it will be safe: The Cave of Pelah.

Someone will have to take it there."

There was no reply, not even a single word from anyone. It was not that anyone was refusing or even afraid. It was only that the suggestion of splitting up, of not staying together, felt, somehow, unexpected and seemed ill advised.

"There is nothing that we can do right now. We will rest here tonight until the storm settles and until Zoësh and Kumél are better, then Ziminiar and Msusi will take the fourth face back to Pelah."

Ross wanted to say something, he *needed* to say something, but he did not want to appear to be questioning Alethia or undermining her in any way. Alethia could see the uncertainty in Ross's eyes. She smiled softly and asked, "What is it, Ross? What do you wish to say?"

"Well, Shu, told me to find the Kleid o'Miht and to never let it out of my sight. I know you may be right, but if I am the one who had to find it, then I am the one who must also keep it safe."

Alethia knew Ross was right. She nodded her head approvingly.

Running through each of their minds was a myriad of thoughts, most of which were worrisome. There was, however, one thought that occupied every mind, especially that of the nephesh. Only one of them was willing to speak of it.

Loham looked up at Alethia and spoke out. "What will we do about Sinistradt and this evil he is planning? How will we stop him?" His voice was quiet, but his mettle was sure, fixed like the temper of iron. The confidence that resonated from him lifted the mood in the cave and every eye locked sharply upon him. He did not feign grit, for it was not in his nature. For some strange reason beyond knowing, Loham came upon a new sense of assurance and with it came the ferocity of lions. He did not doubt, whatsoever, that they could overcome this approaching threat.

Alethia honestly answered him, "That, I do not know, but we will find a way."

A quiet somber hush fell over the company. Softly, like a whisper, Seerae began to sing to the troubled hearts of her friends. Like the thick, sweet flow of honey from its comb, the melody poured into the dark void surrounding the cave:

Don't be long gone, gone from my eyes

Don't be long gone away
I am here I am waiting for you
Waiting here all alone,
If ye go to da land of our father
The land thut bae far, far and so near
Will you come, come to your daughters
Come with smile and with cheer.

Outside of the cave, the strength of the storm had begun to wane as if it was tired and lying down to rest for the night. A luminous, full, bright moon pushed its light through the thinning clouds and shone on the rushing waters of the stream nearby. A black shadow flew over the stream and landed on the corpse of Gubrone. Soon, another shadow flew by and descended on the dead body. One of the corvuses looked at the other and called out. The other corvuses looked around and then spread their wings and flew up into the night as the song of Seerae filled the air:

For we be lonely, lonely without you
Waiting for you to come near
If ye go off to da land of our father
Tell him we are still here
Tell him we are waiting and watching
Waiting and watching for him to appear.

The End

Alan Delahay

Glossary of Names and Terms

Aion, The River – Eternal waters.

Alaya Mountains – A large range of mountains in Pardis

Alethia – Daughter of Eloh. Keeper of truth.

Amik – Friend of Eloh. From the Latin term, Amicus, meaning friend.

Anima – City in Assuk, where Eloh lived. From the Latin term, Anima, meaning life.

Annum – One year.

Antisuyo Mountains – A range of mountains in the realm of Tirnan.

Apostas – Deserters from Attar. Fallen Kerolus are neither joined to Eloh nor Attar. At times, they assist Ross.

Ardu Needles – A towering rock formation of spires where the cave and domain of Sinistrad was hidden.

Assuk – The realm of Eloh or the land of Eloh.

Atramentous Valley, The – A valley named after the term atramentous, meaning black, inky or ink-like.

Attar – The Archkerolus who led a rebellion against Eloh. According to Canaanite mythology, Attar was the Morning Star who tried to dethrone Baal, but failing, he descended and ruled the underworld. A type of Satan.

Aurora Path – The way of light whereby the souls of the lost are carried to the city of Anima and to Eloh.

Bauble – A small insignificant item, unimportant and toy-like. A showy trinket, like a jester's scepter.

Bikkja – An old Norse word for female dog or bitch.

Biritum, The Valley of – From the Aramaic term biritum/birit narim. It refers to the land east of the Euphrates River or Mesopotamia, the land between the Euphrates and Tigres rivers.

Blackstock – A marsh plant with long sharp needles on its stems.

Blue-winged Sturnellas – A small songbird, much like a meadowlark.

Carascians – Formerly Helions. Descendants of the Cementars. They were raised by Eloh after the destruction of the Cementar clans. The Carascians were the citizens of Assuk. Each of their souls and minds were one, much like Eloh's, until the curse of Attar caused them to become two separate beings, the Sapiens and the Nephesh.

Cardinal Directions – North - Norð, Norõn - Northern
South - Suð, Suõn - Southern
East - Ushus, Ushun - Eastern
West - Wes, Weson – Western

689

Northwest - Nor-wes
Southwest - Su-wes
Northeast - Nor-ush
Southeast - Su-ush

When the use of the direction is used with "ward" such as "westward":

Norward

Suward

Ushward

Wesward

Cave of Gubrone – The stronghold of Gubrone, deep in the core of a cave in the Valley of Souls

Cave of Pelah – The burial location of the body of Amik. Derived from the Cave of Machpelah, the believed burial site of the biblical Adam.

Cementars – Ancient stonemasons of whom Amik was a descendent.

Charroahan Tree – Large, deciduous tree that grew along the rivers and in the wetlands. Like a cottonwood tree.

Corvus/es – Blackbirds of the mist, like crows.

Crepuscular – Of or relating to the twilight. Also, active in the twilight.

Cubit – Length of measure. 1 cubit equals about 18 inches.

Custos – Gallue guards who were stationed on the way to the Valley of Souls.

Dakoons – Gallues with wings and talons, who have the breath of fire.

Dakkrahs – Weak, subservient creatures. Rodents and scavengers that were timid, smelly and diseased.

Daniel Yager – Best friend of Ross.

Dhital, Nepal – Ross began his trek to Machapuchare from this village.

Diffoosh, The Well of – A deep well, in the Cave of Gubrone, filled with water that was bitter and smelled of sulfur.

Dukwán – A wooden instrument, like a flute or a duduk, played by the Nephesh.

Eadoun Springs – The source of the Aion River.

Eeolythah – Gigantic stone sentinels that came alive when offered blood sacrifices. They were the guardians of the secret caves of the Gallues.

Eleetrum Shard – A shiv shaped from one of Attar's bones and was used to mark the Gallues.

Eleetrum Wound – The wound made from the Eleetrum Shard. The wound carried by Gubrone.

Eloh – Husbandman over all of Pardis and friend to Amik.

Elohan Essentia – The spirit of life.

Eon – The bathing pool of the Kerolus; these waters were poisoned by the malice of Attar.

Eve Bannister – Fiancée of Ross.

Falls of Jaroh – Waterfall coming from the Pool of Levitus

Gallues – The minions of Attar; fallen Kerolus.

Gamlak – An Archkerolus.

Gates of Abyssus – Massive iron gates forged by Remmel and Sargel to lock the pit that imprisoned Attar and the Gallue armies.

Geddan Valley – A valley in the Alaya Mountains. The location of the war between Eloh and Attar.

Gershom Forest, The – A sanctuary forest in the realm of Shuk

Glo – A luna-tulwyth who befriended Msusi.

Gray Strigidae – A large, gray raptor in the owl family gifted with special abilities to spy and to hear secrets. The sight of them meant an omen of danger.

Gubrone – An Archgallue who ruled one of the 12 domains of the Valley of Souls.

Haemus, The Plain of – A vast plane-land in Shuk, extending from the Telohm Mountains to The Great Sea.

Helions – Now Carascians.

Hidook – A renegade Gallue who aided Huzesh; possessed power over the corvuses and other small creatures in Shuk.

Hoddosh – A snitch who traveled with Morak.

hOmsut – A natural stone fortress outside the Valley of Biritum where Livia and her family found refuge from Attar.

Huzesh – A Gallue who ruled over the Realm of the Mist in the Telohm Mountains.

Ibon, Yellow-breasted – A small bird, like a sparrow.

Illysian Gorge – The abyss that separated Gershom Forest from the rest of Shuk. The word, Illysian, came from the Greek word Elysian. The Elysian field was a paradisiacal land of plenty where the heroic and righteous dead hoped to spend eternity.

Impastious Gorge – The chasm caused by the River Aion, that divided Shuk from Tirnan.

Impetus Mountains – Mountains in Assuk where the Eadoun Springs were found.

Incantus Dominus – The incantation of the master. A spell spoken by Gubrone over the dakoons.

Isinglass – Muscovite Mica; a transparent and reflective rock material.

Jaarah Falls – A waterfall fed by the Pool of Levitus.

Jaroh – The Kerolus spy who found the lair of Attar.

Jekkid – A Gallue tracker skilled at hunting the Nephesh.

Julie Blair – Mother of Ross.

Jupnie – An ancient breath or prophecy that never fails to be fulfilled.

Kantu – The gray strigidae that spied on The Twelve.

Kerolus – Celestial winged warriors of Pardis and friends of Eloh.

Kleid o' Miht – Key of Power given to Amik and stolen from him by Attar. Kleidi from Greek, meaning key and miht from Old English, for might.
Kleid o' Rewellen – Key of Power or Rule. Rewellen from Middle English, meaning power or rule.
Klamata, Pass of – Pass above the Valley of the Souls. Klamata from Greek, meaning tears.
Kumél – An aposta that traveled with Ross and assisted him on his journey.
Kveech Mountains – A volcanic range of mountains where the Cementar clan lived and were destroyed by a volcanic eruption.

Levitas, Pool of or Levitas – A pool of water in the high mountains of Shuk where the droplets of water rise from the surface of the pool and hang suspended in the air, almost like carbonation. Those who step into the pool become suspended on the surface of the water and are physically changed so that their souls appear and can be seen. This is a place of transformation.
League – Measure of distance. Approximately 3 miles.
Leumys – A Luna-Tulwyth who aids Loham.
Livia – A Carascian and the wife of Amik
Loham – The Nephesh of Ross.
Lucleem – A Gallue hunter who searched for the foreigner.
Luna-Tulwyth – A small, flying creature that glows with moonlight even when there is no moon. From the Welsh term Tulwyth Teg or Fairy. Luna is from the moonlight.
Lyzop – The leader of the four Gallues who hunted the Nephesh with Morak.

Msusi – A Nephesh who helps Ross.
Mallaeus – The Archkerolus who forged the Kleid o' miht. Mallaeus from the Latin word malleus, meaning hammer.
Massagt Gorge – Narrow chasm through the west Telohm Mountains, where the River Chimosh flows to the sea.
Mate – A Nephesh whose Sapien is still living.
Mēgs or Mēglydaim, The – The Hunting beasts of the Archgallues on Shuk. They hunt the Nephesh and bring them into captivity in the Valley of Souls. Mega from Greek for large, Lycon from Greek for wolf, daimonion from Greek for demon.
Mentis – The former term for Sapien.
Meredith Yager – Mother of Daniel.
Milech – An Archkerolus.
Mitch Yager – Father of Daniel.
Molissk – A Gallue hunter who searched for the foreigner.
Monadnock – (məˈnædnɒk/ or inselberg) An isolated rocky hill, knob, ridge, or small mountain that rises abruptly from a gently sloping or virtually level surrounding plain. Wikipedia.com
Moon – A measure of twenty-nine to thirty days. Approximately one month.
Morak – A Gallue hunter and tracker. Formerly Korak.

Mount Buresh – The volcanic mountain where the body of Norzaaq was cast.

Mount Ducapita – The ancient mountain where Attar fled from Eloh, also known as Machapuchare.

Mount Sagar – Jaroh's location when he blew the Horn of War. The short name for Sargarmatha or Mount Everest.

Mount Soteria – The Mountain of Deliverance where the Horn of Shukeer was found.

Narcude – The eldest son of Amik. He sent his Nephesh into Shuk as a snitch for Attar.

Ne m'oubliez pas – The French phrase of "forget me not' or 'don't forget me'.

Nephesh – The soul or essence of a bodied person of Shuk. The souls of the Carascians from Tirnan living in Shuk. A person's life or vital breath.

Noorak – A Gallue slave to Tukkir.

Norman Blair – Father of Ross.

Norzaaq – The Nephesh Snitch of Narcude.

Ocktush – The corvus serving Chiddush and tasked with acquiring the Eleetrum Shard.

Orphan/Waif – A Nephesh whose Sapien had died.

Papio – A creature much like a baboon.

Pass of Borak, The – A treacherous mountain pass above the Atramentous Valley.

Pass of Ardu – A secret passage that lead out of the Valley of Souls from the north (Norõ).

Palm – A length of measure that equaled about 4 inches.

Pokhara, Nepal – The village where Ross began his journey to Machapuchare.

Popinus Tree – A high altitude evergreen tree like the Bristle Cone Pine.

Psang – The sherpa who guided Ross and Eve to the base of Machapuchare.

Puggin – A small, burrowing rodent much like a mole or a ground squirrel that looked like a cross between a wild pig and an aardvark. It was about the size of an average dog.

Quavak – One of Jabodaan's Gallue slaves.

Quoio Tree – A giant evergreen tree much like the giant redwoods.

Remmel – An Archkerolus who was faithful and true to Elo. He was mighty in battle.

Ross Blair – A sojourner in a foreign land.

Sapien/s – The will, intellect and reasoning of the bodied people of Tirnan. From "homo sapien".

Seasons:
•   Spring - Bloom

-     Summer - Shine
-     Fall - Blush
-     Winter - Frost

Sargel – An Archkerolus who was gifted with visions.

Seerae – Eve's Nephesh who traveled with Ross and his group. Her name originated from the Tigrinya language meaning Eve.

Seir – An Aposta.

Shamar – The Infinite Manifestation of truth and knowledge. A spirit of authenticity and truth.

Shim – One of the luna-tulwyths that helped Ross and the company.

Shu – Son of Eloh who aids Ross

Shuk – The realm of the souls.

Shukeer, The Horn of – From the Islamic word shukr which meant the responsiveness of God. The Horn of Shukeer was also called the Horn of Deliverance. It was considered by the inhabitants of shuk to be a myth, for only the descendants of Amik could use it to call upon the help of Eloh and the Kerolus armies of Assuk.

Sidhe (side-he) – The realm of the dead.

Simtu – A blue, living mark, like a tattoo, which was worn by the Carascians. The term originated with the ancient Egyptians; borrowed from the Aramaic term, sěnîta, which was an ink marking or a tattoo.

Snitches of Shuk, The – Spies of the Archgallues, fallen Nephesh traitors who traded in information and in their own kind.

Snowpetal – A small, white flower that grew where Ross walked and bloomed when the snowflakes fell.

Sufrar – One of Gubrone's Dakoons.

Sun – One day or twenty-four hours.

Sunnop – A snitch that traveled with Morak.

Tarterniem – A metal, also known as titanium, used to make the spears of the Kerolus.

Teercus, The River – River in Shuk that flows through the Plain of Haemus to the Great Sea.

Telohm Mountains – Mountain Range in Shuk.

Tenush – A primitive lute, like a viola, that belonged to Ziminiar.

Thelion/s – Now Theoscian/s.

Theoscian/s – Formerly Thelion/s. Masters of the realm of Pardis such as Eloh, Shu and Alethia. The name originated from the Gaelic terms theos which meant god and cian which meant ancient.

Tiffany Blair – Ross's sister.

Trouveur (French) – A minstrel, songwriter, balladeer or poet.

The Twelve – Archgallues or Chief Gallues.

1.   Gubrone

2.   Tukkir
3.   Unattah
4.   Jabodaan
5.   Sinistradt
6.   Puttinash
7.   Borash
8.   Rutunick
9.   Chiddush
10.   Mootthont
11.   Nernishut
12.   Zeshkant

The River Chimosh – A wide, raging river that flowed through the central region of the Valley of Souls that acted as a boundary between the norõ region and the two suõ regions.

The Way of Jaroh – A secret stone path behind the Falls of Jaroh that led to the Pool of Levitus.

Tirnan (teer-nan) – The realm of Amik. It was overtaken by Attar and his minions.

Tormut – One of Gubrone's dakoons.

Triakis – Black granite object that possessed Attar's song. An oracle of song given to Amik.

Tuak River – A river that ran through Gershom Forest.

Tulleye – A luna-tulwyth who helped Alethia and Kumél.

Tushun – A region near the Telohm Mountains that was known for its imposing boulder field that spanned many leagues.

Ufrasis, The River – River Flowing through the realm of Tirnan.

Utuks – The evil spirits or demons who worked against the Tirnanites and sometimes possessed them.

Uuduk – The slave Gallue who served Sinistradt.

Valley of Dolus, The – The place where Attar gathered the minions. Dolus came from the Latin term for treachery.

Venustas Woods – The place on Assuk where Eloh lived and the site of the city of Anima.

Veritas, The Well of – (The Well of Truth) A chamber where the archives of history were held and where Alethia lived.

Veroot – The slave Gallue of Sinistradt who stole Ross's ice axe from Gubrone.

Waif/Orphan – A Nephesh whose Sapien has died.

Xanthis – Yellow vines with broad leaves.

Zemorthra Falls – Ancient water falls of the Aion River that flowed into the Impastious Gorge.

Ziminiar – The Aposta who told Ross the secret to binding Attar.
Zoësh – A Nephesh who traveled with Ross and Kumél. They often helped each other. Zoe came from the greek term meaning spiritual life or life. Zoe also came from the Hebrew term meaning Eve.

General Notes:
A legend (Latin, legenda, "things to be read") is a narrative of human actions that are perceived both by teller and listeners to take place within human history and to possess certain qualities that give the tale verisimilitude. Legend, for its active and passive participants includes no happenings that are outside the realm of "possibility", defined by a highly flexible set of parameters, which may include miracles that are perceived as actually having happened, within the specific tradition of indoctrination where the legend arises, and within which it may be transformed over time, in order to keep it fresh and vital, and realistic. A majority of legends operate within the realm of uncertainty, never being entirely believed by the participants, but also never being resolutely doubted.

Appendix A
Kerolus and Gallue Dialectic Vocabulary

Because the kerolus and gallue characters speak with a heavy brogue dialect, this partial vocabulary list is provided to assist the reader in the interpretation of the characters' dialogue. The following vocabulary list should be considered as only partial as there are many uses of words by the kerolus and gallue characters, which may not be in this list. As well, there are many words that have different meanings within the context of the dialogue between the characters. The reader should interpret any meanings within such a context, should there be the use of two words having the same spelling yet, within the context, having different meanings or uses. Most of these distinctions are recognizable within the context of the dialogue.

It is important to note that from character to character there may be slight variations in the use of words from the standard use of speech and dialect.

A

A' - As
Aenuff - Enough
Aer - Ear
Aesy - Easy
Aet - Eat
Afaered - Afraid
Afore - Before
Afta - After
Agan - Again
An, Un - And
Anoter - Another
Ar - Are
Arse - Ass
Aye - Yes

B

B'gun – Begin
B'gunun - Beginning
B'hin - Behind
B'laeve – Believe
B'lung - Belong
B'side/s - Beside/s
B'traed – Betrayed
Bae - Be, Is
Bcom/Bcoms - Become/Becomes
Bes - Best
Bot - Both
Bout - About
Brang – Bring
Buk - Back
Bun – Been

C

Canna - Cannot/Can't
Chidin – Chiding
Claen – Clean
Claer – Clear
Com - Come
Covnant – Covenant
Cud - Could
Cumpny - Company
Cun - Can

D

D' - Do
D'saeve - Deceive
D'sease – Disease
Da -The
Dae - They
Dangrus – Dangerous
Dar - There
Deir - Their
Des – These
Dis – This
Doin - Doing
Dose - Those
Douh - Though
Dud - Did
Dufrant - Different
Dunna - Don't/Do not

E

Eary – Every
Ee - He
Eean - Even
Eem - Him
Ees - His
Er - Her

F

Fael - Feel
Faer - Fire
Faether/ Da - Father/ Dad
Fallun - Fallen
Fare - Fear
Fin - Find
Finin – Finding
Firs - First
Forgut/Forgutin - Forget/Forgetting
Forner - Foreigner
Foun - Found
Frae – Free
Fraedom – Freedom
Frum - From
Frun/s - Friend/s
Fur - For

Furgivness – Forgiveness

G

Gae – Go
Gaein – Going
Garduns – Gardens
Gud – Good
Gut – Get

H

Ha/ Huv - Has, Have
Hae/ Ha – How
Hae - High
Haelp - Help
Haer - Hear
Haerd - Hard
Haert - Heart
Haertbreak – Heartbreak
Hare – Here
Hun/s - Hand/s
Huppae – Happy

I

Iern – Iron

J

Jesin - Jesting
Jus – Just

K

Kae - Key
Kaep - Keep
Kin - Kind
Kull/Kulled - Kill/Killed
Kupt - Kept

L

Lard/s - Lord/s
Laeve – Leave
Lik - Like
Liv/Livs - Live/Lives
Luft - Left
Luk - Look
Lund - Land
Lung - Long
Luse - Loose,

Lose
Lut - Let
Luts - Let's

M

Ma – May
Maad – Made
Mae – Me
Maen – Mine
Maen/Maen'n - Mean/Meaning
Maet – Meet
Maet – Might
Mu – My
Mubae – Maybe
Muk - Make
Mumry – Memory
Mumries – Memories
Mun – Mind
Muny – Many
Mur - More
Mus – Must
Muttar – Matter

N

Naer - Near
Nah - Now
Nam - Name
Nae'er - Never
Nae/No - No
Naed – Need
Naedin – Needing
Nare – Neither
Nut - Not
Nutin – Nothing

O

O' - Of
O'er - Over
Ol' - Old
Ony - Only
Ony - Any
Onyting – Anything

P

Problum – Problem

Q

Quik – Quick

R
Raedy – Ready
Rael - Real
Raelm – Realm
Raely – Really
Res - Rest
Rugret - Regret
Rumumbar –
Remember

S
Sae – See
Saecret - Secret
Saek – Seek
Sael/Saels -
Self/Selves
Saen – Seen
Saes – Saw
Serf/s -
Servant/s
Shae – She
Shud – Should
Shunt -
Shouldn't
Shunt - Should
not
Skaem/Skaemin
-
Scheme/Schemi
ng
Slaep – Sleep
Somon/s -
Someone/s
Somting –
Something
Spaek - Speak
Splat – Split
Spuld -
Spilled/Spilt
Stat - Start
Sun – Send
Sur - Sure
Swaet – Sweet

T
T'/ Ta - To
T'gaer - Together
Tae - Too
Tam - Time
Thun - Then
Thum- Them
Thunk - Thought
Thut - That

Ting/s - Thing/s
Tink – Think
Tis - It's
Tol - Told
Trae - Try
Traed - Tread
Trus - Trust
Tun – Tend

U
Uf - If
Ufter – After
Um – Them
Un - In
Unner - Under
Unsaer/s -
Answer/s
Usk - Ask
Ut – It

V
Vary – Very

W
Wae – Away
Wae – Way
Wae – We
Waer - Was
Waer – Were
Waern't - Was
not/ Were not
Wais – Waste
Waitin – Waiting
Wanna - Want
Weel - Well
Wery - Worry
Whae - Why
Whaer - Where
Wit - With
Wud - Would
Wull - Will
Wun – When
Wunnar -
Wonder
Wunt - Went
Wut – What

X

Y
Ye, Ya - You
Yer - Your
Yersaelf -
Yourself
Yur - You're/ You

are

Z

Appendix B
The Elohan Script or Alphabet

The Elohan Alphabet is derived from the English alphabet in that each letter has an upper case and a lower-case form and is expressed from A – Z. The Elohan script is made up of these letters in, in many cases, does not spell out an entire word or phrase. In many of the cases illustrated in the book, the Elohan letters represent a word or a mark or a symbol or they are written so as to cryptically express a message, promise or prophecy written, engraved, carved or illuminated.

A	a	B	b	C	c	D	d	E	e
F	f	G	g	H	h	I	i	J	j
K	k	L	l	M	m	N	n	O	o
P	p	Q	q	R	r	S	s	T	t
U	u	V	v	W	w	X	x	Y	y
Z	z								

The mark of Eloh - for example is the word Eloh in the Elohan script. Each of the letters, E,L,O,H are carefully arranged to create the mark or symbol of Eloh.

Appendix C
Elohan Writings, Promises and Prophecies

The Mark of Eloh:

From the Pit:

Translated to the common tongue the inscription read:

"Out of the darkness and void a way has been made; the light of Eloh will lead you away from the shadows and into a new world. Let this hope guide you, that a day comes when your brokenness will be healed and when Pardis will be whole once again. There is one who is coming, of the line of your father; he will walk the Aurora Path and pierce the heart of the cruel masters, with a spear stained in Theoscian blood. In that day, you will see a new moon standing in the full light of day. Then you will know that the time is near, when you will return to the realm of Eloh."

Inscription over the Cave of Pelah:

Translation:

"Open wide ye gates of Pelah to the Lamp of Veritus who comes to comfort the sorrows of Amik. He will be pierced by the darkness, and the oil of light will pour out upon the shadows, preparing the way for Eloh."

The Inscription on Loham's Dukwán:

Translation:
"Every breath breathed here is to every hearer a breath of its master Attar."
Script around the bezel of the Kleid o'Miht:

Translation:
"The Power of The Kleid o'Miht Shall Only Obey The One to Whom Eloh has Given It and Shall Not be Circumvented In Any Wise."

Script in the Isinglass:

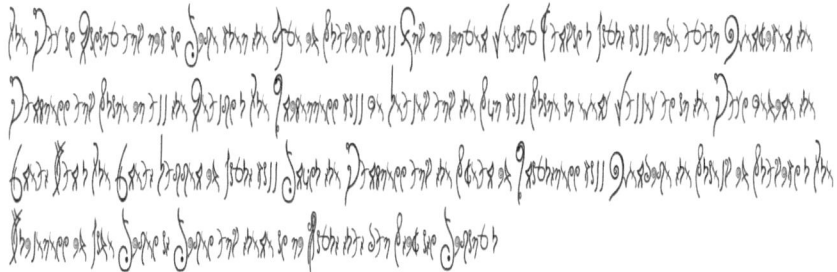

Translation:
"The day is rising and now is come, when the age of shadows will end, no longer vexing Pardis. Light will once again overpower the darkness and shine on all the realms. The brokenness will be healed, and the sun will shine in every valley as in the days before the Great War. The great hammer of light will crush the darkness and the spear of brightness will overcome the shield of shadows. The wholeness of life comes, it comes, and there is no might that can stop its coming."

About Alan Delahay

Alan Delahay grew up in the shadow of the Rocky Mountains, which formed in him a passion for wilderness and mountain climbing. Alan is a writer, photographer, and poet-philosopher, influenced by authors and poets such as Eldridge, Chesterton, Buechner, and Bronte. Their work and style of writing is evident in the detail and thoughtfulness of Alan's writing.

In 2007 Alan finished his first book, "Deep Water." This nonfiction explored the ageless bond between the wild and the soul. It was never published, though sections of the book were later released on his blog. Alan never imagined writing a fantasy novel. Urged by a close friend to consider writing fiction, he found unexpected inspiration to write this debut novel - "The Legend of Eloh."

For 25 years Alan was vice president for a real estate and property development company. Alan is married, has two daughters and lives in the Midwest.

adelahay.com
thelegendofeloh.com